THE BRIGHT SILVER STAR

THE
BRIGHT
SILVER STAR

DAVID
HANDLER

THOMAS DUNNE BOOKS
ST. MARTIN'S MINOTAUR
NEW YORK

THOMAS DUNNE BOOKS.
An imprint of St. Martin's Press.

www.minotaurbooks.com

Library of Congress Cataloging-in-Publication Data

Handler, David, 1952–
The bright silver star / David Handler.—1st ed.
p. cm.
ISBN 0-312-30714-4
1. Berger, Mitch (Fictitious character)—Fiction. 2. Mitry, Desiree (Fictitious character)—Fiction. 3. Motion picture actors and actresses—Crimes against—Fiction. 4. African American police—Fiction. 5. Film critics—Fiction. 6. Policewomen—Fiction. 7. Connecticut—Fiction. I. Title.

PS3558.A4637B73 2003
813'.54—dc21   2003050619

First Edition: November 2003

10 9 8 7 6 5 4 3 2 1

FOR PAMELA BOND,
WHO WELCOMED US HOME

The Bright Silver Star

PROLOGUE

JULY 25

ONE OF THE THINGS that almost no one knew about him was that he was an awful driver. The worst. Not only was he easily distracted from the road in front of him but his eyesight was bad. Especially at night. Especially on narrow, unlit country roads.

Especially when he was stoned off of his gourd, had his foot jammed hard to the floor, and didn't care whether he kept on living or not.

A dense river valley fog hugged low to the ground in the heavy stillness of the summer night. Whenever the twisty road dipped down into a gully the fog became so thick he could see only his head-lights before him in the mist, his wipers swishing back and forth, back and forth. Briefly, he would rise back up out of it, catching occasional snapshot glimpses as he tore along—of granite ledge crowding right up against the narrow shoulder. Mountain laurel and hemlocks. A guardrail where the shoulder dropped right off, the rain-swollen Eight Mile River rushing by a hundred feet below. The distant lights of a remote, lonely farmhouse. Then he would plunge back down into the moldy, overripe fog.

And into his own nightmare.

He hurtled right down the center of the road. If anyone happened to be coming toward him it would all be over. But there was no one else out after midnight on the Devil's Hopyard Road. Just him, with Neil Young cranked up full blast on the CD player. An old album with Crazy Horse called *Everybody Knows This Is Nowhere*, which had to be the single most hopeless, painful album that had ever been recorded at any time by anyone. The man made Nirvana sound like the Cowsills.

It fit his mood much too perfectly.

He hunched low over the wheel, left hand gripping it tightly, right hand groping on the seat next to him for the pint bottle of syrupy peppermint schnapps that lay next to his cell phone. It had been his best friend back when he was in junior high school. He drank it whenever the Bad People came.

He took a deep gulp as he came tearing around a curve, tires screaming, and suddenly two of them were standing right before him in the middle of the road. He swerved to avoid them, scraping the guardrail, a harsh, grinding sideswipe that startled him and sent sparks flying through the air. He did not stop to take a look at the damage he'd done to the car. He did not care about this car or any car. He kept right on going.

He had to keep on going. He was a man on a mission.

And the knowledge of what he was about to do gripped him with such panic that neither the schnapps nor the joint he'd smoked could even begin to help. He was sweating. His hands trembled, his breathing was shallow and quick. But he had no choice. No way out. And he knew this. And it hurt. God, how it hurt.

I have at long last met my soul mate, my one and only love, only it so happens that this person is not my wife. And so tonight I must say good-bye.

Honestly, he could not even believe he had gotten himself into this. How could he fall in love with someone else? God, it was all just so pathetically middle-aged and tawdry. But none of that mattered anymore. All that mattered was that it did happen and he had to end it right now.

He drove, suddenly spotting two more Bad People ahead of him in the mist, darting for cover in the brush. He sped his way past them, knowing full well he could not lose them. Whenever he felt frightened and lost and alone, they came.

He had started calling them the Bad People when he was no more than four and he'd lay awake at night with his heart pounding, waiting for them to come. They lived inside of his bedroom wall. He could hear them rustling around in there when they were coming out, and he could see them if he flicked on his light real fast. They were tiny creatures with horns and tails and hooves that made little clip-clop noises on the wooden floor. They had slimy purple skin, eyes that were narrow yellow slits, teeth that were sharp and dripping with saliva. He did not know why they had chosen him. He only knew that they meant him grave bodily harm.

And that no one else on earth could see them. Just him.

He remembered crying out for his mother when they came. Often, she would ignore him—just leave him alone with his terror. But sometimes she would come and sit there on the edge of the bed so they couldn't get at him. Dab at his damp brow with a wadded tissue. *My good little boy*, she would call him. *My good strong boy*. But then she would leave and there would be only him and the Bad People and the fear.

They did hide during daylight hours. But his fear was with him from sunrise until sundown. Always, it was with him. If only people knew just how hard it was for him to get through each and every day without giving in to it. But they didn't know. No one did.

They see me but they don't see me. No one knows me. No one.

He drove. Somehow, he made it all of the way to the end of the deserted road, where the entrance to the falls was. The state park closed after sunset. A barrier was lowered to keep people out of the parking lot. He pulled over onto the shoulder of the road and shut off the engine and the music. His was the only car there. He was the first to arrive. He sat there for a long moment, hearing the steady roar of the waterfall, his agitation mounting. He needed to hear a sane voice. It was imperative. He lunged for his cell phone and called Mitch. They hadn't known each other for long. But Mitch actually *understood* him—who he was, who he wanted to be. Plus he wanted nothing in return. Only honesty. And this was unusual. Hell, this was unheard-of.

Although right now the voice on the other end of the phone just sounded groggy and disoriented. "H-Hello . . . Whassa? . . ."

"I'm sorry if I woke you. I just wanted you to know something."

"Okay . . . Uh, sure . . ." Mitch sounded semialert now. "Where are you?"

"I'm on Sugar Mountain, with the barkers and the colored bal-loons."

Long silence. "Wait, give me a second. I know what that's . . . Neil Young, right?"

"You are."

"What's that whooshing noise? Are you hanging out in a men's room somewhere?"

"Not exactly."

"What time is it anyway?"

He sat there breathing in and out, feeling much less fear now. More an overbearing sadness. "It's too late. The damage is done. The hangman says it's time to let her fly."

"*What* hangman? What the hell are you talking about?"

"Good-bye, Mitch."

"Wait, don't—!"

He flicked off the phone and hurled it out his open window, hear-ing it clatter to the ground. Got out of the car and staggered his way blindly down the footpath toward the falls, clutching the schnapps bottle in one hand and a book of matches in the other.

It was so dark he kept stumbling over the loose rocks and exposed tree roots. He lit a match, squinting. Ahead were the picnic tables where they'd made love that first night. It all started here. And *there* was the walkway to the top of the falls. During the day, people came from miles around to see the waterfall, to photograph it and wade in the cold, clear pools at its base, to eat their gray, greasy junk food and drink their carbonated sugar water and do the other normal, stupid things that normal, stupid people did.

He staggered on. A wooden guardrail hugged the edge of the cliff, smelling of creosote. Wire mesh was stapled to the posts to keep small children from slipping under the rail and falling to their death. He lit another match. Now he stood before the warning sign that read: *Let the Water Do the Falling. Stay Behind This Point.*

He paid no attention. Climbed right over it and out onto the flat shelf of granite ledge, directly over the falls. This was *their* place, the secret haven where they came to make feverish, forbidden love, night after night, as often as they dared. They were alone here. Just them and the water and the darkness.

The bare granite was slick from the fog and the spray. And it was a bit cooler here. But still hc was sweating. He crouched here on the ledge; feeling the full power of the river as it tore right past him into the darkness of space, smashing down onto the smoothed hollows of granite a hundred feet below, swirling and foaming and cascading before it bottomed out into a river once again. He did think about hurling himself right off the ledge right now, sparing himself the pain of what was about to come. But he could not will himself to do this, no matter how much he wanted to. The words had to be spoken.

And so he waited in the fog for his one true love to come.

He didn't hear the other car arrive over the roar of the falls. Or hear the quick, sure footsteps until they were very close to him. He couldn't see the shimmer of golden hair or the shiny, trusting blue eyes. He didn't need to. He could see everything with his own eyes shut, just as his lips knew the achingly soft, sweet lips that were now kissing him, kissing him.

"Hey, baby," he said as they sat there in each other's arms. They didn't have to raise their voices as long as they stayed very close.

"God, I'm so glad you're here. I wasn't even sure you'd make it tonight."

"I said I'd be here, didn't I?" he responded lightly, hearing the quaver of insincerity in his own voice. "Want some peppermint schnapps?"

"Ugh, no."

"Why wouldn't I be here?"

"You sounded funny on the phone. Was *she* standing there?"

"Not really." He groped in the darkness for a hand, clutching it tightly, knowing that once he said the words he had to say that he would never, ever feel its caresses again. "But I do have something kind of heavy to lay on you . . . about you and me."

"What about us?"

"We can't do this anymore," he blurted out.

"W-What are you saying to me?" They were no longer holding

hands. They were apart, now and forever. "You don't want to *be* with me anymore?"

"No, I *do* want to be with you. That's not the point."

"Then what is?"

"That it's over. That it . . . it has to be over."

"Just like that? You're insane!"

"I know this," he admitted, hearing only the roar of the falls for a moment.

Until he heard a gut-wrenching sob. "My God, do you actually think that you can just snap your fingers and the love's not there anymore? Like it's some kind of a-a choice? Paper or plastic? Smooth or chunky?"

"Look, it's not *you*, okay?" he said, his own voice rising helplessly. "It's *me*. I can't keep doing this. It's not going to be easy to stop. In fact, I think this is the hardest thing I've ever had to do in my whole life. But I have to do it."

"But *how*? We'll still see each other every day. How can we pretend that nothing's happened?"

"We've been pretending that ever since we got involved."

"You mean, ever since you came after me, don't you?"

"I warned you about me from the very start," he shot back, growing defensive now. "I told you what would happen."

"You told me you'd break my poor little heart. You didn't tell me you'd stab me in the chest with a dull knife and . . . and why are you *doing* this to me?" Now he heard another sob in the darkness. "God, listen to me. I sound like a pathetic old lady."

"No, you don't. You sound great. You *are* great. And I wish we could go on like this forever. I swear, I've never been this happy in my whole life."

"Only because your whole life is a lie. You are living a lie."

"Hey, your marriage is just as dead as mine."

"This isn't about me. It's about *you*."

"I know, I know. . . ." He breathed in and out, his chest beginning to ache. "I just can't keep chancing it like this. Not in Dorset. People are bound to find out, and when they do they'll talk. It's what they live for—to talk about people like us."

"So let them. Who cares? I don't."

"Well, I can't risk it. I won't risk it."

"Every day you get out of bed there's risk. Without risk, you're as good as dead."

"Right now, I wish I was," he confessed.

"Screw you and your self-pity. You're not the one who's getting hurt here—I am. And I hate you. Do you hear me? I *hate* you!"

"Look, this doesn't have to end badly," he said soothingly. "It just has to end." He drained the schnapps bottle and set it down on the stone next to him, climbing unsteadily to his feet. He'd said what he had to say. Now all that was left was the ugliness, the words that hurt.

"Wait, where do you think you're going?"

"Home."

"What about *me?*" They were both standing now. "Don't you realize how much *I've* risked?"

"Yes, I do," he said, even though it was not nearly the same. Not even close. "And, believe me, this is better for you, too."

"God, you are so totally full of shit. Our lives were dead until we found each other. We've got something special together. How can you turn your back on that. How can you walk away?"

Now the sob was coming from his own throat. "I *have* to. You know I do."

"I don't know anything—except that I *won't* let you walk away from me. I'll . . . I'll tell her about us. I swear I will."

He stood there in choked silence, realizing that he was trapped in a love he could not get out of. No way out. No good way, anyhow. And now it began to creep into his mind—the terrible thing he had been trying not to think about. Which was that this secret place of theirs, this private, perfect perch where they made love, was also a private, perfect place to kill. And, worse, that he was totally capable of doing it.

I am one of them. I am one of the Bad People.

Maybe he had known this all along. Maybe that was why he'd been so freaked out all evening. Because he was coming here to murder the great love of his life and he damned well knew it.

He stood clenching and unclenching his fists, preparing himself for what he was about to do. "I have to think about my future," he explained.

"You say that as if you have one."

Which he didn't.

"No, don't!" he cried out as he felt himself suddenly being shoved toward the edge of the cliff.

And it was all so unexpected, so ferocious, so *unthinkable* that he had no chance to hold his ground. He did try, in that desperate last fraction of a second, to cling to the slick stone, digging at it with his fingers and his toes like a wild, desperate animal. But now he was pitching over backward into the blackness with his arms waving wildly and the roar of the falls growing louder and now the roar was coming from out of him as his head *smacked* into something hard. And everything went from black to red.

As he lay there on the rocks, he thought he heard a sob coming from somewhere far away, but that may have been his own last groans he was hearing. He felt no pain, no fear, no regret—only a powerful rush of relief.

I am free of them. I am free of the Bad People. They can go torment someone else now, because they can't have me. Not anymore. Because I am free . . . I am free . . . I am . . .

EIGHTEEN HOURS EARLIER

CHAPTER 1

THERE WAS NO LOLLYGAGGING in the feathers on Big Sister Island. Not in July. Not when the sun came beaming through the skylights in Mitch's sleeping loft at five-thirty in the morning. Not a chance. These days, Mitch Berger, creature of the darkness, got up when the sun got up.

And he loved every glorious minute.

He loved the cool, fresh breezes off Long Island Sound that wafted through his antique post-and-beam carriage house no matter how hot and sticky the day was. He loved the blackberries that grew wild all over the island and the fresh vegetables that he had brought to life in his own garden. He loved mowing his little patch of lawn with an old-fashioned push mower, which had to be one of the great lost pleasures of the modern age. He loved parking his pudgy self in a shell-backed aluminum garden chair at sunset, cold beer in hand, waiting for Des to come thumping across the rickety wooden causeway in her cruiser. He loved the bracing dips in the Sound they would take together. He even—and this was the truly amazing part—loved those disgustingly healthy dinners of grilled fish, brown rice and steamed vegetables she would cook for them.

If he didn't know any better Mitch would have sworn he was turning into somebody else.

Every day he learned something new about the sun-drenched natural world around him. Goldfinches are attracted to sunflowers, hummingbirds to the color red. The male osprey stays behind to teach the fledgling how to fly while the female migrates south on her own. Many of these things he had learned from Dodge Crockett, unofficial head of the unofficial walking club Mitch had fallen in with at the beginning of the summer—four local men who hiked the three-mile stretch of beach that ringed the Peck's Point Nature Preserve every morning at seven so as to exercise, to bird watch and to chew each other's ears off.

There was no getting around this: Mitch Berger, lead film critic for the most prestigious and therefore lowest paying of the three New York city metropolitan dailies, was in a male bonding group. Or so Des called it. Mitch simply described it as four Dorseteers who liked to walk together, eat fresh-baked croissants and discuss life, love, and women—three subjects they freely admitted they knew nothing about.

Besides, today he had a serious career-related matter to discuss with Dodge.

At the sound of Mitch stirring around in the kitchen Quirt came scooting in the cat door for his breakfast. Quirt, who was Mitch's lean, sinewy hunter, liked to sleep outside during the summer on a bench under the living room bay window. Clemmie, his lap cat, still preferred the safe confines of the house, but slept downstairs in his armchair as opposed to upstairs on Mitch's bed, snuggled into his collarbone. Mitch had grown accustomed to her being there at night and missed her terribly, but he had also come to understand cats and the high priority they placed on their own comfort. When autumn blew in, and Clemmie felt the need for Mitch's considerable body warmth, she would return to his bed as if she'd never left.

Right now, she yawned at him from his chair and stretched a languid paw out toward him, which was her way of saying good morning.

Mitch was otherwise alone this morning. Des had taken to spending three or four nights a week with him, the rest at her own place overlooking Uncas Lake. Bella Tillis, her good friend and fellow rescuer, had moved in with her on a trial basis, which meant Des could stay over with him and not fret over her own furry charges.

While Quirt hungrily munched kibble Mitch squeezed himself a tall glass of grapefruit juice. As he drank it down he stood before his living room windows that overlooked the water in three different directions, savoring the quiet of early morning on his island in the

Sound. A fisherman was chugging his way out for the day. Otherwise, all was tranquil. Mitch dressed in a faded gray T-shirt and baggy khaki shorts. Shoved four blue tin coffee mugs in his knapsack, along with an eight-ounce plastic water bottle filled with that see-through low-fat milk Des had him drinking—he himself vastly preferred whole milk of the chocolate variety. But Des was absolutely determined that Mitch take off some excess poundage this summer. And a determined Des was no one to trifle with. Ever since she'd turned his kitchen into a No Fry Zone he'd gone down two whole waist sizes.

He started out the door, binoculars around his neck, and headed down the footpath lined with wild beach roses and bayberry toward the causeway that connected Big Sister with Peck's Point. The island had been in the Peck family since the 1600s. It was forty square acres of blue-blooded paradise at the mouth of the Connecticut River just off Dorset, the historic New England village. There were five houses on the island, a decommissioned lighthouse that was the second tallest in New England, a private beach, dock, tennis court. Mitch had been only too happy to rent the converted caretaker's cottage, and to eventually buy it. During the cold months he'd had the whole island to himself. Right now one other house was in use—Bitsy Peck, his garden guru, was living in the big Victorian summer cottage with her daughter, Becca.

Not a day went by when Mitch didn't tell himself how extraordinarily lucky he was to be here. He'd been a total wreck after he lost his beloved wife, Maisie, a Harvard-trained landscape architect, to ovarian cancer when she was barely thirty. He had needed somewhere to go and heal. And it turned out that somewhere was this place. Slowly, he *was* healing. Certainly, Des Mitry's arrival in his life was a huge reason why. So was his determination to plunge himself headlong into new experiences—for Mitch Berger, a socially challenged screening room rat, walking in the sunshine every morning with three men who he'd only recently met qualified as a huge leap into the unknown.

He could see them waiting for him there at the gate as he crossed the narrow quarter-mile wooden causeway—a trio of middle-aged Dorseteers in sizes small, medium, and large. Will Durslag, who towered over the other two, was the fellow who'd brought him into the group. Will and his hyperkinetic wife, Donna, ran The Works and Mitch was a huge fan of their chocolate goodies, or at least he had been until Des put him on his diet. Standing there in his tank top and baggy surf shorts, knapsack thrown carelessly over one broad shoulder, thirty-four-year-old Will looked more like a professional beach volleyball player or Nordic god than he did a jolly chef. He was a tanned, muscular six foot four with long sun-bleached blond hair that he wore in a ponytail. Early one morning, Mitch had encountered him on the bluff hiking with Dodge Crockett and Jeff Wachtell. Introductions had been made, a casual invitation extended. Next thing Mitch knew he was not only joining their little group every morning but looking forward to it.

It was a loose group. If you were there at seven, fine. If you couldn't make it, that was fine, too. No explanations required. There was only one rule: you could not take yourself too seriously. Any subject was a legitimate topic of conversation. The group had no name, though Mitch was partial to the Mesmer Club in tribute to *The Woman In Green,* one of his favorite Basil Rathbone Sherlock Holmes films. Not that he had bothered to mention this to any of them—they would not understand what he was talking about. They had not, for example, grasped the origin of the *Rocky Dies Yellow* tattoo on his bicep.

"Good morning, men," he called out to them.

"Another beautiful day in paradise," said Dodge, his face breaking into a smile.

"*Ab-so-tootly,*" piped up Jeff, an impish refugee from a major New York publishing house. Jeff ran the Book Schnook, Dorset's bookstore.

They set out, walking single file down the narrow footpath that edged the bluffs. Beach pea grew wild alongside of them. Cormorants and gulls flew overhead. Dodge set the brisk pace, his arms swinging loosely at his sides, his shoulders back, head up. Mitch fell in behind him, puffing a bit but keeping up. When he'd first joined the group, Mitch could barely cut it. He was definitely making progress, although his T-shirt was already sticking to him.

Dodge was far and away the oldest of the group. Also the wealthiest. He came from old Dorset money, had been a second-team All American lacrosse player at Princeton, and remained, at fifty-four, remarkably vigorous and fit. Dodge was also the single most rigidly disciplined person Mitch had ever met in his life. So disciplined that he never needed to wear a watch. Thanks to his strict, self-imposed regimen of daily activities Dodge always knew within two minutes what time it was. What made this especially amazing was that Dodge had never held a real job in his life. Didn't need to. And yet he was never idle. Each day he awoke at six, walked at seven, lifted weights at eight, read *The New York Times* and *Wall Street Journal* at nine, attended to personal finances at ten and practiced classical piano at eleven. After lunch, the remainder of his day was given over to meetings. Dodge was president of the local chapter of the Nature Conservancy as well as commissioner of Dorset's historic district. He served on the Wetlands Commission, the executive board of the Dorset library, and the Youth Services Bureau. Some years back, he had also put in two terms as a state senator up in Hartford. A few of the old-timers around John's barbershop still called him Senator.

And yet, Dodge was no tight-assed prig. Mitch had heard him do some pretty amazing things with "Great Balls of Fire" on that Steinway of his. Mitch enjoyed being around the man every morning. He was good company, a good listener, and somehow, he made Mitch feel as if walking with him was the highlight of his day. Dodge also possessed a childlike excitement for life that Mitch truly envied. Hell, the man's whole life was enviable. He had health, wealth, a beautiful renovated farmhouse on ten acres overlooking the Connecticut River. He had Martine, his long-legged, blond wife of twenty-six years who, as far as Mitch was concerned, was merely Grace Kelly in blue jeans. Between them Dodge and Martine had produced Esme, who happened to be one of the hottest and most talented young actresses in Hollywood.

And the reason why Mitch needed to speak to Dodge this morning. Because this was by no means a typical July for Dorset. Not since Esme Crockett and her actor husband, combustible blue-eyed Latino heartthrob Tito Molina, had rented a $3 million beachfront mansion for the summer. Tito and Esme, each of them twenty-three years old, were the biggest thing happening that summer as far the tabloids were concerned. She was a breathtakingly gorgeous Academy Award winner. He was *People* magazine's Sexiest Man Alive, not to mention a man given to uncontrollable bouts of drinking, drugs, and rage. Just within the past year Tito had served two stints in drug rehab, thirty days in a Los Angeles County jail for criminal drug possession, and been sued twice by tabloid photographers for his violent behavior toward them in the street outside of the couple's Malibu home. Their arrival in Dorset had sparked debate all over the village. Esme was one of Dorset's own and the locals were justifiably proud of her. This was a girl, after all, who'd gotten her start on stage in the Dorset High production of *Fiddler on the Roof*. From there she'd starred in a summer revival of Neil Simon's *I Ought to Be in Pictures* at the Ivoryton Playhouse, where she was spotted by a top New York casting director. He was searching for a young actress to play an underaged Roaring Twenties gun moll in the next Martin Scorsese crime epic. Esme won not only the part but an Oscar for Best Supporting Actress. Now she was one of Hollywood's top draws.

But Dorset also cherished its decidedly *un*-Hampton low profile, and Esme and Tito had brought a media army with them, along with stargazers, gawkers, and more gawkers. The village was positively overrun by outsiders, many of them rude and loud—although none ruder or louder than Chrissie Huberman, the high-profile celebrity publicist who the golden couple had imported from New York to run interference for them.

"Oystercatchers at three o'clock, Mitch!" Dodge called out, pausing to aim his binoculars at the rocks down below. Dodge had a bristly gray crewcut, tufty black eyebrows, and a round face that frequently lit up with glee. He was no more than five feet nine but powerfully built, with a thick neck, heavy shoulders, and immense hands and feet. He wore a polo shirt, khaki shorts and size-15 hiking boots. "Two of them, see? They almost always travel in pairs."

Mitch focused his own glasses on one of them. It was a big, thick-set bird with a dark back, white belly, and the longest, flattest orange bill Mitch had ever seen. "Wow, a cartoon shorebird. What a hoot."

"Not to mention a dead ringer for my uncle Heshie," said Jeff as they resumed walking. "I wonder if he cheats at cards, too." Jeff was an odd little puppy of a guy in his late thirties who had a habit of sucking in his cheeks like a fish whenever he was upset, which was pretty much all of the time lately—he was in the middle of a rather ugly divorce. Jeff had moppety red hair, crooked, geeky black-framed glasses, and freckly, undeniably weblike hands. He also happened to walk like a duck. Jeff possessed even less fashion sense than Mitch. Right now he had on a short-sleeved dress shirt of yellow polyester, madras shorts, and Teva sandals with dark brown socks.

"Raccoon poop at nine o'clock," Dodge warned them so they wouldn't step in the fresh, seed-speckled clump on the edge of the path.

The path cut down through the bluffs toward the beach now, and they started plowing their way out to the end of the Point's narrow, mile-long ribbon of sand. It was a very special ribbon of sand. At its farthest tip was one of the few sanctuaries in all of New England where the endangered piping plovers came to lay their eggs every summer. There were two chicks this season. The Nature Conservancy had erected a wire cage to protect them from predators. Also a warning fence to keep walkers and their dogs out. One of the walking group's assignments every morning was to make sure that the fence hadn't been messed with in the night. Kids liked to have beer parties and bonfires out there and sometimes got rowdy.

"You know what I was thinking about this morning?" Dodge said, waving to an early morning kayaker who was working his way along close to shore. "I've traveled all over the world, and yet I would never want to live anywhere but here. Why is that?"

"Open up your eyes, Dodger," Jeff said. No one else in the group called him Dodger—so far as Mitch knew, no one else in the world did. "It's awful damned pretty here."

"If you ask me," said Will, "it's Sheffield Wiggins."

"Old Sheff Wiggins? My God, I haven't thought of him in ages." To Mitch and Jeff, Dodge said, "He used to live in that big saltbox across from the Congregational church."

"You mean the cream-colored one?" asked Jeff.

"That's not called cream, my friend. That's called Dorset yellow."

"I've seen that same color all over New England. What do they call it if you're in, say, Brattleboro?"

"They call it Dorset yellow."

"Okay, I think we're drifting off of the subject," Will said.

"You mean this wasn't a story about paint?" Mitch said.

"Yes, what *about* Sheff? He's been dead for an honest twenty years."

A faint smile crossed Will's lean face. He was a good-looking guy with a strong jaw and clear, wide-set blue eyes. Yet he seemed totally unaware of his looks. He was very modest and soft-spoken. "Sheff's sister, Harriet, called my mom about a week after he died. This was in January and the ground was frozen, so they had to wait until spring before they could bury him. My dad used to dig the graves over at the cemetery, see." Will was a full-blooded swamp Yankee whose late father had done a variety of jobs around Dorset, including serving as Dodge's gardener and handyman. Will was only a kid when he died. Dodge gave Will odd jobs after that and became like a second father to him. The two remained very close. "Anyway, Harriet called my mom to tell her that Rudy, Sheff's parakeet, had died—"

"Honest to God, Will," Jeff interjected. "I can't imagine where this story is going."

"She wanted to know if my mom would keep Rudy in our freezer until the spring so that he and Sheff could be buried together."

"You mean in the same casket?" asked Mitch, his eyes widening.

"I do."

"And did your mom? . . ."

"She did. And, yes, they are. Buried together, that is."

"How old were you, Will?" Jeff asked.

"Ten, maybe."

Jeff shuddered. "God, having that parakeet in my freezer all winter would have given me nightmares. What color was it? Wait, don't even tell me."

"My point," Will said, "is that Harriet Wiggins thought nothing of calling up my mom to ask her. And my mom didn't bat an eyelash. *That's* Dorset."

"In other words, everyone in town is totally crazy?" asked Jeff.

"I like to think of it as totally sane," said Dodge as they trudged their way out to the point, the sun getting higher, the air warmer. The tide was going out. Dozens of semipalmated plovers were feeding at the water's edge on spindly little legs. "Martine was talking about you last night, Mitch."

"She was?"

"They desperately need tutors over at the Youth Services Bureau. All sorts of subjects—history, English, math."

For weeks, Dodge had been trying to convince Mitch to join up with some local organization or another. Already, Mitch had turned down a chance to become recording secretary of the Shellfish Commission. Not the sort of thing he could see himself doing. It seemed so Ozzie Nelson. But Mitch was coming to understand that getting involved was part of the deal when you lived in a small town. Will Durslag served on the volunteer fire department. Jeff was a literacy volunteer.

"We have a bunch of really talented kids in this town, but they're just not motivated. Would lighting a fire under one of them be your kind of deal?"

"Maybe. I mean, sure."

"Great. I'll get you an application."

This man was relentless. Still, Mitch greatly admired his commitment. Mitch could hear a helicopter zooming its way toward them now across the Sound, moving low and fast. A news chopper from New York. All part of the Esme-Tito circus. Another day, another breathless new inquiry. Here was yesterday's: Did she or didn't she just have a boob job? Inquiring, very small minds wanted to know.

Mitch sped up so as to pull alongside of Dodge, the other two falling in behind them. "I wanted to give you a head's-up," he told him, puffing. "My review of Tito's new movie is in this morning's paper. I panned it. I hope that won't be awkward for you."

"Don't worry about Tito. He's much more levelheaded than people give him credit for. Besides, I'm sure you were your usual tactful self."

"Tactful is not exactly the word I'd use."

Tito's movie, *Dark Star,* was in fact Hollywood's hugest, loudest clunker of the summer, an ill-conceived $200 million outer-space epic that the studio had held back from its Fourth of July weekend opening because preview audiences were laughing out loud in all the wrong places. It was so disastrously awful that Mitch had called it "The most unintentionally hilarious major studio bomb since *Exorcist II: The Heretic.*" He went on to say, "Tito Molina has such a pained expression on his face throughout the film that it's hard to tell whether he wants to shoot the aliens or himself."

"I really like this kid," Dodge said. "I didn't expect to, not after everything I'd read about him. But I do. And I don't just say this because he's my son-in-law. He has a broken wing is all. Can't fly straight to save his life. That doesn't make him a bad person. You'd like him, Mitch. I sure wish you'd reconsider my invitation."

Dodge wanted him to join them for dinner one evening. Mitch didn't think that socializing with performers was a good idea for someone in his position. "I'd love to, Dodge, but it wouldn't be appropriate."

"Sure, I understand. I just think you'd enjoy his company. He's one of the most intuitively brilliant young men I've ever met."

This in spite of Tito's famously troubled childhood in Bakersfield, California. Tito's father, a Mexican migrant worker, was killed in a bar fight when Tito was seven. His Anglo mother, a schizophrenic, was in and out of state mental hospitals until she committed suicide when he was thirteen. He took to living on his own after that, often in abandoned cars, and survived by dealing drugs. His big break came when a Britney Spears video was being shot at the Bakersfield high school that he'd recently dropped out of. A girl he was dating auditioned for a bit role. He tagged along with her. The video's director was looking for a bad boy from the wrong side of the tracks to play the bare-chested object of Britney's sweaty affections. One look at Tito's intense, smoldering good looks and he got the part. The video was such a hit on MTV that Tito shot straight to teen dream stardom, acting in a succession of edgy teen angst dramas—most notably the highly successful remake of the greatest teen angst drama of them all, *Rebel Without a Cause,* in which he stepped into James Dean's almost mythic shoes and, somehow, made them his own. It was Esme who was cast in the Natalie Wood role. They fell in love on the set, fueling the picture's on-screen heat, and married shortly thereafter.

Inevitably, critics were labeling Tito as his generation's James Dean. Mitch was not one of them. He believed that labels were for soup cans, not artists. He only knew that when Tito Molina appeared on-screen he could not take his eyes off him. Tito had an untamed animal quality about him, an edge of danger, and yet at the same time he was so vulnerable that he seemed to have his skin on inside out. Plus he had remarkable courage. Mitch was completely won over after he saw him conquer Broadway as Biff Loman to John Malkovich's Willy in an electrifying new production of Arthur Miller's *Death of a Salesman*. As far as Mitch was concerned, Tito Molina was simply the most gifted and daring actor of his generation—even if he had just stumbled badly with *Dark Star*.

"He and Esme are like a pair of special, golden children," Dodge said. "When I see them together, hand in hand, I think of Hansel and Gretel on their way through the woods to grandmother's house. They absolutely adore each other, and she's been able to help him some with his rage. And their publicist, Chrissie, really does try to put a smile on his public face. But it's a challenge. He's just such an intensely unhappy person."

"He's an actor," Mitch said.

"So is Esme, and she's not like that. She's a sweet, big-hearted girl.

A total innocent. I just . . . I hope he doesn't hurt her. He isn't faithful to her, you see."

"How do you know this?" Mitch asked, glancing at him.

"I just do. You can always tell—like with Martine," Dodge said, lowering his voice confidentially. "She's not faithful to me. She has a lover."

"I'm so sorry, Dodge," Mitch said, taken aback.

"These things happen over the course of a marriage," Dodge said, his jaw set with grim determination. "I sure wish I knew what to do about it. But the unvarnished truth is that I don't."

"Well, have you spoken to Martine about it?"

"Hell, no. What good would that do?"

"Communication is a positive thing, Dodge."

"No, it's not. As a matter of fact, it's highly overrated."

They were nearing the tip of Peck's Point now. The osprey stands that the Nature Conservancy had erected out in the tidal marshes were no longer occupied. The ospreys had nested and gone for the season. Mitch did spot two blue herons out there. And the two rare, precious dun-colored piping plover chicks were still in residence in their protective enclosure, tiny as field mice and nearly invisible against the sand.

He and Dodge inspected the cage and warning fence as Jeff and Will caught up with them. A fence stake had worked its way out in the night. Dodge pounded it back down with a rock as Mitch swabbed his face and neck with a bandanna, wondering why Dodge had chosen him to confide in about Martine. Why not Will? The two of them were so much closer.

Mitch opened his knapsack and got out the mugs and plastic milk bottle, his stomach growling with anticipation. From his own knapsack Will produced a thermos of his finest fresh-brewed Blue Mountain coffee and a bag of croissants he'd baked before dawn. Will was up every morning at four to oversee his extensive baking operation. The beach constituted his only break from the punishing fourteen-hour shifts he worked.

There were two driftwood logs with plenty of seating room for four. Jeff filled the tin mugs from the thermos. He and Will took their coffee black, Mitch and Dodge used milk. Dodge passed around the croissants. Then they all sat there munching and watching the killdeer and willets poke at the water's edge for their own breakfast.

Mitch chewed slowly, savoring each and every rich, flaky bite. His diet restricted him to one croissant, and he wanted to make the most of it. "Honestly, Will, you're a true artist. What's your secret, anyway?"

"Nothing to it," Will said offhandedly. "I've been making these ever since I was working in Nag's Head. My partner in those days gave me the recipe."

"You two owned a place together there?"

"No, not really," he replied.

Which Mitch had learned was typical of Will, who was perfectly friendly and polite but could be rather vague when it came to career details. Mitch knew he'd attended the Culinary Institute of America and had led the Have Knives, Will Travel life of an itinerant chef up and down the East Coast before he hooked up with Donna, who was working in the kitchen of the same Boston seafood place at the time. Donna was from Duxbury. After they married, Will brought her home to Dorset and they'd moved into the old farmhouse on Kelton City Road that he'd inherited from his mom. This spring they had pooled their considerable skills to open The Works, a gourmet food emporium that was housed in Dorset's abandoned piano works. The food hall was the biggest piece of an ambitious conversion of the old riverfront factory that included shops, offices, and luxury water-view condominiums. Dodge had helped finance the venture, and it was proving to be a huge success. Already it had attracted Jeff's Book Schnook.

Jeff could not have been more different than Will—every detail of his life was fair game for discussion, whether the others wanted to get in on it or not. The little man was a walking, talking ganglion of complaints. Inevitably, these complaints centered around his estranged wife, Abby Kaminsky, the pretty little blond who happened to be the hottest author of children's fiction in the country—America's own answer to J. K. Rowling. Abby's first two Carleton Carp books, *The Codfather* and *Return of the Codfather*, had actually rivaled the Harry Potter books in sales. Her just-released third installment, *The Codfather of Sole*—in which Carleton saves the gill world from the clutches of the evil Sturgeon General—was even threatening to outsell Harry.

Unfortunately for Jeff, Abby had dumped him for the man who'd served as her escort on her last book tour. Devastated, Jeff had moved to Dorset to start a new life, but an ugly and very public divorce settlement was looming on his personal horizon. At issue was Abby's half-boy, half-fish hero. There was a lot about Carleton that struck people who knew Jeff as *familiar*. Such as Carleton's moppety red hair, his crooked, geeky black-framed glasses, his freckly, undeniably weblike hands, the way he sucked his cheeks in and out when he was upset. Not to mention his constant use of the word *"ab-so-toot-ly."* Though Abby vehemently denied it, it was obvious that Carleton was Jeff. As part of their divorce settlement, Jeff was insisting she compensate him for the contribution he'd made to her great success. Abby was flatly refusing, despite what was sure to be a punishing public relations disaster if their divorce went to court. To handle the publicity fallout, Abby had hired Chrissie Huberman, the very same New York publicist who was handling Esme and Tito. As for Jeff, he was so bitter that he refused to carry Abby's books in his store, even though she outsold every single author in America who wasn't named John Grisham.

"Hey, I got a shipment of your paperbacks in, Mitch," he spoke up, chewing on his croissant. Mitch was the author of three highly authoritative and entertaining reference volumes on horror, crime, and western films—*It Came from Beneath the Sink, Shoot My Wife, Please* and *They Went Thataway*. "Would you mind signing them for me—you being a local author and all?"

"Be happy to, Jeff. I can stop by around lunchtime if you'll be there."

Jeff let out a snort. "Where else would I be? That damned bookshop is my whole life. I'm there twelve hours a day, seven days a week. I even sleep right over the store in a cramped little—"

"Two-bedroom luxury condo with river views," Will said, his eyes twinkling at Mitch with amusement.

"Plus I have to drive a rusty old egg-beater of a car so the locals won't think I'm getting rich off of them," Jeff whined.

"Which, correct me if I'm wrong, you're not," Mitch pointed out, grinning at Will.

"Damned straight I'm not," Jeff said indignantly. "Listen to this, I had to give an old woman her money back yesterday. It seems I recommended a thriller to her and she hated it. Oh, she read every single word of it all right, but she pronounced it garbage. Stood there yelling at me in my own store until I paid her back. It was either that or she'd tell all of her friends that I'm a no-good bum. Barnes and Noble can afford to be so generous. Me, I'm barely hanging on. I don't know what I'll do if things don't pick up."

"But they *will* pick up," Dodge told him. "You're already building customer loyalty and good word of mouth. Start-up pains are perfectly normal. The Works felt them, too, and now it's doing great, right, Will?"

After a brief hesitation Will responded, "You bet."

Which Mitch immediately found intriguing, because if there was one thing he'd learned about Dorset it was this: Often, the truth wasn't in the words, it was in the pauses.

"Sometimes I feel like I'm not even in the book business at all," Jeff grumbled. "I'm in the *people* business. I have to be pleasant to strangers all day long. Yikes, it's hard enough being pleasant around you guys."

"Wait, who said you were pleasant?" asked Mitch.

"By the way, Dodger, Martine did me a real solid—she's so popular with the other ladies that as soon as she joined my Monday evening reading group they all wanted in. I may even add a Tuesday reading group, thanks to her. Best thing that's happened to me in weeks. You'd think with all of these media people in town I'd be selling books like crazy, but I'm not." Jeff drained his coffee, staring down into the empty mug. "Did I tell you they're trying to buy me off?"

Mitch popped the last of his croissant in his mouth. "Who, the tabloids?"

"They want me to spill the dirt on Abby. Every time I say no they raise the ante—it's up to two hundred and fifty."

"*Thousand?*" Will was incredulous.

"And I've got plenty to spill, believe me. Hell, I've known her since she was typing letters for the children's book editor and I was the little pisher in the next cubicle."

"You're still a little pisher."

"Thank you for that, Mitchell."

"My Yiddish is a little rusty," Dodge said. "Exactly what is a pisher?"

"She loathes kids, you know," Jeff said. "Calls them germ carriers, poop machines, fecal felons ... She hates them so much she even made me get a vasectomy. I can't have children now."

"I thought those were reversible in a lot of cases," Will said.

"Not mine," Jeff said. "My God-given right to sire children has been snipped away from me—all thanks to the top children's author in America. Nice story, hunh? And how does the little skank repay me? By boning that—that glorified cab driver, that's how. I swear, every time I see a box of Cocoa Pebbles I get nauseated."

Mitch and the others exchanged an utterly bewildered look, but let it alone.

Dodge said, "Any chance you'll take them up on their offer?"

"I'm flat broke, man. I might have to if she doesn't give me what I want."

"Which is ... ?"

"Twenty-five percent of the proceeds from the first book. My lawyer wants me to aim for the whole series, but that would be greedy. I'm not being greedy. I just . . . I deserve *something*, don't I? I nursed that book along, night after night. I read every early draft, helped her refine it and craft it months before she ever submitted it."

"Plus you *are* Carleton Carp," Mitch added. "That ought to be worth something."

"I am not a fish!" Jeff snapped, sucking his cheeks in and out.

Dodge, the human timepiece, climbed to his feet now, signifying that it was time to start back for his eight o'clock weight training. Mitch wondered if the man was ever late.

"You'll never do it, Jeff," Mitch said. "You'll never sell out Abby to the tabloids."

Jeff peered at him quizzically. "Why have you got so much faith in me?"

"Because you still love her, that's why. No matter how upset you are, you could never hurt her that way."

"You're right," Jeff admitted, reddening slightly. "Abby's the only woman I've ever loved. I'd take her back in a flash. Answer me this, Dodger, what's the secret?"

"To what?" Dodge asked.

"You and Martine have been together all these years, you've got a terrific thing going on—how do you do it?"

Mitch watched closely as Dodge considered this, the older man's face betraying not one bit of what he'd just revealed to Mitch. "Jeff, there are so many things that factor into it," he answered slowly. "Shared values, common interests and goals. Affection, respect, tolerance. But if I had to narrow it down to one word, it would be the same one that's the secret to a happy friendship."

"What is it?" Jeff pressed him.

Dodge shot a hard stare right at Will Durslag before he replied, "The word is trust."

CHAPTER 2

"DODGE IS HAVING AN affair," Martine Crockett informed Des in a soft, strained voice as the two of them crouched next to the over-stuffed, foul-smelling Dumpster behind McGee's Diner on Old Shore Road, waiting for the kittens to show.

Des drew her breath in. Martine had never confided anything even remotely intimate to her before. Now this, a bombshell out of nowhere. "Who's the woman?"

"I don't know," Martine answered miserably. "I don't want to know."

It was just before dawn, which was happy meal fun time in the world of strays. Esme, Martine's famous daughter, was crouched in wait on the other side of the Dumpster with Des's roommate, Bella Tillis. It was Esme who'd spotted the two hungry kittens nosing around the trash bin late last night when she and Tito had pulled into McGee's for a late meal of fried oysters after a night spent drinking tequila shooters on the beach. Somebody had dumped the kittens there, most likely. Summer people did that. Esme had decided that she *had* to adopt them, and since Martine was the unofficial queen of Dorset's rescuers, the four of them were out there now with their dog cages, trying to lure the poor, starved things in with jars of Gerber's strained turkey. A length of string was tied to each cage door. Once a kitten was inside, they could yank the cage door shut behind it.

The predawn often found Des, Bella, and Martine staked out near a Dumpster somewhere, strings in hand, discussing life, love, and men—three subjects they freely admitted they knew nothing about. They made for an oddly mismatched trio. One tall, cool, late-forties WASP from old Philadelphia money. One round, feisty, seventy-six-year-old Jewish grandmother from Brooklyn. And Des Mitry, a highly gifted artist who was twenty-nine, black, and Dorset's resident Connecticut State Police trooper. Throwing a bona-fide Hollywood movie star into the mix just added more flavor. Not that the girl looked like much at this hour. It was obvious to Des from her puffy eyes, disheveled hair, and soiled clothing that Esme Crockett hadn't been to bed yet.

Unexpectedly, Martine had suggested that her famous daughter and Bella team up together. Obviously, it was so she could drop her bombshell on Des. But why had she?

Des studied her there in the early morning light. Martine was a strikingly pretty blue-eyed blond with good, high cheekbones. The age lines in her tanned face were like the gentle creases in fine leather. She wore her shiny, silver-streaked hair cropped appealingly at her chin, a hair band holding it in place. She wore a pink Izod shirt, khaki shorts, and a pair of spotless white Keds. Martine was almost as tall as Des, who was a legit six feet tall in her stocking feet, and she was very active. Played golf several times a week at the country club, swam for an hour a day at the beach club. It showed. Her figure was excellent—shoulders broad, hips narrow, her long legs toned and shapely.

At first, Des had had some trouble warming up to her. Martine was still very much the belle of the debutante's ball, a privileged white aristocrat who'd never wanted for anything. All she'd had to do was smile and it all came right to her, just like mumsy and daddy had promised. It was all just so *easy* for someone like Martine Crockett. Des had her problems with such women. She, well, hated them. Couldn't help it. But now that she was resident trooper of Dorset, which boasted even more millionaires per square mile than Easthampton, she was coming in contact with a whole lot of them. And she really did need to give them the benefit of the doubt. Besides, she genuinely liked Martine, who was unaffected and caring and sweet. She rescued feral strays, volunteered at the Shoreline Soup Kitchen, and the Dorset Day Care Center. Plus she was bright, perceptive, and good to talk to when you were camped out behind a stanky Dumpster waiting for a feral animal to show.

And now her husband was cheating on her, thereby confirming Bella's old axiom: Most rescuers are ladies with good hearts and bad husbands.

This had certainly been Des's own story. "How do you know he's having an affair?" she asked, crouched there in her tank top and gym shorts.

"I can tell. You can always tell, can't you?"

"Yes, I suppose you can."

Not that Des had been able to herself. Not when it came to Brandon. They were living in Woodbridge at the time, a leafy suburb of New Haven. He was in the U.S. Attorney's office. And she, the Deacon's daughter, was flying high on the Major Crime Squad out of Meriden. After Brandon left her, Des crashed. Bella, the no-bull Yale faculty widow next door, recruited her as a rescuer. And saved her. Woodbridge was now in both of their rearview mirrors. When Des started her new life here in Dorset Bella unloaded her own big barn of a house and came with her. It was working out fine. Between the job, the art academy, and the doughboy, Des wasn't home much. Plus Bella was a fastidious housekeeper, great cook, funny, independent, and thoughtful. True, theirs was not what other people might consider a typical living arrangement, but quite honestly Des couldn't think of a single thing about her life these days that was typical.

"How long has this been going on, Martine?"

"A few weeks," she replied, wringing her hands. She had strong hands with long, graceful fingers. She painted her nails pink. "I'm sorry to be burdening you with this. I just, I feel you're someone who I can talk to. I don't have anyone else."

Des pushed her heavy horn-rimmed glasses back up her nose, frowning. Martine Crockett had a million friends, women who she'd known a lot longer than she'd known Des. Why not confide in one of them? One possibility jumped right out.

Because it *was* one of them.

"You won't tell anyone about it, will you?" she asked Des urgently. Now she seemed sorry she'd brought it up.

"Of course not. But what will *you* do?"

Martine raised her chin, and said, "Oh, I've moved on."

"I see," said Des, although she flat out didn't. Moved on meant what—that she'd gotten past it emotionally, taken a lover of her own, loaded up a van with her most precious possessions? God, these Dorset people could be so cryptic sometimes. No one just *said* what they meant.

Esme moseyed over toward them now, looking sleepy and bored. She was a blond like Martine with flawless porcelain skin and the same good, high cheekbones. Her hair was a wild, frizzy mane of curls that cascaded halfway down her back. To Des, Esme still looked very much like a child. Her heart-shaped face bore soft, slightly malleable remnants of baby fat. Her big blue eyes held wide-eyed innocence. And her hands were a girl's hands, chubby and unblemished by time or work. Esme Crockett was famous for her mouth. It was a pouty, highly erotic mouth with a short, upturned top lip that made her look as if she were in a constant state of sexual rapture. She was also famous for her figure. She was a good deal shorter than Martine, perhaps five feet six, but so ripe and voluptuous that she looked positively illicit in the outfit she had on—a deep V-necked halter top cropped at the belly to show off her gold navel ring, super-low denim cutoffs slashed way high up on her thighs and cheap rubber flip-flops. "Where *are* they, Mommy?" she demanded petulantly. "How long do we have to wait for them?"

"Hours, sometimes," Martine answered.

"Sometimes they don't even show at all," Des said.

Esme flopped down carelessly next to Des on the pavement, reeking of tequila and sweaty girl. She was highly unkempt, in contrast to her spotless, stay-pressed mother. Her hair was unclean, armpits unshaven, ankles soiled. Des noticed that she also had splotchy bruises around her upper arms, as if someone had grabbed her and squeezed her hard. Also a number of scratches on her neck and shoulders.

"Girl, what happened?" Des asked her, as Bella joined them. "Did you get in a fight?"

Esme immediately reddened. "It's not what you think."

"Me, I'm thinking Tito beats the crap out of you," said Bella, who did not know how to mince words.

"No, never. We just get *physical* sometimes when we're, you know . . ."

"Getting physical?" asked Des.

She nodded, glanced awkwardly at her mother, who bristled noticeably.

"I never did understand that," Bella said flatly. "If Morris ever put a welt on me when we were in the throes of connubial passion he would have found his bags on the front porch in the morning, packed and ready to go."

"He'd never *hurt* me," Esme insisted, a defensive edge creeping into her voice. In the flesh, she didn't seem nearly as bright or mature as the characters she played on screen. "I bruise easy, that's all. Honest."

"I believe you," said Des, who believed no such thing. Not with Tito Molina's reputation for violent eruptions.

"I wish they'd get here." Esme sighed, scratching irritably at a mosquito bite on her thigh. "This waiting thing sucks."

"Patience is everything in life," Bella said. "Allow me give you an example. When I was your age I desperately wanted to look like Elizabeth Taylor. Which, God knows, I did not. But guess what?" Bella raised her bunched fist of a face to the sky, preening. "*Now* I do, see?"

Esme gaped at her blankly. "Not really."

"Time, tattela," Bella explained. "It's the great equalizer."

"Do you still date men, Bella?"

"When the occasion arises. Lord knows, the men don't. But you have to be very, very careful when you get to be my age."

"Careful how?"

"One of Morris's dearest friends, Velvel, started wooing me last year. Very cultivated man. A renowned mathematician, seventy-four years old. Before I'd so much as let him give me a peck on the cheek I had to, you know, check him out," Bella said waggling her eyebrows at Esme.

"Wait, check him out how?"

"I made a date to go dancing with him, okay? Waited for a nice slow dance, got out him out there on the floor . . ."

"And? . . ."

"I gave him a good hard whack on the leg. *That's* when I heard it."

"Heard what, Bella?" Now Martine was curious, too.

"The slosh," Bella replied. "You hear a slosh it means the man's wearing a catheter bag. You don't want nuttin' to do with him."

Esme smiled at her, a smile that lit up her entire face. "Bella, you are the coolest."

"That's me, all right, the queen of cool." Bella stood there staring down the front of Esme's halter top at her considerable cleavage. "So did you have your boobs done or what?" she asked her bluntly.

"No way. These are all mine. Want to feel them?"

"Not necessary."

"That whole deal was just Crissie doing what she does," Esme explained.

"Which is what exactly?" Martine demanded.

"She plants the denial before there's ever a story."

"So as to create the story?" asked Des.

Esme nodded. "That way she keeps the tabloids fed and off of our backs."

"That woman is so crass," Martine said. "Honestly, I can't tell if she's part of the solution or part of the problem."

"None of it's real, Mommy. It's just some tabloid trash about tits."

"Those are *your* tits they're talking about. And I don't care for it. Or Chrissie."

"Yeah, I kind of sensed that," Esme shot back. They had a definite mother-daughter thing going on. "But don't blame me. Tito's agent hired her. He had to. That's how the business is—if we don't give them *something* then they just make up stuff about how our marriage is in ruins or whatever. It's not like we're real people to them. We're just characters in some twisted interactive soap opera. They shout things at Tito, you know. To bait him."

"What things?" asked Des.

"They tell him I'm a slut. That I'm having sex with Ben Affleck or Derek Jeter or Justin Timberlake, anyone. They're hoping he'll lose it so they can sell a picture of him attacking them. They try to climb over the wall of our Malibu house. They follow us when we leave. It's horrible. If the public knew what really went on, they'd freak. But since it's the press they somehow think it's all noble and decent."

"Those people aren't the press." Bella sniffed.

"No, they totally are," Esme insisted.

Des couldn't disagree. She'd seen the tabloids in action when she'd worked murder investigations. "Do you two keep a bodyguard around?"

"Tito won't live that way. He wants to keep it real, or at least try. He figures, how can you hold on to your street edge when you live like royalty?"

"You can't," Des concurred.

"Besides, Chrissie's staying in the guesthouse while we're here, so she keeps them at bay. And the road we're on is private. The beach association has a gate, and they can't get past that. Or at least they aren't supposed to."

"If they do, let me know," Des said.

"I would, Des, except Tito's deathly afraid of the police. He has *so* many childhood scars." Esme let out a soft laugh. "But, hey, who doesn't, right?"

Martine stiffened at this last comment, Des noticed.

"Everyone thinks they know us, but they don't. Especially Tito. Nobody knows Tito."

"So tell us something we don't know about him," Bella said.

"Seriously?" Esme tossed her head, running her hands through her mane of golden hair. "He's the most deprived boy I've ever met, okay? Growing up, he went without so many things that the rest of us take for granted. Like pets—he's never, ever had one. I mean, God, he'd never even had a Christmas tree until he met me. You should have seen the joy in his eyes when we decorated our very own tree last Christmas." Recalling it, tears began to spill out of her own eyes right down her flawless cheeks. "All the things I took for granted growing up. A nice home, friends, parents who I believed I could trust . . ."

Des felt that there was something deliberately pointy about the words Esme used to describe her parents. Crouched there beside her on the pavement, Martine definitely seemed ill at ease.

"Tito never knew any of those things. That's why he's so *out there* as an actor. It's like he's experiencing everything for the first time."

Des thought she heard some small movements now in the forsythia bushes out behind the Dumpster. "We better get on that other trap," she whispered, tiptoeing around to the other cage and grabbing on to the string attached to its door.

Esme joined her. "Here, let me," she whispered, holding her hand out to Des.

That was when Des noticed the thin white lines on the inside of her wrist. Both wrists, in fact. On-screen, the makeup artists were able to cover them over. But up close and in person Des saw them instantly for what they were. Esme Crockett had tried to slit her wrists at some point in her past. Des found herself wondering what could possibly have driven someone so lovely, gifted, and privileged to want to end her life?

"Shhh, hear them . . . ?" she whispered, clutching the string anxiously.

Des did hear the tiny mewings. And now she could see the two of them coming out of the brush together. They were mixed gray, no more than four or five weeks old.

"Aren't they the sweetest?"

Des didn't like the unsteady way they were moving.

"Hi, babies," Esme cooed as they edged hungrily toward the baited cage, moving closer and closer. "Come get your breakfast. . . . Come on, babies. . . ."

Until they were inside the cage and Esme had yanked the door shut behind them.

"In the house!" Des called out, latching it shut.

Bella and Martine immediately joined them.

"I can't wait for Tito to see them!" Esme cried excitedly, clapping her hands together with girlish delight. "We're going to name them Spike and Mike."

Martine stood there looking down at them in grim silence. So did Bella.

"What, don't they look like a Spike and a Mike?" Esme asked.

What they looked like, all three rescuers knew only too well, was a pair of very, very sick little kitties. Their eyes were rheumy, their noses caked with pus, coats scabby and oozing with sores. Feline influenza, most likely. It was very common in the summer. If left untreated, it often led to pneumonia.

"They look awfully sick to me, honey," Martine said gently. "I think we'd better take them to the vet."

"What do *you* think, Des?" Esme asked.

"I don't meant to be your dream killer, but I think you should prepare yourself for the worst."

Esme let out a gasp of horror. "You mean he might put them to sleep?"

"They're very sick, tattela."

"It was real nice of you to alert us," Des added. "You've done them a solid, because they're *so* miserable."

"Mommy, *noooo*!" Esme threw herself into Martine's arms, weeping.

"We'll get you another pair," Martine promised, hugging her tightly.

"I don't *want* another pair! I want Spike and Mike! They're ours! We found them!" Now Esme released her mother, swiping at her eyes with the back of her hand. "Sorry, I don't mean to be such a baby. This is just so sad. And it's not their fault."

"Me, I'd like to take a baseball bat to whoever dumped them here," Bella growled.

"We do everything we can, honey," Martine said. "We get them neutered. We find homes for as many as we can. But the truth is that there are just too many kittens and not enough people to love them."

"Now, if you'd like to adopt a couple of good, healthy ones," Des offered brightly, "we can certainly help you out."

Esme tilted her head at Des curiously. "You mean you have some at your place?"

"We, uh, happen to have a few." Twenty-eight at last count. "Come on over, girl. Check'em out."

"No, no," Esme said abruptly. "I mean, thanks, but I don't think so."

Martine Crockett took her daughter by the hand now and led her back to Martine's 1967 silver Volkswagon Beetle convertible. They got in and drove off. Des and Bella loaded the cage with the sick kittens into the back of Bella's Jeep Wrangler with its personalized CATS22 license plate.

"What do you think?" Des asked her.

"I think Dr. Bill will put them down as soon as he lays eyes on them."

"No, I mean about *her*."

"Who, the great Esme Crockett?" Bella let out a hoot of derision. "I think she has the worst BO I ever smelled in my entire life."

Why did Martine tell her about Dodge's affair?

Des couldn't imagine. Being human, she also couldn't help wondering who the other woman was. She didn't say anything about it to Bella on the way home—she'd promised Martine she'd keep quiet, and she did. But it was certainly on her mind as they dropped off Spike and Mike with Dr. Bill, knowing full well they'd never see those two helpless kittens again. It was still on her mind when they pulled into her driveway in gloomy silence. She and Bella always felt lousy when a rescue mission turned out sour.

Bella marched straight inside to scrub the kitchen floor and listen to one of her Danny Kaye records, which was what she did when she was blue. Des hung out in the garage for a while with the Pointer Sisters, Mary J. Blige, Bootsy Collins, Master P, Jay-Z and the others that they *had* rescued. She cooed at each of them, stroking the ones who'd let her. Some, like Method Man, just hissed. No problem. He'd come around. Des was patient. She made sure they all had food and water, then went upstairs.

Des had bought and renovated a snug little cottage tucked into a hillside high above Uncas Lake. Mostly, she'd bought it for the sunlight. The living room, which she'd turned into her studio, had floor-to-ceiling windows overlooking the shimmering lake. Her kitchen and dining area were very airy and open, with French doors leading out onto the back deck, which had a teak dining table and chairs, and a dynamite view. The deck practically doubled her living space during warm months. There were three bedrooms, all of them small. The spare room was where Des worked out with twenty-pound dumbbells five mornings a week. Her weight room door was closed currently and there was a steady chorus of meows going on in there. Their five in-house cats were unable to resist the allure of a wet kitchen floor—whenever Bella was in scrub mode she herded them in there.

Des kept a portrait that she'd drawn of Mitch hanging over her bed. She'd drawn it when she was still trying to figure out how she felt about him. He looked very lost and sad in the portrait. He didn't look nearly so sad now. It was the only sample of her art that was visible anywhere in the house. She did not display her haunting portraits of murder victims that were her life's work and her way of coping with the horrors of her job. These she kept tucked away in a portfolio.

She did not like to look at them after she'd finished them.

Right now, Des snatched a graphite stick and Strathmore eighteen-by-twenty-four-inch sketch pad from her easel and started across the house with them as Mr. Danny Kaye was busy singing "Madam, I Love Your Crepes Suzette." Or make that shrieking. Des did not understand that man's appeal. Apparently, you had to be Jewish, old, and from Brooklyn in order to dig him. Also, possibly, deaf.

"I put your breakfast out on the deck," Bella called to her from the kitchen floor, where she was on her hands and knees, scrubbing away like an old-time washerwoman.

"You didn't have to make me breakfast, Bella."

"I did so," Bella shot back, scrubbing, scrubbing. There was a sponge mop, but she wouldn't go near it. "Otherwise you'll tromp all over my wet floor with your big feet."

"They are not big. They're *long*." Twelve and a half double A, to be exact. "Besides, Mitch likes them—especially my toes."

Bella made a face. "*Genug shen!*" Which was Yiddish for *No mas*. "I don't want to hear these things about you two."

"Don't blame me, girl. You're the one said I should snag me a Jewish gentleman."

"And did I steer you wrong?"

"Nope. Just don't tell him that—I don't want his ego swelling." Des tilted her head at Bella curiously. "Real, if I stick around long enough will I *ever* dig Danny Kaye?"

Bella puffed out her cheeks in disgust. "No one appreciates true talent anymore."

"Oh, is that what you call it?" she said sweetly.

"If you want to put on your Jill Scott, go ahead. It's your house."

"It's *our* house. And I'm just woofing on you." Des started out of the kitchen, then stopped. "We can't save them all, Bella."

"I know that," Bella said tightly.

Des went out onto the deck, closing the French doors behind her, and sat down at the table in front of her Grape Nuts, skim milk, and blueberries from Mitch's garden. It was a drowsy, humid morning. A young couple was paddling a canoe out on the lake, their giddy laughter carrying off the water as if they were right there next to Des. Otherwise, it was quiet enough that she could hear the cicadas whirring.

As she ate, she flipped through her drawing pad, looking at her latest work. Her figure drawing professor at the Dorset Academy of Fine Arts, a brilliant and maddening guru named Peter Weiss, had urged Des to take a complete break from her crime scene portraits this summer and draw nothing but trees, an exercise that he claimed would prove highly beneficial to her. He wouldn't explain why this was so, merely said, "You'll find out what I mean." Leaving Des to solve the mystery on her own. She'd tried to do what he said. Spent the past six weeks working on trees and trees only.

And, so far, the results had been a total disaster.

Page after page of her drawing pad was filled with one crude arboreal rendering after another. Her lush, midsummer oaks and maples looked like stick figures topped with meatballs. Her evergreens resembled television aerials. It all looked like something an eight-year-old kid would do. She'd tried graphite stick, vine charcoal, conte crayon, pen, pencil. The results were all the same: *dreck*.

Bella had been the soul of tact when Des showed them to her. "I like everything you do," she said.

Mitch, who was always brutally honest, had said, "Jellystone National Park—they look exactly like the background drawings from the old *Yogi the Bear* cartoons. Remember Yogi and Boo Boo?"

To which Des replied, "Back slowly out of the room while you are still able to."

Knowing full well that he was right. For some reason she kept drawing her way *around* the trees as opposed to getting inside of them. She wasn't *grasping* them. She'd tried to learn her way out of her personal abyss. Pored over book upon book by arborists and nature photographers. Studied the Connecticut shoreline's grand masters such as Childe Hassam, George Bruestle, and Henry Ward Ranger, landscape painters whose works she admired tremendously. But it was no use. Not any of it. She could not translate what her eyes saw into lines and contours and shapes. Her trees were two-dimensional, lifeless, and crude, her drawing hand stubbornly blind.

She slammed her sketch pad shut, boiling with confusion and frustration. Because there was no instruction manual for this, no road map that could direct her to her inner soul. There was only her. The wisdom was within her.

The enemy was within her.

All she could do about it now was punish herself physically. She stormed back down to her weight room. Out went the cats, in came the crazed artist. First, she stretched for twenty good minutes on her mat, freeing her mind, feeling the blood flow through her as she worked the kinks out of her lithe, loose-limbed body. Then she did one hundred push-ups and two hundred sit-ups. Then she hit the irons—two full circuits on her pressing bench with the twenty-pounders, two sets of twenty-four reps each time around. Pushing herself. Working it, working it, working it. Pump, breathe . . . Pump, breathe . . . Muscles straining, veins bulging, the sweat pouring off of her. Pump, breathe . . . Pump, breathe . . . Pump, breathe . . .

Why did Martine tell her about Dodge?

Des could not imagine. These blue-blooded locals genuinely perplexed her. They did not believe that the shortest way between two points was a straight line. They did not believe in lines—only negative space. And she did not know what to do about this. Mitch raved about Dodge Crockett day and night. Should she break it to him his new walking buddy was a snake? Or should she keep it to herself?

She made it through her last set of reps on adrenaline and fumes, and collapsed on the bench in a heap, gasping. She gulped down a bottle of water, then showered off.

Des spent very little time in front of the bathroom mirror these days. She wore no war paint. She needed none. She had almond-shaped pale green eyes, smooth glowing skin and a wraparound smile that could melt titanium from a thousand yards. She kept her hair so short and nubby that it was practically dry by the time she'd put on her summer-weight uniform and polished black brogans. She strapped on her crime-girl belt, complete with top-of-the-line SIG-Sauer semiautomatic handgun, and called out good-bye to Bella. Then she jumped into her cruiser and headed out.

Des lived in was what was considered a mixed neighborhood by Dorset standards, which meant it enjoyed a highly diverse white population. There were tidy starter houses owned by young professional couples. There were rambling bungalows bursting with multiple generations of blue-collar swamp Yankees. There were moldering summer cottages rented by old-timers from New Britain who played bocce out on their lawns. Right now her mail carrier, Frank, was out walking his golden retriever, and a pair of young mothers were on their way to the lake with a brood of kids, complete with pails, shovels, and water wings. They all waved to Des as she drove past. She raised a hand in response.

Summer was her busy season. Dorset's seaside renters nearly doubled the town's year-round population of less than seven thousand, plus the inns, motels, and campgrounds were filled to capacity. More people meant more traffic and more trouble. So did the warm weather. During the cold months, people did their drinking and their fighting behind closed doors. Now it all spilled out onto the front lawn. Dogs barked, tempers flared, neighbors started throwing punches at one another. It could get a little ugly.

And then, dear God, there were the tourists.

First, she headed for the historic district. The lawn in front of the old library on Dorset Street was being set up with chairs for a noon summer concert by Dorset's town band, which was quite accomplished if you happened to be into oompah music. Des rated their sound one solid notch below Danny Kaye on her own personal hit parade. The concert was part of a full day of quaint small-town activities. Crafts stalls were being erected next door on the lawn in front of Center School, where local artisans would be offering their handcrafted candles and soaps, their driftwood sculptures and wind chimes made of seashells and bits of broken glass. Des pulled in at town hall to see if there was anything of interest in her mail slot—there wasn't—and to work on Mary Ann, First Selectman Paffin's new secretary, a lonely widow who desperately needed to adopt two healthy, neutered kittens and just didn't know it yet. Then she resumed her patrol of the historic district, with its lovely two hundred-year-old homes, steepled white churches and graceful old oaks and sycamores. Trees again. Trees, trees, and more trees . . .

I should just give up and move to the damned desert.

The art academy was located in the historic district, in the old Gill House. So were the better galleries and antique dealers, the cemetery, firehouse, John's barbershop with its old Wildroot sign and barber pole.

It was only when she got to Big Brook Road and made a left that she returned to the twenty-first century. Here was Dorset's shopping center, which had an A & P, pharmacy, bank, hardware store, and so on. Across the two-lane road from it were the storefront businesses like the insurance and travel agencies, realtors and doctors. It was all exceedingly underwhelming. There was no ostentatious display of signage allowed in Dorset. No Golden Arches, no big box stores, no multiplexes. Most businesses were locally owned.

As a rule, the business district was quite laid back, too. Not much traffic, plenty of parking. It was possible to get around even during the summer. But not this summer. Not with Tito and Esme in town. News vans were crowded into parking spaces wherever they could find them. Des could spot crews from at least a dozen Connecticut and New York television stations, not to mention CNN, Fox News, *Entertainment Tonight*, and *Inside Edition*. News choppers hovered overhead. And the sidewalks were positively bursting with sunburned tourists cruising back and forth in the bright sun, back and forth, hoping to catch just one glimpse of *them*.

Madness. It was just plain madness.

As she nosed her way around, making her presence felt, Des came upon a genuine traffic jam at Clancy's ice cream parlor. Cars were at a total standstill. Drivers were even honking their horns, which was unheard-of in Dorset. She flicked on her lights and veered over the yellow line so she could get around to it. When she reached Clancy's she discovered a whale-sized white Cadillac Escalade double-parked out front with its doors locked. Its owner had simply left it there and walked away, blocking the entire lane of traffic. No one else in town could get by.

Des hopped out, straightening her big Smokey hat, and took a closer look. The big SUV had New Jersey plates. No special handicapped tag, no media or law enforcement markings. Just a selfish, thoughtless owner. Shaking her head, she got busy filling out a ticket. She was just finishing it when a middle-age guy with an expensive comb-over came sauntering toward her licking a double-scoop chocolate ice cream cone that he really, truly did not need. His gut was already straining hard against his tank top. It didn't help that he was wearing shorts. His skinny, pale legs just made his stomach look even bigger. Summer clothing was very unforgiving.

But not as unforgiving as the resident trooper of Dorset, Connecticut.

"Hey, I just went inside for a second," he protested when he caught sight of her. "One second."

"Sir, that was a very expensive second."

"Now you just hold on," he ordered her, as more drivers honked their horns. "You're *not* giving me a ticket over this."

"Oh, I most certainly am. You've created an unsafe situation, and you've inconvenienced a lot of people. Next time, park in the lot."

"The lot was full."

"Next time, wait," she said, as pedestrians began to gather around them, gawking.

"But everyone does it."

"Not in my town they don't."

"I don't fucking believe this!"

"Please watch your language, sir."

"You've got a real attitude, haven't you, doll?"

"Sir, I am not a doll. I am Master Sergeant Desiree Mitry of the Connecticut State Police, and you are illegally parked." She tore off the ticket and held it out to him.

He refused to take it. Just stood there in surly defiance, his ice cream melting under the hot sun and running down his wrist. Too often, Des had discovered, people on vacation were people at their worst. In their view, the world pushed them around seven days a week, fifty weeks out of the year. When they got their two weeks off, they felt entitled to shove back.

"Take the citation, sir," Des ordered him in a calm, steady voice. "Take it and relocate your vehicle at once. If you don't, I will place you under arrest."

"What is it, Tommy?" His slender frosted-blond wife was approaching them now, two appallingly fat little kids in tow, both eating ice cream cones. "What's wrong?"

"Aw, nothing," he growled, snatching the ticket from Des disgustedly. "You give some entry-level person a little taste of power and right away they bust your balls."

Des knew all about this. "Entry-level person" was a code phrase for *N-e-g-r-o*. But she had learned long ago not to mix it up with jerks. It wasn't as if they got any smarter if she did. She simply flashed her mega-wattage smile, and said, "You folks have yourselves a real nice vacation." And stood there, hands on her hips, while they piled back in their SUV and took off.

Once the traffic flow returned to normal she got back in her own ride and continued on down Big Brook Road, making her rounds, her mind still working it, working it, working it . . .

Why did Martine tell her about Dodge?

Chapter 3

Why did Dodge tell him about Martine?

Mitch couldn't imagine. And it weighed on his mind all morning. It was there while he logged some quality loud time on his beloved sky blue Fender Stratocaster, doggedly chasing after Hendrix's signature opening to "Voodoo Chile," deafening twin reverb amps, wawa pedal and all. It was there while he helped Bitsy Peck move an apple tree to a sunnier spot in her yard, in exchange for unlimited access to her corn patch. It was there while Mitch steered his bulbous, plum-colored 1956 Studebaker pickup across the causeway toward town: Why had the older man chosen to confide in him this way? It wasn't as if the two of them were that close. Not like, say, Dodge was to Will, who was practically like a son to him. So why had he? Only one possible explanation made any sense to Mitch:

Because it was Will who was sleeping with Martine.

True, Martine was fifteen years older than Will. True, Will was supposedly happily married to Donna. But there was no denying that Martine Crockett was still a major babe. And Will was an exceedingly buff younger man. Plus Will had grown up around Martine, meaning that he'd doubtless harbored moist, Technicolor fantasies about her since he was thirteen. What healthy young boy wouldn't have? Certainly, this would explain why Dodge had flashed such a hard stare at Will on the beach this morning.

Because it was Will who was sleeping with Martine.

Mitch was supposed to meet Des for a low-fat lunch at The Works, but as he reached Old Shore Road he noticed that his gas tank was almost half empty. Probably ought to fill up at the Citgo minimart on his way, he reflected. A very nice, hardworking young couple from Turkey, Nuri and Nema Acar, had recently taken over the operation, and Mitch liked to throw his business their way. So did a lot of the local workmen, whose pickups were nosed up to the squat, rectangular building like a herd of cattle.

Mitch pulled up at the pump and hopped out. The Citgo was that rarest of modern-day phenomena, a full-service station. But only tourists and summer people sat there in their cars and waited for Nuri to pump their gas for them, clad in his immaculate short-sleeved dress shirt and slacks. True locals got out and pumped it themselves. When Mitch was done filling up he went inside to pay his money and respects to Nema.

Just like the half dozen other guys who were gathered there at her counter, their tongues hanging out.

Lew the Plumber was there. Drew Archer, the town's best cabinetmaker, was there. So was Dennis Allen, who serviced the village's septic tanks. Mitch knew those three well enough to say hello to. The others he knew by sight. They were Nema's regulars, just like Mitch. Could be found there at the Citgo almost every morning between the hours of ten-thirty and eleven. Although not a one of them referred to the place as the Citgo.

They called it the House of Turkish Delights.

Because the Acars offered way, way more than the usual minimart menu of candy, soda, and Lotto tickets. They offered Nema's own homemade native pastries and deliciously strong, sweet Turkish coffee. Her baklava was the best Mitch had ever tasted. She also made boreks, which were triangles of layered, wafer-thin pastry filled with chopped nuts and cinnamon. And lalangas, which were fried pastry dipped in syrup and brushed with powdered sugar. The lalangas were especially popular with the workmen who'd grown up on fried dough, a regional delicacy.

The House of Turkish Delights was Dorset's best-kept secret. The local workmen, who considered The Works a yuppified tourist trap, had staked it out as *their* place. And so they told no one about it. Mitch sure as hell didn't. He didn't dare tell Will that he was buying pastry from his competitor, and he couldn't breathe so much as a word to Des—every time he inhaled the air in there he was breaking his diet.

The Acars were the first native-born Turks ever to live in Dorset. They were in their early thirties. Nema was tiny and slender, with large, lustrous dark eyes that reminded Mitch of the '50s film actress Ina Balin. Always, she wore a Muslim headscarf. Nuri was courtly and unfailingly polite. Almost but not quite unctuous. The two of them were from Istanbul, where Nuri had graduated from Bosporus University with a degree in mathematics. Nema told Mitch they had emigrated to America because their parents didn't approve of the marriage. Mitch couldn't imagine why they didn't, since any two people who could work side by side fourteen hours a day and never stop smiling clearly belonged together.

"And how are you today, Mr. Berger, sir?" Nema said to him as Mitch pointed directly to the lalanga that had his name on it.

"I'd feel a lot better if you'd call me Mitch."

"Very well, but you are a naughty, naughty boy, Mr. Mitch."

"God, don't tell me a certain resident trooper stopped by."

"No, no. I was reading your review in this morning's newspaper, of *The Dark Star*, and you almost made me spit up my orange juice." Nema let out a devilish little cackle. "Most amusing and yet insightful."

He thanked her and hopped back into his truck, waving to Nuri, who was filling the tank of a minivan that had New York plates. Then Mitch resumed his trip into town, devouring his gustatory no-no in hungry, fat-boy bites.

It was not easy to find a parking place near The Works. Not with all of the news crew vans and tourists taking up every available curb-side space. Mitch had to leave his truck in the A & P parking lot and hoof it two blocks. The traffic on Big Brook Road was unbelievably hectic. Some nut in an immense white Cadillac Escalade almost ran him down when he tried to cross the street. Honestly, he would not mind when Labor Day arrived and everyone left. Because Dorset didn't feel like Dorset right now. It felt like a resort town crowded with hyperactive strangers. And this upset Mitch's new sense of order in his life. New York was his place for rushing around on noisy streets that were teeming with people. Dorset was his place for quiet reflection. Briefly, he wondered if he was feeling bothered this way because he was becoming rigid and middle-aged.

He decided this could not be possible.

Dorset's sprawling 130-year-old piano works had provided jobs for generations of highly skilled local workers until it shut its doors in the 1970s. Often, there had been talk of leveling the abandoned riverfront factory. Instead, Will and Donna Durslag had rescued it. Not a small undertaking. They'd had to sandblast its red brick, reroof it, repoint the mortar, restore the windows—and that was just the shell. Inside, the 148,000-square-foot factory had no plumbing or wiring, no heat, no nothing. But the architect and contractor who'd tackled the job were tremendously talented, and the transformation was remarkable. The old brick eyesore was now a lively European-style food hall with stalls selling fresh, locally grown produce and eggs, cheeses, olives, fresh-baked breads and desserts, pizza, gelato, fresh fruit smoothies. There was a coffee bar that stayed open until ten at night. There were nuts and grains sold in bulk, coffee beans, teas, spices. There was a butcher, a fishmonger, a deli counter offering salads and sandwiches and take-home meals like veal piccata and meat loaf.

An informal eating area anchored the center of the hall with tables and chairs where people could meet for a sandwich or read the newspaper over a cup of coffee. An arcade housed shops like Jeff's Book Schnook and a wine store. Several of the retail spaces still hadn't been leased yet. There were condominium apartments that faced right out onto a newly constructed riverfront boardwalk. These were mostly occupied.

Mitch did not see Des there yet so he stopped in to sign books for Jeff, as promised. A glass wall separated his shop from the food hall. The first time Mitch had walked in the door of the Book Schnook he knew instantly that it was every publishing person's dream bookshop. It felt more like a private library than it did a place of business.

The space was two stories high with towering dark-wood bookcases. Rolling library ladders allowed customers to reach the higher volumes. A spiral staircase led up to a wraparound loft where there were even more books. Jeff had filled his place with cozy armchairs and brass reading lamps. There was a huge fireplace in the old red brick exterior wall, and tons of little nooks and crannies where customers could browse for hours in front of the windows as sailboats scudded past on the Connecticut River. Often, some very tasty music was playing. Right now, Ella Fitzgerald was singing Cole Porter.

Jeff's shelving system was beyond quirky. Nothing, but nothing, was alphabetical. His own favorite authors were arranged near the front on a wall of shelves he called Store Picks. It was a fluid and eclectic array, subject to his latest whim. This week, his picks included the contemporary novelist Richard Ford, British-born travel writer Jonathan Raban, the late food essayist M.F.K. Fisher, the bleak '50s hardboiled crime writer Jim Thompson, Dorothy Parker, Emily Dickinson, Philip K. Dick, Wallace Stegner and H.L. Mencken.

Popular sellers that Jeff didn't like but had to offer were stashed way up on the second-floor shelves. If it was Mary Higgins Clark that a customer wanted, or a copy of *The Corrections* by Jonathan Franzen, Jeff made them go climb for it. It was his store and his system. And it was just about the choicest bookstore Mitch had ever been in. Jeff had everything a bookseller could ask for.

Everything except for customers. The Book Schnook was deserted. And so silent after the din of the food hall outside that Mitch felt as if he'd just entered a shul.

The little guy in his crooked black-framed glasses was dusting stock in hushed solitude when Mitch got there, sucking his cheeks in and out in a decidedly carplike manner. Jeff's shopkeeper outfit wasn't much different from his hiking outfit. He still wore shorts and sandals with dark socks. Only his shirt was different—Jeff had on an oversized Book Schnook T-shirt adorned with a portrait of Dan Quayle and the store's motto: A Mind Is a Terrible Thing to Lose.

"Hey, Mitch, good to see you!" he exclaimed, dashing back to his storeroom. He returned a moment later toting two cartons of Mitch's paperback reference volumes. They began unloading them onto a library table. "You're doing me a real favor, man. Believe me, I need all of the help I can get."

"Jeff, I'm an author," Mitch chided him gently. "You're the one who's helping me."

He got started signing the books, passing each one along so Jeff could slap an Autographed by Author sticker on its cover. As they worked their way through the stack a boy of twelve or so came in the door, looking very intimidated.

"What can I do for you, buddy?" Jeff called to him encouragingly.

"I-I was just wondering if the new *Codfather* book came in yet," he stammered, his voice soaring several octaves.

"I don't sell that garbage in my store," Jeff snarled in response. "Try Borders. Try Amazon. *Anywhere* but here, got it?"

Which sent the little kid scurrying out the door in bug-eyed terror.

"I can see you're really working on your people skills," Mitch observed.

"*Ab-so-tootly*," Jeff responded with great sincerity. "The old me wouldn't have mentioned those other outlets at all." On Mitch's doubtful look he added, "Mitch, we have to measure our progress in inches. I learned that from my dear sweet mother, right along with another heartwarming chestnut: 'You'll never amount to anything.' That's why Abby dumped me, you know. She thinks I *want* to fail because deep down inside I think I deserve to. Didn't want to be around my vibe anymore. Said it was contagious. What do *you* think?"

"I think that you have a beautiful shop and you should be very proud."

"You really think so?" he asked Mitch imploringly.

Needy. That was the word to describe Jeff Wachtell.

"I really do," Mitch assured him.

Pleased, Jeff began moving Mitch's signed books to a prominent spot by the front door. Mitch browsed a bit. Among Jeff's Store Picks he spotted a paperback copy of *Horseman, Pass By,* the slender first novel by Larry McMurtry that Martin Ritt had made into the movie *Hud*. Mitch had lost his copy and had been meaning to reread it, so he brought one up to the counter and paid Jeff for it.

As Jeff rang it up he started sucking his cheeks in and out again, peering at Mitch uncertainly. "Mind if I ask you something else? I just scored Abby's tour itinerary from her Web site, and she's making her way straight through Connecticut this week on her way to Boston. She's already stopping at C. C. Willoughby and Company in Sussex, right? And her publicist, Chrissie Huberman, is here in town with Esme and Tito, right? Would it be out of line for me to ask her if she'd maybe schedule Abby to stop *here*? Abby sure would bring in the customers."

"Jeff, you don't carry any of your wife's books, remember?"

"I could have fifty copies of *The Codfather of Sole* here by noon tomorrow," he said in a determined voice. "All I have to do is pick up the phone."

Mitch raised his eyebrows at him. "This is a tectonic shift for you."

"Dead on," he acknowledged, adjusting his glasses. "But I need to make certain allowances if I'm going to survive in this business. What do you think?"

"I think this is a very healthy development."

"No, I mean about me approaching Crissie."

"Why don't you just talk to Abby?"

Jeff shook his head vigorously. "We only speak through our lawyers—at a cost of three hundred and fifty bucks an hour. Saying 'Hi, how are you?' runs me twenty-nine ninety-five."

"I guess it couldn't hurt. The worst thing Chrissie can do is say no, right?"

"Right," Jeff agreed, a bit less than convinced. "Thanks, man."

Mitch headed back out to the food hall with his book. It was lunchtime and the place was teeming with hungry Dorseteers, the din of their voices rising up toward the skylights. A lot of them were lined up at the deli counter. Mitch took his place at the end of the line, watching Donna merrily take phone orders, chat up customers, and move the line along with a smooth assist from Rich Graybill, the young chef they'd brought in to help manage the place. Will was busy horsing a huge basket of baguettes over from the bakery. All three of them were moving at an astonishing speed. It takes superhuman energy to work in the food trade, Will once told Mitch. Mitch believed it.

As he got closer to the counter, Mitch carefully studied the enticing platters and bowls on display in the refrigerated case, his stomach growling.

Now Donna was serving the young woman in line ahead of him. "What can I get you, Marilyn? God, I love your hair. Who did it? I've got to go see her. Mine looks just like a Brillo pad. . . . Shut up, it does so."

Mitch liked Donna a lot. She was peppery and funny, and she held nothing back. Always, her pink face was lit with a warm, genuine smile. She liked being who she was. Donna was a bit on the short side, nearly a foot shorter than Will, and more than a bit on the chubby side. And her hair did look like a Brillo pad, frizzy and black with streaks of premature gray. She wore a blue denim apron with The Works stitched across it, as did everyone who served food there.

"Hey there, stretch, what can I get for you today?" she asked, squinting at Mitch through her wire-rimmed glasses with feigned astonishment. "Time out, Berger, is that *you*? My God, you're nothing but skin, bone, and wrinkled khaki." Donna had a pronounced Boston accent, the flat, Southie kind. "How much weight have you lost this summer, fifteen pounds?"

"Ten pounds . . . well, nine."

"That's a lot, Mitch," Will said, unloading his basket of baguettes.

"Not enough to satisfy a certain resident trooper."

"Oh, what does that scrawny gazelle know about poundage?" Donna shot back. "Me, I like a full-bodied man. A man whose ass is bigger than mine. That's all any woman wants."

"So that's it," Will joked. "I always wondered."

"Okay, I'm getting mixed signals here," Mitch told her. "You and Des have to get on the same page."

"Not a chance. She's the one who sees you naked. I just sell you food. Not that I wouldn't like to trade places."

"Donna, are you making a play for me in front of your husband?"

"It's okay, Mitch, I'm used to it," Will said, smiling at her.

Mitch studied their playful banter closely, wondering if Will *was* cheating on her with Martine. He had no idea. None.

Donna said, "If you're *not* going to whisk me away to Bermuda on your yacht then you'll have to place an order. This is a business, Berger. I can't just stand here all afternoon talking dirty."

Mitch went for the grilled shrimp Caesar salad, an onion minibaguette and a fresh-squeezed orange juice. He placed it all on a tray and ambled over toward an empty table, pleased to see that people at three different tables were intently reading his review of *Dark Star* in that morning's paper. Mitch enjoyed watching people read his work. He was not alone in this—it was just about every journalist's guiltiest pleasure. He sat and opened his book, keeping an eye on the big glass doors to the street.

Des came striding through them a few minutes later and made her way lithely across the bustling food hall, a supremely relaxed smile on her face as her eyes alertly took in everyone and everything in the place. She was becoming an exceptionally good resident trooper, Mitch felt. She was confident, helpful, and straight with everyone. People in town genuinely respected her. Plus there was a refreshing absence of head games with Des. She didn't try to bully or intimidate anyone. She didn't need to. Whatever came along, she knew she could handle it.

Mitch loved the way her face lit up when she caught sight of him seated there. Loved the special smile that she reserved for him and him alone. As she started toward him he wondered what would happen to him if she were not in his life right now. He would go right down the drain, that's what.

But she must never know this—she thinks I'm the one who has it all together.

They did not kiss when she got to his table. Des had an ironclad rule about Public Displays of Affection when she was in uniform.

But there was no avoiding the way they glowed in each other's presence. Just as there was no missing the curious glances that they got from neighboring tables. Because they were a different kind of couple, no question. And when you're different people wonder about you. The glances didn't bother either of them one bit. They knew how happy they were together.

"Hey, bod man," she said, her pale green eyes shining at him from behind her horn-rims.

"Back at you, Master Sergeant."

"I'm going to fetch me some lunch."

"Lucky me," Mitch said brightly.

She cocked her head at him curiously. "How so?"

"Now I get to watch you walk away," he replied, rubbing his hands together eagerly. Among her many attributes, Des Mitry possessed one of the world's top ten cabooses.

"Dawg, would you be talking trash at me?"

"I'm sure trying."

"You'd better behave yourself before I perform a strip search."

"Could I please get that in writing?"

She let out a big whoop and headed over toward the deli counter, her big leather belt creaking, her stride long, athletic, and totally lacking in self-consciousness. She wasn't showing off her form. Didn't need to. Des knew perfectly well what she had. She kidded around with Donna for a minute, then returned with a Greek salad and an iced tea, and sat across from Mitch, her brow furrowing intently. She had something unsettling on her mind. He knew her well enough to know this.

Mitch raised his orange juice in a toast. "Here's looking at you, kid."

"Wait, wait, I *know* this one! We watched it together. Humphrey Bogart, right?"

"In? . . ."

"Um, was it *The Maltese Falcon*?"

"Almost, it was *Casablanca*. But you were *so* close that we're going to give you one of our very fine consolation prizes."

"Which is? . . ."

"Me."

"And if I'd won—what would I have gotten then?"

"Me."

"Sounds like I can't lose," she said, attacking her salad hungrily. "Looks like I've got me some catching up to do, though. I see you've already had your dessert. I'm guessing something from the doughnut food group."

"Wait, what are you talking about?"

"Powdered sugar on your collar, boyfriend."

He glanced down at the collar of his short-sleeved khaki shirt. There were indeed tiny flecks of white there. "I can't put anything over on you, can I?"

"Don't even try. I'm a trained detective. Besides, I know you. Whenever you're upset about something you break your diet."

"I'm not like you, you know," Mitch said defensively. "I can't survive on such a drastically reduced food intake. Pretty soon you'll have me subsisting on a handful of vitamin pills, just like the Jetsons."

"Well, at least you've moved off of Yogi and Boo Boo," she said tartly.

"I sure do wish you'd let me take that one back."

"Not even. You told me the truth. That's what I need to hear if I'm going to get any better. Hell, that's why I keep you around."

"So that's it."

Des gazed at him steadily from across the table. "What's going on, baby?"

"You first."

"Me first what?"

"Something's bothering you, too, isn't it?"

"No way. You broke your diet—you go first."

"Okay, I can accept that. But we have to keep this between us, okay?" Mitch leaned over the table toward her, lowering his voice. "Dodge Crockett dropped a neutron bomb on me this morning—Martine is having an affair."

"My, my," Des responded mildly. "Isn't *this* interesting."

56

Mitch frowned at her. "You're not reacting the way I thought you would at all. You seem . . . relieved."

"Only because I am," Des confessed. "Real, Martine told me this morning that *Dodge* was having an affair."

"No way!"

"Oh, most definitely way."

"Well, who with?"

"She didn't say. Why, did he? . . ."

"No, not a word," Mitch said, electing to keep his hunch about Will to himself. At least for now.

"Well, this is certainly tangled up in weird," she said, taking a gulp of her iced tea. "I wonder why they've dumped it on us."

"Why pick the same morning?" Mitch wondered. "And why pick *us*?"

She considered it for a moment, her eyes narrowing shrewdly. "I hate to say this, but part of me feels like we're being moved around."

"Moved around how?"

"She told me about Dodge's affair so she could get out in front of any rumors about her own. This way, if word leaks out that she's seeing someone, people will say 'The poor dear had no choice—Dodge has been cheating on her for months.'"

"You think he told me about her for the very same reason?"

"It's a theory, Mitch."

"But that would mean they're expecting us to blab this all over town."

"Not very flattering, is it?"

"Not in the least," Mitch said indignantly. "Dodge told it to me in confidence. I'd never run out and tell everyone in Dorset that Martine is . . . Wait, what am I saying? This isn't Dorset, it's Peyton god-damned Place." He paused, poking at the remains of his lunch with his plastic fork. "Do you think they'll stay together?"

Des shrugged her shoulders. "This may be totally normal behavior for them. Some couples get off on the jealousy. It lights their fire. Hell, for all we know this whole business could be nothing more than air guitar."

"As in they're not really playing?"

"What I'm saying."

"Is that what you think is going on?"

"Boyfriend, I wouldn't even try to guess."

"Neither would I," said Mitch, who had learned one sure thing about Dorset since he'd moved here: no one, absolutely no one, was who he or she appeared to be. Everyone was fronting. That didn't necessarily mean you didn't like or admire people like the Crocketts, it just meant you didn't know them. They didn't let you. "The Crocketts seemed like the perfect couple, too."

"There is no such thing," Des said with sudden vehemence. "And there's no such thing as the face of a dying marriage either." She was drawing on her own painful breakup with Brandon, Mitch knew full well. "If they choose to, a couple like the Crocketts can hide what's really going on from *everyone*."

"So what are we supposed to do now?"

"Besides keep our mouths shut? Not a thing. Not unless they ask us for help." She finished her salad and shoved her plate away. "I did me some hanging with Esme this morning."

"What's she like?"

"Sweet, childlike—at times it seems like nobody's home."

"That's why they call them actors. They're not like you and me. They're instruments. When they aren't performing they're no different than the cello that you see lying on its side in the orchestra room, waiting to be picked up and played."

"If that's the case then why does everybody worship them?"

"They don't. They worship the fantasy that's up on the screen. The performers just have a bit of the stardust sprinkled on them, that's all. It's all about the fantasy. People vastly prefer it to reality, which is depressing and painful and filled with really bad smells. Reality they already know plenty about." Mitch gazed at her searchingly. "Des? . . ."

"What is it, baby?"

"Let's not play games like that with each other."

"Games I can deal with. You sleeping with another woman, that's something different." She drained her iced tea. "Damn, I'm thirsty today."

"Want me to get you a refill?"

"What are you trying to do, spoil me?"

"That's the general idea."

"Yum, I could get used to this idea."

He grabbed her Styrofoam cup and climbed to his feet. "Excuse me, weren't you going to say something?"

"Such as? . . ."

"Such as how lucky you are—you get to watch me walk away."

Des let out her whoop. "Word, you are the only man I've ever been with who can make me laugh."

"Is this is a positive thing?"

"Boyfriend, this is a huge thing."

"Well, okay. Remember now, no wolf whistles." He yanked up his shorts, threw back his shoulders and went galumphing back to the counter for a refill.

"Well, well," Donna said to him teasingly. "The resident trooper certainly has you well trained."

"Nonsense. We like to do favors for each other."

"I think that's very nice," spoke up Will, who was working a baked ham through the meat slicer. "Don't listen to my wife, Mitch. I certainly don't."

"I'm just jealous," she said. "The last time Will fetched something for me was . . . actually, Will has *never* fetched anything for me."

Mitch was watching her refill the iced tea when he suddenly heard *it*—the reverent hush that comes over a room when someone famous walks in. It was as if a spell had been cast over the entire food hall. The boisterous beachgoers and tourists all fell eerily silent, their mouths hanging half-open, eyes bulging with fascination. All movement ceased.

Mitch swiveled around, his own eyes scanning the hall. It was Tito and Esme, of course. They were walking directly toward the deli counter, hand in hand, with Chrissie Huberman running interference. The celebrity publicist wore an oversized man's dress shirt, white linen pants, and a furious expression—because the three of them were *not* alone.

"A little *space*, guys!" Chrissie blustered at the herd of photographers and tabloid TV cameramen who were dogging their every step, crab-walking, tripping over each other, shouting questions, shouting demands as Tito and Esme did their best to pretend they weren't there. Chrissie threw elbows and hips to keep them at bay. She was no one to mess with. She was a strapping, big-boned blond with a snow-shovel jaw and lots of sharp edges. Also the hottest client list in New York. Everything about Chrissie Huberman was hot, including her own image. She was married to a rock promoter who ran an East Village dance club. "Damn it, give us some room to breathe, will you?" she screamed, as the golden couple strode along toward the deli counter, just like two perfectly normal young people out for a perfectly normal lunch.

Hansel and Gretel, Dodge had called them.

Esme had cascading blond ringlets and impossibly innocent blue eyes. Her features were so delicate that Mitch had once called her the only woman on the planet who could make Michelle Pfeiffer look like Ernest Borgnine. She wore a gauzy shift and, seemingly, nothing underneath it. Her breasts jiggled with every step, the outline of her nipples clearly apparent through the flimsy material.

Tito Molina was not a big man, no more than five feet ten and a wiry 165 pounds. And yet his physical presence commanded just as much attention as that of his fantastically erotic young wife. Tito had the edginess of a pent-up bobcat as he made his way across the food hall, that same sexually charged intensity that Steve McQueen once had. The man smoldered. He was unshaven, his long, shiny blue black hair uncombed, and was carelessly dressed in a torn yellow T-shirt, baggy surfer trunks, and sandals. No different from half the young guys in town. And yet he looked like no other guy. No one else had his incandescent blue eyes or flawless complexion that was the color of fine suede. No one else had his perfectly chiseled nose, high, hard cheekbones, and finely carved lips. No one else was Tito Molina.

"Here you go, Berger. . . . ." Donna was holding Des's iced tea out to him. Mitch was still staring at the golden couple. "Earth to Mr. Berger, Mr. Mitch Berger . . ."

"Sorry, Donna," he apologized, taking the cup from her as Tito and Esme arrived at the counter with Chrissie and their tabloid retinue.

Mitch was starting his way back toward his table when he suddenly felt a hand on his arm. It was Tito's hand.

"Did I just hear what I thought I heard?" Tito's voice was tinged with a faint barrio inflection. "Are you that film critic guy?"

"That's me," Mitch said to him, smiling. "That film critic guy."

"Okay, this is good," Tito said, nodding his head up, down, up, down. He was so wired that sparks were coming off of him. "I wanted to let you know what I thought of your review in today's paper."

"Sure, all right," Mitch said, keeping his voice low. He did not want to get into a very public shouting match with Tito Molina. Neither of them would come away the winner. "Go ahead and tell me what's on your—"

Mitch never got another word out—Tito coldcocked him flush on the jaw. The punch connected so fast Mitch didn't see it coming. Just flew straight over backward, the back of his head slamming hard against the floor.

"Tito, *no!*" Mitch heard Esme scream as he lay there, blinking, dazed. "Tito, stop it!"

Now Tito was astride Mitch with both hands wrapped around his throat, trying to squeeze the very life out of him as the tabloid cameramen crowded around them, catching every last bit of it. "How do you like *my* review, hunh?!" the young star screamed at him, pelting Mitch with his spittle. "You *like* it?!"

Mitch could not respond. Could not, in fact, breathe.

Not one of the cameramen tried to pull the actor off of him. They were too busy egging them on.

"You gonna let him get away with that, Mitch!?"

"Throw down, Mitch! Go for it!"

The folks who'd been shopping and eating were getting in on it, too, clustering around them as if this were a street theater performance. Tourists filmed the fracas with their camcorders as Tito continued to choke him, Mitch lying there on the floor like a rag doll, his limbs flailing helplessly. No one seemed to care that he was actually about to die.

It was Will Durslag who vaulted over the counter and yanked the lunatic off him, grabbing Tito roughly by the scruff of the neck. "Let him go, man! Let him go, right now!"

"Get your hands off of me!" Tito spat, struggling in the bigger man's grasp.

"Tito, stop!" Esme sobbed, tears rolling down her cheeks. "Please! . . ."

Now Des had muscled her way through the crowd to Mitch, crouching over him with a stricken expression on her face. "Are you okay? Need an ambulance?"

"No, no, I'm fine," Mitch croaked. "Never better." He sat up slowly, gaacking much the same way Clemmie did when she was trying to bring up a six-inch fur ball. His Adam's apple felt as if someone had just driven a dull spike into it. And his jaw felt numb. He fingered it gingerly, opening and closing his mouth. Everything still seemed to work. "How come I'm . . . all wet?"

"You're sitting in my iced tea."

Will was still going at it with Tito. "I want you out of my market, man!"

"Go to hell!" Tito snarled back at him.

"No, *you* go to hell! You are in *my* place and *I* make the rules here!"

"All right, gentlemen, let's chill out," Des barked, stepping in between the two of them. "Mr. Molina, you need to get a hold of yourself at once, are you comprehending me?"

Tito didn't respond. Esme and Chrissie immediately surrounded him, Chrissie murmuring soothing words at him while Esme hugged him and kissed him.

"Please step back, everyone," Des told the crowd. "Please step back now. And I want these damned cameras out of my face!" she roared angrily.

Miraculously, the paparazzi beat a hasty retreat. Des had explained this phenomenon to Mitch once: no one, not even the lowest tabloid whore, wants to be around a sister when she's armed and pissed.

Esme and Chrissie seemed to be calming Tito down now. He stood there nodding his head obediently as he listened to them, his shoulders slumped, eyes fastened on the floor.

"How are you feeling, Mr. Molina?" Des asked him.

"I'm cool," he said quietly, running a hand through his long, shiny hair. "Everything's cool. No big."

Now Chrissie hurried over to Mitch and said, "God, Mr. Berger, I am *so* sorry about this. If there's *anything* I can do to make it right, just name it."

Mitch sat there in the cold puddle of tea, fingering his jaw. "I'm fine."

The commotion had brought Jeff Wachtell out of his store. "Mitch, I saw the whole thing if you need a witness."

"I'm *fine,*" Mitch repeated.

"Can you walk?" Des asked him.

"I can try," he said, struggling unsteadily to his feet.

"Okay, good, my ride's outside," Des said. "We'll sort this out at the Westbrook Barracks together."

"Whatever you say," Tito said with weary resignation. "You're the man."

"Wait, what's to sort out?" Mitch asked.

Des raised an eyebrow at him, clearly wondering if he was punch-drunk. "The paperwork, Mitch. You have to swear out a formal complaint before we can file criminal assault charges."

"No way," Mitch said hastily. "That's absolutely not happening."

Tito gazed at Mitch, stunned.

He wasn't the only one. Des moved over closer to him, hands on her hips, and said, "What do you *mean*? That man just had his hands wrapped around your throat."

"He was only trying to make a point."

"Yes, that's he's a homicidal lunatic. Guess what? He succeeded."

"Des, we had a simple professional disagreement. He sucker punched me and I slipped on an ice cube. It was really no big deal."

"Mitch, he tried to kill you! You can't let him off the hook just because he's famous."

"I'm not."

She shook her head at him. "Okay, then I don't understand."

"This is already going to be bad enough, media-wise. Do you have any what idea what'll happen to me if it actually heads to court? I'll become a tabloid freak. I'll never be taken seriously as a critic again. My reputation will be ruined. My *life* will be ruined. This is my worst nightmare, Des. Just forget about it, *please*."

"I can't," she said stubbornly. "I'm not satisfied."

"Fine, then tell me how to satisfy you," he shot back.

"Yes, please, Des," Esme said pleadingly as the tabloid cameramen quietly, inevitably, rolled back in like the tide, the shoppers crowding in behind them.

Des stood there in judicious silence for a moment, chin resting on her fist. "Okay, I want you two men to smack meat."

"You want us to *what?*" Tito asked incredulously.

"Shake hands, or I'm running you both in."

"You're kidding, right?" Mitch said to her.

"I said it and I meant it. I don't tolerate fighting in my town. This is Dorset, not Dodge City."

"True enough," Mitch said. "But we're not in the Cub Scouts anymore, Des. We're a pair of grown men and—"

"Smack meat!" Des snapped. "Or we're going for a ride."

Mitch shrugged his shoulders and stuck a hand out. Tito Molina shook it, his own hand smaller and softer than Mitch was expecting. The media horde duly recorded it for posterity.

"What do you have to say, Mitch?" one cameraman asked him.

"Not a thing," Mitch answered curtly. "I spoke my piece, Tito spoke his."

"Sure you don't want to take a poke at him?"

"What do *you* say, Tito?" another paparazzi called out.

"Get your own damned life," Tito snarled, instantly tensing all over again. "Stop living off of mine, hunh?"

"All right, let's go!" Des said, herding them away.

The scene was over. The cameramen headed for the doors, anxious to run with what they had. The shoppers dispersed.

"Hey, Chrissie!" Jeff called out to the publicist, who was fending off the autograph seekers in Esme's face. "Can I have a quick word with you?"

Chrissie shot an impatient glance his way, then a slower double take. "Wait, I know you. . . ."

"I'm Jeff Wachtell, better known as Mr. Abby Kaminsky."

Chrissie smirked at him faintly. "Oh, sure, and I should be standing here talking to you because . . . ?"

"I was just wondering if you could convince Abby to swing by for a signing at the Book Schnook," Jeff said, sucking his cheeks in and out. "She'll be coming right past Dorset on her way to and from Boston, and it sure would help me out a lot. What do you say, will you ask her?"

Chrissie raised her jutting jaw at him. "This is like a joke, right?"

"No, I'm perfectly serious."

"Jeffrey, let me see if I can draw you a picture. My client wishes to see you stripped naked, hung by your thumbs—actually, not your thumbs but a much, much tinier part of your anatomy—and slowly pecked to death by hungry birds."

"Does that mean no?"

"It means," Chrissie replied, "that she thinks you are the lowest, most contemptible creature on the face of the earth. If I so much as mention to her that I bumped into you today she'll need a cold compress and a Valium. You ruined her life. She detests you. Am I getting through to you now?" And with that she turned on her heel and ushered Esme toward the door.

"Maybe this is a bad time," Jeff hollered after her in vain. "Could we talk about it later?"

Tito made a point of hanging back, sidling his way over toward

Mitch with the predatory stealth of Jack Palance in *Shane*. Des was about to intercede but Mitch held up his hand, stopping her. He did not want her fighting his battles for him.

"Just one more thing, critic guy," Tito said to him, his voice low and murderous, blue eyes boring in on Mitch's. "I don't want to see you in here again. If I do, I'll mess you up for real. And I don't care if your bitch is around to protect you or not, *understand?*"

It had been a long time since Mitch had been in this position. But as he stood there in The Works, nose to nose with Tito Molina, Mitch was right back in Stuyvesant Town all over again, a porky twelve-year-old going jaw to jaw with Bruce Cooperman, the playground bully who wouldn't let him pass through the gate to the basketball court. Mitch had known what he had to do then and he knew what he had to do now. He stared right back at him and said, "This town is where I live, and you don't tell me where I can or cannot go. If you want to fight, we'll fight. But we won't do it in front of the cameras. We'll do it somewhere quiet. You'll probably win, since you're such a tough guy, but I do outweigh you and I promise you that I'll put every pound I possess into messing up your precious face. By the time we're through people won't know you from Hermione Gingold, *understand?*"

Tito glowered at him in lethal silence for a long moment—until he broke into sudden, side-splitting laughter. Uncontrollable hysterics. "God, that was so cool," he finally managed to say, gasping. "Thanks for that moment, man. I'll have to use it in a scene someday."

"It's all yours," Mitch said, wondering just how much of Tito's erratic behavior was for real and how much was simply designed to keep people off-balance and afraid. He couldn't tell. Could Tito?

"Tito?!" Esme called out to him from across the food hall. She and Chrissie were waiting at the door. "Come on, let's go!"

Tito waved in acknowledgement and started toward her.

"One more thing," Mitch said, stopping the actor in his tracks.

"What is it *now*, man?" Just like that he'd switched over to irritation.

"This kind of stuff is really beneath you."

"You know dick about me, man."

"I know you're better than this. Much better."

Tito considered Mitch's remark for a long moment, tugging thoughtfully at his lower lip. Then he abruptly spat on the floor at Mitch's feet and stormed off.

"Then again," Mitch said to himself softly, "maybe you're not."

CHAPTER 4

THE CITGO MINIMART WAS three miles down Old Shore Road from the village, past McGee's Diner, past Jilly's Boatyard, just before the turnoff for Peck's Point. There were some summer bungalow colonies clustered another couple of miles down the road, so the Citgo usually did a thriving business this time of year. Right now, Des found only a couple of pickups parked outside as she pulled up in her cruiser and got out. Right now, she found trouble.

Their big plate glass window had been smashed to bits.

Most of those bits were scattered inside all over the floor, Des discovered as she strode through the open door, crunching them under her feet. Some pieces remained framed in place, their sharp jagged edges exposed. A young workman was using a rubber mallet to tap them onto a tarp he'd laid on the pavement outside.

The owners of the station, the Acars, were visibly upset. Behind the counter, Mrs. Acar, a tiny woman in a headscarf, was trembling, her dark eyes wide with fright. Her husband was busy sweeping up and acting extremely brisk and take-charge. Also really unhappy to see Des. He wouldn't so much as look at her.

It wasn't either one of them who'd placed the call to her. It was the young workman, a customer.

"I got me some plywood I can let you have, Nuri," he said. "Until you can get a new piece of glass, I mean."

"That would be very kind of you, Kevin," Mr. Acar responded, glancing up at him. Which meant he could no longer pretend that Des wasn't standing there in the doorway "Good afternoon, Trooper. How may I help you?"

"You can tell me what happened here."

"This happened," Mrs. Acar responded, placing a smooth, round, granite stone on the counter. It was about the size of a man's fist. In her tiny hand, it looked huge. Someone had painted 9/11 on it in red paint. "It struck very near to my head," she said, pointing to a dent in the Sheetrock wall behind her. "It was fortunate we had no customers in line at the time or they might have been hit, with dire consequences."

"As you can see, no one *was* hurt," Mr. Acar spoke up, forcing a tight smile onto his face. "The window is easily replaced. So there is no trouble."

"Did either of you see who threw it?"

"We saw nothing," he replied crisply. "It was one of our quiet moments. I was in the back room replenishing some supplies for the men's lavatory. And Nema was—"

"Where were you, Mrs. Acar?" Des asked, not liking the way he was trying to stampede her. The man was a bit too anxious for her to pack up and go.

"Restocking my case," Nema replied, indicating the glass case next to the cash register, which was filled with exotic homemade pastries.

"You didn't see it happen?"

"I heard the crash of broken glass. And I ducked. I saw . . . nothing," she said, glancing meekly at her husband. "Then I heard a car pull away very rapidly, a screech of tires. That is all."

"Did you get a make or license number of the car?"

"No, this was not possible. It was gone before I could get a look."

"Which way was the car heading when it left—back toward town?"

"The other way, I believe. I am not positive."

Des went to the door and glanced outside. On this stretch of Old Shore there were no businesses on the other side of the road, just an overgrown tangle of vines, creepers, and wild berries. About a hundred yards past the Citgo, heading away from town, there was a sharp left turn onto Burnham Road, a narrow, residential lane that snaked its way through some old farms and ended up back in the village. Whoever did this most likely turned there and was gone in a flash. Probably two kids in a pickup—one drives, the other crouches in back and throws the stone. Swamp Yankees, if she had to guess. Indigenous lost boys with a hate thing for immigrants. Especially immigrants who were operating a successful new business.

"Have you folks had any trouble like this before?" Des asked Mr. Acar.

"No trouble at all, Trooper," he answered. "Everyone has been very welcoming. And, while your presence is greatly appreciated, I wish you'd not pursue this matter any further. It will only draw more attention toward it, which we do not consider desirable. We shall happily bear the cost of replacing the glass. As you can see, this gentleman is already helping."

Des shoved her horn-rims up her nose, and said, "Look, I understand where you're coming from, Mr. Acar—"

"Please, call me Nuri," he purred, smiling at her ingratiatingly. More than ingratiatingly. The man was starting to ogle her long form right in front of his wife.

"Nuri, a crime has been committed here," she said, her stomach muscles tightening involuntarily. The smarm wasn't just undressing her with his eyes, he was licking her. "I have to file a report—that's my job. Furthermore, the message on that stone is an obvious reference to the attack on the World Trade Center. We've got a task force operating out of the state's attorney's office that specializes in hate crimes such as this."

"But who would hate us?" he asked her imploringly. "We are Turkish people, peaceful people. Turkey is America's good friend."

"You and I know that, but the morons who did this may not be too up on their international coalitions. Besides which," she added, glancing at Nema's headscarf, "you *are* Muslims, and that makes you different. Some people don't care for different. I happen to know a little bit about what that's like. I also know that when this kind of thing happens, it doesn't just hurt you, it hurts the entire community. Look, let me show you something, okay?"

She went back out to her cruiser and fished around in her briefcase for the four-by-seven laminated Hate Crime Response Card that the

Connecticut State Police had developed in conjunction with the Anti-Defamation League. When she returned with it the Acars were talking heatedly to one other. They broke it off at once. Des had a definite feeling that Nema was more anxious to cooperate than her husband was. Clearly, he didn't want to involve the law at all. How come? Was something else going on here—say, somebody running a protection racket on him?

"Please, listen to this," she said, reading to them from the laminated card. "It defines a hate crime as 'a criminal act against a person or property in which the perpetrator chooses the victim because of the victim's real or perceived race, religion, national origin, ethnicity, sexual orientation, disability, or gender.'" Des glanced up at the Acars, who were staring at her now in tight-lipped silence. "That's why the task force needs to be brought in. They know the different hate groups and how they operate. They'll know if someone's been pulling this elsewhere around the state. It might be part of a pattern."

"Foolish boys," Mr. Acar sniffed at her dismissively. "Just a prank by foolish boys."

"You're probably right," Des said, although she did have some nagging doubts. Why during daylight? Early afternoon was not the local bad boys' usual hour for committing random acts of stupidity—late night was. "But this way we'll know for sure, okay?"

"As you wish," Nuri Acar said with weary resignation.

A customer in a BMW pulled up at a gas pump out front. Mr. Acar darted outside to help, grateful for the chance to get away from her.

Des was just as happy to see him go. One of the things in life that she was truly bad at was being civil to people who she thought were creeps. *Get along.* That was the Deacon's motto, and he had ridden it all the way to the tippity toppity—deputy superintendent of the Connecticut State Police, highest-ranking black man in the state's history. But Des was not her father, and that was why she wasn't working homicides anymore. At age twenty-eight, Des had been Connecticut's great nonwhite hope—the only black woman in the state to make lieutenant on the Major Crime Squad. She had produced, too. Outperformed every single man in the Central District.

Except she didn't *get along* with the so-called Waterbury mafia—the inner circle of Italian-American males who pretty much ran things in the state police. They liked to have their big, fat egos stroked, especially by the pretty girls. Des hadn't played along, hadn't respected them. And they could tell. And when the chance came to knife her, they had.

"May I offer you a coffee?" Nema asked, smiling at her uncertainly. "A baklava, perhaps?"

"I'm all set, thanks," Des said, as Kevin began hammering the plywood into place over the broken window.

"I regret the circumstances, but I am so pleased to meet you at long last. Your friend is my friend, after all."

"My friend?"

"Mr. Mitch Berger," Nema said. "He is a fine, fine man. And one of my very best pastry customers."

"I'll just bet he is," Des said, her eyes scanning the case of sweets. Some were covered with powdered sugar, just like the powdered sugar he'd had on his collar at lunch. So this was where he came to blow huge holes in his diet. It did occur to Des, standing there at the counter, that Mitch was at heart a fat little boy and always would be. Still, if this was the worst kind of lie he was capable of then she was lucky and she damned well knew it.

"Such a modest gentleman," Nema added. "No airs, despite his prestigious position with the newspaper. And quite the gourmet. Very discerning."

"That he is." Des did not mention his penchant for eating potloads of his god-awful American chop suey, or that she had once found a box of Great Starts microwave sausage-and-egg breakfast burritos in his freezer. She did not want to shatter any illusions, or slow Nema down. The lady was working her way up to telling her something.

"Nuri does not mean to be difficult," she finally said, clearing her throat uneasily. "We wish only to blend in. Surely you can understand that."

"Absolutely," Des said, because she could understand. She just couldn't blend in. "Your husband said he was in back when it happened. You were here behind the counter?"

"Yes, that is right."

"Sure there's nothing else you want to tell me, one friend to another?"

Nema glanced nervously out the glass doors at her husband. "No, nothing."

Clearly, the lady was holding back. She was also frightened. Of what? Who? "Well, if you remember anything . . ." Des handed Nema her card and urged her to give her a call, knowing she never would. Then she bagged and tagged the rock, which would go to the Westbrook Barracks along with her report. The task force would take it from there.

Still, it wouldn't hurt to do a bit of canvassing.

Mr. Acar was washing the BMW's windshield. She tipped her big hat to him politely. He acknowledged her gesture with an equally polite wave. She got into her cruiser and eased it down Old Shore to that quick left onto Burnham, where she parked on the shoulder and got out. She knelt and inspected the pavement carefully for fresh skid marks. Saw none.

Three old farmhouses were clustered there on Burnham not far from Old Shore Road. No one was home at the first house. At the second house she managed to wake up a young man who'd worked the overnight shift at Millstone, the nuclear power plant in Waterford. He hadn't heard anyone speeding by his house in the past hour and was very grumpy about saying so.

Des approached the third house with some reluctance. This one belonged to Miss Barker, an elderly spinster who had called Des twice in past weeks with dire emergencies. A prowler who turned out to be a meter reader from Connecticut Light and Power, and a suspicious-looking hoodlum dumping toxic waste in the marsh who was, in fact, a marine biologist with the Department of Environmental Protection. Still, Miss Barker wasn't a bad person, just lonely and scared. And she missed nothing that went on out on her street.

It took the old girl a while to get to the door. She didn't move very well, which was why Des hadn't tried pressing a kitten on her—she was too likely to trip over it and fall. She was a slender, frail thing with Q-Tip hair, partial to pastel-colored pantsuits. Today she was pretty in pink. The scent of Miss Barker's heavy, fruity perfume wafted out of the doorway with her. She wore so much of it that Des got lightheaded if she went inside the house.

"Sure, it's those darned kids," she responded promptly after Des had explained the purpose of her visit. "They all come tearing around that corner too fast. Especially at night. I hear their tires screeching when I'm lying here in my bed. I'm afraid of what'll happen, dear, I don't mind saying. One of those fool boys is going to smash right into the side of my bedroom some night. The explosion will kill me dead in my bed. Incinerate me sure as I'm standing—"

"This would have happened within the past hour, Miss Barker," Des said, trying to rein her in.

"We ought to have a speed bump out there to slow those boys down, but do you think they listen to me at town hall? I've only been paying property taxes here since 1946, never missed a single payment."

"Miss Barker, did you hear any screeching tires within the past hour?"

"Why, yes, right in the middle of *All My Children*, which I don't know why I still watch. Loyalty, I guess. Not a very popular virtue anymore, is it?"

"Did you see what type of vehicle it was?"

"I absolutely did not *see* anyone," Miss Barker said with a sudden flash of indignation. "So, naturally, I would not have the slightest idea what type of vehicle it was. How could I?"

Des peered at her in surprise. This was a lady who always butted in, never out. Why the dumb act? First Nema Acar, now her. What was this? "Well, did it sound more like a car or a truck?"

"More like a car," she replied after a moment's hesitation. "The pickups have those huge tires now with the big treads that make so much noise. Why do they *need* such huge tires? My daddy drove a truck his whole life, never a single accident, and his tires were just normal, proper tires." Miss Barker paused, her pale pink tongue flicking across her thin, dry lips. "But I really couldn't say *anything* for sure."

Des didn't press her any further. Just thanked Miss Barker for her time and started back toward her cruiser, puzzled and frustrated. So much so that she could feel the beginnings of a deep blue funkadelic haze coming over her.

My job is pointless and stupid. My entire existence is pointless and stupid. I am wasting my life.

She knew the real reason why she was feeling this way. Sure she did. But knowing why didn't make her feel one bit better.

She got back in her ride and cranked up the air conditioner and sat there glowering through her windshield at the huge old sycamore that grew in Miss Barker's front yard. It was so splendid and lovely that it actually seemed to be mocking her with its presence. Either that or she was going totally nutso. She lunged for her cell phone and called her short-relief man. Whenever she needed a save, she reached out for him. As his phone rang, Des sat there wondering what would happen to her if Mitch Berger were not in her life right now. She would go right down the drain, that's what.

But he must never know this—he thinks I'm the one who has it all together.

His phone machine answered. She waited, waited, waited for the beep and said, "Hi, it's me."

And he picked up. "I'm here," he said hurriedly. "I've just been getting a gazillion calls from the media about Tito."

"They're making a big deal out of it?"

"Big doesn't begin to describe it. *Brokaw's* people called me for a quote."

"How's your jaw?"

"Actually, it feels very similar to that molar implant I had done last year. The only difference is that was administered by a board-certified oral surgeon."

"Well, if it makes you feel any better I just met some huge fans of yours."

"Oh, yeah, who?"

"The Acars, Nuri and Nema." Total silence from his end. "She said you're just about her best customer."

"Well, sure," Mitch said slowly. "I fill up my truck there all the time."

"You are so busted, boyfriend."

"Busted," he confessed guiltily. "I throw myself on your mercy, Des. You must be so disappointed in me."

"No, baby, I'm not," she said, easing up off of the gas pedal. Because he could be so much worse. He could be Brandon. "You're my boy. All I want is you, no matter what size you are—large, extra-large, jumbo, economy. . . ."

"Okay, you made your point, Master Sergeant. I'll tell you one thing—I'm going to get Nema for this."

"Cut her a little slack. She's had herself a bad day." Des told him what had happened to their window.

"Oh my God, that's awful. Truly detestable. You wouldn't think . . ."

"You wouldn't think what?"

"Nothing. I was just about to say 'You wouldn't think something like this could happen here,' but I stopped myself because any time something bad happens in a small town the bystanders always say 'This is more the kind of thing you'd expect to happen in New York City.' And, as a New Yorker, I always get hopping mad. Things like this go on everywhere, because there are total assholes everywhere. Will you catch who did it?"

"That's up to Hate Crimes, but if I had to guess I'd say yeah."

"They're a smart crew?"

"They are, plus the people who go in for these types of crimes tend to be genuinely stupid. Real, I think Nema knew more about it than she was letting on."

"Why would she hold out on you?"

"Because her husband told her to."

"You don't like him, do you? You think he's oleaginous."

"Damn, is it that obvious?"

76

"Only to me, girlfriend." From the first day they met Mitch been able to read her mind. Des had never understood how. "I'm glad you called—I was just going to call you and tell you to press your white flannels."

"You just said what?"

"We've been invited to the highly exclusive Dorset Beach Club for dinner tonight, lovey," he said, putting on his best Locust Valley Lockjaw. Which was not good at all. It traveled by way of Canarsie, where his parents were from. "Esme told Dodge what happened between Tito and me. Dodge thought if he got all of us together for a cookout and a swim it would help chill things out."

"And Tito's down with this?"

"Esme said she'd get him there. Dodge is inviting the rest of the Mesmers so as to defuse any possible tension."

"The Mesmers?"

"That's the name of our walking club."

"I didn't know that."

"They don't know it either. I'm bringing corn. Will and Donna are bringing everything else. You like them, right?"

She did like Donna. Will was polite but a bit reserved. Some of the locals were like that. Hell, most of the locals were like that.

"Jeff will be there, too."

Jeff Wachtell she could live without. Des thought he was a whiner, plus he walked like a duck. "I thought you didn't like to socialize with movie people."

"That's absolutely true. But under the circumstances I think this is something I need to do. Tito and Esme are going to be around for a while. I don't want to get into a fight with this guy every time I try to go to the store."

Which was why Des had wanted to march the actor straight to Westbrook in handcuffs. But she held her tongue. They'd been over this already.

"So are you game? I was kidding about the white flannels—it's casual."

"Thanks, baby, but I don't think I'm up for that tonight."

"You're still mad that I didn't press charges against him, is that it?"

"No, no. It's not about you. I need to draw tonight, that's all."

"It'll happen, Des," he said encouragingly. "You just have to be patient."

"Damn it, doughboy, don't you *ever* get tired of being so supportive?"

He didn't respond. Just gave her back a big dose of stung silence.

Now she sat there cursing her bad self. When she was frustrated she could go bitch cakes and then some. All the more reason she should be alone tonight. "That's exactly what Professor Weiss told me," she acknowledged. "He said I'd get it, and that the process would make me stronger. But it's just not happening."

"So why don't you talk to him some more about it?" Mitch said, his voice a good deal cooler than it was before she bit his head clean off.

"I can't."

"Why not? Who is he, the Dalai Lama?"

"I have to figure it out myself, that's all. I just wish I knew *how*. I keep, I don't know, thinking this bolt of inspiration will strike me or something."

"Tex in the stamp stalls, sure."

"Tex in the what?"

"In *Charade*, when James Coburn is walking through the stamp stalls in the Paris park and suddenly, kerchunk, the whole plot falls right into place."

"Damn it, Mitch, this is not some fool movie!"

"I do know that," he shot back. "And I know something else—that I've already had my bellyful of childish, self-absorbed, pain-in-the-asses today, thank you very much."

Des drew her breath in, stunned. He'd never spoken to her this way before. Not ever. "You're right, baby," she said. "My miss. I'm sorry. Really, really sorry."

But she was too late.

Mitch Berger, the kindest, sweetest love of her life, had already hung up on her.

CHAPTER 5

MITCH WAS NOT HAPPY that Des wouldn't come with him to the beach club.

In fact, he was so not happy that he decided he'd better get off the phone awfully damned now. His jaw ached. His mood was vile. And he didn't want to say anything that he might really regret. He found it hard to believe she was so self-centered she couldn't see that he was in the midst of a monstrous professional crisis and that he needed her by his side—not going on and on about her damned trees.

His situation could not have been more of a nightmare. The twenty-four-hour cable news channels were already broadcasting video highlights of The Fight by the time he got home to Big Sister Island. The digital photos of Tito with his hands wrapped tightly around Mitch's throat were out all over the Internet. There was Tito astride him like a wild beast, teeth bared, ready for the kill. There was Mitch pinned helplessly underneath him, looking like some form of slow, terrified water mammal.

It was America Online's top news story of the day. The headline on the service provider's main screen read "Tito Lowers Boom on Highbrow Critic."

The arts editor of Mitch's paper, Lacy Mickerson, had e-mailed him twice and left an urgent message for him on his phone machine. Dozens of his fellow critics from around the country had sent e-mails as well, many humorous. He would respond to them at some point, but right now he was too busy fending off calls from one media outlet after another. Everyone wanted a comment, a quote, something, anything. The very same tabloid TV vans that had been following Tito and Esme all around Dorset were now pulled up on Peck's Point at the gate to the Big Sister causeway, desperate to get out there and film *him*. Mitch was having none of it. He did not want to comment. He did not want to appear on camera.

He was not an entertainer. He was a critic.

Or at least he used to be.

He sat at his desk, an ice pack pressed against his jaw, and called Lacy back.

"Honestly, Mitch, I thought your review was *gentle* compared with a lot of the others I've seen," she said after he'd given her his version of what happened. Among her many attributes Lacy was fiercely protective of her critics. "Hell, this film has been positively trashed by everyone. People are walking out in droves. Why did he pick on you?"

"Because I was there," Mitch grunted, adjusting his ice pack. It didn't help with the pain, but it gave him something to do. "He's a genuinely talented actor. I feel sorry for him, actually."

"Well, I don't. I've seen these so-called bad boys come and go over the years." Lacy was in her late fifties and claimed to have bedded Irwin Shaw and Mickey Mantle in her youth, not to mention Nelson Rockefeller. "They *all* have talent. It's what they do with it that counts."

"What do I do, Lacy? What's my next move?"

"You shut it down," she said firmly.

The two of them cobbled together a brief statement that would be posted immediately on the newspaper's Web site—just as soon as Lacy ran it past someone with a larger office and, possibly, a law degree. It would also appear on the lead arts page in tomorrow's paper. The statement would serve as Mitch's one and only response to the attack:

> *This newspaper's chief film critic, Mitchell Berger, and the actor Tito Molina engaged in a spirited creative disagreement yesterday afternoon in a popular eating establishment in Dorset, Connecticut. Mr. Berger feels the matter is fully resolved. He believes that Mr. Molina is a gifted artist with a wonderful career ahead of*

him and he looks forward to his future film work with as much
excitement as ever.

After he and Lacy were done Mitch swallowed three Advils and spent the rest of the afternoon ducking phone calls. His phone machine got quite a workout that day.

He did pick up when Dodge called. And was pleased that Dodge wanted to broker a peace deal at the beach club. It seemed like a genuine solution. Dodge was smart and tactful. He'd make the perfect intermediary.

As for Des, well, Mitch hoped she'd figure out what she needed to figure out—and soon—because when she was stuck in the deep muck she had a way of dragging him down there with her, whether he felt like going or not. And that could be awfully damned hard to handle sometimes.

Not that love was ever supposed to be an easy thing.

When it came time to leave he dressed in a white oxford button-down shirt, khaki shorts, and Topsiders. He had a welt on his jaw and red finger marks around his throat, otherwise he looked fit, casual, and terrific. It was a warm, hazy evening with very little breeze. The sun hung low over the Sound, casting everything in a soft, rosy glow. He threw a pair of swim trunks and a towel into the front seat of his truck, then moseyed over to Bitsy Peck's garden with a galvanized steel bucket to pilfer a dozen ears of corn.

It was Will who'd taught Mitch the best way to cook corn—plunge the fresh-picked ears directly into a bucket of water, soak them for at least a half hour, then throw them on the grill to steam in their husks.

Bitsy was busy digging up her pea patch with a fork, dressed in cutoff overalls and a big, floppy straw hat. She was a round, bubbly little blue blood in her fifties with a snub nose and freckles, and just a remarkably avid and tireless gardener. Hundreds of species of flowers, vegetables, and herbs grew in her vast, multileveled garden. Actually, Bitsy's garden looked more like a commercial nursery than it did somebody's yard. When Mitch first arrived on Big Sister she had gleefully stepped into the role of his garden guru. The lady was a fountain of advice and seedlings and composted cow manure. Mitch liked her a lot.

Although lately she hadn't been nearly as upbeat as usual. Not since her twenty-three-year-old daughter, Becca, a ballet dancer, had come home to mom and the massive three-story shingled Victorian summer cottage where she'd grown up. Becca had gotten herself addicted to heroin out in San Francisco, and had just finished a stint at the Silver Hill Rehab Clinic in New Canaan. Mostly, the two ladies kept to themselves. Hardly left the island at all, and seldom had guests. Bitsy went grocery shopping every couple of days. Otherwise, Mitch would find her toiling diligently in her garden refuge from dawn until dusk.

Becca was out there working with her right now, weeding a flower bed in a halter top and shorts, her own efforts rather distracted and halfhearted. Mitch had seen old photographs around the house of Becca in her full ballerina getup. She had been a slender and graceful young swan of a girl. Truly lovely. But that was before the needle did its damage. Now she was a gaunt, frail shell of a woman with haunted eyes that were sunk deep in their sockets and rimmed with dark circles. Her long brown hair was twisted into tight braids that looked like two lifeless hunks of rope.

Mitch smiled and said hello to her. Becca mouthed "Hello" in polite response, although scarcely a whisper came out. She was painfully quiet. This, too, was the needle, according to Bitsy, who said Becca had been the most outgoing, popular girl in her high school class. Looking at her now, Mitch found it hard to believe.

"So sorry about all of those press vans at the gate today, Bitsy," he said, toting his bucket over toward her corn patch.

"They didn't bother us one bit," Bitsy assured him.

"Well, they sure bothered me."

Bitsy swiped at the perspiration on her upper lip, leaving a smear of mud behind. "My, my, aren't you all fresh scrubbed and smell-goody," she observed with motherly pride as he began stripping choice ears of corn off their stalks and plunging them into his bucket. "And here we are like a pair of sweaty farm animals, aren't we, Becca?"

"Yes, Mother," Becca responded faintly.

"What's the occasion, Mitch?" Bitsy asked, her good cheer a bit forced.

"I've been invited to the beach club. I'm kind of anxious to check the place out, actually. No one's ever invited me before."

"And who did, dare I ask?"

"Dodge Crockett."

Becca immediately dropped her trowel, which clattered off a low stone retaining wall onto the ground. She stared down at it briefly, but didn't pick it up. Just walked away instead—straight into the house, her stride still uncommonly graceful.

Bitsy watched her go, biting down fretfully on her lower lip. "She doesn't like to talk about Dodge."

"I noticed. How come?"

"I'm worried about that girl, Mitch. She spends too much time alone. It's not good for her. She needs stimulation. I wish Esme would come see her."

Mitch glanced at her curiously. "They know each other?"

"Oh my, yes. They were best friends when they were girls. The great Esme Crockett practically grew up out here. Slept over almost every night during the summer. There were slumber parties and pillow fights, and poor little Jeremy was *so* in love with her." Becca's younger brother, a senior at Duke, was away serving a summer internship in Washington. "He'd follow her around like a gawky little puppy. The house was full of kids and laughter then," Bitsy recalled fondly. "Not like now." She went back to her forking, throwing every fiber of her body into turning over the soil. "I didn't realize you and Dodge had become buddies."

"We walk together every morning. I like him a lot."

"People do think very highly of Dodge," she allowed, nodding. "There was even talk about the party running him for lieutenant governor some years back. I suppose it's just as well they didn't."

"Why do you say that?"

"Yes, he's a bright, enthusiastic fellow, all right. More than willing to do his part around town. So is Martine, who is so generous with her time, always ready to throw herself body and soul behind a good cause. And such a decorative creature, too." Now Bitsy trailed off, glancing up at Mitch uncertainly. "Just promise me one thing. Promise me you won't be too taken in by them. Will you do that for me, Mitch?"

"Okay, sure," Mitch said, frowning at her. "But why?"

"Because they're cannibals," she said quietly. "They eat people."

The Dorset Beach Club was located at the end of a narrow and perilously bumpy little dirt road that snaked its way back through a half mile of marsh and wild brambles off of Old Shore Road. It was a private dirt road. No sign on Old Shore marked its presence. In fact, the roadside brush was so overgrown at the beach club turnoff that if you weren't looking for it you would never know it was there.

Which, this being Dorset, was the whole idea.

In fact, Mitch wasn't even sure he was bouncing his way down the right dirt road until he reached a grassy clearing filled with beat-up old Ford Country Squire station wagons, Mercedes diesels, and Subarus. Then he knew this had to be the beach club—in Dorset, the richer they were the junkier their ride. Only the working poor drove shiny new cars.

At the water's edge sat a modest, weathered gray shingled cottage-style clubhouse that looked as if it had been built in the 1930s. Mitch got out, corn bucket in hand, and made his way around to the beach-side on a raised wooden walkway, passing through a portal directly into a different time and place. Here, on a wide wooden dining porch beneath a striped blue awning, Mitch found properly attired club members being served their proper lobster dinners by hushed, respectful waiters in white jackets. Proper attire for men was apparently defined as a madras sports jacket and Nantucket red pants. Proper attire for women was anything Katharine Hepburn might have worn to a summer concert under the stars in, say, 1957. A rather tinny sound system was playing soothing, vaguely Polynesian-sounding music. Not a single one of these members was under the age of seventy. Actually, not many appeared to be under the age of eighty. They seemed lifelike enough, although none of them actually spoke and all of them moved in slow motion, as if this were a dream. Standing there on the walkway with his bucket, Mitch had the astonishingly powerful feeling that this *was* a dream, that none of it was real, just his own Jewish schoolboy fantasy of what a private club like this might have been like in bygone days.

Mitch had experienced these paranormal phenomena several times before since he'd moved to this place. He'd taken to calling them Dorset Interludes.

Dodge had instructed him to continue past the dining porch to the long wooden veranda that faced the sand. Here there were showers and changing stalls, a cold drink stand and other amenities for beachgoers. Umbrella tables and built-in barbecue grills were provided for members who wanted to cook out and eat right there on the beach. It was all pretty unassuming considering just how exclusive the beach club was. Three letters of recommendation and a certified check for $10,000 were required—and that was the easy part. The hard part was that the membership roll capped out at a strict maximum of two hundred families, meaning that in order to get in you had to know people and then those people had to die. Not that it looked as if it would necessarily be a long wait, given the median age of the members who were politely gumming their lobster and corn back there on the dining porch.

Of course, the main attraction of the club was the beach itself—and a very nice, wide stretch of clean white beach it was, the sand so immaculate it looked as if it were raked hourly. No trash, no doggy poop, and above all, no beer-bellied pipe fitters from New Britain with their loudmouthed wives and squalling kids. Only the right sort of people were to be found on this beach. People who *belonged* here. Mitch didn't and he never would and he knew this. But he plodded his way toward the barbecue grills anyway, footsteps thudding heavily on the wooden walkway. He was not here to fit in. He was here to bury the hatchet with Tito Molina.

The Crocketts had commandeered two umbrella tables at the far end of the veranda, where they were sharing a pitcher of iced margaritas with Will and Donna and Jeff. Tito and Esme hadn't arrived yet. A big spread of cheeses and crackers was laid out on the table. No one seemed to be touching any of it. They were too busy drinking and talking, their eyes bright, voices animated.

"Hey, it's macho man," called out Donna, who was the first to spot him.

"Mitch, you look like you just went three rounds with Roy Jones Jr.," observed Will.

"How does the jaw feel?" asked Jeff, who sat huddled under the umbrella with a beach towel over his exposed knees. Being a redhead, he burned easily.

"It's really not so bad as long as I don't smile, talk, or eat."

"Where's our resident trooper?" asked Dodge as he refilled everyone's glasses. The pitcher was already half empty—they'd gotten a serious head start.

"I'm afraid she couldn't make it."

"That's an awful shame," clucked Martine, who was stretched out languorously on a lounge chair in the sun, looking tanned, terrific, and not a day over thirty-five in her snug-fitting black one-piece swimsuit. Martine's hips were slim, her legs long, shapely, and smooth. She glanced fondly up at Dodge as he brought her a refill, stroking his arm with tender affection. Then she turned her inviting blue-eyed gaze on Mitch, drawing him effortlessly toward her. "But I'm so glad *you* could join us."

"Wouldn't miss it," said Mitch, his mind straying back to that word Bitsy Peck had just used to describe the Crocketts—*cannibals.* "Beautiful evening, isn't it?"

"Beautiful," she murmured, gazing at the soft glowing sky over the Sound.

"It will be raining by midnight," Dodge predicted. "My left knee aches—old lacrosse injury."

"Darling, I always thought it was your right knee," Martine said teasingly.

"It's *always* been the left," he kidded back.

"Oh, goody, Berger brought corn," observed Donna, her eyes gleaming at Mitch. She already seemed a bit tipsy. "Some men bring flowers and champagne, others bring hog feed. Speaking as one of the hogs, I say thank you."

"Speaking as another one of the hogs, I say you're welcome." Mitch delivered the bucket to Will, who was building a fire in one of the grills out of seasoned hardwood chunks and mesquite. Dressed in a tank top, nylon shorts and leather flip-flops, Will could easily be mistaken for the club's lifeguard. To Mitch he also seemed a bit less lighthearted than the others. Distracted, maybe. Was it being around Martine when both her husband and his wife were around? Mitch wondered.

"Seriously, Mitch, how is your jaw?" he asked with genuine concern.

"Seriously, it hurts like hell. I really don't like getting hit."

"But you're okay to eat?"

"Oh, I'll manage," said Mitch, his stomach growling as he checked out their dinner—racks and racks of baby back ribs, potato salad, red cabbage slaw, fruit salad, brownies.

"For what it's worth, I've known Esme since she was in pigtails," Will said. "She's always had good instincts about people. If she likes somebody, there's some good in there."

"I believe it."

"Care to try a margarita, Mitch?" asked Dodge.

"I'll settle for a beer, thanks." Mitch fetched a Dos Equis out of the cooler, popped it open, and settled into a deck chair with it. "This is nice here," he said, taking a long, thirsty gulp.

"You'll have to be our guest more often," Martine said lazily, crossing her ankles. "We vastly prefer it down at this end. You'll find all of us club rebels down here. That dining room crowd is *so* stuffy." A cell phone rang in the canvas tote bag next to her. She reached for it. "I'll bet that's Esme. She's *always* late. . . . Hi, sweetie," Martine said into the phone, nodding her blond head at them. "We're all here waiting for you. . . . It's lovely out, although Daddy is absolutely convinced it's going to rain. His right knee's acting up."

"Left knee," Dodge interjected, grinning at her.

"Sweetie, when are you two—?" Now Martine's face fell, her brow furrowing. "What do *mean*, you're not . . . No, I absolutely *don't* understand. This is very important. You *know* it is. Tito needs to— Esme? Esme, are you still there? . . ." Martine flicked off the phone, sighing, and tossed it back into her bag. "She couldn't get him to come. They quarreled about it and he drove off in a huff. Everything with them is such a battle, Dodge. I wish we could do something."

"They have to work it out for themselves," Dodge said. "It's their marriage."

Now Mitch heard sharp footsteps coming their way.

"Oh, great, here comes Little Mary Sunshine," muttered Jeff.

Chrissie Huberman was marching toward them, the wooden veranda shuddering under each of her onrushing strides. The publicist's face was set in a determined scowl, her fists clenched. She did treat Dodge and Martine to a great big toothy smile when she arrived at their table. "Hi, Mr. and Mrs. Crockett!" she exclaimed, all sugar and spice for the parents of a prized client. But then Chrissie abruptly whirled, stuck her finger in Mitch's face and snarled, "Don't you *ever* try to pull something like this again! I *forbid* it, you hear me!"

Mitch took a sip of his beer and said, "I hear you, Chrissie. But I have no idea what you're talking about."

"Like hell you don't," she raged. "You're trying to feed off of Tito behind my back. No way! You want face time with my client then you come through me! I protect those kids. I bleed for those kids. And there will be no secret sessions with Tito Molina as long as I'm—"

"Before you go any further," Mitch interrupted, "it's my duty to inform you that you're way off base."

Chrissie tilted her head at him mockingly. "Tell me this wasn't a secret meeting."

"It really wasn't, Chrissie," Dodge spoke up. "It was simply an informal get-together between family and friends."

"Of which *you* are neither," Martine said to her pointedly.

"Honestly, all I want is for this situation with Tito to go away," Mitch said.

Chrissie let out a derisive laugh. "Yeah, right. I know all about you, Mitch Berger—how you're the Mother Teresa of film critics. Won't do the junkets, won't accept gifts. Well, guess what? I don't believe any of it. What Tito did to you today is *every* critic's wet dream. You're no different than the rest. You *all* want a taste," she jeered at him, grabbing her own crotch for lewd, crude emphasis. "You want it so bad you can't stand it."

Mitch gazed at her in stunned silence. They all did. Heads were even starting to turn all of the way back at the dining porch. It was safe to say no one had ever seen such a public display of behavior by a female at the fabled Dorset Beach Club. Certainly not by one over the age of three.

"Young lady, I would like you to go," Martine said to her between gritted teeth. "This club is for members and their guests only. You will kindly take your potty mouth and leave right now."

"Are you trying to tell me this seedy dump is *private?*"

"Get out of here, Chrissie," ordered Will, moving over toward her. "Get out or I'll throw you out."

"Fine, whatever. Just remember what I told you," she warned Mitch.

"Not a problem. I don't think I'll be forgetting this for quite some time."

Satisfied, Chrissie stormed off, her footsteps clunking on the veranda. Heads turned to stare as she went charging past the dining porch.

"Well, it's been quite some day for histrionics," Mitch said wearily. "Sorry about that, folks."

"No need for you to be sorry," Jeff assured him. "Not your fault."

"Not in the least," echoed Dodge.

"That woman thinks everyone else in the world is exactly like her," Will said, gazing after her. "Greedy, two-faced, and conniving. And when you try to explain to her that you're not, she calls you a goddamned liar right to your face. She couldn't get away with that if she was a guy. She'd get punched."

"You should have given me the signal, honey," Donna said, putting up her dukes fiercely. "I would have had no problem decking her."

"She has a hard job," Dodge said. "That's not to defend or excuse her."

"What she has is a personality problem," Martine argued. "I wish Esme would get rid of her."

"She didn't hire her," Dodge said. "Tito's agent did."

"Fine, then I wish Tito would get rid of her."

"Hey, let's not let her ruin our party," Dodge said, forcing a smile onto his face. "Why don't you folks take a swim while we start the chow?"

"I think I will," said Mitch. Although in his case "float" would be the operative word. A true child of the pavement, Mitch hadn't known how to swim at all when he moved to Dorset. But thanks to diligence and hard work, he'd taught himself how to float on his back—the main thing was to relax and trust in his own considerable natural buoyancy. As he started his way toward the changing stalls with his swim trunks he discovered Jeff was tailing him, stride for stride. "Going to take a dip, Jeff?"

"Not exactly . . . I wanted to ask you something personal," Jeff said, sucking his cheeks in and out. "Would you go talk to her for me?"

"Talk to who, Jeff?"

"Abby—when she's at C. C. Willoughby on Thursday. She's just got to come sign books for me, Mitch. I *need* this, or I swear I'll go under. Chrissie totally blew me off, and Abby hung up on me as soon as she heard my voice."

"What makes you think she'll speak to me?"

"She'll at least hear you out. She doesn't *hate* you. Will you do it, Mitch?"

Mitch really didn't want to get involved in Jeff's marital problems. But the little guy seemed so desperate and alone that he didn't know how to say no. "Can I think it over?"

"Does that mean yes?"

"It means I'll think it over."

"Sure, sure," Jeff said with great relief. "Mitch, you're a real pal. I don't know what I'd do without you. Honest."

Mitch continued on behind the open-air showers now to the weathered knotty pine changing stalls, which were grouped on either side of a center aisle, maybe fifty of them in all. Each stall was about three-by-five feet, with a door that was cropped a foot short at top and bottom for ventilation. Mitch's stall was bare except for a wooden bench and a few pegs to hang clothes on.

He emerged a moment later in his baggy surf shorts, and padded back out to the veranda. Martine was already swimming laps in a roped-in area out by the float. There was no one else out in the water. Will and Dodge were busy laying the ears of corn around the edge of the fire, which was getting good and hot. Jeff was seated back under the umbrella in the shade.

Now Donna joined Mitch, wearing a generously cut one-piece suit and a self-conscious look on her round face. Donna was no long-stemmed bikini babe—she was stubby and short-waisted, and she knew it. "Berger, is that you?" she joked, groping blindly at the air before her. She had removed her wire-rimmed glasses for the swim.

"It is."

"How do you like my new hot girl suit?" she asked, modeling it with a dainty curtsy. She was definitely feeling her margaritas.

"I like it fine. You ready to go in?"

"Absolutely, but you have to go in ahead of me. I don't want you staring at my big butt."

"But this way you get to stare at mine."

"That's right, honey." she giggled, swatting his arm with her hand.

The tide was out, the bottom sandy and soft. It fell off gradually as they slogged their way out, the water calm but surprisingly chilly.

It was still only about chest deep as they neared the float, where Martine continued to swim laps back and forth, the hazy sunlight glistening on her smooth, tanned flesh.

"What's up with that Rocky Dies Yellow tattoo?" Donna asked, peering at his biceps. "Are you some kind of a Stallone boy toy?"

"No, Cagney."

"Oh, sure, that's from the end of *Angels with Dirty Faces*. I love that movie."

"I didn't know you were into old movies." Mitch's eyes continued to follow Martine, her stroke so effortless and graceful that she barely made a ripple in the water.

"Mitch, there are more layers to me that you can possibly imagine. I'm like a really good lasagne Bolognese—but I'm also old-fashioned."

"How so?"

"I believe that when you go swimming with one girl you shouldn't be staring at another."

"I wasn't staring."

"Were."

Mitch lowered his voice. "What do you think of her?"

"That's a funny thing to ask," Donna responded slowly. "I *should* hate her guts."

Mitch widened his eyes at her. "Really?"

"Oh, totally. There's never been a day in her life when she wasn't pretty, popular, rich, could have any boy she wanted. And look at her now, she's pushing fifty and she's still built like I was when I was *never*. Which is, like, so not fair." Donna paused, letting out a sigh. "But the truth is that she's a real doll, and she's been nothing but nice to me since I moved here. Why are you asking?"

"Just curious."

"And does Trooper Mitry know you're just . . . curious?"

"Not that kind of curious."

"Yeah, right."

Donna headed farther out now, so that the water was up over her head and she had to paddle a little. Back on the veranda, Dodge was busy working the grill. Will was busy staring out at the two of them—so intently that Mitch couldn't help wondering if he was jealous. Jeff was still seated by himself at the umbrella table, shoulders slumped.

"What's up with our Mr. Wachtell tonight?" Donna wondered, squinting back at the shore. "He seems somewhat bummed."

"He's got money worries."

"Hey, who doesn't?"

"Come on, The Works is an incredible success story."

"Incredible," she agreed. "Just as long as you don't look too close."

"What's that supposed to mean?"

"Mitch, let me put it to you this way—what am I doing right now?"

"You're, well, you're at the beach club. You're in the water. You're . . ."

"*Work* with me here, Mitch," she said impatiently.

"Okay, I've got it—you're treading water."

"And what happens if I stop paddling?"

"You sink to the bottom and drown," he replied, nodding. "But how can that be? Your place is mobbed morning, noon and night."

"Overhead," Donna answered simply. "We owe the butcher, the baker, and the candlestick maker. Our payroll is huge. Our debt load is huge. Everything we hold near and dear is tied up in The Works, including the note on our house. Long term, Dodge is convinced we've got a winning idea. He thinks we can even franchise it all around New England—anywhere there's an abandoned mill. But short term, we are just total kitchen slaves. This is the first time I've had fun in I don't know how long."

Martine started back in toward shore now, waving at them as she swam past, her smile dazzling and white.

"I wasn't kidding this afternoon, Mitch," Donna said, coloring slightly.

"About what?"

"Sailing off to Bermuda with you." Her eyes were locked on to his now.

Mitch swallowed. "What about you and Will?"

"Don't look too close at that either."

"You're having problems?"

"I don't know what we're having," she confessed. "Things just haven't been the same since we went into business together. But, hey, enough with the Oprah-babble. I'm trying to seduce you, handsome. Do you want to sail away with me or not?"

"This is the margaritas talking," Mitch said lightly.

"No, it's all me. I'm dead serious."

"I don't have a sailboat, Donna. I don't even know how to sail."

"Do you know how to swim?"

"Why do you—?"

She dunked him hard, pushing him underwater with both hands. He surfaced, sputtering, and paid her back. And the fight was on, the two of them frolicking and shrieking like a pair of twelve-year-olds. When they'd laughed themselves out Mitch noticed that Will was waving at them to come in. Dinner was ready.

As they waded in Dodge got busy lighting a dozen or so citronella candles to ward off the mosquitoes. Donna wrapped a towel around herself and made straight for the grill to see how everything was doing.

Mitch rinsed off under one of the open-air shower heads and padded back to his changing stall, where he stripped off his wet trunks and toweled himself dry, feeling tingly and invigorated. As he dressed he heard someone's footsteps clomp past him on the decking toward a neighboring stall. He heard a stall door slap shut. Then he heard something else.

He heard a man whisper, "Not *here*—someone will catch us!"

And a woman whisper, "I don't give a damn! *He* does what *he* wants. Why can't I?"

Mitch froze, drawing his breath in.

"You're insane!" the man whispered, groaning softly. "We can't just . . ."

"I *want* you," she gasped. "Hurry! Give it to me *now*."

Mitch could not recognize them by their furtive whispers. But there was no mistaking what he heard next—the quick, heavy breathing, the slapping of bare flesh against bare flesh, the steady, rhythmic creaking of the wooden floorboards. The two of them were having it off in there together like a pair of sex-starved high school kids.

And then there was silence.

Mitch immediately tiptoed to the back of his stall and climbed up onto the built-in bench. From this vantage point he'd be able to see over his cropped stall door when they headed back out to the veranda. He was being a snoop and he knew it. But there was no way he was not going to find out who these lovers were.

A few moments later he heard their stall door swing open on rusty hinges. And footsteps, leather sandals clacking against the decking. Martine Crockett walked past, calmly straightening herself. She'd changed into a polo shirt and shorts, and she was striding a bit unsteadily, but she looked as cool, collected, and fresh as she always did.

Mitch waited, breathless with anticipation. After a moment a man emerged, looking flushed and shamefaced.

It wasn't Will Durslag.

It was Jeff. Martine's lover was Jeff Wachtell.

Ab-so-tootly.

The party was still going strong at ten o'clock when Mitch decided to say good night.

A dense fog had settled in, signaling that the rain wasn't far off. His jaw ached and his head was spinning. All he wanted to do was go home, take three Advils, and crawl right under his bed. He could not look at either Jeff or Martine throughout dinner. And yet he was also unable to stop picturing the two of them together, groping each other's naked, tumid flesh in that changing stall. Nor could he turn off the quiz show that was broadcasting nonstop inside of his mind.

Question: Could this GET any weirder?
Answer: Please, God, no.

Mitch felt so whipped by the time he'd steered his way across the fog-shrouded causeway for home that he didn't even bother to turn on the living room lights. Just made straight for the kitchen, where he replenished the cats' kibble bowl, fished an ice pack out of the freezer, and swallowed his Advils, hearing the mournful call of the foghorn on the Old Saybrook Lighthouse across the river. He was halfway up the steep, narrow stairs to his sleeping loft when something undeniable and truly frightening suddenly occurred to him.

He was not alone in his house.

Noises. He distinctly heard noises. The clinking of a glass. A cough.

His heart racing, Mitch flicked on a light and discovered Tito Molina sitting there in his one good chair, drinking up his scotch. Clemmie dozed contentedly in the actor's lap.

"Geez, Tito, scare people much?" he demanded.

"I like sitting in the dark," Tito answered, his blue eyes blazing at Mitch defiantly.

Mitch stood there in guarded silence, wondering what the combustible young star wanted. And whether he should be afraid for his life. Should he try to call Des? Should he arm himself? What with, the fireplace poker? He ended up just standing there, his eyes falling on Clemmie. "She hasn't sat in my lap all summer."

"Animals take to me. I'm one of them." Tito took a gulp of Mitch's scotch, the glass trembling so violently in his hand that it clinked off of his teeth. The man was wrapped beyond tight.

Clemmie awoke with a yawn, jumped out of Tito's lap, and wandered off toward the kitchen. Mitch watched her go, jealous in spite of himself.

"That guitar of yours is a piss," Tito said, his eyes falling on Mitch's Stratocaster. "Play me something."

"Kind of tired right now, Tito. What is it you want?"

"To talk."

"Okay, sure." Mitch sat on the edge of his loveseat, keeping the coffee table between them. He'd made that himself by bolting a discarded wooden storm window onto a leaky old rowboat. He was very proud of his coffee table. "But how did you get here?" he asked, snugging the ice pack against his jaw.

"What, you think because I'm Chicano I don't know how to use a damned phone book?"

"Of course not. I didn't see a car parked at the gate, that's all."

"I swam out. My ride's back at the town beach."

Tito's hair was indeed wet, Mitch now noticed, as were the yellow nylon shorts that he was wearing. The orange-and-blue T-shirt he was wearing was dry. It was one of Mitch's T-shirts. In fact, it was Mitch's treasured and exceedingly threadbare New York Mets 1986 World Series T-shirt. He'd owned that shirt since he was in high school. And Tito had gone and helped himself right to it.

"That wasn't very smart of you," Mitch told him. "People have drowned trying to swim out here—the river currents can be treacherous. That's how the island got its name. Back before they built the causeway they used a little ferry boat, and it capsized and a Peck daughter washed out to sea." Mitch stared at the young actor, wondering what it would be like to be *so* handsome. Everyone in the world wanted to look like Tito Molina—and yet his unparalleled good looks hadn't brought him anything even remotely close to happiness. "It would have been better if you'd buzzed me. I'd have raised the gate for you."

"How could you do that, man? You weren't here."

"I was at the beach club. I thought you'd be there, too. I thought we'd have a chance to talk then."

Tito didn't respond. Just poured himself some more of Mitch's scotch, his hand wavering unsteadily.

Mitch abruptly rose and marched into the kitchen for his emergency stash—the family-sized squeeze bottle of Hershey's chocolate syrup that he kept hidden under the sink behind the laundry detergent and furniture polish, away from Des's disapproving eyes.

"What are you doing in there?" Tito called to him.

Mitch returned with the syrup and sat. "Just getting comfortable," he replied, squirting a generous shot of it onto his tongue.

"You have really disgusting personal habits, man," Tito observed, curling his lip.

"Hey, you pick your remedy, I'll pick mine."

"Fair enough," the actor conceded. "I hear you're hooked up with the trooper lady."

"So what?"

"So nothing. I'm envious, that's all."

"You're married to the sexiest woman in America and you envy me?"

"Totally. Yours is the real deal. The way that she took charge of our situation today. Charged right in, no fear . . ." Tito gazed out the window, his knee jiggling nervously. "That was so cool."

"Esme said you'd be at the beach club tonight."

"She shouldn't have. I told her I wouldn't go." He drank some more scotch, his finely sculpted features tightening. "She's my Miss America, know what I'm saying? All she needs is the damned crown and that . . . what's that thing they wear across their boobies, says where they come from?"

"A sash?"

Tito nodded. "Right. But she doesn't listen to me when I tell her things. I'd never go near a place like that. It's filled with dead men walking. I start hanging at their damned beach club with them then I'm not *me* anymore, know what I'm saying?"

"Yes, I think I do."

"Okay, what did you mean by that?" Tito demanded suddenly.

Mitch shook his head at him, perplexed. The man was an absolute master at keeping people off-balance. "By what?"

"This afternoon, you said I was better than this. What did you mean?"

"It doesn't exactly require a translation."

Tito gazed at him searchingly. "I'm just a poor dumb beaner, jack. I need one, okay?"

Tito Molina sure needed *something*. He seemed to be consumed by inner disquiet. Mitch just didn't know what it was he needed, or why he seemed to feel he needed it from him.

Mitch settled back on the loveseat with his syrup bottle, listening to the foghorn. "I was there on opening night when you were in *Salesman*. I saw it happen, Tito. I saw you blow Malkovich right off of that stage. You're the real deal. You have the talent and looks and pure unadulterated star quality to do whatever you want. They can't stop you. And that's rare. One, maybe two actors in a generation have what you've got. Newman had it. Redford had it. Right now, there's you and there's only you. For me, it's as if you're holding a fortune right in the palm of your hand and instead of investing it wisely you're pissing it away on crap like *Dark Star*, and I wish like hell you wouldn't."

Tito threw down another hit of scotch, shuddering. "Sometimes it's like a trade-off. You've got to do that stuff so they'll let you do what you really want."

"I understand that," Mitch said. "But what is it that you really want to do?"

"Man, I don't know," he replied, staring gloomily down into his glass.

"I don't believe that. You know exactly what you want to do."

Tito peered up at him suspiciously. "Okay, so maybe I do. What I want . . . I want to make a movie about my father. It would be, like, a way to understand where I come from, know what I'm saying? See, he was just this really angry, screwed-up juicehead and he died—"

"In a bar fight, I know."

"I'd play him myself, see. And Esme would play my crazy mother. I've written the script. Most of it, anyway. And I want to direct it myself, too, which means I'd have to raise the money myself, which my agent totally hates. But that's okay, because I don't think I'll be straight with myself until I do this. I *need* to do this." He glanced at Mitch uncertainly. "You're a smart guy. You know about things. Word up, what do you think?"

Mitch stared back at him for a moment. Now he knew why Tito Molina was here, what he wanted. Tito was an actor. He wanted Mitch to direct him. "I think you should do it."

"Really?"

"Absolutely, because you're passionate about it. You should always work on whatever you're most passionate about. Otherwise you're just another meat sack, wasting your time, wasting your life . . ." Mitch applied more syrup to his tongue. "Unless you can't afford to do it, that is."

"Hell yes, I can afford it. They gave me twenty mil for *Dark Star*. That's my going rate now. I'm in the club, man. But, see, my agent wants me and Esme to do this romantic comedy together, *Puppy Love*."

"I'll probably be sorry I asked you this, but what's it about?"

"I play a young veterinarian from the wrong side of the tracks," Tito replied woodenly. "She's a high-class breeder of champion basset hounds. We meet. We fall in love. We fall out of love. We—"

"Say no more. Please." It sounded like a feel-good sapfest, the kind where exhibitors ought to post a sign at the box office reading Diabetics Enter at Own Risk. "Do you like the script?"

"No, I hate it. It's just this bunch of cute, fake moments, strung together like beads. Totally Hollywood, if you know what I mean."

"Oh, I know exactly what you mean."

"But it's a go project. The studio's behind it."

"And Esme?"

"She'll do it if I will. But I don't know, man. I feel like . . ." Tito ran a hand over his face, distraught. "I feel like I don't have any real say in what happens. Like I'm not an actual person, just a character in a movie that somebody else is creating. None of it's real. I'm not real. Esme's not real. Esme and me, Chrissie and me . . ."

"What about Chrissie and you?" Mitch asked, frowning.

"Nothing, man. Forget that. Would you read the pages I've written?" he asked Mitch nervously.

"I'd be honored," replied Mitch, who found himself discovering the same thing about Tito that Dodge had. Mitch liked the guy. He didn't expect to, but he did. There was genuine boyish innocence to him that came through in spite of that twitchy anger. "Mind you, this means I won't be able to review it when it comes out. Hey, wait, is this all just an insidious ploy to disqualify me?"

"No way," Tito insisted. "I'm not that clever, man. I swear it."

"In that case, I'll be happy to read your pages. Drop them by any time."

Tito sat there staring out the window for a long moment. "I don't know, it's all just so . . ." He trailed off. Briefly, he seemed very far away. Then he shook himself and drained his scotch. "I'm in the middle of something bad. Something I got myself into. And I can't get out of it."

Mitch watched the actor curiously. Was he still talking about *Puppy Love* or had he moved on to something else? Mitch couldn't tell. "You can get out of anything if you really want to. You're in charge of your own life, Tito. You have the power."

"What power, man? I don't even know who I am."

"Do you want to know?"

"Yes, absolutely."

"Trust me, that puts you way ahead of most people."

Now Tito jumped to his feet, so suddenly that Mitch found himself flinching. It was an involuntary thing, and if the actor noticed it he didn't let on. "Gotta go. Big thanks, man."

"For what, Tito?"

"The T-shirt," he replied, flashing a smile at him.

"I wouldn't mind getting that back, if you think of it."

"You can have it right now," Tito said easily. "I'm all dried off."

"No, go ahead and wear it home. It's damp out. You might catch cold. Besides, it looks so much better on you."

Tito went to the door and opened it, pausing there in the doorway. "Sorry about this afternoon."

"It's forgotten, as far I'm concerned. Can I give you a lift back to your car?"

"Naw, I'm cool. I'll take that bridge thing back. The walk will do me good. Later, man."

Mitch flicked on the porch light and watched Tito Molina melt soundlessly into the fog just like Sinatra did after he delivered the Arabian pony to the young lord in *The List of Adrian Messenger*, one of Mitch's favorite thrillers in spite of George C. Scott's awful English accent. Quirt was curled up on a tarp under the bay window, his eyes shining at Mitch. Mitch said good night to him, then flicked off the light and went back inside, breathing deeply in and out.

He hadn't realized it, but he had been holding his breath practically the entire time since he'd walked in on Tito.

He crawled right into bed, Clemmie snuggling up against his chest for the first time in weeks. Mitch didn't know if this was her trying to atone for being disloyal to him or whether she just felt cold. And he didn't much care. He was just grateful to have her there. Exhausted, he lay there stroking her tummy and listening to her purr. And now the rain started to patter softly against the skylights over his bed. Mitch lay there with Clemmie, listening to it come down and growing sleepier by the second. Soon, they had both drifted off.

His bedside phone jarred him awake. He didn't know how long he'd been asleep. It didn't seem like very long. He fumbled for it, jostling Clemmie, who sprang from the bed and scampered downstairs. "H-Hello . . . Whassa? . . ."

"I'm sorry if I woke you. I just wanted you to know something."

"Okay . . . Uh, sure." Mitch sat up, recognizing the voice on the other end despite the steady, persistent roar in the background. "Where are you?"

"I'm on Sugar Mountain, with the barkers and the colored balloons."

"Wait, give me a second, I know what that's . . . Neil Young, right?"

"You are."

"What's that whooshing noise? Are you hanging out in a men's room somewhere?"

"Not exactly."

"What time is it anyway?"

"It's too late. The damage is done. The hangman says it's time to let her fly."

"*What* hangman? What the hell are you talking about?"

"Good-bye, Mitch."

"Wait, don't—!"

No use. The line had already gone dead.

Mitch lay there trying to figure out what on earth had just happened. Briefly, he wondered if he'd simply dreamed the whole conversation. He decided there was no sense to be made of it now. He was just too damned tired. So he rolled over and fell immediately back to sleep.

Until another phone call awakened him. This time it was Des. It was dawn now and a steady, driving rain was pounding the skylight over Mitch's head.

"Baby, I'm sorry to wake you—"

"No, no. I'm glad you called," he assured her, yawning. "I didn't feel good about how we left things yesterday. I shouldn't have hung up on you."

"Mitch . . ."

"I was just having a bad day. I understand that you have to obsess. If you don't, you won't get anywhere."

"Mitch . . ."

"So was that our first real fight? Because if it was I don't think it was that bad, do you?"

"Baby, please listen to me. . . ."

Something in her voice stopped him now. "Why, what is it?"

"I'm on my way up to the Devil's Hopyard. The ranger's found a body at the base of the falls. A jumper, apparently."

The hangman says it's time to let her fly.

Mitch's heart began to pound. "God, I should have known. The *falls*, damn it. That's what I was hearing. . . ."

"When?" she demanded. "What do you know about this?"

"It's him, isn't it?" he said, his voice filling with dread. "It's Tito."

She didn't need to answer him. Her silence said it all.

Mitch closed his eyes and let out a groan of sheer agony.

His own worst nightmare had just taken a giant leap into pure horror.

CHAPTER 6

THE ROAD UP TO the Devil's Hopyard State Park was intensely twisty and narrow. Des's cruiser very nearly scraped the mountain laurel and hemlocks that grew on either side of it as she steered her way toward the falls, the wet pavement steaming in front of her as the sunlight broke through the early morning haze. Already, she had her air conditioning cranked up high. The Hopyard was situated in Dorset's remote northeast corner. Very few people lived up here. She spotted a farmhouse every once in a while. Mostly she saw only granite ledge and trees, trees, trees.

The road dead-ended at the entrance to the falls, where a uniformed park ranger was waiting for Des next to a green pickup. Due to funding cuts, many of the state parks made do with summer interns, most of them college students. Kathleen Moloney, the trimly built blond who met Des, was exceedingly young and fresh faced.

Des nosed up alongside of the pickup and got out, her horn-rimmed glasses immediately fogging up in the warm, humid air. Des had to wipe them dry with the clean white handkerchief that she kept in her back pocket.

One other vehicle, a scraped-up black Jeep Wrangler, was parked there in the ditch next to the gate.

"It's just awful," Kathleen said to her over the steady roar of the falls, her voice cracking. "I've *never* seen anything like this. I was making my routine morning swing through the park, you know? I didn't even know what I was looking at when I first saw him. I swear, I just thought it was a bundle of old clothes."

"I'm sorry you had to see it," Des said to her sympathetically. Finding a jumper was definitely pukeworthy.

Des paused to take a closer look at the Jeep. The scrapes were fresh—loose flecks of black paint came right off on her fingers. A mud-splattered cell phone lay on the wet ground a few feet away on the driver's side. Before she did anything else Des bagged it and stashed it in her trunk. Then she opened the Jeep's passenger door and poked around inside. She spotted no suicide note. She did find a car rental agreement stuffed in the glove compartment, made out to Tito Molina. She returned it to the glove compartment and closed the Jeep back up.

"Let's go have us a look, Kathleen, okay? And if you start to feel the least bit funky, just sing out. We don't have any heroes in this unit."

The young ranger smiled at her gratefully and ushered her inside the gate on foot, where there was a parking lot adjoined by picnic grounds. At this spot, they were up above the waterfall. "It's happened before," she told Des as they walked. "A pair of lovers jumped off together back in the '80s. And there was a teenaged boy high on drugs a couple of years ago. I was warned. But I still . . . I wasn't ready for this."

"Trust me, no one is," Des said as they arrived at a guardrail that was posted with a sign: *Let the Water Do the Falling. Stay Behind This Point.*

"I think I know where he jumped from. We can take a look before we go down, if you'd like. Just watch your step."

Des followed her over the guardrail and out onto a bare outcropping of rock, stepping carefully. The granite surface was slick and mossy, and the soles of her brogans were not ideal for rock climbing. An empty pint bottle of peppermint schnapps lay there. She eyeballed it to see if he'd left a suicide note rolled up inside of it. He hadn't. Beyond that, she kept her distance, not wanting to compromise the scene. From where she stood she saw a few spent matches. No muddy shoeprints on the granite. Not that she expected any. The night's rain would have washed them away.

"You can see him from here." said Kathleen, crouching near the edge of the outcropping.

Des inched over beside her and peered over the side of the sheer granite face. Mostly, what she saw was the swirling white foam of the river as it came crashing down onto the smooth, shiny gray a hundred feet below. But then her eyes did make out a small patch of color—a figure in an orange T-shirt and blue jeans that lay there down on those rocks.

"Okay, Kathleen, I've seen enough."

They retraced their footsteps back to the guardrail and made their way down a narrow footpath to the base of the falls. It was a steep and demanding descent. The path was not only mucky from the rain but was crisscrossed with exposed tree roots. Des wished she had on hiking boots like the ranger did.

Tito Molina had landed faceup on the boulders that were next to river, his eyes wide open. His arms and legs seemed grotesquely shrunken inside of the T-shirt and jeans he had on. He looked like a small boy dressed in a man's clothing. His famous, chiseled face had crumpled in upon itself, like a high-rise building after the demolition man has imploded it. Blood and brain matter had oozed out onto the rocks from under his shattered head. The back of his skull seemed to have borne the brunt of the impact, which Des found a bit surprising. So did the direction he was facing—his feet were pointing *toward* the outcropping that he'd leapt from. She stood there looking at him for a long moment, feeling that old, familiar uptick of her pulse. She hadn't felt it for a while. Not handing out traffic tickets to obnoxious tourists.

Briefly, her eyes lingered on the T-shirt Tito was wearing. It was a New York Mets 1986 World Series T-shirt, a shirt that she swore she'd seen Mitch wear. In fact, it was one of his prized possessions. Why on earth would Tito Molina be wearing it?

Now she tilted her head back and gazed up, up toward the top of the cliff, which loomed straight overhead. Rooted there in a fissure in the granite face, perhaps ten feet beneath the rock outcropping where they'd found the schnapps bottle, Des could make out a small, hardy cedar tree clinging for life. Tito's fall had snapped off one of its limbs. The raw wood stood out like exposed bone against the darkness of the stone. She stared at the tree, transfixed, certain that it was trying to whisper something crucial to the suffering artist deep inside of her. But whatever it was she couldn't comprehend it. Didn't speak the right language. Didn't even know any of the words. Didn't know. Didn't know . . .

"I didn't move him or anything," Kathleen said, raising her voice. The roar of the falls was even louder down here. "I couldn't bring myself to get near him."

"You did right, Kathleen."

"I have a tarp in my truck. Should we cover him?"

"We don't want to go anywhere near him," said Des. "That's the medical examiner's deal. What we do need to do is secure this scene. Are the other entrances to the park open yet?"

"No, I always open this gate first."

"Well, that's a help," she said, knowing full well that once word of this got out the paparazzi would be coming over, around, and through any gate they could find. "I need for you to stand guard over the body while I radio in. No one, but no one, comes near it, okay?"

"I guess so," she answered, visibly uncomfortable.

"You don't have to look at him, Kathleen. Just stay here with your back toward him. Anyone gets close, you chase 'em off. I'll be back with the cavalry just as soon as I can. Can you do that for me?"

The young ranger nodded at her gamely.

"You the man, Kathleen."

Des hiked back up to her ride and radioed the Troop F Barracks in Westbrook for as many cruisers as they could spare, then the medical examiner's office for a team of investigators. Based on her own observations, Des also made the decision to reach out to her old unit, the Central District headquarters of the Major Crime Squad in Meriden.

Then it was also up to her to notify the next of kin. As the morning sun broke bright and hot over the trees, she phoned Martine, figuring the news might go down easier if Esme heard it from her mother.

"Martine, we have a situation up here at the Hopyard," she said, keeping her voice calm. "It's Tito. We found him at the base of the falls."

"He's . . . dead?" Martine's voice was a frightened whisper.

"He is. Can you inform Esme?"

"Absolutely. We'll be up there right away."

"I'm not so sure that's a good idea."

"She'll need to see him, Des. She'll insist. I won't be able to stop her."

"I understand. That being the case you might want to bring Chrissie along for the ride."

"Why would we do that?" Martine asked, her voice turning chilly.

"It's going to be a total zoo."

"Yes, you're absolutely right. I wasn't even thinking. I'm just so . . ." Martine sighed mournfully. "Why would Tito *do* such a thing? He was so talented and loved. That poor, beautiful boy."

"Martine, you'd better prepare Esme for something else. . . ."

"What is it, Des?"

"Tito's not beautiful anymore."

The first trooper to arrive on the scene established a perimeter by shutting down the narrow Hopyard Road all the way back at Route 82. More cruisers started arriving soon after that. Des directed them to the other park entrances, and sent a trooper down the path on foot to take over for Kathleen. A medical examiner's van pulled up next and a pair of brisk, efficient investigators in blue jumpsuits hopped out. Des directed them to the body. Then the crime scene technicians started arriving in their cube vans, followed closely by a slicktop with two Major Crime Squad investigators in it.

The investigator behind the wheel was a woman of color. A short, muscle-bound man was riding shotgun. Des knew this man only too well—Rico "Soave" Tedone had been her sergeant back when she was a lieutenant on Major Crimes. Soave was one of the Brass City boys, kid brother of a capo in the state police's so-called Waterbury mafia. When they'd knifed her, it was Soave who'd wielded the blade. At the time, she had hated him for it. Not that he was a bad person, just immature, a work in progress, a *man*. Now that Soave was a lieutenant and Des was Dorset's resident trooper, their relationship had thawed considerably, so much so that when he'd finally gotten around to marrying his high school sweetheart, Tawny, Des had been invited and actually gone to the wedding.

"Yo, Des!" he called to her warmly as he climbed out of the slick-top, flexing his body-builder's muscles inside of his shiny black suit. He always wore black. Thought it made him look classy. In truth, it made him look like a chauffeur.

"How are you, Rico?"

"Never better," he said, grinning at her.

Marriage did seem to agree with him. He looked cheerful and relaxed. Possibly even a bit jowly. And he'd finally shaved off his dead caterpillar of a mustache, Des was happy to note, although he had not lost his nervous habit of smoothing it with his thumb and forefinger. Except now all he was smoothing was bare skin.

"What have you got for us, Des?"

"Got you one dead movie actor."

"He jumped?"

"Very good question, wow man. Happily, I don't have to answer that. You do."

Soave's partner started toward them now, dressed in a sleeveless lime green knit top, tan slacks, and chunky boots that gave her a couple of inches on Soave. She was a good five feet nine and built like a rottweiler with jugs. Huge jugs.

"Now, here's a meeting I've been looking forward to," Soave said eagerly. "Des Mitry, give it up for my new partner, Yolie Snipes."

Des had heard about Yolie Snipes on the grapevine. The boys called her Boom Boom because of what she had going on inside of her shirt. She was half-Cuban, half-black, and all player—young, tough and street smart.

"God, this is just such a thrill for me," Yolie exulted as she pumped Des's hand. She wore her nails short and painted them purple. Her grip was like iron. "Where I come from you are a legend and it is such an honor to even be on the same investigation as you." She talked extremely fast and her voice seemed to come all the way up from her diaphragm. "Word, girl, I have been wanting to meet you *forever*."

"Glad to know you, Yolie," Des said, a bit blown away by her motor. Yolie Snipes was a girl in a hurry. She had a latina's creamy mocha skin and gleaming brown eyes, but her big lips and wide-bottomed bootay spelled sister all the way. So did the braids. She had a thin one-inch scar across her left cheek that looked as if it had been done by a razor, maybe a box cutter. She wore silver studs in her ears, no makeup or lipstick. She was bigged up—had a weight-lifter's rippling arms. She wore the portrait of a woman's face tattooed on her left biceps with the initials *AC* written underneath it.

"Walk this back for us, Des," Soave said. "You have some concerns about the body?"

"I do, although we all know that this was a man with his share of personal problems. And it certainly plays suicide. Looks as if he drove his Jeep up here late last night, got himself drunk, and threw his bad self off a cliff."

"Damned crazy fool," Soave said disapprovingly. "Here's a young guy pulling down millions, is married to a world-class hottie. Why go and do that?"

"It wasn't making him happy, Rico."

"Did you find a note?"

"No, I didn't. But I did bag his cell." She popped her trunk and handed it over. "He placed a call on it from right here at around one-thirty." They could learn the exact time from his cell phone record. "The words he used sounded an awful lot like good-bye."

Soave glanced at her curiously. "You know who he called?"

"I do. It was Mitch."

"Who, Berger?" Soave had always been bewildered by Mitch's presence in her life. "Are you telling me he and Tito Molina were tight?"

"Not exactly. Tito went after him yesterday."

"Sure, sure, I saw it on the news last night," Yolie spoke up. "Tito whooped this movie critic's ass on account of he gave him a bad review."

"You're not saying that's why he killed himself, are you?" Soave asked. "Because Berger hurt his little feelings?"

"No, I don't believe so," Des replied, wondering if Mitch was thinking this.

"Well, what did he say to Berger?"

"You can get the exact words from him. He's waiting to hear from you."

"Okay, good," Soave said. "What else have we got?"

"Tito's ride." Des pointed out the Jeep's freshly scraped paint job.

"Could be this happened earlier in the day," Yolie suggested, kneeling for a better look. "If they phoned in an accident report then the car rental people will have a record of it. Then again, he might have sideswiped somebody on his way up here last night. I'll see if anyone reported it, maybe canvass those farmhouses down the road. Could be somebody heard him hit a tree or something."

This was a sharp one, Des observed. Her mind broke down all of the angles in a flash. "There's an empty bottle of peppermint schnapps up at the top of the cliff. Also some spent matches. I didn't see anything else."

"Yolie, why don't you go have a look?" Soave said. "I'll check out the body with Des."

"I'm on it." Yolie immediately went charging off.

"It's real slippery up there," Des called after her. "Watch your step."

"I always do," Yolie Snipes responded, smiling at her over her shoulder.

"She's an eager one, isn't she?" Des said as she watched her make her way across the parking lot, big bottom shake-shake-shaking. Des could only imagine what was happening to the girl's front end.

"Twenty-four-seven," Soave agreed, smoothing his former mustache. "You slap her down, she bounces right back up. That's Boom Boom. She makes me feel middle-aged, you want to know the truth."

"Rico, you *are* middle aged," Des informed him as they started their way down the footpath to the base of the falls.

"Between us, the wife can't stand her. Thinks she's a scheming slut bomb. Not true. This is a good kid. Tawny's just jealous, you ask me."

"Does Tawny have any reason to be?"

"Hell no," Soave said indignantly. "I'm a happily married man. Me and Tawny just put in an offer on our first house. Besides, Boom Boom's hooked up with my cousin Richie."

"The one who works Narcotics?"

"The two of them are real tight. You know what they're calling her up at the Headmaster's House?" Soave glanced at her slyly. "The next Des Mitry. How do you like that?"

She didn't. It made her feel like she'd retired to Boca Raton or died.

"I'm telling you, Boom Boom's the complete package," he said, stepping his way carefully over the bare roots in the path. "Plus I never have to worry about her drowning."

Des shot a cold look at him in response.

He immediately reddened. "Sorry, Des, you know how I backslide when I've been away from you."

"I do know that, Rico. But I still keep hoping for a miracle."

Tito was in the middle of his final photo shoot as they scampered down onto the rocks. The assistant ME was photographing the star from every possible angle before they transported his body to Farmington for the autopsy, which was automatic whenever there was an accidental or unexplained death.

"What a stupid waste," Soave said, shaking his head at the dead actor disgustedly. "Okay, what are you selling, Des?"

"I'm not *selling* anything, Rico. I just wanted to point out something about the way he landed."

"What about it?"

"The back of his head took the brunt of the impact. That's not consistent with a swan dive. He should have landed facedown, not up."

Soave considered this for a moment, his wheels starting to turn. "So he somersaulted in the air, end over end."

"If that were the case then his head would be where his feet are. He's turned completely the wrong way around, Rico."

"You're right, he is." Soave furrowed his brow thoughtfully. "Maybe the water shifted him around after he landed."

"The man's dry, and there's no blood anywhere else. He's lying right where he hit."

"So he spiraled in the air. That would explain it. The wind can do that."

"There was no wind last night."

"What are you saying, Des?"

"That the position of his body is consistent with someone who was standing with his back to the edge of the cliff and then pitched over backwards. *Or* got pushed."

He peered at her, his eyes narrowing. "Still can't get used to the slow lane, can you? You want back in the game."

"I am totally fine right where I am, Rico. I just thought I'd share my professional concerns with you before you call it. But if you want to blow me off that's totally fine by me."

"Come on, don't get all huffy."

"I do *not* get huffy. I get riled. I get pissed. I get—"

"Whoa, I agree with you, okay?" Soave said, holding his hands up in a gesture of surrender. "It don't read right. That makes it a suspicious death. And that's how we're going to play it." He ordered the crime scene technicians to proceed with maximum care, and to relay that up top to Yolie. Then they started their way back up the path toward the gate. It was becoming very hot out. Soave was perspiring heavily. "Good catch, Des," he said, swiping at his face with a handkerchief. "Thanks for the heads-up."

"You're very welcome," she said crisply.

"You're in a lousy mood this morning, know that?"

"I don't mean to be, Rico. These are my people. I know them."

"There's going to be a major media feeding frenzy, am I right?" he asked, his voice filling with dread.

"There is," she said, thinking that this was a new sign of maturity on his part. Earlier in his career, he'd been supremely hyped at the prospect of getting his face on television. But now that he'd gone before the bright lights a couple of times, he knew just how hot they could get. And had the burn marks to prove it.

"I'm giving them no labels on this one," he said, steeling himself out loud. "I don't say suicide. And I for damned sure don't say murder. Neither of those words comes out of this man's hole. Not once. All I say is it's an unexplained death and that we're still gathering information."

"They'll try to get you to confirm that it's an 'apparent' suicide," Des said. "You say—"

"I say that nothing is 'apparent' at this time."

"Even though they'll go right ahead and call it that anyway."

"Damned straight."

By the time they got back up to the gate the TV news vans were already stacked ten-deep on the shoulder of the road. Cameramen and reporters had swarmed the entrance to the park, shouting questions and demanding answers. The uniformed troopers could barely hold them back.

"How did they get past that roadblock?" Soave wondered.

"They're like mice, Rico. All they need is a quarter-inch crack of daylight and they're in."

Now they heard a car horn blaring. It was Martine's VW Beetle convertible. She was trying desperately to get through the horde, but couldn't. Esme finally leaped out of the car a hundred yards short of the gate and ran barefoot the rest of the way. Chrissie Huberman jumped out in hot pursuit. The press people let out a shout. Their cameras rolled.

"I want to see him!" Esme sobbed as she reached Des, the tears streaming down her porcelain cheeks. "I *have* to!"

"I really wouldn't do that, honey," Des said, as Soave stood there gaping at the beautiful young actress.

"Tito, why did you *do* this?!" she cried out, her stage-trained voice carrying over the roar of the waterfall. "Tito, where are you? *TITO?!* . . ." Esme fell to her knees, sobbing hysterically.

Chrissie knelt beside her, tears streaming down her own face, Des noticed.

And that wasn't all Des noticed. Something new about Esme's look caught her eye: The actress was sporting a great big fat swollen lip this morning.

Somebody had recently punched Esme Crockett in the mouth.

"Girl, I heard *so* much about you when I was coming up," Yolie Snipes gushed from the seat next to her as Des piloted her cruiser back down the narrow Hopyard Road. "First sister to investigate homicides in state history, cover of *Connecticut* magazine when you were twenty-three—I can't believe I'm riding in the same car with you."

"You're being too kind," said Des, who was never comfortable with flattery. "Where'd you grow up, Yolie?"

"The Hollow," she grunted. Frog Hollow was Hartford's most burned-out ghetto. It was nowhere. "My mom died of an overdose a year after I was born."

"And your dad?"

"Never even knew who he was. Everyone I came up with was inmate-bound, me included, but my aunt Celia made sure I got out."

"AC?" asked Des, referring to the portrait on her arm.

Yolie's face lit up. "That's right. She kept me together, body and soul, until I got me my four-year ride to Rutgers."

"You played ball, am I right?"

"It's all that," she acknowledged. "My total dream was to play the point for Coach Geno at Storrs. He scouted me, too, but there was no way I was going to beat out Suzy Bird for playing time. Not in this life. So I moved on down the road to Piscataway, played for Coach Vivian. And we scratched and we clawed and we won us a few. Got my degree in criminal justice. Came back home, took the test, and here I am."

They passed through the roadblock at Route 82, waving to the trooper who was stationed there, and Des started toward the shore now, cruising among the lush green gentlemen's farms with their fieldstone walls and two hundred-year-old houses set way back under canopies of maple trees.

"I never worked a town like this before," Yolie confessed, gazing anxiously out her window at the moneyed countryside.

"You'll do fine. The people here are no different than people anywhere else. They just have longer driveways and better manners."

"Can I ask you for some advice, sister to sister? It's about Soave. . . ."

"What about him?"

"He's a decent man, but my read on him is he won't be moving up. What I mean is, he's got the juice but not the smarts. Am I right about that?"

"He's a good officer," Des said tactfully. "Don't underestimate him."

"I'm not. I'm just, at this point in my career I'm looking to hook up with people who I can learn from. And I'm thinking I've gotten just about all I can out of Soave. I don't mean to sound cold. Just being honest, know what I'm saying?"

"Sure, I do," said Des, thinking that Soave would probably be reporting to Yolie Snipes in a couple of years.

"I might put in for a transfer to Narcotics," she went on. "Or maybe the gangs task force. The street's where I can do the most damage. I *know* the street. That sound like a smart move to you?"

"It does. Just bear in mind that he'll be really insulted. He's thin-skinned."

"Who, Soave? Shut up!"

"And he does have the juice, like you said. Trust me, you do not want that little man for an enemy. Those Waterbury boys are strictly about family and we are *so* not related."

"You saying he'd trash me?"

"I'm saying be careful," Des replied as she cruised into Dorset's business district. Big Brook Road was quiet. The vacationers were still in bed. She turned onto Old Shore at the traffic light and headed for Big Sister.

"This Mitch Berger we're talking to—he's your boy, right?"

"That's right."

"How is that?"

Des glanced at Yolie curiously. "How is what?"

Yolie raised an eyebrow at her. "The pink of things."

"So far so good."

"Myself, I've never road tested a nonbrother."

"I thought you and Soave's cousin Richie . . ."

"No, we're just friends. He'd like to get with me, but I'm not playing that game right now. I'm just so damned tired of getting hurt. Word, are they any nicer?"

Des shrugged. "They're still men."

"Soave had him a major chubby for you, you know."

"He *told* you that?"

"Didn't have to. I can see it in his eyes whenever he talks about you. And he talks about you a lot."

"Well, it never went anywhere, if that's what you were wondering. Strictly his chocolate fantasy—you know how that goes."

Yolie nodded her braided head. "I am, like, uh-hunh. They all want to find out what it's like to get with Sheena, Queen of the Jungle. What do they think, that we hang from the chandelier by our ankles?"

"What, you mean you don't?"

Yolie let out a hoot. "Girl, you've got you a bad self. We're going to be okay."

"Yolie, I never had any doubts."

Des turned off Old Shore at the Peck's Point Nature Preserve. The preserve was open from sunup till sundown. There were footpaths, bike paths, a green meadow that tumbled its way down to the tidal marshes, where the osprey nested. The moisture from the night's rain shimmered on the tall meadow grass in the morning sunlight.

Yolie gazed out the window with her mouth open, overwhelmed by the serene beauty of the place.

Des had grown so accustomed to it that she forgot sometimes just how spectacular it was. She eased her way slowly along the dirt road, passing a couple of joggers who were out with their dogs. The road ended at the barricaded causeway out to Big Sister Island. Des had a key to raise the barricade. Slowly, she eased across the rickety wooden causeway, seeing Big Sister through Yolie's eyes as Yolie took in the lighthouse, the historic mansions, the acres of woods and private beach.

"Shut up, girl! No wonder you dig him—man's got his own private island."

"It's not all his."

"Who *is* this man?"

"He's just someone who happens to know everything there is to know about every single movie that's ever been made in the history of the planet."

"Sounds like a geek."

"That he is—but he's my geek."

Des pulled up in the gravel driveway outside his cottage. Mitch was on his knees in his vegetable patch, weeding with furious intent. Quirt sat right by his side, keenly interested in every clump of fresh soil Mitch was turning over. The lean orange tabby came running to greet Des when he heard her get out. Rubbed up against her ankle, talking up a storm. She bent over and scratched his chin as Mitch got up off his knees, swiping at his sweaty brow, and ambled toward them.

He looked sad and confused and hurt. In fact, he looked exactly the way he had the very first time Des laid eyes on him, the day he'd found that man's body buried in this very vegetable garden. The only thing different about him now was his red, swollen jaw.

"Hey, Master Sergeant," he said to her, his jaw clenched tightly shut. It must have stiffened on him in the night.

"Hey, baby," she said gently, putting her hand on his rather damp shoulder. What she wanted to do was hold him tight, make it all go away. "Say hello to Sergeant Yolie Snipes—she's Rico's new partner."

"We came to ask you some questions about Tito Molina, Mr. Berger," Yolie said to him solicitously. "Are you okay with that?"

Mitch was fine with it. "Let's go inside and get a cold drink. Sorry I sound so funny, Sergeant. I feel just like Al Pacino in the first *Godfather* after he got punched by Sterling Hayden. Remember that scene in Brando's study when Michael tells Sonny *he's* going to be the trigger man in the Italian restaurant? The camera moves in on him slooowly as he sits there, commanding the attention of all of the men in the room, and that's when it dawns on you that *he's* the new godfather. Man, that was great moviemaking."

He shlumped inside the house ahead of them, Yolie pausing to whisper, "Girl, does he talk about movies *all* the time?"

"Only when he's awake."

"You didn't tell me he was so cute. He squeak when you squeeze him?"

Des smiled at her. "That's not all he does."

That morning's New York newspapers were stacked on Mitch's desk, the *Daily News* and *Post* featuring identical page-one photographs of Tito astride Mitch with his hands around his throat. Already it was old news.

"Have you been getting a lot of calls from reporters?" Des asked him.

"I wouldn't know. I unplugged the phone after I spoke to you."

He washed his hands and face in the deep, scarred kitchen sink, then poured each of them a tall glass of iced tea with sprigs of mint from his garden. He handed them around, then flopped down in his one good chair as Des and Yolie took the loveseat. "Whew, it's sticky as hell out there this morning," he said, breathing heavily. "I apologize if I smell like a plow horse, but I'm learning that physical work helps me when I'm down."

"I head straight for the weight room myself," Yolie spoke up, her head swiveling as she took in the view of the Sound from three different directions. She was, Des observed, very uneasy here in Mitch's cottage. Also very anxious to make a good impression on the Deacon's daughter. So anxious she was slouching a tiny bit as she sat there beside Des, just enough so that her immense breasts were less of a temptation for Mitch to stare at. Des knew why—Yolie did not want Des thinking that she'd been waving them in her boyfriend's face. This was an aware, careful girl. A girl who missed nothing.

"Mitch, we need to talk about that phone call you got from Tito," Des said, shifting them into business gear.

"Yeah, okay," he agreed, sipping his iced tea carefully. Some of it dribbled down his chin anyway. "I hadn't been asleep very long. In fact, it seemed as if he'd just left."

"Whoa, he was *here* last night? You didn't tell me that part."

"Yeah, he was sitting right here when I got home from the beach club."

"How did he get out here?"

"He swam out, which should have told me something right away."

"Why is that, Mr. Berger?" Yolie asked, gulping down some iced tea.

"Call me Mitch, would you? You're scaring me with that mister stuff."

She flashed a quick smile at him. "Done, Mitch."

"The tide was coming in," he explained. "It's dangerous. Anyone who tries that can't be thinking straight."

"You couldn't have known what he'd do," Des told him. "Besides, it's too soon to say what did happen. We don't know yet."

"I should have known," he repeated stubbornly.

"Did you give him your Mets T-shirt to wear?"

"He sort of borrowed it. I'm never going to see that shirt again, am I?"

"You wouldn't want it back, believe me."

"Please tell us what happened when he was here," said Yolie, politely taking over the inquiry, pad and pen in hand.

"Nothing," Mitch replied, shrugging. "We talked."

"It was a friendly talk? You were vibing?"

"We totally were," Mitch said, his voice filling with regret. "He told me he wanted to make a movie about his father's life. He said he'd already written most of it. He asked me if I'd mind reading it. I said I'd be happy to."

"What time did he leave here?"

"Eleven or so."

"Was he high?"

"You mean on drugs? I don't think so. He did drink a lot of my scotch, but he was plenty coherent. I offered to give him a ride back to his car. He said he was okay to walk."

"Where was his car?"

"He left it back at the town beach parking lot."

"How long does it take to walk there from here?"

"I've never timed it, Sergeant. A good half hour, maybe forty-five minutes."

Yolie jotted this down in her notepad. "That would put him in the parking lot by around midnight?"

"Yeah, I guess."

"Did he mention Esme to you?" Des interjected.

"He said she was his princess. He said she should be wearing a tiara and sash."

"She showed up just now at the falls wearing a fat lip," Des told him. "Did he say anything about them fighting? That he'd struck her, anything like that?"

"No, not at all. The only negative thing he had to say about Esme was that she sometimes didn't listen to him. But he wanted her to play his mother in the movie he was writing. He wouldn't have mentioned that if they were having serious problems, would he?" Mitch paused, sipping his iced tea distractedly. "Tito also wanted some advice from me."

"What about?" Yolie asked.

"Sergeant, I've been asking myself that very same question ever since Des called," Mitch confessed, running a hand through his curly black hair. "We were talking about his career, okay? There was this movie called *Puppy Love* that his agent wanted him to do, and Tito really didn't want to do it. And then he told me he felt trapped. Being a total idiot who doesn't know how to keep his big mouth shut, I told him that if he was caught up in something he didn't want to be in that he had the power to get out of it."

"Sounds fair to me," Yolie said.

Mitch shook his head at her miserably. "What if he wasn't talking about his career anymore when he said that? What if he was talking about *life*? Think about it, he's sitting here, this unstable, deeply disturbed actor. . . . What if he was trying to tell me that he wanted to end it all? Don't you realize what I did? I gave him the green light. Look at what happened—as soon as left here he drove straight up to the falls and jumped right off a cliff." Mitch slumped in his chair despondently. "God, I may as well have pushed him."

"Don't go there, Mitch," Des ordered him.

"Can you tell us about this phone call you got from him?" Yolie said.

"I was in bed asleep," Mitch said hollowly. "He sounded . . . He was just really down. He said that it was too late. Then he started talking about the hangman. 'The damage is done. The hangman says it's time to let her fly.' That's from a Neil Young song."

"Neil Young." Yolie repeated. "He's that weird old hippie guy, right?"

Mitch stared at her coldly. "He's not weird and he's not old."

"Do yourself a solid, girl," Des advised her. "Stay away from pop culture entirely."

"Mitch, what did you take that to mean?" Yolie pressed on.

"At the time, nothing. But now . . . now I take it to mean that he was about to commit suicide, don't you?" Mitch got up out of his chair and went over toward the windows, standing with his back to them for a long moment. When he turned to face them, his eyes had filled with tears. "I'm the last person on earth who spoke to him," he declared, his voice rising with emotion. "If only I'd said something else, *anything* else. Maybe the right words would have changed his mind. Maybe he'd still be alive."

"I repeat," Des said to him sharply. "Don't go there!"

"Des, I'm already there! And I don't know how to deal with it. How do I live with myself from now on? How do I look at myself in mirror every day? I *killed* him, don't you get it? I killed Tito Molina!"

Chapter 7

As soon as Des and that chesty new sergeant of Soave's cleared out Mitch threw his Power Book and some blank notepads into his day pack. Put down a three-day supply of kibble and water for Clemmie and Quirt. Closed up the house, jumped in his truck and fled.

He did not tell Des he was leaving. He only knew he had to get gone.

He made a quick stop at the House of Turkish Delights for baklava and good, strong coffee. One look at Nema Acar's face when he walked in and Mitch could tell she'd heard the news about Tito's death plunge on the radio.

One look at Mitch's face and she could tell he didn't want to talk about it.

"You got your window replaced," he observed, his voice sounding a bit husky.

"We did, yes," Nema said brightly. "And we were visited by the Hate Crimes officers. They said our misfortune does not correspond with anything presently in their database. Mitch, they don't know if they will find these people."

"They *won't* find them," Nuri said insistently as he came out from the back room with a bucket and mop. "I have told you this many times. And did you listen to me? No, you did not."

Nema's mouth tightened, but she said nothing in response.

"I made very clear to them my feelings," he went on, speaking to Mitch now. "They offered to station a cruiser here for one, perhaps two, weeks, as protection. I told them no, thank you. I do not wish to frighten away my customers, do I? This is a business matter, and therefore I shall raise it with the Dorset Merchants Association."

Mitch was definitely experiencing the tension between the Acars that Des had mentioned. And he most definitely did not want to get caught in the middle.

He pocketed his change and got out of there as fast as he could, devouring his baklava as he drove to the Old Saybrook Amtrak station. Here he caught what the locals called the Toonerville Trolley, the poky little Shoreliner train that connected up the beach towns with New Haven, where the Metro-North commuter train into Grand Central could be picked up. It was a two-and-a-half-hour trip altogether.

The morning rush hour had passed so he had a seat to himself. His Power Book could run for up to six hours on its battery. He immediately fired it up, drained his coffee, and got to work.

First, he made notes. Tried to remember every single word Tito Molina had said to him as he sat there in Mitch's chair, drinking his scotch. Every mannerism, every inflection. Tried to summon up the phone call that woke him in the night. Then he moved on to his other recollections, such as how exhilarated he'd felt that night he'd seen Tito on stage in *Death of a Salesman*. He wrote about the high point of Tito's movie career, *Rebel Without a Cause*. He wrote about Tito's unfulfilled dream to film his father's life story. When he changed trains at New Haven Mitch kept right on writing. He had to keep on writing—until he could get to the city and find some real relief for what ailed him. Mitch wrote and he wrote, stitching all of his recollections and impressions together now into a cohesive essay. So totally absorbed in his work was he that he was surprised when he discovered they were already arriving at the station at 125th Street. The trip had flown right by.

When his train pulled into the belly of Grand Central he caught the Times Square Shuttle, rode the Number 1 subway train down to Fourteenth Street, and hoofed it the rest of the way home, slowing his pace to a crawl in the fetid noon heat of New York City in July. The street tar was as soft and gooey as fresh-baked brownies underfoot as he crossed Hudson Street; the heat positively radiating off of the cars idling at the intersection. He paused at the little market on

Hudson Street to buy a fresh pint of chocolate milk, then headed for his place.

Mitch maintained a parlor floor-through in a nineteenth-century brownstone on Gansevoort between Greenwich and Washington Streets in the West Village's old meatpacking district. Once, the apartment had belonged to Maisie and him. It was their place. Right now, the place was dim and stuffy and smelled like either very old cheese or very dirty socks. He cranked up the window air-conditioners front and back, flicked on his coffeemaker, and put on Taj Mahal's "Phantom Blues" good and loud. He sorted through his bills and catalogues distractedly for a few minutes while the coffee brewed and the apartment cooled. Then he poured himself a mug of strong coffee, laced it with two fingers of rich chocolate milk, and plunged back into his essay.

When he had finished polishing it he phoned Lacy.

"Young Mr. Berger," his editor said brightly. "I wondered when I'd hear from you."

"I'm responsible for his death, Lacy."

"What are you talking about? The first set of wire stories are labeling it 'an apparent suicide.' "

"I could have prevented it. I gave him some advice. Bad advice. And now he's dead. He was the best damned actor of his generation and he's dead. He deserves a critical tribute in tomorrow's paper, Lacy. His career was so much more than tabloid tiffs and that stupid *Dark Star*. His real story needs to be told. *I* need to tell it. What do you think, am I being too self-indulgent?"

"What I think, darling boy, is that you're the only arts critic I've ever worked with who actually wonders whether someone would be interested in what he has to say. Don't you realize that there are one million avid readers who can't *wait* to read your final take on Tito? They will gobble up every single word. Go for it, Mitch, do you hear me? Give me something."

"On its way," he announced, e-mailing her the file.

Then Mitch went off in search of his relief.

He found it exactly where he had found it ever since he was a small boy. Most of the favorite childhood haunts were long gone now—the New Yorker, the Regency, the Little Carnegie, the Bleeker Street Cinema. Skyrocketing rents and the advent of video rentals had driven them out of business. Fans could watch the old movies in their own homes now. And that was well and good. But for Mitch, the movie up on the screen was only one aspect of his viewing experience. He loved being inside of the theater itself. The world made sense to Mitch when he was in a movie theater after the lights went down. It wasn't merely his refuge from the painful disorder of the outside world. It was his natural habitat.

In the darkness of a movie theater, Mitch Berger came alive.

A precious few sanctuaries still remained scattered here and there across the five boroughs, if you knew where to go. And on this steamy July afternoon Mitch knew exactly where to go—to a matinee double bill of *The Deadly Mantis* and *Them!* at the Film Forum on Houston Street.

He was practically alone there in the blessed darkness. No one sat within ten rows of him as he sank into a seat, loaded down with sandwiches, pickles, potato salad, cookies, candy, and soda. He unwrapped a sandwich and got busy chomping on it, sore jaw or not, as Craig Stevens got busy examining those very curious tread marks in the snow outside the demolished arctic lookout station. And so, as *The Deadly Mantis* played out on the screen, Mitch found his solace.

Until suddenly someone tall and slim slid into the seat next to him and whispered, "Is that corned beef I smell?"

"No, it's pastrami," he whispered back, stunned. "What are *you* doing here?"

"Looking for you, doughboy," Des replied. "What did you think?"

"But how did you know where to find me?"

"I know you, that's how. Besides, this isn't my first stop. I've already been to the American Museum of the Moving Image out in Astoria—"

"Naw, I wasn't in a Bergman mood. Want a half sandwich?"

"Uh-uh. Then I stopped at the Thalia, where they were running a Laurence Olivier retrospective."

"Yech, he was a poseur. How about a piece of pickle?"

"Damn, there sure are a lot of white men in this city who look like you and go to films by themselves in the middle of the day. And here I'd thought you were unique. What *are* we watching? Look out, that's one gigantic bug!"

"It's a praying mantis," Mitch whispered excitedly, as the two of them sat there with their heads together. "This is actually a classic cautionary tale about the effects of nuclear radiation on nature. They're saying that we shouldn't mess around with powers we don't understand, because really bad things can happen. We have to be humble. Can't think that we know everything."

She glanced at him curiously. "Are we still talking about this movie?"

"Well, yeah," he replied, frowning. "Hey, want a Mallomar?"

She leaned over now and kissed him with an urgency that surprised Mitch. "You scared me, baby."

"I'm sorry, Des. I didn't mean to. I just had to get away."

"I know that," she whispered, squeezing his hand. "My ride's double-parked out front. I need for you to come back out into the world, okay? I have some important things to tell you."

"Are we going to come back in and watch the rest of the movie?"

"No, we're not."

He gathered up his food and followed her up the aisle and out into the hot sun, blinking at the bright light and colors. Horns honked. Tires screeched. People shouted. People rushed. The world was never a more vivid place than it was in that first moment after emerging from a movie theater into daylight.

The interior of her cruiser was already hot and stuffy. Des turned on the engine and cranked up the air conditioning to high. Now that he was able to get a good look at her Mitch realized that the love of his life looked exceedingly frazzled and upset.

It was me. She was worried about me.

"We won't get toxicology results for several days, so we have no idea how stoned Tito was or wasn't," she informed him, sitting there with her hands on the wheel, shoulders squared inside her uniform. "But the medical examiner's autopsy has turned up some indications that are not entirely consistent with suicide as the cause of death."

"*What* indications, Des?" Already, he could feel his heart beginning to race.

She turned her steady, green-eyed gaze on him, and said, "They found moss and lichen under Tito's fingernails, which were severely torn. And the tips of his sandals were scuffed. A crime scene tekkie went back with a long-range lens to check out the side of the cliff, and the moss that's growing six feet or so from the top has definitely been disturbed. All of which indicates that the man was hanging there, scrabbling and kicking, before he went over."

Mitch gulped. "He was murdered, is that it? Somebody pushed him."

"Slow down, cowboy," Des cautioned him. "Nothing is obvious yet. If you want to spin it that he jumped, there's still a perfectly plausible explanation."

"Which is? . . ."

"That the man changed his mind at the very last second. Tried to save him himself, failed, and over he went. Which would also explain the position of his body when he landed."

"Oh."

"Except for one other interesting piece of information our canvassing turned up," Des continued. "A lady who lives in one of those farmhouses on the Devil's Hopyard Road says she heard a car sideswipe the guardrail near her house sometime around one in the morning. It's a harsh, god-awful noise. She knows it well. She claims the car was heading in the direction of the falls. This would correspond with the fresh scrapes we found on Tito's Jeep, okay? Now here comes the interesting part—she couldn't get back to sleep. Was still up at about two-thirty, heating up some milk in her kitchen, when she heard another car speed by. Only this car was heading back down to Dorset from the falls. It's a dead-end road, Mitch. That means somebody else was up there when Tito died."

"His killer," Mitch declared.

"Or a material witness, at the very least. Not that we've found any physical evidence to support it. The rain washed all of the shoe prints away. The only fingerprints on the schnapps bottle were Tito's. The only tire tracks in the ditch belonged to his Jeep. Of course, somebody could have just left their car in the middle of the damned road at that time of night." Des paused now, her face tightening. "There's one other ingredient we have to stir into the mix . . . Esme Crockett's fat lip."

"You think Tito hit her, don't you?"

"Somebody sure did."

"How did she explain it?"

"She hasn't. She's in seclusion. Too distraught to talk, according to her big-time New York doctor. Her big-time New York lawyer says he'll make her available for questioning tomorrow. In the meantime, I need for you to come back to Dorset with me."

"What for, I've already told them everything that I . . ." Mitch trailed off, swallowing. "Wait, they don't think *I* killed him, do they?"

"Rico doesn't know what to think. At this point, he just wants to learn whatever he can."

"Is that new sergeant of his any good?"

"Boom Boom? She's got her some game."

"Why do they call her Boom Boom?"

"You trying to tell me you didn't notice?"

"Seriously, Des, am I a suspect?"

"You're a material witness. The last person who had contact with him."

"Other than his killer, you mean."

"Assuming that's how it plays out," she countered. "Real life, the autopsy report supports either suicide or homicide. Let's say it's suicide. . . . He left no note, which doesn't fit the pattern. But he did call someone—you. He didn't plan it out very carefully, putting his business affairs in order and so forth. Again, that doesn't fit the pattern. But, hey, he was an actor, not a notary public. Okay, now let's turn it around, say somebody killed him. . . . Where's the stanky?"

Mitch frowned at her. "The stanky?"

"I'm thinking of a murder I worked a couple of years back. A housewife up in Newington. It played suicide right on down the line—except we had us a husband who'd removed five thousand from a joint account the day before his wife died. He had a girl-friend. He had three different post office boxes in his own name. He just plain stank of it, understand?"

"Yes, I do."

"You said Tito told you he was into something that he wanted to get out of, right?"

"You are."

"Could he have been talking about something *romantic?*"

Mitch considered this. "He sure could have. Of course, Des! He was meeting someone up there for a tryst. He wanted to break it off, and she didn't, and so she killed him. Wait a minute—he made some vague reference to Chrissie Huberman last night. I jotted it down when I was making notes this morning. I remember him saying, 'None of it's real. I'm not real. Esme's not real. Esme and me, Chrissie and me . . .' And I said, 'What about Chrissie and you?' And he quickly changed the subject. I assumed he was talking about Chrissie's influence on his career. But maybe the two of them were involved. That would certainly explain why Martine hates her so much. Although why on earth he'd get mixed up with Chrissie when he's got Esme Crockett—"

"Don't try to understand other people's love lives. You'll get nowhere."

"Well, if this does turn into a murder investigation I just hope the tabloids don't come after *me.* We did have that brawl at The Works and I could be construed as a—" Mitch broke off, gazing miserably across the seat at her. "They can do that, can't they? They can actually turn me into the prime suspect."

"Baby, they've got a license to do anything they damned please."

"But Tito called me from the falls," Mitch pointed out. "His cell phone record will show exactly what time that was. How could I have killed him if I was talking to him on my phone moments before he died?"

"Okay, there are a couple of holes in that," Des answered. "The time of death is never that precise. Twenty, thirty minutes either way is well within the margin of error. You could have had that phone conversation, then driven up there and pushed him."

Mitch sat there massaging his tender jaw, not liking this. "What's the second hole? You said there were two."

"There's no proof it was *you* who he spoke to. Someone else could have answered your phone while you were on your way up to the falls to kill him. Anyone who was in your house at the time."

"You're right. God, I *am* a suspect, aren't I?"

"Boyfriend, if I didn't love you I'd be taking a cold hard look at you. You have motive, opportunity, and no alibi. Unless, that is, do you have an alibi?"

"What kind?"

"Was someone else with you at the time of his death?" she asked tonelessly.

"How can you ask me something like that? You know I was alone."

"I know only what you tell me."

"Okay, I'm *telling* you I was alone."

"Okay, fine," she said shortly.

Mitch gazed out the window at the sidewalk. Two smartly dressed young professional women walked by together. Both were talking on cell phones, though presumably not to each other. "Des, do I need to hire a lawyer?"

"You're a material witness, not a suspect. But I do have to bring you back, understand?"

"I understand."

"Good, then let's ride. We split now, we can still beat the rush hour traffic." Des put the cruiser in gear and eased it along Houston Street, heading west toward Varick. "Will this get me to the West Side Highway?"

"Can't we go back in the morning?"

"Why would we want to do that?"

"Because we never spend any time here together. I want to eat spinach fettuccine with you at the Port Alba Café."

"Yum, sounds totally off the hook," she responded as they came to a dead stop at Varick. The intersection was gridlocked—trucks, vans, horns. "But now isn't the right time."

"It's never the right time," Mitch grumbled, because there was something else going on here. She considered his apartment Maisie's turf. She would not stay over. She would not keep any clothes there. "I left my computer and stuff at my place."

"So we'll stop on the way," she said easily.

"Des, we should stay over tonight. This is something you need to do."

"We are never going to move," she said distractedly as the signal went from red to green to red, the gridlock failing to budge. "Okay, why do I *need* to do this?"

"Because you're lost, that's why."

She drew back, scowling at him. "Is this about those damned trees?"

"You can't find your way, and it's making you crazy. Making you a big nonfat pain to be around, too, I have to point out. Because I can't lie to you."

"Maybe sometimes you should," she said menacingly.

"If I did then you wouldn't believe me when I said no one else was at my place last night, would you?"

"Well, no."

"And you *are* sure, aren't you?"

"Well, yes."

"Then believe me when I tell you this—you need New York."

Des let out an impatient sigh, drumming the steering wheel with her long, slender fingers. "Mitch, I live in the country. That's where the damned trees are, remember? This is the city, nothing but pavement and broken glass and, God, I hate this traffic."

"That's why you don't appreciate it. You have to put away your car keys. New York is for walking and looking and listening. You're bombarded by more of everything when you're here—more beauty, more ugliness, more excitement, more jeopardy. That makes you more alive. And *that* sharpens your senses. Des, this will work for you. I'm sure of it. Have I ever steered you wrong?"

"Totally. You promised me that *Written on the Wind* was a good movie."

"It's a camp classic. The apex of Douglas Sirk's career. You just have no appreciation for kitsch, that's all."

"I consider this an asset, not a liability."

"Besides, Dorothy Malone won an Oscar for Best Supporting Actress."

"Which one was she?"

"The blond nymphomanic. Interestingly enough, she went on to play Constance Mackenzie in the TV version of *Peyton Place*."

"Wow, what goes around comes around. Your brain is like a continuous loop, you know that?"

They finally cleared the intersection and she went barreling west toward Hudson, honking at a bike messenger who strayed into her path.

"There's something else I should warn you about," he added. "Sex is better in the city."

"If it gets any better I'll have to be sedated," she said, flashing a quick smile at him. "I can tell you're starting to cheer up—you're getting your mojo back."

"I have mojo?" Mitch asked, brightening.

"Oh, most definitely." At Hudson she took a hard right and floored it, heading uptown toward his apartment. "Look, when this Tito business gets cleared up, and I get me a day off, maybe we'll give it a try. *If* we can go dancing, that is."

"Dancing?" he repeated, frowning at her. "In public?"

"I'm saying it."

"No, no. I don't do that."

"What do you mean, you don't do that?"

"Have you ever seen me engaged in the physical act of dancing?"

"Now that you mention it, no."

"It's not a pretty sight, Des. I have a spongy bottom, poor flexibility, no actual moves to speak of. Trust me, you don't ever want to see me dance."

"Got to dance, doughboy."

"What, this is a package deal?" he demanded, wondering just exactly how this whole situation had gone so horribly wrong so fast.

"Package deal."

"You don't play fair."

"I don't have to, I'm a girl. And you're my boy. And I want to see you out on that dance floor, shaking what your mama gave you."

"Fine, if that's what it takes to get you here, I'll do it. Because nothing, but nothing, is more important to me than your art. Not even my own personal dignity." Mitch paused, squaring his jaw at her grimly. "I just hope that you realize the sheer, unmitigated horror of what you're letting yourself in for."

CHAPTER 8

ETHEL MERMAN VERY NEARLY bounced Des right out of her bed.

This was all about Bella and her digitally damned remastered cast album of *Annie Get Your Gun*. As far as Des was concerned, waking up to Ethel Merman singing "I Got the Sun in the Morning" was like coming to at the epicenter of an earthquake that registered 5.1 on the Richter scale.

Groaning, Des put on her horn-rims and staggered downstairs barefoot in a tank top and gym shorts. She felt groggy and stiff all over after spending most of yesterday driving to and from New York. Her eyes were bleary and puffy.

The coffee was brewing in the kitchen, where Ethel was even louder. That damned woman's vibrato could shatter a plate glass window as far away as Delaware. Bella, who had to be clinically deaf, was parked at the dining table, eating her All-Bran and leafing through that morning's New York papers.

Their in-house cats all came scampering, hoping to convince Des that Bella had failed to give them a morning treat. Des knelt to pet them before she called out, "Morning, Bella!"

"Good morning, Desiree," Bella yelled back to her.

"Um, haven't you got your Ethel cranked kind of high for a woman whose roommate packs a loaded semiautomatic weapon?"

"My bad." Bella immediately went charging into the living room to turn it down. "That's what my grandson, Abie, always says. 'My bad, Grandma. My bad.' The boy starts Harvard next month and he talks like a three-year-old. Would you rather listen to someone else?"

"I think I'd like to ease into today with a little silence, if you don't mind."

"Not at all." Bella shut off the stereo and sat back down. "Very nice piece about Tito Molina by your handsome Mr. Berger in today's paper," she said, stabbing at it with her stubby finger. "It has a lot of heart."

"Mitch felt real bad about what happened, plus he was a genuine fan of the man's work." Des poured herself some coffee and took a sip, scanning it over Bella's shoulder. "What do they have on the investigation?"

"That Lieutenant Tedone isn't ruling out homicide. Neither is the medical examiner." Bella licked her thumb and flipped her way back to the front page. "Here it is. . . . 'The medical examiner is characterizing the circumstances of Mr. Molina's death as questionable.' Is that true?"

"Reasonably," Des responded, yawning. "What do the tabloids have?"

Bella's face dropped. "You don't want to know."

Des immediately spread the *Daily News* and *Post* out on the table for a good look. Both featured page-one photos of a hysterical Esme Crockett arriving at the gate to Chapman Falls with her fat, bloodied lip. The *News* was awash with speculation about the lip. Sex was the culprit. They even quoted an unnamed source close to the golden couple as saying, "They liked it rough." Des wondered just exactly who this source was. The *Post,* meanwhile, was already trying to link Mitch to Tito's death: "Although Mitchell Berger is not considered a suspect at this time, an unnamed source added, 'Obviously, the authorities want to learn everything they can from him.'" Which definitely made it sound as if they thought he was hiding something. Who *was* this unnamed source?

And how can I get my hands around his or her throat?

"Nu, what happens now?" Bella asked eagerly.

"Another day in paradise," Des replied, burying the tabloids under Mitch's paper so she wouldn't have to look at them. The cats roughed up her area rugs in much the same way after one of them had puked on the floor. "Thought I'd start out with another tour of Jellystone with Yogi and Boo-Boo."

"Okay, I'm nodding but I don't actually understand what you're saying."

"Then I'll put on my uni and saddle up. Got me some parking tickets to write."

"Desiree, what do *you* think happened to Tito?"

It was a hazy, humid morning, the sky the color of dishwater. Des went over to her windows overlooking the lake and slowly stretched out her hammies, feeling the tightness in her legs as she bent down to touch her toes. "What I think," she said, "is that it's not my job to think about those things anymore."

"But you must have an opinion. You can't just turn it on and off like a faucet."

"Can, too."

The doorbell rang now. Des padded to the door and opened it.

It was the Crockett girls.

Esme with her wild, uncombed mane of blond hair and her raw, bruised lower lip. The actress wore a pair of military fatigue pants, a tube top, and a somewhat dazed expression on her lovely young face.

Martine held her firmly by one arm, a brave, determined smile creasing her own face. "Go ahead and tell her, sweetie. Tell Des what you've decided."

"The kittens," Esme announced to Des in a trembly voice. "I want to see the kittens. Can I?"

"You totally can," Des assured her. "I never turn away a prospect. We were just having some coffee. Can I pour you ladies some?"

"We're all set, thanks," Martine said, the thin soles of her chic patent leather sandals clacking smartly on the polished wood floors as she strode in. "Good morning, Bella!"

She and Bella launched into cheery chitchat as Esme fell to her knees and started playing with Missy Elliot, Christie Love, and the rest of the in-house crew.

"Hi, there," she cooed, stretching out on the floor with them. "Hi, girls."

"Some of them are boys," Des pointed out. "That big orange stud standing directly on your hooters is Kid Rock."

"Figures." Esme giggled, stroking him gently.

Martine looked around at the house admiringly. "You've done wonders with this place, Des. It's absolutely darling."

"I like the light," said Des, who had never before in her life known someone who used the word "darling" to describe, well, anything.

"Your boyfriend's article was real nice," Esme said to Des. "But he was wrong about Tito's script, you know."

"How so?"

"There are no pages. They don't exist. Never have. The project was all just a fantasy. A lovely, lovely fantasy."

"Des, may I be frank?" Martine cut in briskly. "Esme felt, we both felt, that it would be a good idea to make her available to you right away this morning. She wants to help the authorities any way she can. And there are some . . . things she'd like to get off of her chest."

"Would this have anything to do with your lip, Esme?"

"It would," Martine answered for her.

Esme was back into playing with the cats.

"I appreciate you coming forward." Des said, starting toward the kitchen phone. "I'll reach out to Lieutenant Tedone and we'll get the ball rolling."

"No ball," Esme said abruptly. "No lieutenant."

Des stopped in her tracks. "You just said what?"

"I want to talk to *you,* Des. I like you."

Des smiled at her. "I like you, too, Esme, but I'm not involved in this investigation. I'm just the resident trooper."

"Mommy, I don't like this now," Esme said, slowly shaking her head from side to side.

"Just take it easy, sweetie. We'll figure something out." To Des, Martine said, "You could be present at the questioning, couldn't you?"

"Could you?" Esme asked her pleadingly.

"I can *request* to be present, if you'd like," Des responded carefully. "But that's strictly the lieutenant's call. Before we go any further, does your lawyer know you're here?"

"She's fired him," Martine answered.

"I *hate* lawyers," Esme lashed out suddenly. "They get paid to lie."

"You don't have to tell Des that," Bella pointed out. "She was married to one."

"What about Chrissie?" Des wondered. "Where is she this morning?"

"Chrissie worked for Tito, not Esme," Martine said frostily. "She's been sent packing as well."

"She's left town?"

"We should be so lucky. She refuses to go, Tito's death being such a huge story and all. But she no longer represents Esme's interests and she's no longer living with her."

"Mommy's moved in with me," Esme said.

"I thought she could use the company. It means poor Dodge has to hold down the fort alone at our place, but he can manage for a few days."

"Des, can't I just talk to *you*?" Esme pleaded once again.

"Yes, can't we do that?" echoed Martine, who seemed real anxious to avoid the standard Major Crime Squad channels herself.

Des wondered why. Was she just being protective of her daughter or was there more going on here? Mitch had told Des all about Martine and Jeff—not that Des had for one second been able to get her mind around it. Had Martine also been sleeping with her own son-in-law? Was *she* the other woman who Tito was meeting up at the falls? Was such a thing possible?

This was Dorset. Of course it was.

"I have to shower and throw on some clothes," Des said. "Bella will take you down to the garage and introduce you to the kittens."

"The kittens!" Esme clapped her hands together like a little child. "I want to see the kittens!"

"Take your time. Get to know them. Then we'll figure something out, okay?"

Bella led the Crockett girls downstairs. As soon as they were out of the room Des phoned Soave and told him to get his ass over there. Then she jumped in the shower.

She was buttoning her uniform when the doorbell rang. She raced to the door and answered it. Bella and the girls were still down in the basement.

"Thanks large for the heads-up, Des," Soave said as he came through the door with his chest puffed out, bulked-up muscles flexing inside his shiny black suit.

"No problem, Rico. I'm just glad you were nearby." They'd set up a temporary command station over at town hall.

Yolie came in a bit more slowly, her brown eyes flicking around at the contents of Des's house with intense curiosity. Today she was wearing a loose-fitting dark blue top made of a synthetic silk that didn't cling so conspicuously to her front end. A conscious choice, Des figured.

"Girl, you *live* here?" Yolie marveled, her voice hushed. "This is sweet! And look at that deck. You can sunbathe *buck* out there if you want to. Mind if I ask, what's the rent on a place like this?"

"I own it."

"Shut up!"

"Rico, is it okay with you if I sit in? Esme might feel more comfortable."

"Cool with me," he said, smoothing his former mustache. "Is there a lawyer?"

"She canned him."

"Even more cool."

"You folks want some coffee?"

"That'd be great, Des," Soave said.

The two of them went out on the deck while Des poured it. The Crockett girls came back upstairs now, minus Bella.

"Bella said to tell you she's taking her 'shtarker' walk," Martine informed her. "Whatever that means."

"Once around the lake," Des translated. "It's three-point-six miles, the last mile uphill."

"So many sweet kittens," Esme said dreamily. "I just love the Pointer Sisters, especially the one with the white paws."

"That's Bonnie. They're a sister act—you want one you have to take all three."

"Can I, Mommy?"

Martine was gazing out at the deck. "That's the officer who was at the falls yesterday," she observed. "And that woman with the braids was there, too."

"What do *they* want?" Esme demanded.

"To talk," Des said gently. "It's going to be fine. I'll be with you."

At the sound of their voices Soave and Yolie came back inside. Soave approached Esme slowly and with tremendous care, as if she were made of fine crystal and were liable to shatter if he squeezed her too hard. "I am incredibly grateful that you could give us some time this morning, Miss Crockett. Anything you can tell us about your late husband will be a tremendous help."

"Where's Tito?" Esme demanded.

"Tito?" Soave was instantly thrown. "The body's . . . He's in Farmington, with the medical examiner."

"When can I bring him home?"

"Soon. A few days."

"Please answer me this, Lieutenant," Martine said. "Is my daughter a suspect?"

"At this point no one is a suspect. We're still trying to determine what happened."

"You're saying you don't know?"

"That's exactly what I'm saying."

"Well, what makes you think Esme knows anything?" she demanded.

"Martine, this is strictly an informational interview," Des said.

"That's right," Soave agreed. "Informational."

"Well, okay, then," said Martine, apparently satisfied.

They sat around Des's dining table. Major Crimes didn't usually tape record informational interviews, although a signed, written statement might be asked for later. For now, Yolie produced a notepad and pen, and parked her rippling bare arms before her on the table as if she were getting ready to arm wrestle somebody.

From across the table, Esme watched her every move warily. The actress sat next to her mother, gripping her hand tightly.

Des had her own eyes on Soave, who took a sip of his coffee and then sat back with his hands clasped behind his head, which told her that Yolie was his inquisitor. Des sat back in her own chair, curious to see Boom Boom's moves.

"How are you feeling today, Esme?" Yolie asked, raising her chin at her assertively. She was nervous around these women. Des could tell.

"Okay, I guess."

"I understand you've been under a doctor's care since Tito's death. Are you presently under the influence of any medication?"

Esme shot a sidelong glance at her mother, then raised her own chin at Yolie. "Why?"

"Just answer the question, please," Yolie said brusquely.

"No, this is the real me," Esme responded, smiling faintly. "You know, I just love your scar."

"You love my *what*?" Yolie said, fingering her cheek self-consciously.

"It makes you look so gangsta."

Now it was Yolie who was thrown. "Um, let's try to stay on subject, okay? Esme, when did you get that lip injury?"

Esme lowered her eyes, coloring slightly. "The other night."

"The night Tito died?"

"Yes."

"Want to tell us how it happened?"

"Well, Tito had been out all evening. He was pissed at me, because I wanted him to go to the beach club with me and he wouldn't."

"Where did he spend his evening?"

"I don't know," Esme replied, twirling her blond hair around her finger.

"You have no idea where your husband was all evening?"

"That's what I just said."

Yolie narrowed her eyes at her across the table. "Was that typical?"

"I guess."

"Well, where did *you* go?" she asked, growing a bit frustrated by Esme's vagueness.

"Nowhere. I stayed home. They were running an *I Dream of Jeannie* marathon on TV Land. Do you like that show? It's the one with the astronaut. I am so into it."

"Were you with her, Mrs. Crockett?" Yolie asked Martine.

Martine shook her head in response.

"Was there anyone else in the house? A maid? Cook?"

"We don't like to live like that," Esme said, making it sound as if Tito were still around, still choosing how to live. "We have some daytime help is all."

"A local widow does the shopping and cleaning," Martine explained. "The realtor set it up."

"Gotcha," said Yolie, jotting down the information in her notepad. "So no one else was around?"

"Well, there was Chrissie," Esme offered.

"Your publicist?"

"*Former* publicist," Martine said.

"She was out in the guesthouse," Esme revealed. "It's over the garage. It has a separate entrance and everything."

"Could she hear what went on in the main house?"

"I really don't know. You'd have to ask her."

"Okay, we will. How would you describe your husband's mood that evening?"

"He was pissed at me. I just told you."

"I'm speaking more generally now. Was he morose or depressed?"

Esme stared at her in astonishment. "He was Tito."

Yolie stared right back at her. "Meaning what?"

"Meaning he told me all the time that James Dean had the right idea—live fast, die young, and leave a good-looking corpse. He *always* talked about doing himself in."

"Did you think he meant it—or was he just styling?"

"Tito was never about styling," Esme shot back defensively.

"What time did he come home that night?"

"Around midnight, I think."

"What happened then?"

"He went straight to our bedroom and put on a pair of jeans instead of the swimming trunks he was wearing. Then he started rummaging around in his closet."

"He was searching for something?"

"Maybe. I guess so."

"Any idea what?"

"No, I have no idea."

"Esme, did he keep a gun in the house?"

"No way. Tito hated guns."

"Okay, what happened next?"

"He said he was going right back out again."

"And what did you say to him in response?"

"That he should stay home with me. I got kind of pissed, and that's when . . ." Esme trailed off, her bruised lower lip quivering.

"That's when he hit you?" Yolie pressed her.

"Yes."

"Did he strike you with his fist or his open hand?"

"With his fist."

"He punched you, in other words."

Esme nodded, Martine stiffening noticeably.

"Did he knock you down?"

"Yes."

"Did you suffer any other injuries as a result?"

"Not really."

"Were you angry?"

"I guess."

"You *guess* you were angry that your husband punched you in the damned mouth? Come on, girl, stop fronting me."

"*Yes*, I was angry."

"And what did you do about it?"

"Nothing! He stormed out the door and I never saw him again— not alive, anyway."

"You've got some bruises and scratches on your arms," Yolie observed. "What's up with those?"

"They're from before," Esme responded, glancing down at them. "He and I . . . we fought a few days ago."

"So he had a habit of knocking you around, is that it?"

"I-I wouldn't call it a habit."

"What *would* you call it?"

"We *fought*, okay? That's what two people do when they love each other. They fight. They care. That's what it means to be in love." Tears began to spill out of Esme's big blue eyes. "I guess you wouldn't know anything about love, or you wouldn't ask me anything so lame and insensitive and stupid!"

Des got up and fetched her a tissue. "If I might just ask one quick question . . ." she interjected, hoping to cool things off.

"Go ahead, Des," Soave said, nodding his head approvingly.

Yolie just stared across the table at her with her mouth open, clearly taken aback by the interruption.

Des sat back down, flashing a warm smile at Esme. "The other day, you told me that those bruises happened during rough sex," she reminded her in a slow, soft voice.

Esme dabbed at her eyes, sniffling. "I know I did."

"So you were lying to me?"

"I was. I'm sorry, Des."

"And that story about your lip in this morning's *Daily News*?"

"Also a lie. I don't even know how it got there, but it's a lie."

"Why did you lie to me about it, Esme? Was it to protect Tito?"

"Yes," she admitted. "I didn't want you thinking just what *she's* thinking." Meaning Yolie. "That he was a bad person. He wasn't bad. He was just messed up."

"Were you ever afraid of him?"

"No."

"Did he ever threaten to harm you?"

"Never."

"Okay, good. I just wanted to clear that up," Des said. "We all know how hard this is for you, Esme, and we appreciate it. You're doing great."

"Really great, sweetie," Martine agreed, squeezing Esme's hand.

"Sorry for the interruption," Des said to Yolie. "She's all yours."

"You two were having marital problems?" Yolie asked, her tone a bit less prosecutorial now.

"Yes, we were," Esme said bleakly.

"Straight up, was Tito seeing someone else?"

Esme's mouth tightened. "Yes, he was."

"For how long?"

"I don't know. I think it started after we came here."

"I see," Yolie said, clicking her pen between her teeth thoughtfully. "Do you know who the woman is, Esme?"

"No, but . . ." Esme trailed off, twirling her hair around her finger again.

"But what?"

"Tito was never faithful to me. Not ever. That's just the way he was."

"And did this bother you?"

Esme shrugged, saying nothing in response.

"What happened after he punched you in the mouth?"

"I told you that already," she replied coldly. "He left."

"This was about twelve-thirty?"

"Something like that, yeah."

"Did he take anything with him?"

"A bottle of peppermint schnapps."

"And what did you do after he left?"

Esme glanced over at her mother, reddening, then looked back at Yolie and shrugged once again, saying nothing.

Soave tilted his head at the actress curiously.

So did Yolie, who leaned forward a bit, her breasts jutting out over the table. "Esme, we believe that Tito died sometime between one-thirty and two. Were you at home at the time of his death?"

"Not really," she answered in a quavering voice.

Now Martine was looking at her curiously, too.

"Esme, where were you?" Yolie persisted.

"Out," she whispered.

"Out where?"

Esme sat there in pouty silence for a long moment before she turned to Des and said, "Do I have to answer that?"

"I would if I were you," Des advised. "They're going to find out eventually. Better all the way around if they hear it from you."

"Well, okay," Esme said reluctantly. "I was with a man."

Martine glared at her with withering disapproval. "You've been seeing someone yourself?"

"Yes, Mommy," she admitted guiltily. "After Tito split, I went to his place."

"And you stayed there with him how long?" Yolie asked.

"Until maybe four in the morning."

"What did you do then?"

"I went home."

"What did you think when you got home and Tito wasn't there?"

"I didn't think anything. I took a shower and went to bed."

"You weren't worried about where he was?"

"No."

"Who is this man, Esme?"

Again the actress turned to Des. "Do I have to say?"

"It's kind of necessary, Esme. Tito's death is still unexplained, and this man is in a position to vouch for you."

"Well, if you say so . . ." Now Esme's face broke into a naughty little smile. "It's Jeffrey Wachtell."

The composed beauty of Martine's face instantly turned harsh and ugly. "Why, you little *whore*!" she cried out, smacking her daughter hard in the face.

Des grabbed Martine roughly by the wrists and yanked her to her feet. "Okay, we're not having any of that in my house!"

"Yo, what the hell *is* this?" Soave wondered, baffled.

Esme scarcely reacted at all. Just sat there, unfazed, as her split lip started to ooze fresh blood. Clearly, this was someone who was used to getting hit. Des had encountered her share of female punching bags before, but they were never rich, pretty, and white. In this regard, Esme was a first for her.

"Why did you come back?!" Martine screamed at her daughter, struggling in Des's grasp. She was a handful, amazingly strong. "You could have gone anywhere in the world—why did you have to come *here*?!"

"Yolie, want to get her an ice cube and a towel?" Des said as she muscled Martine toward the French doors.

"Got it," Yolie said, springing into action.

"You did it on purpose, didn't you?! You *wanted* to hurt me!"

"What if I did?" Esme shot back, sneering at her.

"You are *sick*!"

"Well, you ought to know!"

"Okay, let's take it outside," ordered Des, hustling Martine out onto the deck.

Soave followed them out there. "So, what, they're *both* boinking this guy Jeff?" he asked, stroking his former mustache.

"So it would seem," Des replied, as Martine began to pace back and forth across the deck, hugging herself, utterly distraught.

"Who is this guy, the stud of the century?"

"Rico, I truly don't know how to respond to that."

He went back inside now, shaking his head. Des stayed with Martine. It felt warm and muggy out there after the coolness of the house.

"How could she do this to me, Des?" Martine sobbed as she continued to pace. "My own daughter—how could she?"

"When you told me about Dodge you didn't tell me that you were seeing someone else, too."

Martine stopped in her tracks. "You sound disappointed."

Des said nothing to that, just gazed at her.

"Our marriage is not exactly healthy these days," Martine confessed. "Dodge goes his way and I go my mine. Jeffrey is . . . not exactly Brad Pitt, I'll grant you. But he's funny and he's sweet and he's the most attentive lover I've ever been with. He bathes me. He reads Emily Dickinson to me by candlelight. He licks whipped cream from between my—"

"Really don't need to hear this part," Des growled.

"Do you have any idea what that's like after twenty-six years of Dodge?" Martine demanded. "Twenty-six years of wham-bam-good-night-ma'am? Jeffrey makes me feel like *me* again. And that sick little bastard has been having it off with my own damned daughter this whole time. I will hurt him for this. I will make a bow tie of his balls and—"

"Martine, I wouldn't say things like that in front of me."

"You're absolutely right," she said hurriedly. "I didn't mean to make threatening remarks. I'm just so *hurt*. I know exactly why she did it, too. To get back at me."

"For what?"

Martine's face darkened, but she didn't answer. Just went over to the railing and faced the lake, her back to Des, posture rigid.

Des studied her there for a long moment. "Martine, were you and Dodge home in bed together when Tito died?"

"I do believe I can see Bella from here," she said, shading her eyes with her hand. "That fierce little bowling ball of a person striding along the footpath at the edge of the water. See her?"

"If Esme was with Jeff when it happened . . ."

"It means that I wasn't," Martine acknowledged. "I was home."

"Was Dodge home with you?"

"It's very pleasant out here, isn't it?" Martine said evasively. "Still, I would have thought there'd be a bit more breeze coming off of the water."

Yolie came out there now to tell them she was done with Esme. Martine asked if she could take her daughter home. Yolie said she could, but only after the lady solemnly promised to behave herself.

Yolie remained with Des after Martine had gone inside. "Girl, is *this* your idea of better manners? Because I can get this for free back in the projects morning, noon, or night."

"I was as surprised as you were."

"Word, did I just choke in there?" she asked, glancing at Des uncertainly.

"No, not at all. It's all okay."

"But you took the ball out of my hands. How come?"

Des kept quiet. It wasn't her place to criticize Sgt. Yolie Snipes.

But Yolie wasn't having that. "Please tell me," she pleaded. "I'm not on my home court here. And I get, like, *no* help from Soave when it comes to how to behave."

"Well, okay," Des said. "You were moving in for the kill, which is fine. But you didn't see that she was on the verge of wigging, which isn't fine. That's a delicate young performer in there. She just lost her husband. If you'd kept at her one minute longer, she would have shut down on you completely."

"Kinder and gentler is not my style."

"I'm not saying it should be. Do what works for you. Keep the funk alive. Just keep an eye on your subject's temperature gauge, too. Know when to back off."

"Yeah, I can be a raw dog sometimes," Yolie admitted, nodding her head. "Especially when I'm uptight. I mean, she's so famous and all. Only, why did she say that to me about my cheek?"

"She's an actress. Everything in her world is make-believe. Pay no attention. You're doing fine."

"Real?"

"Real."

"Big thanks," Yolie said gratefully. "Ready to go?"

"Go where?" asked Des, frowning.

"Interviews. Soave wants you along, since you know the people."

"Okay, sure." Des started back inside, then stopped. "Oh, hey, you didn't give up anything to the tabloids yesterday about Mitch, did you?"

"Who, me?" Yolie let out a huge laugh. "Not even. Soave won't let me anywhere near the press. 'One voice, one message,' he always says. Between us, I think Tawny's on the receiving end of a big happy whenever that little man sees himself on television. Why are you asking?"

"Just curious," Des said, smiling at her. "Come on, girl. Let's do Dorset."

CHAPTER 9

IT WAS SUCH A sultry, sticky morning that there wasn't even a breath of breeze out on Big Sister. Mitch could barely make out the Old Saybrook Lighthouse through the haze as he stood at his windows, drinking his morning coffee and listening to the shrill whine of the cicadas in the trees. The Plum Island workboat was chugging its way out, the Sound as calm as a bathtub. But no summer yachtsmen were setting out for a day's sail. There was no point in leaving the boatyard when the weather was like this.

He hadn't slept well. For one thing, Clemmie was way unhappy about him traipsing off to New York that way. She made her displeasure known by bounding across his bed like a playful faun every half hour all night long. In Clemmie World, this was known as payback.

Not that Mitch would have been able to sleep anyway. Not after he'd made the mistake of checking the Web sites of the New York tabloids to see what they'd be featuring about Tito's death in their morning editions.

Garbage, that's what.

Snide quotes from unnamed sources implicating him in Tito Molina's death. Dirty hints that he knew more than he'd let on, possibly even had something to do with it.... *Obviously, the authorities want to learn everything they can from him....* Why on earth did someone, anyone, think he was holding out? Mitch didn't have the slightest idea. But he did find it deeply, deeply disturbing. Despite his own best efforts, he was being turned into a featured player in this ongoing media sideshow.... *And costarring chubby, good-natured Mitch Berger as the thinking man's Kato Kaelin* ... And now he had no control over what was happening to him. Zero. None.

And so he'd tossed and he'd turned all night long as the ceiling fan stirred the warm, steamy air around his sleeping loft and Clemmie periodically leaped across his stomach, yowling. And he was up well before dawn, getting shaved and dressed. Naturally, as soon as he started stirring Clemmie curled up in his chair and went fast to sleep, one paw over her eyes to block out the rising sun.

Mitch didn't log on to his computer. He didn't want to read any more stories connecting him to Tito's death. He didn't even want to look at his own story about Tito in this morning's paper.

What he wanted was to get his life back.

He was looking forward to his daily hike with the Mesmers. He could use a good honest dose of Dodge Crockett's upbeat reassurance, Will Durslag's croissants and quiet strength, even Jeff Wachtell and his kvetching.

But there was no Dodge waiting there in the haze when he trudged his way across the causeway with his birdwatcher's glasses—just big Will and little Jeff.

"Hey, man, we missed you yesterday," Jeff called to him cheerfully.

"I had to wait around for the police."

"Do they seriously consider you a suspect?"

"I seriously don't know. But I didn't push Tito off any cliff."

"We all know that," Will assured him, standing there with his knapsack filled with fresh-baked goodies. "Real nice article you wrote about him, Mitch."

"Thanks, Will," Mitch said, peering down the misty path in search of Dodge. "Don't tell me our captain's actually late."

"Maybe Dodger ought to buy himself a wristwatch," Jeff cracked.

"Sure, let's chip in and get him one," Mitch joined in, still trying to fathom the concept of the little guy and Martine naked together. He couldn't imagine what went through Jeff's mind every morning as he walked along next to Dodge, stride for stride, knowing that he was shtupping the man's tall, blond beauty of a wife behind his back. How did he feel—gleeful, superior, guilty, all of these things?

"Dodge is *never* late," Will said, frowning. "I don't know where he is."

"He must be tied up with Esme this morning," Mitch said. "Don't you think?"

"No, I don't," Will said. "When I talked to him on the phone last night he said Martine was going to stay with her for a few days, and that he'd see us out here in the morning."

"So something came up," Jeff said. "Come on, men, let's march. I've got a full morning of unpacking ahead of me."

Will didn't budge. "If something came up he would have called me," he said stubbornly. Will always carried a cell phone on their walks in case Donna needed to reach him. He pulled it out of his back pocket and punched in Dodge's number and waited as it rang, an intent expression on his face. "Machine," he grunted, shaking his head. He left no message. "This is really not like Dodge, I'm telling you."

Mitch studied Will curiously. "Do you have a feeling something's wrong?"

"I really don't know," Will said with obvious concern. "But he *was* all by himself last night."

"Does he have a health problem that we don't know about?" Jeff asked. "A heart condition or something?"

"Hell no," Will responded. "He's in great shape."

"Then what's the big deal?"

"I just think we should go take a look, that's all. Make sure he's okay."

"If that's what you want," Mitch said. "You know him best."

"Well, I think you guys are wasting your time," Jeff argued. "This is the only break I get all day. Me, I'm going to walk our walk." And with that he marched off down the path, toes pointed outward in an exceedingly ducklike fashion.

They took Mitch's truck, Mitch helping himself to a warm croissant as he eased his way down Peck's Point's rutted dirt path to Old Shore Road. Will bounced along next to him, big and broad shouldered, his lean face etched with worry as he gazed out the windshield at the road. Mitch found himself wondering why. What did Will know that he wasn't sharing?

"I think I've figured out your secret," Mitch said, munching.

"My secret? . . ." Will seemed startled.

"Your great-tasting croissants. I know how you do it."

Now Will's face broke into a lopsided grin. "Okay, Mitch, take your best shot."

"Butter," he declared.

"What about butter?"

"My theory is that when something tastes really, really good it generally has something to do with extra butter. A whole lot of extra butter. Would you say I'm right or wrong?"

"Mitch, you are not wrong," Will conceded, laughing.

"You see?" Mitch exclaimed triumphantly. "I knew it."

The Crocketts lived on ten acres of lush green meadow and marshland overlooking the Connecticut River on Turkey Neck Road, an exclusive little lane that twisted its way along a narrow peninsula off of Old Shore Road. The land had been in Dodge's family for many generations. Mile Creek ran along the edge of the property, which was enclosed by fieldstone walls that dated back to the 1820s, when the land was first cleared for farming.

As Mitch pulled in at their driveway, Will asked him to stop so he could hop out and see if Dodge had retrieved that morning's *Wall Street Journal* from their mailbox. Dodge had. Then Will climbed back in the Studey, gazing down the long gravel drive at their rambling, natural-shingled house. Long ago, it had started out as a modest summer bungalow. Then it had been winterized. Then modernized. Then added on to—a music room for Dodge's piano, an office, a gourmet kitchen with French doors that opened onto a blue-stone terrace overlooking the tidal marshes.

"My dad used to plow this driveway when it snowed," Will said, slamming his door shut behind him. "I'd come with him sometimes. It was always early in the morning, freezing cold. God, I loved those mornings. He had an old truck like this one, and the heater never worked."

"This one doesn't work either," Mitch said to him encouragingly.

He enjoyed hearing Will's Rockwellesque remembrances of his youth.

"One year, when I was twelve, two feet of pure white powder fell overnight," Will recalled fondly as they rumbled up the drive toward the house. "It was a bright blue morning, and when we got here there was this snowman, must have been twelve feet high, standing right in front of the house. Dodge had built it for Esme in the night. She was tiny then, three or four. It had a carrot for a nose, coals for eyes, a scarf, hat, the whole nine yards. Most amazing thing I'd ever seen. Even my dad couldn't get over it. H-He died just a few months after that, cancer of the pancreas. Went real fast. The amazing thing is I've been down this driveway a million times since then, but every single time I pull in here I flash right to that morning, that snowman, riding next to my dad in that cold truck." Will hesitated, glancing shyly over at Mitch. "Do you ever do that—live inside of your memory that way?"

"God, yes. There are certain street corners in the West Village, every time I see them I think of Maisie and start to mist up. There are restaurants I haven't gone back to since she died. Fire Island is off-limits. The Mohonk Mountain House up in New Paltz is flat-out haunted, so is Tuscany, where we spent our honeymoon. Hell, I almost had to give up our apartment."

"But you didn't, right?"

"No, I did something much smarter than that—I came to this place. That's how I met Des. And you and Dodge."

"Dodge is a rock. If it hadn't been for him, I'd never have made it after my dad died. Martine, too. I owe both of them so much."

Will obviously cared deeply about the Crocketts, Mitch reflected. So why had Dodge glowered at him that way on the beach? And if they'd been so good and kind to Will, why had Bitsy Peck called the two of them cannibals?

The garage door was open, Dodge's diesel wagon parked inside. Mitch pulled up by the front porch and killed the engine. It was very quiet, so quiet he could hear the flapping of gull wings overhead.

"Want to ring the bell?" he asked Will as they got out.

"Let's check around back. They usually leave the kitchen door unlocked."

A wrought-iron dining table and chairs were set up out on the terrace to take maximum advantage of its view of the tranquil tidal marshes. A juice glass and coffee cup, both emptied of their contents, sat there on the table. So did the *Wall Street Journal*, a set of car keys, a pair of sunglasses, Dodge's birdwatching binoculars, Dodge's sun hat . . . everything but Dodge.

"This is really weird," Will said fretfully, trying the French door to the kitchen. It was locked. "I don't like this at all."

They put their noses to the glass, shielding their eyes against the sun's glare with their hands.

Will let out a gasp. "Oh no . . ."

Dodge was sprawled out on the tile floor behind the kitchen's center island. Mitch could make out only the lower part of his body—his hiking shoes and shins. But he could definitely hear faint whimpers of pain coming from in there.

"Better call nine-one-one, Will."

Will had other ideas—he threw his big shoulder against the glass door with all of his might and shattered the whole damned frame. As the lock gave way he stormed inside, Mitch on his heels. But what they barged in on was not Dodge writhing in pain on the floor.

Because Dodge was not alone.

He was going at it with someone there on the kitchen floor, his hiking shorts bunched down at his knees. The naked woman was slender and pale and appeared to be quite young, although frankly Mitch couldn't tell much about her because she had a canvas gunny sack over her head, the drawstring pulled tight across her throat. The whimpers that they'd heard were hers. She was pinned there beneath Dodge on her hands and knees, her wrists lashed together around a leg of the massive maple chopping block next to the stove.

As Mitch and Will burst inside Dodge tumbled back against the counter in surprise, reaching for a dish towel to cover himself. He lay there, his chest heaving, sweat pouring from him as Mitch and Will stood there with their mouths open, too flabbergasted to speak.

"W-We phoned," Will finally stammered dumbly. "When you didn't answer we got concerned."

"No reason to be," Dodge assured him with remarkable calm. "Another opportunity presented itself this morning, that's all. What with me bunking alone and all."

From the floor next to the chopping block, the woman bucked and strained against her wrist restraints, moaning incoherently inside of that gunny sack over her head. Mitch stood there, shuddering with revulsion. He felt as if he'd just walked in on a porn film that had been custom-tailored for ranking members of the Gestapo.

"There's nothing unusual going on here, men," Dodge pointed out, in response to Mitch's look of sheer horror. "Just two adults having consensual sex."

What Mitch wanted to do was run right out the door. Go straight home and wash out his brain with soap and water. But he didn't. Instead, he crossed the kitchen floor and knelt next to the woman, who was so slender her ribs and vertebrae were plainly visible.

She recoiled in animal fright when he touched her.

"Sshh, it's okay," he whispered, gently removing the bag from over her head.

Her eyes were wild with panic and she was gagging for air—some kind of black material had been stuffed into her mouth. Her panties, Mitch discovered as he reached in and pulled them out. She immediately began gulping down huge lungfuls of air, her breathing rapid and ragged. Mitch dug his pocketknife out of his shorts and cut through the leather cord that bound her hands together. Her thin cotton summer dress lay in a heap next to her on the floor. Mitch helped her on with it.

Then he held his hand out to her, and said, "Come on, Becca, I'll take you home."

Chapter 10

"I DIDN'T HEAR TITO smack her around," Chrissie Huberman insisted. "I didn't hear *anything*—and you can't make me say I did."

"We're not trying to, Miss Huberman," Yolie said back at her, somewhat helplessly. "We're trying to figure out what happened that night."

"Well, don't look at me, okay? And if *I'm* the best you can come up with as a suspect then you are just totally brain challenged."

"You're not a suspect," Soave said, trying to cool the publicist's jets. As if he or anyone else could. "We're investigating an unexplained death."

"Can you boys and girls even *deal* with a case this hot?" she wanted to know. "You should consider bringing in an outside consultant. I can pick up the phone and get you a retired NYPD chief of detectives here by three o'clock. He'll be up to speed by the five o'clock news. You want me to make the call?"

"What we want," Des said slowly, "is for you to relax and answer the questions that are put to you."

"Fine, whatever," Chrissie blustered, puffing out her cheeks.

They were grouped around a conference table in the spare conference room of Dorset's musty-smelling town hall. The Major Crime Squad computers were up and running in there, and a couple of uniformed troopers were busy working the phones. Outside, there was total insanity—news vans with satellite transmitters lined up every which way on Dorset Street, reporters and cameramen waiting in a noisy, impatient cluster out on the curb for their twelve o'clock feeding.

Chrissie sat erect at the end of the table, dressed in a yellow silk blouse, white linen slacks, and suede loafers. Her hands were placed palm down on the table, fingers spread wide. She had big hands and wrists. She was a big woman, tall, rangy and very sure of herself. She was not pretty, but everything about her manner suggested that if you didn't think she was then you'd been seriously misinformed.

"At present, we're still trying to fill in the blanks," explained Soave.

"What if I told you I'd like to have my lawyer present?" she demanded, glaring at the three of them.

"That's totally your right."

"Not necessary," she said dismissively. "I have a law degree myself."

"I thought you were a publicist," he said, frowning.

"That doesn't mean I can't be well educated, does it?" Chrissie raised her longish nose in the air, sniffing. "You know, this building smells an awful lot like my grandmother's house in Great Neck. What am I . . . Wait, that's *moth balls* I'm smelling, right? And something else . . ."

"Ben-Gay," Des informed her quietly.

"*Definitely* Ben-Gay," she exclaimed. "God, I would have been up all night wondering about that. Thank you, Trooper."

"You're very welcome."

Yolie said, "We understand from Esme that you're planning to stay around Dorset, even though she's terminated your services."

"If by that you mean I was fired, I wasn't," Chrissie said smoothly. "Esme can't fire me. I didn't work for her—I worked for Tito. And now is when he needs me the most. His whole legacy as a screen star is on the line. The lasting image that audiences around the world will have of Tito Molina is being cast right at this very minute. I will not quit on him. Too much is at stake."

"Pretty big story for you, too, I imagine," Yolie suggested.

"What are you trying to do, girlfriend, fit me for a hooker hat?" Chrissie snarled at her angrily.

Yolie drew back, a bit overwhelmed by this savvy, hard-shell New

York image broker. Clearly, this would go down as a learning day in Boom Boom's personal diary. "I'm just wondering why you're still around."

"I'm *around* because I cared about that kid," Chrissie said. "Both of them, actually, whether Esme believes it or not. She's a helpless little lamb. If I don't stay in town she'll be slaughtered by those predators out there. Who else does she have watching her back? Her aging preppy bitch of a mother? Besides, I have another client passing through this area today, so it made no sense for me to go back to New York. I'm bunking at the Frederick House Inn for a few days."

"How did you manage that?" Des asked her curiously.

"How did I manage what?"

"It's the peak of the summer beach season. Plus every tabloid reporter in America is in town. How did you get a room there on such short notice?"

"No biggie," Chrissie said offhandedly. "A writer for the *Daily News* swapped me her room for an exclusive."

"What exclusive would that be?" Des asked.

Chrissie looked down her nose at her. "You don't really care about shop talk, do you?"

"Just answer the question, please," Des persisted, as Yolie watched them go back and forth, content to be riding the bench for now.

Chrissie shrugged her shoulders. "Okay, sure. I fed her that rough sex spin to explain Esme's split lip. Kinky sex between two beautiful stars the public will eat up. Wife beating they will not—bad for Tito's image."

"Not to mention Esme's lip," Des said. "So *you* were the informed source close to the golden couple. Girl, you have you some skills. I'm impressed."

"I work hard for my clients," Chrissie said simply.

"Most definitely. But now you've got to show us the love, too."

"What are you talking about?" Chrissie wanted to know.

"I'm talking about you sitting here telling us that you couldn't hear what went on that night between Tito and Esme. That's just not going to get it done, is it, Lieutenant?"

Soave shook his head gravely. "Not even maybe."

"But it's the truth!" Chrissie protested.

"Tell us what you heard, Chrissie," Des said, raising her voice at her. "Give us some news we can use."

"Look, it's a big, big piece of property. There are acres of lawn in between the guesthouse and the main house. They're nowhere even near each other."

"Where were you earlier that evening?" Soave asked.

"I went out to dinner with a couple of reporter friends. Got home at about ten-thirty, climbed into bed, and worked the phone."

"Who were you talking to at that time of night?"

"My other clients, for starters. They're my babies. I have to tuck them into bed. And I called Gunnar, my husband. We talk every night when I'm away. Then I, let's see, I talked to Tito's agent on the coast, then a guy I know at *Daily Variety*. What can I tell you? I live on the phone. I was too wired to sleep, so I took a Valium."

"How often do you need to do that?" Yolie asked her.

"Are we here to talk about my personal shortcomings?" Chrissie shot back.

"Please answer the question, Miss Huberman," Soave said.

"Fairly regularly, okay? I get kind of wound up. Maybe you noticed."

"And you heard no yelling going on between Tito and Esme?" Yolie pressed her doggedly.

"For the thousandth time—no."

"What about cars?" Des asked. "Did you hear any cars come and go?"

Chrissie thought about this for a second. "I did, now that you mention it. The driveway there is gravel, and it makes a definite crunching noise. Somebody pulled in about eleven-thirty, maybe twelve. Then went out again a few minutes later. Another car took off not long after that."

So Chrissie was corroborating Esme's story, Des reflected, that Tito had come and gone in a huff and that she, Esme, had then gone running to Jeff Wachtell. "We're placing the time of Tito's death at between one-thirty and two," Des said, shoving her horn-rimmed glasses up her nose. "You were in bed?"

"Asleep," Chrissie replied, nodding. "I dropped off at around one."

"Alone, yes?"

"Alone, yes," she answered frostily. "Next thing I knew Esme was in my bedroom screaming about how the police had just found Tito, and I had to hit the ground running in six different directions at once. It's been like that ever since."

"She doesn't seem all that crazy about you," Des said. "Esme, I mean."

"She doesn't have to be."

Des stepped into the batter's box now and swung from her heels. "Would that have anything to do with the fact that you were sleeping with Tito?"

Chrissie wouldn't take the bait. "Why, what did she tell you about us?" she asked, not the least bit flustered.

"Not one single thing."

"Then how do you . . . Oh, I get it. Tito must have told someone. He wasn't real discreet, to put it mildly." Chrissie fell silent for a moment, staring down at her hands on the table. "Esme probably did know, yeah. And my personal rule of thumb is whatever she knows, Mommy knows."

"How long had you two been involved?" Des asked.

" 'Involved' isn't the word for it. Tito didn't get involved. The boy was strictly a midnight rambler. Showed up bombed on my doorstep late one night."

"And you let him in?"

"Are you kidding me? He was the sexiest man in America. Who was I not to? And in answer to your next question—Gunnar and me, we're not about being possessive. So this was not a major deal, okay?" She paused, lowering her voice confidentially. "Neither was Tito, for that matter. In the sack, I mean. Besides, we only slept together a grand total of four times. Three, technically. The last time he couldn't even rise to the occasion."

"Too bombed?"

"Too *something*. Don't ask me what. The boy didn't exactly confide."

"Was he upset about it?"

"Well, he wasn't thrilled, if that's what you mean."

"This is a very interesting angle, Des," Soave spoke up. "I am liking this large."

"I heard that," Yolie agreed, nodding her braided head.

Chrissie's eyes immediately widened. "Whoa, do not even go there," she said, her voice rising with urgency. "Tito did *not* toss himself off of that waterfall because of me. This is ancient history I'm talking about. Five, six months ago. It happened when I was staying with them out in L.A. And he never, ever knocked on my door again after that. We've been strictly business ever since. And in case you're thinking I'm some kind of a Sally Home Wrecker, forget that, too. Their marriage was already a joke."

"You saying he got around?" Yolie asked her.

Chrissie let out a sharp bray of a laugh. "Don't put it all on him. Esme more than kept up her end. And that girl's taste in men isn't the greatest, believe me. She's a slut for big dumb clods. That's the real reason why Tito wouldn't have bodyguards around. She was always giving 'em some in the pool house."

"This made Tito jealous?" Des asked, leaning forward.

"Totally," Chrissie affirmed. "Understand this about Tito Molina. He was a genuine rebel—angry, soulful, gifted, all of that. But when it came to women he was strictly old school. He wanted to chase puss whenever he felt like it, and he wanted Esme waiting patiently at home for him. And if she talked back to him, *wham*, right in the kisser. Trust me, she wasn't going to take that from him much longer. A few more months at most. The marriage was toast. That's why Tito's agent was so anxious for them to make *Puppy Love*. It was going to be their last big payday together. I am talking north of thirty million between the two of them. But it was absolutely vital that they start filming it right away."

"Vital for who?" Des asked.

"For everyone," Chrissie replied, bristling. "We are talking about two mega-stars. When they work, hundreds and hundreds of other people work. And I'm not talking about the glamour people. I'm talking about the assistant wardrobe girl and the guy who drives the catering truck. These people depend on that work to feed their families. And I'm talking about the fans. The millions of young people who wait in line for hours in the rain just for a chance to see those two up on screen together." Chrissie broke off, her eyes glittering at Des defiantly from across the table. "You think we were *using* them, don't you? You think we were manipulating poor little Tito and Esme for our own selfish personal gain. Well, you're wrong. I happen to know actors better than you do, and do you know what they fear the most in life? *Being ignored*. If those two had made *Puppy Love* together, it would have been sheer tabloid heaven—just like Taylor and Burton in *Cleopatra*. And, believe me, they both would have loved every single crazy minute of it." Chrissie sighed, her voice heavy with regret. "But now it's never going to happen."

"Tell us what Tito was up to since they arrived in Dorset," Yolie said.

"Okay, sure," Chrissie said easily. "What would you like to know?"

"Were you aware that he was seeing someone?"

"I assumed he was. He slipped out a lot late at night."

"Who was she?"

"You're assuming it was one particular she. It's more likely that there were several women."

"Can you give us a name? One name?"

Chrissie shook her head. "I don't do that. I don't gossip about a client."

"Shut up," Yolie exclaimed. "What do you call what you were just doing?"

"Dishing like nobody's business, you ask me," Soave said, nodding.

"I was not. I was talking about Tito and me. I mentioned no other names. Go ahead, look it up in your notes." Now Chrissie focused her gaze on Des. "How come you haven't asked me who *Esme* was seeing?"

Des didn't respond.

"It's because you already know his name, am I right?"

Again, Des didn't respond.

"I see, so you get to ask questions and I don't." Chrissie heaved her chest, exasperated. "Then let me put it to you this way—are you at least taking a good, hard look at Mitch Berger as your killer?"

"Why do you say *killer?*" Soave fired back. "We're investigating an unexplained death, remember? Or do you know something we don't know?"

"I know that he's very well connected." Chrissie stared right at Des as she said this, purposely trying to push her buttons. "I know that he and Tito really threw down at The Works."

"Tito threw down," Des corrected her. "Mitch hit the deck."

"All the more reason for him to come after Tito that night," Chrissie went on. "The man was publicly humiliated. Guys hate that. It drives them nuts. Seriously, shouldn't you be talking to him?"

"We *have* talked to him," Yolie blurted out.

"Really, what did he say?" Chrissie asked eagerly, smelling a choice morsel she could feed to the hungry horde outside.

"We're talking to everybody," Soave said brusquely, shooting a warning look at his young partner. Boom Boom still had a lot to learn about the Chrissie Hubermans of the world.

"And I sure do hope I don't pick up the paper tomorrow and read that we're focusing our attention on him," Des added in a low, steely voice. " 'According to a high-level source close to the investigation.' "

"You have to admit it makes a good story," Chrissie said.

"Good for who, girl?"

"You do your job, I do mine."

"I'm down with that, only maybe you ought to pull into Jiffy Lube and get your value system checked."

"What's *that* supposed to mean?"

"That you are not going to pump up the volume by trashing

Mitch Berger," Des told her. "If you try that I will come after you and I will put you in the hospital."

"You're a law officer," Chrissie objected. "You can't threaten me that way."

"This isn't the badge talking. This is me. Do we understand each other?"

"Sure, whatever. I mean, God, it's so obvious that you people have nothing."

"We're talking to everybody," Soave repeated coldly. "We're especially interested in Tito's lovers."

"Well, don't look at me," she said. "A meaningless fling—that's all we had, I swear. Why would I lie to you about it? I have no reason to."

"You have every reason to," Des countered. "Not only were you and Tito involved but you have no one to vouch for your whereabouts at the time of his death."

Chrissie sat there in heavy silence for a moment. "You're right, I don't. So I can't help you *or* myself. Live and learn. The one night when it would have paid for me to drag a warm body home, I have to hop into bed with my cold hard cell phone. There's a valuable lesson to be learned here."

"What lesson is that, Miss Huberman?" Soave asked.

"If you don't watch out, being a good girl can get you in a whole lot of trouble," she replied. "Now can I get the hell out of here? I have a client who needs me."

CHAPTER 11

"Why would Becca let Dodge treat her that way?" Mitch asked Bitsy Peck as the two of them sat there in rocking chairs on her shaded porch, gazing out at the dead calm Sound. "What was she even doing there?"

"Mitch, that man has always had a peculiar power over her," Bitsy replied, sipping her iced tea. "It's something I had to face up to a long time ago. When it comes to Becca, Dodge is leaning on an open door. She's weak and she's pliable and she so wants to please him. He was her first, you see."

"Her first lover?"

"Love had nothing to do with it," Bitsy said bitterly.

Becca hadn't said a word the whole way home in Mitch's truck. Just sat there in between Mitch and Will, staring out the windshield as if she were in a trance. And she smelled bad—rank and coppery, like a handful of moist, dirty pennies. Will was very quiet himself. He seemed terribly upset by the scene they'd walked in on.

As for Mitch, he could not get over that this shell-shocked, twenty-three-year-old recovering heroin addict was Dodge's idea of a lover. True, Becca was a consenting adult, as Dodge had taken pains to point out. But strictly in a legal sense. In a human sense, she was a lost little girl. What was she to Dodge—someone who he cared about? Or merely a limp rag he could tie up and plug to his heart's content? Mitch had no idea. How could he?

He obviously didn't know Dodge Crockett at all.

When he pulled up next to Will's van at the entrance to Peck's Point, Mitch told Becca he'd be right back, then hopped out with him, and said, "Will, did you have an idea that this was going on?" Keeping his voice low.

"I don't know what you mean." Will unlocked his van and got in.

"You seemed so worried about Dodge not showing up. Did you know about him and Becca?"

Will didn't respond. Just started up his engine and sat there behind the wheel, a remote and silent keeper of secrets.

Mitch found himself wondering what those secrets were. What else did Will know about the man? How much was he holding on to?

"Don't judge him, Mitch," Will said, putting his van in gear. "The man's not perfect, but here's some news for you—none of us are."

Then he'd driven off and Mitch had taken Becca across the causeway to Big Sister, where a silver VW Beetle was parked outside of the Pecks' sprawling summer cottage.

Esme was seated there cross-legged on the veranda in a string bikini, calmly shucking peas with Bitsy, her signature mane of tousled blond hair tied back in a ponytail. Mitch couldn't get over how much the beautiful actress resembled a ten-year-old child as she sat there intently popping open the pea pods, her pink tongue flicking distractedly at her raw, swollen lip. She had a girl's tiny, delicate ears and snub nose, a girl's blond peach fuzz on her tummy. But she was not a girl. She was a lithe, voluptuous woman who had cheekbones the camera loved, an Academy Award to call her own, and a very famous, very dead husband.

As he stood there looking at her, Mitch noticed that Esme Crockett also had thin, faint white scars on the inside of each of her wrists.

"Hey, girlfriend!" the actress called to Becca, smiling at her warmly. Until, that is, she spotted the thousand-yard stare coming from her old school chum. Then Esme said no more—just put down the bowl of shucked peas, hopped nimbly to her bare feet, and led Becca inside the house by the hand.

"She wasn't . . . isn't on drugs, is she, Mitch?" Bitsy had asked him first thing, her eyes wide with fright.

"I don't believe so, no."

"Well, that's a relief. I only worry about that girl every minute of every day. I don't suppose you feel like telling me what happened to her, do you?"

Mitch hadn't felt like telling her one bit. "What brings Esme by?"

"The poor dear's having such a hard time, what with the police and the media and the grief. She needed a bit of a breather," Bitsy said, fanning herself with her floppy straw hat. "We've been sitting here shucking peas and making girl talk, just like we used to."

Esme came padding back out onto the porch, alone. "Becca's taking a hot shower," she said, reaching for a man's white dress shirt to throw on. "I'd better get going. Mommy will freak out if I'm gone for long."

"I'm sorry about Tito, Esme," Mitch said.

"I know you are," she said coolly. "Everyone is."

"What I mean is, I liked him."

Esme glanced at him searchingly, as if she were noticing him for the first time. "Thank you." Then she went over to Bitsy and kissed her on the forehead. "I love you, Bits."

"I love you, too, sweetheart," Bitsy said affectionately. "Come back any time. You're always welcome."

Then the actress had headed off and Bitsy had asked Mitch, once again, what had happened to Becca. And so Mitch told her, Bitsy's round cheeks mottling with anger as he detailed where and how they had found her.

"Dodge has always had a thing for teenaged girls," Bitsy revealed to him now as they rocked back and forth, the floorboards creaking under them. "Some men can't be trusted with other men's wives. Dodge Crockett can't be trusted with their daughters. That's why they couldn't run him for lieutenant governor—he's left too many tender young virgins in his wake."

"Like Becca?"

"Like Becca. And now he wants her again, apparently. And if that man nudges her off of her road to recovery, I swear I will load up one of father's old hunting rifles and shoot him down like the wild dog that he is. I don't care if I go to jail for the rest of my life."

"Don't talk crazy, Bitsy."

"Mitch, I'm telling you the God's honest truth."

A long black cigarette boat filled with sunburned summer people went tearing by the island, leaving an incredible roar of noise in its roiling wake.

"God, I wish they'd outlaw those horrible things," she observed irritably. "What kind of morons ride around in them anyway?"

"Morons who like to make a lot of noise."

"Why on earth would they want to do that?"

"So that people like you will notice them. Otherwise, you wouldn't." Mitch glanced at her curiously. "Exactly how old was Becca when she and Dodge first got together?"

"She was of legal age, eighteen. It wasn't statutory rape, just unsavory. And drugs were involved. She was high on pot half the time, and eager to try anything new. He took advantage of her poor judgment to grab himself a piece of fresh young girl. I'd like to point out that Becca wasn't in any serious trouble before that, Mitch. She was just a headstrong girl who liked to kick up her heels. It wasn't until after she got mixed up with Dodge that she got into heroin."

"I wondered why you called him a cannibal before. Now I know why."

"Mitch, you don't know the half of it," Bitsy said darkly.

Mitch rocked back and forth in guarded silence, wondering what else there was. Part of him hoped she'd spill it, part of him hoped she wouldn't. Because there were some things about people that you were better off not knowing, he had come to realize.

Bitsy took a long, slow drink of her iced tea before she said, "It was that golden summer when the girls turned fifteen. They were inseparable, those two. Esme was such a sweet girl, Mitch. A sunny, happy girl who loved to swim and windsurf. And so pretty that there were always lots of boys around. Nice boys, good boys. All of them so healthy and bright, full of enthusiasm. Mind you, she and Becca both had huge crushes on Will Durslag, who was lifeguard at the town beach in those days. All of the girls did. He was a great big handsome boy—an *older* boy. They were like pesky kid sisters to him." Bitsy let out a long, pained sigh. "God, that seems like such a long, long time ago. . . ."

"What happened that summer, Bitsy?"

She rocked back and forth, her brow furrowing. "I'm not even sure I should tell you this. But I feel like you're family, and I've always trusted you to do the right thing. You have to promise me you'll never, ever tell a soul about this. Except for Des. I know you confide in her. But no one else, okay?"

"Okay . . ."

"Esme was Dodge's first, Mitch," Bitsy said quietly.

Mitch swallowed. "Freeze-frame, are you saying? . . ."

"I'm saying he started sexually abusing his own fifteen-year-old daughter that summer. The change in Esme's personality was noticeable and truly alarming. She became gloomy and distant. She looked unwell. She . . . even tried to take her own life."

Those scars on her wrists. Mitch discovered he was scratching at his own wrists now, as if something were crawling around under his skin. He stopped himself, squirming in his seat.

"I honestly don't think Esme would have survived if she hadn't found her way into acting," Bitsy went on. "Acting was her escape. It got her away from this place. Away from *him*."

"Did she ever press charges against him?"

"No, never. All she wanted to do was go far, far away. And she did. She hasn't been back here since she finished high school. Not until this summer."

"What about Martine?"

"What about her?"

"How could she stay married to him? How could she stand by him?"

"By refusing to believe it. She insisted that Esme was making it all up. That she was merely trying to *hurt* her father."

"So she was a full-time resident of the state of denial?"

"Denial is not uncommon under such circumstances, Mitch. The alternative is simply far too horrible to contemplate. Esme's silence was also quite typical. She was afraid to tell anyone. The only reason I know about it is that the night before she left for New York she finally told Becca everything. And Becca told me."

Just another day in paradise, Mitch reflected as he rocked back and forth on Bitsy's porch. One more slice of family life in this Yankee eden called Dorset. "Why did Esme come back now? Why did she bring Tito here?"

"I honestly don't know, Mitch."

"Maybe the wounds have finally healed."

"Wounds like those never heal."

"I'm thinking that one other person may know about this. . . ."

"Such as who, Mitch?"

"Will Durslag."

"You're not wrong," Bitsy concurred, shoving her lower lip in and out thoughtfully. "Will's role in life has long been to clean up the sobbing, broken messes that Dodge leaves behind. He delivers the parting gifts, mends the broken hearts. There was an au pair girl on Turkey Neck Road some years back, a lovely Scottish girl. And when she got pregnant it was Will who claimed responsibility and paid her way back home. Even though everyone *knew* she was Dodge's little beach blanket plaything. Will has always stuck by him. He so looks up to Dodge."

"My God, how can he?"

"Because he was so young when he lost his own father. Dodge is all he has as a role model."

"Some role model."

"Besides, it's not as if he hasn't profited from their little arrangement. Dodge put him through the Culinary Institute of America, after all. And Dodge has bankrolled The Works."

"Between us, Donna told me they're barely getting by."

"Between us, I'm not surprised to hear that," Bitsy said, raising an eyebrow at him. "Dodge is seriously cash strapped these days."

"How do you know this?"

"I know it because there isn't a plumber or an electrician in Dorset who will work for them anymore. The word is out—the Crocketts don't pay their bills. Martine has bounced so many checks at the beauty parlor that Rita won't let her set foot in the door unless she has cash on her."

"But how could this happen?"

"The NASDAQ, that's how. Dodge risked everything he had on tech stocks. When the dot-com bubble burst, so did his entire portfolio. The man's not a wise investor."

"But he seems so, I don't know, on top of things."

"Well, he's not, believe me. He's run through two considerable family fortunes in the past twenty years, his and Martine's. That house of theirs is mortgaged to the rafters. All he has left is The Works. If *it* doesn't succeed, he and Martine may actually be out on the street."

"Amazing," said Mitch, who was beginning to wonder if there was any one single facet to Dodge's life that wasn't a complete sham.

Now he heard footsteps on the floorboards of the veranda and turned to see Becca standing there barefoot in a sleeveless white cotton nightgown, damp and fragrant from her shower. Her wet hair was combed out straight and shiny. She looked very young and innocent. "I think I may lie down in my room for a while, Mother," she said softly.

"Of course, darling," Bitsy said, mustering a reassuring smile.

"Thanks for the save, Mitch," Becca said with a shy smile of her own.

"No problem. That's what neighbors are for."

"He told me he still cared about me. That he thought about me a lot and missed me."

"So you've been seeing him?" Bitsy asked her pointedly.

Becca lowered her eyes. "Maybe a little," she admitted, scuffing at the floorboards with her big toe. She had a dancer's feet, knobby and calloused. "We went for a walk on the town beach together the other night."

"Was this the night before last?" Mitch asked her curiously.

"Well, yeah. It was raining. We walked and talked for hours in the rain. It was nice. He was very sweet."

"What time did you meet him there, Becca?"

"Why do you want to know that?"

"Because it might be important."

"Midnight. I met him at midnight. You were in bed asleep, Mother."

"This morning, too, I imagine." Bitsy was not pleased that Becca had been slipping out on her this way.

"I'm an adult, Mother."

"You absolutely are."

Clearly, they had boundary issues, which were of no concern to Mitch. What did interest him was that Becca Peck was apparently walking on the beach with Dodge at the time of Tito's death. This being the case, where was Martine? Who could vouch for her?

"I-I thought it would be different this time," Becca said haltingly. "I thought *he* would be different. I was wrong, Mitch. And by the time I realized it, it was too late to stop."

"You don't have to explain yourself to me, Becca."

"No, I need to. I just can't imagine what you must have thought when you walked in on us. What you . . . must be thinking of me right this very minute."

"I'm thinking that you got played. It can happen to anyone. Believe me, you're not alone. Not by a long shot."

"I'd like to repay you somehow."

"You don't have to do that either."

"Can I make you lunch one day? I'm a decent cook, if you don't mind vegetarian."

"It's true, she is," Bitsy chimed in encouragingly. "She's taught me all sorts of inventive ways to use my zucchinis."

"Sounds great."

Becca padded back inside now, leaving them alone there on the veranda. They rocked back and forth in silence for a long moment.

"What are the chances she'll stay clean?"

"Not good," Bitsy answered flatly. "You have to like the person who you see in the mirror every day, and Becca doesn't. She needs to feel good about herself again. Find something she can care about. For years, it was dance. But she's stopped dancing and she hasn't come up with anything to take its place. That's what she needs in her life right now—*not* a degrading affair with a man who preys upon her own sense of worthlessness. She tells herself Dodge treats her that way because she *deserves* to be treated that way. It isn't so, Mitch. She's sweet and she's lovely and she's never been a harm to anyone in this world but herself." Bitsy trailed off, fanning herself with her hat. "Something you'll learn when you have children of your own—and I sincerely hope you will, because you'll make a wonderful father—is that you can't protect them from their own mistakes. All you can do is love them."

"Why do you think I'd make a good father?"

"I believe the word I used was 'wonderful.'"

"Well, why do you?"

"Because you care about other people. A lot of couples who have children don't. Too darned many."

"Tell me about Martine."

"What do you want to know about her?"

"Well, she must at least be aware that Dodge chases after young girls."

"Of course she is."

"How can she tolerate it?"

"Mitch, the most important thing to remember about Martine Crockett is that she's a crushed flower."

Mitch glanced at her curiously. "A crushed what?"

"That's an old Miss Porter's expression. I guess no one uses it anymore. It means that she's, well, she was a great beauty who married unwisely. And has paid dearly for it ever since with a life of regret, resentment, and muted desperation. It means . . ." Bitsy hesitated briefly, her chest rising and falling, round cheeks reddening. "It means that she's Dorset's town tramp. Has been for a good twenty years. And I can never forgive her for that, Mitch. Not because I give a good goddamned whose husband she's sleeping with—and, believe me, I can think of a dozen without even breaking a sweat—but because she was that poor girl's mother and she let it happen. Instead of protecting Esme from that awful beast, she was out chasing after her own selfish pleasures. And when she was presented with the horrible truth, when Esme *told* her what Dodge was doing to her, she simply chose not to believe it. And look what happened to her beautiful little girl, Mitch. Look what happened to *my* girl. My b-beautiful, sweet—" Bitsy broke off with a sudden choked sob and went barreling into the house with her hands over her face, her straw hat falling from her head and fluttering to the veranda floor.

She didn't want Mitch to see her cry. Crying was something that was done behind closed doors. Bitsy was very old-fashioned.

Mitch picked up her hat and hung it from a hook outside the door, then trudged home by way of the lighthouse on the island's narrow, rocky strip of beach, his hands in his pockets and a hollow, sick feeling in the pit of his stomach. Quirt was taking a nap in the shade under the butterfly bush by the front door. Clemmie was nowhere to be seen.

There were several more phone messages from news outlets wanting to talk to him about Tito's death. These he ignored. There were also three messages from Dodge. *"Mitch we need to talk. . . . Mitch, I really don't want to leave things this way. . . . Mitch, please call me. Mitch. . . ."*

These Mitch carefully erased. He did not call Dodge Crockett back.

C. C. Willoughby and Co. was situated smack-dab in the center of the quaint little main drag of quaint little Sussex, a highly desirable shoreline commuter town sandwiched in between Greenwich and Cos Cob. At latest count, a hefty 38 percent of the homes in Sussex were valued at more than $1 million apiece. Pristine white colonial mansions, immaculate green lawns and shiny new silver Lexus SUVs abounded. No handyman specials, no weeds, no clunkers. It occurred to Mitch, as he tootled his way slowly through town in his old Studey, that he had entered a world apart, a world where virtually no one was not rich, blond, slender, and stylish. At least Dorset had a few middle-class working stiffs who were misshapen, dark, and shlumpy.

Well, at least it had *him*.

Most of the shops were located in vintage brick row buildings. The parking out front was on the diagonal, just like in that Connecticut village in *Bringing Up Baby*, the one where Cary Grant and

Katharine Hepburn stopped to buy meat for Baby. There was a movie theater that played foreign films for mature audiences, a barbershop, dry cleaner, a coffee shop called The Beanery. There were chic boutiques selling things like really expensive baby clothing and kitchenware.

And there was C. C. Willoughby and Co., which had started out in the space where the village hardware store had once been and had proven to be such a success that it had spread not only upstairs but to the buildings on either side of it. C. C. Willoughby was the rarest phenomenon in the book business—an independent bookstore that made money. Book lovers didn't just come to C. C. Willoughby to shop, they came to spend the whole day. And they came from all over the state of Connecticut. This made it a must-stop for best-selling authors on tour. Most of the big names, from Tom Brokaw to Toni Morrison to Abby Kaminsky, author of the Codfather Trilogy, held signings there on their way from New York to Boston.

Mitch couldn't even get near the place on this particular July afternoon. People were lined up by the hundreds to get in the door and meet Abby. Many of these people in line were children wearing pointy Carleton Carp fish-head costumes. As he drove by them in search of a parking space, it dawned on Mitch that they looked disturbingly like a legion of very short Ku Klux Klansmen in town for a rally.

He wondered if anyone else had every noticed this before.

He ended up parking in a municipal lot three blocks away and strolling back. He entered through the bustling café, which was connected to the gift shop, where high-end stationery, soaps, and scented candles were sold. The herbal scents filled the entire bookstore. Mitch had always thought a bookstore should smell like, well, books. Not like lavender. Still, he admired C. C. Willoughby. He admired anyone who could turn a profit selling books. Most of the vast downstairs was reserved for current hardcover fiction and nonfiction. Abby was signing copies of her new novel upstairs, where the children's books were. The line of kids and their parents waiting to meet her snaked all the way down the stairs and out the front door.

Mitch squeezed past them and tried to get to her by way of an adjoining room. But the doorway was intentionally blocked. All he could manage was a peek of her seated there at a table, greeting her fans one by one and signing copies of *The Codfather of Sole*. Abby was a chubby little blond in a cream-colored linen suit. Flanking her were Chrissie Huberman and Abby's escort, a six-foot-four inch slab of granite who favored the goatee and shaved head look. Mitch supposed it was intended to make him look menacing, and as far as he was concerned it worked.

There was no way Mitch could approach her now. None.

So he waited outside on a bench across the street, nursing an iced cappuccino from the café while he tried to keep his mind off of the horrifying image of Dodge and his own teenaged daughter in bed together. He could not do it. The image would not fade away.

A half hour later, Abby finally emerged out front with Chrissie. The two women chatted for a minute as Abby signed books for a few more grateful young readers. Meanwhile, her escort made his way over to a black town car parked two doors down, unlocked it, and waited there for her, holding a rear door open. Mitch was on his feet now, inching his way steadily closer. Abby and Chrissie exchanged a hug, then Chrissie went back inside and Abby started toward the car. As soon as she'd climbed in the escort slammed her door shut and got in behind the wheel.

This was when Mitch yanked open her door, jumped in beside her and said, "Abby, we need to talk."

"Hey, what do you think you're doing!" she objected angrily.

"I'm sorry, but this was the only—"

"Back off, Mr. Stalker Nut!"

"I'm not a stalker, I'm—"

"Yo, who is this guy, Abby?" her escort demanded, twisting around in the front seat and seizing Mitch by the collar of his rumpled button-down.

"Wait, I *know* him. . . ." Abby shook a manicured finger at Mitch now. "I've seen your picture in the paper. You're—"

"Mitch Berger," he gasped.

"Right," she exclaimed. "And you're all mixed up in this Tito Molina mess with Chrissie. . . . Let him go, Frankie." Frankie complied. "I know who this man is, although I don't have the slightest idea what he wants. What *do* you want, Mitch?"

"It's about Jeff," Mitch said, straightening his collar. "I'm a friend of his."

Abby's face fell. "Oh, I see."

Abby Kaminsky was a little bitty thing, barely five feet tall. And there were two things Mitch knew about her right away. One was that she was someone who had been told that she was adorable for as long as she could remember. The other was that she was someone who had always fought her weight. For some reason, Abby reminded Mitch of Muriel Bloom, the teacher who he'd been madly in love with when he was in the fifth grade. Something about her heart-shaped face, milky complexion, and startled blue eyes. Abby wore her frosted blond hair in a smartly styled bob. Her makeup, lipstick, and nail polish all came together in a way that indicated a professional had supervised her entire look—right down to the linen suit she wore, which accentuated her generous curves rather than fighting with them.

On the seat next to her were a box of Cocoa Pebbles kids' cereal and a water bottle. She reached for the water bottle, her eyes studying Mitch carefully. "Look, I have to be in Boston. I don't have time for this—whatever *this* is."

"It'll only take a few minutes," Mitch promised. "Have you eaten lunch? I happen to know they make a superior BLT at The Beanery."

"God, cookie, you know the way right to my heart."

The Beanery was narrow and dark. The floors were of well-worn wood, as were the high-backed booths, which had several generations of initials carved into them. Since it was after two o'clock, no one else was in there eating lunch. They took the booth next to the front window. Frankie stayed outside, leaning against the town car with his big arms crossed, glowering at Mitch.

"Don't mind him, Mitch," Abby said, hanging her linen jacket on a coat hook by the door. She wore a sleeveless white silk camisole underneath. Her bare arms were round but well toned, as if she'd been going to the gym regularly. "He's just very protective. And we had a brief, a-a *thing*, so he gets all hormonal."

"You're not with him any longer?" Mitch asked, recalling how enraged Jeff had been over their affair.

"I don't stay with anyone for very long. Listen, I have to go wash my patties. I've just spent the past hour shaking hands with my you-know-whos. Do you have *any* idea where those fingers of theirs have been? In their mouths, in their noses, in their . . . God, it's too horrible to even think about." She paused, looking Mitch up and down. "I'm going to take you on faith. Order me a BLT and a chocolate shake."

He ordered the same for both of them from the elderly waitress as Frankie continued to glare at him through the window.

"That was so terrible about Tito," Abby said when she returned to their booth, sliding in across from him. "It must feel weird knowing you were the last person on earth to speak to him before he jumped."

"Actually, that may not be what happened. He may have been murdered."

"*You* didn't kill him, did you?" she demanded breathlessly, her big blue eyes widening. "Please tell me it wasn't you, Mitch. You've just jumped into my town car. You're notorious. You're desperate. You've got the wounded teddy bear thing going on. Already I have a mad crush on you."

"It wasn't me," Mitch said.

"Oh, thank God."

The waitress returned now with their shakes, fussing over Abby, who she obviously recognized.

Mitch tasted his. It was frosty and good. "But until they do know how Tito died, I won't get over this. I need to know if I could have saved him."

"Mitch, I wouldn't blame myself, I were you. Tito Molina didn't know up from down. That was one hurtin' puppy."

Mitch gazed at her curiously. "You sound as if you knew him."

"I did." She took a gulp of her shake, the tip of her pink tongue flicking at the residue on her upper lip. "We had a brief, a-a *thing*."

"Really, when was this?"

"Before I left on my tour. Would you believe I've been on the road for over six weeks? I've hit twenty-three cities in forty-nine days, not that I'm counting or anything. My face is breaking out for the first time since the Reagan years. I have no life and no one to talk to except for Frankie, who is not exactly Mr. David Halberstam, in case you didn't notice. These past few nights have been the first nights I've slept in my own actual bed since, like, Memorial Day. When I woke up my first morning home, I didn't recognize my own room. I couldn't even remember what city I was in. That's when you know you've been on tour too long. And already I'm back on the road again, two nights in Boston and . . ." She trailed off, suddenly realizing that she hadn't answered Mitch's question. "Chrissie brought me by Tito's hotel for breakfast one morning. He was in New York to meet with some British playwright, and the studio was hoping he'd agree to be the voice of Carleton for the film version of *The Codfather*. He ended up passing, but he wanted to hear my thoughts about the character before he committed."

Mitch nodded. The first Carleton movie was a state-of-the-art animated production that had been two years in the making. It was going to be its studio's big Christmas release. Freddie Prinze Jr. was providing the voice of Carleton.

"I thought he was very sweet," Abby went on. "And after Crissie took off, I found myself upstairs in his hotel room, naked. Scout's honor, I boinked Tito Molina—little Abigail Kaminsky from Margate, New Jersey, thunder thighs and all. Honestly, I was so nervous I felt just like I do when I'm at the gynecologist's office. My little hands and feet were all clammy, and I couldn't stop shaking. But he was very gentle and considerate."

The waitress arrived with their sandwiches now. "Miss Kaminsky, my granddaughter *ab-so-tootly* loves your books," she said as she set down their plates. "Could I get your autograph?"

"You *ab-so-tootly* can!" Abby responded sweetly, scribbling her name on a napkin and handing it to her. "Tell her I said hi!"

"Oh, I will." The waitress scurried off, thrilled.

They dove hungrily into their sandwiches, two chubby people who prized their eats.

"You sure do know your sandwiches, Mitch," Abby proclaimed after several bites, licking mayonnaise from her manicured fingers. "This is the best BLT I've ever had. What's the secret?"

"The tomatoes are right off of the vine, I think. Makes all the difference." Mitch sipped his shake distractedly, his mind racing. Could Abby somehow be a player in this? "How long were you and Tito an item?"

"We weren't," she said flatly. "It wasn't that kind of a deal at all. It was strictly a one-shot matinee. The proverbial quickie. Besides, like I told you, I don't stay involved with anyone for long."

"Not even Jeff?"

Abby reddened instantly. "Jeffrey Wachtell broke my poor heart into a million pieces. I gained twenty pounds after we split up. I couldn't write a single word. I couldn't leave the house. All I could do was eat and cry. I cried and I cried. I still cry myself to sleep every night. Look at me, Mitch—I'm rich, I'm famous, I'm buffed to within an inch of my life. Believe me, this is as fantastically cute as I'm ever going to look. And I can't remember the last time I went out on an actual date." She shot a brief, disdainful glance out the window at Frankie, who appeared to have fallen asleep on his feet, rather like a barnyard animal. "What's wrong with me anyway? Am I that disgusting?"

Mitch went back to work on his sandwich. "You're just worn down from your tour, that's all. You'll meet someone real soon."

Abby smiled at him coyly. "You really think so?"

"I do. And I'll tell you something else—Jeff's out of his mind."

She reached across the table and put her hand over his. "Come with me to Boston, Mitch. Have dinner with me tonight. Stay over with me."

"I can't, Abby," he said, staring down at her soft little hand.

"Why not?"

"Well, for starters, I've known you for less than an hour."

"Sometimes it happens that way," she said, squeezing his hand tightly.

"Plus it would not be a good idea for me to leave the state right now."

"I can vouch for you. I'm famous. I'm credible."

"*Plus* I'm involved with someone."

"Damn, I knew it. The good ones are always taken." Abby released his hand and took a long gulp of her shake, peering at Mitch over her fountain glass. "So how do you know Jeffrey?"

"We walk together on the beach every morning."

"How is he?" she asked, her nostrils flaring. "Not that I care."

"Still in love with you, or so he says."

Abby let out a shrill, mocking laugh. "Yeah, right," she said scornfully. "Listen to me, Mitch, the single most important thing to remember in regards to Jeffrey and women is that every single word out of his mouth is a lie. And the little putz gets away with it, too. You know why? Because he happens to be among the world's greatest swordsmen. You wouldn't know it look at him, but it's true. Jeffrey has absolutely spoiled me for other men. That's my curse. I swear, when I was there in that hotel bed with Tito Molina all I kept thinking was 'God, if only he were Jeffrey Wachtell.' That's crazy, isn't it?"

"Not if you still love the little guy."

"I *hate* the little guy! The little guy is despicable. The little guy is . . ." She fell silent, dabbing at her mouth with her napkin. "I understand he has a mother-daughter tag team thing going on now—he's boinking Esme Crockett *and* her old lady at the same time. Chrissie told me all about it. You look surprised, Mitch. Don't be. That man is the craftiest little pussy hound imaginable. Even beautiful women instinctively get all motherly and protective toward him. They can't help themselves. Half of the time *they* seduce *him*— despite knowing he's absolutely no good for them. Believe me, I'm the expert. I paid the price in the worst possible way." Abby sat back in the booth, hugging herself with her bare arms. "I'm the one who walked in on him boinking my own baby sister, Phyllis, in our own bed in our own apartment. Mitch, you have no idea how violated I felt. How dirty."

"I'm sorry, Abby."

"So am I," she said, shivering. She had goose bumps up and down her bare arms now. "That's why I won't give him a nickel of my earnings. He's not the injured party, *I* am."

Mitch got up and fetched her linen jacket for her.

She snuggled back into it gratefully, studying him with her startled blue eyes. "I don't know what Jeffrey's told you about our settlement battle. . . ."

"That he's asking for twenty-five percent of the proceeds from the first book. He claims he was involved early on in the creative process, and therefore should participate in it."

"Not in a million years." Abby sniffed. "Never."

"I don't blame you at all. Still, you have to admit that, well, Jeff *is* Carleton, isn't he?"

"Carleton is fiction," Abby shot back, bristling. "Carleton is *my* creation. Jeffrey had nothing to do with him. Not one thing!"

"Are you *ab-so-tootly* sure of that?"

"And he does *not* own the copyright to that *stupid* expression! No one does. I was free to use it. And I'll keep on using it for as long as I damned please. Carleton is *not* Jeffrey Wachtell. How could he be? Carleton isn't a liar. Carleton doesn't whine about every single thing twenty-four hours a day, seven days a week. Ask yourself this: Can you imagine Carleton hosing his wife's sister?"

"No, of course not. Carleton's not old enough. He's still a little boy. Or fish. Or . . ."

"Carleton is *good* is what he is," she asserted. "Carleton is honest and brave and true. And I will bankrupt Jeffrey Wachtell with lawyer fees before I ever give him one shiny nickel of my proceeds." Abby took a deep breath and let it out slowly, silently mouthing a ten-count. Jeff was way under her skin, no two ways about that. "How is his bookstore doing, anyway? Chrissie told me it's a real dump."

"Not true. It's a lovely little store. Although he is struggling to get by."

"Good."

"In fact, that's the reason why I'm here—he was wondering if you would stop in and do a signing. You'll be passing right by Dorset on the interstate, and he could really use the boost."

"Not a chance," she replied sharply. "After Boston I'm in Bar Harbor, then Martha's Vineyard, then home. I am not stopping at some neighborhood bookshop in some out-of-the-way village no one's ever heard of. It's not worth my while, Mitch. How many books could he move—fifty? I just sold ten times that this afternoon."

"Still, you could do it if you really wanted to."

"It's true, I could," she admitted. "But you've put your finger right on it, Mitch. I really, really, don't want to."

"It sure would help him out, Abby."

Abby cradled her chin in her palm, gazing at him in wonderment. "Cookie, have you been totally ignoring every single word I've been saying to you?"

"Absolutely not."

"Then answer me this—why on earth would I help Jeffrey out?"

"Because you still love him. And he still loves you. You two should be looking out for each other, not trying to draw blood."

"You're sweet, Mitch, but you're living in a make-believe world. In real life, people who hate each other really do hate each other."

"You want real life? A tabloid has offered Jeff a quarter of a million dollars for dirt on you."

"Dirt?" Abby immediately paled. "What dirt? What has that weasel been telling you about me?"

"That you hate kids so much you made him get a vasectomy."

"That was his idea, not mine," she said heatedly. "He's the one who's terrified of parenthood. I want to be a mother more than anything in the world. Don't you think I'd make a good mother?"

"I honestly don't know."

"Well, I do, because I know what's in my heart. Besides, the procedure he had is totally reversible. God, I don't *believe* he's trying to peddle such crap! Wait, what am I saying? Of course I do. This is *Jeffrey* we're talking about."

"My sense is that he really doesn't want to dish, Abby. In fact, I don't believe he will. But he's in a tight spot financially."

Abby recoiled, shaking her finger at him. "Wait one lousy minute. Now I know why you're here—you're trying to strong-arm me! Sure, that's it. You came here to tell me that if I don't show up at his crummy store he'll go to the tabloids. You're his stinking messenger boy, aren't you? Tell me I'm wrong, Mitch. Go ahead!"

"Okay, you're wrong. The thought never even occurred to me."

"Maybe it didn't," she conceded. "But I can guarantee you that it occurred to him."

"Abby, that's really not how I read the situation."

"Then you'd better go get your eyes checked, cookie. I know Jeffrey. I know how his mind works. And he's telling me, through you, that if I don't do this for him he'll sell me out."

"But he swore he wouldn't," Mitch pointed out. "He told me you were the only woman he's ever loved, and that he'd take you back in a second."

"And you *believed* him?" Abby demanded incredulously.

Mitch drained his milkshake and slumped there in the booth, suddenly feeling profoundly deflated and used up. "Abby, I honestly don't know who to believe anymore."

"If I were you," Mitch advised, feeling the gentle lift and dip of the swell beneath him, "I'd do some checking up on Abby Kaminsky's whereabouts the past couple of days. Or, more specifically, nights."

"Jeff's ex-wife?" asked Des, who was floating on her back next to him, wet skin gleaming in the moonlight. "Why is that?"

"Because she slept with Tito Molina."

"No way. Her, too?"

"Scout's honor."

"You think she might be involved in this?"

"She's certainly in the mix. Quite the humid little pepper pot, too."

The two of them were enjoying a late-night skinny dip off Big

Sister's private beach. The water was bracing and the night air had turned gloriously crisp and clear. Overhead, the moon was full, the stars bright.

Mitch had spent much of the evening seated there on his favorite beach log, gloomily sampling the bottle of peppermint schnapps he'd bought out of morbid curiosity. It tasted awful, in his opinion. Strangely familiar as well, although he could not imagine why. Des had pulled up outside his carriage house at around ten o'clock and joined him on the beach a few minutes later, clutching two cold Bass ales and two towels.

He had never been happier to see her in his life.

As they floated there naked in the moonlight, the lights of the town a glow in the distance, Mitch reminded himself just how lucky he was to be here on this night with this woman. It was the one positive thing he had taken from losing Maisie the way he had—not a day went by when he took the good things for granted.

"How did you happen to meet up with said humid little pepper pot?"

"Jealous?"

"I'll ask the questions, mister."

"Jeff asked me to look her up. He wants her to sign books at his store."

"Since when do you do Jeff's bidding for him?"

"Since everything stopped making sense. I need for this to make sense."

"It may not, Mitch. A lot of times things just get more and more confusing."

"That's not what I need to hear tonight, Des. Tonight I need to hear that life is nothing but one big long Frank Capra movie. And I actually detest Frank Capra—with the possible exception of *Dirigible* with Jack Holt and Fay Wray."

"My miss," she said, flashing a smile at him. "And thanks for the heads-up. I'll pass it along to Rico."

"Abby's been sleeping with her escort, too—a big goon named Frankie. I don't know his last name, but he might be worth looking into. Meanwhile, get this, Jeff's actually been two-timing Martine with her very own—"

"With Esme. Yes, I know."

"Esme told you?"

"She had to. Jeff's her alibi. And, believe me, the news came as a real unpleasant surprise to Martine. I had to pull her off of the girl."

"What did Jeff say about it?"

"He backs Esme up all the way. At the time of Tito's death, she was getting busy with him at his condo. Yolie and I confirmed it with him this afternoon."

"Hmm, that means each of them is the other's alibi. . . ."

"Where do you think you're going with that?"

"Nowhere," Mitch said, as they floated along. "Except, well, what if Esme and Jeff killed Tito together?"

"Why would they?"

"Revenge. He hated Tito for getting it on with Abby. Esme hated him because he beat on her and cheated on her. Do we know for a fact that Tito's killer acted alone?"

"Mitch, we don't know anything for a fact," she said wearily, glancing over at him. "You cast an awesome glow in the moonlight, you know that?"

"You've obviously never gone skinny-dipping with a white boy when the moon was full."

"No, I'm serious, Mitch. Check out your stomach—you look like you've swallowed something radioactive."

"Only because my stomach happens to be sticking up out of the water," Mitch growled at her. "But thanks for pointing it out to me, slats."

"What I'm here for, doughboy," she said sweetly. "Got anything else for me?"

He fed her the highlights of his morning. How he and Will had walked in on Dodge and Becca having rough sex together. How Becca had told him she and Dodge were taking a midnight stroll on the beach together when Tito died, meaning that he had someone to vouch for his whereabouts—and Martine very likely didn't.

"Why would Martine want to kill her own son-in-law?" she wondered.

"Maybe she was romantically involved with Tito, too. Maybe he broke her poor, cheatin' heart. It makes about as much sense as Martine and Esme both having extramarital affairs with Jeff Wachtell. I mean, once you get your mind around that unwholesome factoid nothing seems out of the realm of possibility, does it?"

"Now that you mention it, no."

"Did Esme know about Jeff and her mom?"

"Totally, judging by the little smirk on her face when she gave out with the news. It was her own special way of inflicting pain on mommy dearest. For what specific reason I don't know."

"I do, Des," Mitch said quietly. And now he told her about how Dodge started molesting Esme when she was fifteen. How Martine had refused to believe her. How Esme had attempted suicide. How Dodge had long been a plague on Dorset's young girls and Will had been his enabler, in exchange for future considerations.

Des listened in stony silence before she said, "Well, that does explain the way Esme reacted this morning when Martine smacked her."

"How did she? . . ."

"Like she'd been getting smacked around her whole life."

"What, you think Dodge beat her up?"

"Believe me, a bright, beautiful fifteen-year-old girl doesn't spread her legs for daddy without a fight. I'm with you, Mitch—she hates her mom for not protecting her. But I don't buy that Martine didn't know what was going on. She knew. That's why she was so anxious to go to the police this morning. Because the longer this drags out, the deeper we'll dig. And she's terrified we'll unearth it. How did you hear about it, anyway?"

"From Bitsy. Becca told her. I don't think anyone else knows, except for Will."

"And possibly Tito. Esme may have told him."

Mitch glanced over at her, wondering where her mind was going. "Bitsy said I could tell *you* this. Does Soave have to know about it?"

"Maybe I can withhold it from him," Des answered slowly. "If it's not vital to the investigation, that is."

He smiled at her. "You're one of us now, you know that?"

"One of who?"

"A Dorseteer."

"Let's not get carried away, doughboy. I said maybe."

"Sure, sure. Are you getting cold?" he asked, paddling gently to stay afloat.

"A little, but I'm okay. You?"

"I'm fine. This is why I maintain the extra layer of subcutaneous fat."

"So that's it."

"*Ab-so-tootly.*"

"Mitch, I want you to promise me you'll never say that word again."

"Promise," he said, grinning at her. "Bitsy did tell me one other thing about the Crocketts—they're so strapped for cash that Martine can't write a check anywhere in town. Apparently, just to round out the whole bogus illusion, Dodge sucks as a businessman." He gazed back ashore at Bitsy's rambling house. There were several lights on upstairs, a porch light downstairs. "She's real worried about Becca being mixed up with him again. Becca's fragile and vulnerable, and there's no way that having some guy stuff your panties in your mouth can be good for your . . . Oh, hell, never mind."

"No, it's okay, baby. What are trying to tell me?"

"I just don't want to be friends with Dodge anymore, that's all."

"I don't blame you. But what about the Mesmers?"

"I won't be walking with them again."

"I'm sorry, Mitch."

"So am I. That was something I really looked forward to doing every morning. But I can't now. Not without my skin crawling. Would you believe Will actually *defended* the guy to me this morning? 'Don't judge him,' is what he said. He and Donna are having some problems of their own, by the way. Donna told me."

"Since when does Donna Durslag talk to you about her marriage?"

"Since she had one too many margaritas at the beach club."

"Sounds like maybe she made her a little play for you, too."

"Jealous?"

"I already told you. I'll ask the questions, mister."

"Des, I don't belong around these people," Mitch confessed. "I gave it my best shot. I tried to be a normal, socialized member of the species. But if this is what passes for normal—"

"Believe me, Mitch, this *is* normal. It's what I deal with every single day of my life."

"Then I'm proud to be a maladjusted geek who sits in the dark by myself all day, staring at flickering images on a wall." He reached for her hand in the water and found it and squeezed it. "When do people stop surprising you?"

"They don't. But the surprise doesn't always have to be an unpleasant one. In fact, when you least expect it, you might bump right into somebody who just makes you feel good all over."

"Are you trying to cheer me up?"

"Actually, that was me flirting with you shamelessly. Not very good at it, am I?"

"That all depends—do you put out?"

"Only for a certain glowing gentleman."

Mitch maneuvered his way over closer to her and planted a salty kiss on her wet, cold mouth. "Am I that gentleman?"

"Could be," she said, her almond-shaped green eyes glittering at him in the moonlight.

"Then as far as I'm concerned, you flirt great. Care to start back in?"

"Hell, I'll even race you back to the house."

"You're on. Provided you promise me one thing."

"Name it."

"Let's steer clear of the kitchen floor tonight, okay?"

"Not a problem, boyfriend."

They dashed back in the crisp night air, teeth chattering, and jumped right into a hot shower together, howling and snorting like a couple of rambunctious little kids. After they'd toweled each other dry they made their way up into Mitch's sleeping loft, where they forgot about everything and everyone and there was only the two of them and it was wonderful.

They were blissfully asleep at 4:00 A.M. under a blanket and a Clemmie when Des got paged. She started rummaging hurriedly for her clothes as the Westbrook Barracks dispatcher gave her the details over her cell phone.

"Wha' is it?" Mitch groaned at her after she'd hung up.

She was already lacing up her shoes. Des could get dressed unbelievably fast. It was her four years at West Point. "Night manager of the Yankee Doodle Motor Court just found . . . There's a woman dead in the tub with part of her head smashed in."

Something in her tone of voice set off alarm bells. Mitch swallowed, fully awake now. "Who is it, Des?"

"Baby, it's Donna Durslag."

CHAPTER 12

IF DORSET POSSESSED WHAT could be truly called a seedy side it was found up Boston Post Road just before the town line for Cardiff, Dorset's sleepy, landlocked neighbor to the north, which benefited not at all from summer tourism and which elderly locals still called North Dorset, even though it had been a separate town since 1937. Here, just past Gorman's Orchards, could be found a tattered strip of businesses operating out of wood-framed buildings that had once been residences. If someone needed to have their sofa reupholstered or their unwanted facial hair removed, they came here. Pearl's World of Wigs, Norm's Guns, and Shoreline Karate Academy were here. The Rustic Inn, a beer joint popular with the Uncas Lake swamp Yankees, was here.

And so was the Yankee Doodle Motor Court, which was a living relic from the bygone days of drive-in movie theaters and poodle skirts. To the casual passerby, it was a wonder that the decaying little bungalow motel hadn't been torn down twenty years ago. It had no swimming pool, was not near the beach or the interstate. There was no apparent reason for anyone on earth to stay there—not unless they were terribly lost or desperate.

But Des knew better.

The Yankee Doodle enjoyed a prized niche in Dorset society—it was the place where married people came to mess around. Des had learned early in her career that every town, no matter its size or degree of affluence, had just such a place for illicit trysts. Mostly, what the Yankee Doodle offered couples was privacy. The bungalows were spaced a discreet distance apart, and the parking spaces were around in back so that people driving by on Boston Post Road couldn't see who was parked there. The management was reputed to be very discreet.

She got there in the purplish light of predawn. Danny Rochin, the sallow, unshaven night manager, came right out of the office to greet her wearing a too-large Hawaiian shirt, slacks, and bedroom slippers. He was a stringy, sixtyish swamp Yankee with a jet black Grecian Formula hair job that looked totally unnatural under the courtyard floodlights, especially in contrast with his bushy white eyebrows. They always neglected the eyebrows. Big mistake.

"Is anyone still staying here from last night?" Des asked him as she climbed out of her cruiser.

"No, ma'am, we're all empty," he replied, eyes bright with excitement. He was missing a few teeth, and his narrow shoulders were hunched against the morning's unusual chill. It had dipped down into the forties, which was a shock to the system in July.

"Let's go have us a look, Danny."

There was blood. The spread on the double bed was spattered with it. So was the wall behind the bed. So were the shades on the night table lamps. Donna's wire-rimmed glasses, which lay neatly folded on one of the night tables, were spattered, too. The bed did not appear to have been used. The covers were still crisply folded, and the pillows had no depressions in them.

The Yankee Doodle was the sort of a place where things like lamps and televisions were bolted down, just in case some low-class guest might be tempted to walk off with them. But Donna's killer had still managed to find something to club her with—a night table drawer. It lay on the rug next to the bed, smashed, splintered and bloodied. Her shoulder bag was on the dresser next to the TV, as was her gauzy summer peasant dress, carefully folded. Also a see-through black nightie, very slinky, very hopeful, very sad.

The bungalow was tiny. There was barely enough space to squeeze around the bed to the bathroom, where Donna was on the floor. From where she stood, Des could just make out her bare feet.

"Did you touch anything, Danny?" Des asked him as he remained outside, pulling nervously on a cigarette.

"Not a thing, I swear. Her purse is just as I found it. I'm not here to steal no twenty bucks from some poor woman's billfold."

"I know that, Danny," she said, flashing a reassuring smile at him. "I'm just trying to assess the crime scene." Now she went farther in for a better look.

Donna was naked on her knees before the bathtub with her big butt sticking up in the air for the whole wide world to see. Not that she was obese but she wasn't a nineteen-year-old runway model either. And the bathroom floor is not the most dignified place to die. Go ask Elvis. There was a foot of blood-tinged water in the tub. By the look of things, her killer had knocked her unconscious with the drawer, dragged her in there and held her head underwater until she was gone. Her center of gravity had tumbled her a bit backward after she'd died, lifting her face up out of the water. There were broken blood vessels around the eyes, and her lips were blue. The bloody wounds to the back of her wet head were readily apparent to Des from the bathroom doorway. There was some blood on the floor, but not much. No bloody shoeprints. The floor had been wiped. Des could not see any bloody towels in there. No towels at all, in fact. He'd taken them with him. Whoever he was, he was careful.

Standing there gazing at Donna Durslag, Des experienced that same mix of despair, horror, and fascination that she always felt when she saw what people were capable of doing to each other. She would need crime scene photos. She would need to get this down on paper. Possibly life-sized, so she could bring forth the full impact of Donna's figure as it knelt there in death. She would draw this. *Had* to draw this. It was how she kept it together.

And to hell with Professor Weiss and his damned trees.

"How often do you run the vacuum in here, Danny?" she asked, starting back around the bed toward him.

"Once a week . . . maybe," he replied.

Meaning there would be tons of hairs in the rug from past guests. Most likely, the tekkies wouldn't even bother with it. But they would for sure check the surface of the bed for hair or fiber transfers, and the blood spatters for a blood sample that was not the victim's. Also the smashed night table drawer for prints, although he'd doubtless wiped that clean same as he'd wiped down the bathroom. Des was certain that they'd find nothing. It smelled like a clean kill all the way.

"Where's her car, Danny?"

"Around in back."

It was faded gray Peugeot station wagon. Locked. Both the passenger seat and backseat were strewn with empty take-out coffee cups and food wrappers. There was one other vehicle parked back there, a red Nissan pickup truck that belonged to Danny.

He led Des back to his office now, where there was a reception counter made out of fake wood, a Coke machine, television, a couple of green plastic chairs. The worn linoleum on the floor was the color of canned salmon. A door marked Private led back to the inner office.

"What time did she check in?"

"Just after ten o'clock," Danny replied, taking his place behind the counter. The man seemed much more at ease now that he was back there, straighter and taller.

"Was she alone?"

"Yes, ma'am."

"Did she sign the register?"

"You bet. We run a clean operation here. No hookers, no minors, no monkey business."

Des glanced at the register—Donna had signed her own name, clear as can be. "Did she pay you in cash?"

"Credit card," he said, his bony hands shaking slightly as he produced the credit card slip for her. She suspected he was in need of a drink. He settled for another cigarette.

"The lady had a husband," Des said, surprised that Donna had made no apparent effort to cover her tracks. "Is this typical?"

"Yes and no," Danny answered, thumbing his stubbly chin shrewdly. "Some of 'em are real careful about keeping their after-hours activities off the household books, others aren't. Depends on who takes care of the bills every month, is how I always figured it."

"Had you ever seen her before?"

"No, ma'am. She was a first-timer. On my shift, anyway, and I been here on overnight for thirteen years."

"How did she seem to you? Had she been drinking? Was she high?"

"She was nervous. A lot of 'em are. Men and women both."

"And what does that generally tell you?"

"That they're doing something they never thought they'd be doing."

Des turned and glanced through the front window at Donna's bungalow across the courtyard. "Did you see him arrive?"

"No, ma'am, I didn't. Got no idea who he was."

"Maybe you saw his car pull in. Think hard, please. This is important."

"I wish I could help you, ma'am, but we're real busy that time of night. Eleven, twelve o'clock is my rush hour. Lots of folks coming and going. Going, mostly. Some drop the key off in here with me. The rest just leave it in the door—the ones who don't want to be seen together by *anybody*, if you know what I mean. Shoot, I must get one suspicious husband in here a week, offering me cash money for the lowdown on his missus."

"And do you give it to him?"

"Hell no," Danny replied indignantly. "Our guests have a right to their privacy. That's why they come here."

Des had happened upon this peculiar phenomenon before—people with tremendous professional pride where you least expected to find them. And why not? Danny Rochin certainly had more class than, say, Dodge Crockett. "That lady got herself pretty beat up in there. You didn't hear them going at it?"

"Well, maybe . . ." Danny cast a longing glance over his shoulder at the office door.

"You want to go take care of what you need to take care of?"

He slipped gratefully into the back room, shutting the door softly behind him. Des could hear a desk drawer slide open and shut. A moment later Danny returned, smelling of whiskey. "I did hear a woman . . . shriek, I guess you could say. And it did come from the direction of that bungalow, number six."

"What time was this, Danny?"

"About one-thirty," he replied. "Look, it may have been nothing. Some couples, they make certain noises when they're . . ." He trailed off uncomfortably, his eyes avoiding hers.

"I'm right with you, honey. Just keep on going."

"So I didn't think much of it—not until I started cleaning out the bungalows this morning and I found her in there. I'm real sorry if I did wrong, ma'am." He seemed genuinely upset. "But I can't go knocking on doors every time somebody lets out a shriek, can I?"

"Don't be so hard on yourself, Danny. There's no way you could have known what was going on in there."

"Do you really mean that?"

"I really do."

"I never had nothing like this happen before on my watch. Worst thing was an attempted rape charge three, four years ago. And that just turned out to be a lover's quarrel."

Outside, Soave and Yolie pulled up alongside of Des's cruiser and got out. Each of them clutching a Bess Eaton take-out coffee container. Each of them wearing an angry glower. Soave's lips were tightly compressed. Boom Boom's chin was stuck out. They'd been spatting. Or they were just getting on each other's nerves. It happened. Partners had to spend a lot of time together. And that's not easy—especially when the case they're working suddenly goes way bad.

Soave seemed relieved to see Des standing there in the office doorway. "Another early start to the day, hunh?" he said, forcing a weary smile onto his face. His eyes were bloodshot, his bulky shoulders slumped with fatigue.

"This could get to be a habit, Rico."

"God, let's hope not."

Yolie couldn't get away from the man fast enough. "I'll check the register, put together a list of guests for us to canvass," she told him hurriedly as she started inside, wearing a bulky yellow cotton sweater that made her entire upper body look huge. "Maybe one of them saw somebody, recognized somebody. . . ." She halted in the doorway, smiling brightly at Des. " 'Morning, girlfriend."

"Back at you, Yolie. You'll find the victim's car behind the bungalow."

"I'm on it."

Des led Soave toward the crime scene, their footsteps crunching on the gravel. As they made their way across the courtyard two more cruisers pulled up, followed by a team of tekkies in a cube van. The uniformed troopers secured the perimeter. The tekkies got busy unloading their gear.

"I swear, that damned Boom Boom is going to drive me crazy," Soave complained. "Right away, she wants to brace our movie star this morning. She's convinced that Esme Crockett's behind all of this. Her and Jeff Wachtell both, since each is the other's alibi."

"That's interesting," Des said. "Mitch went there, too."

Soave glanced at her coldly. "So, what, Berger's backstopping my investigation now?"

Des let that one slide on by. "What did you tell her, Rico?"

"I told her we don't have enough yet. This is *Esme Crockett* we're talking about, not some gang-banger. She can hire the best team of criminal defense lawyers in the world. We have to get all our ducks in a row before we go anywhere *near* her."

Des had to smile at this. When they were a team it was always Soave who was Mr. Great Big Hurry, Des who was Ms. Go Slow.

"So guess what she says back to me."

"Rico, I can't imagine."

"She says I'm not secure enough in my manhood to accept her input. That I feel, quote, sexually threatened by her performance on the job, unquote. *And* that she finds it hard to respect me. Can you believe that?"

"She possesses what my good friend Bella Tillis calls moxie. Got to like that in a girl."

"*You've* got to like it—I don't. She's busting my balls, Des."

"She's hungry, Rico. Better that than a slacker, don't you think?"

He shook his head at her. "Somehow, I *knew* you'd take her side."

"Chump, I'm not taking anyone's side," Des shot back angrily. "And I have an excellent idea—solve your own damned personnel problems, okay?"

"Real sorry, Des," he apologized, reddening. "I didn't mean that. I'm just, I got like two hours of sleep last night and this case is now totally out of hand. I appreciate your input. Really, I do."

They arrived at the bungalow. Soave went inside to take a look at Donna's body on the bathroom floor, his face tightening. "Did you know her?"

"I did. This was a nice lady, Rico. A professional chef. She ran The Works with her husband, Will."

"If she was such a nice lady what was she doing here?"

"Playing in the dirt."

"Who with?"

"I wish I knew. As questions go, that's the big kahuna."

The crime scene technicians wanted to squeeze in there and start taking pictures.

Soave made way for them, moving back outside. "No, Des," he countered. "The big kahuna is how does this fit into the Tito Molina death?"

"You think the two are connected?"

"Don't you? Two violent deaths three days apart in a town this size—they can't be unrelated, can they?"

"I agree, Rico. Although there was no effort to make this one look like a suicide."

"That could have been dictated by circumstances," he suggested, taking a noisy slurp of his coffee.

"Again, I agree. But why did Donna pay for the room with her damned credit card? What kind of way is that to sneak around?"

"Des, I can't get my mind around what's going on here, can you?"

"Not even."

"Tito Molina and Donna Durslag are both dead and there *has* to be a reason why," he mused aloud, smoothing his former mustache. "You know what I keep coming back to? I had me a very wise loot once who had this saying: 'It's never complicated. It's about money or it's about sex. Or it's about money *and* it's about sex. But it's never complicated.'" He paused, grinning at her. "She was a wise person, that loot."

"Still am, wow man. Don't kid yourself."

They stood there in silence for a moment. A car drove by on Boston Post Road, the driver slowing for a look before he sped past.

"Any chance Donna was romantically involved with Tito?"

"I doubt that, Rico. If she was mixed up with Tito then what was she doing here last night? Or, more precisely, *who* was she doing here last night?"

"You have a point there, Des."

"Then again, so do you."

"Which is? . . ."

"That Donna wasn't so nice. She slept around on Will. Mitch did tell me they were having marital problems. Let's say she *was* involved with Tito. Say Tito wanted to break it off, and she didn't, and she killed him in a jealous rage. Maybe someone else, someone close to Tito, figured it out and paid her back last night."

"Like who?" he wondered.

"Then again," she went on, "it's not as if her killer brought a weapon along. He had to use a drawer to beat on her."

"Meaning we could be looking at a spontaneous crime of passion," Soave said, nodding.

Yolie came charging across the courtyard from the office now. She took a look inside the bungalow at Donna, then reemerged, grim-faced.

"Rico, we'd better notify Will," Des said.

"Would you mind delivering the news?"

"Not a problem. I can try to feel him out while I'm there, if you'd like. He might know who her boyfriend is."

"Go for it," he urged her.

Yolie joined them now, hugging herself tightly with her big arms. She was either cold or freaked by the sight of Donna. Both, maybe. "Check it out, are we thinking it was a man who did her?"

Soave shot a blank look at Des, then turned back to Yolie, and said, "Why, where are you going with this?"

"That bed wasn't slept in," Yolie replied. "Her nightie was never worn. They can't say for sure until they swab her, but it sure doesn't *look* like she had sex before she died."

"So he killed her before the two of them got busy." An impatient edge crept into Soave's voice. "So what?"

"So if there's no evidence she had sex with him then there's no evidence it was a *him*," Yolie answered, her own voice getting sharp.

"She's right, Rico," Des agreed. "A reasonably strong woman could have done this."

"Maybe Donna was waiting for her boyfriend to show," Yolie continued, encouraged by Des's backing. "Maybe her boyfriend's jealous woman showed up first and decided to take care of business."

"All possible," Soave conceded. "But how would she know that Donna was shacked up here?"

"Easy," Des said. "She listened in on another phone extension when they made the date. Or intercepted their e-mail. Or maybe she just followed her here."

"*Or* how about if the woman and the boyfriend were in on it together?" Yolie offered eagerly. "What if it's a *couple* we're after—a jealous, desperate woman and her boy toy? Esme and Jeff. First they killed Tito, now Donna."

Soave immediately let loose with an exasperated groan.

Yolie lowered her eyes, pawing at the gravel with her boot. "Well, what do *you* think, Des?"

"Yolie, it's not totally out of left field," Des answered guardedly, not wanting to get caught in between them. "Esme doesn't come across as a major-league schemer, but she *is* an actress and great beauty. For the sake of argument, let's say she could manipulate Jeff into killing Tito for her. It still comes back around to this: What's so damned special about Donna Durslag?"

"Okay, I'm not hearing you," Yolie said, frowning at her.

"Then you need to take a deep breath, count to ten, and listen up," Des explained. "When it came to Tito and other women it was strictly take a number, the line forms on the right. That boy slept with everyone. Esme knew this. In fact, she was plenty busy herself. So say he and Donna *were* sleeping together—why would Esme suddenly care?"

"Maybe Tito wanted to divorce her and marry Donna."

"Get outta here!" Soave erupted. "He's going to dump one of the world's top hotties for that butterball in there? No way!"

"Life is not a P. Diddy video, Rico," snapped Des, who was immediately sorry. Right away, she was caught in their crossfire.

"Now, what's that supposed to mean?" he demanded, flexing his shoulders defensively.

"It means," Yolie shot back, "that love is about more than a tight butt, *dawg*."

"Hey, I know that, Yolie."

"Sure didn't sound like it, *dawg*."

"Can we please move on?" Soave said angrily. "Because I'm about solving these murders, not arguing sexual politics with you all morning, okay?"

"Cool by me," Yolie huffed. "I'm not about arguing. That's not what I'm standing here doing."

"Have you got anything local for us?" he asked Des abruptly, clearly desperate to scramble his way back to safer ground.

Des fed them what she'd learned from Mitch about Dodge Crockett walking on the beach with Becca Peck when Tito went over the falls, thereby putting Martine in the same apparent category as Chrissie Huberman: without an alibi. "You might also look into the whereabouts that night of another Chrissie Huberman client, Abby Kaminsky, who happens to be Jeff Wachtell's estranged wife."

Yolie perked right up at the mention of Jeff's name. "What about her?"

"She had a fling with Tito."

"Shut up!" Yolie clapped her hands together excitedly. "I am loving this."

"That's good work, Des," Soave echoed. "Anything else we should know?"

"Not that I can think of," she said tonelessly, twirling her big Smokey the Bear hat in her fingers.

"Okay . . ." Soave narrowed his red-rimmed eyes at her, sensing that she was holding on to something else. They knew each other too damned well. Plus she was not the world's greatest liar.

"Any idea where this Abby is?" Yolie asked.

"Boston, I think. Chrissie will have her exact itinerary. I can check with her if you'd like."

"I want you to do more than that, Des," Soave said. "I want you to go interview her."

"Whoa, Rico, I'm resident trooper, remember? I don't do road trips."

"I know that, but me and Yolie are going to be buried here all day, and I don't have time to run all of this by somebody new. And, look, I'm really up against it, okay? They're going to muscle me out of the way if I don't score in the next twenty-four." So he was feeling the hot breath of the bosses on the back of his neck, Brass City family ties or not. "I need you on this one, Des. You know the players. You've got the game skills. Will you come off of the bench for me?" he pleaded, his voice catching slightly. "I'd be unbelievably grateful. I really, really would. Honestly, I don't know what I'll do if you say no. . . ."

"Damn, Rico, pull on over to the curb and park it, will you?" Des said, flashing a grin at him. "All you had to say was please."

Will Durslag's mother had left him a farmhouse up on Kelton City Road, a bumpy dirt road that forked off Route 156 just past Winston Farms. Des piloted her cruiser along it slowly, realizing that Mitch had been totally right last night.

I am a Dorseteer now.

When put to the test, she had put the interests of the locals ahead of Meriden. She'd seen no vital need for Soave to know that Dodge had sexually abused Esme and so she hadn't shared it. And this was something entirely new for her. She'd heard plenty of shocking news on the job before. But hearing it about people who she knew—this was fresh. So was withholding it from a colleague. Not that any of this should have surprised her. She was well aware now that being resident trooper required a whole lot more moral dexterity than she'd realized going in. Nothing about her new job was black or white. Each day brought a brand-new shade of gray.

The Durslag place was at the very end of Kelton City Road, down a rutted, muddy driveway. It was a rundown circa 1920 two-story farmhouse on three acres of stony ground. The porch sagged. The roof sagged. Everything sagged. There was a jack under one corner of the foundation, and a blue tarp was stretched over a section of the roof that needed replacing. Numerous windowpanes were cracked, the glazing crumbling or missing entirely.

Will and Donna had started paving the driveway at some point, but after they'd done the stretch between the house and the wood-shed they'd stopped. A portable basketball hoop was set up there, and their catering van was parked alongside of it. Will hadn't left yet—for his morning beach walk or work or anywhere else.

Des pulled up behind the van and got out, smelling tangy wood smoke in the chill morning air.

At the sound of her cruiser Will came out the door onto the rotting porch. "Do you know something, Des?" he called out anxiously, running his hands through his lanky hair. Dressed in a sweatshirt and cutoffs, he looked like a college kid home for the summer. "Where is she? I've been up all night worried sick."

"Let's go inside and talk, Will," she said, starting her way up the steps.

"Why, what do you know?"

The front parlor was small, dingy, and damp. There was a Victorian loveseat upholstered in purple silk brocade shot so full of holes that the stuffing was spilling out. There was an armchair with a blanket thrown over it. There were stacks of old magazines and newspapers. There was dust and there were cobwebs. Whatever they were, the Durslags were not tidy housekeepers. Will had a fire going in the old potbellied Franklin stove, which gave off some welcome warmth against the chill in the room.

"I've been calling *everywhere*," he said fretfully. "I even called nine-one-one to see if there'd been an accident on the highway. Where *is* she, damn it?"

Des smelled coffee in the kitchen. "How do you take your coffee, Will?"

"Black, why?"

The kitchen was a whole different scene—bright and sunny and cared for. It was a spacious farmhouse kitchen equipped with a commercial Viking range, Subzero refrigerator, and a massive butcher block island. Well-used copper pots hung from a rack overhead. A paint-splattered dining table was set before sliding glass doors that overlooked the woods. Clearly, this was the room where they spent their time. Des found a cup in the cupboard, filled it from the coffeemaker and came back to the parlor with it, hating what she was about to do to this man.

Will had lifted the lid of the stove and was feeding the fire with stubby logs, his movements edgy and urgent. "I'm sorry it's so cold in here this morning. This house has absolutely no insulation, and this wood's kind of damp. It's been so humid out."

"You'd better sit down, Will."

"How come?" he asked, looking at her warily.

"It's bad news about Donna. I'm sorry to tell you that she's been found murdered."

Will sank slowly down onto the loveseat. "Oh no, this can't be . . . It *can't.*"

"Here, drink this," she said, holding the coffee out to him.

He didn't reach for it. Just sat there, dazed.

"Will? . . ."

Again, he didn't respond. Just sat there goggle-eyed, his breathing quick and shallow. He was a big strapping guy but size meant nothing when it came to shock. At West Point, Des had seen rock-hard specimens of fearless fighting manhood faint dead away over a flu shot.

She darted into the kitchen and rummaged under the sink for some ammonia. Came back, uncapped it and waved it under his nose.

Will barely reacted to the first two whiffs. After the third whiff he recoiled from her, his eyes starting to clear. Then the recognition of the news set back in. "Oh, God," he gulped. "She was my soul mate, my *everything*. What am I going to do?"

"You're going to drink your coffee, and we're going to talk. Come on, take this. The caffeine will help."

Obediently, he reached for it and took a sip, his chest rising and falling. "How did it happen?"

She sat in the armchair facing him and crossed her long legs. "The details aren't pretty."

"I don't care," he said, his eyes searching her face. "Tell me everything. I *need* to know."

"She was found at the Yankee Doodle."

Will's eyes widened in surprise. "The motel?"

"She checked in there last night at about ten o'clock. She was meeting somebody, Will. Whoever he was, he knocked her unconscious and he . . ."

"And he what?" Will demanded.

"Drowned her in the bathtub."

"No, this can't be," Will groaned, rocking back and forth on the sofa. "You've made a mistake. Take another look. It's got to be somebody else, not Donna."

"It's Donna. I saw her with my own two eyes."

He drank some more coffee, clutching the mug tightly in both hands. "Will they have to cut her open? Please tell me they're not going to do that."

"I don't believe that's called for," Des replied. "Have you got someone who can stay with you, Will? You shouldn't be alone at a time like this."

"I have no one," he replied woodenly. "Just Donna—and now she's gone."

"May I use your phone?"

He didn't respond. Barely seemed to hear her.

Des went in the kitchen and called Mitch, who promised he'd be right over. Then she returned to Will and sat back down. "Mitch is going to hang out here for a little while, okay?"

"Who did this to her, Des?" Will demanded suddenly. His shock had given way to raw anger. It often happened this way. "Who murdered my Donna?"

"We don't know yet. You can help us out. If you're up to it, I mean."

"Of course, but how?"

"By answering some questions. I have to warn you, this might be rough."

"You can ask me anything. I don't give a damn. I've spent the whole night going crazy. She didn't come home. She never, ever did that before."

Des took out her notepad and pen. "Do you have any idea where else she was last night?"

"She had her meeting of the Dorset Merchants Association. They get together for dinner twice a month."

Will's mention of the Merchants Association set off a faint flicker of recognition in the back of Des's mind. "Where do they usually meet?"

"At the Clam House. There's a back room for club meetings." The Clam House was a seafood restaurant adjacent to the Dorset Marina, popular with boaters and tourists. "It usually runs from seven until about nine."

"Did she typically go without you?"

"Yeah, the association was her deal. We've always divided up the workload according to our strengths. Donna was good at working the room. She liked it, even. Me, I'm a cooker. I belong in the kitchen with my pots and pans."

"Were you expecting her home after that?"

"Not directly, no. She had to meet somebody about a catering gig on her way back."

"Any idea who that was?"

Will furrowed his brow in thought. "She may have told me their name, but I'm drawing a total blank. Things are always just so hectic. It was a cocktail party. A bon voyage thing. That's all I remember."

"Where did she keep track of her appointments? Could she have input it somewhere?"

Will smiled very faintly. "No, no, she hates . . . she hated computers. But it ought to be written down in her date book. It's black leather."

"This would be in her shoulder bag?"

Will nodded his head, swallowing.

"Okay, good," Des said, knowing full well that it wouldn't be written down. That there was no catering gig. It was simply the little white lie she'd told Will to buy herself enough time to stop off and screw her boyfriend. "What time did you get home last night, Will?"

"I rolled in about nine-thirty. I was expecting her by ten, ten-thirty. We always stayed in touch by cell phone. If she knew she was going to be later than that she would have called. I tried calling her about eleven. When she didn't answer I started to worry. I phoned our late man, Rich Graybill, to see if she'd stopped by The Works. Rich is usually there until about midnight, cleaning up and getting things set up for the morning. But he said he hadn't seen her."

"Tell me more about him. What's his story?"

"Who, Rich? He's a young guy, good guy. Lives with his girl-friend, Kimberly. She's one of our pastry chefs."

"Her last name?"

"Fiore."

"What did you do after that, Will?"

"Paced around a whole lot," he confessed. "Kept calling her cell phone. Kept getting more and more worried. Like I said, I called the state police to see if there had been any accidents. I can't even remember what time I did that. . . ."

"Not important." And even if it were they would have logged his call.

"At one point I actually decided to go look for her at The Works. I thought *maybe* she'd decided to get an early start on tomorrow's baking. Which makes no sense, because if that's where she was she would have called me. But I was just so desperate. I couldn't just sit here, you know?"

"Yes, I do."

"I left her a note on the kitchen counter in case she got home while

I was out." He loped into the kitchen and returned with it, gazing down at it as if it were the last piece of concrete evidence that Donna and their marriage and their life had ever existed. Gently, he placed it on the coffee table for Des to see. He'd scrawled it in pencil on a piece of lined yellow paper: "Don-Don—I'm out looking for you. Where are you? Be home soon. Love, Willie Boy"

"When I got back here, she still wasn't home," he added quietly. "And I've been sitting up ever since."

"Will, there are some things I need to ask that might seem pretty cold and hurtful. But I need to ask them, and you need to answer them. If you can, that is."

"I understand." He sighed, flopping back down on the loveseat. "Fire away."

"Was Donna involved with someone else?"

Will glared at her, his jaw clenching. For a second, he looked like a vengeful Viking warrior. Then he relaxed, his gaze dropping to the worn rag rug at Des's feet. "We had our troubles," he admitted. "All couples do. Especially when they're together twenty-four hours a day. But I swear to you, I wasn't sneaking around on Donna with another woman. That's the God's honest truth."

"I understand." Des was patient with him. The man was blown away. "And what about Donna? Was she seeing someone?"

He looked up at her miserably. "You want to know if she had a boyfriend—the short answer is yes."

"Who is he, Will?"

"No idea. She never told me. In fact, we never so much as discussed him. But I knew. There were these hang-ups on the phone all the time when I'd answer it. There were the errands she'd run during the afternoon—she'd be gone for an extra hour without any explanation, and be real anxious to take a shower as soon as she got home. I'd notice scratches and bruises on her body that she wasn't real specific about explaining. She . . . she acted different, smelled different, *was* different. I don't know what else to say, except that when you've been married to someone for a while you can just tell."

"How long had this been going on?"

He shrugged his broad shoulders. "Three, four months."

"Her not coming home last night," Des said. "Did it occur to you that—?"

"That she was with *him*? Sure it did. Except that she never, ever did that to me before. She never just disappeared for a whole night. I mean, she didn't want me to know about it, okay? Me or anyone else. Dorset's a small town. Everyone knows you. If you're sneaking around in this place, you have to be incredibly careful." Will reached for his half-empty coffee cup. "One other thought did cross my mind," he admitted, sipping from it. "I thought maybe . . . that she'd run off with him. Left me for good. Our bank has one of those automated eight-hundred numbers you can call day or night to find out your current balance. I called it to see if she'd withdrawn anything from our joint checking account."

"Had she?"

"No."

"You say you kept a joint checking account. Who paid the monthly bills?"

"Me, usually."

"So you would typically see her credit card statements?"

"I guess," he replied, frowning. "Why?"

"Will, Donna paid for the bungalow at the Yankee Doodle with her Visa card. Is this something that would have caught your eye when you sat down to pay the bills?"

"Most likely. I mean, yeah. Definitely."

"What would you have thought when you saw it?"

"Well, I know what sort of a reputation the place has, if that's what you're asking me."

"Maybe she was planning to intercept next month's statement and pay it herself. Does that seem reasonable?"

"Des, why does *any* of this matter?"

"Because her behavior last night wasn't typical, that's why. Like you said, she'd been so careful to hide this affair from you, and yet she showed up at the Yankee Doodle at ten o'clock. She *had* to know she'd get home late enough to set off alarm bells with you. Now, why did she do that? And why didn't she pay cash?"

"Maybe she was *out* of cash," he replied helplessly. "Maybe she was feeling horny and reckless. Who knows, she may have been drunk as a skunk."

"Did she have a problem with alcohol?"

"No! I'm just trying to . . ." Will broke off into heavy silence. "I honestly don't know what she was doing there at that hour, okay?"

"Okay, Will," Des said gently.

She heard the rumble of an engine outside now and went to the window. Mitch's old plum-colored pickup truck was bouncing its way up the dirt drive. She went out onto the sagging porch to greet him, her gallant, uncombed love, her pudgy white knight in his frayed oxford button-down and shlumpy khaki shorts.

"How is he?" he asked, giving her a quick bear hug.

"Not so good."

"God, I am hating this," he murmured glumly. Then he took a deep breath and went charging in the front door with a smile forced onto his face, Des on his heel. "Whoa, it's like a meat locker in here, Will," he exclaimed, rubbing his hands together. "Your place is just as bad as mine. Zero insulation, am I right?"

Will scarcely seemed to notice Mitch. Just sat slumped there on the loveseat, lost in his grief.

Mitch clomped over to the stove to warm his hands, glancing at his friend uncertainly. "I'm really sorry about Donna."

The mention of her name seemed to rouse Will. "Thanks, man," he said hoarsely. "How . . . was the beach this morning?"

"I didn't walk," Mitch replied.

"Yeah, me neither." Will ran a hand over his face, his eyes filling with tears. "I don't think I'm going to make it, Mitch. I really don't."

Mitch came over and put his hand on Will's shoulder. "That's exactly how I felt when I lost Maisie. I know it doesn't seem like it right now, Will, but you're going to make it. It'll get a little better every day, I promise you."

"I can't even *see* tomorrow," Will confessed. "All I can see is that I'm all alone. Donna was my *everything* . . . my best friend. My soul mate. My partner."

Mitch drew back from him, startled.

Des couldn't imagine why. Perhaps he had once said those very words himself about Maisie. "I'll be heading out now, Will," she spoke up.

Will nodded absently, saying nothing to her.

She motioned for Mitch to join her out on the porch.

He did, closing the door softly behind him. "Whew, this is not going to be a lot of fun."

"Not even close," she said, putting her big hat back squarely on her head. "Just wanted to let you know I'm heading up to Boston now."

"You going to talk to Abby?"

"Yeah."

"Give her my regards. And, hey, if you go through Cambridge on your way back, stop at East Coast Grill and pick up a large quantity of their eastern North Carolina shredded pork, okay? We can have it for dinner when you get home. Trust me, it's outstanding."

She cocked her head at him curiously. "Man, how can you think about barbecue at a time like this?"

"I'm not like you. Food is all I think about when I'm upset, remember?"

"That's not something I forget, believe me."

"East Coast Grill," he repeated. "It's on Cambridge Street, just off of Prospect. Anyone will be able to give you directions. And, please, whatever you do, don't take that damned Ninety-five the whole way up. Get off at exit seventy-four, take Three-ninety-five through Norwich and then change to the—"

"Mitch, I *know* how to get to Boston from here."

"Promise me you won't take Ninety-five," he said urgently.

"Why is my route so damned important?"

"Because there's a fatality on that highway at least three times a week and I love you and I don't want to lose you."

She utterly melted. Never had a man made her go gooey the way this one did. She leaned over and kissed him softly on the cheek. "Okay, I promise."

"I don't get it, Des," he said, shaking his head in bewilderment. "Why would someone want to kill Donna? What the hell's going on here?"

"Boyfriend," she sighed, "I wish I knew."

As Des steered her cruiser back down Route 156 she gave Yolie a heads-up on her cell phone about Donna's so-called catering gig and her black leather date book. Des also fed her the name of the Durslags' late-shift man, Rich Graybill. Yolie agreed that he was definitely someone worth talking to. She said she'd also hook up with his girlfriend, Kimberly Fiore, to see if Kimberly backed up what time Rich got home.

Before Des got onto the highway for Boston she pulled in at the Acar's minimart and got out to fill up her gas tank.

Nuri came out at once to do it for her, dressed in his customary white shirt and slacks. "Good morning to you, Trooper," he said politely. His eyes were not nearly so polite. Once again, they were working their way over and around every single inch of her body. "Shall I fill it up?"

"Yes, please," she responded, shuddering slightly. She felt positively creeped by this man. She spotted Nema inside through their sparkling new front window and waved to her. Nema waved back, smiling broadly. "Have you had any further problems, Mr. Acar?"

"Not a one, as I anticipated," he replied, starting in on her windshield with a soapy squeegee. "Everyone has been most supportive. Most particularly my fellow members of the Dorset Merchants Association, who have agreed to offer a cash reward of one thousand dollars to anyone who can provide useful information regarding the identity of these vandals."

Des leaned against the side of the cruiser with her arms crossed. "You folks had your monthly meeting last night, am I right?"

"That is correct," he said, clearing the soap from the window with careful, precise movements. "At the Clam House. The surf-and-turf combo is particularly delicious, in my opinion."

"Did you happen to see Donna Durslag there?"

"I sat right next to her," he said easily. No hesitation or tinge of color to his cheeks, no nervous glance over his shoulder at his wife. "Very nice lady, Mrs. Durslag. So full of personality. Jolly is an appropriate word for her, is it not?"

"So she seemed in good spirits to you?"

"She did. Very upbeat and pleasant."

"What did you two talk about?"

"Nothing very specific. Local business concerns. Tourism and so forth."

"Do you remember what she had on?"

Now Nuri Acar glanced at her curiously, aware that her interest in Donna was more than casual. "A white dress, I believe. It was not anything fancy."

"Like a peasant dress?"

"If you wish."

"Did she happen to say anything about where she was going afterward?"

"I don't believe so, no." Nuri dumped the squeegee back in its soapy tub and returned to the gas pump nozzle, gripping it tightly as he finished filling her tank. "Why do you wish to know so much about Mrs. Durslag?"

"What did *you* do after the meeting broke up, Mr. Acar?"

"I came back here to help Nema. We stay open until ten."

"What time did you get here?"

"Perhaps nine-fifteen," he said, as the nozzle clunked to a halt. Her tank was full. "That will be twenty-two dollars even, please."

"You came straight here?" she asked, handing him her credit card.

Nuri took it from her, scowling. "What is the point of this, young lady?"

"Mr. Acar, if you have anything at all to tell me, it'll go down a whole lot better if you do it before rather than after."

"After *what*, may I ask?"

"After I say out loud that Donna Durslag was murdered last night."

Nuri's eyes widened. "My goodness gracious. By who?"

"By her boyfriend," Des replied, raising her chin at him. "Whoever he is."

"I was not involved with that woman," he shot back. "And I resent your insinuation."

"I insinuated nothing. You asked me a question, I answered it."

"How dare you doubt my veracity?" he demanded, highly indignant. Or staging one hell of an imitation, especially for someone who was so overtly smarmy. "I am a respectable businessman. A married man. How dare you?"

"I simply have a job to do, Mr. Acar."

"Then you have a filthy, horrible job. A proper young lady would not hold such a job. She would not." Glowering, he turned on his heel and sped inside to run her credit card. Service without a smile.

Des got back in her cruiser and waited calmly for him to return.

When he did, he refused to make eye contact with her. She was too far beneath him.

"I carry a pooper-scooper, Mr. Acar," she explained as she signed the credit card slip. "I'm the girl who cleans up after the other human beings. You're right—sometimes it's not a very nice job. We're not a very nice animal. In fact we're the cruelest, most thoughtless animal on the planet. I try not to let it get to me, but, wow, some mornings it just turns me all upside down." She tore off her copy and handed his back to him, treating him to her biggest smile. "You have yourself a good one, okay?"

Abby Kaminsky lived plenty large when she was on tour.

The best-selling children's author had herself a condo-sized suite on the ninth floor of the highly choice Four Seasons Hotel on Boylston Street, complete with a drop-dead view of the lush green Public Garden, the Common, and Beacon Hill. It was a bright, crisp New England afternoon, the sky a deep blue, the clouds puffy and white. Off in the distance, the Charles River shimmered in the sunlight.

"It's like I told you on the phone," Abby chattered gaily as she showed Des in. "I am insanely busy today. I can only give you a few minutes. I have two bookstore appearances, a radio call-in show, and then I'm talking fish with the *Zoom* kids." Jeff Wachtell's estranged wife was a bustling, impeccably groomed little thing with a frosted head of architecturally designed, stay-put hair that made her seem a bit taller than she really was, which was barely five feet tall. "A stylist will be here in twenty minutes to make me gorgeous. It's just a really tight, tight day."

"Understood," Des said. "I appreciate you squeezing me in."

There was a fruit basket and a bouquet of flowers in the living room. There was a portable wardrobe rack full of Armani linen suits and silk blouses. There was a life-sized cardboard cutout of Abby clutching her new Carleton Carp book under a balloon caption that read: *Go Fish!*

And there was a goateed no-neck seated on the sofa, drinking a diet soda and staring at a rerun of *Baywatch* on the television.

"This is my escort," Abby said. "Frankie, say hello to Resident Trooper Mitry. She's come here all the way from Dorset, Connecticut."

Frankie gave Des a brief nod, barely bothering to look her way. He was too busy maintaining his cultivated air of bad-assdom.

One whiff and Des could smell yard all over him. "Glad to know you, Frankie," she said pleasantly. "Your last name is? . . ."

He glowered in silence for a long moment before he said, "Ramistella."

"You work out of New York?"

"Bay Ridge."

"What's your address?"

He gave it to her, peering up at Des now with eyes that were heavy lidded and immensely hostile. "Why so many questions?"

"Behave, Frankie," Abby ordered him. "She's just doing her job. You need to leave us alone now, okay? Go take a walk or something. And have the car ready for me downstairs at two sharp."

He got up very deliberately, turned off the TV, and started for the door.

"Oh, hey, cookie?" Abby called after him. "Take my cutout, will you?"

Grimacing with disdain, Frankie carried the cardboard Abby out of the room under his arm, shutting the door softly behind him.

"Can I get you anything from the minibar, Trooper?" Abby asked her. "Water, juice?"

"I'm all set, thanks."

Abby sat on the sofa and kicked off her little pumps, one stocking leg folded under her, a box of Cocoa Pebbles kids' cereal cradled in her lap. She reached inside for a handful and munched on it. "Want some? What am I saying? Of course you don't. Pebbles are my own thing," she explained merrily. "Can't help myself. Now what can I do for you?"

Des took off her hat and sat in an armchair across the coffee table from her. "You can tell me where you've been the past couple of nights."

"Sure, I can do that," Abby said easily, chomping on her cereal. "Only let me ask you something first—why do you want to know this?"

"Because we're trying to ascertain the whereabouts of anyone and everyone who was involved with Tito Molina."

"Oh, sure, I get it," she said, nodding her head of hair. "You found out that I had a little, a-a *thing* with Tito. Did Chrissie tell you? No, wait, it was your boyfriend, wasn't it? It was Mitch."

Des didn't bother to answer her.

"It's okay, Crissie's told me all about Mitch and you. And now that I've met you both I must say you are the last two people in the world I'd guess would *ever* end up in the feathers together. I mean, talk about an odd couple. You're black, he's Jewish. He's a critic, you're a cop. You're skinny, he's . . . not." Abby wagged a manicured finger at Des, her big blue eyes gleaming. "You know, you two would make a terrific pair of fish."

Des let out a laugh. "I'll make sure to pass that one along to him."

"No, no, I'm serious. I've been wanting to get more racial for some

time. The inner city kids need role models. And you're so tall and gorgeous and self-assured. Seriously, I am adoring this. May I use you?"

"I can't imagine anything more flattering—just as long as you
don't name me something like Hallie Butts."

"Cookie, I am *stealing* that!" Abby squealed with delight. "You
are so lucky, you know that? Mitch is one you'll never, ever have to
worry about. Trust me, I personally road tested him."

"Road tested him?"

"I came on to him like gangbusters yesterday," she confided, girl to
girl. "Did everything but dive under the table and go for his zipper
with my teeth. See, when I'm tour I can get a little, you know, horny.
But I could not generate so much as a mild whiff of interest out of
him. That one is a keeper, believe me."

"Oh, I believe you," Des said, wondering what America's parents
would think if they found out that their kids' favorite author was a
little bit nutty and a whole lot slutty. "So about your activities these
past couple of nights . . ."

"Okay, sure." Abby folded her little hands in her lap and took a
deep breath, collecting herself. "I got home to New York from my
tour the day Tito died. I was on the six P.M. flight from Los Angeles."
She gave Des the name of the airline and what time it had left L.A.

"Was Frankie with you?"

"He sure was. I can't travel alone anymore. Too many kids want
to talk to me and touch me. Puh-leeze . . ." Abby shivered, fanning
herself with fluttering fingers. "A limo met us at the airport to bring
me home. Frankie helped me shlep all of my stuff upstairs—I had to
take a ton of clothes."

"Where do you live?"

She gave Des her address on Riverside Drive. It was a doorman
building on the corner of West Ninety-first Street.

"What time did you get settled in?"

"Maybe eight."

"Did Frankie stick around?"

"No, he took the limo on home."

"And how did you spend your evening?"

Abby got up suddenly and padded over to the window in her stocking feet, silent as a kitten on the plush carpet. "I realize this is going to sound terrible, but I can't lie to you because I happen to be the soul of honesty—except for when I'm not. You do believe me, don't you?"

"I really couldn't say. So far, you've told me jack."

"You're absolutely right," Abby admitted, letting out a nervous laugh. "The truth is, I was in Dorset. I-I've been in Dorset a lot lately."

Des leaned forward in her chair, watching Abby closely. "Doing what?"

Abby went over to the minibar and pulled out a small bottle of Perrier and opened it. "Sitting parked outside of Jeffrey's condo in my car," she replied, taking a dainty sip.

"What are you, stalking him?"

"God, no. I'm not parked out there with an Uzi or anything. Just a box of Cocoa Pebbles and a pair of b-binoculars." She paused, reddening. "Okay, maybe I'd better explain myself."

"Maybe you'd better."

"I just . . . I wanted to see for myself who he's sleeping with. I need to know. And I am so humiliated to admit this out loud to you that I could just about crawl under that sofa. I mean, how pathetic am I? But it's the truth. I've been sitting in my damned car every night, watching that little weasel entertain one gorgeous woman after another and crying my poor baby blues out."

"Have you been in direct contact with him?" Des asked, shoving her horn-rimmed glasses up her nose.

Abby returned to the sofa and sat back down. "Define direct contact."

"Well, does he know you've been watching him?"

"*God*, he'd better not. I would just die if he found out."

"You haven't spoken to him?"

"Of course not. Why would I?"

"Because you still love him, that's why."

"I do *not* still love him," Abby said angrily.

"Tie that bull outside, as my good friend Bella Tillis likes to say. A girl does not sit in her car all night with a pair of binoculars unless she feels the love."

"Okay, so maybe I feel it a little," Abby admitted reluctantly. "That's really beside the point."

"And the point is? . . ."

"That I'm telling you the truth. Check with my garage on Broadway and Ninety-second. They'll tell you what time I took my car out and when I brought it back. It's a black Mercedes station wagon. I've practically been living in it since I got back. Night after night I sit there—until dawn, when I drive back. What a rotten drive that is, too."

"Have you been making it alone?"

"Of course. Who else would sit there with me all night like some nut?"

"Frankie would."

"I am not involved with Frankie. We *were*, very briefly. But not anymore. I've been alone. Just little me."

Which meant that Abby Kaminsky had no one to vouch for her, Des reflected. No one who could say she hadn't pushed Tito Molina off that cliff. True, she was a tiny thing. But the element of surprise can add a good deal of muscle. And that granite ledge was plenty slick. Only, what about Donna Durslag? Why would Abby want to see *her* dead?

"You do believe me, don't you?" Abby asked, watching her uncertainly.

"I don't disbelieve you," Des responded. "How about you tell me what you saw while you were parked out there?"

"Sure, okay, I can do that. I saw, let's see, I saw Esme Crockett show up there the first night."

"This is the night Tito died?"

"Correct. She got there at around midnight. I could see her and

Jeffrey sucking face through the kitchen window—until he turned the lights out and they did God knows what unspeakable things to each other in the dark. She left at about four in the morning."

Which backed up what Esme and Jeff had said. "And the next night?"

"Her mother showed up at around eleven."

"Did Martine stay the night?"

"She was there less than ten minutes," Abby said gleefully. "Tossed a major hissy fit on the front porch. She even threw a flower pot at Jeffrey."

"She'd found out he was two-timing her with Esme," Des ventured.

"You got that right, cookie. And what a mouth that bitch has on her. She's standing out there screaming at the top of her lungs about how she's going to make a bow tie out of his balls. Unbelievable! Then she took off in a huff."

"And what did you see last night?"

"Last night I was here in Boston," Abby said hastily. "But . . . why are you asking?"

"Because someone else got murdered last night, that's why."

"Really, who?"

"Donna Durslag."

"Oh, sure. She owned The Works with her husband."

"You knew her?"

"By name. Jeffrey rents his space from them."

"So you're saying you *weren't* watching his condo last night, am I right?"

"That's right," Abby said, lowering her eyes.

"Don't disrespect me, girl. If you took your town car out of the hotel parking garage last night, I'll know. If you rented a different car, I'll know. If you so much as walked out that lobby door, I'll know. I have the means. I have the skills. I have the—"

"Okay, okay, no need to get all huffy on me."

"I do *not* get huffy."

"I *was* at Jeffrey's last night," Abby conceded. "I was staked out just like the other two nights—from eleven till about four. I took the town car."

"Why lie to me about it?"

"Because I'm embarrassed," she wailed plaintively. "Wouldn't you be embarrassed? I mean, God, this is *so* humiliating."

"Who visited Jeffrey last night?"

"No one, I swear."

"Did he go out?"

Abby shook her head. "He was there by himself all night."

"Did you think about knocking on his door?"

"Not a chance."

"Why not, was Frankie with you?"

"Look, I'd rather not involve Frankie in this, okay?"

"That's not an answer."

There was a tapping at the suite door now.

Abby let her breath out, clearly relieved by the interruption. "Would you mind getting that, cookie?"

Des got up and went to the door and opened it.

A frail young man with a concave chest and a two-day stubble of beard stood out in the hallway clutching a pair of battered metal carrying cases. "I'm here for Abby," he announced.

"Come in, Gregory!" Abby called to him as she bustled over toward the desk. "I'm afraid I'll have to cut this off now, Trooper. Gregory has to do my mouth."

"That's fine," Des said. "I got what I came for. Where will you be tonight?"

Abby frowned at her. "Right here in Boston, why?"

"Just checking. You're a happening little girl. Liable to turn up anywhere."

"Well, I'll be here. That's the truth. And I always tell the truth."

"Except for when you don't," Des said, smiling at her. "Right, I heard that."

One of the doormen down in the lobby gave Des directions to the

East Coast Grill. Her cruiser was double-parked out front. She got in and called Yolie on her cell phone to tell her what she didn't want to hear—that Abby Kaminsky backed up Esme and Jeff's story.

"Did you believe her?" Yolie asked, sounding thoroughly dejected.

"Yolie, I honestly don't know. She's rich, wiggy, in love. Anything's possible. What have you got?"

"So far, not a damned thing. None of the guests at the Yankee Doodle saw our boy come or go. And, Lordy, were they not happy to be questioned. Kimberly Fiore backs up her boyfriend, Rich Graybill. He got home from his late shift at The Works by midnight. Word, we are *nowhere*," she grumbled at Des.

"Hey, we'll lick this, Yolie. You keep that chin up for me, okay?"

"Girl, I am *all* about that," Yolie vowed before she hung up.

Des started up her cruiser and glanced in her rearview mirror, spotting big Frankie. He was seated at the wheel of the black town car parked behind her in the hotel's loading area, glowering at her with as much menace as he could muster. Definitely a yard face. The man had done time. She was positive.

As she pulled away, Des ran a check on him on her digital radio. She got her answer before she'd made it across the Charles into Cambridge on the Massachusetts Avenue Bridge. Frank Ramistella had wriggled his way out of two assault charges when he was in his late teens, then served three years of New York state time for armed robbery. As far as the law knew, he had been clean for the past six years.

All well and good, Des reflected as he steered her way toward Central Square. The man was still hired muscle. And he was way into Abby. He'd do what that little blond asked him to, even if it meant pushing Tito Molina off a cliff. But that still begged the question about Donna. What possible reason could Abby have for wanting Donna dead?

This question Des could not answer.

And it troubled her big-time. Actually, this whole case did. Because the more she learned the more confused she got. In truth, she wasn't getting any closer to figuring this one out at all.

In truth, her damned fool head was reeling.

CHAPTER 13

"Um, okay, tell me again why we're sitting here like this?"

"Because I have a feeling, that's why," Mitch explained to her for the umpteenth time.

"You have a feeling," Des repeated from next to him in the darkness. She was still in uniform, her collar opened, sleeves turned back.

"I do. I have a definite, undeniable feeling."

"Oh, it's undeniable, all right."

They were sitting in his pickup a hundred yards up Turkey Neck Road from Dodge and Martine Crockett's driveway, their bellies full of barbecue. Carriage lanterns framed the driveway entrance, bathing it in a dim, golden glow. Across the darkened meadow, lights were on inside the house. It was just past eleven. Warm, sticky air had moved in from the south as the afternoon had given way to evening, bringing low clouds and fog with it. Now it was humid and still and the cicadas were whirring. In the distance, Mitch could hear the foghorn on the Old Saybrook Lighthouse.

"What's more, you need my help," he added. "You've got two murders that don't seem to connect with each other except for the simple fact that they must. And you're totally flummoxed by it— you, Soave, Yolie, all of you."

"Well, you're not wrong there," she growled at him.

"Would you like to know why you're so flummoxed?"

"One way or the other, I have a feeling you're going to tell me."

"Because all three of you think inside the box. I'm not being critical, mind you. I'm just saying that you're encumbered by the rules and procedures of your job, and I'm not. This allows me to function as a freer thinker. You might even think of me, well, as a visionary."

Des reached over in the dark and squeezed his hand. "Baby, I'm not going to have to hit you, am I?"

"What you'll be doing, before this night is over, is thanking me."

"Mitch? . . ."

"Yes, Des?"

"*What* damned feeling?!"

"That we've let our heads get turned by all of this sex. We've got so many Dorseteers hopping in and out of bed with each other that we don't know who loves who, who loathes who, who might want who dead. . . . Are you with me so far?"

"You're talking, I'm listening."

"Okay, good. We've got Abby, Chrissie, and Martine all without alibis for the night Tito died. Two of them had been romantically involved with him. The third was his mother-in-law. Now, we don't know why Donna Durslag had to die. Therefore we have no idea which one of those three had any interest in killing her. But here's something that we *do* know—that Dodge Crockett is a sick, bad, morally depraved guy."

"I won't disagree with you there."

"Let's say that this qualifies him to be our prime murder suspect, okay?"

"That's a bit of a leap, but go ahead and run with it."

"We know that he's home alone tonight. He told me so this morning. So all we have to do now is wait and he'll show his hand."

"What hand?"

"Something is going to happen tonight," Mitch declared with total certainty. "I'm telling you, I can feel it."

"Whoa, time out, cowboy—*this* is your feeling?"

"Well, yeah. Put yourself in his shoes, Des. It's not as if a perverted sociopath like Dodge is going to spend his night watching *Send Me No Flowers* on American Movie Classics. Not that it's a bad movie, mind you. Rock Hudson and Doris Day were an underrated comedy team, and Paul Lynde absolutely goes to town as a funeral home director who loves his work just a bit too—"

"Okay, I *am* going to have to hit you."

"Someone is going to visit Dodge tonight. Or he's going to go see someone."

"And? . . ."

"And that's our chance to find out what he's really up to and who he's up to it with. If he leaves, we follow him. If someone comes by, we tiptoe our way to the house and put our noses to the glass. It's smart, it's simple, and it'll work. What do you say, Master Sergeant, am I right or am I right?"

Des sat there in the darkened silence for a long moment before she said, "You do know that this particular move is straight out of the Hardy Boys, don't you?"

"Maybe it is," he admitted. "But it was a darned effective maneuver when they'd exhausted their other options. Besides, Frank and Joe cracked a number of Fenton's toughest cases."

"You do know that was fiction, don't you—for little boys?"

A possum moseyed its way out of the brush and up the Crocketts' driveway, its long, slinky tail trailing along behind it. Truly one of God's ugliest creatures, Mitch observed. Right up there with the lowly woodchuck. Just one of the many new things he had learned since he moved to Dorset. "You think this is a stupid idea, is that it?"

"Actually, I'm sitting here thinking you make a shocking amount of sense."

"So what's the problem?"

"For starters, I think you have you a personal vendetta thing going on. You admired Dodge and he's turned out to be a total sleaze and now you want him to fry. Your judgment is clouded, Mitch. That's not to say I disagree with you. The man is bad news, and he should pay for what he's done to Esme and Becca and who knows who else. But that doesn't necessarily make him a murderer. Just a sleaze."

Mitch considered this for a moment. "Okay, what else?"

"I also think there's an exceptionally good chance that we're going to sit here until four in the morning and have nothing to show for it except stiff necks."

It *was* awfully quiet. They hadn't seen so much as single passing motorist since they'd been parked there.

"Maybe, but at least we're together." He leaned over and kissed her smooth cheek. "You don't mind that part, do you?"

"No, baby, I don't mind," she said, her own knowing lips finding the sweet spot under his ear, the one that turned him into a quivering mass of man Jell-O.

"Did I remember to thank you for stopping at East Coast Grill?" he murmured, finding her mouth with his.

"Three times . . . This makes four."

"I'm overwhelmed. I've never had a woman bring me pork before."

"If I'd known you were this easy I'd have done it a lot sooner," she said, groaning softly. "But you'd better pass me some of that coffee. I've been up since before dawn."

Mitch poured her some from the thermos he'd brought, thinking about what she'd said. Because she wasn't wrong. Not one bit.

He did want it to be Dodge.

They'd had words that morning at Will's house. Mitch hadn't needed to stay there with Will for long. As soon as Des took off the poor guy headed straight for the phone to call his father figure. Dodge's arrival was Mitch's official cue to leave. Mitch was in no mood to hang around with that man.

Still, their paths crossed out on the front porch as Dodge came bounding up the steps, looking all tanned, virile, and fit, a manila folder tucked under one arm. "Mitch, I'm so glad you're here," he said, face etched with concern. "This is just such an awful business. Why would anyone want to hurt Donna?"

"I really don't know, Dodge."

"How is our boy holding up?"

"Our boy is pretty shook."

"We missed you out there this morning," he said, eyeing Mitch carefully. "The tide was out. It was beautiful."

"I couldn't make it," Mitch said, rather stiffly.

"Sure, sure." Dodge seemed stung by Mitch's chilly response. "Oh, hey, I've got something for you," he said, holding the manila folder out to him. "This is the application for that teen mentoring program over at the Youth Services Bureau. They'd love to have you if you can spare an hour a week."

Mitch reached for it gingerly. He did not actually wish to touch anything that Dodge had touched. In fact, he felt a form of visceral revulsion just standing on the same porch with him.

After an awkward silence Dodge said, "I'm sorry you had to walk in on my . . . private moment with Becca yesterday."

Mitch said nothing. He knew that the older man was waiting for him to put his mind at ease. But Mitch didn't particularly feel like doing that.

"I can tell that you're still upset," Dodge persisted.

"Dodge, I really don't want to talk about this right now. Why don't you go inside? Will needs you."

"It's wasn't what it looked like, Mitch. Becca and I have a real history together. We go way back."

"Kind of like you and Esme?" Mitch snapped, immediately regretting it. He should have kept his mouth shut.

Dodge didn't lose his composure. He simply looked Mitch straight in the eye and said, "I don't know what you've been hearing, or from who, but I love my daughter, and I would never, ever hurt her. Anyone who says otherwise is a liar."

"You never touched her?"

"I'd like to have an opportunity to discuss this further with you, Mitch. Martine will be with Esme tonight. I'll be home all evening. We can have a drink on the terrace and talk it through, okay? Maybe by then you will have cooled off."

"Dodge, one thing keeps puzzling me—why'd you tell me that Martine was having an affair?"

"Because she was," he said. "And because you and I are friends. Or at least I thought we were."

"Okay, right, I get it now," Mitch said, nodding his head. "*I'm* the one who has the problem."

"Mitch, we all do things that we don't understand and we can't control," Dodge offered as explanation. "Things that we feel bad about. That's what makes us human beings. Our only real failure is when we don't make the effort to understand one another. Will you at least try? Will you do that much for me?"

"Sure, I'll do that much, Dodge," he replied grimly, seized by the horrifying certainty that his friend had just confessed to killing Tito Molina and Donna Durslag.

And then Mitch had said good-bye to him and headed home to prowl Big Sister's tidal pools alone with his hands in his pockets. He pruned his tomato plants, mowed his lawn, picked wild blackberries and beach plums. He was fine as long as he kept moving. Until at long last Des returned to him from Boston, one-quart tub of shredded pork in hand.

And now they sat there together in his truck, Des sipping coffee and stabbing holes in his theory. "What about the fact that Dodge has an alibi for when Tito was murdered?"

"His alibi is Becca," Mitch pointed out. "I don't mean to sound cold, because I like Becca, but if Dodge can convince her to get down on all fours with a bag over her head, he can convince her to fib for him."

"I'll give you that one," she responded. "But answer me this—why would Dodge want to kill Tito?"

"Maybe he didn't. Maybe it was the other way around. Let's say Tito found out about Dodge and Esme. Maybe Esme told Tito, okay? And let's say Tito called Dodge out on it. Think about what Tito told me at my house that night. He said he'd gotten himself into something bad, something he couldn't get out of. This certainly fits the bill, doesn't it? *'The hangman says it's time to let her fly,'* Maybe Tito was telling me that Dodge was about to pay for his sins."

"Except that Dodge got the best of him up there," she mused aloud. "Is that what you're saying?"

"Well, why not? There's no actual proof that it was a woman who pushed Tito off of that cliff, is there?"

"Not one bit," Des said. "Only answer me this, boyfriend. Why did Dodge turn right around and kill Donna? What's the connection?"

"Maybe there isn't one. Maybe it was just some rough sex that got out of hand. It happens."

"No sale. You can't tell me that he *accidentally* happened to kill his second person in three days."

"Look, I saw with my own two eyes what this guy is capable of doing to women. Frankly, it's a miracle that more of them haven't died while they were getting freaky with him."

"This wasn't getting freaky, Mitch. Donna was brutally, violently murdered. I am talking about walls spattered with blood."

"Was there a lot of blood?"

"There was enough. Why, what's the significance of—?" Des broke off suddenly, drawing in her breath.

Mitch sat right up, hearing the same sound she had—a car starting. It came from across the Crocketts' meadow. Headlights flicked on now in front of their house and, slowly, the lights turned and made their way down the long gravel drive toward them. Mitch recognized the flatulent burble of the car's diesel engine. It was Dodge's old Mercedes wagon.

It was midnight and Dodge was heading out.

"I don't believe this," Des muttered at him.

"And I don't believe you doubted me," Mitch exclaimed triumphantly. "If I were a less secure person I would actually be hurt."

"Hush!"

The Mercedes was nearing the carriage lamps at the entrance to the drive. From where they sat, it was impossible to tell if Dodge was alone in the car. For that matter, it was impossible to be sure that it was Dodge who was behind the wheel. As the Mercedes paused at the road, Mitch reached for his key in the ignition.

Des stopped him with a warning hand. "Not yet. Let him get rolling first."

Dodge pulled out and headed toward Old Shore Road, leaving plumes of diesel exhaust in his wake. Mitch waited until he'd gone around a bend before he started up the pickup and put it in gear.

"No headlights," Des cautioned him. "Just zone in on his taillights."

Mitch took off after the Mercedes in the blackness. Fortunately, there were occasional streetlamps to mark his way. Otherwise he would have driven into a ditch for sure.

Old Shore Road was deserted at that time of night. The Mercedes was about a half mile ahead of them, chugging in the direction of town, its headlights casting a soft, film noir glow in the foggy mist that reminded Mitch of the opening sequence of *The Killers*, when William Conrad and Charles McGraw are pulling into that sleepy small town in search of the Swede. All that was missing was the ominous Miklos Rozsa score.

Mitch chugged along after it at a steady forty-five.

"Don't get too close," Des said anxiously from next to him, her knees jiggling with excitement. "Give him room."

He grinned at her. "Want to take the wheel, Master Sergeant?"

"Heck no. You're doing great."

"You miss this, don't you?"

"Miss what?"

"The hunt. You are loving this. I can see it in your eyes."

"Doughboy, it is pitch-black in this cab."

"So maybe I'm imagining it."

"So maybe you ought to keep your imagination on the road. Careful, he's slowing down. . . . Watch it!"

Mitch hit the brakes, coming to a dead stop. Up ahead, Dodge was pulling into the Citgo minimart, even though it was closed up for the night. The illuminated sign was dark, the big floodlights out. There was only the night-light that the Acars left on inside when they went home. Nonetheless, Dodge drove around in back, where the rest rooms and trash bins were, and shut off his lights.

"Man, what the hell is he doing?" Des wondered as they idled there.

"Meeting somebody?"

Des jumped out, shutting her door silently behind her. "Catch up with me real slow," she said to him through the open window. "Hit your lights when I signal you, got it?"

"Got it."

She was off and running now, streaking her way toward the min-imart, her knees high, her arms pumping. Mitch eased along behind her, seeing her backlit by the night-light inside. Now he could see her cutting across the parking lot toward Dodge's car, raising an arm high over her head. Now he could see her lowering it. . . .

And now Mitch flicked on his headlights.

And there stood Dodge Crockett intently spray-painting 9/11 WTC on the side of the minimart in two-foot-high red letters.

"Hold it *right* there, Mr. Crockett!" Des bellowed at him angrily.

First, Dodge froze. Then he hurled the aerosol paint can at her. Then he tried to run, which was futile—Des was faster than he was. He scarcely got twenty feet before she overtook him and threw him roughly to the pavement, jamming her knee into the small of his back. She slapped a handcuff on him and dragged him over to the rear service door, which had a heavy steel handle on it, and cuffed him to that. Then she called for a cruiser on her cell phone. She also got the Acars' home number and put in a call to them.

Mitch climbed out of the truck and walked slowly over toward Dodge, his eyes hungrily searching Dodge's face in the headlights for some insight into what was going on in this man's mind—this man who he had looked up to and confided in and thought of as a friend.

Dodge did not hang his head in shame or defeat. He remained unbowed and unapologetic, the same way he had when Mitch and Will had walked in on he and Becca.

"A cruiser will be here in five," Des announced, pocketing her phone.

"How about the Acars?" Mitch asked.

"No answer. I left a message on their machine."

Mitch frowned. It was after midnight—kind of late for them to be out. Then again, maybe they didn't pick up after they went to bed. A lot of people didn't.

"This finally makes some sense," Des said, staring coldly at Dodge "I get it now."

"You get what?" wondered Mitch.

Dodge wasn't saying a word.

"Why Miss Barker got weird on me," she explained. "The old girl clammed right up when I asked her if she'd seen anybody drive by her house after that rock got thrown. Same with Mr. Acar, who was way too anxious to button it all up. Because it wasn't any stupid kids who were messing with him. It was *you*, Mr. Crockett, and you're someone who still matters in this town. Miss Barker knew it was you—she recognized your car. And Mr. Acar knew because you'd warned him, hadn't you? You'd told him what might happen if he didn't back off."

Mitch turned to Dodge and said, "Why have you done this? What did the Acars ever do to you?"

"They've cut our morning take-out trade in half, that's what," Dodge spoke up, his voice calm and matter-of-fact. "They're absolutely killing us with those Turkish pastries of hers. The locals haven't come anywhere near The Works since she started selling them. I begged Nuri to give us a break. I said to him, look, you've got a thriving gasoline business. Kindly leave the food trade to us. He refused. I even offered to buy the damned pastries from him myself and sell them at The Works. Again he refused. He just wouldn't listen to reason. Those Acars are unbelievably stubborn people."

"So, what, you're trying to scare them into leaving town?" Mitch asked.

"I'm *trying* to protect my investment. This is business I'm talking about, Mitch. People play for keeps. Believe me, some fellow who was truly ruthless would have burned this damned place to the ground a month ago and never lost a night's sleep over it. We will have to shut down half of our bakery operation if they don't back off. As far as the banks are concerned that's a red flag. I won't be able to raise any more capital. I won't be able to meet my overhead. The Works will go into receivership, and I'll be cleaned out. I'll lose everything."

"In other words, the Acars are smart businesspeople and you're not."

"Don't judge what you don't understand," he shot back gruffly.

"Actually, I understand you perfectly, Dodge," Mitch said.

"You're the single most arrogant egomaniac I've ever met. You think the rules that apply to other people don't apply to you. That you can do whatever you want to whomever you want, up to and including your own daughter. Well, you're wrong, and it's amazing to me that you've lasted all of these years without finding that out. I guess you're just a sheltered small-town boy. But let me just ask you this—why did you have to push Tito off of that cliff? And how did Donna qualify as competition? It seems to me she was one of your biggest assets."

"Now, you wait one minute." Dodge's eyes widened. For the first time he seemed genuinely rattled. "I've stepped over the line a tad, I'll grant you that."

"You're granting us jack," Des snapped. "We caught you in the act."

"I threw a rock through a window," Dodge acknowledged readily. "I sprayed some graffiti on a wall. But that's all. You can't pin those murders on me. I had nothing to do with them. I am not a killer, I swear."

"All I know," Mitch said, "is that Donna told me not to look too closely at her business or her marriage. And now she's dead and you're out here trying to put a hardworking immigrant couple out of business."

"Where were you last night, Mr. Crockett?" Des asked him.

"I was home all evening."

"Alone?"

"Very alone. I don't seem to be too popular these days."

"I can't imagine why," she said, raising her chin at him. "Were you romantically involved with Donna?"

"Of course not," Dodge replied. "Donna Durslag didn't sleep around. She wasn't the type. Believe me, I know about these things."

Mitch started to say something back but before he could get the words out something went *ker-chunk* inside his head and he just stood there with his mouth open, dumbstruck. Because it hit him now—the thing that had been staring right at him all along. The thing he'd completely ignored.

And now Mitch stood there in the Citgo parking lot with his head spinning. It was spinning when the cruiser that Des had summoned pulled up and an immense young trooper climbed out. It was spinning as Des went over the charges with the trooper. It was spinning as she uncuffed Dodge from the door handle and put him in the backseat. It was still spinning when he and Des stood there watching the cruiser take Dodge away to the Troop F barracks in Westbrook.

"Are you okay, boyfriend?" Des asked, examining him with concern. "You look a little blown away."

"Des, I've figured it out. . . ."

"Figured what out?"

"Who killed Tito and Donna."

"Well, are you going to tell me about it?"

"Of course, only there's absolutely no way to prove it. No conventional way, that is. Des, I'm afraid that this is going to call for some more, well, visionary thinking."

She stood there with her hands on her hips, scowling at him. "Mitch, you have *got* to be kidding me."

"What do you mean by that?" he protested innocently.

"I *mean*, I know that look on your face. You look just like a fat little boy who is about to stick his fat little hand in the cookie jar."

"Okay, first of all I resent the repeated use of the F-word—"

"You want to set some kind of a trap. And you want *me* to watch your back, don't you? Tell me I'm wrong. Go ahead, tell me."

"Well, it worked once before, didn't it?"

"You ended up in the *hospital* before."

"I didn't mind. The wound healed fast, and I got all of the ice cream I could eat. Not to mention tapioca."

"Mitch, it cost me my damned job on Major Crimes."

"And look how much happier you are. Look at how much fun we have together, day in and day out." He strode resolutely back to his truck now and got in, waiting for her join him.

Des followed him reluctantly and climbed in, her eyes shining at him. "Mitch, I'm being serious now, okay? Please, please don't do this—whatever *this* is."

"I have to," he insisted, pulling out onto Old Shore Road and heading for home.

"Why, damn it?"

"Because somebody has been killing people who I care about. You guys can't put a stop to it. I can. And there's absolutely no need for you to worry about me. I can handle myself. I'm perfectly capable of . . ." Mitch frowned, glancing over at her. "What was that noise you just made? I distinctly heard a sound come out of you."

"That was sheer human anguish!" she cried out. "I am involved with a crazy person. You are insane!"

"Am not. I'm just a concerned Dorseteer who's had enough."

"Kindly tell me this, Mr. Had Enough—what am I supposed to do about Rico and Yolie? What do I tell them?"

"Not a thing. If they have so much as a hint of prior knowledge then it's entrapment. That's one of the truly valuable things I've learned from hanging with you, Des."

"Mitch, it's entrapment if *I'm* involved!"

"But you're not. You're simply backing my play in case it all turns sour. They can't fault you for being in the right place at the right time. Perfectly legitimate."

She glowered out the windshield in seething silence. "You're going to do this no matter what I say, aren't you?"

"If you don't want in, just say so. I promise I won't hold it against you."

"You know what I should do? I should cuff you to that steering wheel right now."

"But you won't," he said, grinning at her.

"Why the hell not?"

"Two reasons. One, because I'm your sweet baboo—"

"You *were* my sweet baboo. Our love is like *so* hanging in the balance right now."

"Two, because deep down inside, where your scrupulously high moral standards live, you know I'm right."

She said nothing in response to that. Just rode along next to him, smoldering, as he steered his truck back to Big Sister.

"I can't do it," she finally said, her voice low and pained. "Not again. I won't be there to help you this time. You're on your own. I'm out."

"That's fine. I understand."

"I *mean* it!"

"So do I."

"Mitch, I can't even begin to tell you how much I am hating you right now."

"I'm awfully fond of you, too, Master Sergeant."

The road up to the Devil's Hopyard was narrow and twisting, and the low, dense fog ahead of him in the headlights made the shoulders seem to crowd right in around his truck.

Mitch drove slowly, alone in the cab except for his microcassette recorder and the pint bottle of peppermint schnapps on the seat next to him. His mouth was dry, his palms moist, even though he kept wiping them on his shorts.

When he arrived at the end of the road he pulled onto the shoulder by the gate, just as Tito had when he'd phoned him to say goodbye. The yellow crime scene tape had been removed, but two overflowing barrels of evidence still remained—the trash that the press corps and celebrity gawkers had left behind. Their empty film canisters, food wrappers, coffee cups and soda cans were spilled out all over the pavement.

Stinking garbage. This was Tito Molina's final tribute from his public.

Mitch shut off his engine, grabbed his things and got out, hearing the roar of the falls, feeling the fear surge through his body. He started down the rocky footpath in the fog, making his way by flashlight past the picnic tables toward a wooden guardrail that smelled of creosote. Here he spotted the warning sign that all of the newspaper accounts had referred to, the one that read: *Let the Water Do the Falling. Stay Behind This Point.*

He climbed over it and started his way carefully out onto the slick, gleaming shelf of ledge, the roar growing louder as the water cascaded right by him, crashing onto the rocks down below. It was cooler up here over the falls. But he was still perspiring, his heart pounding as he inched his way slowly out onto the promontory.

Mitch sat now, hugging his knees with his arms, and flicked off his light, alone there in the wet, roaring darkness. And terrified. He would be feeling way more sure of himself if Des were backstopping him, no question. Not that he blamed her for saying no. She had to think of her future. He knew this. But he also knew that she was his safety net. Walking this particular tightrope without her made the trip a whole lot more daunting. He took a sip of the peppermint schnapps, realizing at long last that what it tasted exactly like was Nyquil—although he doubted that a slug of peppermint schnapps would put him to sleep in ten to twelve minutes with drool dribbling down his chin.

In fact, he doubted he'd be asleep for a long, long while.

The waterfall masked all distant noise. Mitch didn't hear the other car arrive. Didn't hear its door slam shut. Didn't hear the footsteps approaching in the darkness—not until they were right there beside him, sure and quick on the slippery granite ledge.

And Mitch heard a raised voice say: "You came alone?"

Mitch reached down and flicked on the microcassette recorder at his feet. It was a powerful little unit. When he'd tested it in his bathroom with the shower and faucet running full blast it could pick up his voice quite clearly from four feet away. "Of course I did," he responded, hearing the quaver of fear in his own raised voice. "I said I'd be alone, didn't I?"

"You said it was urgent, and that I should meet you up here. Why here?"

"Because this is your special place. You feel safe up here. I think I can see why. It's comforting being surrounded by so much darkness and water. You're totally free to be yourself—the self that you hide so well from everyone in the daylight." He took a gulp from the bottle. "Want some peppermint schnapps?"

"I've never liked the stuff. Since when do you?"

"Oh, I don't."

"Then why'd you bring it?"

"As a tribute."

"Does anyone else know we're here, Mitch?"

"Not a soul."

"Why are we?"

"Because we're friends. I want to help you."

"You said on the phone that you know. *What* do you know?"

Mitch reached for his flashlight and flicked it on, its beam illuminating the lean, taut face of Will Durslag. "I know that you loved Tito and you killed him. I know you loved Donna and killed her. But I don't know why, Will. I need to know why."

Will's eyes turned to narrow, frightened slits. He looked like a wild, desperate animal crouched there in the torchlight.

Mitch flicked it off, plunging them back into the darkness. They'd been doing better there. "We talk about lots of things when we walk on the beach together. Can't we talk about this?"

"Sure, Mitch," Will finally said, his voice heavy with sadness. "Let's do that. It'll be good to talk about it. Maybe I won't feel so scared."

"I can't imagine why you're scared. You've got away with it all. There are no witnesses. And the only physical evidence is in your Franklin stove."

"My Franklin stove . . . ?"

"Sure, that's why you made that fire in your parlor this morning. Not because of the chill, but because Donna's blood got all over your clothes. Plus there were the towels you mopped up with. I'm thinking you must not have been wearing rubber-soled shoes when you killed her—rubber stinks out loud when it burns. You must have had on your leather flip-flops. I suppose you could have buried the stuff, but a fire made a lot of sense." Mitch glanced over at him in the darkness. "What are you scared of, Will?"

"Myself. I'm not in control of *me* anymore. My God, I even killed my own wife. That's generally considered to be pretty despicable behavior."

"Generally."

"Tell me, Mitch—how did you know?"

"You told me yourself."

"I did?" Will shot back in surprise. "When?"

"On the beach the other morning, when I asked you about your croissant recipe. You mentioned you'd gotten it from your partner in, I think you said, Nag's Head."

"Yes, that's right."

"When I asked you if you meant *business* partner you said no. But you didn't clarify what you did mean. Just kind of left it hanging there."

"So? . . ."

"So I work with words for a living, Will. Guys our age usually use the word 'girlfriend' when we're discussing a significant romantic partner. Unless, that is, we're going out of our way to be non–gender specific. Unless, that is—"

"Unless we're gay," Will said.

"I didn't think much about it. Not until this morning, when you used the word again in connection with Donna. That's when it dawned on me that you're bisexual. And that *you* were the one getting it on with Tito—who, like you, had relations with both men and women."

"No," Will said emphatically. "You're wrong on both counts."

"Okay, tell me how."

"For starters, we weren't 'getting it on.' That suggests something quick and sweaty in the backseat of a parked car. It wasn't like that, Mitch," he insisted, his voice growing painfully earnest. "It was real love. I was ready to devote my life to him. Give up Donna. Give up everything. We were in love, Tito and me. And Tito *wasn't* bisexual. He was one hundred percent bitch—his word, not mine. Oh, sure, he got married to Esme. And he could perform sexually with women, up to a point. He *was* one hell of an actor, after all. But his heart was never in it. Tito was gay from the time he was a barrio boy, Mitch. He kept telling me: You have no idea what it's like to be a bitch in the barrio. The scorn you face, the contempt. He *hated* being gay. That's why he became an actor—so he could become someone else, *anyone* else. That's why he got high all of the time. And that's why he was always trying out so many different women. He kept hoping that one of them would 'cure' him, as if what he had was a disease. God, he was *so* nineteenth century."

Mitch sat hunched there on the damp granite, recalling that both Abby and Chrissie had pointed out how disappointing the lovemaking with Tito had been. Chrissie even told Des that the screen idol hadn't been able to perform at all the final time they'd slept together.

"Tito was a tortured soul, Mitch. He couldn't be himself. They wouldn't *let* him be himself."

"Who wouldn't, Will?"

"The powers that be, that's who. You of all people should know why."

Mitch nodded his head. "You're right, Will, I do. It's the final frontier. And no one, but no one, has ever been able to cross it."

There was a very short list of bankable Hollywood leading men— the $20-Million-Dollar Men they were known as, by current wage standards. Actors whose name above the title guaranteed a picture instant financing. There were seldom more than a half dozen such actors at any one time. Right now there were the two Toms, Cruise and Hanks, Harrison Ford, Robert De Niro. And, until a few days ago, Tito Molina. These leading men all had very different qualities. But they all had one very important trait in common.

They were not gay. They were never gay.

There *was* no such thing as an openly gay Hollywood leading man. The mass audience simply would not accept him. If anything, gay actors had been driven even deeper into the closet than they had been in the Rock Hudson days, when everyone in the business knew but the public didn't. There was too much tabloid money out there now. Too much ugly fascination in the stars' private lives. Not to mention AIDS awareness. The merest whisper about a lingering respiratory infection or unexplained weight loss could completely short-circuit an actor's rise to stardom. Mitch had seen it happen.

"Will, how was it possible for him to keep his sexual identity a secret?"

"By marrying a great beauty," Will replied. "By sleeping around with a million women. By never being happy one single day of his life."

"You're the first man he slept with since he got famous?"

"No, of course not. He had others. But he hadn't been with a man since he married Esme. Mitch, he was deathly afraid of falling into the clutches of an opportunist. So he was always very careful to choose the right type."

"Which was . . . ?"

"The married type. Men with children and roots in the community. Men who had just as much interest in keeping it quiet as he had. Tito never, ever cruised the bars. Never picked up anyone. Never *told* anyone. Not his agent, not Chrissie—"

"What about Esme? Did *she* know?"

"Never. His marriage to her was the greatest acting performance of Tito's life. Not that he hated her or anything. He genuinely liked Esme as a person. And they belonged together in a weird sort of way. They were both so confused and vulnerable. I mean, God, that poor girl is *so* screwed up after what Dodge did to her."

"How could you let Dodge get away with that, Will? How could you cover for him?"

"I had to."

"Why, because he was like a father to you? That doesn't justify it."

"You don't understand, Mitch. I had no choice." Will fell silent, shifting around next to him on the ledge. "I hit a pretty bad patch after my dad died. Got into some real trouble. I-I stole a car and accidentally ran somebody down in East Dorset. An old lady. I almost killed her, Mitch. Dodge was a state senator then. He went to bat for me. Kept the newspapers out of it. Got the charges dropped. My record is clean, and I have Dodge to thank for that. I *owe* him, okay? And I will always be loyal to him. He's big on loyalty. He's big on trust. Can you understand that?"

"I guess I can," Mitch said, recalling the steely way Dodge had stared at Will on the beach when he'd said the word "trust."

"Esme could never make Tito happy," Will went on. "She never knew why. And it was a source of tremendous pain for her. He felt bad about that, because he was hurting her and he knew it. But there was only one person on the face of the earth who could make him truly happy, Mitch, and that person was me. With everybody else, he was just acting."

"How do you know he wasn't acting when he was with you, too?"

"Because it was *real*, damn it!" Will cried out, enraged. "We *loved* each other!"

"How long were you two together?"

"We met the day he and Esme arrived in town. The Crocketts had us over for dinner and . . . and we just stared at each other across the dining table all evening long. Couldn't take our eyes off of each other. God, Tito had the most beautiful eyes. He made the first move, out on the patio after dessert. I'll never forget those first words he said to me, not for as long as I live. He said, 'I'd better warn you—I'll break your heart.' I said I'd take my chances. And he *did* break my heart—because he loved being a star more than he loved me. It wasn't just the money. It was being *Tito Molina*. He wouldn't give it up for anything, Mitch. I was willing to sacrifice my marriage, my business, everything I'd ever worked for. I was willing to throw it all away for him. But he wasn't willing to do that for me." Will let out a heartbroken sob. "And now he's dead and, God, I miss him so much."

"You should have thought of that before you killed him."

"I *didn't* think, don't you see? I lashed out in a blind rage. I just couldn't stand to lose him. Tito was my true soul mate, Mitch. Someone like that . . . it only happens once in a lifetime."

"It can happen twice, if you're real lucky."

"I loved him, Mitch. And he loved me. Just not enough. He wouldn't leave Esme for me. He wouldn't risk his career for me. That's what he came up here to tell me that night. That he had to b-break it off."

Mitch uncapped the peppermint schnapps and took a swig. "I didn't know what he was mixed up in, Will, but he did tell me he felt trapped. I urged him to get clear of whatever it was. So whatever he said to you that night—it was partly my fault. I should have kept my mouth shut."

"Don't blame yourself, Mitch," Will said to him insistently. "Tito broke it off because he wanted to break it off. And when it came time to do it he was ice cold. Do you want to know what he said to me? He said, 'This doesn't have to end badly, it just has to end.' Like he was talking about a service contract on a kitchen appliance. I wouldn't listen. I couldn't imagine not being with him. I begged him. He refused. We argued. And now I'm all alone."

"Will, how much did Donna know?"

"She knew that I'd been involved with men, if that's what you mean. Not a big deal, as far as she was concerned. Not until lately, that is."

"Since you'd met Tito?"

"I started coming home from work later and later. My physical interest in her fell way off. She kept asking me, 'Who is it?' And I said 'You don't have to worry, it's nothing.' And then one night she caught Tito dropping me off at The Works after we'd been up here together. My own fault. It was late. I thought she'd already gone home for the night. I was wrong. She said, 'What are you doing with *him?*' And I said, 'We're friends.' And she said 'Since when?' Donna was no dummy, Mitch. She knew what was going on. She was hurt. And she was afraid. She started drinking a lot more than usual. And flirting. Trying to make me jealous. I saw her getting all frisky with you at the beach club."

"That was the night you killed him. Did she know about that, too?"

"She put two and two together," Will acknowledged. "She started acting very guarded around me, very uneasy. I didn't think she'd turn me in. She did love me, after all. But I *was* afraid that she'd get involved with someone else. You, maybe. And that one night she'd have herself a little too much to drink and blab my little secret. This is Dorset, Mitch. The most dangerous weapon here isn't a gun, it's a whisper. I couldn't risk it. I couldn't take that chance."

"So you killed her."

"I suggested we try to rekindle our romance at the Yankee Doodle. We'd been joking about the place for ages. She loved the idea. She even bought herself some sleazy black lingerie for our little tryst. We made it all into a game. We arranged to meet there a half hour apart, just like a pair of illicit lovers afraid of being found out. She got there first."

"And she paid for the room with her credit card," Mitch said. "She didn't try to keep it off the household books, or disguise her identity. She didn't have to, because the man who she was meeting was her own husband. Dodge was right about her, you know. He put his finger right on it—Donna wasn't the type to sleep around."

"I couldn't risk it," Will repeated vehemently. "When I spoke to Des this morning I reversed our roles. I told her it was Donna who was slipping out on me. All a lie, of course. There was no boyfriend. And no catering gig after the Merchants Association dinner. I made all of that up. I parked our van behind a beauty parlor just down the road from the Yankee Doodle. I didn't want anyone to spot it in the motel parking lot. That was the one thing I couldn't chance. I brought along a change of clothes as part of our game, and I left nothing behind. Not even the towels I used to wipe the blood off of my hands. I burned it all when I got home. Towels, clothes, my flip-flops—just like you said. And then I got busy acting like the concerned husband. I called our late man, Rich. I called the state police. And I waited there for someone to knock on my door to tell me Donna was dead. Des, as it turned out. I think I was pretty convincing as the grieving widower. I learned a few pointers about acting from Tito. The main thing he told me is you have to *believe* the dialogue. I believed it, all right. I believed every damned word of it."

"How could you do it, Will? How could you murder Donna that way? Tito I can comprehend. It was a momentary spasm of anger. But Donna's death was something that you plotted out really, really carefully. How could you?"

"I *told* you, I'm not in control of myself anymore!" he cried out. "I loved Donna, don't you see? And now I'm all alone and I'm scared and I'm desperate and I—I don't want to go to prison for the rest of my life. *That's* why I had to kill her. If she'd told anyone, I'd be finished."

"You *are* finished, Will. It's all over now. Come on, let's go do the right thing, okay? Let's go call Des. I'll be by your side the whole way, I promise." Mitch fumbled around in the dark for his tape recorder, shut it off and stuck it in the back pocket of his shorts. Then he grabbed the schnapps bottle and climbed to his feet, flicking his flashlight beam on Will. "Tell me something—was it any easier?"

Will remained crouched there on the granite ledge, staring out into the fog-shrouded blackness. He seemed very calm now, very at peace with himself. "Was what easier?"

"Killing Donna. It's supposed to be easier to murder someone if you've already killed once before."

"No, that's a Victorian myth, same as thinking you can be 'cured' of being gay. Just because you've killed once doesn't mean that you've gone over to the dark side, Mitch. I hated what I did, and I'll be haunted by it for as long as I live." Will looked up at him now, blinking in the torchlight. "Quite honestly, I don't think the third time will be any easier either."

It happened so fast.

Will lunged at him with such sudden ferocity that Mitch's flashlight went clattering to the rocks and rolled right over the cliff, plunging them back into darkness as they wrestled with each other there on the slick granite ledge, slipping and sliding. Will trying with all of his might to push Mitch over the edge. Mitch trying with all of his own might to stop him.

"Will, don't do this!" he gasped, struggling to dig his heels in. He did have heft on his side, and a lower center of gravity. But Will had a distinct advantage of his own—he was insane. "You *have* to turn yourself in."

"Never," he gasped back at him.

They fell to the ledge now, rolling around there on the narrow shelf of rock, punching and kicking and clawing for their very lives. And there was only them and the roaring water and the blackness of certain death a hundred feet below.

Will was back up on his feet, kicking blindly at Mitch in the dark, smashing him in his ribs, his shoulder, his neck.

Mitch scrambled away, groping desperately in the dark for a stone, a weapon. His fingers found the schnapps bottle—but Will's powerful hands found his throat. And Will was choking him and choking him. And Mitch was fighting for breath as he raised the bottle high over his head, gasping, gagging, until with the very last bit of power that was left in his body Mitch smashed Will Durslag hard in the face, shattering the bottle and pitching the taller man over backward, right over the cliff.

Which would have been fine by Mitch except for one thing—Will was still holding on to him by his shirt.

And so as he went over Mitch went over, too, his own legs flailing wildly in space as Will hung there in midair, clutching on to him for dear life. Mitch tried in vain to grab on to the moss, to the wet stone, something, anything. Feeling Will's weight pulling him down, down the sheer edge of the cliff, moss coming away in his fingers, bare stone refusing to yield him even the merest finger or toehold as he slid and he slid and he—

Until with a sudden rip Mitch's shirt gave way in Will's hand and Will was gone, screaming, into the blackness of the night, his roar and the roar of the waterfall merging into one.

Freed of Will's weight, Mitch clung there to the sheer side of the cliff for a brief, gravity-defying instant. But now he could feel himself falling again, scrabbling, kicking, trying to put on the brakes. Except there was nothing to hold on to and it was all happening too fast and he was going and he was going—until his hand *just* wrapped itself around a spindly tree branch, halting his fall.

And now he was hanging there by one arm, his body swinging free in the air, and there was only enough time for one final realization.

I am never going to see Desiree Mitry again. I am going to die. I am going to die. I am going to . . .

Chapter 14

Des had to be so damned careful.

As much as she wanted to floor it straight for the falls, she didn't dare. Couldn't take the chance that Will Durslag would spot her cruiser at the gate and wig out. Because there was absolutely no telling what that man was liable to do to him. Assuming that Mitch was right and it *was* Will who'd killed Tito and Donna. Maybe Mitch was totally wrong about his walking buddy. Maybe Will could convince him of this. Maybe he and Will would have a perfectly pleasant conversation, shake hands, and go their separate ways.

Then again, maybe not.

She used an entrance that was way over on the other side of the park, at Witch Meadow. Kathleen Moloney drove over from her cabin to raise the gate for Des. The young ranger had to wonder why Des needed to get into the park at one o'clock in the morning. But she was too sleepy to act genuinely interested, and she did not offer to tag along.

Des made do with her parking lights as she sped through the fog-shrouded park on a narrow service road, asking herself why she was letting herself get dragged into this fool gambit of Mitch's after all. Even though she'd sworn up and down that she wouldn't. Even though his impulsive desire to make things right sometimes seemed as if it came straight out of those old Hollywood movies of his, as opposed to the real world. Even though not one bit of this was smart or sane.

Why, damn it?

Because he was her boy, that's why, and he was what he was. She could not change him. She could only love him, even when he acted crazy. And if *anything* happened to that pudgy pink butthead tonight because she wasn't up there watching his back she would never forgive herself.

She would just die.

She left her cruiser a quarter mile up the service road from the river, hearing the roar of the falls now. She made it the rest of the way on foot, stumbling her way along the footpath in the darkness. She did make sparing use of her flashlight, holding it low to the ground, pointed straight down. But once she'd reached the guardrail she did not dare use it at all. Plunging herself into utter blackness, she climbed over the rail and crept slowly out onto slick bare granite, the river roaring as it raced by her, her eyes and ears straining for some sign of human life. But it was no use. She was blind and she was deaf. It was straight out of a nightmare.

Except this was no nightmare. This was real.

All she needed was a hint of where they were. One hint. A breath of a voice. A trace of movement. But as she crept slowly forward in her crablike crouch, there was nothing. Not one thing . . . Wait, was that the sound of glass breaking? No, her ears were playing tricks on her. It was nothing. She couldn't even be sure they were here at all.

Not until she heard a man's bloodcurdling scream.

It came from very close to her—no more than ten feet away. And now all bets were off and she was up on her feet with her flashlight out, charging toward the edge of the cliff, waving her beam around the granite promontory.

Except there was no one.

They were gone. Both gone.

She was all alone up there—just her and a broken liquor bottle that glistened on the granite. Peppermint schnapps.

Des felt a clutch in her chest. It was pure, animal anguish. She very nearly went over herself. Because she did not want to live. But she held back, standing there frozen, unable to believe, to think, to *breathe*. Until at last she drew in her breath in big ragged gulps and called his name out into the black void below her. *"MITCH!!"* she cried in helpless desperation. *"MITCH!!"*

"D-Des . . ."

She barely heard it over the roar of the falls. It was the weakest of gasps.

"*D-Des* . . ."

From below her. It came from right below her.

She inched her way over to the very edge and shined her light straight downward—directly into the two poached eggs that were Mitch Berger's terrified eyes. The man was swinging there in midair ten feet below her, clinging by his white-knuckled hands to a spindly little cedar that grew out of a crevice between the rocks. It was the very same tree that Tito had snapped when he fell.

"You *came*!" he groaned. "I-I knew you would. . . ."

"I knew that you knew," she called down to him, trying to keep her voice calm. "Where's Will?"

"Dead!"

"That's not going to happen to you, baby. I won't let it, hear me? Just hold on. I got you. Just hold on. . . ."

She had no rope. And no time to run back to her car for one. He'd be dead in a matter of seconds. Swiftly, she whipped off her black leather garrison belt, jettisoned her holstered SIG-Sauer and cell phone, and knotted the tongue around her wrist, yanking it tight. She propped the flashlight up against a stone, pointing downward, and edged her way as far down the sheer granite face as she could without losing solid hold.

Bracing herself, Des dangled the belt buckle out to him. "Reach for it!"

He tried, waving an arm in feverish desperation at the belt buckle as it wavered there in the air above him.

But it was no use—the other end of the belt was still a good two feet shy of him. If only she had a fifty-inch waist. But she didn't. That left her with one last option. It wasn't a good one, but it was the only one she had.

She had to surrender her solid hold. Climb her way down that bare, vertical granite toward him, fingers and toes searching for crevices and holds in the slick stone. "Hang on, baby!" she called to him as she edged down closer, inch by precarious inch. "I'm here!"

"Des, my arms are g-getting . . ."

"I am *not* hearing that!" She dangled the belt out to him once more. Damn, still another foot to go. And not a thing to grab on to. "You *can* hold on. Just one more minute. One minute. Say you'll hang on for me. Come on, say it!"

"I'll . . . I'll hang on. . . ."

She edged lower, clinging to the side of the cliff by her fingers, clawing at the moss with her nails as the river tore on by her, pelting her with cold spray. She could not even think about how she was going to climb back up there with him. One impossibility at a time. "Hang on, I got you," she told him, keeping her voice steady. "You're taking me dancing, remember? I've been waiting for this. Think I'm going to let you weasel out now?" Reaching her belt down to him. *Damn*, still six more inches. Edging lower, surrendering a halfway decent toehold for *no* toehold, seeing him real clearly now in the flashlight's beam, his hair glistening from the spray, his hands trembling around the branch that was the only thing between him and death. The branch that was bending and straining against his weight. "What was the name of that place again?"

"*What* place?"! He was panting wildly, as if he'd been running all out for miles. It was exhaustion and it was panic.

"Where you're taking me dancing."

"T-Tavern . . . The Tavern."

One more good foothold was all she needed. One more. She reached down with her foot, poking blindly, kicking, until finally she made contact with the base of the tree that Mitch clung to. Her shoe was right next to his hand, bracing her there. "They got them a DJ?"

"Just a jukebox . . . Des, I c-can't . . ."

"It's okay, we're all good now," she said, her voice brimming with confidence. "I've got you. Here we go. . . ." Des readied herself, breathing in and out, realizing with a shocking degree of clarity that it was for this singular moment in her life that she had done all of that work. Every weight she had lifted. Every mile she had run and hiked and biked. The four years of iron-willed training at West

Point. All of that was preparation for this moment, this mountain, right here, right now. And she would need all she could bring. Every bit of strength. Every bit of heart. It all.

Because she was about to take on two-hundred pounds of man.

With her left arm, Des dangled the belt out to him. "Grab it, Mitch."

"I *can't!* We'll both go down!"

"No, we won't."

"We *will!*" he cried out, panting. "I'll p-pull you right down with me. Kill us both. Just let me go. . . ."

"I *can't* let you go!" she sobbed, the tears beginning to stream down her face. She could not stop them from coming. She did not even try. "I don't want to be alive unless you are, too. Then I *will* die, don't you get it? Now give me your damned hand, you fat son of a bitch!"

He made an angry lunge for the belt and grabbed hold, the suddenness of his weight very nearly yanking her right off the mountainside. But she held on, wet fingers clinging to wet granite, fingernails breaking, her shoulder feeling as if it were about to pop out of its socket.

But she had him. Now all she had to do was tow him back up one-handed. Nothing to it. Cherry pie. Great big slab of it, à la mode.

Slowly, Des began the agonizing climb back up that sheer cliff to safety, the veins in her neck bulging as she reached up with her right arm, grabbing an uncertain fingerhold, and pulled him up along with her by her left, the muscles in her legs and lower back powering them upward, inch by precious inch. An animal groan of pain coming out of her as she willed them back up. The pain in her shoulder growing so intense that she was positive she could not hold him one second longer, that she *had* to let him go. Or die. She was beginning to feel light-headed now, almost delirious. The mountain was starting to waver and shift on her, like a ship at sea.

"What's our . . . song?" she panted, terrified she was about to pass out.

"Our . . . *what?*"

"Got to have . . . song . . . How's Aretha?"

"Fine . . . by me . . ." he answered, kicking wildly against the side of the cliff. Somehow, he found a toehold in a crevice, freeing some of his weight from both of their shoulders for a precious moment.

Gasping, she clung there, soaking wet, every muscle in her body quivering, knowing she had to keep moving. Forcing herself to keep moving. "Here we go, baby. One more time." Climbing upward again. Gaining a fingerhold, losing it, slipping back down, grabbing on to the wet granite for dear life. And trying it all over again. "Your favorite Aretha . . . ?"

"Has to be . . . 'Respect.'"

"Me, too. Oh, God!" she groaned, as the pain in her shoulder grew even more unbearable. "Tell me about . . . the food."

"Des, we can't. . . ."

"We *can!*" she screamed, inching farther upward toward the dim glow that was her flashlight's beam. "Tell me . . . what we'll eat."

"Spinach . . . fettuccine."

"Love me . . . I love me the pasta. Must be part Italian."

"No, can't be. You're already . . . part Jewish. Bella said so."

One inch, then another. Until at last he could finally swing a leg up over that branch he'd been hanging from. He straddled it, his chest heaving.

She clung there, her face hugging the cold granite as if it were a goose-down pillow. Her shoulder felt dead now. *She* felt dead— ready to surrender to the black void below. She had nothing left. Not one bit of energy. She couldn't make it. *They* couldn't make it.

Mitch worked his foot up under himself, bracing it against the base of the little tree. Then he knotted the belt tightly around his wrist, the better to hold on. "Just a couple more feet and we're there," he said with a sudden rush of bravado. "Two, maybe three. We're going to make it, right?"

Now he was trying to spur her on, even though both of his arms had to be ready to fall off. But he could tell that she was losing it.

"Almost there," she croaked, slowly tilting her head upward, raising her eyes. She could see the flashlight up there. Five feet away. Might as well be five miles. "You . . . still my boy?"

"You know I am. Know something else? Your gas tank isn't empty. You've got two more gallons left."

She tried to smile but was too weak. "I-I do?"

"You come with an emergency reserve tank. I read about it in your owner's manual. Listen to me . . . Des, are you listening to me?"

"Y-Yeah?"

"My turn to do the heavy lifting now. Soon as I get both feet up under me. All you have to do is move us up two more inches. Then I can push you the rest of the way, okay? Can you give me two more inches?"

Groaning, she started to climb again, positive her fingers were about to break right off at the knuckle. And now he had both feet under him on that little tree and he was pushing her upward instead of pulling her down, lifting her up, up, up the side of the cliff just like when she was a little girl and the Deacon would take her for a ride up on his shoulders, laughing and singing. And Des was grabbing for the top now and she was safely up and she was—

Until suddenly there was an awful cracking sound and that little tree gave way.

And Mitch was hanging on to her for dear life again, nothing under him besides blackness and death. But she could brace her knees against solid stone now, and he was making it up, up, and over and they were both collapsed there, alive, covering each other's faces with kisses, grateful for life, grateful for each other, grateful.

They lay there for a long time, soaking wet, too exhausted to stir. The awful pain in Des's left shoulder didn't subside at all. She couldn't move the arm one bit.

"Admit it," she finally said weakly. "Admit that you're glad I made you lose those ten pounds."

"I will never, ever doubt you again," he groaned, sprawled there beside her. "Only, what do I do now?"

"About what?"

"I just killed a man."

"Don't go there, Mitch. Will Durslag did that to himself."

"No, that's not what happened," Mitch said with sudden vehemence. "You didn't see it, Des. I smashed him in the head with a bottle. I killed him."

"*Before* he killed you. Which, by the way, he almost did."

"I know, but—"

"No *buts*!" Des said angrily. "Just forget about any *buts* and you listen to me, okay? You will need a story for Rico. And if you don't stake one out and stick to it you'll be looking at the inside of a criminal investigation. Will Durslag murdered two people, and he tried to murder you—it was kill or be killed, understand? Say you understand!"

"What are you so upset about?"

"Because I just saved your fool life and I am *not* going to throw you back. I worked too damned hard."

He was silent for a moment. "Okay, I understand."

"Thank you." She reached over with her good arm and stroked his face. "You got his confession, right?"

"Tape recorder's in my back pocket. Or it was. I don't have enough strength to see if it's still there."

"Roll over."

He rolled over on to his side and she smacked his butt with her fist, striking something squarish and hard. "It's going to be okay. I can work with Rico." Now she fumbled around for her cell phone.

"Hey, Des?"

"What is it, bod man?"

"Have I told you recently how much I love you?"

"It's okay, I don't mind if you tell me again. I've had a pretty hard night."

The sun woke her early. There was no sleeping late on Big Sister. Not in July. Not even with the aid of multiple painkillers.

The morning was warm, but there was a fresh, lovely breeze off the water. Mitch made the coffee and poured them each a cup. She got herself into a tank top and gym shorts and they went strolling barefoot together on the island's narrow beach, sipping their coffee, neither of them moving very fast. They were the walking wounded. Des wore a sling on her left arm and bandages around all five fingers on her drawing hand. Mitch's right cheek was scraped raw, and he had an angry welt on his neck where Will had kicked him. Will had also kicked him in the ribs, cracking two of them.

When they returned to his cottage he picked blueberries for their cereal while Des chilled in a lawn chair drinking iced tea with her long, bare legs stretched out before her and Quirt sprawled out on his back underneath her, his tail swishing happily in the grass. She was on medical leave for at least a week. She had nowhere to go and nothing to do. She could think of worse ways to do nothing, and worse places to do it.

Soave came rumbling over the wooden causeway just past nine, Yolie bringing up the rear in Des's cruiser. They had taken a preliminary statement from Mitch last night at the falls. Soave had not acted the least bit leery. Perhaps a bit blown away.

Yolie had been a lot blown away. "Shut up!" she kept exclaiming as she listened to Mitch's story.

The EMS people had hiked down by flashlight and found Will Durslag dead on the rocks in almost the same exact spot as Tito Molina had been. Will was even lying on his back the same way as Tito. Same head trauma. Same everything. It was eerie just how exactly he had followed the great love of his life into death.

Since it was the middle of the night and Des needed medical attention, Soave had held off on taking a more detailed statement until the morning, when Des assured him it would all start to make sense. Then she had accepted EMS transport to the twenty-four hour Shoreline Clinic in Essex. Mitch followed in his truck.

Everyone was very nice to her at the clinic. A chatty technician x-rayed her shoulder. A kindly nurse plunged her torn, bloodied fingers into a disposable basin of warm soapy water. The orthopedist who was on duty scrutinized her X-ray and pronounced it an anterior subluxation, which was physician-speak for a partially dislocated shoulder. There was some ligament damage, but the bones within the joint were not fractured. He assured her she would not need surgery and would soon be as good as new. After injecting her with a muscle relaxant he manipulated her shoulder back into place, gave her a sling to wear, and told her she might need physical therapy to restore her normal range of motion and strength. He also warned her that when a shoulder has popped out once there's a greater likelihood that it will pop out again under similar circumstances. Not a problem, Des assured him. She had no intention of ever again clinging to the side of a cliff with a grown man hanging from her arm.

It wasn't until she was signing her release forms that Mitch happened to tell the orthopedist that he was experiencing sharp pains whenever he breathed. That was when they x-rayed him and found the cracked ribs. Which they did not tape. They just told him to take it easy.

There was a twenty-four-hour pharmacy in Old Saybrook where they were able to get their prescriptions filled. By the time they got back to Mitch's place her shoulder was starting to ache again. She swallowed a pain pill and climbed into bed with an ice pack, sleeping off and on. Clemmie stayed glued to her hip the whole night, watching over her carefully. Cats were amazing that way. They always knew when you were hurting. Des just hoped Mitch didn't resent this, since he was prone to jealousy in regards to Clemmie, thereby demonstrating that he still didn't totally understand cats.

He himself had stayed downstairs watching a tape of his favorite boyhood comfort film, *The Beast from 20,000 Fathoms*, and putting away an entire box of Entenmann's chocolate chip cookies that he'd had squirreled away somewhere.

Now Des remained on her lawn chair, gazing at the sailboats out on the Sound, while Soave and Yolie went in to talk some more with Mitch and listen to the tape recording of his last conversation with Will Durslag.

Soave strolled back outside first, smoothing his former mustache, and came over and crouched beside her, carefully averting his eyes from her shapely bare legs. "I'll tell the media we've been made aware of the existence of a confession," he said slowly. "Meanwhile, we'll go hard after some physical evidence to backstop it. Could be we'll find remains of burnt clothing in his Franklin stove with traces of Donna's blood DNA on them. Maybe even find one of his hairs on the bedspread at the Yankee Doodle. That'll at least put him at the scene. As far as Tito goes, I don't think we'll ever come up with anything solid." Soave paused now, shaking his head at her. "You were right again."

"I was?" Des shifted her sling, wincing. "How so?"

"It *was* about sex."

"It was about love, Rico. Makes the world go around."

"Your boy says that it was all his own idea to arrange a meet with Durslag—and bring his tape recorder."

"True enough."

"*And* that you were up there without his knowledge and just happened to be in the right place at the right time to save his fat, sorry ass."

"He said that?"

"Everything but the fat, sorry part. What were you doing in the park at that time of night anyway?"

"Nosing around. Some local kids have been holding pot parties up there."

"Uh-huh." Soave narrowed his eyes at her shrewdly. "Me, I'm figuring it's a good thing he didn't tell you his plan in advance—because then it sure might have smelled like the E-word."

"The E-word?" Des gazed at him dumbly. "Oh, you must mean entrapment. *Hell* yeah. Smart of him not to do that."

"You wouldn't think they'd teach him stuff like that at film critic's school."

"Man's a big-league journalist, Rico," she pointed out.

"Yeah, well, your big-league journalist seems a little shook up, you want to know the truth."

"He saw a man die last night. Almost lost his own life in the deal. He's not used to that."

Soave stood back up now, swiping at his shiny black trousers, and let out a sigh. "I have to tell you, Des, my life is a whole lot simpler when you're not in it."

"Yeah, but you miss me so much you can't hardly stand it," she said, smiling up at him. "Can you work with this, Rico?"

"We can work with it," he said, which was his way of finally indicating to her that they were two people who really were there for each other. "And I still say you have the best legs in the whole damned state. Did you notice I didn't stare at them once?"

"I did, Rico. And I was impressed. You're a nascent feminist."

"Okay, I don't know what that means, but I'm looking it up."

"You do that, wow man."

He started back to his car as Yolie emerged from the carriage house with Mitch. "Girl, I left your keys in the ignition," she said, coming over to Des.

"Great, thanks."

"I've, um, decided to stick it out a little while longer with Soave."

"Glad to hear that. You keep your eyes and ears open, you can learn a lot."

"Dig, I'm not sure that what I learned on this one belongs in any how-to manual," Yolie said, crossing her rippling arms in front of her boom booms.

"Why, what did you learn?"

"You're *supposed* to assemble the facts until they point you at the truth, check? But this one's ass backwards. The truth's already a done deal and now we're going looking for the facts."

"In Hollywood they call that retrofitting," Mitch piped up.

"Retro-*what*?" Yolie shot back, cocking her head at him.

"You insert an earlier scene as story foundation for the climax you ended up improvising on the spot."

Yolie peered at him in confusion. "Sure, whatever . . ."

Des said, "Word, it's the stuff they don't teach in the manual that makes you wise." She stuck her bandaged hand out to her. "Stay in touch, Yolie. Put a shout on sometime, hear?"

"I hear," said Yolie, clasping it gently. "It was all good, Des. I'm wishing we can do this again."

"That's something else they don't teach you."

"What is?"

"Be careful what you wish for, girl. Because it just might come true."

CHAPTER 15

NURI ACAR WAS METHODICALLY brushing a thick coat of tan-colored primer over the graffiti Dodge had spray-painted on his wall when Mitch pulled into the minimart for his morning fix. Nuri must have been on his second coat by now, because the red paint was becoming all but invisible to Mitch's eye.

"That doesn't look bad at all, Mr. Acar," he said encouragingly.

"It will be fine." Nuri smiled at him broadly. He seemed more at ease than Mitch had ever seen him. "All we have wished for since we arrived in Dorset is to be good neighbors. I am so glad that this matter is resolved now. I wish I knew how to thank you, Mitch."

"Not necessary."

"No, it absolutely is. Nema and I have decided that from now on we will accept no money from you for coffee or pastry. Gasoline only."

"That's insane. I can't let you do that."

"Mitch, you must allow me to show my appreciation. To deny me is to insult me."

"Well, okay, but the resident trooper won't be happy about this. She's very particular when it comes to my caloric consumption."

"She is one very tough lady, our resident trooper," Nuri observed quietly, his mouth tightening.

"Tougher than you can possibly imagine."

"But she is also what you call a 'straight shooter.' And I respect her for that."

"Good," said Mitch, smiling. "Now I'm the one who's glad."

They shook hands, Mitch wincing slightly as Nuri gave his arm a hearty yank. The ribs felt okay unless Mitch made a sudden movement or, God forbid, sneezed. Then it felt as if someone were jabbing him with a boning knife.

Mostly, he was still just really resentful that Clemmie had chosen to stay up in the loft with Des after they got home from the clinic instead of on the sofa with him. He'd been hurting, too, after all, and wasn't she *his* cat? Didn't he feed her and tidy up her gaaacks? Where was the fairness in this? Where was the loyalty?

Deep down inside, Mitch figured he still didn't totally understand cats.

He tried to slip one past Nema and pay her for his baklava and coffee, but she wouldn't go along.

"Your money is no good here, Mitch," she clucked at him.

"You knew, didn't you, Nema?" Mitch said to her. "You saw Dodge throw that rock through your window."

"I did, yes," she admitted reluctantly.

"Why didn't you say anything?"

"We were afraid," she replied, lowering her large, dark eyes.

"Of what?"

"Mr. Crockett is part of the hierarchy. A man with connections. Who knows, he could get our business license revoked. Possibly even get us deported. So Nuri felt it is best to keep quiet."

"And you went along with him."

"He is my husband," Nema said, as if that answered everything.

For her, it did.

From there Mitch piloted his truck up Old Shore Road to the post office, munching on his baklava. He bypassed Dorset Street entirely so as to avoid the media crush at town hall, where Soave was busy putting out information about Will Durslag's death. Thirty-six hours after the fact, Des's former sergeant was still playing it very close to the vest until the forensics people up in Meriden finished sifting through those ashes in Will's woodstove. Soave had still not made public Will's tortured love affair with Tito Molina. All he was saying was that Will had been found dead at the base of Chapman Falls, that they were in possession of his taped confession, and that an investigation was proceeding.

He had not mentioned one word about Mitch's involvement in Will's death. This was fine by Mitch.

When he arrived at the post office he fetched his mail from his box and was starting back outside with it when Billie, the jovial old girl who worked behind the counter, called out, "Hey, Mitch, I got something for you. Been holding on to it." She reached down under the counter and produced a torn, overstuffed ten-by-thirteen manila envelope. "Somebody dropped this in our mailbox out front the other night," she explained, her eyes gleaming at Mitch with keen interest.

Mitch took one look at the envelope and immediately knew why. It had originally been addressed to Tito Molina—from a talent agency in Beverly Hills. Someone had crossed out Tito's name and box number, and hurriedly scribbled Mitch's name across the top. No box number or address for Mitch, no postage, no nothing. The envelope wasn't even sealed shut.

"You owe me a buck sixty-five, my dear," Billie said apologetically.

Mitch paid her and went back outside and got into his truck, his heart racing as he sat there staring at the envelope. He opened it. Inside he found a fat sheaf of lined yellow legal pages covered with crude, almost childlike handwriting.

On the first page a note had been scrawled in the margin: "Mitch, hope you like it. But *please* be honest—Tito"

It was his unfinished screenplay. He'd called it *The Bright Silver Star*.

Mitch devoured it at once, seated there in the post office parking lot. What he read turned out to be the heartfelt story of a sensitive, special little Chicano boy named Ramon who sees imaginary creatures he calls the Bad People and fears they are about to murder him in his sleep. Ramon has an Anglo mother who lives in her own dream world. His Chicano father, a day laborer, can't understand either one of them. Enraged, he lashes out in a violent drunken outburst, beating Ramon's mother half to death before he packs up and clears out.

Mitch found *The Bright Silver Star* brutal yet surprisingly delicate and poignant. It reminded him quite a bit of *The Glass Menagerie* by Tennessee Williams. In fact, it was written more as a play than a movie. The action, such as it was, consisted of a series of conversations that took place over a single day in a squalid two-room apartment.

There were no exteriors, no camera directions. Tragically, there was also no second act. Tito had managed to write only the first fifty or so pages, leaving the crisis in little Ramon's family life unresolved. Even so, this glimpse into the private hell that was Tito Molina's childhood was so painful that it very nearly brought tears to Mitch's eyes.

He was still sitting there in the cab of his truck, totally decked, when Martine Crockett pulled up next to him in her silver VW Beetle convertible, her golf bag tossed across the backseat. Mitch was pretty hard to miss there in his '56 Studey half ton, but Martine did her best anyway, scrupulously avoiding eye contact with him as she got out and strode inside, her gait long and assertive.

Mitch took a deep breath and followed her in. He found her waiting in line to buy stamps from the vending machine. A couple of her lady friends were asking her how Dodge was doing.

"He's home, he's fine," Martine replied with a brave smile. Her face was composed, her gaze clear. "*We're* fine. It's all just a terrible misunderstanding."

Warm hugs were exchanged, lunch invitations extended. They weren't shunning her. She was one of *theirs* after all, a cherished member of the inner circle, and by repudiating her they'd only be repudiating themselves. If she wasn't afraid to show her face in public, they weren't afraid to stand by her.

Mitch found this rather amazing, but he shouldn't have. This was Dorset, where appearances mattered. Hell, appearances ruled.

And then her friends were gone and Martine was alone. She stiffened at the sight of Mitch standing there.

"How is he, Martine?" Mitch asked.

"Anxious to clear his name," she answered tightly. Martine started to say something more, stopped herself, then plowed ahead. "He was very hurt that you turned against him, Mitch. I guess where you come from people define friendship differently."

"Martine, how much did you know?"

Martine paid for her stamps and tucked them into her purse. "About what?"

"About Dodge and Esme."

"I have no idea what you mean."

"Yes, you do."

"Look, I don't know what she or anyone else may have told you—"

"Yes, you do."

"You've been lied to, Mitch. And you've chosen to believe those mean, ugly lies instead of the simple truth."

"Which is? . . ."

"Esme has always enjoyed a warm, wonderful relationship with her father. And she . . . And they . . ." Martine's lower lip quivered, her flawless blond composure starting to crumble. For one brief second, Mitch thought she might give in to the horrifying reality of what her husband had done to their daughter. But she didn't. When it came to the fine art of keeping up appearances, Martine Crockett was a master. "They have nothing but love for each other—not that I expect someone like you could ever believe something decent or good about a man like Dodge."

And with that she turned on her heel and marched stiffly out of there, leaving Mitch convinced of something he had never really believed about people before. Not until this very moment, standing in the Dorset post office.

When someone can't accept the truth about the person who they love, they don't accept the truth. They accept the illusion instead.

They have to.

The news about Abby Kaminsky's unscheduled appearance at the Book Schnook got out incredibly fast.

Kids wearing carp heads were lined up all the way out the door of the bustling food hall into Big Brook Road for the chance to buy an autographed copy of *The Codfather of Sole*. The Works was still doing a bang-up lunch trade, Mitch couldn't help but notice. Rich Graybill was running the show for now.

Inside the Book Schnook, Abby was seated at a table in front of a giant *Codfather of Sole* poster, signing copies and chattering gaily with her excited young readers. Chrissie Huberman was near at hand, watching over her protectively. It was Chrissie who was responsible for the huge, last-minute turnout. She'd not only blitzed the local radio stations with ads but had hired a private plane to pull a sign along the shoreline beaches all the way from Madison to New London. Thousands upon thousands of beachgoers had seen the message.

Jeff was bustling back and forth between the cash register and the stockroom, his manner lively and animated. "Hey, it's my main man Mitch," he exclaimed brightly. "Did you walk this morning?"

"No, did you?"

"Couldn't. I had to drive up to the warehouse in Springfield for copies of Abby's book. Otherwise they wouldn't have gotten here in time." He deposited an armload on the table next to Chrissie. She immediately began opening them to the title page for Abby, who was signing books and shaking hands with the brisk, focused efficiency of an assembly line worker. Jeff started back to the cash register, where parents and kids were stacked up six deep. "Mitch, I don't know how to thank you for this. You're a true-blue friend."

"You have a slightly different take on me than Martine does."

Jeff gulped. "Shhh, not so loud," he pleaded, shooting a nervous glance over his shoulder at Abby.

Mitch lowered his voice. "What's the official story, are you and Martine finished?"

"There was nothing *to* finish. Reports of our 'affair' have been greatly exaggerated. And I would appreciate it if you'd never, ever mention that woman's name in my presence again."

"Whatever you say, Jeff." Now Mitch moseyed over to Abby to say hello.

"How are you, cookie?" Abby said to him as she signed and shook, signed and shook.

"Surprised to see you here. Pleasantly so."

"No big. I called Chrissie from Boston last night and we decided it was something we actually could squeeze in."

"And why not?" Chrissie deftly arranged an open book in front of Abby as the next eager kid in line stepped up. "It shows what kind of a classy, above-the-fray person you are."

"And you were right, Mitch," Abby added. "It's a lovely little store. Jeffrey even laid in a supply of Cocoa Pebbles for me. Can you believe he remembered?"

"Where's Frankie, out in the car?"

Abby's saucer eyes widened in panic. "Listen, I barely knew that yutz, understand? And, besides, he's history."

"She fired his tight, hairy buns last night," translated Chrissie.

"I've decided to travel a little lighter from now on," Abby acknowledged, her eyes following Jeff as he scampered back into the stockroom for another load of books. "Maybe I should help him with those. He gets back spasms if he shleps too much weight."

"You stay here and sign—I'll shlep." Chrissie dashed off to help him.

"You may be seeing a bit more of me in Dorset from now on, Mitch," Abby confided.

"Working on a new book?"

"A new venture," she replied, graciously handing over a signed book and moving on to the next kid. "You might even say I'm looking out for my own interests by being here today. This whole operation is going into receivership, and my business manager thinks it has a really huge upside if some new investor is willing to take it on."

"And that investor is you?"

"Why not? I love food, I love New England. . . ."

"And they've barely scratched the synergy surface here," Chrissie said, setting down a huge load of books. "My God, I can see Emeril Legasse and Jacques Pepin giving cooking demonstrations out there while Jeff's selling copies of their cookbooks in here. In fact, I can see *you* here, Mitch."

"Me?"

"Sure, dinner and a movie with Mitch Berger, noted New York film critic. What do you think?"

"We'll talk," he replied. To Abby he said, "So you'll be Jeff's landlord?"

"Partner is more like it," she said.

"We're not divorced yet, Mitch," Jeff pointed out as he dumped another load of books in front of her. "Technically, we're still husband and wife."

"Technically, we still are," Abby allowed.

"I *knew* it—you two are going to end up back together again, aren't you?"

"Not a chance," protested Jeff. "Word of honor, Mitch. That could never, ever happen."

"Not in a million years," Abby chimed in, blushing furiously. "Like, *ab-so-tootly* never."

Esme was building a huge sand castle with Becca on the beach near Big Sister's lighthouse. Bitsy was watching them from her covered porch, fanning herself with her floppy straw hat. The day was bright and hot, with very little breeze.

"She's hiding from the press," Bitsy told Mitch as he stood there next to her, observing the two of them out there in their string bikinis, working away. "I don't blame the poor thing. She can stay here as long as she wants to, as far as I'm concerned."

"How long will she?" Mitch wondered.

"You'll have to ask her that."

He went down the wooden steps to the beach and plowed through the hot dry sand toward them. They were on their hands and knees before their rising castle, both of them filled with laughter and high spirits. From fifty feet away, they looked like a pair of impudent, playful fourteen-year-old schoolgirls full of lollipop dreams. From closer up they were the very picture of innocence lost—two battle-hardened veterans who between them had logged enough years on the dark side for ten lifetimes. Becca was nothing but skin and bone, with dark circles under her sunken eyes. Esme had that fat, scabby lip to go with the expression of dazed confusion that wracked her delicate, lovely face. Her eyes were those of a woman who was now completely lost and fearful.

"This is quite some castle," Mitch observed, because it was. A good five feet high, with turrets, towers, and a fine, deep moat.

"Are you going to help us?" demanded Becca, wetting her hands in a water pail. "Or are you just going to stand there like a big boss man?"

Mitch promptly flopped down on his knees and started scooping out more sand for the moat. "How long are you planning to stick around, Esme?"

"Until they release Tito's body," she answered quietly as she continued molding the castle walls with her hands. "I want to take him back to Bakersfield and bury him with his parents."

"That's a really nice idea," Mitch said. "Listen, there's something important I need to talk to you about. The night Tito died, do you remember when he came home and was rummaging around in his closet before he went back out?"

Esme didn't respond for a moment. Just kept fashioning the castle wall with her shapely hands. "I remember," she finally said in a voice that came from somewhere on the other side of the ocean.

"It was his script he was getting. He must have mailed it to me on his way up to Chapman Falls that night. I just got it today. It really does exist, Esme."

"How is it?" Becca asked eagerly. She seemed vastly more excited about Mitch's discovery than Esme, who'd scarcely reacted at all.

"I have to tell you, I was pretty knocked out by it. Honestly, it's terrific. He called it *The Bright Silver Star*."

Esme sat back on her haunches now, swiping at the hair in her face. "I never once saw him working on it. He must have done it when I was asleep." She let out a heavy sigh, her breasts straining inside the tiny bikini top. "Tito did get up a lot in the middle of the night. The poor thing had such awful nightmares."

"I have it back at my house," Mitch said, climbing to his feet. "I'll go get it for you right now."

"No, don't," Esme said abruptly. "I mean, please don't. Tito wanted you to have it."

"It's your property, Esme."

"He gave it to you."

"But this is something of great value. You can get a lot of money for it."

"I don't want it. I don't even want to read it. It will just make me sad. I'm tired of being sad, Mitch. Can't you understand that?"

"Sure I can. Only, what am I supposed to do with it?"

"Something good," she said simply. "Something decent. You're a smart man. You'll know what to do."

"Getting a little dry here," Becca announced, taking their empty water pails down to the water's edge to fill them.

"Can we talk about something personal?" Mitch asked Esme.

"If you'd like."

"Did you know that Tito was gay?"

The actress peered at him curiously. "You must think I'm a total bimbo, asking me that."

"No, not at all. It's just . . . Will told me that you didn't know."

"Will was wrong."

"He said that's what Tito told him."

"Then Tito lied to him," she said, her voice growing heated now. "I *always* knew he was gay. It was obvious. Gay is gay."

"And yet you stayed together," Mitch said. "Why?"

"I loved him. Is that so hard to understand?"

"Not to me," said Becca, returning now with the water pails. "I think you guys were really great together. And I always will."

"Besides," Esme added, her face darkening, "after what I went through with Daddy dearest, Tito and me just seemed kind of . . ."

"Kind of what, Esme?"

"Normal."

"How much did Tito know about that?"

"Not a thing."

"Why, were you afraid of what he might do to Dodge?"

"No, not really."

"Then what was it?"

"That was the past," Esme explained. "I don't like to go there—there's never anything back there that's any good. So I never, ever look back. Only forward."

"Is that why you never went after your dad?"

"You mean like call the law on him or something?"

"No need to do that," Becca spoke up, her own sunken eyes getting a steely look. "His current punishment is much worse."

Esme nodded her head in grim assent.

"What punishment is that?"

"Daddy has to live with himself," said Esme.

"Each and every day," Becca added.

Mitch let this one go. He didn't tell them that Dodge seemed to have no regrets, no remorse, no functioning conscience at all. Esme and Becca both needed to believe that he did, and Mitch wasn't about to take it from them. They had so little else to cling to. "Esme, why did you come back here this summer?"

"I thought Dorset would be good for us," she replied, shrugging her soft shoulders. "I was wrong."

A pair of kids on jet skis went hurtling past them now, shrieking with high-decibel delight. Mitch sat back on his ample haunches, watching them. "Look, maybe we ought to talk about Tito's script again in a few days," he suggested.

"No, Mitch," Esme said. "I don't ever want to talk about that again. Just promise me one thing, okay?"

"Of course. Anything."

"His fans deserve to know who Tito really was. Tell them. It can't hurt him now."

"What about you? It can hurt you."

"No, it can't," Esme said softly as she continued working on their castle, her wet hands fashioning its walls higher, higher, and still higher. "Nothing can hurt me anymore. Not a thing."

CHAPTER 16

"Hey, Tina — long time no see."

"Mitch, it has been *too* long!" Tina's round, pink face lit up with motherly delight as she planted wet kisses on both of Mitch's cheeks. She was a chubby, bustling little strawberry blond in her fifties. "Now tell me," she commanded him, gazing up, up at Des. "Who is this lovely creature?"

"Say hello to Desiree Mitry."

"Welcome to my restaurant, Desiree."

Des smiled at her. "Thank you, I've heard a lot about it."

The Port Alba Café was on Thompson Street a block below Washington Square Park, next door to a shop where men sat playing chess with each other. It was a tiny café—no more than a dozen tables, all but one of them filled. Young families with small children were eating there. Several couples. One very dignified old man in a white suit who sat alone, sipping an espresso. There was a mural of a fishing village on one wall, a tiny bar with glasses in an overhead rack. The ceiling was of stamped tin. Wonderful smells were coming out of the kitchen.

Des had on a dress for the first time in ages, a sleeveless little yellow knit thing that clung to her hips and bootay for dear life. She wore sandals with it, gold loops in her ears, her grandmother's pearls, a bit of lipstick. She had even painted her toenails, which she almost never did. But this was a special night. She was out on a genuine New York City date with the man she loved.

Mitch wore a white oxford button-down, khakis, and Mephisto walking shoes, which was the same damned thing he always wore. But for this occasion his shirt and trousers were actually pressed and his mop of curly hair combed. He looked positively grown-up.

Tina seated them at the empty table by the window and brought them a bottle of chianti, a loaf of warm, crusty bread, and a platter filled with little plates of antipasti—grilled sardines, white beans in extra-virgin olive oil, marinated calamari salad, fresh buffalo mozzarella with basil leaves and tomatoes. After Tina had poured them each a glass of wine she went to fetch her husband, Ugo, a grave, scrawny little man who was the chef. Ugo solemnly shook hands with Mitch and asked him if he wanted the usual.

"For two," Mitch said, beaming at Des. "If that's okay with you."

"What I've been waiting for, boyfriend."

Ugo disappeared back into the kitchen.

Mitch reached across the table and took her hand. "You are a total hottie, you know that?"

"Um, okay, I'm thinking maybe I should put on a dress more often."

"That's funny, I'm thinking about taking it off of you."

"You're awfully frisky tonight, sir. Happy to get away from Dorset?"

"I'm just excited about spending the night here with you," he said, attacking the grilled sardines.

Des spooned some calamari onto her own plate and dove in. "That was our deal. And a deal's a deal, right?"

"Whatever you say, Master Sergeant."

Des gazed over at the mural of the fishing village, loving it even though she was fully aware that Professor Weiss would pick it to pieces. The proportions, angles, placement of cast shadows—all were wrong, wrong, wrong. "So this was your place, am I right? You and Maisie."

Mitch lowered his eyes, nodding.

"You haven't been back here since she died, have you?"

"No, I haven't." His eyes met hers now. "Is this okay, us coming here?"

"Mitch, it's more than okay. It's an honor."

They had gone through the entire antipasto platter and a half bottle of wine by the time Ugo emerged from the kitchen with a battered copper skillet full of spinach fettuccine. Tina laid warm plates before them and he spooned it out. Ugo had a whole Alfredo thing going on in there with the homemade green pasta and fresh spinach—lots of cream, butter, and melted cheese. Total sin. Especially when Tina was done grating even more cheese onto it.

She hovered there anxiously as Des tasted it. "You like?"

"No, I love." Truly, it was the best pasta Des had ever eaten. It positively melted in her mouth.

Thrilled, Tina left them to it.

"Have you figured out what to do with Tito's script?" she asked Mitch as they ate.

"I'm going to publish it," he replied. "I'll write an introduction that expands on the article I wrote after he died. I'll go into the real deal of what happened to him, complete with the transcript of Will's confession. Esme wants it that way. Whatever money it earns will go into a college scholarship fund for kids in the barrio where Tito grew up. And if someone wants to buy the movie rights, the same deal applies. Sound good?"

"Sounds real good, Mitch."

"Des, what do you think will happen to Dodge?"

"You mean with the law? My guess is he'll cop to malicious mischief, get off with six months probation."

"No jail time?"

"I wouldn't think so. He *is* a pillar of the community, after all," she pointed out dryly.

Mitch sat back from his plate. He had a troubled look on his face. "I'm thinking I don't believe in what I believed in before."

"Which was? . . ."

"Dodge is a really, really bad guy. He's done horrible things to Esme, to other girls, to his business competitors, his friends. He gets a slap on the wrist and is basically free to dust himself off and start all over again. Will, meanwhile, was a decent guy who fell in love with the wrong person, lost his head, and now he, Tito, and Donna are all dead. Where is the justice here?"

Des patted her mouth with her napkin and said, "First of all, you're wrong. Will wasn't a decent guy, he was a stone-cold killer."

"And Dodge?"

"Total human scum, I'll grant you."

"So where's the justice?"

"You don't win them all. That's why I have such a clean kitchen floor."

"Okay, you just lost me."

"Bella gets down on her hands and knees and she scrubs when she's upset. You watch old movies about giant bugs—"

"Not always. Sometimes they're about giant crustaceans."

"And I draw pictures, or at least I used to. I don't know *what* to call the stuff I draw now. Actually, I do—I call it crap. My point is, we all deal in our own way. That's real life."

"Well, it sucks," he grumbled, sipping his wine.

"Sometimes it does. Other times, it can be pretty damned perfect."

"Like when?"

She put her hand over his and squeezed it. "Like right now."

The Tavern was on Horatio and Washington, right around the corner from Mitch's apartment. It had sawdust on the floor and very little in the way of decor. In past days, it had been a saloon favored by the neighborhood's big burly meatpackers. Now it was filled with bright, boisterous young writers, artists, actors and grad students. A lot of them hadn't paired off yet and were assembled in groups. A lot of those groups were mixed. Des saw black faces, Asian faces, all sorts of faces.

It was not, repeat not, a proper dance club. But it was a place he liked and it did have a jukebox. Since he'd insisted on buying dinner she got the drinks while he edged his way warily over to the juke, a look of sheer dread on his face.

She was at the bar fetching them two frosty mugs of New Amsterdam draft when she heard that opening blast of horns—the one that belongs to no other song than "Respect," followed by that slamming guitar riff, and then by the lady herself. And now Aretha was singing about what *she* needed. And Des was gliding her way across the bar toward Mitch, their eyes locked on to each other, and there was no one else in that crowded place, just them. She put their beers down on the juke and raised her arms up high into the air, bumping hips with the boy, feeling the music and the wine and . . . and . . . *Damn,* what *was* he doing with himself? Passing a kidney stone? And where was he going with those two clumsy feet of his? Did he not even *feel* the beat?

But, hey, he was dancing his dance and no one was staring or caring. And he was so damned cute.

Besides, it wasn't long before they were back at his place and they were in each other's arms in his big brass bed. He was still worried about her shoulder but she kept telling him not to be. They made sweet love deep into the night while the sirens and the car alarms serenaded them, and the refrigerator trucks outside the packing houses *beep-beep-beeped* as they backed up and the cabs went *tha-thunk-ker-chunk* over the steel plate Con Ed had put over the hole in the street.

And for some strange reason there was a special urgency that had never been there before for either of them. Together, they found something new and even more fantastic that night in Mitch's bed.

"Now you've felt it," he murmured at her as the early light of dawn approached, Mitch stroking her face gently. Truly, he was the most loving man she'd ever been with.

"Felt what, baby?"

"The energy of the city."

"I thought that was the energy of you and me."

"Maybe we had a little something to do with it," he admitted, immediately falling into a deep sleep with his mouth open.

Des was wide awake herself. Something about being here in his apartment made her feel all wired. She threw on a T-shirt, padded barefoot into the living room and flicked on a lamp, gazing around at his place. She was definitely uneasy here. It was Maisie's place. He'd tried to scour it of her presence after she died. He had told Des this. But there was still a lot that smacked of *her.* Like the exquisite, matching leather loveseat and club chairs positioned just so. And those vintage brass lamps with green glass shades. And the genuine Stickley library table that he used as a desk. Out on Big Sister, the man used an old door on sawhorses. Des's trained eye also caught the small things he had missed, like a fat volume entitled *Simplified Site Engineering* that was shoring up one end of the radiator cover.

Standing there, Des felt a sudden, powerful urge to be somewhere else.

She slipped back into the bedroom for her gym bag. Put on her shorts and running shoes, pocketed Mitch's spare keys and let herself out the door. It was not quite 6:00 A.M. but the cobblestoned street was awake and active. A half dozen meatpackers were going home after their night's work, exhausted but rowdy. An executive type in a spotless seersucker suit was walking his Jack Russell terrier and scanning the *Wall Street Journal*. A young Latino man, stripped to the waist, was working under the hood of his parked car, a sheen of sweat on his bare shoulders, a can of Budweiser within arm's reach. An old lady in the brownstone across the street was watching him from her second-floor window, her arms resting on a cushion on the windowsill, the smoke from her cigarette curling lazily up into the early morning sunlight that slanted low across Gansevoort from the east.

Des found herself lingering there on the stoop of Mitch's building, staring at that lady, that sunlight, that man working on his car. To her surprise, her pulse began to quicken and her fingertips tingled. This was the same sensation she felt whenever she walked into the studio at the art academy—an overwhelming sense of being in a special, hallowed place. Des had never experienced this while standing outside on a street before. Not anywhere.

She headed out, suddenly giddy with excitement. The Chinese laundry down the street was already open. So was the corner grocery store, where a young boy was hosing down the sidewalk and a milk truck was making a delivery. She bought herself a coffee and sipped it as she began walking through the close-knit neighborhood of family-owned brownstones, her eyes open wide, soaking in every detail. The building super who was out bagging the trash, muttering to himself. The housewife in her bathrobe who was moving her car from the no-parking side of the street before she got ticketed. The wasted rock 'n' rollers in black leather climbing out of a cab from their night out, reeking of cigarette smoke and patchouli.

By now it was nearly seven, and some folks were heading off to work. Des followed them, swept along by their urgency. Found herself on Fourteenth Street at the entrance to the subway. Bought a token. Rode the Number 1 train all the way up to Times Square and back, gazing at all of those faces across the car from her, faces representing ten, twenty, thirty different nations and races and ethnic groups. Young faces and old faces, the hopeful and the homeless, students, laborers, and millionaires, all of them standing there shoulder to shoulder, gripping the handrail, clinging to their own individual dreams.

Des was gone for hours. There was a bagel place near Mitch's corner where she bought fresh bagels and two more coffees on her way back. Then she went back down Gansevoort to Mitch's building, the one that had that scrawny London plane tree growing out front in a cutout in the sidewalk. A low iron rail had been positioned around it to keep dogs from peeing on it. It was not an easy life for a tree in the city. As Des started up Mitch's steps she paused, noticing just how tenaciously the plane tree's shallow, exposed roots clung to the soil— exactly like the knuckles of those subway riders she'd just seen— fighting for its place, fighting for its life, fighting for its . . .

And that's when it hit her. Why she hadn't been able to draw them.

Trees weren't things made out of twigs and leaves. They were living, breathing creatures. Their trunks and branches weren't wood, they were muscle and sinew and bone. *That's* what that poor little cedar had been trying to tell her, the one that had been clinging to the side of the cliff at Chapman Falls—until it died saving their lives up there that night.

Trees weren't *things*.

Breathless, she darted inside for her sketch pad, rushed back out and sat down on the stoop, resting it on her bare knees, graphite stick in hand. She started with quick gesture drawings of the plane tree. Except she wasn't drawing a tree anymore—she was drawing a nude figure model who was posed there for her in the morning light, reaching high for the sun. Des drew and she drew, her stick flying across the page.

She barely heard Mitch when he moseyed out and joined her there, yawning and blinking "What time did you get up?"

"Never went to sleep," she replied, as an old lady went by with a grocery cart.

"Morning, Mrs. Fodera," Mitch called to her. "Lovely day."

"Eh," the old lady grunted, waggling a hand.

He sat next to Des on the stoop and opened a coffee, glancing over her shoulder at her pad, not saying another word.

"Do you ever get tired of being so smart?" she asked him.

"Nope, it stays fresh pretty much all the time," he replied, biting into a bagel.

"Mitch, I've been thinking about something. . . ."

"Uh-oh, this sounds serious."

"It is. I'd like to start spending more time in New York than I have been."

"Are you kidding me? I've been begging you to."

"Wait, there's more," she warned him, swallowing. "I'd maybe even, you know, keep a few . . . some of my clothes here. Can you handle that?"

"Would any of these clothes be little yellow dresses?"

Her eyes locked on to his. "I mean it, Mitch. Can you?"

"That all depends," he said gravely. "Would I have to dance in public again?"

"Try that one more time and I'll bust you myself."

"In that case, girlfriend, I think we can work something out."

THE GOOD MOTHERS

THE
GOOD
MOTHERS

*The True Story of the Women Who Took on
the World's Most Powerful Mafia*

ALEX
PERRY

wm

WILLIAM MORROW
An Imprint of HarperCollins*Publishers*

Originally published in the United Kingdom in 2018 by HarperCollins UK.

FIRST EDITION

Maps by Martin Brown

Library of Congress Cataloging-in-Publication Data

Names: Perry, Alex, author.
Title: The good mothers : the true story of the women who took on the world's most powerful mafia / Alex Perry.
Description: New York, NY : William Morrow, 2018. |
Identifiers: LCCN 2018000498 (print) | LCCN 2018013643 (ebook) | ISBN 9780062655639 (ebook) | ISBN 0062655639 (ebook) | ISBN 9780062655608 (hardback) | ISBN 0062655604 (hardcover)
Subjects: LCSH: Mafia--Italy. | Women and the mafia--Italy. | BISAC: TRUE CRIME / Organized Crime. | BIOGRAPHY & AUTOBIOGRAPHY / Criminals & Outlaws.
Classification: LCC HV6452.5 (ebook) | LCC HV6452.5 .P47 2018 (print) | DDC 364.106092/520945--dc23
LC record available at https://lccn.loc.gov/2018000498

ISBN 978-0-06-265560-8

18 19 20 21 22 RS/LSC 10 9 8 7 6 5 4 3 2 1

For the good daughters

and for Tess, always

CONTENTS

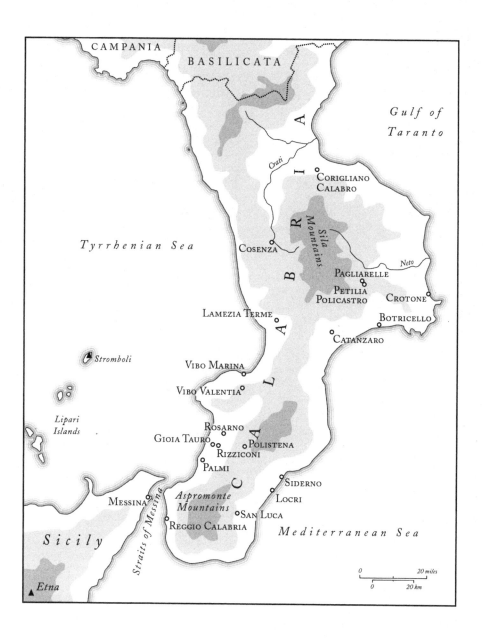

AUTHOR'S NOTE

To assist the English-language reader, I have used anglicized place names: Florence, not Firenze, for example. By contrast, I have observed Italian custom when it comes to individuals' names. Maria Concetta Cacciola, for instance, becomes Concetta, or 'Cetta, at the second mention. In another difference from Anglo-Saxon custom, Italian women retain their fathers' surnames after marriage. Thus Lea Garofalo kept her name after she married Carlo Cosco but the couple's daughter was called Denise Cosco.

ACT ONE

A Vanishing in Milan

I

—————

THE SYMBOL OF Milan is a giant serpent devouring a screaming child.[1] The first city of northern Italy has had other to-
tems: a woolly boar, a golden Madonna, and, more recently, the
designer labels that make Milan the fashion capital of the world.
But the eight-hundred-year-old image of a curled snake sinking
its fangs into the writhing, blood-soaked body of an infant has remained its most popular emblem, adorning flags and bas-reliefs on
the city walls, the Alfa Romeo badge, and the Inter Milan jersey. It's
an oddly menacing standard for a people more normally associated
with family and food, and a strangely crude one for a city whose artistry reaches the sublime heights of da Vinci's *The Last Supper*—and
most Milanese generally profess ignorance of its meaning. In more
candid moments, however, some will confess they suspect that the
image owes its endurance to the way it illuminates a dark truth at
the heart of their city: that the dynamism and accomplishment for
which Milan is famous depends on, among other things, whom you
are prepared to destroy.

In the four days they spent in Milan in late November 2009 before her father killed her mother, then erased any trace of her from
the world, Denise Cosco could almost believe her family had tran-
scended its own special darkness. Denise was seventeen. Her mother
was Lea Garofalo, a thirty-five-year-old mafioso's daughter, and her
father was Carlo Cosco, a thirty-nine-year-old cocaine smuggler.
Lea had married Carlo at sixteen, had Denise at seventeen, wit-

nessed Carlo and his brother kill a man in Milan at twenty-one, and helped send Carlo to the city's San Vittore prison at twenty-two. Denise had grown up on the run. For six years, from 1996 to 2002, Lea had hidden herself and her daughter away in the narrow, winding alleys of the medieval town of Bergamo in the foothills of the Alps. Lea had made it a game—two southern girls hiding out in Italy's gray north—and in time the two had become each other's world. When they walked Bergamo's cobbled streets, an elfin pair holding hands and curling their dark hair behind their ears, people took them for sisters.

One night in 2000, Lea glanced out of their apartment to see her old Fiat on fire. In 2002, after a scooter was stolen and their front door set alight, Lea told Denise she had a new game for them—and she walked hand in hand with her ten-year-old daughter into a carabinieri station, where she announced to the startled desk officer that she would testify against the mafia in return for witness protection. From 2002 to 2008, mother and daughter had lived in government safe houses. For the past eight months, for reasons Denise understood only in part, they'd been on their own once more. Three times Carlo's men had caught up with them. Three times Lea and Denise had escaped. But by spring 2009, Lea was exhausted and out of money, and she told Denise they were down to their two last options: either they somehow found the cash to flee to Australia, or Lea had to make peace with Carlo.

If neither was likely, reconciliation with Carlo at least seemed possible. The state had dropped its efforts to prosecute him using Lea's evidence, and while that infuriated her, it also meant she was no longer a threat to him. In April 2009, she sent her husband a message saying they should forgive and forget, and Carlo appeared to agree. The threats stopped and there were no more burned-out cars. Carlo began taking Denise on trips around the old country in Calabria. One September night he even talked Lea into a date and they drove down to the coast, talking into the early hours about the summer they'd met, all those years before.

So when in November 2009 Carlo invited his wife and daughter to spend a few days with him in Milan, and Denise, her hand over the phone, looked expectantly at her mother, Lea shrugged and said OK, they'd make a short break of it. Lea's memories of Milan in winter were of a cold, dismal city, the trees like black lightning against the sky, the icy winds tumbling like avalanches through the streets. But Denise would love Milan's shops, Lea and Carlo needed to talk about Denise's future, and ever since the summer Lea had found herself wondering about Carlo again. Twenty years earlier, he had held her face in his gorilla hands and promised to take her away from the mafia and all the killing—and Lea had believed him chiefly because he seemed to believe himself. Lea still wore a gold bracelet and necklace Carlo had given her back then. There was also no doubt that Carlo loved Denise. Maybe Denise was right, thought Lea. Perhaps the three of them *could* start over. The idea that Carlo's new geniality was part of some elaborate plot to catch her off guard was just too far-fetched. There were easier ways to kill someone.

LEA GAROFALO HAD outclassed Carlo Cosco from the start. Carlo had earned his position with the clans, but Lea was born a mafia princess, a Garofalo from Pagliarelle, daughter of east coast 'Ndrangheta aristocrats. Carlo was as broad and handsome as a bear, but Lea was altogether finer, her natural elegance accentuated by high cheekbones, a slim frame, and long, thick, curly dark hair. Carlo's stuttering grasp of Italian and his sullen, taciturn manner were never more noticeable than when he was with Lea, who spoke with the sophistication of a northerner and the passion of a southerner, laughing, arguing, and crying all in the same five minutes. In any other world, it would have been the natural order of things for

Lea to have walked out on Carlo a few years into their marriage and never looked back.

At least Carlo was making an effort not to gloat, thought Lea. He had a friend drop around one hundred euros for the train tickets to Milan. When Lea and Denise pulled into the city's central station, Mussolini's opulent glass-and-marble monument to northern order and power, Carlo himself picked them up in a black Audi and took them to the Hotel Losanna, a cozy backstreet place a block from the Corso Sempione, Milan's Champs-Élysées, and a short walk from their old family apartment on Viale Montello. And for the next four days, Carlo refused even to discuss the past. He didn't mention the 'Ndrangheta or how Lea had broken omertà or the way she almost destroyed everything for which he and his brothers had worked. Instead, Denise said the three of them enjoyed a "quiet and pleasant" mini vacation, the kind of family holiday they'd never had. Milan's Ferrari showrooms and Armani stores were a million miles from the goat pastures of Calabria, and Carlo seemed happy for his wife and daughter to enjoy it. With his coat tugged around his shoulders in the Milanese style, and Lea and Denise in jeans and thick down jackets, the three of them wandered the canals and the polished stone piazzas, eating pizza and cannoli and window-shopping in the nineteenth-century galleria across from Milan's flamboyant Gothic Duomo. Carlo paid for everything: clothes for Denise, dinners for the three of them, coffees and gelatos. Carlo even fixed it for the two women to get their eyebrows done at a beauty salon owned by his friend Massimo. Another time, when Lea was out of hash, Carlo summoned a cousin, Carmine Venturino, and made sure she didn't pay.

It wasn't perfect, of course. Denise was busy nurturing a teenage addiction to cigarettes and an aversion to heavy Italian food. Carlo, seeing his wife and daughter for only the second time in thirteen years and noticing how alike they were, couldn't help but be transported to the day, nineteen years earlier, when sixteen-year-old Lea had eloped with him to Milan. Meanwhile Lea was struggling to hold her nerve. She'd asked Carlo not to tell anyone she was in Milan but already he'd gone ahead and introduced her to Massimo and Carmine—and Carmine, for one, seemed more than just a friend to Carlo. She also had the recurrent feeling that they were being followed.

Lea found herself turning to an old habit. Denise's mother had long needed a joint or two just to get to sleep at night and, as the butts Denise found in their room attested, she was now also smoking steadily through the day. Sleep and peace were good, of course, and a real rarity for Lea. But you had to wonder at the wisdom of getting stoned around Carlo, a mafioso who had spent the last thirteen years chasing her across Italy trying to kill her.

Still, the trip went better than Lea might have feared. Initially, she had asked Denise to stay with her when Carlo was around because, Denise said, "if I was there, nothing was going to happen to her." Soon, however, Lea felt safe enough to be left alone with her husband. On the night of November 23, Denise went to bed early, and Lea and Carlo ate out alone. If the years had tightened Lea's nerves, time seemed to have relaxed Carlo. He was now a barrel of a man, with thick ears, a close-shaven head, and a boxer's nose, but his manner was gentle and attentive. When Lea mentioned Denise's plan to go to Milan University, Carlo offered to keep an eye on her. When Carlo volunteered that he'd set aside €200,000 for his daughter and Lea scolded him for the tens of thousands he'd spent trying to track them down—"and for no reason, because you always arrived too late!"—Carlo, unusually, took the slight well. After he paid the bill, Carlo took Lea on a drive through the city, the pair of them gliding through the empty streets in silence, just taking in the sights and each other's company. So distracted was Carlo that he ran a red light, delighting Lea, who was treated to the sight of the big mafioso trying to wriggle out of a ticket.

Watching them together in those days—Lea smoking and laughing, Carlo rubbing his bruiser's neck and letting a smile soften his frown—Denise said you could see they had been in love once. You might even believe it would work out for the three of them. The three of them "ate together as a family," Denise said later. Carlo was showing them how "caring and kind" he was. And there was no denying Lea still had it. Even without a cent in her pocket, and despite everything that had happened, her mother was still a rare and beautiful thing, a Calabrian forest sprite with the same pure spirit that had marked her out from every other girl in Pagliarelle all those years ago. Carlo, Denise felt sure, had to be falling for Lea again. "I had absolutely no bad thoughts about my father," she said.

LEA AND DENISE's last day in Milan was November 24, 2009. The two women were planning to take the 11:30 P.M. sleeper back to Calabria. In their room at the Losanna, Lea and Denise packed. To help take the bags to the station, Carlo brought round a big gray Chrysler he had borrowed from a friend.

As he loaded their cases, Carlo asked Denise whether she'd like to eat that evening with her uncle Giuseppe, her aunt Renata, and their two boys, eighteen-year-old Domenico and Andrea, fifteen. Denise should grab the chance to spend time with her family, said Carlo. A night alone would also give her parents the chance to discuss a few last things.

Denise agreed. She and Lea then walked into town to do some final shopping. It was an overcast day, only just above freezing, and a dull chill echoed off the granite buildings. CCTV later showed Lea in a black jacket with its furry collar turned in and Denise in a thick white jacket with her hood up and a black backpack over the top. Mother and daughter wandered around the arcades, warming themselves in cafés and grabbing lunch at a McDonald's, just happy to be out together in the city and, for once, not looking over their shoulders.

An hour after dark, just before 6 P.M., Denise called Carlo. She and Lea were near the Arch of Peace in Sempione Park, not far from the hotel, she said. A few minutes later, Carlo arrived in the Chrysler, flicked on his hazard lights, and reminded Denise through the driver's window that she was expected for dinner with her cousins. Lea, who had already gotten in the car, didn't want to go. Even if she was getting on better with Carlo, she wanted nothing to do with his family. Carlo suggested he drop off Denise, then return to take Lea out for a quiet dinner. After everyone had eaten, Carlo and Lea would pick Denise up again and all three of them would head over to the station. The women agreed. "See you at the station, Mama," said Denise to Lea, as she jumped into the car. "Later," replied Lea, getting out. "I'm going to have a drink."

Carlo drove Denise to No. 6 Viale Montello on the edge of Milan's Chinatown. A large, grubby six-story walk-up of more than a hundred apartments arranged around a drab internal courtyard, No. 6 Viale Montello had once belonged to the Ospedale Maggiore, one of Europe's first public hospitals when it opened in 1456. But the place had fallen into disrepair and was later abandoned, and in the 1980s the 'Ndrangheta from Pagliarelle had taken it over as a live-in hub for their heroin and cocaine business. The ground floor was now filled with half a dozen cheap Chinese stores—groceries, laundries, *tabacs*—whose metal shutters were decorated with extravagant graffiti. Most of the apartments were home to immigrants from China, Romania, Albania, Poland, Eritrea, and Nigeria, tenants whose own uncertain legal status ensured they were no friends of the law. The rest was given over to around a dozen mafia families. Carlo, Lea, and Denise had lived in one apartment in the early 1990s. Carlo's elder brothers Vito and Giuseppe were still installed in others with their wives and children. It was to these rooms that tons of cocaine and heroin were transported every year before being repackaged and shipped north into Europe.

Carlo left Denise with her aunt Renata at 6:30 P.M. at Bar Barbara, a Chinese-run café on Piazza Baiamonti at the end of Viale Montello, then drove off to fetch Lea. Denise ordered an espresso. Renata said dinner was minestrone and cold cuts. Denise told her aunt she wasn't all that hungry, so she and Renata went to an Asian supermarket a few doors down to buy her a small tray of sushi. Denise tried to pay but Renata wouldn't hear of it.

Looking back, Denise would say it was around then that the make-believe stopped. Back at her cousins' second-floor apartment in Viale Montello, Denise ate her sushi alone. Then she sat with Renata, Domenico, and Andrea as they had their soup and meat in front of the TV. It was far from the family get-together Carlo had described; her cousins were in and out all evening. Her uncle Giuseppe wasn't even home, which was doubly strange as there was a big game that night, AC Milan away at Barcelona. There was something else, too. When Denise had spent time with Renata before, she remembered thinking that her aunt was a jealous wife, always calling Giuseppe to ask where he was, who he was with, what he was doing, and when he was coming home. That night, Denise noticed, Renata didn't call Giuseppe once.

Denise, who after years on the run had developed a sixth sense for these things, began to feel something was off. Around 8 P.M. she called her mother. Lea's phone was unobtainable. That was odd, too. Lea always made sure her phone was charged. Denise sent her mother a text. "Something like 'Where the hell are you?'" Denise said later in court.

The big game started at 8:40 P.M. Barcelona scored quickly. Denise texted Lea a couple more times. Still no answer. Renata told Denise not to worry about smoking in front of the family—no one would tell Carlo—and as the evening wore on, Denise found she was chain-smoking. Her cousins groaned as Barcelona scored a second goal just before halftime. Sometime after 9 P.M., just when Denise was beginning to feel truly unnerved, Giuseppe stuck his head around the door, registered the score and Denise's presence, then left again. A few minutes after that, Denise's phone rang. It was Carlo. He would be over in a few minutes to pick up Denise to take her to the station. She should wait for him downstairs at her uncle Vito's first-floor apartment.

Denise kissed her cousins and her aunt good-bye, then took the stairs to Vito's. Carlo hadn't arrived so Vito's wife, Giuseppina, made coffee. It was after 9:30 P.M. now—more than three hours since Denise had last heard from her mother—and she was fighting a rising sense of panic. After a while, Vito appeared at the door. Behind him, down the corridor, Denise caught a glimpse of her father at the entrance to another apartment. She hadn't even known Carlo was in the building. Instead of fetching her, he was talking to his brother Giuseppe and two other men. Carlo glanced at his daughter, and called over that she should wait for him in the car. Denise went down to the street and found the Chrysler. Lea wasn't in it. By now, it was 10 P.M. When Carlo got in, Denise asked him immediately: "Where's my mother?"

"I left her around the corner," replied Carlo. "She didn't want to come in and see everyone."

Carlo drove in silence to a street behind Viale Montello. Denise regarded him. He looked upset, she thought. The way he was driving, barely focusing on the road. "*Scossato*," she said later. Shaken.

When they turned the corner, Lea wasn't there. Denise was about to speak when Carlo cut her off. Lea wasn't waiting for them, said Carlo, because what had happened was that Lea had asked him for money and he had given her two hundred euros, but she had screamed at him that it wasn't enough, so he had given her another two hundred and she'd stormed off anyway. They hadn't eaten dinner. Actually, said Carlo, he hadn't eaten at all.

Carlo fell silent. Denise said nothing.

"You know what your mother's like," said Carlo. "There's nothing anyone can do."

Carefully, Denise asked her father, "Where is my mother now?"

"I've no idea," replied Carlo.

Denise thought her father was a terrible liar. "I didn't believe him for a nanosecond," she said. "Not one word." All his kindness over the last few days, all the opening doors, fetching coats, and driving them around—his whole Milanese bella figura act—all of it was gone. Carlo appeared to have regressed. He seemed raw, almost primal. He wouldn't even look at her. And suddenly Denise understood. The dinner with her cousins. The calls to Lea that wouldn't go through. The endless hanging around. The urgent discussion between the men in the apartment opposite. Lea had been right all along. Denise, who had begged her mother to let them go to Milan, had been catastrophically wrong. "I *knew*," said Denise. "I knew immediately."

Denise understood two more things. First: it was already too late. Denise hadn't spoken to her mother for three and a half hours. Lea never turned off her phone for that long and certainly not before telling Denise. *It's done*, thought Denise. *He's already had time.*

Second: confronting her father would be suicide. If she was to survive, in that moment she had to accept Lea's fate and fix it in her mind not as possible or reversible but as certain and final. At the same time, she had to convince her father that she had no idea about what had happened, when in reality she had no doubt at all. "I understood there was very little I could do for my mother now," said Denise. "But I couldn't let *him* understand *me*." Inwardly, Denise forced her mind into a tight, past-tense dead end. "They've done what they had to do," she told herself. "This was how it was always going to end. This was inevitable." Outwardly, she played herself as she might have been a few minutes earlier: a worried daughter looking for her missing mother. The speed of events helped. It was absurd, even unreal, how in a moment Denise had lost her mother, her best friend, and the only person who had ever truly known her. She didn't have to pretend she was struggling to catch up. She even had the feeling that if she willed it hard enough, she might bring Lea back to life.

It was in this state, with Carlo in a daze and Denise acting like there was still hope in the world, that father and daughter drove all over Milan. "We went to all the places we had been," said Denise. "Where we'd had a drink, where we'd eaten pizza, the hotel where we had stayed, over to Sempione Park. We went to a local café, a shopping center, the McDonald's where we had lunch and the train station, where my father bought two tickets for my mother and me. We went all over the city. I was phoning and texting my mother all the time. And of course, we found nothing and nobody."

Around midnight, just after the train to Calabria had departed, Denise's phone rang. Denise was startled to read the word "Mama" on the screen. But the voice on the other end belonged to her aunt Marisa, Lea's sister in Pagliarelle, and Denise remembered that she had borrowed her cousin's phone before leaving for Milan.

Gathering herself, Denise told Marisa that Lea was nowhere to be found and that they had just missed their train back to Calabria. "Have you heard from her?" Denise asked her aunt. "Did she call you?"

Aunt Marisa replied she had missed a call from Lea sometime after 6:30 P.M. but hadn't been able to reach her since. Marisa was calling to check that everything was all right. Denise replied that Lea's phone had been dead all night.

"They made her disappear," Marisa told Denise, just like that, with Carlo sitting right next to Denise in the car.

"She was so matter-of-fact," Denise said. "Like she assumed we all expected it. Like we all felt the same."

Denise and Carlo kept driving around Milan until 1:30 A.M. Finally, Denise said there was nowhere else to look and they should file a report with the police. Carlo drove her to a carabinieri station. The officer told Denise she had to wait forty-eight hours to make out a missing person's report. With Carlo there, Denise couldn't tell the officer that she and Lea had hidden for years from the man standing next to her, so she thanked the officer and they returned to Renata's, where her aunt opened the door half asleep in her dressing gown.

Renata was surprised to hear Lea was even in town. "We came up here together," Denise explained. "We didn't tell you because we didn't want to cause any trouble." The three of them stood in the doorway for a second. Denise found herself looking at her father's clothes. He'd had them on all evening. It had been in that jacket, thought Denise. That shirt. Those shoes.

Carlo broke the silence by saying he would keep looking for Lea a little while longer and headed back to his car. Renata said Denise could sleep in Andrea's room. To reach it, Denise had to walk through Renata and Giuseppe's bedroom. "I could see Giuseppe wasn't there," she said later. "And I ignored it. I ignored everything *for a year.* I pretended nothing had happened. I ate with these people. I worked in their pizzeria. I went on holiday with them. I played with their children. Even when I knew what they had done. I had to be so careful with what I said. They were saying my mother was alive even after I hadn't seen her for more than a year. I just made out like I didn't know. But I knew."

II

___

IN CALABRIA, LEA Garofalo's disappearance needed no explanation. The mafia even had a term for people who, one day, just vanished: *lupara bianca* (white shotgun), a killing that left no corpse, seen by no one. In Pagliarelle, the remote mountain village on the arch of Italy's foot where Lea and Carlo were born, people knew never to speak Lea's name again.

They wouldn't be able to forget her entirely. Lea's modest first-floor studio, its shutters and drainpipes painted bubblegum pink, was only yards from the main piazza. But the four hundred villagers of Pagliarelle had learned long ago to live with their ghosts. In three decades, thirty-five men and women had been murdered in mafia vendettas in Pagliarelle and the nearby town of Petilia Policastro, including Lea's father, Antonio, her uncle Giulio, and her brother Floriano. In such a place, in such a family, Lea's disappearance could seem inevitable, even a kind of resolution. Years later, her sister Marisa would look up at Lea's first-floor window from the street below and say: "Lea wanted freedom. She never bowed her head. But for people who follow the 'Ndrangheta, this choice is considered very eccentric. Very serious. You want to be free? You pay with your life." Really, Marisa was saying, there was nothing anyone could do.[1]

Alessandra Cerreti knew many of her colleagues shared that view. When she arrived in Calabria from Milan seven months earlier as the province's newest magistrate, she had been struck by how many Calabrians still accepted the 'Ndrangheta as an immutable fact of life. Outside southern Italy, the mafia was regarded as a movie or a novel, an entertaining, even glamorous legend that might once have held some historic truth but which, in a time of more sophisticated concerns such as financial crises or climate change or terrorism, felt like a fable from a bygone era. Not so in Calabria. Like their more famous cousins in Sicily and Naples, the 'Ndrangheta had been founded in the nineteenth century. But while the Sicilians, in particular, had seen their power steadily eroded by a state crackdown and popular resistance, the 'Ndrangheta had grown ever stronger. The organization was still run by its original founders, 141 ancient shepherding and orange-farming families who ruled the isolated valleys and hill towns of Calabria. Its foot soldiers were also still quietly extorting billions of euros a year from Calabria's shopkeepers, restaurant owners, and gelato makers—and murdering the occasional hardheaded carabinieri or judge or politician who stood in their way. What had transformed the 'Ndrangheta, however, was a new internationalism. It now smuggled 70 to 80 percent of the cocaine in Europe. It plundered the Italian state and the European Union for tens of billions more. It brokered illegal arms deals to criminals, rebels, and terrorists around the world, including several sides in the Syrian civil war. By the prosecutors' count, by 2009 the 'Ndrangheta's empire took in fifty countries, a quarter of the planet, from Albania to Togo, linking a mob war in Toronto to a lawyer's assassination in Melbourne, and the reported ownership of an entire Brussels neighborhood to a cocaine-delivering pizzeria in Queens, New York, called Cucino a Modo Mio (I Cook My Own Way). By the dawn of the second decade of the new millennium, the 'Ndrangheta was, by almost any measure, the most powerful criminal syndicate on earth.

If ruthless violence was the fuel of this global empire, astounding wealth was its result. The prosecutors' best guess was that every year the organization amassed revenues of $50 billion to $100 billion,[2] equivalent to up to 3.5 percent of Italian GDP, or twice the annual revenues of Fiat, Alfa Romeo, Lancia, Ferrari, and Maserati combined. So much money was there that cleaning and hiding it required a whole second business. And so good had the Calabrians become at money laundering, pushing billions through restaurants and construction companies, small offshore banks and large financial institutions, even the Dutch flower market and the European chocolate trade, that Alessandra's fellow prosecutors were picking up indications that other organized crime groups—Eastern Europeans, Russians, Asians, Africans, Latin Americans—were paying the 'Ndrangheta to do the same with their fortunes. That meant the 'Ndrangheta was managing the flow of hundreds of billions or even trillions of illicit dollars around the world.

And it was this, the 'Ndrangheta's dispersal of global crime's money across the planet, that ensured the Calabrians were in everyone's lives. Millions of people lived in their buildings, worked in their companies, shopped in their stores, ate in their pizzerias, traded in their companies' shares, did business with their banks, and elected politicians and parties they funded. As rich as the biggest businesses or banks or governments, 'Ndrangheta moved markets and changed lives from New York to London to Tokyo to São Paulo to Johannesburg. In the first two decades of the new millennium, it was hard to imagine another human enterprise with such influence over so many. Most remarkable of all: almost no one had ever heard of it.

THE 'NDRANGHETA—PRONOUNCED *un-drung-get-a*, a word derived from the Greek *andranghateia*, meaning "society of men of honor and valor"—was a mystery even to many Italians.[3] In truth, this ignorance was due as much to perception as deception. Many northern Italians had trouble even imagining wealth or achievement in the south. And the contrast *was* striking. The north had Florence and Venice, prosciutto and parmigiana, Barolo and balsamic, the Renaissance and the Enlightenment, AC Milan and Inter Milan, Lamborghini and Maserati, Gucci and Prada, Caravaggio, Michelangelo, Pavarotti, Puccini, Galileo, da Vinci, Dante, Machiavelli, Marco Polo, Christopher Columbus, and the Pope. The south had lemons, mozzarella, and winter sun.

This was, Alessandra knew, the great lie of a united Italy. Two thousand years earlier, the south had been a fount of European civilization. But by the time the northern general Giuseppe Garibaldi amalgamated the Italian peninsula into a single nation in 1861, he was attempting to join the literate, the industrial, and the cultured with the feudal, the unschooled, and the unsewered. The contradiction had proved too great. The north prospered in trade and commerce. The south deteriorated and millions of southerners left, emigrating to northern Europe, the Americas, or Australia.

In time, the provinces south of Rome had come to be known as the Mezzogiorno, the land where the midday sun blazed overhead, a dry, torpid expanse of peasant farmers and small-boat fishermen stretching from Abruzzo through Naples to the island of Lampedusa, 110 kilometers from North Africa. For much of the south, such a sweeping description was a clumsy stereotype. But for Calabria, the toe, it was accurate. The Romans had called it Bruttium, and for 300 kilometers from north to south, Calabria was little more than thornbush scrub and bare rock mountains interspersed with groves of gnarled olives and fields of fine gray dust. It was eerily empty: more than a century of emigration had ensured there were four times as many Calabrians and their descendants outside Italy as in their homeland. When she was driven out of Reggio and into the countryside, Alessandra passed a succession of empty towns, deserted villages, and abandoned farms. It felt like the aftermath of a giant disaster—which, if you considered the centuries of grinding destitution, it was.

Still, there was a hard beauty to the place. High up in the mountains, wolves and wild boar roamed forests of beech, cedar, and holly oak. Below the peaks, deep cracks in the rock opened up into precipitous ravines through which ice-cold rivers raged toward the sea. As the incline eased, woods gave way to vines and summer pastures, followed by estuary flats filled with lemon and orange orchards. In summer, the sun would scorch the earth, turning the soil to powder and the prickly thorn grass to roasted gold. In winter, snow would cover the mountains and storms would batter the cliffs on the coast and drag away the beaches.

Alessandra wondered whether it was the violence of their land that bred such ferocity in Calabrians. They lived in ancient towns built on natural rock fortresses. In their fields, they grew burning chili and intoxicating jasmine and raised big-horned cows and mountain goats that they roasted whole over hearths stoked with knotted vine wood. The men hunted boar with shotguns and swordfish with harpoons. The women spiced sardines with hot peppers and dried trout in the wind for months before turning the meat into a pungent brown stew. For Calabrians, there was also little divide between the holy and the profane. On saints' days, morning processions would be followed by afternoon street feasts at which the women would serve giant plates of *maccheroni* with *'nduja*, a hot, soft pepper sausage the color of ground brick, washed down with a black wine that stained the lips and seared the throat. As the sun began to sink, the men would dance the tarantella, named after the effects of the poisonous bite of the wolf spider. To the tune of a mandolin, the beat of a goatskin tambourine, and a song about thwarted love or a mother's love or the thrill of a hot spurt of blood from a stabbed traitor's heart, the men would compete for hours to see who could dance fastest and longest. "The Greece of Italy," said the newspa-

pers, though in reality that was an insult to Greece. Unlike its Ionian neighbor, southern Italy's legal economy hadn't grown since
the millennium. Unemployment among the young, at more than one
in two, was among the worst in Europe.

THE SOUTH HAD experienced one kind of development, however.
Many southerners saw Garibaldi's creation of a northern-dominated
Italian state as an act of colonization. Already damned for who
they were, they cared little for northern opinions of what they did.
Across the Mezzogiorno, from the birth of the Republic, brigands
were commonplace. Some organized themselves into family groups.
In the century and a half since unification, a few hundred families
in Naples, Sicily, and Calabria had grown rich. And as criminal rebels who claimed to be secretly subverting an occupying state, they
used the intimacy and loyalty of family and a violent code of honor
and righteous resistance to draw a veil of omertà over their wealth.
Even in 2009, Calabria's crime bosses still dressed like orange farmers. It was only in the last few years that the Italian government
had begun to grasp that these brutish men, with their bird-faced
women and reckless sons, were among the world's great criminal
masterminds.

There was, at least, no mystery to who ran the 'Ndrangheta.
The south's lack of progress was social as much as material. Tradition held that each family was a miniature feudal kingdom in which
men and boys reigned supreme. The men granted their women little
authority or independence, nor even much of a life beyond an existence as vassals of family property and honor. Like medieval kings,
fathers paired their girls off as teenagers to seal clan alliances. Beatings of daughters and wives were routine. To men, women were desirable but feckless, not to be trusted to stay faithful or direct their
own lives but to be kept strictly in line for their own good. Women

who were untrue, even to the memory of a husband dead for fifteen years, were killed, and it would be their fathers, brothers, sons, and husbands who did it. Only blood could wash clean the family honor, the men would say. Often they burned the bodies or dissolved them in acid to be sure of erasing the family shame.

Such a perversion of family would have been extraordinary in any time or place. It was especially so in Italy, where family was close to sacred.[4] The severity of the misogyny prompted some prosecutors to compare the 'Ndrangheta with Islamist militants. Like ISIS or Boko Haram, 'Ndranghetisti routinely terrorized their women and slaughtered their enemies in the service of an immutable code of honor and righteousness.

So, yes, Calabria's prosecutors would say, the life of an 'Ndrangheta woman like Lea Garofalo was tragic. And, yes, the 'Ndrangheta's inhuman sexism was one more reason to destroy it. But that didn't mean the women were much use in that fight. Almost from the day in April 2009 that Alessandra arrived from Milan, many of her colleagues told her the women in the mafia were just more of its victims. "The women don't matter," they said.[5] When they heard of Lea's disappearance, they conceded the news was heartbreaking, especially for those who had known Lea and Denise in witness protection. But Lea's death was merely a symptom of the problem, they insisted. It had no bearing on the cause.

Alessandra disagreed. She claimed no special insight into family dynamics. Alessandra was forty-one, married without children, and her appearance—slim, meticulously dressed, with short, straight hair in a sharp, boyish part—emphasized poise and professionalism. When it came to The Family, however, Alessandra argued that it was only logical women would have a substantial role in a criminal organization structured around kin. Family was the lifeblood of the mafia. Like an unseen, uncut umbilical cord, family was how the mafia delivered nourishing, fortifying power to itself. And at the heart of any family was a mother. Besides, argued Alessandra, if the women really didn't matter, why would the men risk it all to kill them? The women *had* to be more than mere victims. As a Sicilian and a woman inside the Italian judiciary, Alessandra also knew something about patriarchies that belittled women even as they relied on them. Most judicial officials missed the importance of 'Ndrangheta women, she said, because most of them were men. "And Italian men underestimate all women," she said. "It's a real problem."

At the time Lea Garofalo went missing, evidence to support Alessandra's views was on display in every Italian newspaper. For two years, the press had filled its pages with the lurid allegations and distinctly conservative attitudes of a state prosecutor in Perugia named Giuliano Mignini. Mignini had accused an American student, Amanda Knox—with the assistance of two men, one of whom was Knox's boyfriend of five days—of murdering her British flatmate, Meredith Kercher. Mignini alleged the two men were in thrall to Knox's satanic allure. Taking his lead from Mignini, a lawyer in the case described Knox as a "she-devil . . . Lucifer-like, demonic . . . given over to lust." Fifty-nine years old, a devout Catholic and father of four daughters, Mignini later told a documentary maker that though the forensic evidence against Knox was scant, her "uninhibited" character and "lack of morals" had convinced him. "She would bring boys home," he mused. "Pleasure at any cost. This is at the heart of most crime."[6]

In the end, Knox and her boyfriend were acquitted on appeal, twice, and the prosecutors castigated by Italy's Supreme Court for presenting a case with "stunning flaws." But at the time of Lea's disappearance, Knox was days from being found guilty for the first time and Mignini's version of events—that an unmarried American woman who had slept with seven men was just the kind of fiendish deviant to have sex slaves murder her roommate—was the accepted truth.

Alessandra didn't lecture her colleagues on female emancipation. In their own lives they were free to hold whatever views they wished, and she wasn't about to let any of them think she was asking for special treatment. But when it came to cracking the omertà that cloaked Europe's biggest mafia, Alessandra argued that the state had pragmatic reasons to care about the prejudice of gangsters. The 'Ndrangheta was as near-perfect a criminal organization as any of them would ever encounter. It had been around for a century and a half, employed thousands around the world, and made tens of billions a year. It was not only the single biggest obstacle standing in the way of Italy finally becoming a modern, united nation, but also a diabolical perversion of the Italian family, which was the heart and essence of the nation. And yet until a few years earlier, the Italian state had been barely aware of its existence. When she arrived in Reggio Calabria, no one at the Palace of Justice could give Alessandra more than rough estimates of how many men the 'Ndrangheta employed or where it operated or even, to the nearest $50 billion a year, how much money it made. The kind of free will and independence that Lea Garofalo had shown, and the murderous chauvinism rained down on her as a result, represented one of the few times the 'Ndrangheta had ever broken cover. At a time when prosecutors were just beginning to understand "how big the 'Ndrangheta had become and how much we had underestimated it," said Cerreti, women informants were an invaluable, untapped source of knowledge with unimpeachable motivations for talking. The 'Ndrangheta's violent bigotry wasn't just a tragedy, said Alessandra. It was a grand flaw. With the right kind of nurturing, it might become an existential crisis. "Freeing their women," said Alessandra, "is the way to bring down the 'Ndrangheta."

III

ALESSANDRA CERRETI WAS born on April 29, 1968, in the eastern Sicilian port of Messina.[1] In twenty-two years away, she'd only rarely visited her hometown. Now she was living in Reggio Calabria, Messina's sister city, three miles across the water, and rarely out of sight of it. She realized she'd never noticed how Messina changed through the day. At dawn, a pink light would lift its piazzas, boulevards, and palm trees out of a purple gloom. At midday, the sun painted the scene in primary colors: blue sea, red roofs, yellow hills, and the white cone of Mount Etna to the south. Sunset was a languid affair, as the wind slackened and Messina sank back into the dusk under clouds edged with orange filigree. Night ushered in a Mediterranean glamour, a fathomless black set off by a necklace of white lights strung like pearls along the coast road.

It was a scene that had drawn artists and writers for generations. Those raised beside the Strait of Messina, however, have long understood that the truth of the place is in what lies beneath. The Strait is a narrow, plunging abyss formed when Africa and Europe collided fifty million years ago and Africa bent down toward the center of the earth. In this underwater chasm, the rushing currents created when the Ionian and Tyrrhenian Seas meet make for some of the most disturbed waters in all the oceans. Boiling whirlpools and sucking vortexes trap yachts and fishing boats. Slewing tides send ferries and freighters skidding sideways toward the rocks. Those peering into the depths can see startled bug-eyed fish, and even sharks and whales, shot to the surface from the seafloor 250 meters below. The swirling winds of the Strait reflect this turmoil, inverting the normal pattern of hot air over cold to create an optical illusion called the fata morgana, in which boats and land on the horizon appear to float upside down in the sky.

On land, human history has mirrored this natural upheaval. Reggio and Messina were founded by Greek colonists whose king, Italos, eventually gave the country its name. But for three millennia, the Strait has been continuously conquered and appropriated, first by Syracusans in 387 B.C., then by Campanians, Romans, Vandals, Lombards, Goths, Byzantines, Arabs, Normans, Hohenstaufen German kings, Angevins, Aragonese, Spanish Habsburgs (twice), Ottomans, Barbary pirates, and reactionary French Bourbons and Bonapartists, before finally, in 1860 and 1861, Reggio and Messina were captured by Giuseppe Garibaldi in the war that unified Italy. The wealth of its occupiers had given Messina and Reggio their ancient, yellow-stone harbors, their Arabic street names, and an early artistry that found exquisite expression in the Riace Bronzes, two sculptures of naked, bearded warriors dating from 450 B.C. discovered by a snorkeler off the Calabrian coast in 1972. But this early globalism also had its costs. It was through the Strait's ports that the Black Death entered Europe from Asia in 1346, going on to wipe out two-thirds of the continent's population. In 1743, by which time humanity's numbers had barely recovered, plague returned a second time, killing 48,000 in Messina alone. Next to those disasters, the deadly earthquakes of 1783 and 1894 were largely forgotten, though not the quake and ensuing twelve-meter tsunami of December 28, 1908, which flattened both Reggio and Messina, killing 200,000 people. Rebuilt entirely, the twin cities were leveled again by Allied bombers in 1943.

Assailed by tempests, consumed by catastrophe, the people of the Strait could be forgiven for thinking they were cursed. Many used magic and folk wisdom to account for their suffering. In the *Odyssey*, Homer had written about two sea monsters that lived on opposing sides of the Strait. Surging out from Calabria, the six-headed Scylla would snatch sailors from the decks of their ships, while from Sicily Charybdis would suck entire boats under the waves with her insatiable thirst. People explained Etna's deadly eruptions by describing the mountain as the home of Vulcan, or sometimes of Cyclops, both of them angry, thundering types with low regard for mortals. The tremors people felt under their feet were said to be the shifting grip of Colapesce, the son of a fisherman who took a deep dive one day, saw that Sicily was held up by a single, crumbling column, and stayed in the depths to prevent its collapse. The floating islands that appeared over Reggio, meanwhile, were thought to be glimpses of Avalon, to which the fairy-witch Morgan le Fay (after whom the fata morgana was named) spirited a dying King Arthur. Up there, too, it was said, was *The Flying Dutchman*, a ghost ship doomed to sail the oceans forever.

Alessandra would carry the feel of the Strait with her all her life. It was there in the way a winter's chill would remind her of the morning breeze off the city docks or how the first days of summer would almost instantly change her forearms from alabaster to honey. It was there, too, in her distaste for the way people often seemed to prefer fiction over truth. While most children were delighted to find themselves growing up in a world of gods and castles in the sky, Alessandra was unmoved. Stories of monsters and fairies were entertaining, but they also obscured the deadly reality of the Strait. Every summer, Messina's coastguardsmen heaved a steady procession of dripping, blanketed stretchers onto the docks. How could these regrettable, preventable deaths be part of some mystical grand plan? There was little logic, either, in the other spurious legends that Sicilians would spin to glorify their island. In 1975, when Alessandra was seven, a twenty-six-year-old from Messina called Giovanni Fiannacca swam to Calabria in thirty minutes and fifty seconds, a record that was to stand for forty years. Alessandra's neighbors proclaimed Fiannacca the greatest distance swimmer in Sicily, perhaps even of all time. The reality, as most Sicilians knew, was that he had timed his crossing to coincide with a particularly strong east–west tide that would have carried a rubber duck to Calabria.

In another life, in another land, Alessandra might have forgiven these illusions and the credulous adults who repeated them. But her home was the birthplace of Cosa Nostra. By the 1970s, the Sicilian mafia was operating all but unopposed on the island. It was a state within a state, extracting taxes via extortion, dividing up public contracts among mafia companies, settling disputes, delivering punishments—and lying, cheating, and murdering to preserve its position. Yet no one said a thing. To inquisitive outsiders, Sicilians would claim the mafia was a fable, a cliché, or even a groundless slur. Among themselves, proponents would characterize it in more mythic terms, as an ancient Sicilian brotherhood built on courage, honor, and sacrifice. Never mind that the mafia itself cooked up these romantic legends and embellished them with more recent folklore, such as their story about how mafiosi rode Allied tanks to liberate Sicily in the Second World War. Never mind that in their hearts most Sicilians knew they were being lied to. Just as the islanders found it hard to accept the indifference shown to their city by Nature and Man, so most preferred not to confront the truth that their fellow Sicilians had grown rich by robbing and killing them.

Alessandra lamented her neighbors' complicity in these deceptions even as she understood it. Decades later, reading sensational newspaper accounts of mafia adventures, she would react the same way she had as a child. The facts about the tyranny and the killing were plain. Why dress them up as something else? What Alessandra truly detested, however, was the way outsiders assisted the mafia's mythmaking. A year after she was born, Mario Puzo, an American pulp magazine writer, sold the screenplay adapted from his book *The Godfather* to Paramount for $100,000. Two years later, Francis Ford Coppola was directing Al Pacino in the movie on location in Savoca, twenty-five miles south of Messina.

The film, one of the most successful of all time, contained elements of truth. The Corleone family *was* a crime syndicate from south of Palermo. There also *had* been a disagreement inside the mafia in the 1950s over whether to enter narcotics trafficking, a dispute that did lead to an internal war. What Alessandra found unforgivable was the way Hollywood used southern Italians' daily tragedy as a device to make its dramas more compelling. She shared none of Coppola's empathy for the men who murdered their wives and girlfriends. She could make no sense of the women, either, passive, giddy creatures who allowed their men to lead them from love to betrayal to an early death. Nor did she recognize any of the film's somber majesty or mournful grandiloquence in the blood that stained the gutters as she walked to school. When Alessandra was ten, two ambitious bosses, Salvatore Riina ("the butcher of Corleone") and Bernardo Provenzano ("the tractor," so called because, in the words of one informer, "he mows people down"), began what became an all-out mafia war by assassinating several Sicilian rivals.[2] The decade and a half that followed, spanning most of Alessandra's adolescence, became known as *la mattanza*, "the slaughter." More than 1,700 Sicilians died. Mafiosi were shot in their cars, in restaurants, as they walked down the street. In a single day in Palermo in November 1982, twelve mafiosi were killed in twelve separate assassinations. Yet through it all, foreign tourists would arrive in Messina asking for directions to the Godfather's village. No, thought Alessandra. This was a hideous, willful delusion. It was a lie. It had to be corrected.

When Alessandra was eight, her teacher asked her class to write an essay about what they wanted to be when they grew up. "Let your minds wander," said the teacher. "You can be anything at all, anywhere in the world." Excited by the chance to escape Messina's violence and fear, most of Alessandra's classmates wrote whimsies about becoming princesses or moving to America or flying a rocket to the moon. Alessandra said she would be staying put. *I want to be an anti-mafia prosecutor*, she wrote. *I want to put gangsters behind bars.*

IT WAS TO pursue her ambition that in 1987, at the age of nineteen, Alessandra took the train north to become a law student. Pulling in to Rome's central station the next day, she found herself in a different nation. But Alessandra quickly assimilated. She graduated in 1990, qualified as a magistrate in 1997, and quickly became a specialist in organized crime. Over the next twelve years, she investigated the 'Ndrangheta's expansion across northern Italy, assisted the prosecution of billion-euro tax evasion in the art world, sat as a judge in a high-profile terrorist recruitment case, and, on a quiet weekend, married a rising anti-mafia carabinieri officer.[3]

No one was surprised that Alessandra married into the job. Few outsiders would tolerate the life of a mafia prosecutor's spouse. The wide autonomy Italy's anti-mafia prosecutors enjoyed in their investigations was about the only freedom they possessed. The constant threat to her life required Alessandra to exist in isolation behind a wall of steel—literally, in the case of her office door and her armor-plated car—and for her to be escorted by four bodyguards twenty-four hours a day. Spontaneity was out of the question; all her movements were planned a day in advance. A normal life—meeting friends and family, eating out, shopping—was next to impossible. "We go nowhere with crowds because of the risk to others," said Alessandra. For the same reason, she and her husband—whose identity she kept secret—had long ago decided against children. "I would have to fear for them," she said. "As we are, I have no fear for me or my husband."

Alessandra didn't relish the sacrifices the job demanded. But she had come to accept them as useful to developing the character she needed to face the mafia. Her response to the mafia's romanticism and glamour remained what it had been in Messina: an insistence on the facts. To some, Alessandra knew, she could seem cold and aloof, living a gray half-life ruled by procedure, discipline, and evidence. She told herself she needed this distance—from mafiosi, from their victims, even from life—to preserve her perspective. Passion and blood and family and tragedy—that was the mafia, and the mafia was the enemy. She had to be the opposite: intellectual, forensic, and dispassionate.

By forty-one, what once had been girlish obstinacy had matured into stoicism and self-possession. In her office in the Palace of Justice, Alessandra kept her desk clear and her office spartan. Besides a photograph of the legendary Sicilian prosecutors Giovanni Falcone and Paolo Borsellino, she hung only a graphite drawing of Lady Justice and a pastel of the Strait of Messina. Among her staff, the young female prosecutor's icy focus was a favorite topic of discussion. She wasn't scared or emotional, as some of the men had predicted. Rather, she was unwavering, scrupulous, and unnervingly calm— *legale*, they said—her rebukes all the more crushing for their dispassion, her smiles all the more disarming for their unexpectedness.

Inside this narrow, monotone life, Alessandra permitted herself a few indulgences. Every August she and her husband took off on a foreign holiday without their bodyguards, telling no one where they were going—"the only time I can be free," she said. On a shelf in her office, she kept a collection of snow globes, sent to her by friends from their travels in Europe. Alessandra also liked to dress well. To court, she wore slim, dark suits over plain white blouses.

To the office, she wore woolen winter shawls with leather boots, or stretch jeans with a biker's jacket, or heels with a sleeveless summer dress, her toes and fingernails painted chocolate in winter and tangerine in summer. This was not about looking good to the world. Anti-mafia prosecutors were rarely seen by anyone. Rather, this was about freedom. To do her job and not be defined by it, to accept its restrictions and not be beaten by them, to face the threats of ten thousand mafiosi and respond with grace and elegance—that was true style and, in a world of male brutality, a display of adamant and unyielding femininity.

THROUGHOUT HER TIME in the north, Alessandra had kept a close watch on the southern battle against the mafia. It had been a long and bloody fight. After the state tried to stem *la mattanza* in the 1980s, judges, policemen, carabinieri, politicians, and prosecutors became targets, too. On May 23, 1992, the mafia detonated half a ton of explosives under an elevated highway outside the city on which Giovanni Falcone, Italy's most celebrated anti-mafia prosecutor, was driving with his wife and three police bodyguards. The explosion was so big it registered on Sicily's earthquake monitors. Hearing the news of Falcone's assassination, his coprosecutor Paolo Borsellino, who had grown up in the same Palermo neighborhood and had always been somewhat in Falcone's shadow, remarked, "Giovanni beat me again." Two months later, Borsellino and five policemen were killed by a car bomb outside the home of Borsellino's mother in Palermo. Six houses were leveled and fifty-one cars, vans, and trucks set on fire.

Falcone's death was to Italians what President John F. Kennedy's was to Americans: everyone can remember where they were when they heard the news. To the tight group of Sicilians like Alessandra who had taken up the fight against Cosa Nostra, the loss of their two champions was deeply personal. At the time, Alessandra was a twenty-four-year-old law graduate in Rome who had just begun training to be a magistrate. Falcone's and Borsellino's sacrifices only made the two prosecutors seem more heroic. "They were the inspiration for a generation," she said. "Their deaths made us stronger." To this day, the two prosecutors remain the titans against whom all Italian prosecutors measure themselves. A picture of either Falcone or Borsellino, and generally both, hangs on the wall of every anti-mafia prosecutor's office in Italy, often accompanied by a famous Falcone one-liner. "The mafia is a human phenomenon and, like all human phenomena, it had a beginning, an evolution, and will also have an end," was one favorite. "He who doesn't fear death dies only once," was another.

In time, even Cosa Nostra would acknowledge that the murders had been a miscalculation. They gave the prosecutors' political masters no choice but to abandon attempts to negotiate a peace with the mafia and try to crush it instead. Tens of thousands of soldiers were dispatched to Sicily. The two prosecutors' deaths also prompted renewed appreciation of their achievements. The chief accomplishment of Falcone, Borsellino, and their two fellow prosecutors, Giuseppe di Lello and Leonardo Guarnotta, was finally to disprove the grand Sicilian lie. After decades of denial, Cosa Nostra was exposed not as a myth or a movie but a global criminal organization, headquartered in Sicily, with extensive links to business and politics in Italy and around the world. The climax of their investigations, the Maxi Trial, saw 475 mafiosi in court, accused of offenses ranging from extortion to drug smuggling to 120 murders.

How had Falcone and Borsellino succeeded? Many of their accomplishments hinged on a new 1982 law, the crime of mafia association, which outlawed a mere relationship with the mafia, even without evidence of a criminal act. That effectively made it a crime just to be born into a mafia family and was aimed squarely at the omertà and close blood relations on which the mafia was built. The new legislation worked. First a handful, then scores, then hundreds of mafiosi turned *pentiti* (literally "penitents"). A host of otherwise innocent family members did the same. From their evidence, Italy's prosecutors were able to construct a picture of Cosa Nostra's internal structure for the first time.

The Sicilians' other innovation was to abandon the mercurial autonomy traditionally enjoyed by individual prosecutors. Independence from political masters, who were often the target of anti-mafia investigations, remained essential. But prosecutors' habitual individualism had often found expression in less helpful fashion, such as fighting each other for position. By contrast, Palermo's anti-mafia prosecutors worked as an indivisible team, the "anti-mafia pool," as they called themselves, which shared information, diffused responsibility, and cosigned all warrants. In that way, they ensured their work was coordinated and efficient, and never depended on the continuing good health of any one of them.

So it was that in the months after the deaths of Falcone and Borsellino, other prosecutors—first Gian Carlo Caselli; then the Sicilians Piero Grasso, Giuseppe Pignatone, and his deputy Michele Prestipino—picked up where their storied predecessors left off. And in a further decade and a half, the Palermo prosecutors and Palermo's elite flying squad largely finished what their predecessors had started. By the mid-2000s, a generation of Cosa Nostra's bosses were in jail, its links to senior politicians were exposed, and its rackets, while they still existed, were a shadow of what they had once been. Capping the prosecutors' success, in April 2006 at a small, sparsely furnished cottage outside Corleone, Pignatone and Prestipino were present for the arrest of Cosa Nostra's remaining *capo tutti*, seventy-three-year-old Bernardo Provenzano, who had been on the run for forty-three years.

ON VISITS BACK to Sicily, Alessandra saw the transformation in her homeland. In the streets of Palermo and Messina, a new popular movement called Addiopizzo (Good-bye *Pizzo*, mafia slang for extortion) united shopkeepers, farmers, and restaurateurs in a refusal to pay protection. Thousands of anti-mafia protesters marched arm in arm through the streets. Cosa Nostra, in its weakened state, was unable to respond. When mafiosi firebombed an anti-mafia trattoria in Palermo, the city's residents found the owners new premises on a busy junction in the center of town where they opened up again and quickly became one of the city's most celebrated destinations. In time, Palermo and Messina could boast city-center shops run by an activist group called Libera (Free), which sold olive oil, sauces, wine, and pasta made exclusively by farmers who refused to pay protection to Cosa Nostra.

But as the war on Cosa Nostra wound down, a fresh threat took its place. During *la mattanza,* across the water in Calabria the 'Ndrangheta had initially toyed with joining Cosa Nostra's war on the state, and even killed a couple of policemen for itself. But the Calabrians soon realized that with the Sicilians and the government so distracted, the strategic play was not to side with Cosa Nostra but to take its narco business. The 'Ndrangheta paid the Sicilians' debts to the Colombian cocaine cartels, effectively buying them out as the Latin Americans' smuggling partners.

Carlo Cosco arrived in the north in 1987, the same year as Alessandra. Carlo's intention was not to fit into northern Italy, however, but to conquer it—and his timing was perfect. The 'Ndrangheta was pushing its drug empire north across Europe. Milan, Cosco's new patch, was a key beachhead in that expansion. And there had rarely been a business like cocaine smuggling in Europe in the 1990s and 2000s. After saturating the U.S. market, South American producers were looking to other territories for growth. Europe, with twice the population of North America and a similar standard of living but, in the 1980s, a quarter of its cocaine consumption, was the obvious opportunity. With the 'Ndrangheta's help, the cartels flooded the continent with cocaine. By 2010, the European cocaine market, at 124 tons a year, was close to matching the American one. In Spain and Britain, the drug became as middle-class as Volvos and weekend farmers' markets.

In the estimate of Italy's prosecutors, the 'Ndrangheta accounted for three-quarters of that. So rich, and so fast, did the 'Ndrangheta grow, it was hard to keep track. On wiretaps, carabinieri overheard 'Ndranghetisti talking about buried sacks of cash rotting in the hills, and writing off the loss of a few million here or there as inconsequential. At Gioia Tauro port on Calabria's west coast, officers were seizing hundreds of kilos of cocaine at a time from shipping containers but reckoned that they found less than 10 percent of what was passing through. A glimpse of quite how big the 'Ndrangheta had grown came in the early hours of August 15, 2007—the Ascension Day national holiday in Italy—when two 'Ndrangheta gunmen shot and killed four men and two boys aged eighteen and sixteen who were connected to a rival clan outside a pizzeria in Duisburg, in Germany's industrial heartland. Northern Europe was apparently now 'Ndrangheta territory.

Italy, and Europe, had a new mafia war to fight. And though its empire was now global, the 'Ndrangheta remained as attached to Calabria as Cosa Nostra had been to Sicily. In April 2008, two of the prosecutors who had humbled the Sicilian mafia, Giuseppe Pignatone, now sixty, and Michele Prestipino, fifty, had their requests for transfer to Calabria accepted. Their friend and ally in the Palermo flying squad, Renato Cortese, went with them. As the three cast around for a team who might do to the 'Ndrangheta what had been done to Cosa Nostra, they realized they faced a problem. Many Italian prosecutors balked at the idea of an assignment to what was universally regarded as both a backwater and enemy territory. In

2008, only twelve of the eighteen prosecutor positions in Calabria were filled, and the province had just five anti-mafia specialists. In Milan, however, Alessandra applied. She was ready to return to the south, she told her bosses. She understood the work would be "riskier" and more "difficult and complicated." That just made it all the more urgent.[4]

IN APRIL 2009, Alessandra and her husband packed up their apartment in Milan and flew south, following the sun down the west coast of Italy. As the plane started its descent, Alessandra saw the Aeolian Islands to the west, then Sicily and the snows of Etna to the south, then the streets of Messina below. As she passed over the broad blue of the Strait, she regarded the white foam trails of the rusty freighters as they rounded the tip of the Italian peninsula and turned north to Naples, Genoa, Marseille, and Barcelona. Not for the first time, it occurred to Alessandra that the lazy arc of this shore would, from a suitable distance, form the shape of a very large toe.

Alessandra's new security detail met her at Reggio airport. They took the expressway into town as a two-car convoy. The road climbed high above the city, skirting the dusty terraces that led up into the Calabrian hinterland. Below were the cobbled streets and crumbling apartment blocks whose names were familiar to Alessandra from dozens of investigations into shootings and firebombings. Somewhere down there, too, were the bunkers, entire underground homes where 'Ndrangheta bosses would hide for years, surfacing through hidden doors and tunnels to order new killings and plan new business.

As they reached the northern end of Reggio, the two cars took an off-ramp and plunged down into the city, dropping through twisting hairpins, bumping over ruts and potholes, plunging ever lower through tumbling, narrow streets before bottoming out just behind the seafront. Once on the flat, the drivers accelerated and flashed through the streets, past abandoned hotels, boarded-up cinemas, and empty villas before turning back up toward the hills and sweeping through the gates of a carabinieri barracks. In its 3,500 years of existence, Reggio had been a Mediterranean power, the birthplace of the kingdom of Italia, a Norman fortress, and a Riviera resort. Now it was bandit country. Entire neighborhoods were off-limits to carabinieri or prosecutors. For Alessandra, home for the next five years would be a bare-walled officer's apartment jammed into the barracks roof with a view of the Strait of Messina.

IV

D ENISE SLEPT FOR an hour and a half the night Lea disappeared.[1] The next morning, November 25, 2009, she ate breakfast with her aunt Renata, walked with her to the kindergarten where she worked, then spent the morning silently smoking cigarettes with Andrea and Domenico in a nearby piazza. In the afternoon, Carlo phoned and told her to meet him at Bar Barbara. On the way there, Denise ran into a cousin from Lea's side of the family, Francesco Ceraudo, who lived in Genoa. She told Francesco that Lea was missing and asked him if he had seen her. Francesco blanched. "Do you know anything?" Denise asked. "Absolutely not," he said, and walked on.

The entire Cosco clan were in Bar Barbara: Carlo, his brothers Vito and Giuseppe, and Aunt Renata. Giuseppe and Renata were playing video poker in the corner. Giuseppe won fifty euros and, clumsily, gave the winnings to Denise. After a while, the carabinieri called Denise on her mobile and said they needed to speak to her. During the call, a squad car pulled up outside. Vito asked what was happening. "Lea's missing," Carlo told him.

The Coscos weren't about to let one of their own go to the carabinieri alone. Vito dropped Carlo and Denise at the station around 8:30 P.M., and father and daughter entered together. Inside, however, carabiniere Marshal Christian Persurich told Carlo he had to talk to Denise unaided. Persurich showed Denise to an interview room. He informed her that in Calabria her aunt Marisa had reported Lea missing. Marisa had also told the carabinieri that Lea had testified against the 'Ndrangheta and that she and Denise had spent time in witness protection. Lea had now been missing for more than twenty-four hours. Persurich needed the whole story. Denise should take her time and leave nothing out. The interview would be strictly confidential.

Denise nodded. "If my mother's missing," she began, "then it's probably because she's been killed by my father."

MARSHAL PERSURICH INTERVIEWED Denise for five hours, finishing just before 2 A.M. Denise emerged to find Carlo pacing the waiting room, demanding that the officers let him read her statement. Seeing his daughter, Carlo confronted her. "What did you tell these people?!"

"You asked us to Milan," Denise replied blankly. "We spent a few days together. You were meant to pick her up. But you couldn't find her. Then we looked for her all over."

Carlo looked unconvinced. Five hours for that?

On the way back to her cousins', Carlo and Denise stopped at a restaurant, the Green Dragon, named after the symbol of Milan. Inside was Carmine Venturino, the cousin who had given Lea some hash to smoke. Carmine had a babyish face and looked like a born truant, and Denise had liked him from the moment she met him at a wedding in Calabria the previous summer. But that night they had nothing to say to each other. After Carmine and Carlo had a brief, hushed discussion, Carlo walked his daughter back to Viale Montello. There, Denise slept in Andrea's room for a second night.

The next morning, Carlo, Denise, and a friend of Carlo's, Rosario Curcio, saw a lawyer in town. Carlo told the lawyer he wanted to see Denise's statements. The lawyer asked Denise what she'd told the carabinieri. Denise repeated what she had told Carlo: that she and her mother had come up to Milan to spend a few days with her father, and Lea had vanished on their last night. She began crying. The lawyer said he could arrange to have Lea's disappearance publicized on national television. There was a show, *Chi l'ha Visto?* (*Have You Seen Them?*), which appealed for information on missing people. "Oh, for fuck's sake!" cried Carlo. The lawyer didn't get it at all. Carlo stood up and walked out, leaving Denise crying in the lawyer's office.

After Denise recovered, she, Carlo, and Rosario drove to a beauty salon owned by Rosario's girlfriend, Elisa. Carlo took Rosario aside for another quiet talk. Elisa asked Denise what was going on. Denise burst into tears once more and told Elisa that her mother had gone missing two nights before. Elisa said that was strange, because Rosario had vanished for a few hours the same evening. They'd had a date, said Elisa, but Rosario had canceled, then switched off his phone. When she finally got through to him around 9 P.M., he'd told Elisa something about having to fix a car with Carmine. It didn't make sense. Why the sudden rush to fix a car? Why at night? Denise was about to say something when Carlo interrupted to say he was taking Denise back to Viale Montello. She slept in her cousin's room for a third night.

The next day, three days since Lea had disappeared, Denise detected an improvement in Carlo's mood. He announced that he and Denise would drive to Reggio Emilia, not far from Bologna, to stay the night with another cousin. They left in the early afternoon. While her father drove, Denise watched silently as the winter sun flashed through the poplar trees like a searchlight through the bars of a fence. How could her mother just vanish? How could anyone be there one minute, and there be no sign of her the next? How would she ever talk to her father again?

In Reggio Emilia, Denise went to bed early while Carlo and his cousin went out for dinner. The following morning, Carlo drove Denise back to Milan, changed cars to a blue BMW, and announced that he and Denise were leaving immediately for Calabria with two other friends. As they were packing, Carmine arrived to say good-bye. Denise was struck by his expression. Stiff and formal, she thought. Something about the way he wouldn't look her in the eye.

From the back seat of the BMW, Denise watched as Milan's grand piazzas and chic boutiques gave way to the flat, gray farmland north of Florence, then the rust-colored hills of Tuscany and Umbria, and finally, as the sun sank into the sea to the west, the towering black volcanoes around Naples and Pompeii. It was dark by the time they crossed into Calabria. Denise felt the road change from smooth asphalt to worn, undulating waves. The car negotiated an almost endless succession of roadworks, then plunged into the steep valley of Cosenza, skimming the cliffs as it wound down into the abyss before hitting the valley floor.

Soon Denise felt the car turn left and accelerate back up into the hills. She registered the tighter turns and the sound of tires scrabbling on loose stones. The cold of the window dried her tear tracks to a salty crust. As the car filled with the smell of pines, the conversation between the three men took on a giddy, jubilant tone. "The only thing in my head was my mother," she said. "I was just sitting in the back, crying. But the others—they were so happy. Chatting and smiling and joking and laughing out loud."

After an hour of climbing, the car crested a mountain pass and began to descend. At the edge of a forest, by the side of a stream, they came to a small village. They were heading to the one place where Carlo could be sure Denise would never speak out of turn again. Pagliarelle.

PAGLIARELLE COMES FROM the word *pagliari*, meaning "shelter." The name commemorated how for thousands of years, as the winter snows melted, Calabria's shepherds would lead their sheep and goats up a track into the mountains and find a stream on whose banks they would graze their animals for weeks at a time. Keeping one eye out for wolves and another on the sea on the horizon, the men would collect pinewood, barbecue goat meat, drink wine, and sleep in a handful of open-sided shacks that they roofed with fir and clay. In the twentieth century, the track leading from the nearby town of Petilia Policastro was tarred, electricity arrived, and the shepherds' rest grew into a modest settlement of gray-stone, red-tiled townhouses gathered around a small central square. The name survived, as did the stream, which was channeled into a fountain in the piazza where Lea's and Carlo's mothers would send them as children to fill buckets for the day.

It was here, high up in the frozen, granite mountains of eastern Calabria, that Denise found herself walking a tightrope of pretense in the weeks after Lea's disappearance. Lea hadn't just been Denise's mother. After so many years alone together, she had defined Denise's life. Now Denise found herself back in the place that her mother had tried to escape for so long, adrift among the people she was sure had killed her. It was impossible to know how to behave. With no body and no funeral, Denise couldn't mourn. Carlo was telling people that Lea had run off, maybe to Australia, and Denise found herself having to make believe that her murderous father hadn't really killed her courageous mother at all but that, rather, her fickle mother had abandoned her husband and only child and jetted off to a new life in the sun. Denise knew the way she looked so much like Lea—the same hair, the same cheekbones—made her an immediate object of suspicion. Worse, Carlo was making so much of Denise's return. After years of problems with his wife and daughter, the boss finally had both his women where they belonged—and he wanted everyone to know. Ten days after Lea's disappearance, Carlo organized an eighteenth birthday party for Denise, inviting hundreds of people from Pagliarelle and Petilia Policastro and even buying Denise a car. When Denise refused to go, Carlo went ahead with the party anyway.

Mostly, Denise spent her days trying to learn from her aunt Marisa, with whom she was now living. Ever since Lea had first denounced the 'Ndrangheta in 1996, Marisa had been forced to pull off a daily performance in Pagliarelle. Convincing an entire village they needed to have no doubts about her had required Marisa not just to tell lies but to live them, too. In her mind, Marisa suffocated any affection she had for Lea and focused instead on the resentment she felt toward her sister for the trouble she had caused. Denise realized she would have to learn to hate her mother, too. "I knew my aunt and her family," said Denise. "I knew how they thought. My idea was to understand their mentality and see if I could also work out how to live there. I didn't want to end up like my mother. I wanted to keep living."

V

D ENISE WASN'T THE only one living a lie in Pagliarelle. Watching Lea's daughter offered the carabinieri one of their best leads for finding out what had happened to Lea. But any reminder of the state's relationship with Lea, or any hint that it might continue with her daughter, would be enough to condemn Denise. The carabinieri decided the state's only visible presence in Pagliarelle should remain the lone village policeman. Unseen and unheard, however, scores of officers would watch Pagliarelle day and night.

Over the years, the challenge posed by the mafia had compelled Italy's security services to innovate. To pursue violent 'Ndranghetisti through mountain terrain had led the Calabrian carabinieri to form a unique Special Forces–style squad, the *cacciatori* (hunters), a unit made up of snipers, bomb-disposal experts, heavy-weapons operators, helicopter pilots, and Alpinists. The sight of a *cacciatori* helicopter gunship flying low over the Aspromonte mountains was a corrective to anyone who doubted the state was fighting a war in southern Italy.

But even the *cacciatori*'s resources paled next to those commanded by Italy's covert intelligence units. Around the world, only a few specialized police units are permitted to eavesdrop on suspects' telephone calls or spy on them electronically. In Italy, a measure of the mafia threat was that all three police forces—the domestic police, the militaristic carabinieri, and the Guardia di Finanza, which specialized in economic crime—had surveillance divisions that employed thousands. In 2009, the Italian state was tapping a total of 119,553 phones and listening to 11,119 bugs. Almost no type of reconnaissance was forbidden. To establish targets' whereabouts, plainclothes officers followed them, filmed them through hidden minicameras and larger zoom lenses set up at a distance—several miles across the valley, in the case of Pagliarelle—and tracked their phones' GPS signals. To find out what the subjects were saying, they hacked their text messages, phone calls, e-mails, and social media chats.

In Reggio, almost an entire floor of the gracious building that served as the city's carabinieri headquarters had been transformed into a humming, indoor field of electronic espionage. At the center was a control room from which chases and operations were coordinated. Around it were twenty smaller offices, each dedicated to a different surveillance operation. Every room was packed with scores of screens, servers, modems, and snaking, thick black wires. Working without interruption in six-hour shifts that ran continuously, day and night, officers in Reggio and an identical team in Milan had been following bosses like Carlo for years. Chosen for their facility with dialects and their ability to inhabit the skins of their subjects, the operators knew their subjects so well they could decipher the meaning of their words from a euphemism or even an inflection in a person's voice. The Calabrian teams also had a particular skill with bugs. They planted devices in cars, homes, and gardens. They bugged a basement laundry whose underground, signal-cutting location made it a favorite 'Ndrangheta meeting place. They bugged an orange orchard where a boss liked to hold meetings, and for the same reason bugged a forest. One time they even bugged a road where one boss took walks, ripping up the asphalt and re-laying it with tar embedded with listening devices.

Such entrepreneurialism brought results. In early 2008, the squad hunting 'Ndrangheta supremo Pasquale Condello, by then fifty-seven and on the run for eighteen years, observed that every two weeks, as though he were on a schedule, Condello's nephew would shake his surveillance in the center of Reggio, swapping from the back of one motorbike to another in a series of choreographed changes. The carabinieri were convinced the maneuvers were in preparation for meeting Condello. One day, an officer noticed that the nephew always wore the same crash helmet. A few nights later, a carabinieri officer punctured the muffler on a car, then drove it up and down outside the nephew's house to cover the sound of a second officer breaking in and switching the helmet with an identical one implanted with a tracer. When it was time for the next rendezvous, the carabinieri followed the nephew through his usual multiride acrobatics, using the tracer, to a small pink house in a back alley on the south side of Reggio Calabria. Surrounded by more than a hundred *cacciatori*, Condello surrendered without a fight.

THIS WAS THE front line on which Alessandra had imagined herself working when she transferred to Calabria. But a staffing shortfall meant that on arrival she was assigned to Reggio as a city judge. Her knowledge of Milan and Calabria and her interest in 'Ndrangheta women notwithstanding, she was forced to watch the Lea Garofalo case unfold from afar.

Still, there were advantages to such a gentle start. For one, the undemanding hours allowed plenty of time to learn the lay of the land. Alessandra kept pace with active investigations by chatting with officers at the carabinieri's headquarters, a short walk from the Palace of Justice. At other moments, she researched the 'Ndrangheta's history. In her office, she assembled piles of case files, carabinieri surveillance transcripts, *pentiti* statements, academic papers, history books, and even accounts of Calabrian folklore.

To a Sicilian like Alessandra, the origins of the 'Ndrangheta felt familiar. The organization was at its strongest away from the big cities in the hundreds of small mountain hamlets like Pagliarelle nestling in the valleys that led away from the coast. As in Sicily, many of these settlements had been the cradle of some of Europe's first civilizations. Alessandra read how paintings of bulls dating from 12,000 B.C. had been found in Calabrian caves. By 530 B.C., Pythagoras was teaching mathematics in Kroton (later Crotone) on the plain below Pagliarelle while the citizens of nearby Sybaris were drinking wine piped to their homes by vinoducts. Like Sicilians, Calabrians had their own archaic language, in this case Grecanico, a Greek dialect left over from the Middle Ages when Calabria had been part of the Byzantine Empire.

Something else that Calabria had in common with Sicily: from the beginning, it was a land apart. Many of the valleys were accessible only from the sea, naturally isolated behind steep mountainsides, thick pine forests, and, in winter, snows that could cut off villages for months. For thousands of years, there had been no one to defend the families who lived in these valleys. They tended olive trees, fished the ocean, and scanned the horizon as invading armies sailed by from Rome, Germany, Arabia, Spain, France, Italy, and America. They were poor, resilient, and resolutely autonomous, and as Italy's north steadily eclipsed the south, their estrangement from the rest of the Italian peninsula only grew. When in 1861 a group of northerners began to send bureaucrats, teachers, and carabinieri into the valleys to proclaim the rule of a newly united Italy, the families repudiated, thwarted, and occasionally killed the colonizers.

At first, the families had no connection to the mafia. The phenomenon of organized crime first emerged in Italy in the 1820s with the Camorra in Naples and then in the 1840s and 1850s with what became Cosa Nostra in Sicily. In both cases, ordinary criminals found themselves in jail with educated, bourgeois revolutionaries who were fighting foreign domination and feudalism, and who often organized themselves in masonic sects. As patriots, the rebels taught the future mafiosi the importance of a righteous cause. As freemasons, they taught them hierarchy, and the power of legend and ceremony.

When Sicily simultaneously unified with the north of Italy and ended feudalism, the ensuing chaos gave Sicily's criminals a chance to put these new lessons to work. Though the northern dukes and generals leading unification described it as an act of modernization, many southerners regarded it as another foreign conquest. Adding to the discontent, the immediate effect of the advent of private property in Sicily was a rash of property disputes. To protect themselves, landowners, towns, and villages set up vigilante groups who, for a fee, protected their assets, hunted down thieves, and settled disputes. To be effective, these groups required men who could intimidate others. Jail-hardened criminals were a natural choice.

Soon these bands of enforcers were calling themselves mafiosi, a term derived from the Sicilian word *mafiusu*, meaning "swagger" or "bravado." Their new name was, in effect, a rebranding. Violent criminals had always been able to inspire fear. The mafiosi wanted respect, too. While they didn't deny a criminal self-interest, the mafiosi insisted theirs was an honorable endeavor: protecting poor southerners from rapacious landowners and an oppressive north. Of course, Sicilians soon learned that the people from whom they needed most protection were the mafiosi themselves. The protection racket was born.

When organized crime reached Calabria a generation or two later, Alessandra read, it had repeated many of the same patterns. Like Cosa Nostra, Calabria's mafia began in jail. One of Calabria's main administrative centers was Palmi, a hill town with views out over the east coast that, as the provincial capital of the Gioia Tauro *piano*, the estuary plain, possessed a police station, a courtroom, and a prison. In the spring of 1888, gangs of hoodlums, many of them graduates of the town jail, began staging knife fights in Palmi's taverns, brothels, and piazzas. As the heat rose with the coming summer, it seemed to stoke a violent hooliganism among the ex-cons, who began rampaging through the streets, slashing citizens with knives and razors, extorting money from gamblers, prostitutes, and landowners, rustling cattle and goats, and even threatening magistrates, the police, and newspaper editors.

In those early days, the prototype gangsters called themselves camorristi, a straight copy of the Naples mafia, or *picciotti*, a word that the British historian John Dickie translates as "lads with attitude."[1] If they were united, it was chiefly by their dandyish style: tattoos, extravagant quiffs, silk scarves knotted at the neck, and trousers that were tight at the thighs and flared at the ankle. In his history of the three big Italian mafias, *Mafia Brotherhoods*, Dickie describes how *picciotto* culture spread across Calabria in months.[2] Like all young male fashions, it might have died just as rapidly had it not penetrated the hill valleys. There the families had little taste for the *picciotti*'s dress. But the remote and defensive interior of Calabria was fertile territory for a movement whose methods were mostly physical and whose distrust of the state was pronounced. And just as they ran everything in the valleys, the families were soon running the *picciotteria*.

A central goal for all mafias was to create a consensus around power. Whenever the question of power arose—political, economic, social, divine—the answer had to be the mafia. It was the peculiar luck of the Italian mafias that circumstances conspired to graft their enterprise onto the most durable of southern Italian power structures: the family. In Sicily, the mafia came to be known as Cosa Nostra, meaning "our thing," and Our Thing was, really, Our Family Secret, an outsmarting of the northern state built on the intimacy and obedience of kin. Likewise in Calabria, the valley families gave the *picciotti* a ready-made hierarchy, order, legitimacy, and secrecy. It was this—loyalty to blood and homeland—that was the foundation of all the horrors to come.

By the turn of the twentieth century, Calabria's street hoodlums had been organized into local cells called 'ndrine, each with its own turf, ranks, and boss. At first, picciotti were useful for small matters: appropriating a neighbor's field for the boss's cows, resisting rent demands from fussing landlords, or extracting protection money from the neighborhood trattoria. Highway robbery, smuggling, kidnapping, and loan-sharking were lucrative earners for more enterprising picciotti. Bosses also took on additional duties like adjudicating property disputes or defending women's honor.

But as the picciotti endured successive crackdowns by the authorities, some wondered how they might turn the tables on the state. If the source of the wider world's power came from money, they reasoned, then maybe the way to attack that outside world was to venture out into it, steal its money, and take its power?

The Calabrian mafia was soon using its money to buy favors from the carabinieri and the judiciary. After that came bribes to political parties, mayors' offices, the state bureaucracy, and the Italian parliament. In time, the families were also able to infiltrate these institutions with their own men. The insiders then defrauded and embezzled, diverting public funds to mafia-owned contracting businesses such as construction firms, refuse collectors, and dockers. Elections were rigged and more allegiances bought. Those who could not be corrupted or intimidated were beaten, firebombed, or killed.

All this felt familiar to a Sicilian like Alessandra. But the Calabrians outdid their peers in two respects. Where the Sicilians recruited from a particular area, the Calabrians relied on family: almost without exception, picciotti were either born into an 'ndrina or married into it. And while the Sicilians certainly spun stories about themselves, the Calabrians dreamed up legends that wove together

honor, religion, family, and southern Italian separatism into an elaborate and almost impenetrable veil of misdirection.

By the early twentieth century, 'Ndranghetisti were tracing their
origins to three medieval knights-errant. These figures crop up in
mafia creation myths from Asia to Africa to Europe.[3] In the 'Ndrangheta version, the knights were Spanish brothers—Osso, Mastrosso,
and Carcagnosso—who had fled their homeland after avenging their
sister's rape. Landing on the tiny island of Favignana off Sicily's west
coast and taking shelter in damp and cold sea caverns, the trio nursed
a sense of righteous grievance and steadfast family loyalty for thirty
long and uncomfortably damp years. Eventually their discussions
became the basis for a brotherhood founded on mutual defense. With
the Honored Society sworn to protect all members, and they it, no
outsider would ever think of shaming the brothers and their families
again. And when the brothers felt ready to take their creation to the
world, Mastrosso traveled to Naples to set up the Camorra in the
name of the Madonna, Osso sailed to Sicily and founded Cosa Nostra
in the name of Saint George, and Carcagnosso took a land between
his two brothers—Calabria—where he established the 'Ndrangheta
in the name of Saint Michael, the Archangel.

The story is, of course, bunk. The Calabrian mafia is not hundreds of years old but barely 150. The story of the three knights also
seems copied from that of the Garduña, a mythical fifteenth-century
Spanish criminal society whose founding legend would have been
familiar to 'Ndranghetisti from the time when Spain ruled Calabria.
The irony is that most historians have concluded the Garduña was
itself a fabrication.[4] This, then, was mafiosi trying to fool others
with a piece of gangster fiction that had, in fact, fooled them.

This was far from the only example of mafia make-believe, however. The 'Ndrangheta's ancient-sounding name did not derive from
a venerable heritage but, as Dickie uncovered, was a modern artifice
that first surfaced in police reports in the 1920s and in newspaper

stories in the 1950s.[5] Alessandra found more recent mafia fictions in
the form of Internet videos ripping off scenes from American gangster movies like *The Godfather* and *Goodfellas* and set to Calabrian folk
songs. The lyrics to these melodies were hardly poetry but no less
chilling for that:

> *Keep the honor of the family.*
> *Avenge my father.*
> *I have to get good with guns and knives*
> *Because I can't stop thinking about it.*
> *The pain in my heart—*
> *It can only be stopped if I avenge my father.*

Then there were the "ancient" rituals. For a boss's son, Alessandra read, these could begin soon after birth. A newborn boy would be
laid kicking and screaming on a bed, a key next to his left hand and a
knife by his right, denoting the state and the mafia. An 'Ndrangheta
mother's first duty was to ensure, with a few careful nudges, that her
boy grasped the knife and sealed his destiny. In *Tired of Killing: The
Autobiography of a Repentant 'Ndranghetista*, Alessandra read about
the early life of Antonio Zagari, the son of an 'Ndrangheta boss who
turned informant in 1990.[6] In his book, Zagari described a probation of two years, during which a teenage *picciotto* was expected to
prove his worth by committing crimes and even killing, as well as
learning by heart the fable of Osso, Mastrosso, and Carcagnosso
and a set of rules and social prescriptions. After that came a formal
initiation ceremony. The ritual began when Zagari was led into a
darkened room in which a group of 'Ndranghetisti were standing
in a circle. At first, Zagari was excluded. The boss addressed the
'Ndranghetisti, asking if they were "comfortable."

"Very comfortable," they replied. "With what?"

"With the rules," said the boss.

"Very comfortable," came the reply once more.

The boss then "baptized" the meeting in the name of the Honored Society "as our ancestors Osso, Mastrosso, and Carcagnosso baptized it . . . with irons and chains." He ceremoniously confiscated any weapons. The congregation confirmed their loyalty to the society on pain of "five or six dagger thrusts to the chest." The boss then likened their common endeavor to "a ball that goes wandering around the world as cold as ice, as hot as fire, and as fine as silk." After the members of the circle affirmed three times that they were ready to accept a new member, they opened their ranks to admit the newcomer. The boss then cut a cross on Zagari's finger so that it bled over a burning image of Saint Michael while he intoned: "As the fire burns this image, so shall you burn if you stain yourself with infamy."

That was the cue for Zagari to take his oath: "I swear before the organized and faithful society, represented by our honored and wise boss and by all the members, to carry out all the duties for which I am responsible and all those which are imposed on me—if necessary even with my blood."

Finally, the boss kissed Zagari on both cheeks, recited the rules of the society, and delivered a homily to humility, the island of Favignana, and blood—which, in case anyone was lost, was the essence of the icy, fiery, silky, and world-wandering ball he had mentioned earlier.

It was a wonder anyone kept a straight face, thought Alessandra. Certainly, the phony medievalism of the 'Ndrangheta's performances made serious historians choke. Dickie likened the "solemn ravings" of its initiation ritual to a scout ceremony that crossed *Lord of the Flies* with Monty Python. One of Italy's most eminent mafia historians, Enzo Ciconte, was just as dismissive of the 'Ndrangheta's "Red Riding Hood fantasies."[7] But Ciconte cautioned that ridiculous did not mean meaningless. "No group of people can last long just by using violence, just by killing, stealing, and rustling—they need some sort of faith or ideology," he said. "The 'Ndrangheta had no tradition. They had to invent one."

It was a good point, thought Alessandra. What mattered with faith was not plausibility but belief. Most of the main religions clung to unlikely myths and holy stories, which they called miracles or acts of God. Few of them were ever hurt by others laughing at them—quite the opposite. More to the point, a lie was just that: a fib, a fiction, a deceit. No one was claiming the 'Ndrangheta's bosses believed it. After all, they were the ones telling it.

A better question was why the 'Ndrangheta chiefs found such decorous fantasies expedient. The answer was to be found in their spectacular rise. However contrived and derivative the cult of the 'Ndrangheta might appear to academic examination, it had gained the organization the loyalty and secrecy of its members, the fear and respect of ordinary Calabrians, and, as a result, a thick cloak of opacity under which it hid from the world. The 'Ndrangheta's stories might have appealed to Calabrians because of their own distrust of the state or their sense of theater, or simply because they were handed down from father to son with the solemn conviction of a sacred truth. The point was they worked. Myth was how the 'Ndrangheta assumed a moral purpose when it was self-evidently immoral, how it colored itself romantic and divine when it was base and profane, and how it convinced others it was their righteous champion even as it robbed and murdered them. Myth was how those inside the organization were persuaded they were following a higher code and those outside it found themselves stumped by even the simplest questions, such as who was who. It was all an enormous lie. But it was a lie that explained how, almost without anyone noticing, a small group of families from the wild hills of Italy's south had become the twenty-first century's most formidable mafia.

———

ALESSANDRA BECAME FASCINATED by the intricacies of the deception. The 'Ndrangheta was an extraordinary puzzle, a multilevel mosaic. From transcripts of tapped phone calls and bugged conversations, she discovered 'Ndranghetisti had their own language, *baccagghju*, a slang based on Grecanico whose meaning was obscure to almost everyone but initiates. Even when they spoke Italian, 'Ndranghetisti used a code of metaphors to disguise their meaning. An 'Ndrangheta family in criminal partnership with another would describe itself as "walking with" that other family. Rather than demand protection money outright, 'Ndranghetisti would request a "donation for the cousins," an allusion to those men in jail whose families needed support. For a boss to describe a man as "disturbing" or "troubling" was for him to pass an oblique but unequivocal death sentence on him. The euphemisms could be highly contorted. *Pizzo*, the word for an extortion payment, was a term whose origins were the subject of academic dispute, but according to one explanation, was the "piece" of ground on which a nineteenth-century prisoner had slept in jail, which were ranked according to their proximity to the boss. Outside jail in the twentieth century, it had come to denote the tribute that a boss expected from real estate inside his territory.

Deciphering the true meaning of 'Ndrangheta speak was a constant struggle. "You have to become more perceptive, more capable of decrypting," Alessandra would tell her husband over dinner in their apartment. "Mafiosi very rarely make a direct threat. Instead, they send messages with a dual meaning." Even the smallest gesture could carry the utmost importance. "They can order a murder just by looking at someone from the prisoner cage in court," she said.

One of the 'Ndrangheta's most audacious lies was its relationship with the church. The 'Ndrangheta was plainly an unchristian organization. But since it came from the most Roman Catholic of lands, it simply insisted the opposite was true. It invoked the saints, especially the Madonna and Saint Michael, the Archangel. It mimicked prayer and church services in its rituals. And it co-opted and bred priests. At Mass, some priests in 'Ndrangheta areas would exhort their congregants to resist outsiders. On saints' days, they directed celebrants to bow statues of the Madonna before the *capo*'s house, while at Easter the honor of bearing statues of Jesus, Saint John, and the Virgin was reserved for *picciotti*. The most stunning example of the 'Ndrangheta subverting Christianity happened on September 2 every year, when crowds of thousands gathered at the small town of San Luca in the Aspromonte mountains for the festival of the Madonna di Polsi. Among the pilgrims were hundreds of 'Ndranghetisti, including the heads of all the clans, who since at least 1901 had used the event as a cover for the 'Ndrangheta's annual meeting, the *gran crimine*. In plain sight, the bosses would sit at a table laden with pasta and goat sauce, present their annual accounts—what they had earned, who they had killed—and elect a new *capo crimine* for the coming year. "The church is very responsible in all of this," Alessandra would say. "It's guilty of some terrible, terrible, *terrible* things."

Though the organization found Christianity useful, Alessandra concluded that at its core the 'Ndrangheta was more of a blood cult. Blood was the bond between the families that were the 'Ndrangheta's strength. The act of spilling blood was also revered as a source of fearsome power. That had led to some unforgiving 'Ndrangheta feuds. The Duisburg massacre of 2007—which police identified as an attack on an 'Ndrangheta initiation celebration when a burned picture of Saint Michael was found in the pocket of the dead eighteen-year-old—was the latest atrocity in a quarrel between two clans from San Luca. The feud had begun in 1991 when a group of boys from one family threw rotten eggs at the window of a bar owned by another. Including Duisburg, nine people had since died. Many more had been injured. To avoid being shot, 'Ndranghetisti in San Luca would hide themselves in the trunk of a car just to travel one hundred yards. Killings were timed for maximum horror. The year before Duisburg, a boss from one clan was paralyzed by a bullet that passed through his spine as he stood on a balcony cradling his newborn son. In revenge, a rival boss's wife was shot dead in her family home on Christmas Day.

Why the ruthlessness? For the 'Ndrangheta, the answer was easy: to instill fear and reap power. For individual 'Ndranghetisti, the question was more vexing. Why be an 'Ndranghetista if your fate was to spend lengthy stretches in prison, inflict unspeakable violence on your neighbors, and, in all probability, die young? Alessandra decided it came back to the lie. The 'Ndrangheta had used its fantasies about honor, sacrifice, loyalty, and courage to build a prison around its young men, trapping them in a claustrophobic sect based on blood and butchery. Pride in the 'Ndrangheta's rural heritage even encouraged some 'Ndranghetisti to imbue their violence with a rustic aesthetic. Pigs often featured. A family targeted for intimidation might discover the throats of all its male pigs had been slit. On one occasion, the carabinieri recorded an 'Ndranghetista boasting how he beat another man unconscious, then fed his living body to his own pigs. The bloodthirstiness could also be literal. More than once, men loyal to an assassinated boss were observed to rush to the scene of the killing, dip their handkerchiefs in the departed *capo*'s blood, and press the dripping cloth to their lips.

ALESSANDRA REALIZED THAT the 'Ndrangheta's cult of blood, family, and tradition also accounted for its oppression of its women. That misogynist tyranny was real enough. Driving through small-town Calabria, Alessandra rarely saw women out of doors and almost never unaccompanied. Nevertheless, it was with a sinking sense of inevitability that she read that the 'Ndrangheta's conservative values were yet another affectation.

As long ago as 1892, the 'Ndrangheta had admitted two women highwaymen into its ranks. John Dickie found court records from the 1930s showing that the *picciotti* once had a pronounced personal and professional attachment to prostitution as both pimps and johns. But it seemed that the 'Ndrangheta later dispensed with prostitution because, though the trade was lucrative, it was built on qualities like infidelity, loose discipline, and double standards, which were inimical to order and control. The closed, buttoned-up, isolated family culture of traditional Calabria, on the other hand, was perfect for organized crime. Family ties were also how the 'Ndrangheta fashioned a global criminal octopus out of the pattern of Calabrian emigration to the United States, Canada, Australia, South Africa, and Latin America in the 1920s.

The more she read, the more Alessandra realized that the 'Ndrangheta's true genius had been in co-opting the Italian family. The more the 'Ndrangheta made itself indistinguishable from traditional, family-based Calabrian culture, the more anyone thinking of leaving the organization had to consider that they would be abandoning all they knew and all they were. For most, it would be impossible to see beyond it.

But by basing itself around family, the 'Ndrangheta hadn't merely been bolstering secrecy and loyalty. It had understood that family itself was a source of corruption. The undeniable love of a mother for a son or a daughter for a father—these were the sorts of bonds that ensured even the most law-abiding broke with principle and the law. Fathers would advantage their families however they could. Children would never betray their parents. Mothers, above all, would do anything to protect their children and wreak terrible revenge on those who harmed them. The 'Ndrangheta was the family augmented and accentuated into a perfect criminal entity. It was, of course, a diabolical transformation. The use of children was plainly child abuse, while to pervert the family in a country like Italy was to poison the soul of a nation. But it was also a masterstroke. If family was the basis of its power, and family was the essence of Italy, then family was how the 'Ndrangheta could corrupt the country.

For such a clan endeavor to work, Alessandra was convinced women had to have a role. And from her reading of case files and investigations, she soon discovered they had several. Women acted as messengers between men on the run or in jail, passing along tiny, folded notes—*pizzini*—written in a code of glyphs and addressed by the use of a code of numbers. If a man was killed or inaccessible in jail, his widow could become his de facto replacement and continue the family business. Some women acted as paymasters and bookkeepers.

Most significantly, women ensured the future of the 'Ndrangheta by producing the next generation of 'Ndranghetisti, raising children with an unbending belief in the code of honor, vendetta, and omertà, and a violent loathing of outsiders who, the mothers whispered, were weak and without shame with their loose talk and looser women. "Without women performing this role, there would be no 'Ndrangheta," said Alessandra. Secrecy and power were the goals. Male misogyny and female subservience, forced or even willing, were the means.

What confirmed women's influence inside the 'Ndrangheta was that, though they were often the victims of its violence, they also instigated some of it. Alessandra was astonished to hear about one mother from the Bellocco clan who outdid all the men for bloodthirstiness. The carabinieri had managed to bug a family meeting convened to discuss how best to avenge the death of one of their men, killed in a clan feud. The men proposed killing every male member of the rival *'ndrina*. Then the woman spoke up. "Kill them *all*," she said. "Even the women. Even the kids." The woman wanted an entire family of thirty wiped from the face of the earth.

There was no way any of it worked without the mothers, thought Alessandra. And to a resourceful and open-minded prosecutor, that held out an enticing possibility. In the twenty-first century, there had to be other Lea Garofalos out there, mafia mothers who were unhappy with their lives and the destiny of their children. The mother, the madonna, was a holy figure in Italy, and the 'Ndrangheta had corrupted her and bent her to its criminal will. Some women inside the organization must have hated the way they were being used. It had to be possible for Alessandra to offer these knowledgeable figures a different life and persuade them to betray their husbands and fathers. And imagine if she could. "It would break the chain," she told her fellow prosecutors. "It would remove the guardians of the 'Ndrangheta's traditions. If they took their sons, too, then they would be removing future soldiers. It would be very special, very important. It would impoverish the entire mafia family. It would undermine the whole culture and the mind-set."

Alessandra was refining her theory. The way to destroy The Family, she was beginning to realize, was through its mamas.

IN JANUARY 2010, Pignatone and Prestipino finally gave Alessandra the job she wanted.[1] From the New Year, she would be lead anti-mafia prosecutor for Calabria's west coast, taking in the villages on the Gioia Tauro *piano*, the town of Rosarno, and the port of Gioia Tauro. She would report directly to Pignatone and Prestipino. She would also have a second prosecutor as her junior, Giovanni Musarò, a thirty-seven-year-old on his first big posting.

Like Alessandra, Musarò was attracted by Pignatone and Prestipino's dynamism. "I was very young, they had this huge experience from Palermo, and they brought with them a completely different way of working," he said. Borrowing from Falcone and Borsellino, Calabria's new anti-mafia team ensured the old model of prosecutors as "lonely heroes" was out, said Giovanni. The new watchword was collaboration. "They put a great effort into creating a team, sharing information with colleagues, and behaving like a democracy," he said. Each member brought different strengths. "Alessandra was driven by ethics and very determined. Pignatone had a great ability to predict events. Prestipino was very clever and very pragmatic. He knew all his investigations and all his investigators. He was able to go to each of us and say: 'Maybe go to Alessandra and you'll find this.' Or 'Maybe go here and ask this investigator, and they'll help you with this.'"

For Alessandra, the prize was her new territory. Palmi, on the southern end of the Gioia Tauro estuary, was where the 'Ndrangheta

was born. A century and a half later, the *piano* remained the heart
of the empire. Though you wouldn't know it to look at the place,
thought Alessandra. The 'Ndrangheta was richer than most global
corporations, and in Rosarno even the most minor 'Ndrangheta family was thought to have three, four, or five million euros stashed away.
Yet somehow in a country of amber cornfields, olive hills, and blue
mountains sprinkled with red-roofed villages and magnificent Roman and Renaissance cities, the 'Ndrangheta had contrived to make
their towns into verrucae of unkempt, concrete ugliness. Touring
Rosarno for the first time, Alessandra felt like she'd arrived after
an apocalypse. Everything looked scorched. The trees were dying
and their leaves orange and brittle. The single park was just chalky
pebbles and dry, spiky weeds. The streets, whose asphalt resembled
spilled lava, were strewn with refuse. Everything was covered with
crude graffiti. And the town was dead. Shops were shut or deserted.
Many of the cinder block houses were unfinished and empty, their
gardens building sites, and their glassless windows as vacant as the
eyes of a skull. In the main piazza, no one sat on the benches, no one
ate in the restaurants. To one side, a children's playground consisted
of a rusted swing, a broken slide, and a shattered piece of concrete
littered with wrappers, cigarette butts, and broken glass. Alessandra could feel it. The fear. The omertà.

Unpicking the paradox of how this desperate place could be home
to such a rich criminal empire was key to the story of the 'Ndrangheta's modern rise. It began at 3 A.M. on July 10, 1973, when a
small gang of 'Ndrangheta toughs from the villages around Gioia
Tauro kidnapped John Paul Getty III, the sixteen-year-old grandson
of the billionaire Jean Paul Getty, from outside his home in Piazza
Farnese in central Rome. The gang held the boy in the Calabrian
mountains for five months. His father, who had been in a heroin-
induced haze at the time his son was taken, initially thought the
kidnapping was a hoax staged by his son to obtain money. The kid-

nappers called the family patriarch, Jean Paul Getty Sr., and threatened to cut off his grandson's fingers unless they received a ransom of $17 million. The elder Getty refused, arguing: "If I pay one penny now, I'll have fourteen kidnapped grandchildren." To press their case, the gang cut off John Paul III's left ear and sent it to a newspaper in Rome. It was accompanied by a note threatening that the second ear would be arriving in ten days unless the ransom was paid. Getty Sr. relented and paid $2.2 million, the maximum his accountants advised him was tax efficient. He loaned the final ransom balance of $700,000 to his son, the boy's father, at 4 percent interest.

John Paul Getty III never recovered from his abduction or his grandfather's indifference. He died at fifty-four, an alcoholic and a drug addict in a wheelchair, having been crippled at the age of twenty-five by a near-lethal combination of Valium, methadone, and cocktails. But for the west coast 'Ndrangheta, these grubby beginnings were the seeds of an empire. They went on to stage 150 more kidnappings. In Gioia Tauro, they used the ransom money to buy construction trucks. 'Ndrangheta men inside local government ensured these trucks were contracted for the building of a steel plant near the Gioia Tauro port. When the government abandoned that project as uneconomic, the trucks went to work on a bigger site: the expansion of the port itself.

State construction contracts—building motorways, high-speed rail links, and even wind and solar farms, while loan-sharking at extortionate rates to force rivals out of business—went on to become a giant, profitable 'Ndrangheta business in its own right. By the time Alessandra was posted to the west coast, a project to widen and repair the arterial highway running from western Calabria up Italy's coast to Salerno had somehow ended up costing the state $10 billion in three decades for what was still little more than a succession of roadworks.[2] The biggest earner, however, was the Gioia Tauro port itself. Once its expansion was finished, the port was the largest container facility in Italy and the sixth largest on the Mediterranean, with a capacity to load and unload millions of containers a year on a quay that ran for three and a half kilometers and was backed by an avenue of towering cranes. The 'Ndrangheta, as the only power in the area, had total control. The group "taxed" every container passing through the port at $1.50 a time. It charged the port operators fees amounting to half their profits, an annual income that ran into several billion dollars. It used the port to send weapons around the world. And in the 1980s and 1990s, during *la mattanza*, it was through Gioia Tauro that the 'Ndrangheta built its cocaine empire.

But aside from a single street of new houses nicknamed Via John Paul Getty in a small town to the south, there was no sign of the 'Ndrangheta's wealth. To the 'Ndrangheta, a facade of poverty was crucial to the lie. It helped it escape the attention of the state and added credibility to its claim to be championing a deprived south against an oppressive north. The 'Ndrangheta went to mulish lengths to service its pretense. When Alessandra first visited Rosarno, Domenico Oppedisano, a seventy-eight-year-old 'Ndrangheta big shot, could still be seen in his battered trilby and dusty suit, driving around in a three-wheeled van and delivering his oranges and lemons to market.

For the 97 percent of Gioia Tauro's population who were not 'Ndrangheta, however, the deprivation was real. Calabria was the poorest province in Italy. Incomes were around half those in the north, unemployment ran at 28 percent, and even in 2009, roasted dormice were considered a delicacy. The provincial government, meanwhile, was so dysfunctional that in 2008, a U.S. embassy fact-finding mission concluded that were it an independent state, Calabria would be a failed one.

As she was driven around the estuary delta between Rosarno and the port, Alessandra found it easy to guess who had ruined it. The area was latticed by a series of two-lane highways connected by a spaghetti of looping off-ramps and roundabouts, a modern industrial grid built with tens of millions of euros donated by the European Union and the Italian government. Economists and bureaucrats in Brussels, it seemed, had imagined a new warehousing zone to support the port that would help reverse the economic fortunes of one of Europe's poorest areas. Initially, 'Ndrangheta construction companies had been happy to take what public money was on offer. Then the 'Ndrangheta squashed the project. Threats, violence, and demands for crippling protection payments had ensured all but one of the international transport and logistics businesses proposed for the site had either closed or never opened. Weeds and thickets of bamboo edged far out into the road. Asphalt roads and concrete bays cracked and splintered in the sun. Giant bougainvilleas surfed out over the walls of empty business parks. Once-luxuriant palms were grotesquely overgrown, their green starbursts turned sickly yellow by a layer of sticky dust. Streetlights were ubiquitous but lifeless, connected to a field of large black solar panels fast disappearing under long grass. Rusted signs, some peppered with shotgun blasts, pointed the way to now-defunct enterprises whose gates were decorated with sun-bleached strings of international flags. In front of one grand entrance, a giant brass globe on a spike stood at a crazy angle, a dream of world domination turning, continent by continent, into a small pile of rusted metal on the ground. The only sign of life was a herd of goats grazing in drainage ditches choked with poppies, buttercups, and pink and purple flowers and, to one side, a tented camp of several thousand African migrants, whom the authorities, or possibly the 'Ndrangheta, had peevishly kept off-site.

The place felt like a war zone. And in a way it was. Covering the entire summit of a hill high above the port was a complex of sprawling villas and gardens once owned by the Piromalli clan, in whose territory the port lay. From here, the Piromallis had surveyed their empire like generals. The state had eventually confiscated the property but, since no one was willing to buy it, the houses and gardens were empty, an obstinate and unmissable reminder of where real power lay. Below the villa walls were a chapel and graveyard filled with baroque 'Ndranghetisti graves. Since it had been built without permits, the local authority had ordered the chapel demolished, only to discover that no local contractor was available to do the work.

In all of Gioia Tauro, a few lone entrepreneurs had taken a stand. One was Antonino de Masi, who in the 1990s decided to diversify the family agricultural machinery conglomerate into transport logistics. The business had foundered under 'Ndrangheta pressure, and de Masi now pursued other ventures, such as marketing earthquake shelters and smokeless pizza ovens, both of which he had invented himself. But he refused to leave his offices. That simple act of defiance had cost him dearly. After receiving numerous death threats, de Masi had sent his family to live in northern Italy. De Masi himself was obliged to move around in an armored car, flanked by two bodyguards. Two uniformed Italian army soldiers with automatic rifles and a camouflage jeep stood guard in his office parking lot. De Masi described himself as "living in enemy territory."[3]

Why would the 'Ndrangheta ruin its own homeland? Because de Masi was right. As a wealthy businessman with the means to pursue his ambition and the courage not to ask the 'Ndrangheta's permission, he was its sworn foe. It wasn't that the 'Ndrangheta hated development. It was that it tolerated no power other than itself. Inside its territory, there could be no intrusion by the outside world and no escape from the world the 'Ndrangheta had created. Education, especially the kind that encouraged free thinking, was discouraged. The sort of exit offered by gainful employment with a figure like Antonino de Masi also had to be crushed. The 'Ndrangheta even restricted physical ways out of the place. There was just one bus a day to Reggio Calabria. Roads built by 'Ndrangheta construction firms didn't connect to provincial highways, or to each other. Bridges over highways and rivers joined nothing to nowhere. The railway that connected Gioia Tauro to Europe stopped 1.5 kilometers short of the port, meaning all the cargo from one of the biggest Mediterranean container ports had to be loaded onto mafia-owned trucks and driven three minutes to the station. This was the suffocating magnificence of the 'Ndrangheta. The point wasn't money. The point was power.

BY 2010, THE Calabrian anti-mafia prosecutors were finally piecing together quite how much influence the 'Ndrangheta had accumulated. Even veterans of *la mattanza* like Pignatone and Prestipino were astonished. Where once the 'Ndrangheta had been outmatched by Cosa Nostra in drug smuggling, it now dominated the entire European trade in illicit narcotics. Cocaine was produced and refined in Colombia, Peru, or Bolivia, transported east, generally to Brazil or Venezuela, and from there across the Atlantic to Europe via the Caribbean or West Africa, before being landed in Holland, Denmark, Spain, or Italy. Though other criminal groups were involved at each stage of its journey as producers and traffickers, the 'Ndrangheta had assumed a position of broker, overseer, and employer across the entire supply chain.

Inventiveness was a consistent characteristic of this empire, especially in trafficking methods. For sea routes through the Caribbean, the 'Ndrangheta or their partners would conceal cocaine under trawlers full of frozen fish or inside tins of pineapple, or by sewing it into bananas or even dissolving it in bottles of whiskey. Another trick was to secrete a load together with duplicate security tags inside a shipping container carrying other cargo. The drug could then be removed after crossing the Atlantic, generally in customs storage or at a refueling stop, and the containers resealed with the copied tags and sent on their way without detection. To further confuse customs agents, two ships might rendezvous in the middle of the ocean and make a further swap between containers.

Aircraft offered further options. On commercial flights—across the Atlantic to West Africa, and from West Africa to Europe—the smugglers used passengers who would swallow up to thirty plastic bags, amounting to a total load of a kilo each. They would then pack as many as forty "swallowers" onto a plane, sometimes using an entire class of African exchange students who could pay for several years at a foreign university with one trip. Plane crews, who generally sailed through customs without checks, were another good option. Mostly the traffickers would enlist individual stewards, but on occasion they recruited entire crews, including the pilots. When private planes were available, freelance pilots flew small props fitted with custom-enlarged fuel tanks at low altitude thousands of miles across the Atlantic from Latin America to touch down in West Africa. A few times, the smugglers had used an aging Boeing 727, which could take ten tons of cocaine at a time and which in 2009 had been found by the authorities in Mali in the middle of the Sahara, abandoned and torched by the traffickers after snapping its wheels on landing. The onward land route through the Sahara to the Mediterranean was perhaps the most dramatic drug lane of all, involving convoys of twenty to thirty 4×4s driving north for four or five days right across the desert, navigating by the stars and refueling at a string of camouflaged outposts.[4]

Once the drugs reached the Mediterranean, they might be taken from Tunisia to Europe on cruise ships or driven counterclockwise around the coast, across Libya and Egypt and on through Israel and Turkey, a journey facilitated by border guards and army officers. To move cocaine across Europe required a high degree of subterfuge. Tons of cocaine were trucked from Gioia Tauro to Holland hidden under flowers destined for Europe's biggest flower market, where florists served a second purpose as 'Ndrangheta money launderers. Payment going the other way was also disguised. Billions of euros in credit might be uploaded to hundreds of online betting accounts. One time, €7.5 million was sent in the form of 260 tons of Lindt chocolates.[5]

The prosecutors knew which 'ndrine were so trusted by the Colombians that they were allowed cocaine on credit. They knew which families had diversified into dealing arms. They'd investigated who used smuggling ships on their return journey to dump hazardous chemicals and nuclear waste by sinking boats off the coast of Somalia. The investigators knew which customs services, armies, rebels, Islamists, officials, ministers, prime ministers, and presidents along the smuggling routes took a cut of the profits. Mozambique's customs, the midpoint on an otherwise little-traveled, entirely Portuguese-speaking route from Brazil to Portugal via Africa, had been bought almost whole. So had the entire government of Guinea-Bissau, a tiny West African state and another former Portuguese colony, where soldiers would clear traffic from public highways to allow narco-planes to land.

What gave the prosecutors most pause was how as the rewards of power had multiplied, so had the struggle for it. As 2010 dawned, West Africa was in the midst of an unprecedented wave of coups, civil wars, revolutions, and assassinations driven by the struggle to get rich from drug smuggling. Surveying the chaos created by cocaine, the prosecutors realized the 'Ndrangheta hadn't just ruined Calabria and undermined the Italian state but had done the same to significant parts of the planet. This lent new urgency to their mission. This wasn't the old story about how drugs messed you up. This was about how the 'Ndrangheta's drugs had messed up the lives of hundreds of millions of people in countries on the other side of the world, places that few Europeans had even heard of.

Nor was even that the most worrying part. By 2010, Calabria's

anti-mafia prosecutors were picking up indications that the 'Ndrangheta's money-laundering operations were undermining the world's
financial markets and even the sovereignty of nations. Giuseppe
Lombardo, a prosecutor who specialized in tracking its money, said
that alongside the 'Ndrangheta's growth had come increased financial sophistication. Faced with a need to launder ever-increasing
amounts of money and observing how the world's stock markets
were increasingly lightly regulated, a few 'Ndrangheta families had
made their first few forays into the world of international finance in
the mid-1980s. A generation later, what had begun as an experiment
in diversification and legitimization was now a giant multinational
asset management business run by 'Ndrangheta lawyers, accountants, and bankers in Milan, London, and New York through a maze
of offshore financial centers that specialized in secrecy and low tax:
Cyprus, Malta, Gibraltar, Mauritius, Switzerland, Luxembourg,
Holland, the British Virgin Islands, and other British dependencies.
The global recession of 2007 to 2009 had been a particular boon. As
legitimate finance dried up, businesses, banks, stock markets, and
even political parties found themselves suddenly short of money.
For the 'Ndrangheta, this credit crunch had proved to be a once-in-
a-lifetime chance to convert criminal power into legal economic and
political might around the world.

The 'Ndrangheta was driven by two motivations. It needed to
safely launder its riches. And it wanted to become so indispensable
to the international economy that tackling it would be an act of
self-harm for any government. According to Lombardo, the 'Ndrangheta had largely succeeded in both endeavors. "They have become
one of the main interlocutors in the criminal field," he said. "But
much more broadly, they have become a world power."

Initially, said Lombardo, the 'Ndrangheta had bought politicians
who offered state protection, and created a network of accountants,
lawyers, traders, and other facilitators inside the banking system,

which allowed the 'Ndrangheta to clean and invest its money. But in a crucial second stage, the 'Ndrangheta had opened its financial structure to organized crime groups around the world: Cosa Nostra and the Camorra, but also Chinese triads, Nigerians, Russians, Colombians, Mexicans, and criminal groups from every part of the planet. "The 'Ndrangheta plays the role of service agent to the other mafias," said Lombardo. "They make this network of financial professionals working for them available to other mafias. And after that, when it comes to finances, all the mafias move together as one big mafia."

That meant the 'Ndrangheta had hundreds of billions of euros at its command. Such a tsunami of money had elevated it to a "fundamental and indispensable position in the global market," said Lombardo, one that was "more or less essential for the smooth functioning of the global economic system." This new centrality afforded the 'Ndrangheta the level of protection it sought. It also offered it an opportunity to indulge in typical mafia behavior— bullying, intimidating, extorting, and blackmailing—on a whole new scale. Lombardo had indications that the 'Ndrangheta regularly manipulated stock prices or markets to its advantage and had even caused mini financial crashes to create buying opportunities for itself.

Most remarkable was what the prosecutor had discovered about the mafia's taste for government debt. "I found a huge amount of capital deployed by the mafia to buy government bonds and Treasury debt," he said. At first, this revelation confused Lombardo. There was no sound financial imperative to buy bonds: yields were typically low and far better opportunities were available in other financial instruments. But then he realized the 'Ndrangheta's motivations were more than merely financial. "They don't need to become any richer," he said. "They're rich enough. But alongside the goal of making money is the goal of limiting national sovereignty." The 'Ndrangheta had always sought to undermine Italian state power and authority. Now it was doing the same across the world. It did this by buying up large tranches of foreign countries' debt, then threatening those countries with dumping their debt and prompting a financial default. A debtor nation's only option was to allow the 'Ndrangheta to use its territory as a base and a money-laundering location. So far, the prosecutors had collected evidence that the 'Ndrangheta had blackmailed Thailand and Indonesia in this way. Lombardo expected China and India to be next. "This is about conditioning the global economic system, conditioning the global citizenry, and conditioning the political choices of nations," he said. "This is how the 'Ndrangheta become the rulers not just of territory in Italy but whole other countries."

Lombardo's investigations revealed the 'Ndrangheta not merely as a menace to southern Italy but as a global monster. Though other mafias were better known, the 'Ndrangheta was the most powerful. In the name of profit and power, it was sowing the seeds of war, chaos, and corruption from Rio to Rotterdam to Reykjavík. It was the dark underside of globalization made real in flesh and blood. Of paramount importance to Italy's anti-mafia prosecutors, however, Calabria remained the key to the entire enterprise. Any big business decision—to expand territory, to enter a new business, to eliminate a rival—was referred back to the old country. In their bunkers buried beneath Reggio Calabria and Rosarno and the orange groves of Gioia Tauro plain, the bosses were deciding the fates of nations. As she read through the latest case files, it dawned on Alessandra that with their new crackdown on the 'Ndrangheta, the prosecutors held the destiny of hundreds of millions of people in their hands.

THE STIMULI TO the Italian state's new campaign against the mafia were various: the outcry at the Duisburg massacre of 2007, the

2008 election of a new government publicly committed to ending the threat from organized crime, and, the same year, the arrival in Calabria of Giuseppe Pignatone and Michele Prestipino. The fight against the mafia was quickly reinvigorated with fresh energy and resources. Over 2008 and 2009 the carabinieri bugged millions of conversations. 'Ndranghetisti still habitually spoke in riddles and metaphors, and in isolation the meaning of any one conversation was obscure. But taken together and over time, the mass of recordings added up to a true revelation: the authorities' first-ever complete picture of the internal structure and dynamics of the 'Ndrangheta.

There were several surprises. Hitherto, the prosecutors had understood the 'Ndrangheta as a loose alliance of family firms, each with its own territory. Surveillance of Reggio Calabria and the surrounding towns and villages revealed that the horizontal structure of hundreds of *'ndrine*, each run autonomously by a family boss, was still the 'Ndrangheta's foundation. But it emerged that above it was a new vertical, unifying hierarchy of eleven ranks. Several *'ndrine* together made a grouping called a *locale* or *società*, managed by a paramount chief, assisted by an accountant and a "head of crime" who oversaw all illegal activities. Above the *locali* were three regional authorities called *mandamenti*, one each for the Tyrrhenian and Ionian coasts and another for Reggio Calabria. Together these three groups made up a council variously called *la provincia* or *il crimine* or—something that made Alessandra do a double take—*La Mamma*. Overseeing all of it was a *capo crimine*, or boss of bosses, who could convene a court, or *tribunale*, of senior bosses to judge a peer accused of transgressing the code.[6] "We'd always thought of the 'Ndrangheta as a lot of local, smaller organizations," said Alessandra. "Suddenly we realized it had a federal structure and was being run almost like a military organization."

In the 1990s, carabinieri had picked up word of an attempt by the 'Ndrangheta to unite the clans. That had ultimately failed. From what the carabinieri were hearing now, this time the reorganization had succeeded. Why? The old arguments in favor of better coordination to improve efficiency and discipline still stood. But in 2009, the carabinieri were detecting a more ominous motivation: to coordinate a concerted assault on the authorities through a series of assassinations and bombings. On October 31, 2009, the carabinieri filmed an especially brazen 'Ndrangheta summit outside Milan at which twenty-two bosses raised their glasses to toast the new city boss inside a memorial dedicated to Giovanni Falcone and Paolo Borsellino.[7] The 'Ndrangheta was abandoning its decades-old policy of discreet infiltration in favor of direct confrontation. Why the change? From what the carabinieri could gather, the 'Ndrangheta felt their hand was being forced. The new push against organized crime had resulted in the arrests of hundreds of mafiosi, including twenty-one of Italy's thirty "most wanted," and the confiscation of assets and businesses worth €9 billion.[8] Though the operations had hurt the Camorra most of all, the 'Ndrangheta knew it was next. Its bosses had decided on an aggressive and unified response.

For Alessandra, one episode captured by the new intelligence was especially significant. Officers watching a mafia wedding in the hill town of Platì on August 19, 2009, between two powerful clans, the Pelles and the Barbaros, were amazed to spot a who's who of the 'Ndrangheta among the two thousand guests. These included bosses not only from across Calabria but also from northern Italy, Europe, and as far away as Canada and Australia. "They came from all over the planet to this tiny little town in the middle of nowhere," said Alessandra. The reason for this unprecedented summit was soon clear. Wiretaps and bugs picked up numerous references to the election of a new *capo crimine*, Rosarno boss Domenico Oppedisano, appointed to spearhead the 'Ndrangheta's war on the state. That seemed to confirm the importance of a well-attended meeting of bosses held a few days earlier in Oppedisano's orange orchard. Two weeks after the wedding, Oppedisano's promotion was formally confirmed at the annual 'Ndrangheta meeting, held at the festival for the Madonna di Polsi at San Luca.

What interested Alessandra was not Oppedisano himself but who he represented. She knew the *capo crimine* was elected by a kind of criminal meritocracy, based on who inside the organization was deemed "most charismatic, most admirable, and most ruthless." The boss had to be someone the entire 'Ndrangheta could agree outdid them all for criminal excellence, a leader who would ensure they wasted no more time and blood fighting each other.

On the face of it, seventy-eight-year-old Oppedisano, with his farmer's tan and a family that was outranked by at least two others in Rosarno, was an eccentric choice. But with her burgeoning knowledge of the clans, Alessandra could see its logic. More than advancing the Oppedisanos, Domenico's new position confirmed the ascendancy of the west coast clans inside the 'Ndrangheta. Specifically, it attested to the dominance of a particular Rosarno crime family to whom Oppedisano was related by marriage. It was this family's domination of the cocaine trade with two other Gioia Tauro families that, more than anything, accounted for the 'Ndrangheta's spectacular growth over the last three decades. Its reputation for ruthless violence ensured that as well as being one of the richest and most powerful crime families in all Italy, it was also one of the most feared. "Through Gioia Tauro, they were running all the drugs and all the arms," said Alessandra.

So spectacular had been this family's progress and so naked their ambition to dominate the 'Ndrangheta, however, that they were resented by almost every other *'ndrina*. An earlier attempt to force the election of their own family *capo* had been fiercely resisted on all sides as an unacceptable affront. The other families might be diminished by comparison, but honor demanded they save face by pretending otherwise. Nominating Domenico Oppedisano was a

shrewd compromise, combining the signature 'Ndrangheta charac-
teristics of strategy and willful delusion.

Still, Alessandra had no doubt who now held power inside the
'Ndrangheta. She had seen video surveillance of family members
toasting Oppedisano with champagne on the night he was elected.
In any new war on the 'Ndrangheta, this family would be target
number one. They were called the Pesces.

VII

LEA GAROFALO WASN'T the first 'Ndranghetista to turn on the organization, nor even the first woman.[1] But she was one of a mere handful of 'Ndrangheta *pentiti*, and only the second woman, and the story of the Pagliarelle mama and boss's daughter who had crossed over to the state had reverberated like a cannon blast around the valleys. Seven years later, Lea was most likely dead. The message that sent to places like Pagliarelle and Rosarno was that there *was* no alternative to the 'Ndrangheta. You leave, you die. It was a disaster for the Italian state's new war on the mafia. What had gone wrong?

Lea's long struggle with Carlo and the 'Ndrangheta was well documented. She had made lengthy statements against the 'Ndrangheta and Carlo three times, in 1996, 2002, and 2008. From these, the picture that emerged of the rural Calabria where Lea and Carlo had grown up was of a lost world, cut off from the rest of humanity by a wall of violent tyranny. For most 'Ndrangheta children, it was enough just to be born in a place like Pagliarelle to know their destiny.

But Lea had been different. Her father, an *'ndrina* boss called Antonio Garofalo, was killed by three brothers from a rival clan on New Year's Eve, 1974, when he was twenty-seven and Lea was just eight months old—and, for Lea, none of it made sense after that. The feud, or *faida*, that her father's murder set off between the Garofalos and the Mirabellis, another Pagliarelle family, lasted all through her childhood until Lea was eighteen. When she was seven, in 1981, Lea's uncle Giulio tried to avenge his brother by opening fire on a Mirabelli funeral. A few months later, Giulio was killed in retaliation. In 1989, when Lea was fifteen, another of her relatives was shot dead, right in front of her and in broad daylight, in the center of Petilia Policastro. That same year, the Garofalos began taking their revenge, killing one of the three Mirabelli brothers. They shot a second in 1990 and the third in 1991, then in 1992 they murdered Mario Garofalo, a cousin who—illustrating the incestuous nature of the feud—worked for the Mirabellis.

Lea's older brother, Floriano, directed much of the bloodletting. He involved his nine-year-old sister, asking her to hide a pistol belonging to their uncle when a police raid was imminent.[2] But despite Floriano's instruction in the duties of vendetta, despite Marisa's warnings about the need at least to pretend, despite all the anger she felt over her father's death, and barely knowing that any other life even existed, Lea couldn't remember a day when she hadn't seen through the lie. "Lea was born into a family where violence was the rule," said her former lawyer Vincenza Rando, known to everyone as Enza. "It was 'Kill one of mine and I'll kill one of yours.'" Lea saw the world differently, said Enza. To her, "the 'Ndrangheta was a cult of death, and Lea was a woman who loved life. The 'Ndrangheta writes your destiny for you. Lea wanted to write her own."

Lea's independence might have come from her mother. Though her mother had married an 'Ndranghetista, she had always worked, mostly as a cleaner at a school in Petilia. "Our mother had a completely different mind-set from people around here," said Marisa. "She was a decent woman." It was Lea's mother who taught her what Lea always used to tell Denise: that education was freedom, and that providing for her family was what gave a woman dignity.

Still, their mother wasn't affectionate, said Marisa. She, Floriano, and Lea grew up mostly in the care of their grandparents, who might as well have been from another century. Of the three children, Marisa said it was Lea, the youngest, who felt their parents' absence most keenly. She was always asking for pictures of her father, who, since she had never known him, she was free to imagine as perfect: caring and loving and cruelly taken from the daughter he adored. As a teenager, Lea had a small "A" for Antonio tattooed onto her hand. While the violence raged on around them, Lea couldn't imagine her father wanting her to spend her life carving out brief moments of peace in a dead-end job as her mother had done. "You don't *live*," Lea told the carabinieri in 2002. "You just survive in some way. You dream about something—anything—because nothing's worse than that life." As Lea grew up, it dawned on her that the freedom she craved would be impossible unless she left Pagliarelle.

Lea's tragedy was that, like many 'Ndrangheta women, she thought love was her way out. When she was fifteen she fell for a village boy she had known all her life, a thick-set bruiser with a flattened nose and cropped hair called Carlo Cosco. Carlo, nineteen at the time, was back from his new life in the north and visiting Pagliarelle for the holidays. What Lea especially liked about him was that he seemed to have no ambition other than to work an honest job and raise a family. And he lived in Milan, "a big city where she could start again," said Enza. Lea and Carlo eloped after a few weeks. When she was sixteen, in 1991, they married and moved to Milan, where Carlo had an apartment in a large, drab building on Viale Montello.

Almost immediately, Lea realized her escape was a mirage. No. 6 Viale Montello was in the possession of the 'Ndrangheta and Carlo turned out to be one of several 'Ndranghetisti using it as a base from which to traffic cocaine and heroin. Lea had rejected the 'Ndrangheta code, but it transpired that her new husband's embrace of it had been so wholehearted, he thought nothing of tricking Lea into marrying him. Worst of all, it emerged that Carlo was working for Lea's brother, Floriano, whose bloodthirstiness in Pagliarelle had propelled him to the head of the Garofalo *'ndrina*. Lea had thought she courted Carlo. Now it occurred to her that Carlo had sought her out—because she was the sister of an 'Ndrangheta boss. Marriage to her had been a promotion for Carlo. For Lea, the love she had imagined would free her had trapped her even deeper.

Lea sank into depression. According to Enza, she made several attempts at suicide. When she got pregnant in the spring of 1991, Lea tried to abort. "She did not want to give her son or daughter the same future," said Enza. In December, heavily pregnant, she left Viale Montello and took a bus to a hospital deep in the country. She gave birth alone, to a baby girl. Lea had imagined she might give her baby up for adoption, somewhere Carlo would never find the child. "But when Denise was born," said Enza, "Lea fell in love all over again. Denise gave Lea a reason to live."

LIKE EVERYONE WHO had worked mafia cases in Milan, Alessandra knew all about No. 6 Viale Montello. A vast and historic building in the middle of the Italian business capital, *il fortino delle cosche* (the fort of the clans) wasn't just a mafia base but a six-story challenge to Italy's claim to be a modern, unified, lawful state. The 'Ndranghetisti paid no rent on its 129 apartments, nor any tax, nor any bills for municipal services like water or electricity. They treated the Renaissance mansion with disdain. A spaghetti of wires hung from its walls and collapsing balconies. Its courtyards and central garden were filled with refuse and rusted, broken appliances. The stairwells and corners stank of urine. Not only was the building a hub of the European drug trade, it was the source of supply for hundreds of Milan's street dealers, especially those in the notorious Piazza Baiamonti, and a focal point for other criminals of every type: enforcers, smugglers, and killers; political corrupters and state contract fixers; wayward policemen, judges, and politicians. And all of it in flagrant plain sight. Viale Montello was an arterial thoroughfare just a kilometer from the city center and yards from a city police station. Unsurprisingly, No. 6 Viale Montello was something of a preoccupation for Milan's anti-mafia prosecutors, who had it under near-permanent surveillance.

For the prosecutors, the relationships inside No. 6 Viale Montello in the 1990s—between brothers, in-laws, and even husband and wife—and the way those dynamics eventually played out became an important early case study of this newly ascendant mafia. It was from watching events there that the prosecutors would be able to assemble a picture of what Alessandra described as a "modern, efficient, present-day organized crime syndicate" whose strength lay in "enforcing a respect for medieval rules." In the end, the prosecutors would conclude that they were fighting a culture, and that in No. 6 Viale Montello they had a peculiarly instructive petri dish. Among the most informative events they watched there was the rise of an ambitious young 'Ndranghetista called Carlo Cosco, and his eventual undoing by his wife.

Carlo's first big step up the ladder had been to marry the boss's sister. On his return to Milan in 1991, the surveillance teams watched as Floriano's lieutenants in Milan, Silvano Toscano and Thomas Ceraudo, duly catapulted Carlo and his brothers, Vito and Giuseppe, to prominence, granting them control of the lucrative dope and protection rackets in Piazza Baiamonti and nearby Quarto Oggiaro. As a medium-level drug smuggler, dealer, and extortionist, Carlo wasn't above manual tasks. Sometimes he would ask his new wife, Lea, to help cut and package heroin, cocaine, and hashish. He asked her for other favors, too, like spying on Antonio Comberiati, a rival 'Ndranghetista who lived in the building with his wife, Gina.

Comberiati was a hothead and troublemaker. His nickname was *il lupo*, "the wolf." He resented most of the families in Viale Montello, seemingly aggrieved by his and Gina's inability to conceive. But he was especially incensed by Carlo's promotion.

One day in February 1994, Lea was dressing Denise, then two, for her first Milan city carnival, when Carlo interrupted to say he had seen Comberiati talking to the Chinese shop owner who "employed" Carlo as a security guard. This arrangement was standard for the men at Viale Montello. Whenever carabinieri asked for proof of occupation, they would be shown contracts of employment claiming a job providing security for the Chinese traders on the ground floor. Carlo was concerned by what might be transpiring between his sponsor and his rival and asked Lea to listen in from the street. Lea soon overheard Comberiati insisting that the store close because it was being watched by the carabinieri. If Carlo lost his "job," said Comberiati, that was too bad.

This was too much for Lea. "I couldn't help myself," she said in testimony years later. "I interrupted and tried to defend Carlo, saying we had a daughter and Carlo had the right to remain there to work." Comberiati, outraged at being confronted by a woman, and his rival's wife to boot, shouted back that he outranked Carlo. Then he threatened to kill Lea for daring to face him. "I'm the boss around here!" he shouted. "I'm in charge! It's my right!"

The fight continued inside the courtyard of Viale Montello. Eventually, Gina and several other women intervened. Lea ran back up to her apartment. Carlo was waiting. He had heard everything. "Don't worry," he reassured Lea. "One day Comberiati will pay."

In the event, it was Comberiati who made the first move. In simultaneous assassinations on the night of November 30, 1994, Thomas Ceraudo was gunned down in Quarto Oggiaro and Silvano Toscano was abducted from his mother-in-law's house in Petilia and killed, his body dumped in a field outside town. Comberiati barely bothered to deny he was to blame. The surveillance teams at Viale Montello reported that he immediately installed himself as the new king of Milan.

But with Carlo's backers dead and Floriano looking weak, Comberiati was daring Carlo to respond. Six months after the double murders, just after midnight on May 17, 1995, Lea was sleeping in bed with Denise when she heard several shots ring out in the courtyard below. When she opened the door, she could see Comberiati's body lying prone on the concrete. It was raining. Gina was screaming for an ambulance and shouting that the killer was still in the building. She started smashing the windows of a Chinese shop in which she was convinced the gunman was hiding. Lea observed her. Then she watched the ambulance and carabinieri arrive. After twenty minutes, Carlo's brother Giuseppe appeared at her door, exhilarated.

"He's dead," said Giuseppe.

"You sure?" asked Lea.

Giuseppe giggled. "The bastard just wouldn't fucking die," he said. "It was like he had the devil in him or something. But, yeah, he's dead now, for sure."

Giuseppe left for his apartment. Carlo arrived seconds later.

"Where were you?" asked Lea.

"Karaoke," replied Carlo.

"Liar," Lea shot back.

Carlo laughed. "Well, then, I've been over at the shop getting a sandwich."

Lea later told the carabinieri that she had surmised that Carlo had stood watch for Giuseppe while his brother shot Comberiati, then the two men had dumped the gun in the street. It made sense for Giuseppe to pull the trigger, said Lea, because he "needed the points." "Carlo doesn't need them," she explained to the prosecutors. "He's already Floriano's brother-in-law. But Giuseppe's no one. A killing like this gives him position. He becomes somebody."

With his rival dead, Carlo's accession, and the elevation of the Cosco family, was complete. Previous generations of Coscos had been goat herders and fruit farmers. Now, through luck and ruthlessness, they were players in an exploding international criminal empire. Carlo himself was right hand and brother by marriage to Floriano Garofalo, one of the most powerful *'ndrina* bosses in all Calabria.

For Lea, however, something died with Comberiati. Her husband had brought violence into the home where she lived with their daughter. Years earlier, she had tried to escape and it hadn't worked. For Denise's sake, she had to try again. Looking at her daughter was like looking at herself in the third person, thought Lea. She could see everything clearly: all the troubles around the two of them and what they needed to do to move past them. "She wanted Denise to have other possibilities in her life," said Enza. "The chance to be part of the cult of life and friendship and respect and to be part of another kind of family."

Lea tried one more time to convince Carlo to leave the 'Ndrangheta. The three of them could begin again somewhere new and raise their baby to be anything she wanted to be, she said. Carlo's response was to beat her. That was the last straw for Lea. "So she decided to go to the carabinieri and tell them all about the drug trafficking," said Enza.

In May 1996, Carlo, Floriano, Giuseppe, and several others were arrested at No. 6 Viale Montello. The operation to detain them—using four hundred men to seal off the street and storm the building—confirmed the Coscos' new status in the European drug trafficking elite. Carlo was transferred to San Vittore prison, on the other side of town.

Though she had played a key role in his arrest, Lea decided she would give Carlo one last chance. In September 1996, Lea, now twenty-two, took Denise, five, to see him in prison. "I want to stay with you," she told him, "but on one condition: you collaborate with the carabinieri and denounce the 'Ndrangheta. When you come out of jail, we can start a new life. Or you continue this life and you will never see me or Denise again."

Carlo leaped over the screen between them and grabbed Lea. He had his hands around her throat by the time the prison guards pulled him off. He expected his wife to stand by him. After all the work and all the blood, Carlo's maneuvering had paid off. He was king of Milan. Now Lea was betraying him and taking it all away: his link to the boss in the old country, his standing in the brotherhood, even his self-respect as a man. Lea had broken the code. There was only one remedy. From that day, said Enza, Lea knew she was living under "a death sentence."

Lea returned to Viale Montello for a final time. She packed a suitcase, then called a friend to drive her and Denise to a convent in Bergamo where they would be safe. Renata, Giuseppe Cosco's wife, saw Lea leave. "I remember the day Lea left Milan well," she said in court fifteen years later. "Lea looked at me with anger. She spat on the ground. She swore she would never again set foot in that shitty place. She yelled that she wanted a different future for herself. A different future for her daughter." And just like that, Lea and Denise were gone.

THE NEXT SIX years were the happiest of Lea's and Denise's lives. Initially, the pair stayed in an Ursuline convent in Bergamo dedicated to the education of women and girls. In Mother Grata, who ran the convent, Lea seemed to discover the parent she'd never had. She began reading for the first time in years, learning about Giovanni Falcone, Paolo Borsellino, and Giuseppe Impastato, a Palermo anti-mafia activist who had been born into a Cosa Nostra family and was assassinated by them at thirty. After a few months, Lea and Denise moved into a small apartment on Via Alfieri, a quiet street of bungalows and two-story houses painted yellow and pink.

Later they moved into town to another small place on Via Mose del Brolo, a dead-end street full of pensioners and students. Lea found work in factories and bars. She met a man. She and Denise adopted a dog. Lea even went skydiving.

Every June, Lea and Denise would go down to Pagliarelle to spend the summer holidays with Marisa and their relatives. Perhaps it was those breaks in Calabria, unmolested by Carlo's men, that lulled Lea into thinking her escape was real. When they were back home, Lea even allowed Denise to visit Carlo in Catanzaro jail, to which he had been transferred from Milan.

But Carlo never had Lea out of his sights. When the officers investigating Lea's disappearance tracked down Salvatore Cortese, an 'Ndrangheta killer who had shared a cell with Carlo in Catanzaro from 2001 to 2003 and had since turned *pentito*, Cortese told them Carlo never forgave Lea. Carlo, he said, was always talking about how Lea had betrayed him and betrayed the 'Ndrangheta. Carlo was especially incensed that she still stayed with her family in Pagliarelle and walked around the village alone and in front of everyone. She was flaunting her freedom, said Carlo. He knew about her affair in Bergamo and suspected, since Lea never came to visit, that the other inmates in Catanzaro had deduced the same thing. Worst of all, her brother Floriano was doing nothing about any of it. Carlo had been wronged and wronged again. It was intolerable. "And," said Cortese, "according to the 'Ndrangheta's rules, Floriano's silence allowed Carlo to appeal to other men of honor for permission to kill Lea."

Nonetheless, killing the sister of a boss was a tricky business. Carlo told Cortese that Lea had to be dispatched in such a way that Floriano would believe she had run off with her new lover. "The plan to physically eliminate Lea Garofalo and get rid of her body by dissolving it in acid grew in Carlo's mind since at least the early 2000s," said Cortese. How, the carabinieri asked, did Cortese know that? Because, Cortese replied, he was among those Carlo asked to help him.

Carlo knew he might fool Floriano but not the entire 'Ndrangheta. If he was to pull off such an audacious killing, he would need approval from higher up. Approaching two bosses in the prison yard, he explained how his honor and that of the wider 'Ndrangheta had been so impugned that it could only be restored by washing it in blood. The two bosses knew Carlo was right. But they had their own clan feuds to pursue. Calculating that Carlo's vendetta would anyway have to wait until he was released from jail, they stalled.

Carlo still held out hope that Floriano would choose his duty over love for his sister. Getting his brothers to set Lea's car alight in Bergamo in 2000 was Carlo's way of reminding Floriano of his obligation. It had some effect. One summer's day two years later, when Lea and Denise were back in Pagliarelle, Lea took Denise to buy a gelato from the shop off the main piazza. Vito Cosco drove up in his car. He was agitated. He told Lea he was tired of taking Denise to see Carlo. Carlo was sick of it, too. It wasn't right, said Vito. Lea had to get in line.

Lea refused. As the argument grew more heated, Floriano, by then out of prison and back in Pagliarelle, arrived. Vito was right, Floriano shouted at Lea. What kind of woman let her husband rot in jail alone? What kind of sister was she to him, Floriano, an 'ndrina boss? Then, in the middle of the square, Floriano held Lea by her shoulders and slapped her across the face for everyone to see. He leaned over his sister, looking as though he was about to strike her again. As he did so, however, he whispered in her ear: "Lea! You have to escape! Because, really, I have to kill you!"

TWICE LEA HAD run from the 'Ndrangheta. Twice it had clawed her back in. For choosing freedom over murderous criminality, her husband wanted her dead, the 'Ndrangheta required it, and her brother had told her he would be the one to do it. Lea felt like the world was closing in on her. On July 29, 2002, a few days after the argument with Vito and Floriano, the door of Lea's grandmother's house was set alight while Lea and Denise were inside. It was an especially blunt 'Ndrangheta message. There was no way out.

Perhaps because it was so unthinkable, the 'Ndrangheta had overlooked one exit, however. The same morning as the fire, prosecutor Sandro Dolce in the nearby city of Catanzaro received a call from the chief of the carabinieri in Petilia Policastro. "He told me that in front of him stood the sister of Floriano Garofalo. She had a ten-year-old girl with her. She wanted to give evidence about a number of facts and events concerning her family. She wanted to break with her past and the environment in which she had been living."

Dolce immediately understood the significance of what he was hearing. In 2002, the authorities knew very little about the 'Ndrangheta. Despite prosecuting several 'Ndranghetisti for their roles in the Pagliarelle feud, their knowledge of what had happened barely extended beyond the body count. Though they had successfully prosecuted Carlo and Floriano for drug trafficking, they also knew little about the structures and hierarchy of the wider 'Ndrangheta. "Up until that time, we had very poor knowledge of the workings of the 'Ndrangheta," said Dolce. "State witnesses are our main source of knowledge for any mafia and we just hadn't got that many from the 'Ndrangheta. The 'Ndrangheta was known, of course—its existence was no big secret—but its internal dynamics were not known."

Dolce knew immediately what he had to do. "I did not go to Petilia," he said. "It's a small town. The fact that she had gone to the carabinieri would have already alarmed people there. So I could not go personally to listen to her statement there. Instead, I had the carabinieri move her urgently to a hotel one hundred kilometers away, and I went to see her there. And I did nothing but listen to her talk for two days."

What particularly impressed Dolce was how different Lea was from the stereotype of an 'Ndrangheta woman. Most were submissive, ignorant, and poorly educated. Lea was assertive, knowledgeable, and articulate. "She had a different outlook," said Dolce. "She was open-minded. She wanted her own life. She did not want to depend on a man or to stay at home. She wanted her independence. She wanted to be the protagonist and the subject in her own life. Lea had grit." Just as impressive, said Dolce, "she was very honest. If she hadn't told us she had been involved in the drugs, we'd never have known."

Lea's testimony began from her father's death when she was eight months old and ran through everything that had happened in the previous twenty-eight years. She spoke about the Pagliarelle feud. She gave an account of all the murders and named all the killers. She detailed how her brother Floriano had shot and knifed his way to the top, and how that had enabled him to take over the protection and cocaine rackets in Milan, especially Quarto Oggiaro. She talked about packaging and distributing cocaine inside No. 6 Viale Montello. She described Antonio Comberiati's murder and how Carlo and Giuseppe had spoken about killing him. Finally, she said she had decided to turn state's evidence because she felt time was running out. Her greatest fear was that someone would break into her house and shoot Denise.

Reading through Lea's statements years later, prosecutors investigating her disappearance were amazed by the detail. Dolce had reacted the same way at the time. "I have had experience of false *pentiti*—men who just say a few things but not everything," he said. "They make a utilitarian choice. They decide to collaborate because they are facing life sentences." But Lea was different, he said. Her collaboration was "more genuine, and more effective. She said everything she knew. She hid nothing. You could feel how her choice had put her through suffering and pain. But she had a very dignified look. She was very determined and proud of what she had done."

The more the new team of Calabrian prosecutors read about Lea, the more they were struck by how, seven years before, in two days of interviews and on her own initiative, Lea had single-handedly proved Alessandra's theory that mothers were the key to undoing the 'Ndrangheta. Lea's testimony amounted to an unprecedented insight into the 'Ndrangheta. Her motivation—to give Denise a better life—was untainted and unstoppable. Lea should have prompted a complete rethink inside the Italian judiciary of the value of women in the fight against the mafia. There was certainly every reason to imagine that July 2002 had been the start of a whole new chapter in the war on the mafia. That made the investigation into Lea's disappearance even more critical. What had happened?

VIII

L EA WAS A beguiling mix of the carefree and the purposeful.[1]
She laughed easily, because life was for living, but she would
erupt if she felt her freedom or Denise's were threatened. She and
Denise would have been safer, she knew, if she had been able to accept the meek, servile existence of an 'Ndrangheta mother and wife.
But to Lea, that meant dying anyway. If the happiness she enjoyed
as a free woman and the possibilities Denise enjoyed outside the
'Ndrangheta were often eclipsed by terror, it was a price Lea felt
they had to pay.

The day Lea walked with Denise into a carabinieri station in
July 2002, she was petrified. Annalisa Pisano, then thirty-four, was
a public defender on call. "There was a list of lawyers to deal with
witness cooperation," she said. "I think they picked me because I
lived close by and I was a woman." Tall with short blond hair and
the businesslike bearing of a young criminal lawyer with her own
practice, Annalisa arrived at the station, rang the bell in the waiting
room, and sat down, unaware that the mother with a small child
sitting quietly next to her was her new client. "But then the carabinieri officer came and said: 'This is the girl who has asked for your
help. She has made the choice to talk.' And we had fifteen minutes
to prepare before the procedure began."

Annalisa remembered thinking how Lea was "so small, so skinny,
and Denise so tiny." She wondered how they would handle the giant
step they were taking. "There's almost no words to describe the

choice Lea was making," said Annalisa. "I could see she was blinded by terror, in a condition of high anxiety and stress. She had an idea about her brother, that he could take some action to reconcile with Carlo and preserve the status quo. But she was trying, like all mothers, to be courageous because she had her daughter with her." Annalisa tried to be sympathetic, telling Lea that she would get help and support from the state. The provincial carabinieri guarding her were no help. "Are you really interested in cooperating?" asked one officer, gruffly. "Because if not, you'll stay here."

The state's first task was to assess whether Lea and Denise were worth protecting. After two days of testimony, Lea was judged genuine, and she and her daughter were granted state protection. The process, bureaucratic and banal, was at odds with the momentous nature of what was happening. This, after all, was how a *pentita* gave up allegiance to family and homeland, abandoned everything and everyone they had ever known, accepted that forever after they would be at war with one of the world's most ruthless mafias, and put their faith in a state that they had been taught to despise from birth.

Initially, Lea and Denise were moved to Ascoli Piceno, a small, quiet province east of Rome. Lea told Denise they were to pretend they were sisters. They'd even had new make-believe names: Alessandra de Rossi and her younger sister, Sara. But Denise kept forgetting the rules, calling Lea Mama or Ma, and after a few weeks, Lea changed their names to Maria and Denise Petalo so that anyone overhearing them could excuse Ma as Lea's nickname.

Though safe from harm, Lea and Denise found their new life hard. They were rarely in one place long enough to put down new roots, moving six times in six years. Lea, for whom freedom meant the opportunity to be gregarious, found the isolation especially difficult. Her one connection to the outside world was a mobile given to her by the prosecutors, which she used to talk to Annalisa. "We spoke every day for the next six years, even on Saturdays and Sundays," said Annalisa. "For all that time, I was her only point of contact on the outside."

Despite the state's efforts, Lea also felt a constant threat around the corner. One day in August 2003, she read in the newspaper how Vito Cosco, then thirty-four, had shot and killed two small-time drug dealers who had insulted him. One of Vito's shots had also killed a two-year-old girl. A fourth victim, a sixty-year-old man who witnessed the shooting, had collapsed and died on the spot. Vito holed up at No. 6 Viale Montello for three days before phoning the carabinieri and telling them to come and arrest him. The newspapers called the killings "the massacre of Rozzano" after the small town outside Milan where they took place.

The Garofalo-Mirabelli *faida* raged on as well. In September 2003, Lea's cousin, Mario Garofalo, was shot in his car at a junction outside Pagliarelle. In June 2005, Floriano, by then forty, was walking to his front door in Pagliarelle when a man stepped out of the shadows carrying a shotgun. Floriano ran. Sprinting through a vegetable plot, he tore across the main road and up a side street. The gunman ran after him and shot him in the back. Floriano fell against a fence. The gunman reloaded, walked up to Floriano, and shot him several times in the face, blowing his head back to a stump.

Though Lea had often lived in fear of Floriano when he was alive, now she was convinced her brother had died because he had refused to kill her. Carlo had been released from prison in December 2003. Floriano's murder eighteen months later couldn't be a coincidence. "It's my fault they killed him," she told Marisa. The guilt destroyed her. Just as bad, in her safe house her protection officers would grin at her and tell her that the threat to her life was gone. They didn't understand anything. Not that it had probably been Carlo who had killed Floriano. And not that with Floriano dead, Carlo now not only ruled the Pagliarelle 'Ndrangheta but had also inherited the task of restoring its honor by killing Lea. The threat to Lea had soared. She took to staying awake through the night and sleeping during the day while Denise was at school. Even then, she kept a knife under her pillow.

Lea was right to be scared. Carlo began his search for her the day he left jail. He dropped by the convent in Bergamo, explaining he was a relative and asking the nuns if they had any contact with his cousin. In November 2004, Gennaro Garofalo, a member of Carlo's *'ndrina* who had once worked as a police auxiliary, showed up at his old station in Monza, asked his old colleagues out for pizza, then casually logged onto the witness protection system to search for Denise's address, which came up as No. 9 Via Giovanni Ruggia, Perugia. Later in court Gennaro would claim he saw nothing sinister in a father's desire to know his daughter's whereabouts. "Carlo always treated Denise well," he explained. "In Pagliarelle, he made sure Denise ate and dressed well. She always had earrings."

Early in 2005, Carlo sent two of his men, Rosario Curcio and Giovanni Peci, to find Lea in Perugia. The address in Via Giovanni Ruggia turned out to be a police station. When the men returned to Carlo empty-handed, he sent them back in a fury. By then, however, word had circulated in Pagliarelle that Carlo was closing in on Lea and a cousin had traveled to Perugia to warn her. Lea and Denise were quickly moved to Florence. But Carlo was relentless. In 2006, he sent another cousin, Genevieve Garofalo, to meet Lea with a message that Carlo wanted to see her and had set aside €200,000 for Denise. "It's a trap," Lea told Denise. "He's trying to get us back to Calabria." Lea was right, no doubt. Still, Carlo's persistence was having an effect. Lea could feel herself increasingly enclosed in a prison of paranoia.

ALESSANDRA HAD ENOUGH experience of witness protection not to be surprised by Lea's experience of it. The system wasn't perfect.

The mafia had always had its men inside the judiciary, who passed it information on the whereabouts of *pentiti*. There was also an inherent contradiction between trying to protect someone and simultaneously giving them their freedom. Sometimes that need for personal liberation led witnesses to put themselves in harm's way. Lea's motivation was always to give Denise a different life. But she also longed to free herself—and she had hardly achieved that. She couldn't go out unaccompanied. She couldn't talk to strangers. She was to live meekly and quietly, dependent on meager handouts. It was eerily similar to 'Ndrangheta life. Some of the officers guarding her seemed to regard her as little more than a lowlife Calabrian hick who'd conned the state and struck it lucky. The truth was that the sacrifices she had made in her fight against the mafia—risking her life, abandoning her family and friends—were far greater than any nine-to-five provincial cop would ever make.

Lea began to push back. She demanded to see her boyfriend from Bergamo. She asked not to be placed in towns with Calabrian populations. She wandered off into town without telling anyone. She refused to accept her protection officers' complaints about her behavior. "Why do I have to defend myself against the state that is supposed to be defending me and my daughter?" she asked. Denise, as a growing girl, was also becoming difficult. "Lea would explain to her daughter why they were moving and why they had to change their names," said Sandro Dolce, the prosecutor, "then the daughter would talk about it at school, and they would have to move again."

As months turned to years, the state began to have doubts about Lea and Denise for other reasons, too. The procedure for mafia turncoats was to keep them closely guarded while their evidence was evaluated and corroborated, and any trials conducted. Only after that would the government give them a permanent new identity, home, and job. But not only was Lea proving tiresome to handle, without other *pentiti* to confirm her evidence, the investigators were having trouble building a solid case against Carlo. Lea's statements, mostly describing what she had heard but not seen, weren't enough on their own to make arrests or secure convictions. "We investigated for a long time but we never found enough confirmation," said Dolce. "Then a colleague replaced me and was very severe in his assessment: how what we had was not enough for arrests, and the silly things Lea did. So in February 2006 Lea and Denise were ejected from the program."

Annalisa immediately won Lea and Denise a temporary reprieve while she appealed the decision to throw them out of witness protection. But Lea was shattered. The state had reneged. It had promised her and her daughter a new life. Then it had betrayed them. She had expected the state to prosecute every crime she had revealed. It hadn't prosecuted any. Worse, by taking her testimony, the state had needlessly exposed Lea and Denise to even more danger than before. The Italian state, Lea decided, was little better than the 'Ndrangheta. The irony was that if Lea had been an actual 'Ndranghetista—if she had taken part in the dealing and the thieving and the killing—she would have been of more use to the authorities. It felt like they were punishing her for being honest.

That July, she phoned Annalisa. "I've changed my mind," she said. "I'm getting out of the program." Denise said later, "My mother decided to give up on the state. She had lost all confidence in them. Our life was exhausting, and for what? Her statements turned out to be useless."

Annalisa, aware that Lea was now suffering increasingly dramatic mood swings, managed to talk her client around. "More and more, she was finding herself lost in a reality that was bigger than her," said Annalisa. "You have to remember she was just a girl, only thirty-two years old. She thought her world and all her plans were collapsing around her." But Lea had already submitted a formal request to leave the program, and until Annalisa could get her readmitted, she and Denise were on their own. It was terrifying, said Annalisa. The state had washed its hands of Lea and Denise. Her mafioso husband was trying to kill her. Lea had no one. "And so," said Annalisa, "it fell to me."

Annalisa did her best. In November 2006, she moved close to where Lea and Denise were living. She became, as she said, "less a lawyer than a mother." But Lea remained volatile and mistrustful. Denise, who turned fifteen in December 2006, was also no longer a girl playing a game of hide-and-seek with her mother but, increasingly, had become a teenager with her own opinions. Lea had shielded her daughter from much of the truth about Carlo. The price of Denise's innocence was that she didn't understand why, now that she and Lea were out of witness protection, she couldn't see her father. "Denise kept asking," said Annalisa. "She would insist, pressing and pressing. Lea would call me every day because she couldn't manage Denise—you know how teenagers are." Annalisa tried to mediate between mother and daughter. Denise responded by demanding that the lawyer find a way for her to meet her father. Annalisa refused point-blank. "I told Denise it was completely unacceptable for her to meet her father. I only had to see the terror in Lea's eyes when the name of Cosco came up. But I think Denise started hating me after that."

Looking for help wherever she might find it, Lea briefly moved with Denise back to Bergamo, where Lea sought the advice of Mother Grata and found a job in a bar. Then they moved to Fabriano, where they had also lived before and Lea had an old boyfriend. At the end of 2007, Lea went to a café in Rome run by the anti-mafia group Libera. She met Libera's president, Don Luigi Ciotti, who put her in touch with a lawyer who volunteered for the organization.

Lea met Enza Rando at her townhouse offices in the center of Modena. The two women were very different. Lea, now thirty-three, was free-spirited and passionate, and the knowledge that she might die any day had given her a determination to live each one as her last. Enza was in her fifties, small, neat, and conservative. But at their first meeting, Lea brought pastries, then sat down and poured out her life story. Almost immediately, Enza loved her. "Lea was beautiful," she said. "Very intelligent and very courageous."

Annalisa had often been hard on Lea, especially when it came to Denise. Though Enza couldn't offer Lea much more than Annalisa, to Lea, after six years in isolation, she was a fresh face ready to listen. And from the moment Enza appeared, Annalisa sensed a new distance between herself and Lea. "There was a change," said Annalisa. "I could tell another lawyer was giving her advice. Something was wrong. I felt I was losing Lea. And I thought it was best to stop right then. Overlaps like that—inconsistencies, conflicting advice—could be very dangerous for Lea."

Heartbroken, Annalisa wrote a letter to Lea, offering her resignation. "In my mind, I was hoping this would shake Lea up and she would change her mind," she said. "We'd had ups and downs, but six years is a long time." Instead, in June 2008, Lea accepted Annalisa's notice.

In September 2008, largely as a result of Annalisa's years of appeals and applications, Lea and Denise were readmitted to the witness protection program. They were moved to Boiano, a small town near Campobasso in central Italy. Denise settled in well at her new school, and soon had a new group of friends. But by now Lea's state of mind had graduated from paranoid to disturbed. She was still staying awake all night, sleeping through the day, and keeping a knife under her pillow. Now she bought a guard dog and began taking lessons in martial arts. Nothing could soften the loneliness, however. She had no friends in Boiano and, with Annalisa gone, no one to talk to. Without government papers giving her a new identity, she also couldn't risk working, lest her name on an employee record identify her whereabouts. "It's all been a pile of crap," she would tell Denise. "Just a giant waste of our lives."

"It was so lonely for her," said Denise. "And without a job, she couldn't be independent, she couldn't provide for us by her own efforts and, for her, this was a real defeat."

One day in April, Lea decided to write to the president of Italy, Giorgio Napolitano:

> *I am a young mother at the end of my tether. Today I find myself together with my daughter isolated from everything and everyone. I lost everything. My family. My job. I lost my home. I lost countless friends. I lost any expectations of the future. I had reckoned on all of this. I knew what I was getting when I made my choice.*

But her sacrifices had been for nothing, wrote Lea. Her statements had led to no arrests and no convictions. She and Denise had suffered for seven years for no reason. And then the state cast them out. Lea wrote that she was losing her faith in justice. "The worst thing is that I already know the fate that awaits me. After poverty comes death. Undeserved and unearned but unavoidable." Who else would make the choice she had? she asked.

"Today, Mr. President, you can change the course of history. I still believe that a person can live with integrity and decency in this country. Please, Mr. President, give us a sign of hope. Help innocent victims of injustice."

But when Lea went to post the letter in Boiano, she spotted a couple on a street corner who seemed to be watching her. The woman was wearing an earpiece. As Lea approached, the woman reached into her bag. Lea thought she was going for a gun. "I didn't believe her," said Denise, when Lea told her later, "but I wasn't there and I didn't see it and my mother certainly believed there was someone who wanted to hurt her. She was very frightened. She decided not to send the letter and told me that we were leaving the protection program once again."

Lea's second request to leave the state program was the final straw for its administrators. They gave her and Denise two weeks to vacate their safe house and advised her never to reapply. Lea and Denise were on their own once more, and this time forever.

LEA, HOWEVER, HAD a new plan. She phoned her sister Marisa and asked her to pass on a message to Carlo. "She basically said: 'OK, I said some things that were inconvenient for you,'" recalled Denise. "'But I retracted everything and there will be no trial and no one will be shamed. So you have to leave me alone and leave my daughter alone.'"

Lea wanted out of witness protection, said Denise, because the process had been "absolutely pointless." The one upside was that if the state wasn't using her evidence, then Carlo had no reason to kill her. She just wanted to return to Pagliarelle and be left alone to quietly bring up their daughter. In return, she said Carlo would get to see Denise whenever he wanted. "She just didn't want to have to worry about her life and my life anymore," said Denise.

Carlo agreed. In a few days, Marisa came to pick up Lea and Denise from Boiano and take them back to Pagliarelle. Lea refused to see Carlo and stayed in the house with the curtains drawn. For Denise, it was the first chance she'd had to see her father in nine years. "He took me for drives, to restaurants, to see his friends, to eat at his house," she said. "He said we should move to Pagliarelle and that I could finish high school down there." Denise said she wanted to finish school in Boiano, where she had friends. She asked Carlo to rent an apartment there, because she and Lea had nowhere to live. Carlo agreed to that, too. After Easter, he and Denise drove to Campobasso, a short bus ride from Boiano, and rented the first apartment they were shown near the school in the old town for one month. Carlo then installed Denise; his mother, Piera; and his nephew, Domenico—Uncle Giuseppe's son—in the apartment. Since he was paying for it, Carlo moved in himself for a few days.

Lea was furious at the way Carlo was insinuating himself back into their lives. She had no choice but to accept his money for her daughter's sake. Nevertheless, while Denise, Carlo, Carlo's mother, and Carlo's nephew slept in the apartment, Lea refused to meet Carlo and spent the nights outside in the car. "We'd slept in the same bed for years," said Denise. "She found it hard."

The pressure eased slightly when Carlo returned to Milan. But the atmosphere in the apartment remained poisonous. On April 24, Lea's thirty-fifth birthday passed without celebration. Another day, she fought with Carlo's mother, Piera, saying she shouldn't be there and that she, Lea, should be taking care of Denise, seeing as she'd managed for seventeen years. Shortly afterward, Lea had to take Piera to the hospital for what looked like hypertension. When Carlo heard his mother was sick, he drove back down from Milan.

The night that Piera was released from the hospital, Lea, worried about her mother-in-law and unable to deny a son's love for his mother, found herself at supper with the entire Cosco family. It was the first time Carlo and Lea had been in the same room for thirteen years. Lea was primed to explode. When Piera yelled that Lea was making her unwell—"she's killing me with her shouting"—Lea, who was holding a bread knife, blew up. What was Piera even doing there? Why were any of them there? What the fuck was *Carlo* doing there? Lea and Denise had done fine by themselves all these years. She waved the knife at Carlo and shouted at him. "You have to go," she said. "Get the fuck out of here right now! Go now! Go now!"

"I was crying through all of it," said Denise. "But my father didn't say anything. He just took the two suitcases he'd brought with him, kissed me on the cheek, and left."

WITHOUT MONEY, LEA and Denise were still dependent on Carlo. They needed him even for small things like fixing the broken washing machine in the apartment. In early May, Denise and Lea went to a four-day pop festival in Rome, returning to Campobasso early on May 5. At 9 A.M., Carlo called Denise to say a repairman was coming that day to fix the washing machine. Denise said OK and went to bed. Lea fell asleep on the couch.

A few minutes later, the doorbell rang. Lea stuffed a knife in her back pocket and answered the door to a clean-shaven man in jeans and a blue jacket with a tattoo down one side of his neck, carrying a toolbox with a Winnie the Pooh sticker on the side. The man said he had come to fix the washing machine. Lea let him in and showed him to the kitchen. She watched him as he pushed a few buttons on the machine. He didn't open his toolbox. He asked Lea how the machine worked. Lea regarded him. "If you have to kill me, do it now," she said.

The man flew at Lea and she pulled the knife from her back pocket. He stuck two fingers down her throat, trying to choke her. Lea kicked him in the crotch. The toolbox fell onto the floor. Upstairs, Denise heard the crash. "I came down and this man and my mother were wrapped around each other," she said. "At first I thought it was my father, because he was dark-skinned and wearing the same jacket my father had."

Denise jumped on the man and started punching and kicking him. She saw his face: it wasn't Carlo. Still, the man seemed to recognize Denise. He looked at her with shock, threw the two women off, and ran for the door. Denise chased him and grabbed him by the throat. "Who sent you?!" she shouted. "Who sent you?!"

"Let me go!" the man yelled, and ran out.

Denise went to help Lea, who was bleeding. The two of them examined the toolbox that Lea's attacker had left behind. Inside were no plumbing tools but, instead, duct tape, wire, rope, scissors, a saw, and latex gloves. Lea called the carabinieri, who interviewed her and Denise and took fingerprints. Once they left, Lea told Denise that though it was important to have an official record of the attack, they couldn't count on the carabinieri to keep them safe. They packed, ran down to Lea's car, and drove to a B&B, taking care to park on a different street. After staying in their room all day and all night, they left early the next morning without paying and drove to the main piazza, where Lea pitched a tent opposite the town hall. They were safer where everyone could see them, she said.

Lea and Denise were convinced Carlo had sent an assassin to kill Lea. Still, when Carlo called, Denise arranged to meet her father in town. "I had no choice," she said. "If a person wants to hurt you or kill you, either you let them or you pretend to be their friend."

When Denise saw Carlo, however, she couldn't control herself. She flew at him. She accused him of trying to kill her mother. Carlo shouted back that the attack had had nothing to do with him.

"But you were the only one to know about the broken washing machine!" said Denise.

"Your phones are tapped!" shouted Carlo. "You were in the protection program! Anyone could have known about the washing machine! Anyone could have sent that guy!"

Denise was caught off guard for a second. Then she said: "I never want to see you again. I'm going with my mom."

LEA WISHED THAT the two of them could have ridden off into the sunset as Denise wanted. But with no money, no state protection, and no lawyer, their only option was to follow their original plan, move back to Calabria, and try again to secure a truce from Carlo. They packed up their tent, caught the train to Calabria, and moved into Lea's mother's house in Petilia, all three women sharing a kitchen, a single bedroom, and a tiny bathroom. Lea replaced the old wooden front door with a new metal one. Aside from walking a few meters to buy cigarettes, she stayed indoors.

For Lea, life in Pagliarelle was more claustrophobic than ever. She had to assume that most of the village might be trying to kill her. She quarreled with the few people she did see.

Denise quickly couldn't stand to be in the apartment with her mother. Almost without realizing it, she found herself falling into the routine of clan life, taking drives into the country with her father when he was down from Milan, eating lunch with him and his friends. In Pagliarelle, there was no way to behave differently. But when she returned to the house with new jeans, new trainers, or a new jacket, Lea, who had raised her daughter to despise materialism, would throw a fit.

What surprised Denise was that Carlo seemed to find the situation just as hard. One day he asked his daughter to go on holiday with him. When Denise asked Lea, and her mother initially agreed only to change her mind at the last minute, Carlo erupted. "On that occasion, I really understood how deeply my father loathed my mother," said Denise. "He insulted her in front of me and said that for my entire life, my mother had made all the decisions for me and that she still did. He couldn't stand that. It was intolerable. He couldn't allow my mother to decide whether or not I spent time with him." Marisa, who overheard, took Denise aside after Carlo left. "He really wants her dead," said Marisa. "He truly hates her."

Toward the end of summer, however, Lea began to think that Carlo might be softening. In September 2009, she asked to meet him and Carlo came to the house. Denise was there. "They were talking for more than an hour, just the two of them," said Denise.

"At one point, I couldn't see them anywhere and I got scared. But when I looked out from the balcony, they were in the garden under a tree, just talking. They waved at me." Lea announced that she and Carlo were going for a drive to Botricello, a small holiday town built around a medieval castle on the coast where they used to go as teenagers. It was already 11 P.M., and she and Carlo didn't return until 4 A.M. When Denise asked Lea the next morning what her parents had been talking about for so long, Lea smiled coyly and said: "You know, old times. Mind your own business."

It might seem strange to others, said Denise, but she believed her parents had loved each other once. Now she began to imagine that they would again. A lot of their conversation that night had been about where Denise should go to university. Lea favored Catanzaro while Carlo was pushing for Milan. Lea was hurt that Denise might want to leave her. "After all she had been through, after everything she had done for me, she said I was being ungrateful," said Denise. Still, it was everyday parent chat. Meanwhile, Denise and Carlo were getting used to each other's company again. "We spoke on the phone, we went to the beach, we ate dinner together," said Denise.

On November 19, 2009, Lea and Denise traveled to Florence. Lea was due in court, accused of a minor assault from years earlier when she had slapped a teenage girl in the street after the girl accused Denise of trying to steal her boyfriend. The case was to be heard on November 20. Enza had agreed to represent Lea. The day before, Denise and Lea went window-shopping in the city. Denise spotted a sweatshirt she liked, but she knew Lea wouldn't have the money for it and worried she would sell the gold necklace and bracelet Carlo had given her to buy it. So Denise called her father. Carlo said new clothes were no problem and suggested that after the case, she and Lea come to Milan and they all go shopping together.

When Enza heard about the plan, she told Lea, "It's a bad idea.

Carlo's trying to kill you." But, said Enza, "Lea was a strong woman and she had decided." Lea told her lawyer, "It's Milan, not Calabria. A big city. People everywhere. I'll never be alone and Denise will be with me. Nothing's going to happen. He wouldn't be able to organize anything in time."

On the day of the court case, Enza managed to negotiate an official reprimand for her client. Hours later, Lea and Denise caught the evening train to Milan. Watching them leave, Enza decided she would try to stop them one last time. "Turn around," she texted her client. "Get off at Piacenza. Libera has a place for you where you can be safe."

As they neared Milan, Lea sent her reply. "Thank you, my lawyer, thank you. But Denise and I have to try to make a life for ourselves. God bless you. God bless us all."[2]

"And that was the last I heard from her," said Enza.

ACT TWO

Rebellion in Rosarno

IX

T WO HOURS BEFORE dawn on the first Sunday of 2010, the rattle of a scooter could be heard curling up through the empty streets of Reggio Calabria. Two figures leaned into the windscreen to protect themselves from the January cold. In front was a slim man in a dark jacket and tight jeans, a dark helmet pushed down over his long hair. Behind him sat a plumper man in jeans and a striped jacket. Despite the speed at which the pair were racing across the icy cobbles, the second man declined to hold on to his companion. Instead in his arms he cradled a bulky canvas bag, almost as though it were a baby.

After following the shoreline for a few minutes, the pair turned away from the sea and climbed up steeply toward the center of the old town. They passed the floodlit walls of the Castello Aragonese, built by the Normans and expanded by the Spanish in the fifteenth century. When the pair reached the castle gardens, the driver executed a wide U-turn, eased off the throttle, and allowed the bike to coast gently over the cobbles back down the hill. After a few yards, he pulled up in front of an imposing metal gate, holding the bike on the slope with his legs and keeping his hand on the accelerator. Behind him the man bent over his bag and pulled his jacket around him as though he were lighting a cigarette. Suddenly there was a spark. Flames licked up out of the bag. The man jumped off the bike and ran toward the gate, swinging the burning bag high and wide like a lasso to avoid the flames. The driver revved the engine and let the bike roll slowly down the hill. The man dropped the bag, ran back to the moving bike, and jumped on, and the pair roared off. Seconds later, the bag exploded.[1]

In the predawn calm, the noise of the blast rolled out across the Strait of Messina like thunder. The noise woke the carabinieri barracks where Alessandra had her apartment. A few hours later at a press conference, a carabinieri commander described the bomb as the kind of crude device—a stick of dynamite attached to a ten-kilo gas cylinder—familiar to anyone with experience of southern Italy's protection rackets. Aside from some damage to a gate and a railing, and a few shattered windows, there was little physical harm done.

That didn't mean the attack wasn't serious. The mayor of Reggio, the chamber of commerce, the president and vice president of the Italian parliament, even Italy's head of state, President Giorgio Napolitano, sent the Reggio authorities messages of solidarity. Italy had declared war on the world's most powerful mafia. The mafiosi had started the New Year by signaling their intention to strike back.

The stakes in this new fight had escalated radically over the previous few months. Thanks to years of surveillance, for the first time the Italian state now had a comprehensive picture of the 'Ndrangheta's structure and its cocaine business. The prosecutors were now confronting the full scale of the mission they had undertaken. Their priority was also clear: Calabria's west coast, the heart of the cocaine business. That explained the bomb's target, detonated outside Reggio's courthouse, the seat of justice in Calabria for as long as the 'Ndrangheta had existed and, in 2010, the offices of Calabria's attorney general, who oversaw the confiscation of mafia assets. If the 'Ndrangheta liked to send messages, this was the group at its most unequivocal: Calabria's prosecutors should end their campaign or face violent consequences. But as Alessandra and her colleagues absorbed the implications of the warning, they drew a second conclusion, too. To provoke this kind of reaction, their crackdown must be having an effect.

There followed other signs that the west coast 'Ndrangheta was feeling the pressure. A week after the bomb, Rosarno erupted in three days of riots. The violence began when a group of 'Ndrangheta teenagers, apparently bored and looking for kicks, fired an air gun into the tented camp behind Gioia Tauro port where more than a thousand West African migrants lived. Hundreds of Africans marched into Rosarno, protesting, burning several cars, and fighting with the police. Rosarno hoodlums armed with iron bars set up roadblocks. At least two Rosarno men tried to run over migrants in the street. More than twenty Africans were injured, many of them beaten and three shot. Eventually, riot police descended. On the orders of the interior minister, they expelled every last African—a total of 1,200 people—from the town. Rosarno and its people, said Minister Roberto Maroni, were the unfortunate victims of "too much tolerance."

But if the Rosarno *picciotti* considered such unashamed racism a victory, they were mistaken. The violence drew condemnation and outrage from across Italy. Pope Benedict XVI urged pilgrims gathered in St. Peter's Square in Rome to remember that "an immigrant is a human being." One opposition leader, Luigi Manconi, said that by expelling the Africans, the authorities had been complicit in creating "the whitest town in the world." The media attention also exposed the wretched hypocrisy of the 'Ndrangheta—who, it turned out, were attacking the very people they had brought to Rosarno to work as fruit pickers for as little as three euros a day. The spotlight on Rosarno also gave Alessandra's office an opportunity to score a very public victory. A day after the violence died down, with the eyes of Italy still on Rosarno, her office arrested seventeen suspected members of the Bellocco clan, the Pesces' main rival in the city, and seized assets of several million euros.[2]

Almost straightaway, the 'Ndrangheta tripped up again. Nine days later in Reggio, hours before President Napolitano arrived to reinforce his support of Calabria's authorities in their new war, a telephone tip-off led carabinieri to a stolen car parked close to his route. The vehicle contained two bombs and two pistols. But what was intended to intimidate quickly managed to do precisely the opposite. The tipster was arrested almost immediately and charged with mafia association. Napolitano's visit went ahead, though now he was able to strike a courageous profile by defying the mafia's threat to his life and, on 'Ndrangheta turf, hailing a "turning point" in the fight against them. As a final insult, by the end of the month Reggio Calabria had been selected as the location for a new Italian agency tasked with seizing mafia businesses and transforming them into Libera shops or offices for policemen, magistrates, or the tax department. As fightbacks went, it felt uncomfortably like humiliation.[3]

But even if the 'Ndrangheta had lost the opening exchanges in its war with the state, the fight was far from over. Alessandra, in particular, was convinced that a crucial weakness in the state's strategy meant it could never win. Pignatone and Prestipino were freethinkers who had no trouble imagining a woman 'Ndranghetista could be as much use as a woman prosecutor. Cerreti described joining their team as finally finding "fertile territory" for her ideas. But among the rank and file, "Italian prosecutors were still not investigating women," said Alessandra. Many rejected outright the idea that women could serve justice in any way at all. ("I mean, *really*, women do have eyes and ears," said Alessandra.) They also refused to see as anything other than exceptional what Alessandra was observing in Rosarno: that by early 2010, 'Ndrangheta men had realized their women were being left alone by the authorities and were starting to give them power. Across the province, at least two women had become clan bosses. Nevertheless, said Alessandra, "it was still very hard for us to make our colleagues believe that women had a role."

Alessandra understood that if many prosecutors and carabinieri were barely able to conceive of a woman 'Ndranghetista, then they would dismiss out of hand the idea of an 'Ndrangheta woman with the strength to rebel against her men. "This was another form of the same prejudice," she said. "The belief that no one, and certainly not a woman, is going to talk about their own family, let alone testify and accuse their own family." She conceded that it would take unusual bravery. But to write it off as impossible was to guarantee it never happened. "When justice shows to people that it is strong and that the state is present and can help you if you want to collaborate," she said, "then you find collaborators appear."

At heart, thought Alessandra, this was a failure of perception. Whenever many of her male colleagues saw women and children, they saw family and nothing else. Most seemed incapable of identifying what a family might represent in a place like Rosarno or Pagliarelle: a living, breathing criminal organism. "The entire structure, the family nature of it, makes it hard for many people even to recognize it as a problem," she said. Once again, Alessandra was confronting the 'Ndrangheta's astute understanding of family. "The part played by family, and by women, makes them so difficult to track." Sometimes she felt that she, Pignatone, and Prestipino were the only ones who could see what was right in front of them: women who were simultaneously mothers, mafiosi, and potential state witnesses. That had been the problem with Lea Garofalo. The state had seen her too simplistically, as a battered wife, a troubled witness, a victim. Only one prosecutor, Sandro Dolce, had grasped everything that Lea was and everything that she offered the state. What Alessandra needed was another 'Ndrangheta mother to change her colleagues' minds.

As it happened, she would have two.

ACCORDING TO THE precepts of clan rivalry, Giuseppina Pesce, thirty-one, and Maria Concetta Cacciola, thirty, were unlikely friends.[4] The Pesces led the most powerful clan in Rosarno, which had ruled the town since the 1920s. The Cacciolas were muscle for their rivals, the Belloccos. The Pesces and the Belloccos sometimes cooperated in business and on occasion their children even married each other. But as the Pesces climbed ever higher up the 'Ndrangheta's new vertical hierarchy, the Bellocco name meant ever less— and the Belloccos hated the Pesces for that.

Giuseppina and Concetta also weren't alike. Giuseppina was tough, an 'Ndrangheta wife who had pushed the men in her family to let her become an 'Ndranghetista in her own right. There were limits on what a woman could do in the organization. Murder and violence were out, and any involvement in extortion, corruption, or drug smuggling was confined to bookkeeping and passing messages between the men. But Giuseppina was dismissive of any man who imagined her to be less than him and communicated her adamant equality in a tomboyish appearance. She wore bulky woolen V-necks over cheap and baggy worker's shirts. She had no time for makeup. Her dirt-brown hair was cut in a scruffy parting at whatever length kept it out of the way, and from under it her brown eyes would stare out at the world with a blankness that conveyed an intimidating intimacy with brutality.

Concetta could not have been more different. She took no part in the men's business, and her knowledge of it extended little beyond gossip about where the bunkers were and who had killed whom. Unlike the Pesces, the Cacciola men didn't accept even a hint of independence or assertion in their women, and they kept Concetta confined to the house for weeks at a time. On the rare occasions she was allowed out, Concetta's own private rebellion was to emerge immaculately dressed, as though she were a busy socialite. She favored tight jeans with unbuttoned blouses that hung loosely across her perfumed chest. Her jet-black hair was styled in a long undulating curl that swept across her forehead, nestled over her ears, and executed a jaunty ski jump on her shoulders. She plucked her eyebrows, waxed her legs, painted her fingernails and toes, and paired dark shades of plum and scarlet on her lips with heavy mascara and a brush of mauve over her eyes. If Giuseppina's appearance implied equivalence to any man, Concetta presented herself as nothing like them.

Despite their differences, Giuseppina and Concetta had been close friends since they were girls. When they were growing up in Rosarno in the 1980s, the town had been a cold, hard place of loveless lives where girls could be beaten just for stepping out of the house unaccompanied. Rosarno was also small, however, and as schoolgirls Giuseppina and Concetta would see each other every day in the playground or on the street. As they approached their teens, their lives also followed a near-identical prescribed course, which—since the town had no secondary school and 'Ndrangheta girls weren't allowed to leave it—meant marriage, quickly followed by motherhood.

Giuseppina finished her education at thirteen. By then, she had already met her future husband, Rocco Palaia, twenty, whose father managed weapons for the Pesce clan. At fourteen, Giuseppina eloped with Rocco, a common event in Rosarno, known as *fuitina*. At fifteen she gave birth to the first of the couple's three children, Angela. By then, Rocco was doing little more than smoking weed and lying around the house all day, so Giuseppina went to work in the family store. It wasn't long before Rocco was arrested and jailed for mafia association.

Concetta had always had it harder than her friend. When she was eleven, her brother Giuseppe caught her playing in the street with a few local boys. He beat her, dragged her home by her hair, and forbade her to leave the house alone again. After that, Concetta never went out for pizza or gelato. "You know my brother 'Peppe," she would say. "If he saw me, you know he'd kill me." When Concetta was thirteen, she met her twenty-one-year-old future husband, Salvatore Figliuzzi, and eloped with him. When she was just fifteen, Concetta gave birth to Alfonso, the first of the couple's three children. Salvatore was also soon hauled off to jail.

By the time of his arrest, Salvatore was already beating Concetta regularly. One day he held a gun to her head. When Concetta complained to her father, he replied, "It's your marriage and your life. You deal with it." Concetta might have expected things to improve with Salvatore in jail. Instead, her father took over the role of violent disciplinarian, slapping her to the ground in the street one day when she returned late from a shopping trip to Reggio. On conjugal visits to prison, Concetta conceived a second child, Tania, then a third, Rosalba, whom she named after her mother.

By their early twenties, Giuseppina and Concetta were alone, married to jailbird husbands, and mothers to three children each. They would meet at the school gates or the doctor's or in the Pesce family minimart where Giuseppina worked, across the street from the Cacciola family home. The two women negotiated their situations as best they could. Concetta had somehow remained "a sunny girl," said Giuseppina years later, through tears. "Strong. She was an optimist . . . She cared so much." As Lea had done growing up in Pagliarelle, Concetta sustained herself with a dream of true love that would take her away from it all. With Salvatore in jail, she began fantasizing that she was not the abused wife of a violent small-time gangster at all but, rather, a woman tragically separated from her love. On prison visits, she would wear scarlet lipstick with thick eyeshadow and frame her face with thick long curls. She wrote Salvatore wistful letters. "I go out in the morning to take the children to school but I have no contact with anyone," she wrote in 2007. "How can I live if I cannot even breathe? If I can't even speak to anyone? My father likes to see me miserable from dawn to dusk. If only I could have a little peace of mind. I'd pay anything, take anything, for a little peace. I don't know how long I can go on without you."

If Concetta survived by retreating into fantasy, Giuseppina endured through sheer will. Like Concetta, she was beaten by her husband. But Rocco would hit Giuseppina not because she was out on her own or because she was looking at other men, or even just because he could, but because Giuseppina insisted on speaking out of turn. "He beat me when I said what I thought," she said. "He attacked me to get me to shut up."

After Rocco went to jail, Giuseppina's father, Salvatore Pesce, told her to confine herself to the home like Concetta. He refused to let her go to college or divorce Rocco or continue her piano lessons. "You're not going anywhere," he shouted. "You'll stay locked up in the house." Giuseppina's way of conserving some autonomy was to join the family firm. Within a few years, she was running messages between bosses in jail, laundering money, and overseeing the collection of *pizzo*. No one had to tell her what to do, she said later. "I lived in this family. I breathed these things, the superiority and the power and the privilege. I knew because I was there. I have always known, since I was a child."

WITH EVERY YEAR that passed, Giuseppina's knowledge of the 'Ndrangheta grew. She knew its power structure intimately. The nominal head of the clan was Giuseppina's uncle Antonino. Since he was in jail, however, others handled day-to-day operations. By primogeniture, Giuseppina's father, Salvatore, should have been the first choice to replace Antonino. But Salvatore had never been leadership material: since he was a boy, his nickname had been U Babbu, the buffoon. The mantle instead fell to Antonino's son and Giuseppina's cousin, Francesco "Ciccio" Pesce, a hothead given to angry and violent outbursts who wielded absolute power in his father's stead.

The 'Ndrangheta was run as an autocracy. But Giuseppina would later insist it was one willingly accepted by its subjects. In the 'Ndrangheta, tyranny was what passed for effective leadership, and what it took to have and hold power. At its heart, however, Giuseppina said an *'ndrina* was a collective. "They decided together, as a family, who took state contracts, who handled extortion, who oversaw the drug trade. That's the strength of the clan—that we are all family members together."

Inside the *'ndrina, picciotti* like Giuseppina were expected to help out however they were needed. Her work gave Giuseppina a comprehensive view of the Pesce empire. The house of her seventy-eight-year-old grandmother, Giuseppa Bonarrigo, often served as a base for operations and a meeting place. There the family would discuss at length the delicate question of how much *pizzo* to charge. The younger men tended to squeeze as much as they could out of everyone, once even extorting tickets for the entire family from a visiting circus. The older men would warn against overdoing it, arguing that driving a business to ruin was in no one's interest. Another point of discussion was how to divide the take. Giuseppina saw many *picciotti* try to resist handing over their revenues to a common family pot, as required. What everyone agreed on, however, was that there could be no exceptions to paying *pizzo*. "An outsider can't say no, because he is afraid," said Giuseppina. "The men would go and ask for money like they were doing people a favor. But everyone knew they couldn't refuse."

Giuseppina got to know other sides of the business. Her father, Salvatore, her cousin Ciccio, and her husband, Rocco, all moved cocaine through Gioia Tauro port and stashed packages in the house, ready for onward transport. Negotiating the interminable roadworks on the A3 from Reggio Calabria to Salerno one day, her brother pointed out which sites belonged to the Pesces and which to other clans. 'Ndrangheta rules also required each clan to have a stash of automatic rifles, shotguns, and pistols. Rocco and his brother had buried the Pesce arsenal around town, wrapping the guns in sheets of plastic and duct tape. "We're prepared for a war," Rocco liked to say.

It was the Pesces' firepower that guaranteed the family was feared or, as they liked to see it, respected. Around town, people would make way for Giuseppina. In restaurants, bills never appeared. In grocery stores, the manager would come out to serve her personally. If she went to the doctor's, she walked straight to the head of the queue and "no one could ever say anything to me because I was part of the family." One time she went to an ear specialist in Gioia Tauro. On hearing her name, the man asked after the health of her niece and her daughter, then knocked his price down to bargain-basement level, saying he wanted to send "his greetings to my uncle and my family."

But if the family enjoyed their local fame, other kinds of attention made them paranoid. The ability of the police and the carabinieri to listen in was unreal. They tapped phone calls, filmed the interiors of houses from several kilometers away, mounted secret cameras outside homes and schools, and planted bugs almost anywhere—in cars, in walls and fireplaces, in orchards and schools, even under stones in Giuseppina's grandmother's garden. The Pesces bought bug detectors to sniff out these devices, as well as jammers to block their signals and scanners of their own to monitor the carabinieri's radios. Still, they were often reduced to whispering and using sign language in their own homes. Ciccio was always telling the others, "Don't talk too much." More than once, his paranoia led him to smash up his phone and television, unscrew every light bulb in his house, and throw everything into the street.

This mistrust forced many a boss into hiding. Most sought sanctuary in secret underground bunkers buried deep in the countryside. It wasn't as bad as it sounded. The bosses would trick out their bunkers with lights, televisions, kitchens, and comfortable beds. Some had their hideouts built into the cliffs to give them a sea view and a sunset. Others enjoyed bucolic locations in orchards or olive groves. Instinctively territorial, however, the Pesces built their bunkers in town, often under their own houses. Before he was arrested in 2005, Giuseppina's father had been hiding for years in a bunker that he'd spent thousands of euros renovating under the floor of Giuseppina's grandmother's house.

IF RESPECT WAS everything to the Pesces, shame was unacceptable for the same reason. The treacherous and unfaithful didn't just need to be killed. They had to vanish from the face of the earth and leave no reminders of the dishonor they had brought on the family.

By 2010, Michele Prestipino was looking into a number of deaths in Calabria, including some officially recorded as suicides, that he suspected were actually honor killings. In one of the most recent, a widow called Dominica Legato had jumped to her death from her balcony in Rosarno in 2007. At least, that was what her son told police. Giuseppina, Concetta, and every woman in Rosarno suspected another version of events, as did the coroner, who found knife wounds on Dominica's hands, suggesting she had been fending off an attack when she fell. A few months later the Rosarno man with whom Dominica was said to be having a relationship also disappeared.

The full fury of the Rosarno 'Ndrangheta's rage could be terrifying. What made it even more disturbing was how the 'Ndrangheta could sustain it. In 1979, when she was twenty-five, the husband of Concetta Teresa Galluci, a mason, died in an accident, falling from the fourth floor of a building he was helping build for the Pesces. Concetta and her husband had had three children. More than a decade later, she began a relationship with twenty-three-year-old Francesco Alcuri. One night in November 1993 in Rosarno, Alcuri was shot nine times in the groin, dying eleven days later in agony. Concetta, now forty, fled for Genoa in northern Italy, where her sister lived. One evening four months after arriving, she opened her sister's front door and was shot in the head. The gunmen then shot the dead woman's seventy-two-year-old mother as she ran into the living room in her nightdress, before killing her twenty-two-year-old niece while she slept in her bed.

The Pesces were deeply secretive about their own family embarrassments. Not for them the scrutiny that accompanied the discovery of a dead body. Long ago, the Pesces had calculated that since Rosarno's graveyard was the most obvious place to dump a body, it would be the last place anyone would look. Up there, buried under the floor in the family's chapel, was Giuseppina's grandfather, Angelo Ferraro, killed for having an affair. Alongside him was Annunziata Pesce, Giuseppina's cousin, who had betrayed her husband and the entire 'Ndrangheta by running off with a policeman. Kidnapped off the street in broad daylight in 1981, she was shot in the neck by the boss, Antonino Pesce, while her elder brother, Antonio, watched. Antonio's reward for his unflinching loyalty? Promotion to a dominant position inside the *'ndrina* for him and his immediate family.

Killings like these left no doubt about the price of betrayal. It was a measure of the desperation of many 'Ndrangheta women that the men kept finding it necessary to carry them out. Perhaps it was inevitable. 'Ndrangheta mothers knew their sons would grow up to be killers and drug dealers destined for prison and an early grave. They knew their daughters would be married off as they had been, barely pubescent, to an older, abusive, criminal husband. They expected to lose their own abusive, criminal husbands to death or jail. Faced with a life in which what Concetta called Rosarno's "stone-hearted men" extinguished all the light and joy in the world, it was hardly surprising that the town's women grabbed what little sweetness they could.

Many of the men seemed to understand this. Their response was not to ease off but to take preemptive action, particularly when, with a husband dead or in jail, an 'Ndrangheta wife found herself alone. Concetta's cousin Giuseppina Multari had been locked up at home as a virtual slave since the day in 2005 that the Cacciola men had killed her husband, their cousin, for being a junkie. When her brother tried to confront the Cacciolas about the way they were treating his sister, he also vanished.

When Concetta's husband, Salvatore, went to jail, her father and brother resolved to prevent her from almost ever leaving the house. But such blinkered conservatism blinded them to the fact that they were living in the twenty-first century, in which friendship—or more—was only ever a click away. "In the land of the 'Ndrangheta, the Internet is an open window in a closed world," said Alessandra. "It introduces women to a free world. It tends to provoke a kind of emotional explosion." A colleague, Roberto di Bella, said he had seen the same pattern repeat with many wives of jailbird 'Ndranghetisti. "They are very young and they are on their own," he said. "But they have the Internet and Facebook and that gives them the chance to communicate with a different world. There are cases of women falling in love with people who treat them like human beings. And with their new horizons opening up for them, they come to understand that they are prisoners in their families. The Internet has opened their lives and their minds."

So it proved with Concetta. "She began to explore the world through the web," said Giuseppe Creazzo, a prosecutor in Palmi who would later investigate the Cacciola family. Concetta found she liked celebrity news: charming people leading beautiful lives. She imagined the famous couples watching sunsets together and going out at night. Soon, said Creazzo, she was looking for friends for herself. She joined Facebook. Slowly, a feeling began to grow inside her. "Every day," said Creazzo, "Concetta felt more and more like rebelling."

By the middle of 2009, Concetta was chatting regularly to a Rosarno man who had moved to Germany. Giuseppina, more assertive, went further than her friend, beginning a clandestine affair with a man called Domenico Costantino, with whom she had worked at a family factory that made crystallized fruit. "He was the first man who ever seemed to care for my children," said Giuseppina. "He was the first man to respect me as a woman, the first who ever loved me."

Almost anywhere else in Europe, either of these liaisons would have merited condemnation or, perhaps, understanding. In Rosarno, Concetta and Giuseppina were risking death. It was a gauge of their loveless lives that both women courted that danger without hesitation.

X

I N PAGLIARELLE, THE carabinieri were watching another illicit romance unfold.[1]

For Denise, a birthday without Lea had been followed by Christmas without Lea, then New Year's without Lea, all of them spent in Lea's apartment, upstairs from Lea's mother. One night, a friend's family took Denise to a restaurant on the coast for dinner—but someone had brought Christmas presents from Milan. Another time, when Carlo took his daughter to the dentist, Denise let herself imagine that it would be the most natural thing in the world for a daughter to ask her father if he had any news of her missing mother. Carlo snapped that Denise needed to get it through her head that her mother had left them. He knew nothing about where she was or what she was doing.

Denise already had a difficult relationship with food. Now she took to binge eating to relieve the stress, gaining twenty kilos in months. If Carlo noticed, he didn't seem concerned. Denise's aunt Marisa took her niece to a clinic but when that proved ineffective, she also offered Denise little other help.

Desperate, Denise turned to the man her father had deputized to keep an eye on her in Pagliarelle. Carlo had given thirty-one-year-old Carmine Venturino orders to escort Denise wherever she went and, above all, to keep her away from the authorities. Carmine would drive Denise around all day. He gave her pocket money. He worked with her in the Cosco family pizzeria in Petilia. When Denise started at a new high school in January, it was Carmine who helped settle her in. Watching all this, the surveillance teams began to feel uneasy. The officers knew Carlo had told Carmine to watch Denise. But this looked like something else.

What made the officers particularly uncomfortable was what they were learning about Carmine's movements on the night Lea vanished. Phone records showed that Carmine spoke to Carlo dozens of times in the hours after Lea disappeared and in the days that followed. Carmine said little of substance in his calls. But his tone had been panicky and his movements erratic. His GPS signal showed him driving outside the city several times in the days and nights after November 24. Recordings of his voice showed he'd been desperate to find the keys to a warehouse and that, once he located them, he kept going back to the place. Besides, thought the officers, Carmine was Carlo's sometime flatmate and one of his key lieutenants. He *had* to be involved.

ON FEBRUARY 3, the carabinieri in Campobasso announced they had enough evidence to arrest Carlo for ordering the attack on Lea in her apartment in May 2009. They detained Carlo just as Denise returned from school. Watching her father being led away in handcuffs, Denise recognized the look on his face as the same he'd had on the night Lea went missing. A newspaper report about Carlo's arrest the next day was accompanied by a picture of another man charged with the Campobasso attack: Massimo Sabatino. The paper said Sabatino was an associate of her father's and was already in prison on a drug charge.

Two months in, the officers investigating Lea's disappearance could be pleased with their progress. They had a prime suspect, for whom they had established motive and opportunity, and from Lea's case files, they had ample documentation to back up their allegations. Handily, Carlo was now also under arrest for another attack on Lea. But the murder case against Carlo also had a giant flaw: no body. Without it, a prosecutor couldn't even say for sure that Lea had died, let alone how.

Then the carabinieri got lucky. Massimo Sabatino, thirty-six, was a career criminal with a long list of convictions for robbery and drug dealing. When he was served his indictment for the Campobasso attack, he was already in San Vittore prison on a charge of dealing heroin after being arrested in December 2009. Slow and poorly educated, Sabatino handed the charge sheet to his friend and cellmate Salvatore Sorrentino, who had been picked up in Milan in January for absconding from house arrest at the end of a five-year sentence for robbery. While Sorrentino digested the document, Sabatino explained to his friend that for a few years he had been working for an 'Ndrangheta boss in Milan called Carlo Cosco. His connection to Carlo was through his sister Rosi, who was engaged to Rosario Curcio, one of Carlo's crew.

One day in April 2009, Sabatino said, Carlo had offered him €25,000 to drive to Campobasso and recover a drug debt from a woman living there. Carlo later refined the plan, saying Sabatino should go disguised as a washing-machine repairman and tie the woman up, drag her to his van, and take her to Bari on Puglia's east coast, where Carlo and his brothers would be waiting. Carlo had also given him fifty liters of sulfuric acid to carry in the back of the van. Sabatino said he had done as instructed but failed to kidnap the woman because her daughter, who wasn't supposed to be there, had appeared from nowhere and jumped him.

Sorrentino said that according to the charge sheet, Sabatino's fingerprints had been found on the washing machine in the apartment. Sabatino agreed that was possible: he'd worn latex gloves but torn them in the struggle with the women. Sorrentino continued that the woman Sabatino had been trying to abduct was a Garofalo, a name familiar to anyone in the 'Ndrangheta. Sabatino claimed he'd never known the identity of the woman. Sorrentino said that according to the indictment, Lea had not only been Carlo's wife but also a *pentita* who had testified against him.

It began to dawn on Sabatino that he was in real trouble. He told Sorrentino that he knew of a second, successful attempt to kidnap Lea in Milan on November 24. Though Sabatino stressed that he had played no part, he assumed Lea was now dead. He added that he had no alibi for either May or November.

Sorrentino agreed it looked bad. Sabatino had to be looking at life. Sabatino swore. Carlo was a motherfucker, he said. He hadn't paid him for the Campobasso job and had refused even to give him money for a lawyer when he was arrested in December.

Sabatino didn't know what to do. But his cellmate Sorrentino did. A day or so later, he sent a letter to the Milan prosecutor investigating Lea's disappearance, offering to relay everything his friend had told him in return for a reduced sentence. The prosecutors, skeptical at first, were reassured when Sabatino was moved to a different cell and his new cellmate made a statement confirming many of the same details. When a prosecutor confronted Sabatino, he lied so badly—initially claiming he was meant to recover a debt from Lea, then claiming he was robbing her, then admitting he was trying to kidnap her—that he managed to solidify the case against himself and Carlo.

To the investigators, the case was beginning to look conclusive. But Sabatino had given them something else, too. According to Sorrentino, Sabatino claimed that the Cosco brothers had also killed two Garofalo men in the past. Sabatino even named Giuseppe Cosco as the shooter in the first killing, which he added had taken place in a Milan apartment block in 1995. Allowing for the distortion of jailhouse hearsay, this seemed to be corroboration of Lea's allegation that Giuseppe Cosco had shot dead Antonio Comberiati at No. 6 Vi-

ale Montello in May 1995. The allegation that the Coscos had killed
a second Garofalo seemed to refer to the 2005 death of Lea's brother
Floriano, a killing that was unsolved. Here, finally, was the evidence
to substantiate Lea's allegations. Disbelieved in life, she was being
vindicated in death.

THERE WAS STILL the mystery of what had happened to Lea, however. In Catanzaro, down on the coast below Pagliarelle, the prosecutor's office had informed Annalisa Pisano that her former client
had disappeared. "They told me clearly that it had to be *lupara bianca*," she said. Though she and Lea hadn't spoken in a year and
a half, Annalisa still felt a strong bond with her. That night, said
Annalisa, "I dreamed of Lea. She was in a warehouse, surrounded
by flames, and she was asking me for help. She was calling me by my
name. 'Annalisa!' But everybody was telling her 'No!'" And every
night from then on, to the day years later when Lea was found, Annalisa had the same recurring dream. "People would ask me: 'How
do you know she has been burned?' And I'd reply: 'Because I see
her. You can believe me or not.' And I am not the kind of person
who believes in these things. But I saw her. Almost every night. She
was on a chair, in a warehouse, surrounded by fire, calling for me.
And at that point, I would wake up."

For Denise, Carlo's arrest only sharpened the questions over her
mother's death. *How* had Carlo killed her? Did he shoot her? Suffo-
cate her? Slit her throat? Did he have one of his men do it? Did she
scream? Was it quick or did he draw it out? Did he torture her? At
what point did Lea know she was going to die? Would Denise know
when her own time came?

While Carlo's arrest should have come as some relief, in Pagliarelle it just made it harder for Denise to maintain the lie. In mid-
February, on the eve of her first visit to see Carlo in jail, the

surveillance team picked up a text message from Denise to Carmine. Denise was losing her mind. The situation was impossible, she said. How could she keep on pretending when her father was in jail accused of trying to kill her mother? How could she face him? "Carmine calmed me," Denise said. "He made me laugh. He made me feel good."

The respite was temporary. When Denise went to Catanzaro jail the next day with her uncle Vito, she wept throughout. Vito tried to be sympathetic but didn't seem to know how. "Crying when your father is in prison and your mother is missing is only natural," he said blankly.

Carmine was waiting for Denise when she returned. Once inside her aunt's house, she collapsed. "It was an hour of crying and eating at the same time," she said later. "I was so desperate. I wasn't thinking about who I trusted and who I didn't. I was desperate for some affection. I cried. I ate. I was shouting out: 'Leave me alone! I have to go to a place where I don't want to go, live in a place where I don't want to live, with people that I suspect? What do you want me to do? Laugh?' What I suffered, nobody can understand." In the end, Carmine just held Denise. They hugged for what seemed like forever. Then they kissed.

Over the next few weeks, the surveillance team watched as Denise and Carmine became inseparable. "She fell in love with this guy and he with her," said Enza. "She was able to open up to him, to speak with him and cry with him." But Denise was also mindful that Carmine was a member of Carlo's 'ndrina. She would ask him over and over again what he knew about what had happened to her mother. "He always said he didn't know and didn't want to know," said Denise. "I never had an answer." Adding to the pressure on Denise, her affair with Carmine was something else she had to keep secret. "Carmine told me to say absolutely nothing to anyone," she said. "If my father knew, he'd be furious. He'd given Carmine the job of accompanying me and controlling me, not dating me. No one could know we were seeing each other. We would meet at midnight in the meadows outside Pagliarelle so that no one would find out."

Unable to express almost any of her thoughts and on constant guard against letting her true feelings show, Denise took to staying silent for most of the day. "I couldn't shout [about] what they had done," she said. "I couldn't cry out: 'You are all killers!'" When the Coscos asked her to write to her father in jail in early March, she agreed, then found she had almost nothing to say.

> *To Dad*
>> *Even if you are away from me, you are still close to me.*
>>> *I love you,*
>>> *Denise*

> *PS Don't worry about me.*
> *PPS I could get you some wild boar if you want. As you can see, like you, I am someone of few words. But what I write here is what I could never say to you. I just want you to be fine.*

On February 25, in a public demonstration of her loyalty to the family, Denise signed a formal waiver giving up her right to witness protection. Secretly, however, she reestablished contact with Enza and other activists in Libera, asking if they could hide her if she left Pagliarelle. On March 5, she also clandestinely met the carabinieri a second time and gave a further statement. For the officers, Denise's new evidence filled in most of the remaining gaps in Lea's life, right up until the last few hours. But for Denise, reliving that night only increased her stress. She couldn't shake the thought that seemed to be getting ever louder in her head: that she should run away from Pagliarelle like her mother.

In early April 2010, when her aunt went away for a few days,

Denise seized her chance. She took the bus to Crotone, then jumped on a long-distance train to the north. After a day, she arrived at a Libera safe house near Turin. "I had to go," she told her hosts. "They wouldn't let me live." Initially, the Coscos didn't notice Denise was gone. But when one week became three, there was no hiding it any longer. On April 23, Vito Cosco drove down from Milan and confronted Marisa and her husband, demanding to know where Denise had gone.

That afternoon, the surveillance team tapped a series of calls between Marisa and Denise. "Vito's been here!" Marisa said. "Wherever you are, you have to be here tomorrow! They say they just want to talk to you. Afterward you can go off wherever you want." Failing to return would be sending a message to the 'Ndrangheta to go screw itself, said Marisa.

"I know I have to go back to talk to these assholes," replied Denise.

"Look, they just want to feel relaxed," said Marisa. "They want to know that you know what you have to do."

"What I have to do?! What I have to do?!" shouted Denise. "I have to keep quiet! I have to be stopped!"

"So fuck them all!" said Marisa. "But we're all so sick of this mess here. And I think once they know where you are and what you're doing, they'll calm down. Vito was going to see your father, but he didn't go because he didn't know what to tell him. Right now, they're afraid that you're back in the program."

"The program your sister was in!"

"They're just afraid, Denise," said Marisa. Denise shouldn't overthink what she had to do. She shouldn't imagine the worst. "They don't care where you are or how you are. They only care about themselves. They only care that no one speaks the truth."

Denise returned to Pagliarelle the next day. Vito, apparently reassured, flew back to Milan. Denise had to wait a week before visiting her father in jail. The prospect of speaking to Carlo once more terrified her as much as it had the last time. She turned to Carmine once again. "I have to wait a week," she texted him. "I know what you think—that I'm wrong—but I just want to have the chance of a different life."

"This is the week you can change things," Carmine wrote back. "No one's standing in the way of the life you want. Just do things right, and the others will relax."

The reality, as Enza discovered years later, was precisely the opposite. Carlo's brothers had kept him closely informed of Denise's behavior. She wasn't getting any better, they told him. When Denise had disappeared, Carlo told his brothers that he had made a decision. If and when she reappeared, she had to die. Carlo added it would be easiest if Carmine did it.

Carmine, ever more in love with Denise, had been half expecting the call. He had already decided to disobey. But now that it had come, the clock was ticking. The boss had given the order that his only daughter, whom he loved, was to be killed. It wasn't a decision he would have taken lightly. But it was one that, given Denise's erratic behavior, he would have concluded was unavoidable. Carlo had to protect the 'ndrina and the 'Ndrangheta. He had to enforce the code. Women were the organization's property and the repository of its honor, to be cherished or disposed of as duty required. Now that he had made the decision, he would want his orders carried out as swiftly as possible. As Carmine's betrayal became apparent to Carlo over the next few weeks and months, he knew Carlo would make him pay dearly for it.

XI

BARELY A DAY after Denise returned to Calabria's east coast, Alessandra made her first strike against the Pesces on the west. In the early hours of April 26, 2010, in simultaneous raids in Rosarno, Reggio, Milan, and Bergamo, code-named Operation All Inside, hundreds of carabinieri moved in on the Pesce empire. They arrested a total of thirty people. Ten warrants were issued for 'ndrina members on the run. Among those accused was clan boss Antonino Pesce, Giuseppina's uncle, who was already in jail. His son and protégé, Giuseppina's cousin Francesco Pesce, was arrested in Rosarno. Reflecting Alessandra's convictions, seven of the detained were women. They included Giuseppina's mother, sister, cousin, grandmother, and great-grandmother, as well as Giuseppina herself.

The charges against the Pesce family included extortion, money laundering, loan-sharking, drug smuggling, mafia association, and two counts of murder.[1] The range of accusations indicated how, inside their dominion of Gioia Tauro and Rosarno, the 'Ndrangheta's hegemony was total. "They completely control their territory and their government," said Michele Prestipino. "People who live there accept that to get something they have to knock on the door of the mafia and that there is no future other than what the mafia sees." The mafiosi's power in Rosarno was at its peak. In a town of fifteen thousand people, the authorities had identified five hundred 'Ndrangheta members and hundreds more associates. That crushing dominance meant a strange kind of peace prevailed. "There is not much need for a lot of violence," said Prestipino. "Everybody knows that if these people want to use violence, they can. They achieve consensus without firing a shot."

The range of assets seized during Operation All Inside was further evidence of the Pesces' reach. While the prosecutors promised heftier hauls to come, even on this first pass they confiscated vehicles, properties, and businesses worth €10 million from one of the poorest areas in Europe. Pesce businesses included a gas station, a car dealership, a food distribution company, and a chocolate distributor whose company documents named Rocco Palaia, Giuseppina's husband, as its owner. A Rosarno radio station, Radio Olimpia, was particularly interesting. The carabinieri had discovered that jailed bosses and *picciotti* were using Olimpia's request show to communicate with each other. Prisoners would ask their family a yes/no question—Is my appeal successful? Were my orders carried out?—and the families would reply by calling in and requesting one of two songs to relay the answer. Giuseppina's fugitive uncle Vincenzo would also call in from time to time and ask the presenter to use his nickname and describe him as a listener "at large." In other words: *I am still in the area; I am still free.*

GIUSEPPINA WAS CHARGED with mafia association, money laundering, extortion, and running messages. She faced more than a decade in jail. That wasn't what troubled her, however. The Calabrian newspapers had reported that she had been detained with a man. Three weeks earlier, she had been warned by her uncle Vincenzo that her family suspected she was having a relationship with Domenico Costantino. Her cousin Francesco had had her followed day and night. Now that she had been found with Domenico in the middle of the night, their suspicions would be confirmed. The family's punishment would far exceed the state's. "In my family, those who betray and dishonor the family must be punished by death," said

Giuseppina. "It is a law." "She was going to die and she knew it," said Alessandra. "She accepted it."

What Giuseppina could not accept was the sudden implosion of her three children's future. She had never been apart from Angela, fifteen; Gaetano, eight; and Elisea, three. Now they were with Rocco's family. With Giuseppina headed for a lengthy sentence, or execution, and probably both, one way or another her children were going to be raised by the 'Ndrangheta. Her son, Gaetano, was a gentle boy especially unsuited for the life now before him. Ahead were years of brutalization. Giuseppina's father, Salvatore, used to joke that when a cousin was giving birth, he'd send flowers for a girl and a .38 for a boy. A few years back, when an uncle had asked Gaetano what he wanted to be when he grew up and the boy, in all innocence, had replied "a policeman," his uncle beat him, then promised to get him a gun to remind him who he was. Giuseppina's fear, she wrote later, was that "they will put a gun in his hands anyway. When I get out of jail, my son could already be in a juvenile detention center. And my two daughters will have to marry two 'Ndrangheta men and be forced to follow them around."

Giuseppina vented her frustration by starting a hunger strike and refusing to talk to prosecutors. But at other times, her spirit seemed broken. She tried to hang herself in her cell a few days after she was arrested. Three months later, by which time she had been transferred to San Vittore prison in Milan, she slashed her wrists with a razor. "There were times when I wanted to die," she said later in court. "I couldn't stand the thought of my children without me. They'd always been with me. I wanted a way out. I was watching my world collapse in on me."[2]

THE PROSECUTORS WERE largely unsympathetic. If an 'Ndranghetista was feeling guilt or paying some other price for her crimes, then they had done their job. This was war. Prosecutors had begun finding gun cartridges leaning up against their windshields. One bullet sent to Pignatone in May 2010 was accompanied by a note that read simply: "You're a dead man." Two of his staff found their cars' wheels had been loosened. Nor could the prosecutors rely on much public support. The same day as the raids on the Pesce clan, police in Reggio arrested Giovanni Tegano, an 'Ndrangheta boss on the run for seventeen years. As he was led from the city's central police station to a squad car to take him to jail, Tegano was cheered by a crowd of hundreds. "Giovanni is a man of peace!" shouted one tearful seventy-year-old woman, to which Tegano smiled and waved back.[3]

The threats against them only reconfirmed prosecutors' determination to bring down the 'Ndrangheta. The pace was relentless. Alessandra and Giovanni Musarò had thirty separate investigations under way against the west coast 'Ndrangheta. "We weren't going to let them breathe," said Giovanni. "They were used to enduring one operation, then having a rest. But we just kept on. Someone would be arrested, they would be replaced, and then we arrested that person, too."

On July 13, in a follow-up from Operation All Inside, the carabinieri staged more raids across the country. This time they were more ambitious. Operation Infinity involved more than three thousand officers and resulted in three hundred arrests across the 'Ndrangheta hierarchy. The standout success was the arrest of *capo crimine* Domenico Oppedisano, now eighty, in Rosarno.

Oppedisano, his gray hair swept back across his head, arrested in the kind of dark gray, open-necked striped shirt you might expect to see on a market trader, conformed to the traditional image of a southern mafioso. But other arrests reflected the organization's more recent sophistication. Around half of the raids took place in and around Milan. Those detained included businessmen, lawyers, bankers, accountants, politicians, policemen, and public health care managers. Pignatone marveled at the range of figures now behind bars and what it revealed about the 'Ndrangheta's ability to "infiltrate such a wide variety of environments." A new cosmopolitan generation of 'Ndranghetisti was emerging, he said, who understood how globalization had opened up the world to illicit businesses as much as it had to legitimate ones. "They are graduates," he said. "They can count on a network of professionals, bureaucrats, and politicians. They can penetrate any part of Italy and anywhere overseas."

Pignatone's junior prosecutors were jubilant. Many had prepared for this moment for years. Alessandra had been waiting all her life. Now the 'Ndrangheta was being hit hard, its bosses arrested, and its precious secrets exposed. "That was the moment we revealed that we knew not only that the 'Ndrangheta existed as a hierarchy and a structure but that it could be proved," said Alessandra. The interior minister, Roberto Maroni, described the raids as a "blow to the heart of the 'Ndrangheta's organisational and financial structure." Oppedisano's arrest was greeted with a standing ovation in the Italian Senate.[4] It was going to be a long war. But the prosecutors had finally shown that they could make the world's mightiest mafia bleed.

THE 'NDRANGHETA WAS a secret criminal organization that oppressed people with inhuman violence. If the Italian state was to win its war with it, if the government was to lift the yoke the mafia had imposed on the people, it had to offer them transparency, legality, and humanity. But in the heat of battle and with the first flush of victory, the last of those, humanity, was being forgotten.

Giuseppina was useful to Alessandra. She represented further evidence to support her theory about women's influence in the

'Ndrangheta. But when Alessandra heard about Giuseppina's suicide attempts, she felt little compassion for a woman whose predic-
ament was entirely her own fault. "I didn't believe Giuseppina was
sincere," she said. "And in fact, she quickly admitted that she wasn't
really trying to kill herself but merely trying to persuade us to help
her reunite with her children."[5]

The same cold-bloodedness was on display in the state's indictment of Carlo Cosco and Massimo Sabatino for the murder
of Lea Garofalo on May 27, 2010. The charge sheet, confidential
at this stage in the Italian legal process, included a detailed reconstruction of Carlo's movements on the night Lea died. But
there was also an extensive account of Lea's relationship with
the witness protection program. To many inside the small group
of lawyers and officials allowed to read it, it made for damning reading. Lea had put her faith in the state, and the state
had abandoned her. It seemed minded to do the same to Denise.
How could Italy expect to beat the mafia if it couldn't even protect those who tried to help it? The state's lack of sympathy
had killed Lea almost as surely as Carlo had. Enza Rando, Lea's
lawyer, was especially critical. "Lea had to make her own way,"
she said. "The state just didn't understand how to make witness
protection work, especially for a woman. Lea had the strength
and weakness of a mother. Brave but at the same time afraid. She
never received the help she needed."[6]

Alessandra bristled at the criticism. She would have preferred
a faultless protection program that led seamlessly to the prosecution and conviction of mafiosi. But people died in war. Sometimes
mafiosi, sometimes carabinieri and prosecutors, and sometimes
witnesses. Lea's death was no reason to show weakness. It was every reason to show resolve. "Prosecutors always get blamed," she
said. "But the facts are that Lea applied for witness protection and

didn't have enough information to justify it. Protection costs a lot of money. If your information is not important or deep enough, you don't get it."[7]

Even if Alessandra was right about the limits on government finances, there was no disputing that the state had failed in one of its primary duties: the protection of its citizens. Lea had crossed the divide to fight on the side of the government, and had lost. As a result, according to the indictment, she had probably been tortured, killed, and dissolved in acid. Why? Because the 'Ndrangheta thought she was theirs to keep or discard as they chose—and because, in the end, the state had done the same. Alessandra might be right that this was a war. But if the state was fighting with the same ruthlessness as the 'Ndrangheta, would the people care who won?

It wasn't that Italy's anti-mafia prosecutors had been born peculiarly unfeeling. It was that they were trained to be. From law school through their training to their years on the job, they had been told that emotion had no place in the service. The mafia was heat and blood. Prosecutors were focus, discipline, and procedure.

But as long as they withheld their hearts from the fight, it was easy to confuse a prosecutor's professional detachment with indifference, or even disdain. The mafia's victims deserved sympathy. Often the best the prosecutors could muster was pity. Cut off from the world, on an endless shuttle between windowless office, bullet-proof car, steel-doored court, and secure apartment, it was easy for a prosecutor to forget that war was ultimately played out in flesh and blood, and often won by capturing hearts and minds. Alessandra dismissed Giuseppina's suffering. She marveled at the emotional decision making that had led Lea Garofalo to her death. "Lea Garofalo went to Milan, where she knew her husband was, even after she had been threatened by him, almost like a form of protest," she exclaimed. Lea had followed her heart, and that had doomed her. Alessandra's considered response was heartlessness. "I study women in the 'Ndrangheta," she said. "I go to conferences about it. It's a subject I'm very passionate about." But no one should mistake intellectual interest for personal attachment. "I don't get involved in these women's lives," she said. "I can't."[8]

XII

THE WAR WAS heating up. In August, a bundle of industrial dynamite was detonated outside the Reggio home of Calabrian attorney general Salvatore di Landro. In early October, an anti-mafia magistrate in Sicily announced that he had intelligence on a secret summit between the leaders of Cosa Nostra, the Camorra, and the 'Ndrangheta at which Italy's three big mafias had drawn up a hit list of assassination targets. On that list was Giuseppe Pignatone. The next week, Pignatone received a phone call at work telling him there was a surprise waiting for him outside. That turned out to be an Eastern European rocket launcher hidden under a mattress. The Italian press began calling 2010 "the year of bombs and bazookas."

Pignatone professed he was encouraged by what he viewed as the actions of an organization in distress. While the threats had to be taken seriously, there was no question of easing off when the crackdown was so clearly being felt. There were more indications that the 'Ndrangheta was being shaken. Ordinary Calabrians were stepping forward to assist the state and that, said Pignatone, "had never happened before." When Justice Minister Angelino Alfano prematurely declared the 'Ndrangheta "fatally wounded," the Calabrian prosecutors winced at his haste. Still, said Pignatone, there was no doubt that "positive results are giving us even more positive results."[1] One development was almost unprecedented, he added. Inside jail, an 'Ndranghetista had begun talking.

———

AT THE BEGINNING of October 2010, the prosecutor's office in Palmi received a letter from San Vittore jail in the center of Milan. San Vittore is Italy's most notorious mafia prison. Thousands of mafiosi have served time there, and most pass through at some stage, including Carlo Cosco, Massimo Sabatino, and Salvatore Riina, the Cosa Nostra boss who ordered the executions of Giovanni Falcone and Paolo Borsellino. Even to write to an anti-mafia prosecutor from inside San Vittore and request a meeting was a risk. But to specify that the meeting must take place without a lawyer—indicating that the inmate was considering talking freely, since mafia lawyers worked for the organization rather than the individual—was so dangerous as to suggest the prisoner was beyond caring. Giuseppina Pesce was already a dead woman walking. Maybe she was thinking of becoming a dead woman talking, too. "If you can make her talk," said Pignatone as he handed the letter to Alessandra, "we'll have done in three years in Calabria what took us thirty years in Palermo."[2]

Alessandra was doubtful. Still, she agreed with Pignatone that Giuseppina was more likely to open up to another woman. And to Alessandra, even the smallest chance of a woman prosecutor unlocking the 'Ndrangheta through the evidence of a woman mafiosa was irresistible.

On October 14, 2010, Alessandra was driven by a security detail through the gates of San Vittore. She was escorted to a meeting room by a prison warden and a marshal. After a few minutes, Giuseppina was led into the room by a prison guard. She walked slowly and hesitantly. Giuseppina had the prison look: wan, with greasy hair, her shoulders hunched like a beaten animal. "She looked at me with such loathing," said Alessandra, "with pride, resentment, and hatred. I represented the state, which was ruining her life."[3]

After this inauspicious beginning, the atmosphere quickly de-

teriorated. Giuseppina blurted out that she wanted to be moved
to a state safe house and to see her children. In return, she would
help them catch some 'Ndrangheta bosses on the run. Alessandra
dismissed the offer out of hand. "She wanted to give us a couple
of names in exchange for her freedom," she said.[4] It was a pathetic
offer—and, in any case, it wasn't how the prosecutors worked. They
didn't negotiate with gangsters. That was how the mafia drew you
in. Alessandra closed her laptop and made to leave.

Giuseppina looked up at Alessandra with alarm. This wasn't
how the meeting was meant to go. Giuseppina's idea had been to
negotiate with Alessandra the 'Ndrangheta way, which was to say,
hard: reveal little of what you have, affect nonchalance about any
deal offered, and eventually extract as much as possible for as little as possible. What's more, Giuseppina was a Pesce. Her family
killed people. Her family was power. She had summoned the state
to see her. And yet here was this woman prosecutor—a woman!—
turning everything upside down and heading for the door.

Alessandra would later admit she was bluffing. Of course she
wanted to know about 'Ndrangheta fugitives. She wanted anything
Giuseppina could give her. But Alessandra was angling for *everything* Giuseppina could give her. The state had painstakingly built
its case against the Pesces and the 'Ndrangheta. The evidence was
good enough for trial. But it could always be stronger. It was all
but inevitable that several mafiosi, including a few kingpins, would
walk. There was so much the prosecutors didn't know or couldn't
prove. Who ran what? Who, precisely, moved how much cocaine?
Who laundered whose money? Who, exactly, pulled the triggers? In
Giuseppina Pesce's head was the evidence that could solve hundreds
of crimes stretching back decades. A full confession would split the
'Ndrangheta wide open, devastating an organization whose power
depended on secrecy. It would transform the fight against the mafia. Most crucially to Alessandra, it would also finally prove—to

the 'Ndrangheta, the judiciary, and all Italy—that chauvinism was toxic, witless, self-destructive folly.

Alessandra, then, was gambling. But as she reached the door, Giuseppina cleared her throat. "Everything I testify to now," she said, "I do it for my children, I do it to give them a different future."[5]

GIUSEPPINA WOULD EVENTUALLY tell Alessandra everything she knew. It took time. Alessandra and Giuseppina began talking inside San Vittore prison. Once the carabinieri retrieved Giuseppina's children from the Palaias, who had been looking after them, and took them to a safe house near Aprilia, south of Rome, where they were reunited with their mother, Giuseppina and Alessandra spoke for several more months. It wasn't just the size and scale of Giuseppina's knowledge. At the beginning, in those first few hours and days, she also delivered it slowly. Giuseppina was still torn between love for her own small family and loyalty to The Family. "She was desperate to be reunited with her kids," said Alessandra. "But it was really hard for her to betray her relatives."[6]

But gradually, as Alessandra offered reassurances about her safety and that of her children, the two women established a rapport. "She *knew* she was going to die," said Alessandra. "She *knew* it would be her brother who killed her. I had to explain to her over and over that it's not normal that if you cheat on your husband, then you have to die."[7] Giuseppina started to relax. There was even a moment on that first day in October when Alessandra saw her eyes shift from terror and confusion to courage and trust. As they talked, Giuseppina became calmer and more confident. Alessandra could feel an almost tangible sense of a beginning, like the first glow of a new era of collaboration opening up right in front of her.

Transcribed, Giuseppina's evidence would eventually run to 1,514 pages. It included diagrams she drew of the 'Ndrangheta hier-

archy, descriptions of rituals, evidence of several murders, and detailed accounts of cocaine smuggling rings, extortion rackets, money
laundering, credit card fraud, and public corruption. "No stone was
left unturned," said Alessandra. "She told me so many things."[8]
Giuseppina's evidence not only backed up the existing cases, it
prompted a raft of new ones. "The whole character of our investigations changed from that moment," said Alessandra. "It was a real
turning point." Based on what Giuseppina told her, over the next
year Alessandra would confiscate a total of €260 million in property
from the Pesces and the 'Ndrangheta, including forty businesses,
four villas, forty-four apartments, 164 cars, sixty plots of land, and
two soccer teams. The number of arrests skyrocketed. Eventually,
Alessandra would be able to bring charges against a total of sixty-
four 'Ndrangheta men and women from the Pesce *'ndrina*, including
two Palaias and fourteen Pesces. Giuseppina revealed the location
of three houses in Rosarno under which the Pesces had built bunkers and pinpointed five other underground hideouts. Even when
she didn't know a bunker's whereabouts, she offered other help. Her
cousin, acting clan head Francesco "Ciccio" Pesce, she said, "liked
women, a lot of women." After she gave Alessandra details of one
girlfriend, the carabinieri followed the woman until she led them to
Ciccio's hideout, which he had equipped with sixteen infrared cameras. Another boss was tracked to a bunker by tailing his friends,
whose names were also provided by Giuseppina.

More than the loss of money or personnel, it was the act of Giuseppina's betrayal that shook the 'Ndrangheta. "Pesce was a name
that creates terror in Calabria," said Alessandra. "This—breaking
the chain, making it possible for women and children to leave the
mafia and be free and safe—it was like a bomb."[9] When news of Giuseppina's betrayal reached Rosarno, their rivals the Belloccos held
a party to celebrate the Pesces' shame. In Reggio, Prestipino and
Pignatone were equally ecstatic. "A woman with the name of Pesce,

an organic member of this fearsome 'Ndrangheta family, a woman from a place where women don't have the same rights as men, she betrays them and moves to the side of the state," said Prestipino.[10] "Immediately, they lose prestige. They lose power. It's devastating. Ordinary people see it's not true that they will always go unpunished. It's not the case that they're invincible. People say: 'They're no longer capable of silencing even one of their own members.' People start having doubts about them."

Just as important, 'Ndrangheta members themselves would start to feel the old certainties erode. "Giuseppina showed everybody that there was an alternative to 'Ndrangheta—that the state could save you and save your family," said Alessandra. "She was living proof that you could leave the 'Ndrangheta. That you could survive it. That you could be free."[11] Prestipino concurred. "'Ndrangheta members start realizing that the 'Ndrangheta life is not irreversible. They have an alternative. Giuseppina is proof to all 'Ndrangheta members and women that a mafia member cannot just quit but can organize their life in a different way. Anyone can do it. This undermines and jeopardizes the consensus the mafia has built. It's an existential crisis."[12]

Giuseppina's motivation for her betrayal was rooted in her desire to give her three children a better life. "I want to change my ways now and take my children with me and try to create a different future for them," she wrote in a testimonial statement.[13] But there was something else, too. She and Alessandra had made a connection. In one sense, they were two women united against a world of violent men. When Alessandra felt Giuseppina was holding back on a sensitive matter—her marriage, her affair, how the Pesce men were—she would ask the male carabinieri officers in the room to leave, so Giuseppina would feel less liable to be judged and able to speak more freely.

Alessandra and Giuseppina were discovering they had more in

common than they initially thought. They were two women with a common enemy, living difficult, isolated, and sometimes terrifying lives. That made them natural allies. More than that, it ensured that both were starved of friendship. Giuseppina, in particular, had broken faith with her entire family and her whole life. "I am alone," she would often tell the prosecutors. Alessandra sensed that Giuseppina needed someone new to rely on. A state that kept its promises. A prosecutor whose word she could believe. A new life, not just security and survival but a full and meaningful existence, even a hope of joy and love.

Perhaps more than Giuseppina knew, Alessandra understood. Almost for the first time in her career, Alessandra began to allow herself to feel something, too. This was not just another case, Alessandra told herself. Departing from a creed she had held on to since law school, she began to see Giuseppina not just as a tool for getting the job done but as an individual with discrete strengths, flaws, and needs. Alessandra saw to it that Giuseppina was never alone and was always able to phone her or her lawyer, day or night. She began visiting Giuseppina even when they had nothing professional to discuss. She was aware she was breaking her own rules. Her relationship with Giuseppina was evolving into something beyond the technical or the objective. At times, Alessandra saw herself as a gondolier, ferrying Giuseppina from her old life to the new. In other moments, she spoke about how she and this young girl were establishing "an umbilical cord."

At the age of forty-two, in the most unlikely of circumstances, Alessandra was becoming a mother.

XIII

I~~N Pagliarelle, Denise~~ was unaware of the prosecutors' progress in the hunt for her mother's killers.[1] She had no idea that her father, Carlo Cosco, had ordered her own death, nor that Carmine was refusing to obey him. Still, pretending to live as a good 'Ndrangheta girl while secretly seeing Carmine and keeping contact with Libera, Enza Rando, and the carabinieri was an impossible balancing act. On September 28, 2010, she visited Carlo in jail. The conversation was awkward and stilted. Denise could sense her charade was wearing thin. "I had no wish to see my father," she said later. "I didn't feel sincere about seeing him."

A few weeks later, on the morning of October 18, 2010, the Milan prosecutor leading the investigation into Lea's disappearance, Giuseppe Gennari, finally released a public indictment for murder against Carlo. Describing Lea's death as an "execution" planned and ordered by Carlo, Gennari said Carlo had organized a van to transport Lea out of the city, secured a warehouse where she would be interrogated and tortured, procured a gun to kill her, and supplied fifty liters of sulfuric acid in which to dissolve her body. Erasing any trace of Lea would allow the conspirators to claim she had run off to Australia, he said. The motive for the killing, Gennari told reporters, was "the statements Lea made to the prosecutors, none of which, for unexplained reasons, were ever used in a trial." Specifically, said Gennari, Lea was killed for her testimony about the murder of Antonio Comberiati. Though Carlo never knew what Lea had told prosecutors, Gennari said he had not wanted to take any chances. In any case, he continued, Carlo believed Lea had to be punished for her disloyalty and the shame she had brought on him. From the moment Lea left witness protection in April 2009, Carlo had been working toward the chance to abduct, torture, and kill her. Gennari added that Carlo had had five accomplices, whom he named as Massimo Sabatino; Carlo's two brothers, Vito and Giuseppe; Rosario Curcio; and Carmine Venturino.

The morning of October 18 in Calabria was warm, one of the last days of summer. Denise and Carmine had driven to Crotone to buy supplies for the Cosco family pizzeria, where both of them still worked. Afterward, they took a ride along the coast to Botricello beach. Their plan was to swim, sunbathe, and perhaps grab a bite for lunch. Around midday, as prosecutor Gennari was speaking to reporters in Milan, the couple watched a line of carabinieri cars drive up along the seafront and pull to a stop. Several officers got out. They started walking across the sand. Denise and Carmine watched them come. Then Carmine sighed, tugged on his T-shirt, and stood with his head bowed, his arms by his sides.

As Denise watched the officers surround her boyfriend, cuff him, slap their hands on his shoulders, and start to lead him off across the beach, she felt the blood drain from her face. Her relationship with Carmine was still a secret. Something in their manner told Denise the officers knew all about it. But she had a sudden intuition about something else, too. She followed the officers as they walked Carmine to a waiting squad car. One man put his arm around her and led her to a different car, where he opened the door for her. "This is one of the men who killed your mother," said the officer. "This is the guy who dissolved your mother's body in acid."[2]

G IUSEPPINA PESCE AND her children were reunited at a safe house near Aprilia on November 5, 2010. Days later, her eldest daughter, Angela, received a package from Rosarno. The carabinieri had spirited away Angela and her brother and sister, Gaetano and Elisea, with such haste that the children had left with just the clothes they were wearing. Now the Palaias, Giuseppina's in-laws, were forwarding their belongings. The children were delighted. Unpacking her sweatshirts and favorite jeans, Angela found her mobile carefully wrapped up in her clothes. She didn't tell her mother.[1]

The calls from Rosarno started almost immediately. Angela's uncles and grandparents would ask her whether she was eating OK. How was she coping without her family? Was she keeping away from those others? For most of the seven months their mother had been in jail, the children had been living with their aunt, Angela Palaia, with whom Angela shared her first and last names. Aunt Angela called almost every day. She would tell her niece that her family missed her. She would promise Angela to buy her this jacket or those trainers once she returned to Rosarno. Sometimes she would say that Giuseppina had made her own decision for her own reasons but hadn't stopped to consider the consequences for her children, who were being ripped away from their family and friends. It was unfair, said Aunt Angela. Unfair, and bad parenting. Witness protection was no life for a teenage girl. Think of everything Angela was missing out on. The Palaias had everything she wanted. What could the state give her that her family could not? "Tell your mother you want to be with us," Aunt Angela would say. "If she wants to go on, she should go on alone. But you come back to us."

Angela was torn. She loved her mother. But she had also become close to her aunt in the time they had lived together. And while Giuseppina had promised her a better life once they were reunited, Angela found it was nothing like that, nor like any life she'd ever known. She was soon arguing with Giuseppina, calling her mother selfish for taking her, her brother, and her sister away from their school, friends, and family. Angela stopped eating. She refused to get out of bed. Her aunt would tell her that it was her mother who was making her ill. And it was all so unnecessary, said Aunt Angela. She promised the family would forgive Giuseppina. Everyone loved her. Everyone loved Angela, Gaetano, and Elisea, too. They were family, after all. The men had a lawyer standing by who would deal with whatever statements Giuseppina had made. Life could go back to normal. It would be as if nothing had happened. Why didn't they all come home? "My daughter started calling me her enemy," said Giuseppina. "She would tell me how good Aunt Angela was to her, how Aunt Angela loved her."

The Palaias' aim was true. Realizing that Giuseppina had started collaborating for the sake of her children, they guessed correctly that she would stop for them, too. At the time, Alessandra had no idea of the secret phone discussions taking place inside the safe house. When she found out later, she conceded that with its keen understanding of family, the 'Ndrangheta had found Giuseppina's weak spot. "Angela was only sixteen and didn't understand her mother's choice," she said. "And everyone knew that without her daughter, Giuseppina would not proceed."

For the 'Ndrangheta, forcing an end to Giuseppina's cooperation was becoming critical. On November 23, 2010, Alessandra staged Operation All Inside II, a series of further raids aimed at dismantling the Pesce empire, this time guided largely by Giuseppina's information. Twenty-four more Pesce clan members were arrested. They included two policemen, a prison guard, and two more women: the twenty-eight-year-old wife of a low-level 'Ndranghetista said to be passing messages between bosses; and Carmelina Capria, forty-seven, wife of clan head Antonino Pesce and, allegedly, the family accountant.

In response, the clan stepped up the pressure on Giuseppina. As 2011 began, the calls to Angela became more frequent. In early March, a second mobile somehow found its way to Giuseppina. She, too, was soon speaking to Aunt Angela. Aunt Angela told Giuseppina that her husband, Rocco Palaia, still loved her, as did the whole family. She tried to reassure her, saying she shouldn't worry about retribution. Everyone made a mistake once in a while. Rocco was prepared to forgive her. What was most important was her children's health. For a sixteen-year-old girl to be apart from her family wasn't natural. It was clearly distressing her. For her daughter's sake, said Aunt Angela, Giuseppina had to stop collaborating, renounce the statements she had made, and come back to Rosarno.

Giuseppina said little in these conversations but neither did she hang up. And as March 2011 passed into April and Aunt Angela continued her emotional blackmail, Giuseppina's brother-in-law, Gianluca Palaia, began relaying precise instructions as to how Giuseppina should end her collaboration. Once she left witness protection, Gianluca told her, the family would find her a lawyer, cover her legal fees, and rent her a new apartment. He arranged for her to receive €3,000, which he described as a gift from "a good man." Like Aunt Angela, Gianluca tried to be reassuring. Don't worry, he said. No one was going to do anything to her. Even Giuseppina's daughter, Angela, tried to persuade her. "You see? You see?" she would say. "Now it's up to you."

Toward the end of March, Giuseppina was granted permission

to leave her safe house for a few hours to meet a lawyer. At a carabinieri station in Aprilia, she met Giuseppe Madia, a defense lawyer
from Rome who had represented mafiosi before and had now been
retained by the Palaias. Madia asked Giuseppina to read a letter to
the prosecutor's office that he had drafted on her behalf. It stated
that Giuseppina's health had suffered from her time in prison; that
the authorities had taken advantage of her fragile state of mind by
forcing her to cooperate; and that her evidence was false and she
was withdrawing it. Giuseppina objected to several claims but eventually agreed to sign. She also accepted Madia's proposal that she
refuse to sign off on the witness statements she had given Alessandra and exercise her right to silence in any further interviews.

Giuseppina copied into her own handwriting the typewritten
letter drafted by Madia, then signed it and dated it April 2. On
April 4, she consented to a carabinieri interview during which she
freely answered all questions. She was, she said later, "caught between two fires." When Madia told the Palaias that Giuseppina
was still cooperating, Aunt Angela, Giuseppina's brother-in-law
Gianluca Palaia, and a third clan member, Angelo Ietto, simply
turned up at her safe house, saying that they were there to give
their cousin "emotional support" at this difficult time. Giuseppina
realized that, once again, her destiny was being decided for her. "I
had made the choice to make my daughter's life better, but collaborating had ended up hurting my daughter," she said. Now she had
to do what her daughter wanted. The 'Ndrangheta were inside her
house, sitting with her children. If she refused to cooperate, they
would take them away forever. "I couldn't betray my children," said
Giuseppina. "I couldn't say no."

On April 11, Alessandra flew up from Reggio to Rome, then
drove down to Aprilia to see Giuseppina. Months of interviews had
been leading to this moment. It was 179 days since Giuseppina had
begun cooperating and one day before the legal deadline by which

Italian prosecutors in any investigation must present their evidence to court. Alessandra was bringing with her close to two thousand printed pages, transcripts of all Giuseppina's interviews over the past six months. Within those pages was the most detailed portrait of the 'Ndrangheta that had ever existed. It was enough to bring down one of Europe's most powerful crime families and blow open a secret, murderous, cocaine-smuggling cabal that had terrorized Italy for 150 years. It was also the fullest possible vindication of Alessandra's intuition about 'Ndrangheta women. She found it hard not to feel a moment of triumph as she set the stack of files down on the table in front of her star witness.

Alessandra explained to Giuseppina that her signature was just a legal formality. All she had to do was sign a covering letter, declaring that the statements that followed were her own words and a true representation of the facts as she knew them to be.

Giuseppina looked at the papers. She told Alessandra she couldn't sign.

"Are you refusing to sign because everything you've told us is lies?" asked Alessandra.[2]

Giuseppina, trying not to look Alessandra in the eye, started to cry. Sobbing, she invoked her right to silence. Stunned, Alessandra packed up her files and said she would leave Giuseppina with her lawyer for a few minutes to consider her options. She returned half an hour later.

"Is this really what you want?" she asked.

Giuseppina began to cry again. "It's not what I want," she said. "It's what I must do for my children." She refused to say any more.

ALESSANDRA TRIED TO carry on as before. On April 16, she arrested Giuseppina's mother, Angela Ferraro, and her sister Marina on charges of extortion and mafia association. The two had been detained a year earlier and released on bail, but with the new evidence from Giuseppina, their offenses were now serious enough for custody. Their detention brought to seventy-four the number of Pesce clan members that Alessandra had arrested in the year since she launched All Inside.

The next day, however, the Pesces hit back. A report appeared in the *Gazzetta del Sud*, the main southern daily, quoting Giuseppe Madia saying Giuseppina had recanted. Alessandra shrugged off the story as typical mafia lies. They just couldn't admit weakness, she thought. The state was winning this war.

On April 21, Alessandra struck again. Once more acting on Giuseppina's evidence, she launched Operation All Clean, this time aimed at the Pesces' finances. Forty-one companies were seized, most of them based in and around Rosarno, including trucking firms, orange and lemon traders, service stations, a sports complex, a sports fishing operation, a plastics firm, and a pizzeria. In addition, the prosecutors confiscated fifty properties—villas, apartments, houses, and garages—fifty-four plots of land, fifty-one cars and motorcycles, and 102 trucks. The total value was estimated at €190 million. "Today we can say with satisfaction that Rosarno is truly free," said Pignatone.

But barely had Alessandra had time to savor her new victory when, on April 26, 2011, she was handed a copy of the Reggio newspaper, *Calabria Ora*. On its front page, the paper had printed what it said was a letter from Giuseppina Pesce to Calabria's attorney general.[3]

> *Dear Mr. Judge,*
>
> *With this letter I want to withdraw all the allegations I made in my previous statements. I resolved to do this not out of fear but out of conscience because I said things that do not correspond to reality. I made those assertions at a time when I was seriously ill and suffering a great deal from being separated from my children.*

The doctors who came to visit me when I was detained witnessed the seriousness of my illness and how severely I was depressed in jail where, out of desperation, I put my own life in danger. I was hoping to see my three children, one of whom has serious health problems. But my hopes did not last long because . . . I was sent on to Milan. That was the moment I realized I would die if I did not make the statements I was expected to make.

I will explain in court how my answers were born of questions loaded with accusations. The more you accuse, the more you are believed. The more you accuse your family, you will be believed even more. I was so sick that I slandered my closest family members with untruth. Fear and illness made me make those statements, which now make me feel nothing but shame in my heart. I feel stripped naked, exposed to everyone, with no thought for my dignity or my loved ones. I feel like I have been used. Now that I feel better, I have found the courage to retract my allegations, even as I fear the monstrous process that I know awaits me. I ask everyone, even those whom I have hurt unjustly, spare me a little understanding and respect for the situation in which I am living.

Sincerely,
Giuseppina Pesce

Calabria Ora added to its scoop with an interview with Madia, the lawyer, under the headline: "Forced to Repent: Pesce Said Whatever the Prosecutors Wanted." The article began with a quote from Madia: "Do you know how many times I have spoken with my client? Once, in a carabinieri station, then nothing. Can you imagine? Today I don't even know where she is."

Madia alleged that Alessandra had "extracted" Giuseppina's testimony by using the "threat" that unless she cooperated, she would never see her children again. "Read this medical report, read what it says about Mrs. Pesce," he told the *Calabria Ora* journalist, handing him a file that he said was signed by Nicola Pangallo, a psychiatrist who interviewed Giuseppina in prison. "The prisoner has particularly serious conditions that do not allow her custody in prison . . . The service agent reports that the prisoner had attempted suicide by hanging. The patient is completely detached from current reality and obsessed by the idea of leaving prison and seeing her children again. When she spoke to her daughter, her daughter replied: 'Is that my mom?' [The patient said]: 'I'm afraid my children no longer recognize me.'"

Dr. Pangallo went on to recommend that Giuseppina receive specialist care in a prison located close to her children, in order to allow more frequent contact. "And where do the prosecutors think the nearest prison to Reggio is located?" Madia asked the journalist. "Why, Milan, of course, a thousand kilometers away." It was after her transfer that Giuseppina had collapsed and begun collaborating, he added. "It's obvious Mrs. Pesce has not told the truth. She only said what the judges wanted her to say. That's why she made these statements."

In an editorial, *Calabria Ora*'s editor in chief, Piero Sansonetti, decried the prosecutors' conduct. "The fight against the mafia, like all exercises of justice, must be conducted within the rules, strictly within the rules, totally within the rules," he wrote. "Otherwise it might land a few blows on the mafia but inflict far greater damage to our legal system and society." Three days later, April 29, which happened to be Alessandra's forty-first birthday, Sansonetti gave a television interview in which he repeated Madia's allegations, demanded a parliamentary inquiry, and accused Alessandra of extortion and blackmail.

It was the start of a yearlong campaign by *Calabria Ora* against Alessandra and the other anti-mafia prosecutors. Throughout Giuseppina would be described not as an individual who had made her own choices but as a disturbed and weak woman who had been used by the prosecutors and manipulated into betraying her family. A week later, Sansonetti wrote another editorial in which he appeared to justify breaking the law and to characterize the 'Ndrangheta as victims of oppression. "To tell the truth, I actually don't care for lawfulness," he wrote. "To respect the law is not always, in my opinion, a merit. I have never sided with the law. Disobedience is a virtue. I tend to think it's right to stand for the weak whoever they are, and whether they're good or bad, guilty or innocent." Over the next few months, *Calabria Ora* published a string of stories castigating the prosecutors. One was an interview from prison with Salvatore Pesce, Giuseppina's father, who criticized the way his daughter had been treated. Giuseppina's uncle Giuseppe Ferraro also spoke to *Calabria Ora*, accusing Alessandra of blackmailing his niece by having the carabinieri kidnap her children and forcing her to make statements under the influence of psychotropic drugs.

It wasn't clear how much of this the Pesces actually believed. The intended audience seemed to be the citizens of Rosarno as much as Alessandra and the state. Still, the judiciary had to respond. The head of Italy's Anti-Mafia Directorate in Rome first denied any wrongdoing, then summoned Alessandra to the capital, where she was ordered to make out a report and explain her actions. A prosecutor in Catanzaro was even deputed to investigate Alessandra for extortion. "This slander campaign went on and on," said Alessandra.

Alessandra knew she was becoming a liability to the judiciary. Even to colleagues who backed her, she was in danger of becoming a cautionary tale: the spectacular rise and fall of the woman prosecutor who flew too high. She had the backing of Pignatone and Prestipino. But no prosecutor could tolerate criticism forever, least of all one on the front line of a war against the mafia.

Alessandra's only hope was to change Giuseppina's mind again. It seemed improbable. But in the months that followed, Alessandra began to fixate on the last conversation she had had with Giuseppina, going over it in her mind time and again. The letter in *Calabria Ora*, in which Giuseppina withdrew her statements, was clearly written for her. But when Alessandra had challenged Giuseppina to declare that her evidence was lies, Giuseppina had refused to speak. She became convinced Giuseppina was trying to tell her something. Refusing to sign wasn't recanting. Giuseppina might only be refusing to sign her statements *at that moment*. Who knew what kind of pressure the 'Ndrangheta was putting on her?

In early May, Alessandra was passed transcripts of bugged conversations between the Pesces. The contents seemed to support the idea that, contrary to Giuseppina's letter, she was far from reconciled with her family. In one exchange on May 5, caught on video, between her brother Francesco Pesce and her grandmother Giuseppa Bonarrigo, Francesco reassured the family matriarch that the Pesce family itself had "nothing to be ashamed of. If she [Giuseppina] screwed up, she did it alone, without anyone else from the family." Besides, Giuseppina's evidence wasn't all that damning, said Francesco. The family had found experts who would testify that she was mentally ill. "She's crazy, crazy," agreed Giuseppina's grandmother. "She did it for the children. Imagine!" Francesco added that Giuseppina's testimony was, in any case, mostly hearsay. Women weren't like men, he said. They just stayed in the home and listened to men talk. All Giuseppina had been able to pass on was what she had heard. It was a problem made in the home, said Francesco, "and we'll solve it. We just have to try to get her home. I'm trying to approach to tell her I have nothing against her, that I love her." At the words "solve it," Giuseppina's seventy-eight-year-old grandmother clasped her neck as though she were being choked.

That conversation would stay with Alessandra. Giuseppina's motivation for talking had always been to give her family a better life. That maternal compulsion meant all was not lost. Giuseppina would still want a new life for her children. She hadn't disavowed her statements, merely set them aside. If she was planning to take her children back to Rosarno, it would only be until she thought it was safe to leave again. Over the months they'd worked together, Alessandra had grown to trust Giuseppina, to care for her, and to respect her. Giuseppina was resilient and resourceful. The more Alessandra thought about it, the more she was convinced Giuseppina was executing a plan by invoking her right to silence. "She's being clever," she told her staff. To the 'Ndrangheta, Giuseppina was trying to appear as though she had been successfully brought to heel. But to Alessandra, Giuseppina was indicating she remained true to the cause. She was still planning to cooperate. She was just biding her time. "She's telling me that what she had said in all those months of interviews was true," said Alessandra.

Still, time was not on Giuseppina's side. As her grandmother's gesture indicated, her family would likely kill her as soon as they could. Since Giuseppina had stopped cooperating, the witness protection service would soon eject her, as they had done with Lea Garofalo—and if Lea's fate was any indication, Giuseppina's death would follow swiftly. However Alessandra was planning to save her star witness, she needed to act now.

Even as she struggled to find a way to rescue Giuseppina, Alessandra found her *pentita*'s example was inspiring another 'Ndrangheta woman to follow suit.[1]

In June 2010, anonymous letters began arriving at the yellow two-story house in Via Don Gregorio Varrà, Rosarno, that Maria Concetta Cacciola shared with her parents. The letters claimed that Concetta was having an affair with one of her Facebook friends. The accusation was absurd. Her friend had been in Germany all the time that Concetta had known him. But Concetta's father and brother, Michele and Giuseppe, didn't hesitate. Shouting, "You filthy animal!" they grabbed Concetta, punched her to the floor, and kicked her until they cracked one of her ribs. Desperate to avoid any public tarnishing of the family name, the two men then refused to let Concetta be treated at the hospital. Instead, they arranged private visits to the house by a doctor related to the Pesces. All this happened in front of Concetta's three children, Alfonso, fifteen, Tania, twelve, and Rosi, six.

It was three months before Concetta was well enough to step outside. Even then, one of her cousins followed her wherever she went. Finding herself alone in the house one day, Concetta called a women's refuge on the other side of Calabria but hung up before anyone answered. Then on May 11, 2011, the carabinieri summoned her to the station in Rosarno. Alfonso's scooter had been confiscated for a minor driving offense, and Concetta needed to pay his fine before it was returned. The twenty-minute walk to the station was the first occasion in months that Concetta had been allowed out of the house on her own.

Concetta entered the carabinieri station and asked to speak to an officer. From the moment Officer Carlo Carli led her into an interview room and closed the door, it all just tumbled out of her. Concetta first asked if Carli knew the reputation of the Cacciola family and her husband, Salvatore Figliuzzi. When Carli said he did, Concetta told him her family had kept her a virtual prisoner at home for the eight years since Salvatore had gone to jail. The situation had become intolerable in the last eleven months, she said. She told Carli the saga about her Facebook friendship with a man called Giuseppe in Germany, the poison-pen letters, and the beating. Her family now never let her out of their sight. As if to underline the point, Concetta's phone soon started ringing. It was her mother, Anna Rosalba Lazzaro, asking where she was. Concetta said she had to leave. At the door of the interview room, she predicted that one day her family would murder her. "If they find out I'm here saying these things, they'll kill me for sure," she said.

Officer Carli wanted to know more. Using Alfonso's scooter as an excuse, he summoned Concetta back to the station four days later. This time, she spoke to a female officer and, feeling less inhibited in front of a woman, told the officer she now wanted to escape her family and Rosarno. She had bought tickets to northern Italy several times but never had the nerve to go through with it. She'd even ripped up her ticket once when one of her cousins followed her into the travel agent's. The thing was, Concetta confided to the officer, her family was right. Calling herself "Nemi," she had begun a second online relationship with "Prince 484," a Reggio man called Pasquale Improta.[2] Initially, it had been innocent. But now it was starting to evolve into an affair. Pasquale was living a few hours away in Naples. When she'd told him about the beating, he'd urged her to go to the carabinieri to ask them to protect her. Concetta wanted to be with Pasquale. She had told her mother she wanted to divorce Salvatore. After all, he had never loved her and had only married her to assist his rise inside the 'Ndrangheta.

Concetta said her father would never let her divorce her husband. But it was her younger brother, thirty-year-old Giuseppe, who really scared her. He had been raised as a true believer, she said, and knew nothing outside the 'Ndrangheta. She had had to warn friends to stay away from her in case Giuseppe suspected they were helping her. The only time she could relax was when Giuseppe went away on business or once when he vanished for a few days immediately after a murder in Rosarno. Even then Giuseppe's wife had taken Concetta aside and whispered to her not to speak freely inside their house because Giuseppe had had the place bugged. "Giuseppe gets these rages," said Concetta. "He could do anything." He was just waiting for proof that she was having an affair, she said. "Sooner or later, he'll come to me and say, 'Come with me.' Then he'll make me disappear."

On May 23, Concetta returned to the station and spoke to Officer Carli again. With each successive visit, she seemed to be building up her courage. This time she gave more details about how her father and brother beat her. She added that she was thinking of leaving for Naples. On May 25, she went to the carabinieri station in Gioia Tauro. On this occasion she ended the conversation by saying she was prepared to make a statement about her family in return for witness protection. When she returned to Gioia Tauro station the next day, her fifth visit to the carabinieri in fifteen days, she found Alessandra and Giovanni Musarò waiting for her.

Concetta told the two prosecutors she could talk for a maximum of ninety minutes. "It was a complicated interrogation," said Alessandra. "We had to know who we had in front of us, why she was talking to us, what she was able to tell us, and whether she was lying. And she was very scared. She had told her family that she had to go to the carabinieri to pay a fine. That gave her more time than usual away from home. But she was worried. She kept looking at her watch."[3]

The prosecutors quickly concluded Concetta was credible. Her knowledge of the Rosarno clans was extensive. She told them details about the murder of Palmiro Macri, sixty-two, shot in a clan feud by a gunman using a Kalashnikov in July 2008 as he drove through Rosarno in his Fiat Panda. She described how a boss called Umberto Bellocco had killed Salvatore Messina, his wife's brother, then blamed the murder on Concetta's cousin, Gregorio Bellocco, something that caused a rift between the Belloccos and the Pesces for years. She told the story of how the Belloccos had extended their protection rackets to the nearby coastal town of San Ferdinando. She pinpointed the location of at least two bunkers, buried under an old factory in Rosarno, and explained how they were equipped with televisions and refrigerators stocked with food and champagne. The bosses' hypocrisy seemed to outrage Concetta. Hanging on the wall where "these men without honor shut themselves up like beasts," she said, would be an image of Saint Pio of Pietrelcina. "I'm speaking about murderers," she added, people who "butcher wretched people that thought they were friends, men they invited to dinner, not killed for honor or the family's sake but just for money and power."

The two prosecutors were struck by Concetta's resolve. "I was very impressed," said Giovanni. "Very often, people like her who go through pain and suffering—they are conflicted. Concetta was terrified but she was also very resolute."[4] When Alessandra asked her whether she would want to take her three children with her into witness protection, Concetta demurred. "I don't want my children to weaken my resolve," she said. "I need to find my strength in the choices I make, then you can go and find them, tell what I've done and why, and they can make their own decision whether to join me or not."[5]

But something about Concetta's story bothered the two prosecutors. Giovanni zeroed in on the reason her father and brother had beaten her. He asked her to explain the anonymous letters. They couldn't just have appeared from nowhere. "Giovanni was pressing her a bit," said Alessandra. "He could see she was lying. She was hiding something."

Concetta said nothing. But when the two prosecutors called a short break, Concetta waited until Giovanni and a male carabinieri officer were talking, then approached Alessandra. "If you wish, I can tell you about my relationship with Pasquale," she said, "but I'm too ashamed to talk in front of the men." Even inside a carabinieri station, negotiating her exit from the 'Ndrangheta, "Concetta was still a victim of the mafia system," said Alessandra.[6]

FOUR DAYS LATER, on the night of May 29, 2011, Concetta stole out of the family home in the middle of the night and ran to a waiting carabinieri car. In her room, she had left a letter for her mother.

Dear Mama,

I do not know where to start. I can't find the words to justify this action of mine. Mama, you're mama! Only you can understand a daughter. I know the pain that I'm causing you. By explaining everything to you, then at least you can explain to everyone else. I didn't want to leave you without saying anything. How many times have I wanted to talk to you? How much did I want to spare you pain? But I failed. And all this pain, I turned it into aggression, and I took it out on the person who, above all, I love the most.

That's why I'm entrusting my children to you. But one thing I beg of you. Don't make the mistakes that you made with me. Give them a better life than I had. Paired off at thirteen, I thought marriage would give me a little freedom. Instead, I ruined my life. Salvatore never loved me nor me him. You know that. So don't make

*the same mistakes with the children, I beg you. Give them space. If
you shut them away, they'll start to behave badly because they'll feel
trapped by everything. That's how you treated me.*

*I can't write much more. I just wanted to ask you to forgive
me, Mother, for the shame I'm bringing you. In the end, I realized
that I was alone—alone among everyone. I've never known luxury
and I never wanted money. But now I have the peace and love and
the satisfaction you feel when you make a sacrifice. This life has
given me nothing but pain. The most beautiful thing in my life is
my children. I keep them in my heart. Give your strength to them.
Don't let their father have them; he's not worthy of them. Take care
of Alfonso. He suffered as a boy and that's why he is how he is. He's
not strong. You need to watch him closely.*

*I will live as long as God allows but I have to try to find some
peace in my heart. Mama, forgive me. Please pray for forgiveness
for all the harm that I'm causing. I'm going to a place where I
can find some serenity. Don't look for me or you'll get into trouble.
I can't speak to you anymore and I can't hug you, I can only
write—but I couldn't leave without telling you I was going and
wishing you well. I have only you and my children in my mind's
eye. I love you, Mama. Hug my children as you always have and
don't talk about them to anyone who's not worthy of them. Ma,
farewell. And forgive me. Forgive me if you can. I know I'll never
see you again. This is how it must be with a family of honor. That's
why you have lost your daughter. Good-bye. I will always love you.
Forgive me, as I, too, pray for forgiveness. Good-bye.*

On the dashboard of the family car, Concetta also left a brief
note for her father and her brother. "I'm going over to my friend
Giusy's," she wrote.

———

FORMALLY ADMITTING A witness to the protection program took months. But Concetta needed immediate protection. The carabinieri took her to a secluded holiday resort, the Colle degli Ulivi, near Cosenza, in the hills above the coastal town of Sibari, two hours' drive north of Rosarno.

The Colle degli Ulivi was a safe, nondescript place, generally used by northern Italian families on holiday. It had three restaurants, a bar, a solarium, a Jacuzzi, and a giant pool, and it offered its guests horse riding, mountain biking, tennis, archery, karaoke, and walks in the hills or down to the beach. At mealtimes, giant buffets would be laid with fruit, salads, and cold meats, or you could order à la carte, and there was every type of wine. Concetta's protection officers stayed on-site but otherwise let her roam as she wanted.

Concetta loved it. She could walk into town or down to the shoreline whenever she chose. In the hotel, as the temperature rose with the onset of summer, the rooms slowly filled with guests: young families, old couples, foreigners. No one knew her. No one knew the meaning of the name Cacciola. There was no shame and no punishment. And Concetta realized that at thirty-one, for the first time in her life, she was truly free.

Pasquale came to visit for a couple of nights. Staff and guests would later recall how Concetta seemed just as happy striking up conversations with perfect strangers, arriving promptly at mealtimes in the hope of meeting someone new. She picked up several lone men over the two months she was there. "In this new environment, she got to know a lot of men," said Giuseppe Creazzo, the prosecutor who would later investigate her case. "She made love with a lot of them. It was a way for her to be alive. It was the best way she knew to communicate."

On June 16, Alessandra drove up to Sibari, and Concetta gave her as much detail as she could on the bunkers. Two days later, Giovanni arrived for a third interview to go over Concetta's earlier evidence. Concetta identified various 'Ndranghetisti from mug shots that Giovanni brought with him and added details of the murders and protection rackets she had described. When Giovanni asked, Concetta reconfirmed in a written statement that she was willing to leave her three children with their grandmother. "I believe they're in no danger," she wrote. "I believe my children don't need the state to protect them."

Concetta struck Giovanni as "more serene and at peace" than when he had last seen her. Importantly, "she was also still determined." Unprompted, Concetta went into fine detail about how the Bellocco clan ran their loan-sharking operation. Two brothers of a friend of hers, Rita Stefania Secolo, had borrowed €600,000 from the Belloccos. Two years later, their debt was €1 million. "Stefania told me that the Belloccos had threatened to kill her brothers if the money was not repaid," said Concetta. "They told her they would take an apartment building owned by her family as part payment. They even shot up a shop on the ground floor and told Stefania they would have killed somebody if the gun hadn't jammed." Stefania ended up living on the top floor of the building, above her old apartment, paying rent to the Bellocco extortionists who had moved in below.

Every day Concetta stayed at Colle degli Ulivi was another small adventure. When the formal approval for her witness protection came through in late July, she was moved to Bolzano in the Alps. But when a new man she brought back to her hotel room turned out to be a former convict, her protection officers moved her again, this time to Genoa on Italy's northwest coast.

IF LEAVING GAVE Concetta a new sense of peace, it created uproar in Rosarno. "Your escape sparked off hell," her friend Emanuela Gentile told her, in a call tapped by the carabinieri. "Your father really freaked out. Your mother went around yelling 'They ruined us,' and was crying and tearing her hair out. Your brother grew a long beard and locked himself far away in a house by the sea out of shame. He never leaves. Now *he* is the prisoner."

Alessandra and Giovanni couldn't help enjoying the ruckus. "It was the fact that she was a woman called Cacciola," said Giovanni. "That was really unacceptable to them. The 'Ndrangheta's reaction to Giuseppina and Concetta was not proportional to the information they gave us—most of it was hearsay, not a murder confession or anything—but to the 'Ndrangheta it wasn't about the information. It was the symbolic value of them turning state's evidence."

Alessandra took particular pleasure in reading the transcripts from the Cacciola family. The carabinieri had tapped their phones and planted a bug in the family car. You could almost hear the 'Ndrangheta shattering. In one recording, Anna Rosalba Lazzaro, Concetta's mother, railed about the female carabiniere in Rosarno with whom Concetta had spoken. "That officer slut!" shouted Lazzaro. "She has a thing going with the judges! She's a whore!" Another time, Alessandra listened as Concetta's mother tried to wrap her mind around her daughter's actions. "She saw nothing in her life," said Lazzaro. "But she never saw the whole truth. She's always been like that. She eloped at thirteen! She's never seen anything in her life, poor devil. And they took advantage of that, those unworthy bastards! Bastards! It's so easy just to talk. You just say your brother told you this, your father told you that, your mother's cunt told you something else." Lazzaro suspected that one day Concetta would send for her children. She found the thought unbearable. "She wants to tear them away from their roots and take them where? How is she going to provide for them? She can't even sweep the floor! No! She must come back home. The carabinieri don't have any actual evidence. In a week nobody in Rosarno will ever speak about these things again."

Michele Cacciola, Concetta's father, was just as disturbed. At home, he would unleash tirades that could last an hour. "This unworthy piece of shit!" he shouted in one episode recorded on July 11, 2011. "I worked twenty years for her!" Michele seemed most upset at his loss of standing. "I had [such] a family that they [the people of Rosarno] were all jealous of me," he yelled. "I enjoyed watching my grandchildren grow. Nobody was happier than me!" Michele saw Concetta's departure not as her bid for a new life but as an attack on him by the state. "These contemptible people, these unworthy bastards, to take a daughter from her father! How is this the law to come at me and take my daughter? Did I start a fight with them? Do they even know who I am? If they have something on me, then arrest me! They are taking daughters away from their fathers!" Not that talking to a mere woman would serve the state's purpose, said Michele. "They wait for her to disgrace me. But what can she know about me? She knows nothing. What can a *woman* know in my house? You think I told my daughter about my fucking business? She knows nothing!"

These 'Ndrangheta men, thought Alessandra. Treat their women like dirt. But one walks away from them, and they fall all to pieces.

Lea Garofalo. The picture is undated but seems to capture Lea in her early twenties, just after she became a mother. The image became iconic. (*http://www.wikimafia.it*)

Lea, on the left, and Denise captured by CCTV in Milan in their last minutes together on the evening of November 24, 2009. (*Milan Carabinieri*)

Alessandra Cerreti, pictured in her office in Reggio Calabria. (*FILIPPO MONTEFORTE/AFP/Getty Images*)

Reggio Calabria, as seen from the hills to the southeast of the city, looking northwest across the Strait to Messina. (*Anna Quaglia/Alamy Stock Photo*)

San Luca. For decades, the 'Ndrangheta have convened an annual meeting on September 2 in this Aspromonte hill village, using a religious festival as cover. (*ROPI/ Alamy Stock Photo*)

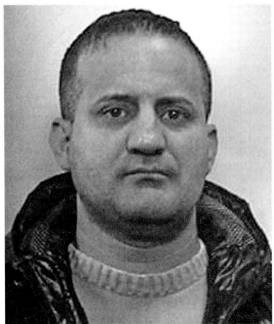

Carlo Cosco in a police mug shot taken after his arrest in February 2010. (*Lanese / Epa/REX/Shutterstock*)

Giuseppina Pesce the day after her arrest in April 2010. (*ANSA*)

Domenico Oppedisano being driven through the streets after his arrest in Rosarno in July 2010. (*Franco Cufari / Epa / REX / Shutterstock*)

Giuseppina Pesce in her mug shot after her arrest. (*ANSA*)

Maria Concetta Cacciola. Confined to the family home for weeks at a time, only one other picture of her has ever surfaced. (*ANSA*)

The gate of the warehouse in San Fruttuoso, Monza, where Lea's remains were discovered in October 2012, three years after her death. (*Fabrizio Radaelli/Epa/REX/Shutterstock*)

Breaking a lifetime of omertà, Carlo speaks in court on April 9, 2013. (*Corriere TV*)

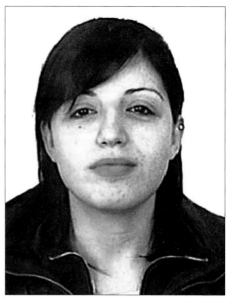

Giuseppina's mother, Angela Ferraro, and sister, Marina Pesce. (*ANSA*)

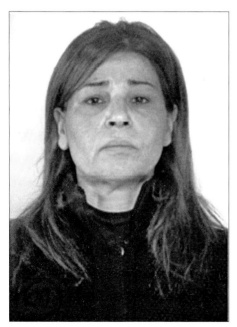
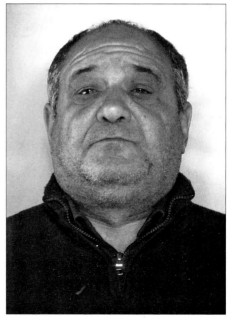

Concetta's mother, Anna Rosalba Lazzaro, and father, Michele Cacciola. (*ANSA*)

Lea's funeral on October 19, 2013. Thousands from all over Italy turned out for a woman who, four years after her death, united the nation against the mafia under the slogan "I see, I hear, I speak." (*Marco Aprile/ NurPhoto/Corbis via Getty Images*)

XVI

As soon as Alessandra was sure Concetta was safe, she switched her focus back to Giuseppina. Since she had stopped cooperating with the judiciary, Giuseppina's options had steadily narrowed. The 'Ndrangheta plan to return her to Rosarno was well under way. Her family had rented her an apartment in Vibo Marina, a small seaside town north of Rosarno, and a judicial order transferring Giuseppina's house arrest there was being drawn up. Alessandra suspected the clan would kill her almost as soon as she arrived. In May, the witness protection service ordered Giuseppina's ejection from the program as an uncooperative witness. There would be a delay before the command was implemented. But as May turned to June, Alessandra reckoned she had days to save her witness.

The order for Giuseppina's transfer to Vibo Marina was issued in early June. On the morning it was due to be executed, June 10, Alessandra received a call from the protection officers at Giuseppina's safe house outside Aprilia. Giuseppina; her boyfriend, Domenico Costantino; and her daughter Angela had gone for a day in Lucca in Tuscany, four hours to the north, leaving her younger children, Gaetano and Elisea, with a babysitter. The officers added that Angela had been threatening for a while to sneak out of the house to go and see a friend in Lucca. When Domenico had driven up from Rosarno a few days earlier, Giuseppina had seized the chance to make her daughter happy one final time. "I was living those days as if they were the last I would ever spend with my children," she said later.

It was the opportunity Alessandra needed. As a collaborator, even one who had stopped talking, Giuseppina enjoyed a measure of freedom. But she still needed permission to travel long distance. By the letter of the law, a trip to Lucca violated the conditions of her house arrest. Alessandra raced to the carabinieri surveillance office in Reggio. En route, she called the Lazio carabinieri's mafia surveillance team. Alessandra told the officer on duty that she needed the carabinieri to intercept Giuseppina on the highway from Lucca back to Aprilia. If Giuseppina could be caught in the act of flouting the conditions of her detention, then Alessandra could have her summarily sent back to prison. A jail cell, explained Alessandra, was now the only place Giuseppina could be sure of staying alive. But they had to catch her first.

No problem, the carabinieri officer replied. What car were they looking for?

Alessandra said that she didn't know the make of the car, its color, or its license plate, or the route it was taking.

That wasn't much to go on, replied the officer.

Alessandra said that was precisely why she was asking for a hundred carabinieri to set up as many checkpoints as possible along the various routes from Lucca. Somewhere in the four hundred kilometers between Lucca and Aprilia would be a car of some description in which would be three people—Giuseppina, her boyfriend, and her fifteen-year-old daughter.

The officer said he would call her back. Minutes later the duty officer in charge of all Lazio's carabinieri, a captain, was on the line. "We wouldn't use a hundred men even for Osama bin Laden," he said.

Alessandra insisted. This one *pentita* could take down the entire Rosarno 'Ndrangheta, she said. "And unless we arrest her right now," Alessandra said, Giuseppina was going to be murdered. Alessandra told the captain she had something that would help: Giuseppina's mobile, whose GPS signal the carabinieri could use to track her. According to the screen Alessandra was watching at that moment in Reggio, Giuseppina had just left Lucca and was now heading to Florence. That meant she would likely be taking the main toll road all the way to Aprilia. The journey would take three and a half hours. That was how long the captain had to save the most important witness ever to testify against the 'Ndrangheta.

The captain said he would try. Within minutes, his men were setting up roadblocks and checkpoints. "We were following her mobile in real time on the screen," said Alessandra, "and I was in constant contact with the carabinieri captain and his officers on the ground." But as Alessandra watched, the dot on the screen approached the first roadblock, then sailed through. Half an hour later, it approached a second, then kept on going as before. Alessandra phoned the captain. "What is going on?!" she yelled. "How come they're getting through?"

The captain, unaccustomed to being shouted at by a southerner, and a woman, told Alessandra that his men were doing their best. She had given them almost nothing to go on. But his men would do what they could.

By now Alessandra was also phoning officers at individual checkpoints, asking them to keep the line open so she could listen to what was happening. One by one, they all reported seeing nothing. The dot on the screen kept moving south. As Giuseppina floated through roadblock after roadblock, the carabinieri captain's attitude changed from defensiveness to despair. When the screen showed Giuseppina approaching Aprilia, the captain told Alessandra it was over. "We've lost her," he said. "We've lost her."

"You have to block *all* the traffic on the highway!" shouted Alessandra. "All of it! Do it right now!"

The captain protested. The screen had Giuseppina at three kilometers away. Only one checkpoint lay between her and the safe house. Alessandra was suggesting that he block one of the main arterial roads in all of Italy when it was already too late. "She's gone, she's gone," he said.

"You do *not* give up, Captain!" shouted Alessandra. "You block the entire highway, you do it right now and you keep this line open! Do it, Captain!"

The officer reluctantly agreed. Alessandra went back to checking the screen. There were a few moments of silence. Then the captain's voice came back on the line.

"*Hold on!*" he shouted.

"Hold on . . ."

"There's a car . . ."

"With a *woman*!"

Alessandra heard a commotion. She guessed several squad cars had encircled the suspect vehicle and brought it to a stop.

There was a moment of silence.

Then a woman's voice shouted: "Don't shoot! Don't shoot! My name is Giuseppina Pesce!"[1]

REGULATIONS REQUIRED GIUSEPPINA be kept in isolation for three weeks. Alessandra wasn't unhappy that Giuseppina would have to stew for a while. She had been desperate to save Giuseppina but that didn't mean she was pleased with her. She had put her faith in this 'Ndranghetista, and the 'Ndranghetista had reverted to type: shutting down, submitting to The Family, resuming omertà. Giuseppina had ground to make up with Alessandra. She needed to know it.

Of course, it was also possible that Giuseppina wouldn't see her rescue as anything of the sort. There was the manner of her capture: men with guns drawn, screaming at her to lie on the ground. And since Giuseppina was back in jail, the authorities had had no choice but to separate her from her children once more and send them back to the Palaias in Rosarno. After all the risks she had taken and the torment she had endured, precisely nothing had changed for Giuseppina. She could be forgiven for questioning the point of it all.

Alessandra was counting on the transformation she thought she had discerned in Giuseppina. When she had first arrested Giuseppina in Rosarno a year earlier, the 'Ndranghetista had been defined by the men in her life: daughter to a criminal father, wife to a violent husband, obedient servant to violent and criminal men of honor. Even Giuseppina's identity as a mother had been defined by the men. Though she loved Angela, Gaetano, and Elisea, she had also accepted that her role, however repugnant, was to prepare them for the 'Ndrangheta.

But in the last year, Giuseppina had broken with all of that. She had become the director of her own life. She had reclaimed her freedom. She had retrieved her children. She had even chosen her own lover. Above all, she had recovered herself—and there was no giving herself away again. She had not, as the Pesce men told reporters, acted as a sick, weak woman. She had not been used by Alessandra. Just the opposite. The first time she went to prison, she had been cowed and terrified and had tried to kill herself within days. Now, back in a cell and away from her children once more, she was calm and in control. A jail cell had a way of stripping everything away. Being reunited with her children was the only thing that mattered, and Giuseppina knew what she had to do to achieve that.

As Alessandra bided her time, she monitored Giuseppina's correspondence. Dispatches arrived every day from Aunt Angela; Giuseppina's mother, Angela Ferraro; her sister Marina; her father, Salvatore; even her husband, Rocco Palaia. Mostly her family congratulated her on ending her cooperation and described the new life that they had prepared for her in Calabria. But by now, Alessandra thought she knew Giuseppina well enough to hope that she wouldn't believe a word. Not that her husband forgave her, not that the Palaias would take good care of her son, not that anything could ever go back to how it was. The likelihood was that the 'Ndrangheta would try to turn her children against her and even persuade her son to kill her. Alessandra felt that by insisting on the pretense, the clan was over-playing its hand. Moreover, as Alessandra saw it, by attempting to give Giuseppina no choice, they were offering her no alternative but to reject them. The only way for Giuseppina to save her children was to stay alive and look after them—and the only way to do that was to reenter witness protection and take her children with her. There was every chance, thought Alessandra, that her family's letters would have the opposite effect from what was intended.

The letters Giuseppina received from Rocco, laced with sarcasm and suppressed fury, were especially useful. "My dear tourist," he began in a letter dated June 15:

> *I hope you are in as good health as I. I thought you were allergic to jail but I see I was wrong. I told you many times to stay in your own place, in your own shoes. But you walked off alone for a holiday in Lucca. Who are these relatives in Lucca that I do not know? I'm not angry with you so much, but with that bastard Mimmo [Costantino] who took you there. What was he doing there? Tell me.*

Rocco wrote that he feared his children were suffering. He couldn't understand why his wife was in Lucca when she was meant to be in Vibo Marina. So much of what had happened was confusing to him, he wrote. "If [only] you were in your place at this time. But you are out." Still, he had advice for Giuseppina on how to set things right:

> *The first thing you need to do is to write to your father and explain the situation. How come you were with Mimmo? I want to know*

as well. After that, if you leave protection, good. If not, I'll see
you on July 12th. We can still return to being a normal family,
as we were before. I hug you and urgently await your news and
explanations. I have forgiven you many times. I hope this is the last.

On June 24, Rocco wrote again. "My dearest love (if I can call
you that)," he began. He then described a prison visit from his
brother, Gianluca Palaia, and their daughters, Angela ("my princess
who fell from the clouds") and Elisea. He assured Giuseppina that,
as a responsible parent, he would make sure the children had money
for clothes. "It doesn't matter that you abandoned me like you did.
Let's leave our arguments until we're both out. Even then, we can
pretend it never happened."

He added that he had to tell her about her friend Maria Concetta
Cacciola:

Do you remember 'Cetta? Who lives near the minimarket? Her
husband is also in prison and she had an affair, possibly with a
cop—something she should rightly be killed for. Anyway, when
she realized her family had found out, what did she do? She called
the police and entered witness protection—and in the family car
she left a note saying she was "going with her friend, Giusy."
They say she's making statements to the authorities now. She
really did it all.

   Your situation, of course, is very different. Everyone's forgiven
you for what you did. Me most of all. But, still, I wondered if this
put you in mind of anyone?

"It was typical mafia style, disguising a threat," said Alessandra
after she read the letter. "'Don't worry. You didn't do what Maria
Concetta Cacciola did, so nothing can happen to you.' Which is exactly the opposite of what he meant."[2] Alessandra sent the letter on

its way. When she received a letter from Giuseppina dated the same day, she knew Rocco's letter had hit its mark.

I am writing to tell you a few things that I feel I have to tell you, and I really hope from the bottom of my heart that you can hear me. After the last time we met, a lot has happened. All that publicity in the media, and all the accusations, and everything that came after. I would love to have the opportunity to explain what happened to you, especially to you, but also to the entire prosecutors' office. This morning I fired the lawyer, Giuseppe Madia, and am currently represented by the lawyer Valeria Maffei. It is my intention, if you are still interested, to resume the path of collaboration. I hope I can regain your trust. Sorry, again, for what happened. I hope I have a chance to apologize in person.[3]

The next day, June 25, Giuseppina wrote again:

I urgently renew my invitation to be heard by you. I want to resume the collaboration that was under way and that I interrupted for the reasons you know. I am willing to finish what I started. I beg you to make it happen before my transfer hearing on July 12—for obvious reasons concerning my personal safety and the safety of those closest to me. I repeat my apologies for my hesitancy. I am keenly aware that I caused great difficulties and wasted so much time.

The turnaround was amazing, thought Alessandra. The prosecutors had done nothing but let the 'Ndrangheta's internal dynamics play out. The clan's threats alone had been enough to propel Giuseppina back to the state. Alessandra's instinct was to give it longer. But Giuseppina was right to be afraid of the July 12 hearing. After it, she would likely be returned to the general prison population, and that would be all the opportunity the Pesces needed.

Alessandra waited a few more days, then sent word that she and Prestipino would see Giuseppina again on July 7.

At the meeting Alessandra was initially defensive. She adopted the same manner she had affected when she first met Giuseppina nine months before: cold and analytical, betraying little empathy or warmth. After all she had done for Giuseppina, she demanded to know how Giuseppina could accuse her of threatening her children. And how could she say that Alessandra had forced her to collaborate?

Giuseppina explained that her "retraction," published in *Calabria Ora*, had been written for her by the Palaias' lawyer. "I was opposed to this letter," she said. "They said this thing had to come out, had to be made public. Everyone had to know that I was not an informant. This would be proof that I wasn't collaborating anymore. They pressured me again and again to write this letter."

It sounded convincing, but Alessandra wasn't done. How could the state trust Giuseppina again, she asked. How could it know if she was genuine this time? The interview went on for hours, with Alessandra demanding Giuseppina explain herself and Giuseppina begging for Alessandra to trust her again. In addition to repairing her credibility as a witness, it seemed just as important to Giuseppina that she mend her friendship with Alessandra. "You have to trust me again," said Giuseppina.

"You have to earn it," replied Alessandra.

After several hours of talking, however, Alessandra was satisfied. She'd had to make sure, but she was now certain that Giuseppina's intention to collaborate once more was authentic. Trust between *pentita* and prosecutor was restored.

GIUSEPPE MADIA, THE Palaias' lawyer, passed word of his dismissal back to Rosarno. To the family, that could only mean one thing: Giuseppina was planning to testify again. Even when the clan had tried to appear gentle and understanding, Alessandra had always felt it straining to contain its crueler instincts. Now it unleashed them. Leading the campaign against Giuseppina was her own mother, Angela Ferraro.

Reading transcripts of bugs placed in the jail where Giuseppina's mother and sister were being held, Alessandra realized Ferraro had stopped referring to her daughter by name. Now Giuseppina was simply "the collaborator" or "the traitor" or "that whore." Like Concetta's father, Ferraro seemed most infuriated by her loss of prestige among other inmates. She set about revenging herself by trying to turn Giuseppina's children against her. On July 13, the day after Giuseppina's resumption of cooperation was confirmed in open court, Ferraro and Marina were visited together in jail by Sara, the third daughter in the family, who was mentally disabled, and Giuseppina's two daughters, Angela and Elisea.

Ferraro quickly told them all to cut all ties with Giuseppina. "She's dead to the family," she said. "If she calls, you don't answer. If you happen to pick up the phone, you have to tell her: 'You're dead to me. You don't exist anymore. For not doing your time in prison, you are the most contemptible, the most despicable.'" Ferraro was working herself into a fury, taking out all her frustration and rage on her grandchildren. "Tell her!" she shouted. "Tell her that her mother told you to pretend that she had died! She doesn't give a fuck about who's now in jail! She doesn't care about anything! When the phone rings, you tell her that her mother told you to forget you even have a mother! Your mother is gone!"

Sara began to cry. "Don't cry, love, don't cry, beautiful," said Ferraro, softening and gently kissing her daughter. "This is just how it is. This is the truth." She produced a letter from Giuseppina and began reading from it. "Forgive me if I am not the daughter you wanted," Giuseppina had written. "I know I've disappointed you.

I know my sister is very angry with me." See? asked Ferraro. Even Giuseppina knew she had done wrong.

Angela said she, too, had received a letter from her mother, asking for her forgiveness and saying that she wanted her children to join her but that they should "do what their heart tells them." Ferraro looked at her granddaughter. Five-year-old Elisea was crying, too. "From now on, it's you, me, and the family. Don't think that I'm not suffering in here. But I'm in here because of my love of family. You know what that means, love of family? It means loving you, loving my grandchildren, loving my children. My other daughter does not want to be in my heart. But that was her choice, not mine. I could never do what she did. Such a disappointment. But you should all go to the beach. Have fun. Mama is just fine here. It's just that I miss you. I miss you all. I miss my home. Let's all hug. We are a nice family. We love each other, no?"

Sara, crying once more, started hitting her hand on the table between them. "She is my sister," she said. "You're bad, and I don't care [what you say]. She is still my sister. She is still my sister."

Marina interrupted angrily. "You have to think of the rest of the family," she told Sara. "We've all cut her off. You have to turn your back on her. You have to be strong. Show me that strength in you that I love so much. Turn away from her."

Reading the transcripts, Alessandra was astonished by the two women's will. "They were ferocious. Brutal. The way they gave orders to the others. 'You must separate from your mother, your sister. You must forget her. She has betrayed the family.'" Among the adults, she said, only Giuseppina's disabled sister seemed to have a soul.

BACK IN ROSARNO, the clan began tormenting Giuseppina's children in earnest. Angela, Gaetano, and Elisea were forced to break all contact with their mother. Their aunt Angela threw them out. Forced to live with Giuseppina's father-in-law, Gaetano Palaia, they found that the family that had once offered their mother thousands of euros for lawyers and rent now claimed there was no money to feed them. They often went without. Elisea began to lose weight and developed leg cramps and insomnia. Gaetano regularly beat the grandson named after him with a belt. One day an uncle took the boy to a games arcade where he was hustled into a back room and set upon by four other older kids, including a seventeen-year-old cousin, as his uncle watched.

Angela was forced to play a part in torturing her mother. On July 18, a bundle of letters arrived for Giuseppina. In them her father-in-law accused her of being too cowardly for prison. Her husband, Rocco, told her, "The road you're taking will not be as easy as you think . . ." Aunt Angela wrote that "after everything we talked about, you were just lying. How happy we would all be if you'd only known your place." Finally, there was a letter from her eldest daughter:

> *Hello, dear mother. How are you? I hope you're fine, though I believe you're not . . . Don't think that I'm not angry with you. You're wrong. I've got it in for you, Mama. I am mad at you for what you're doing. I know you're missing us and we're missing you, but does it make any sense to make the same mistake twice? . . . And now you can't change back again. This is your choice, and I respect it, but you need to know that you are doing this only for you, not for us. You are just hurting us by taking us away from everyone else, as well you know . . . You know that I will not come [to live with you]. You gave me the chance to choose and I did. I don't want to live that life again. I would have liked to be with you because I love you, and because you are my mom, yet I cannot do this. Making this choice twice . . . you're spitting in the pot you*

eat from. I'm not telling this to be mean. I'm telling you this so you understand this is wrong. I don't know what they promised you and honestly I don't care. I wish to ask you a question, and for you to think it through. Is what they promised you more important? Or is your family, and our happiness, more important to you? If it is our happiness, and your family, then don't take this step. If you are more interested in what they promised, then it means that you are thinking only of yourself. I can't take it anymore, believe me. You ruined my life and I am only 16. Instead of having fun, I have to have this shitty life, only because of you, and you know it, Mama . . . Just leave me alone, please. I'm leaving you mom. Sorry for these words but this is what I think and what I want. I love you mom, but you should know that what you are doing is wrong.

The letter nearly broke Giuseppina's heart. It might have shattered it entirely but for one phrase: "spitting in the pot you eat from." That didn't sound like Angela or any sixteen-year-old Giuseppina knew. It was too old-fashioned. Too 'Ndrangheta.

The following week, a second letter came from Aunt Angela, urging Giuseppina to acknowledge that her son, Gaetano, was lost to her. From now on, he would be brought up by her in-laws. "He's terrified," she said. "I asked him about visiting you and he says he doesn't want to. He wants to stay here. I think moving him away again would just be more trauma. He would suffer even more. Try to think of your boy's happiness."

Four days later, on July 27, 2011, there was a second, short note from Angela. She was writing in secret, she said. Her mother should forget her earlier letter. The words had been dictated by her uncles.

It was not my doing. It wasn't what was in my heart.
Mom, I want to be with you.

I do not want to live with anyone else.
You're my mom, and without you, I am nothing.
Whatever choice you make, I will follow.

It was what Giuseppina desperately needed to hear. It was all she needed, too.[4]

XVII

Mafia prosecutors are realists, not optimists.[1] Still, there was no doubt that the spring and summer of 2011 were a heady few months for Calabria's Anti-Mafia Directorate. Giuseppina Pesce's testimony had dealt the 'Ndrangheta a devastating blow, and though the clan had fought back, Alessandra's intervention had saved both Giuseppina's life and the case. Hundreds of 'Ndranghetisti were in jail. Hundreds of millions of euros in assets had been confiscated. Giuseppina's example had then inspired a second 'Ndrangheta mother, Maria Concetta Cacciola. The panicked reaction in Rosarno seemed to indicate that the clans feared being undone by an avalanche of feminine assertion.

Moreover, any west coast 'Ndranghetista tempted to dismiss Giuseppina and Concetta as anomalies only had to look over the mountains to the east to see how women were humbling the 'Ndrangheta there as well. After Carmine's arrest, Denise Cosco had left Pagliarelle, moved to a safe house in Turin run by Libera, reunited with Libera lawyer Enza Rando, and formally reentered state witness protection. Initially, said Enza, Denise was "destroyed" by the knowledge that she had fallen in love with one of her mother's killers. But in protection, Denise slowly began to remake herself. She held on to the memory of what Carmine and she once shared. "Fake love can still be true love," she insisted. But a memory was all it would ever be. "It doesn't matter now," she said. "The arrest brought things to an end."

Denise found new purpose helping prosecutors prepare the case against the Pagliarelle clan. "I have no pity," she said of Lea's accused killers in a statement released by Enza on the eve of Carlo Cosco's trial. "I don't care who is my father or who is my boyfriend. I don't even know what I feel more: hatred or anger. These people should get life. Or maybe just killed in the street. Until I hear in court that these people will pay for what they did, I have no life."[2] Denise elaborated on her state of mind in an interview with Libera's information service. "I want to live like any other normal twenty-year-old in the town where I was born, with my friends. I am a young woman and I want to be free to study and get a degree in Oriental languages. I don't want to hide. Only the men and women of the 'Ndrangheta should have to hide away, not justice witnesses. We did our duty. I want to live. I want to love. I want to be free to be happy, for my mother's sake if nothing else."[3]

Denise's defiance, continuing her mother's fight even after Lea had been murdered by her father, and giving hours of sworn testimony against the man she loved, attracted the attention of the national press. The city of Milan decided to join Denise in a parallel civil action against her father's *'ndrina*, symbolically uniting Italy's most progressive city with Italy's women against Italy's mafia. When Carlo, his brothers Giuseppe and Vito, and Massimo Sabatino, Rosario Curcio, and Carmine Venturino went on trial in Milan on July 6, 2011, the hearing was attended by hundreds of students. They filled the public gallery and held vigils for Lea in the street outside. In opening remarks that resonated with almost every woman in Italy, Enza described Denise as a "proud witness," once forced by the men of her family to live in silence, now reclaiming her "freedom to choose her own life." The case against her father and the other men of the 'Ndrangheta, said Enza, was the "start of new hope, and a new life."

These were giddy times to be an Italian prosecutor, and even an Italian woman. Looking back years later, Alessandra could even remember thinking that they might last.

AFTER HER TRANSFER to Bolzano on July 22, 2011, Concetta found herself in another strange town, free but alone. It was seven weeks since she had seen or spoken to her three children. Overwhelmed, suddenly, by an almost physical maternal need, Concetta e-mailed her twelve-year-old daughter, Tania. "And of course, the girl tells her grandmother," said Giuseppe Creazzo, the anti-mafia prosecutor who would later investigate the case. "And the family uses the girl to reestablish contact with Concetta and try to persuade her to come home."

The carabinieri missed the first call between Concetta and her mother, Anna Rosalba Lazzaro. By the time of the second, on August 2, Concetta was in Genoa, and the Cacciolas' plans were well advanced. Concetta had followed Giuseppina's example when she walked into a carabinieri station. The Cacciolas duly decided to copy the Pesces' methods to blackmail her into returning to them.

In that call of August 2, her mother told Concetta that she and her father, Michele Cacciola, would be arriving in Genoa that evening to pick her up. As a witness, rather than a *pentita*, Concetta was not bound by any restrictions on her movements. Within hours, the carabinieri were listening to a conversation inside the family car as the Cacciolas headed south for Calabria with Concetta in the back seat. Like the Pesces, Concetta's parents pursued two avenues of persuasion: promising their daughter everything would return to normal if she came home, and insinuating harm to her children if she did not. Unfortunately, Concetta did not have Giuseppina's steel. Confronted by parental authority, she was soon telling her mother and father everything that she had told the prosecutors.

"You told them about murders?!" exclaimed Lazzaro at one point. "Oh, the disgrace!"

"The sacrifices I've had to make for you, 'Cetta!" shouted Michele. "How you have dishonored me!"

Then Michele seemed to remember the plan. "Don't worry. I forgive you," he said, trying to sound calm. "You can't wrong family. You're blood. You're safe. You'll see. You'll say you know nothing. You'll say everything you said is not true. And in ten days, you'll be safe and quiet in Rosarno and no one will talk about you anymore."

After a lifetime of abuse from her father, Michele's uncharacteristic attempt at paternal understanding spooked Concetta. Then Michele revealed he had somehow obtained her phone records. He said he knew about her calls to her boyfriend, Pasquale Improta. That was even more worrying, thought Concetta. How could he possibly forgive that?

When the Cacciolas broke the journey for the night at Lazzaro's family home in Reggio Emilia, Concetta announced she would go no further and called the carabinieri. The following morning a pair of officers arrived to pick her up and drive her back to Genoa. Michele Cacciola and Rosalba Lazzaro continued on to Calabria. But now that they had found a way to reach their daughter, they weren't about to give up. En route they kept up the pressure in a series of phone calls.

"'Cetta, listen to me!" said her mother. "You must tell the truth. You must say you knew nothing about what was going on. You have to drop everything."

Between calls, the carabinieri could hear Concetta's mother and father discuss a plan to deliver their daughter to an 'Ndrangheta lawyer who would hand her a prepared statement to sign, as the Pesces had done with Giuseppina. It was her mother who, in another call to Concetta, hit on her daughter's weak spot. "Tomorrow morning, you call the lawyer," she said. "This is how you get what you want. This is how you get me to send you your children."

Concetta went quiet, and the line went dead. The carabinieri were stunned. Whatever her differences with the 'Ndrangheta, Concetta had always respected family. She was a dutiful daughter and a good mother, and it was her faith in the maternal bond that had persuaded her that she could safely entrust her children to her mother. She had paid dearly for her trust over the years. Now her mother was using it against her, in all likelihood to try to send her to her death. What kind of person would do such a thing? What kind of mother?

Concetta called her mother back a few minutes later. She sounded broken.

"Wait, Mom, just let me talk, and then you talk," she said. After her mother assented, Concetta continued.

"I get it," she said. "I get it already. Already I can't do anything else. I just couldn't talk right then because I was near those people who want to arrest you. Understand?"

Concetta's mother moved quickly to reinforce her position. "I don't care about them," she replied. "*O cu nui, o cu iddi.*" (You're with us, or you're with them.)

"Yes, I know," answered Concetta.

"You have to do this, 'Cetta! Tonight, I spoke with the lawyer. You understand? Tomorrow you go to the same lawyer. We've already paid him."

"I know, I know."

"Tomorrow! The same lawyer. Vittorio Pisani."

"OK."

"Swear to me, 'Cetta! You'll do this tomorrow!"

"Yes, I'll call him. I'll call him tomorrow."

"If you don't call him tomorrow, you can forget about me, 'Cetta. I'm destroyed here."

"Stop it, Mother. Enough. Leave me alone."

"Swear to me! Tomorrow morning! You don't understand, 'Cetta. The ones you are with. You're making the men crazy! You call the lawyer tomorrow morning!"

"All right, Mom. All right. Please stop."

"If you do everything the lawyer says, then the children will be with you again. You don't want to come home? Fine. You go to your aunt Angela's or your aunt Santina's or wherever you want. But you make the choice. Us, or them. And you shut up!"

Three days later, on August 6, Concetta called her friend Emanuela Gentile. To the surveillance team, the change in Concetta's tone was dramatic. A few days earlier, she had sounded free and confident. Now she was in pieces. "You know, Emanuela, the one mistake I made was to call home that one time," she said. "If I hadn't called, I would have continued on the same path. But I called, and I weakened."

Concetta told Emanuela about her talk with her mother and father. "They know everything I've been doing," she said. "They even have printouts of my phone calls."

Emanuela said she'd heard that Concetta's father and brother had visited Pasquale Improta at his home in Reggio. "Your brother's sick in the head," she said. "He's relentless."

"My father told me he wouldn't let Giuseppe lay a finger on me," replied Concetta. "He even started to cry. He told me: 'I forgive you.' But I'm afraid, Emanuela, I tell you. I'm scared. Even if they're telling me, 'Come back, daughter, come back,' you know how these families are, especially my family, especially the men. They don't forgive. They don't forgive injuries to their honor. My father has two hearts. One for his daughter and one for his honor."

Something was sure to happen to her if she went home, Concetta said. It had to, though probably not immediately, she thought. "They'll wait," she said. "If they already have you there, in their place, they don't need to hurry. But does it make sense for me to go home and live just a year, maybe a year and a half?" She couldn't make up her mind. "In one way, I'm thinking I should just do it, you know? Go home. Take the risk. Because I *have* to go back, Emanuela. I have to. They won't send my children to me."

"*Mamma mia!*" exclaimed Emanuela. "They're keeping your children from you?"

"I asked for them but they haven't sent them. And they won't. Because they know that if they send my children to me, their daughter is lost to them forever."

In another call, to Pasquale Improta, Concetta tried to prepare her boyfriend for what lay ahead. "If I go home, I'm finished," she said. "I understand that. I know how it will end. They don't forgive offenses to honor or dignity—and I injured both."

"Concetta," Pasquale replied, "can I tell you something? You're too good. Too good."

"Too stupid," joked Concetta.

"Too good. They broke your ribs. Other women wouldn't even call them."

"It scares me to go home, I tell you."

"If it scares you, Concetta, then don't go. If you go, you'll pay."

"Well, that's for sure."

Maybe because he wasn't 'Ndrangheta himself, or maybe because he wasn't a father, Pasquale didn't seem to get it. He imagined Concetta still had choices. Concetta couldn't make him understand. Before she hung up, however, she made sure to take time over her good-byes. "Pa," she said, "until my last breath, I will love you. Good night, my love. Good night. I love you."

ON AUGUST 8, Concetta wrote a note to her protection officers, saying that she had spoken to her mother, who was on her way to Genoa with her uncle Gregorio and her eldest daughter, Tania. Concetta explained that she couldn't bear not to see Tania.

In fact, Concetta had initially tried to resist. Her surveillance officers heard her on the phone trying to stall Lazzaro, saying she needed to check with the carabinieri before she agreed to meet. "Who do you need to call, 'Cetta?" her mother shouted back. "Why do you need to ask anyone? Do you hear your daughter?"

On the line came the sound of a small child crying and screaming. Lazzaro was holding the phone toward Concetta's youngest daughter, Rosalba, seven, named after her grandmother. The girl was in tears. "She's dying without you, 'Cetta!" she said.

"Tell her not to worry," said Concetta softly.

"Tell her to be quiet?" replied Lazzaro. "'Cetta, she's dying here."

"OK, OK. Tell her I'm close by. Tell her I'm coming."

"You meet us on the other side of town!" Lazzaro ordered, and hung up.

The following morning, when Concetta's protection officers went to her hotel room, they found the door open with the keys in the lock. Inside, her suitcase was gone.

THE SURVEILLANCE TEAM wouldn't hear Concetta's voice again for more than a week. That wasn't because she hadn't been talking, however. Three days after arriving back in Rosarno, Concetta secretly recorded a statement at the Cacciola family lawyer's office in town. The recording, including one brief interruption, lasted eleven minutes and seven seconds:

> My name is Maria Concetta Cacciola, today is August twelfth, 2011, and I want to clarify what happened to me this May.
>
> During a visit to the carabinieri barracks, I told them I had some problems with my family. My family had received some anonymous letters. At the time, I was in a bad way. I

was jealous. My husband was in prison. Then these letters came and I held up my hands to what they said, and my family shut me in my home, telling me I couldn't go out or have friends. I was angry at my family. I wanted to make them pay. So I told the carabinieri: "Maybe I can help you. I have problems with my parents and my family. I'm afraid that my father and my brother are going to do something to me."

Initially, they did not take me away. But a few days later, they told me that I should talk to their superiors and the carabinieri commander came to see me. And that's how it happened. I said whatever I needed to say in order to get away from home. I was confused. But my reasoning was to make them pay. I was so angry.

Two days later, they told me they had agreed to take me into custody and they met me again at the barracks. There was a car ready, and two magistrates were there to talk to me. At first, I was confused. But then, because I wanted to leave, I said things that weren't true and which hadn't happened. Because I just wanted to go away and make them pay for my suffering. Finally, one magistrate said to me: "It's Friday. Get ready to leave here on Monday."

In fact, they came to get me on Saturday. They took me to Cosenza. Three days later, the two magistrates came back and began pressuring me about my family. And I, because I was still furious with them, I again accused my father and my brother.

I was a month and a half in Cosenza. From there they took me to Bolzano. But by the time I got to Bolzano, I wanted to retract because I realized that out of anger I had said things that weren't true. It was all just things that I had read in newspapers or heard people talking about, and just because I was so enraged I accused my father and brother of being involved even when they were not. I realized I was in the wrong. I realized that because I was so angry, I was accusing people who had nothing to do with anything. It wasn't right. I wanted a lawyer. But they told me I couldn't have one because witnesses weren't allowed lawyers under the law. I told them I wanted to return to my family. But they told me: "Don't go back to your family. We are your family now. Your family won't forgive you if you go back now. If you thought they wanted to kill you before, imagine what they'll do now they think you have a relationship with us." And I was afraid, knowing what I had done and how gross an injury I had inflicted.

In Bolzano, I talked to my daughter by e-mail. After that, I spoke to my mother. I wanted to know what my mother thought of what I had done. In Bolzano, I also met people who might have recognized me. At that point, I was moved immediately to Genoa. They told me: "You can't have any contact with people you know."

From Genoa, I called my mother again and told her I missed her and wanted to see her. I spoke to my mother and my father, too. And now I really knew what I had done! My mother came to Genoa but the state told me I couldn't have any contact with my family. When I got into the car with my dad, however, I realized he had already forgiven me for the mistakes I had made. We reached Reggio Emilia. I was scared of going back to Calabria, though not of my father, and of my own free will I left again with the carabinieri for Genoa. They asked me: "Are you sure you haven't told your family that you're staying in Genoa?" I said I hadn't, even though I had told my mother.

I had also told my mother that I wanted to talk to a lawyer. From Genoa I called a lawyer, Vittorio Pisani, telling him

I was confused because the state had told me that if I hadn't been represented already in the process then I couldn't start now. Anyway, the state told me to stop calling the lawyer, and added that I was stubborn, that I shouldn't call my family, that I should turn off my phone and everything else. I didn't agree. And I called my mother again, asked her to come back up to Genoa, and she came with her brother and my daughter and I left Genoa of my own free will. Now I have decided to appoint the lawyers Gregorio Cacciola and Vittorio Pisani to represent me . . .

At that point the recording cut, then resumed:

I've now been back at home for three days with my father, my mother, my brother, and my children. Finally, I have found the peace . . .

"—that I have been looking for," prompted a female voice in the background.

. . . that I have been looking for. I should add that I have written a letter to go with this recording. In the future, I hope to be left alone, out of contact with anyone and with no one contacting me.[4]

On August 13 and 14, Concetta's surveillance officers picked up two text messages she sent to Pasquale Improta using a phone she had managed to hide from her family. In them, she told a different story. She said she was a prisoner of her family in the yellow house on Via Don Gregorio Varrà once more. This time, however, "they brought lawyers to make me retract," she wrote. "They made me say that I was using drugs, that I was angry. My brother won't speak to me. Their coldness is terrifying. I don't want to stay here, Pa. I don't see how any good will come of this."

Concetta asked Pasquale to pass a message to Chief Marshal Salvatore Esposito at the carabinieri headquarters in Reggio Calabria. She wanted to return to witness protection, she said. This time, she had to take her children with her. "I feel caged here," she wrote. "What can I do?"

Pasquale passed on the message. On August 17, Concetta spoke to the carabinieri several times to confirm she wanted to reenter witness protection. Just before 11 P.M. she called Marshal Esposito in Reggio. After confirming for himself that Concetta wanted to return to the program, Esposito asked how best to extract her and her three children. "Can you leave the house?" he asked. "Even later tonight?"

Concetta said no. She asked if Esposito could send officers to arrest her to make it look as though she were being taken against her will. "It's so difficult here, with my father and my brother," she said. Even outside the family, she explained, "there are also those around them, people know what happened. Word that I've been speaking to the carabinieri is spreading."

"Are you afraid of moving or of the repercussions?" asked Esposito.

"Both!" replied Concetta.

Eventually, Esposito and Concetta agreed that she would call when the time felt right—that night or the following morning—and that Esposito would dispatch a car immediately. It would be with her fifteen minutes after her call, Esposito said. "Call any time," he added. "We'll be waiting."

In Reggio's Palace of Justice, Alessandra was also waiting. It was August, the daytime temperature was breaching 100°F, and the entire country was on holiday. Pignatone, Prestipino, and Giovanni Musarò were all away. Only Alessandra remained. "The situation appeared to be calm with Cacciola," said Giovanni later. "There was a wiretap of her talking to a friend in which she said that she knew she would be killed—but not soon. She was talking about a year, a year and a half, because it would be stupid to kill her immediately. And anyway, Concetta was going to be back in protection soon. So we felt safe."

The next day, August 18, in a conversation recorded by a bug inside the Cacciola car, Concetta told her mother she had spoken to Chief Marshal Esposito. She added she intended to return to witness protection.

"'Cetta, no!" screamed Lazzaro. "No! Absolutely not!"

"You told me everything would be different!" shouted Concetta.

"I was resigned to you leaving us," replied Lazzaro. "But now I'm not. No! I won't accept this!"

"Mom, I have to finish what I started," said Concetta.

Half an hour later, Concetta phoned the carabinieri once more and told them she was in a dilemma. It was impossible to leave the house without being accompanied by her mother. On the other hand, if she left with her and her mother returned home without her, then her mother would face dire consequences. Eventually Concetta agreed with the carabinieri that the solution was to wait for everyone in the Cacciola house to fall asleep that night, then usher her children out into the street and into a waiting carabinieri car. They would do it around 1:30 A.M. Four hours later, Concetta called back to say her youngest, Rosalba, had a fever and everything had to be put off for a day or so.

Reading the transcripts, Alessandra was exasperated. "We were all waiting for her call to come and pick her up. She had called and said: 'I want to come back.' The barracks were all ready for her and her children. I'd even asked the carabinieri to come back from their holidays. So we were just waiting. And then this back-and-forth. Honestly, at that point, we thought that she was playing with us.

We discovered that the part about her daughter being sick was a lie. Her children were at the beach. Concetta just did not have a clear mind. She was changing it constantly. Some days she reached out to us. Some days she didn't. There was such indecision. We really wanted her to make up her mind and make a final decision, a choice. But we thought that at least she had the situation under control. And I think perhaps she herself thought she had more time."

THE NEXT DAY, August 19, Alessandra and the carabinieri waited by the phone in case Concetta changed her mind once again. No call came.

On August 20, Alessandra and the carabinieri gathered again to resume their vigil. "The whole team was there on alert, waiting for her to give the word and we'd go in and get her. But we couldn't do anything until she gave us the go-ahead. By law, since she was a witness, we weren't allowed to charge in and break down the door. She had to open the door for us. And she just couldn't open that door."[5]

At 6:40 P.M. on August 20, 2011, Concetta's father, Michele, arrived at Santa Maria Hospital in the town of Polistena, twenty minutes from Rosarno. Concetta was immobile in the back seat of the family Mercedes. She had burns around her mouth and foam spilling from her lips.

In emergency admissions, Dr. Fortunato Lucia confirmed that Concetta had no pulse. As staff at the hospital called the police, Dr. Lucia attempted to resuscitate her using CPR. The paramedics handed the doctor a red, one-liter plastic bottle of hydrochloric acid, which they said Concetta's family had found next to her in the family basement. Dr. Lucia tried to put Concetta on an intravenous drip, but without a pulse it wouldn't take. By the time a police patrol arrived at 7 P.M., Dr. Lucia had pronounced Concetta dead.

ACT THREE

Italy Awakes

XVIII

MARIA CONCETTA CACCIOLA's death certificate identified her as having been born three decades earlier, a few miles south of the hospital in which she died.[1] It listed her as living ten miles to the west in Rosarno. Born in Calabria. Lived in Calabria. Died in Calabria. As her family had promised her, it was as though the past four months had never happened.

Word of Concetta's death reached Alessandra and the carabinieri in a call in the early evening from the local police. The officer said the indications were that Concetta had drunk a liter of hydrochloric acid in the basement of the Cacciola family home. For the second time that year, Alessandra found herself momentarily overwhelmed. "It was terrible for everyone," she said. "No one had imagined it would end so finally, so completely. We were all ready to pick her up. It was very hard to come to terms with."[2]

Giovanni took Alessandra's call on holiday. He was speechless. Years later, he would say, "You can't let the work become personal. But the story of Maria Concetta Cacciola was terrible, really hard to bear. She hadn't even been arrested and had no convictions. She was just a witness."[3] It was the tragedy of Concetta's death, the way it seemed almost mythically predestined, that most disturbed Giovanni. "Maria Concetta Cacciola was a character from a Greek play," he said. "She went back even though she was aware she would be murdered. She went back out of love for her children. This almost symbiotic relationship that she had with her mother, the love letter she wrote to her—there is something beautiful about it. Beautiful, and unacceptable."

Giovanni and Alessandra knew only too well the effect Concetta's story would have on the small towns and hill villages of Calabria. "It was what had to happen," said Concetta's father, Michele, in an aside recorded by the carabinieri two days later— and the prosecutors knew every Calabrian would be thinking the same. Lea Garofalo was dead. Giuseppina Pesce had been forced to retract in public. Now Maria Concetta Cacciola was gone, too. This was what happened to women who betrayed the 'Ndrangheta. There was no escaping fate. The 'Ndrangheta *was* invincible. "If this phenomenon of women testifying had gathered momentum with Giuseppina, it was going to come to a sudden stop with Maria Concetta Cacciola's death," said Alessandra. "By contrast with Giuseppina, Concetta was a symbol that the 'Ndrangheta *could* get to you."

The evening Concetta died, the carabinieri sealed off the basement at 26 Via Don Gregorio Varrà in Rosarno where she was found. They seized mobile phones, a computer, Concetta's diary, and several letters addressed to her husband, Salvatore. When they questioned Michele, he told them he had returned home after 5:30 P.M. and had called for Concetta but couldn't find her. He eventually discovered her lying on the floor of a bathroom in the basement. Next to her body was an empty plastic bottle. Asked why his daughter might have killed herself, Michele exploded and refused to answer. Concetta's mother, Anna Rosalba Lazzaro, was more forthcoming. Concetta, she said, had taken her own life out of shame. "She felt bad. She said things that she had no knowledge of. She couldn't face those she had accused." Concetta's family had "fully supported her" after she returned home, added Lazzaro. They knew she had been unwell. After all, she had a history of it. She had pined for her absent husband for many years. She had also taken diet drugs obsessively. These things had affected her mind.

Giovanni dismissed Lazzaro's interview out of hand. "It was clear that something had happened that we didn't know about," he said. The prosecutors knew Concetta was at long-term risk from her family. Like Concetta, they had calculated the family wouldn't harm her so quickly after her return, since suspicion would immediately fall on them. On the other hand, they also knew Concetta had told her mother that she would shortly be returning to the protection program. Maybe the family decided they had to kill her while they could.

Because there was no doubt that Concetta had been murdered. Every gastroenterologist said drinking a liter of hydrochloric acid was impossible to do voluntarily. The human reflex was to choke and vomit after just a sip. The pain was unbearable. The acid would eat through the stomach wall. Unconsciousness would be swift. The coroner would later report that Concetta had died of a heart attack and respiratory failure but only after the acid had burned her throat, stomach, pancreas, and lungs. "It's simply not something you can do by yourself," said Giovanni.

The method of Concetta's death also had the 'Ndrangheta written all over it. Acid was a favorite 'Ndrangheta tool for traitors. They used it on the dead, to erase every shameful trace of a collaborator's body, and they used it on the living. In December 2010, Reggio council's budget manager, Orsola Fallara, had given a press conference in a downtown restaurant at which she admitted making suspicious payments and keeping irregular accounts—and, hours later, was found dying in her car after drinking acid.[4] In March 2011, another 'Ndrangheta wife, thirty-eight-year-old Tita Buccafusca, had run into a police station near Rosarno clutching her young son and offering to testify—and a month later her husband, an 'Ndrangheta boss called Pantaleone Mancuso, reported that she had committed suicide by drinking acid.[5] Mouths that spoke out of turn were rubbed out. Concetta's death was part of a pattern.

For the prosecutors, there was one anomaly in the case, however. Concetta had told them that her family never left her alone, especially since her return to Rosarno. But on the day she died, her father, mother, and brother had all been out of the house. "That seemed quite strange," said Giovanni. It suggested not just careful planning but also the involvement of a third party.

ON AUGUST 23, three days after Concetta died, the Cacciola family delivered a formal written complaint to the prosecutor's office in Palmi. Following the script established by the Pesces, Concetta's parents accused Alessandra and Giovanni of taking advantage of a woman in a frail mental state. Concetta had walked into the carabinieri station in May 2010 "depressed" and in "pathological distress," they said. The carabinieri had seen her weakness as an opportunity. They had promised her a new life, "which turned out to be a living hell, taking her away from her family."

By this view, Concetta, like her friend Giuseppina before her, was a pathetic creature. The complaint claimed that none of what she had done was by conscious choice. She had not elected to create a new life for herself and her children. She had not rejected her family and the 'Ndrangheta. She had not, above all, asserted her free will and reclaimed her independence from her parents and her husband. Rather, according to the Cacciolas, she had been pitiably weak and easily led. This daughter, this woman, had been dazzled by the state's perfidious offers of a better life. In return, her feeble mind had conjured up the kinds of stories about her family's criminality that she imagined the prosecutors wanted to hear. Concetta had soon come to her senses, realized her mistake, made contact with her family again, and eventually succeeded in escaping the authorities' clutches. Once back in the bosom of her "loving and attentive" family, she had confessed to everything, especially the "invented allegations" she had made against her kin to "ingratiate herself with the prosecutors." Happily, she had finally found the peace of mind that she had sought in her family's loving forgiveness and acceptance. Understandably, however, the shame had proved too much. The whole sorry saga could be heard in Concetta's own words by listening to the attached tape cassette or reading the attached transcript. The Cacciolas expected a reply forthwith from the prosecutors and the carabinieri, explaining their disgraceful conduct.

Even then, the Cacciolas weren't done. The same day they filed their complaint, Anna Rosalba Lazzaro wrote a letter to the *Gazzetta del Sud*, the main southern Italian newspaper, complaining that in their report on Concetta's death, the *Gazzetta* journalists had described her as having grown up in "an environment pregnant with the negative values of the 'Ndrangheta." "That's simply not true," wrote Lazzaro. "On this particular issue, I challenge anyone to show that my house has ever held discussions about criminal matters that have affected or involved the members of my family. I want to add that my husband and I dedicated our lives to giving our children the best civic education possible."[6] The next day, *Calabria Ora* splashed on an exclusive interview with Lazzaro, which it headlined: "You Drove My Daughter to Suicide!"[7] On its inside pages, *Calabria Ora* hammered home the message that Concetta's death was inevitable. "Chronicle of a Suicide Foretold" was the paper's banner headline.

It was unbelievable, thought Alessandra. The Cacciolas had blackmailed their daughter into returning to them, then stood by as she was executed. Now they were painting her killing as a tragedy for which the state was to blame, while using her death to mend their criminal reputation. At no point had they expressed sorrow or love or any feeling other than outrage at the wrongs done to them. They hadn't even buried Concetta. Had there ever been a family so unspeakable as the Cacciolas of Rosarno?

XIX

THE 'NDRANGHETA HAD reasserted itself in spectacular fashion.[1] Once more their challengers were dead or in disgrace. Just as Alessandra and Giovanni had been required to answer questions about the Giuseppina Pesce case, now they had to account for their handling of Maria Concetta Cacciola. The editor of *Calabria Ora*, Piero Sansonetti, celebrated the state's humiliation in a series of editorials. "The season of cooperation is over," he wrote.

In Milan, the six defendants on trial for the murder of Lea Garofalo seemed emboldened by events to the south. Their lawyers argued that the case against their clients should be dismissed outright. No body, no murder. Lea, they said, was actually living by the beach in Australia. "I hope she gets tired of Australia and does us the honor of appearing in this court," said one.[2] Their clients were innocent not just of killing Lea, they claimed, but of any criminality. Carlo's brother Giuseppe said he was a shoemaker. Vito said he was a builder. Rosario Curcio said he ran a solarium. Carmine Venturino asked to be excused from answering questions in court because he only spoke Grecanico, not Italian. Carlo had somehow managed to convince the legal aid authorities that his income was a mere €10,000 a year, thereby qualifying him for state assistance. He said he was mystified by the entire process. "It's not fair that I'm sitting here," he said. "I'm an honest person. My mother taught me to respect and love the family. My daughter wrote me letters in prison saying she loved me and missed me and wanted to be with me again. I had nothing to do with Lea's disappearance. I, too, want to know the truth about what happened."[3]

The defense paraded a succession of villagers from Pagliarelle through court to testify to Carlo's decency. Most claimed to have barely known Lea. When one prosecution witness, a friend of Carlo's and resident at Viale Montello, repeatedly failed to show up at court, the defendants laughed and whooped. "Maybe he's in the attic," came one shouted suggestion. A lawyer for Giuseppe further muddied the waters by declaring that his client had not spoken to his brother Vito in years, making a nonsense of any conspiracy between them.

There were, however, signs of tension between the defendants. From the start, Massimo Sabatino sat apart from the other men in the caged dock. "Shame on you!" Venturino hissed at him one day as they were being led away for the night. "Shame on me?!" Sabatino yelled back. "It's your fault I'm doing six years! If I get my hands on you, I'll rip your head off, you piece of shit!"

The defendants also seemed to lose some of their initial confidence as the weeks progressed and prosecutor Marcello Tatangelo painstakingly took apart their denials. Traces from their phones showed all of them had been busy moving around Milan and its outskirts and in each other's company for the three hours after 6:30 P.M. when Lea Garofalo was last seen alive. The carabinieri had unearthed a friend of Carlo's who said he had lent Carlo the keys to his grandmother's apartment. It was here, said Tatangelo, that Lea had been taken to be tortured, then shot with a bullet to the neck, before her body was disposed of outside the city. When Salvatore Cortese, Carlo's old cellmate, testified about Carlo's burning desire for revenge on Lea, Carlo couldn't contain himself. "What are you saying?!" he shouted. "What's this about getting permission from the bosses to kill Lea? He's making it up! I had nothing to do with anything!" When Sabatino's confession to his

cellmate, Salvatore Sorrentino, was read out, it was Sabatino's turn
to shout. "I never said those things about Carlo!" he said. "It's not
true that I said they were bastards and I wanted to kill them!
You're making it up! I agree with everything these men say."

Finally, Denise was called on to testify. A screen was erected in
court so her father could not see her. Denise wore a hooded top to
further conceal her face. Sensing his daughter a few yards away, Carlo
stood, walked to the front of his cage, and placed his arms through
the bars. In a clear voice and without hesitation, and in testimony that
lasted two full days—September 20 and October 13, 2011—Denise
told the story of her mother's early life and their years on the run
and in the protection program. "We were like sisters," she said. "It
was almost like we grew up together. We swapped clothes. We liked
the same music." For seven years, she added, she had no contact with
Carlo.

"That's a fact," said Carlo audibly.

Denise frowned. "Can you request that person to keep quiet?"
she coolly asked the judge. "It's disturbing."

Denise went on to recount her mother's attempts to make peace
with Carlo. She described the attack in Campobasso in May 2009,
prompting Sabatino to stand and pace up and down inside the cage.
Only once did Denise break down. When one lawyer rebuked her
for accusing the defendants of murder when there was no body and
no murder weapon, she cried: "She can't be allowed to say that! It's
been two years since I saw my mother!"

In the face of such raw emotion, the defense lawyers tried to con-
jure up some sympathy for the defendants. "I know in my heart that
my client is innocent," said Maira Cacucci, Carlo's lawyer. "Just one
look in his eyes and you'll understand." Francesco Garofalo, a Calabrian lawyer representing Carmine Venturino and Vito Cosco, fell
back on a familiar defense: the unstable nature of women. "Why
all these attempts to sanctify Lea, who was born and raised by

the 'Ndrangheta?" he asked. "She was a crazy woman, as her own daughter has described. Lea Garofalo wanted to go to Australia. What better time than after leaving her daughter with her father? That is what happened here!"

Nevertheless, the defense's histrionics did little to deflect what was starting to feel increasingly certain: that all six men would eventually be found guilty of murder. But as the trial wound toward its conclusion, on November 23, the eve of the second anniversary of Lea's disappearance, disaster struck. Out of the blue, the presiding judge, Filippo Grisolia, was appointed chief of staff at the Ministry of Justice. The trial would have to be abandoned, then restarted. What was more, the statutory limit on detention in custody meant any new trial would have to finish by July 28, 2012, eight months away. The trial had already taken five months. It wouldn't be hard for the defense to spin out a new trial past the deadline. At that point, Carlo and his entire *'ndrina* would walk free.

XX

T HE 'NDRANGHETA HAD always relied on fictions.[1] One of the
biggest was that it could not be challenged, and never by a
woman. Lea Garofalo, Giuseppina Pesce, Maria Concetta Cacciola,
and now Denise Cosco had all exposed that lie. The 'Ndrangheta's
response was uncompromising. The women had to die. And their
stories had to be rewritten.

Alessandra and Giovanni were now confronting the possibility that after their early triumphs, the clans were succeeding, at
least in public perception. The Lea Garofalo investigation might
have revived several old cases and injected new life into the fight
against the east coast 'Ndrangheta, but there was no resuscitating
Lea. Likewise, despite Giuseppina's decision to start cooperating
again, the last public memory of her was that she had recanted.
As for Concetta, she had died and then, in a mafia masterstroke,
had retracted from beyond the grave. Now, with the very public
collapse of the trial against Carlo Cosco and his men, it seemed the
clans had gotten lucky with Denise, too. "The truth is that there is
no more important or fundamental investigative tool than the *pentiti*," said Giovanni Musarò. The prosecutors had had four women
pentiti. None had emerged unscathed. The 'Ndrangheta had used
Concetta's death, in particular, as a warning. "When the Cacciolas
wrote their denunciation of the prosecutors, they weren't thinking
of their daughter," said Giovanni. "They were ensuring that this
never happened again. It went beyond Cacciola. It was a message

to all Calabria. So, yes, at that time, you can say things were not in our favor."

On reflection, however, it was possible to view the 'Ndrangheta's vehement crushing of any opposition as a sign of weakness. Its absolutist intolerance of freedom seemed to stem from an appreciation of how, once released, it was almost impossible to contain again. And, despite the clans' efforts, Giuseppina and Denise were still breathing. Both also seemed strengthened by the resolve they had discovered in the gale of the 'Ndrangheta's oppression. In Milan, Denise had already faced her father once in court and was telling prosecutors she could do it again. As for Giuseppina, the death of her friend appeared to have had the exact opposite effect from that intended. Giuseppina told Alessandra she had no doubt that the 'Ndrangheta had forced Concetta to drink acid. Her friend's killing made her realize how close she had come to the same fate herself: she had been mere hours from her own return to Calabria when Alessandra arrested her. "You saved my life," she told Alessandra. "If you hadn't stopped me, my children would now be taking flowers to the cemetery, like 'Cetta's."

The realization seemed to release Giuseppina from any last doubts. On August 23, three days after Concetta's death, a letter from Giuseppina arrived at the Palace of Justice in Reggio Calabria, addressed to Alessandra, Pignatone, and Roberto di Bella, head of Reggio's juvenile court. "I know you already know my story," Giuseppina wrote, "but here I wish to start from the beginning."

After six months of imprisonment, on October 14, 2010, I expressed my desire to the prosecutor Dr. Cerreti to pursue this course of action, driven by my love as a mother and my desire to lead a better life, far away from the environment where I was born and lived. I never thought about doing that to obtain reductions to my sentence. It was also never my intention to tease anyone. I only did this because I was, and remain, convinced that this is the right

*choice, since because of our husbands' and relatives' life choices, we
have endured a life full of pain and, above all, cowardice and fear
of consequences. In reality, each of us should have the power . . . to
choose between right and wrong.*

*Maybe I should have done this earlier, before being dragged into
[this situation] . . . My hope is that we still have time and that I
can act so my children can have a better life—a life of principle
and freedom of choice. I also hope that many people like me who are
in situations like mine will find the courage to rebel. I have found
the strength to take this important decision and defy a fearsome,
powerful, and unforgiving family, in the full knowledge of the risk
to me and those I love. Finally, I am doing it.*

*There were times when I thought my choice had been hasty and
not properly thought through. I have been fragile. The courage that
I had back on October 14, 2010, deserted me. The bond between
my children and their family also bewildered me. I began to think
I had no right to deprive them of their father. I told myself neither
I nor they could escape that life. It all weighed heavily on me. And
after discussing with my partner, who disagreed, I decided I would
arrange for [my children] to go back to Calabria. I would have my
own battle in court, with a good lawyer to defend me. In my mind,
giving back their freedom to my children was the fairer solution.
But I was dying inside. It wasn't what I wanted. It was just what I
imagined was right for them.*

*And, of course, there were the newspapers. What was written,
day after day, made me look like a victim instead of someone
in command of their own decisions. The letter I had to send to
the judge . . . that made me feel even worse: all those lies, this
impression of me that was created that was not me. I had to swallow
that as well, not because anyone was forcing me to but because I felt
that, like in the movies, there was a story I had to maintain—and
that if I wasn't going to be a collaborator anymore but was one day*

going to be returning to Calabria, then maybe [those stories] would
be a shield protecting my children and myself from the prejudices of
my family and my people.

Driving back from Lucca with Domenico, I realized the
importance of my motivation to cooperate. My children's future.
My love of a man who loves me for who I am and not for my last
name. Today, while I may have lost credibility as a collaborator,
all these experiences have strengthened me as a woman. Even more
important, they have restored my confidence in myself. I feel now
that maybe I wasn't so selfish, after all. Perhaps if I had been more
courageous, today I would already be at the beach with Domenico
and my children. I gave them the freedom to choose. It is true that
I have always prioritized my love for my children, their health and
peace. And my children and Domenico chose me. They are the ones
who really love me. However many times I change my mind, they are
there for me, thank God.

That's why I believe my collaboration will make a real change,
for many people. I wish to tell you that I'm not crazy, like they
said. I tell you all these things so you can really see the person in
whom you placed your trust. I never told any lies. I just had a
moment of confusion. I patiently await your reply, aware of my
mistakes.[2]

As her staff and colleagues read the letter, Alessandra was
pleased to note that they lingered, silently reading every line. Man
or woman, they were moved. Though she'd never show it, Alessandra was, too. In a world of deception, here was clarity. Instead of
hate, here was love. Gone was fear. Here was strength.

AFTER GIUSEPPINA'S LETTER, events moved fast. In early September, she gave Alessandra a comprehensive account of how her former

lawyer, Giuseppe Madia, and the editor of *Calabria Ora*, Piero Sansonetti, had coordinated the drafting and release of her retraction letter. (Madia told Giuseppina he had had to approach Sansonetti because the editor of Calabria's small, local daily "was the only one willing to publish it and adopt our cause.")

On September 15, Giuseppina received another letter from her husband, Rocco. At first, he admonished her. "I know you've started making *coccòdeo*," he said, using the Italian for "cock-a-doodle-do." "I do wonder why you've ruined all our lives, including your own, just to be with the children?" Perhaps sensing Giuseppina's renewed determination, however, he soon switched to a plaintive tone. "Please, don't make me look bad," he wrote. "I don't think I'm asking for the moon. There is no morning that I don't wake up and think of you. Sadly, this is how things have turned out. My family is broken. But I leave you with an embrace, and the hope that God will enlighten you."[3] A year earlier, Rocco's meekness might have swayed Giuseppina. Now it merely confirmed that she had emerged from their marriage the steelier of the two, and it further hardened her purpose.

She was unmoved, too, five days later on September 20, when the first trial to result from Operation All Inside concluded in the sentencing of eleven members of the Pesce *'ndrina*. Giuseppina's uncle Vincenzo and her cousin Francesco Pesce, who had been found hiding in a bunker on August 9, received the heaviest sentences: twenty years each for mafia association and other crimes; and a total fine of €70 million, of which €50 million was to compensate the citizens of Rosarno for decades of murderous oppression and €10 million each was to go to the Ministry of Interior and Calabria's regional authority.[4]

The sentencing began a bewildering few days of public humiliation for the Pesces. The next day, September 21, the carabinieri took Angela, now sixteen, Gaetano, nine, and Elisea, five, from their grandparents' home and delivered them to the protective custody of the juvenile court.[5] On September 22, Alessandra formally announced in court that Giuseppina was once more cooperating with the authorities.[6] On September 23, at her own request, Giuseppina appeared in court in Palmi by video link to hear charges put to clan head Antonino; her husband, Rocco; her mother, Angela Ferraro; and her sister Marina.[7] On September 27, Giuseppa Bonarrigo, the family grandmother, chained herself to the gates of Rosarno town hall, where she was photographed by journalists protesting the innocence of her sons.

The public dishonoring of the Pesces was far from over. On October 4, Giuseppina's in-laws, Gaetano, Gianluca, and Giovanni Palaia, were arrested, quickly followed by aunt Angela Palaia and Angela Ietto. On October 13, Alessandra seized another eight Rosarno companies worth a further €18 million, bringing the total value of confiscations from the Pesce empire to €228 million.[8] A week later, on October 21, Alessandra announced that besides Giuseppina, she had a second 'Ndrangheta woman ready to testify: Rosa Ferraro, a cousin from Genoa taken in by the Pesces as a domestic helper after she was thrown out by her husband.[9] The following day, 110 'Ndranghetisti who had been arrested during the mass raids of July 2010 were sentenced to terms of between two and sixteen years.[10]

The climactic disgrace came on November 25, the day the Pesce clan maxi-trial formally opened. Sixty-three 'ndrina members were accused. More than fifty were present in court, including several Pesces, Palaias, and Ferraros, along with fifty defense lawyers. Those already serving sentences in jail, like clan head Antonino and Giuseppina's husband, Rocco, attended by video link. A handful of Pesces remained on the run. They would be tried in their absence.

Procedure demanded that Alessandra read out the charges to the accused and submit the evidence gathered from years of investigation, including Operations All Inside, All Inside II, All Clean, and

Crimine. The evidence ran to 65,000 words, the length of a book. Running through it all would take several weeks, and a full trial was not expected to start until May 2012.

That first day did not go as expected, however. The defendants already knew they were being tried by a woman prosecutor on a woman's evidence. The news that Giuseppina would be joined by a second woman from the Pesce household had come as a shock. As they were led in, the men were surprised to see that, in addition, an unusually large proportion of the court officials, carabinieri, and even lawyers and reporters on duty that day were also women. When the judges entered, one president and two assistants, the 'Ndranghetisti were astonished to see three more women: Maria Laura Ciollaro, Antonella Create, and, taking the president's seat, Concettina Epifanio.

To the 'Ndrangheta men, it must have felt like a conspiracy. "No! No!" they shouted. Pointing at Alessandra and taking the name of another male prosecutor in the case, they yelled: "We want di Palma! We want di Palma! Not that! Not *that!*"

State and court officials would later insist there was no plot to unsettle the Pesces. The selection of staff and judges was a matter of neutral procedure. In particular, the three women judges had presided over the case since its inception. Nor was there any question that Alessandra had to lead the prosecution in court since she had led the investigation that preceded it. That didn't mean that the officials couldn't enjoy the defendants' discomfort. "When they saw us all in the court, they began screaming and shouting at me and my colleagues," said a smiling Alessandra. "They were humiliated to be in front of so many women—to be judged by women, to them something less than a man." To Alessandra and Giuseppina, listening by video link, there was something in the men's outraged reaction that suggested they knew, perhaps for the first time, that the tables were being turned. Alessandra described their shouts of indignation

as something close to music. "A symphony of women's liberation!"
she laughed. "Divine justice for these men!" Prestipino, who also
denied any hand in the unusual number of women in court, was
similarly jubilant. "Think of how many women in Calabria live the
same lives as Giuseppina Pesce and Maria Concetta Cacciola," he
said. "Now they have something, an example, some symbolism, to
hold on to." Alessandra noted how across court Giuseppina's mother
and sister, Angela Ferraro and Marina Pesce, remained seated and
silent throughout. There was perhaps no better representation of
the injustice in their own lives than watching their men howl at
the sight of an assembly of modern, professional women sitting in
judgment over them.[11]

XXI

Giuseppina Pesce wasn't the only one spurred to action by the death of Maria Concetta Cacciola.[1]

In Reggio Calabria, the youth courts had long been the poor cousin of their adult equivalents. The juvenile justice chief, Roberto di Bella, felt that was shortsighted. Like Alessandra, di Bella reasoned that the 'Ndrangheta was, above all, a family operation. "Since World War II, the same families have controlled the territory," he said. "Whether it's smuggling heroin or cocaine or business or politics, this culture, this phenomenon, is born of family and goes from father to son. It's hereditary. It's dynastic." Somehow, the Italian judiciary had contrived to focus on the fathers but forget their wives—and their children. This was despite di Bella's own experience in Calabria. In two decades in Reggio, he had dealt with more than a hundred serious crimes committed by 'Ndrangheta children. "We had extortion, robbery, kidnapping, and more than fifty cases of homicide or assisted homicide!" he said. "Kids who used Kalashnikovs. Kids who took part in clan feuds. Kids who were assassins. Kids who killed carabinieri."

Di Bella's experience also taught him that sending 'Ndrangheta children to detention mostly confirmed them on a path to more crime and incarceration. Once inside, they were fated to become killers and bosses, and before long wind up back in jail or dead. "These children start to breathe this 'Ndrangheta culture from the moment they are born," he said. The brainwashing was constant, and effective. By the age of twelve, an 'Ndrangheta child would spit whenever they saw a policeman. As teenagers, they would learn to exercise power "not just over children but over adults, too." By eighteen, they were beyond rescue. Sometimes hatred for the state was literally ingrained in them. Di Bella had found some children with tattoos of individual carabinieri officers on their feet "so they can tread on them twenty-four hours a day."

Di Bella had a gentle manner, and his neatly parted dark hair and gold-framed glasses suggested a small-town doctor or provincial academic or even a priest. And his work, it was clear, was a calling. One case in particular had stayed with him. In 2002, a sixteen-year-old scion of a Calabrian clan had been detained for possessing a gun and resisting arrest. "The serial numbers had been filed off the gun and there was a bullet in it," said di Bella. He surmised that the boy was preparing for his first murder. He knew the family well. The boy's father had been murdered when he was eleven. Di Bella had already sent three of his older brothers to jail. They were, he said, "one of the most violent and bloody 'Ndrangheta clans."

Throughout his trial, the boy made a show of appearing tough, said di Bella. "His eyes were like steel. He did not betray his emotions." In the end, di Bella felt he had no option but to send him to join his brothers for several years in juvenile detention. Several months into the boy's sentence, however, di Bella received a phone call from the director of the youth prison. The boy was unwell. "He was suffering from sleeplessness," said di Bella. "He had stomach disorders that were stress related. He needed to speak to a male role model but he had none."

Di Bella had the boy brought back to court for reassessment. He found him a shadow of his former self. "He no longer had eyes like ice," he said. "He was bewildered. He had a lot of fear. He was distressed—strongly distressed—because of the murders and the mafia wars and the people he had lost, including his father." Di Bella realized the boy's defenses were down and he could talk to him directly. "So I told him clearly that he had to leave his 'Ndrangheta family. I said he would be murdered or be put in prison, like his father and brothers. And this boy said to me, for the first time: 'I want to leave.' He did not hide that his family was 'Ndrangheta. He asked me to help him leave them at the end of his sentence."

Di Bella promised that he would do what he could. A few months later, however, he was transferred away from Calabria. Several years after that, the court registrar in Reggio got in touch to tell him that the boy, now out of prison, had come looking for him at the court in Reggio. "He had been waiting for me for over a year until someone told him I was no longer there," said di Bella. The magistrate was consumed by guilt. There was no question that he and the state had failed this boy, a child after all, with the simple misfortune to be born into circumstances beyond his control but who, from the depths of his turmoil, had reached out for their help.

When di Bella returned to Calabria in 2011, he discovered the boy, now a man, was back in prison, convicted of mafia association. "He sent me a greeting from the psychological clinic where he was being treated," he said. "A few months later, I heard his elder brother had been arrested once again. This all sat with me."

On his return to Calabria, however, di Bella was heartened to discover that the fight against the 'Ndrangheta had been transformed. Pignatone, Prestipino, Alessandra, and the other prosecutors had brought new energy and new ideas to the struggle. They had forged a new consensus. In Alessandra's words, "The 'Ndrangheta is a very complicated phenomenon that defies a single solution. We need to take action on several different levels at the same time." Alessandra, particularly, had been instrumental in refocusing minds on the internal family dynamics of the 'Ndrangheta. That, too, made sense to di Bella. The youth courts, he felt, had much to contribute to this new direction.

If di Bella had any remaining doubts about the need for change in his own court, they vanished when, one day in Reggio, he found himself judging the children of the children he had judged a generation earlier. Here was undeniable proof that the 'Ndrangheta and the justice system were locked in never-ending conflict. The 'Ndrangheta would keep thieving, maiming, and killing. The carabinieri and the judges would keep throwing them in jail. It was systemic, perpetual failure. "We were all *inheriting* the 'Ndrangheta," said di Bella. And if targeting an 'Ndranghetista when he was young was one of the ways to end this eternal battle, and all the blood and prison and death it wrought, then di Bella felt it was his duty to seize the moment.

WHEN HE READ the files on Maria Concetta Cacciola's death in August 2011, di Bella sensed his chance had arrived. "Concetta's children were used as a tool to make her come back and retract," he said. "Her parents made Concetta listen to her six-year-old crying 'I miss Mommy' on the phone." It was an unambiguous case of child abuse in the service of criminality. A few weeks later, di Bella read the transcripts of a bugged conversation between Concetta's sixteen-year-old son, Alfonso, and his father, Salvatore Figliuzzi. In the transcripts, Alfonso accused his grandparents—Concetta's parents—of treating his mother so badly that "they practically killed her. You lost a wife. I lost a mother. Nothing would have fucking happened if it hadn't been for Grandpa and his jealous rage." Here was another 'Ndrangheta boy crying out to be rescued from his family. One way or another, the state had failed Concetta. Di Bella couldn't allow it to fail her children. "After Concetta's death, we decided to try a very different approach," he said.

Di Bella's first move was to have the carabinieri remove Giuseppina's and Concetta's children from their grandparents. This twin seizure from two of the most prominent 'Ndrangheta families in Rosarno sparked immediate fury. Di Bella received threatening letters. The Calabrian newspapers ran interviews with fathers and mothers from Rosarno accusing him of breaking up families and stealing children out of sheer vindictiveness. Apparently in all seriousness, some accused him of trying to brainwash their children in the same way the Nazis abducted and indoctrinated their enemies' children during World War II.

Di Bella was unmoved. He had found legal justification for the seizures in international law, particularly the United Nations Convention on the Rights of the Child. "It says that a child's family has to respect their freedom, their rights, and their peace," he said. "None of that is respected by the mafia." The convention became di Bella's basis for a new policy for handling the children of *pentiti* so they could no longer be used to blackmail their mothers. "Now, whenever there is a woman who collaborates, the officers inform the court about the children so we can intervene and get the children to the woman. This avoids the dangerous vacancy of authority over the children, which the 'Ndrangheta tries to exploit."

Di Bella realized the convention had far wider applications, too. What he had been fighting all these years was not, as his colleagues sometimes excused it, the simple bad luck of being born into a southern mafia family or even some traditional version of *patria potestas*, the customary power of a father. The convention was unequivocal. What was happening inside almost every 'Ndrangheta family was illegal child abuse. "When we are talking about a child of twelve and his father is taking him to the beach to learn how to shoot a gun, the convention says it's our duty to intervene," said di Bella. "A father under house arrest teaching his twelve-year-old how to strip a gun or move a Kalashnikov from one house to another—we have an obligation to intervene there, too. A man who is a fugitive for twenty years with his children, forcing them to miss their education—we have the same obligation. All the cases where crimes are committed by children or parents relying on children, or if we have children extorting on behalf of their parents, or when a child is taken somewhere to shoot traffickers and witness a drug fight, or when they use their children as killers during clan feuds—in all these cases, when there is tangible and concrete detriment to the child, the convention says we have an obligation."

The same duty of care applied to 'Ndrangheta mothers schooling their children in mafia life, the very life force of the 'Ndrangheta. The convention recognized a parent's right to educate their child. But that was subordinate to the child's right to be protected from prejudice and abuse, physical or psychological; and to their right to a responsible education aimed at preparing the child for a tolerant, peaceful, legal life. 'Ndrangheta children didn't have any of that. They didn't have much of a childhood, full stop. "You take a seventeen-year-old 'Ndrangheta boy and ask him what music he listens to and he'll reply 'the tarantella,'" said di Bella. "He doesn't know Lady Gaga or Madonna. It's such a strict, narrow upbringing. They can't see further than their own family and their own little town."

Di Bella began to believe that the greatest problem with an 'Ndrangheta upbringing was the way it stunted a child emotionally. At an early age, children learned to hide and control their feelings, lest they betray themselves or others. They internalized the code, which forbade almost any individual expression or identity. And while they formed almost no relationships outside the 'Ndrangheta, inside it, as their friends and relatives were steadily murdered or were put in prison or went on the run, they became ever more lonely. "There is no one to tell the child the right road to take and no individual will to choose a different road," said di Bella. "The young man doesn't even contemplate it because he doesn't know a different reality exists. For children growing up in these little mafia towns, the cult of the 'Ndrangheta oppresses everything and everyone." No surprise, said di Bella, that court reports on 'Ndrangheta children showed psychological devastation. "Their symptoms are similar to Vietnam veterans," he said. "They are inhibited. They all have this strong sense of anguish and anxiety. Their dreams are full of nightmares. And they are alone."

Taken together, di Bella concluded, the "mafia family system" was itself "prejudiced against the welfare of children." "A mafia education, mafia indoctrination by the parents, the perpetration of crimes by the child, the physical danger to children," said di Bella, "all these are detrimental to the mental and physical integrity of the children and contravene the fundamental rights, liberties, and principles of the UN charter. The primary victims of the 'Ndrangheta are their own children."

The Family had always been an immoral perversion. Now it seemed it was illegal, too.

DI BELLA WAS proposing deprogramming 'Ndrangheta children, a matter in which the judiciary had no expertise. When he raised the subject with social workers and psychologists, they recommended not just taking the children away from their parents but trying to offer them a normal adolescence. Growing up was, at heart, about discovering freedom. Freedom was what the 'Ndrangheta denied its children, and that was why they turned out the way they did. If the state wanted to change them, said the psychologists, it should place younger children with families far outside Calabria who would let them attend school and hang out with friends and make the conventional choices of any child growing up. Once they were old enough, the children could stay in a hostel where they would be required to attend school. They should be allowed contact with their parents but, crucially, the power to direct their lives should rest with the children themselves. The advice made sense to di Bella. "These children come from small worlds where everything is 'Ndrangheta," he said. "Their inexorable destiny is to be killed or end up in jail. A desire to choose a different path is never contemplated because they don't know the alternatives. You can't desire another world if you don't know it exists."

The hope, said di Bella, was that if children were allowed to experience a conventional upbringing, a new idea would take hold in their minds: self-determination. "Our idea was to let them know there is a better world out there with different rules," he said. This was "a place where you can be free. Where there is love and affection. Where there is no need for violence or killing in order to let other people understand what you're thinking. Where there are equal rights for men and women. Where prison is not a medal you get on your chest. And where you can try out your personality free from the surname you have." What the authorities would be attempting, said di Bella, was a kind of "cultural infiltration." They would insert the children into everyday Italian life and let it gently subvert them. "The 'Ndrangheta infiltrated us," he said. "Now we were going to infiltrate them right back."

In court, instead of custodial sentences, di Bella began ordering 'Ndrangheta children to be separated from their families in another fashion. He sent many of the older teenagers across the Strait, to a hostel attached to a church high up in the hills above Messina. The program was run by a young Sicilian psychologist, Enrico Interdonato, who had made a specialty of the mafia. Interdonato would take his charges out for pizza and to nightclubs. When he took one boy to a bookshop, he was astonished to learn it was the first time the boy had ever visited one.

Initial results were mixed. One boy, Francesco, arrived with a propensity for violence and a set of rock-hard prejudices against women, immigrants, the police, and the state, which were only slightly softened by the time he left. But another boy, Riccardo Cordì, from the 'Ndrangheta stronghold of Locri, was transformed. Riccardo's father, an 'Ndranghetista, had been killed when he was a boy. His brothers were all in jail. Riccardo himself had been headed the same way, appearing in di Bella's court after being arrested for stealing a police car, and then again for fighting.

After a year at the hostel in Messina, that destiny no longer appeared certain. After he turned eighteen and left the hostel, Riccardo wrote a letter that was published in several newspapers.

> *Dear Editor,*
>
> *I am a boy of Calabria, I come from Locri and my name is Riccardo Cordì. On March 7, 2011, I was arrested by the police in Locri for the theft and damage to a car owned by the railway police. In July 2011, I was charged with another instance of assault. But the court in Reggio decided to send me away from Locri to see if I could leave behind these experiences. It was the start of my journey.*
>
> *When I arrived in Sicily, at first it was not easy to be alone and away from home. But everything changed when I began to see a psychologist in Messina who guided me toward the discovery of a new life. I did things, met people, and visited Rome, Milan, and other places that I had never seen. One morning, I went to see the sea with the psychologist. We could see Calabria, my land. But for the first time, I could see it from another perspective.*
>
> *I decided then and there that my life would be different. I want to return to Locri, but I do not want any more problems with the law. Not because I can't handle it but because I want to live in peace. I want to be clean. Before this experience, I believed the state did not care about the people. The state was just this thing that took you away from home, without you ever knowing when or if you would return. But in recent months, I have met a different state.*

This state didn't seem to want me to change. Rather, it tried to
understand who I was.

  And who am I, really? A boy of eighteen. A boy like any other.
I was very small when my father was killed and I saw my brothers
go to jail. I want a different future for myself. That doesn't mean
that I renounce my family. My brothers will always be my brothers
and Calabria will always be my land. But now a new road lies
before me and I choose it for myself with my own free will. The state
has given me this chance. I can choose what I do when I grow up.
I can choose what job I do to get by in the city. I can stand tall. I
have no idea if I'll succeed but I'm going to try—because something
has changed for me. I changed. And I can change further. Others,
too. There are so many guys like me who need the state to support
them as it supported me. Right now, they don't believe this state
exists. But I know, and I write this letter so that others can know,
too. The road is still steep. But a happy ending, I now know, is not
just a dream. It can be real life.[2]

Interdonato, Riccardo's psychologist, said even Riccardo's family, who were 'Ndrangheta through and through, seemed to accept that the state wasn't harming their boy and might even be opening up some new horizons to him. Interdonato and Riccardo still talked every day months after Riccardo had left the hostel. One morning, Interdonato turned on his phone to find Riccardo had sent a picture of himself with a small baby. "He married his girlfriend this year and they had a son," said Enrico. "Family is at the center of Italy's history. The mafia took those values and *extremized* them until it became a kind of psychological abuse. But Riccardo is beginning a new family. He's writing a new history."

XXII

A LESSANDRA AND GIOVANNI were still haunted by their inability to prove that Maria Concetta Cacciola's death was murder.

They had plenty of circumstantial evidence. For one, Concetta had never seemed suicidal. On the contrary, said Giovanni, "Concetta was organizing to leave her family again. She had her love affair. The wiretaps showed she and her lover were planning their future together."

There was also the physical impossibility of drinking a liter of hydrochloric acid by choice. Though initial forensics suggested Concetta had killed herself, a pathologist later found bruises on her neck and other marks on her arms consistent with someone holding her down while a second person held her mouth open, possibly with a funnel, and poured acid down her throat. In addition, the autopsy revealed Concetta had taken no sedatives to dull the pain. She'd felt everything. Presumably, surmised the prosecutors, because she was meant to.

Alessandra and Giovanni were also sure Concetta's family was behind her killing. That was the 'Ndrangheta code. Every family cleaned up its own mess. Alessandra still thought Concetta's indecision, and her belief that it would be months before the family acted, had given the Cacciolas the opportunity they needed. "This lack of determination, taking too much time," she said. "Maybe this was fatal to her."

There was a further possibility, however. Maybe the Cacciolas *had* planned to wait but had stepped up their plans after Concetta told her mother she was returning to the protection program. In that scenario, Concetta's mother, Anna Rosalba Lazzaro, would have been key. "Maria Concetta Cacciola still felt love for her mother," said Giovanni. "That's why she told her she was going back into witness protection. But Lazzaro was a classic mafia woman, tasked with preserving the clan. She was the one who said: 'You're either with us, or with them.'"

Precisely who killed Concetta, however, remained a mystery. "We can say she was murdered," said Giovanni. "The question remains: by who? Her mother and father left the house that afternoon. It wasn't them. Something else happened but we still don't know what."

If the two prosecutors couldn't say who killed Concetta, they couldn't charge anyone with her murder. They decided that even as they would continue trying to prove a case of homicide, they would prosecute the Cacciolas on a lesser charge. Article 110 of the Italian criminal code specified that "when more than one person participates in the same offence, each shall be subject to the penalty prescribed for such offence."[1] Article 580 made it illegal to help or instigate suicide, an offense punishable by between five and twelve years in prison.

Charging the family with pressuring Concetta into suicide would still show that in twenty-first-century Italy no one could expect to assist their daughter's death, to conspire in it, and get away with it. And it was a case Alessandra and Giovanni could readily prove. Concetta had told them how the family had beaten and threatened her. From wiretaps, they had the Cacciola family on tape discussing how to force Concetta to retract. They also had them using her children to blackmail her into returning to Rosarno. In the recording of her retraction, a second woman's voice could be heard coaching her.

Two months after Concetta's murder, they had her sixteen-year-old son, Alfonso, blaming Concetta's parents for his mother's death. Finally, the Cacciolas themselves were saying that their daughter had died of shame. There was some poetic justice here, thought Alessandra. The Cacciolas were so blinded by the cult of the 'Ndrangheta and their loyalty to the code that they hadn't realized they were effectively admitting an offense. Concetta had felt no shame on her own. Whether she had killed herself or been murdered, it was the shame poured on her by the family that had made her death inevitable.

During the last few months of 2011, Alessandra and Giovanni steadily built their case against the Cacciolas. By February 9, 2012, they were ready. That morning, as the prosecutors released their indictment to the public, the carabinieri arrested Concetta's parents, Michele Cacciola and Anna Rosalba Lazzaro, in Rosarno and issued a warrant for Concetta's brother Giuseppe, who was detained two months later in Milan. All three were charged with conspiracy to force Concetta to perjure herself and to commit suicide. The carabinieri called the arrests Operazione Onta, or Operation Shame.

The arrests made the press the next day. "Driven to Suicide by Her Own Family" read a front-page headline in *Il Quotidiano della Calabria*, the province's main paper.[2] What caught Alessandra's eye, however, was a lengthy accompanying editorial by the paper's editor, Matteo Cosenza. For the first time in an Italian newspaper, Cosenza linked the cases of Concetta, Lea, and Giuseppina as elements of the same essential story. "Giuseppina Pesce, Maria Concetta Cacciola, and Lea Garofalo had the misfortune to be born into a terrible world," he wrote. "Despite tremendous suffering, these women decided to break with their families and to choose the path of legality and justice." All three women had paid dearly for their courage, wrote Cosenza. All had plunged their lives and the lives of their children into dark turmoil. Two of the women had died. Cosenza continued:

Some say we exaggerate when we talk about the 'Ndrangheta
and its penetration of Calabria's society and institutions. They
say it doesn't exist. These cases remind us of the truth. All honest
Calabrians must follow these women's example in their daily lives
and stand up to the 'Ndrangheta. Do it for yourself! Do it for
the young, who deserve a different future in this wonderful land!
It's almost impossible to imagine how someone can make a change
after being born into an 'Ndrangheta family—someone who sucks
arrogance and lawlessness from their mother's breast and who can't
even conceive of a world of civil coexistence, tolerance, respect, and
happiness. That's why we must bow before Giuseppina, Concetta,
and Lea. Despite everything, they were able to grasp that they were
living among evil and find the courage to say: "Enough! Stop! We
and our children must live in peace, not in perpetual war!"

They paid a high price. They will pay a higher one if we forget
them. Calabrians, don't turn away! Let's become the beautiful,
strong Calabria we all want! We know the evil among us. Step
by step, we will rid Calabria of this great malevolence and redeem
ourselves in the eyes of our children, and of the world.

Alessandra could scarcely believe what she was reading. Her
big idea had always been to crush the 'Ndrangheta by freeing its
women. For years, it had been a private obsession. Over the last
two years, month by month, man by man, she had slowly persuaded
her colleagues. With the backing of Pignatone and Prestipino, and
each successive case—first Lea, then Giuseppina, then Concetta—
the strength of her argument had grown. Concetta's death, in particular, had given Giuseppina renewed determination and spurred
Roberto di Bella to rethink everything he was doing at Reggio's
juvenile court.

But Alessandra could never have predicted a newspaper campaign against the 'Ndrangheta, calling on all Calabrians to take the

three women as their standard-bearers. Two years earlier, crowds had blocked the road in Reggio to cheer 'Ndrangheta boss Giovanni Tegano as he was led away to jail. Only a year earlier, *Calabria Ora* had launched its campaign against Alessandra. Now, suddenly, here was everything she had been working toward, all her intuition from growing up during *la mattanza* in Sicily, the summation of her years of study and research, the mountain of evidence she had amassed detailing how 'Ndrangheta women were oppressed and how a tiny few had fought back—all of it, on a newspaper front page, in an article calling for something close to revolution. It felt miraculous. "*Il Quotidiano* created, for the first time, a public debate about the women in the 'Ndrangheta," she said. "And suddenly people all around us were talking about how the 'Ndrangheta had been corrupting our lives all these years. It was a real, immediate change."

It occurred to Alessandra that what she had resisted for so many years—sentiment, empathy, emotion—was precisely what *Il Quotidiano* was using to stir up its readers. To a prosecutor, the 'Ndrangheta's women were a technical tool with which to unlock Europe's biggest criminal conspiracy. To a newspaper editor, the story of the three good mothers was an epic tragedy to rouse a people. And *Il Quotidiano*'s reporters had been industrious. Across the inside pages, they laid out every element of the story for their fellow Calabrians to read. A report on the arrest of Concetta's parents was accompanied by articles on the Pesce investigation ("Pesce Clan Hit with 11 More Arrests") and the Garofalo case ("Garofalo Trial: One Defendant Threatened"). The letter Concetta left for her mother when she went into witness protection was reprinted in full, as was her recorded "retraction." There were backgrounders on the clans of Rosarno and eulogies to the two dead women from members of parliament. There were even descriptions of the three bunkers about which Concetta had testified.

The common thread that ran through the coverage was the heroism of Lea, Giuseppina, and Concetta and the imperative for all Calabrians to follow their example. At heart, wrote Cosenza, this was a tale about three mothers who had understood their families were a curse on Calabria and who had defied centuries of violent misogyny—whether mafioso, Calabrian, or Italian—to save their children and their homeland. This was about sacrifice and pain, abuse and terror, blood and acid—and a dream of a new future. And now, said Cosenza, it had to be about the millions of Calabrians, men and women, who would join the rebellion the women had started. Cosenza even set a date for Calabria's revolt: March 8, the Festa della Donna, International Women's Day. On that day, he demanded that all true Calabrians celebrate Lea, Giuseppina, and Concetta. By doing so, he wrote, they would finally reclaim their freedom.

By coincidence, March 8, 2012, was a date already looming large on Alessandra's calendar.

That spring Thursday was sentencing day in the last of the maxitrials resulting from the 2010 raids against the 'Ndrangheta. More than two hundred men and women from across Italy had already been convicted and sentenced to a total of several thousand years in jail. Hundreds of millions of euros in property and assets had been seized. Entire crime families had been taken down and whole criminal empires dismantled. Now, in a caged dock inside a bulletproof and bombproof court in Reggio Calabria, a final 127 'Ndranghetisti would be judged and sentenced, among them bosses from every significant 'ndrina as well as Domenico Oppedisano, the *capo crimine*.

Alessandra knew that whatever happened, the 'Ndrangheta would endure. Despite the convictions and confiscations, the organization retained thousands of men in its employ and hundreds of billions of euros in assets. The bosses could still rule their businesses from jail, even commanding clan feuds and overseeing international expansion. Every prosecutor knew that however hard they worked to bring the 'Ndrangheta to account, tens of thousands of crimes, including hundreds of murders, would remain unsolved.

But there was no doubt that Calabria's prosecutors had shaken the 'Ndrangheta in a historic manner. The organization's most precious weapon, its secrecy, had been shattered. The century-old myth about a band of southern Italian Robin Hoods was in pieces. No longer would anyone nurse the illusion that the Calabrian mafia was a bunch of brigands with blunderbusses and trousers held up by baling twine who rustled goats and kidnapped provincial grocers. At last, the 'Ndrangheta had been exposed for what it was: a violent, unified, modern criminal conspiracy based in Calabria that threatened every country in the world.

This day had been decades coming, since long before Falcone and Borsellino or *The Godfather* or the night in July 1973 that the sixteen-year-old grandson of a billionaire stayed out late in Rome. The investigation that led to the maxi-trials had taken years and involved tens of thousands of policemen, carabinieri, prosecutors, and judges. It had necessitated the biggest surveillance operation ever mounted in Italy, amounting to a total of 25,000 hours of tapped phone calls and 83,000 hours of video and audio. The result of all this work was a prosecutors' picture of the 'Ndrangheta that was comprehensive and, to most of Italy, Europe, and the rest of the world, nothing less than dumbfounding. Whether measured by the tens of billions of euros it earned every year, or the grip it exerted over the illicit global markets for narcotics and weapons, or the political corruption it fomented from Melbourne to Montreal, or even the way it subverted financial markets and national sovereignty around the globe, Calabria's prosecutors had exposed the 'Ndrangheta as the world's most powerful and dangerous mafia.

What especially pleased Alessandra was that the greatest injury to the 'Ndrangheta had been performed by the investigations into Lea, Giuseppina, and Concetta. Their cases revealed the organization not as some fairy tale about wandering knights and righteous honor but a grotesque, illiterate, make-believe murder cult that practiced merciless and bloody cruelty, twisted family in the service of greed, and delighted in crushing freedom, love, and hope. "More than just the arrests, it was the loss of image and the injury to their legend," said Alessandra. "It really wounded them."

EACH MORNING FROM February 10 until March 8, *Il Quotidiano* ran a front-page banner featuring pictures of Lea, Giuseppina, and Concetta. Each day, it sent reporters to cover how ordinary Calabrians were joining the fight against the 'Ndrangheta. The prosecutors and women's groups were among the first to pledge support. They were followed by companies and trade unions, schoolchildren and university students, political parties and town mayors. After that came youth groups and pensioners' associations, trattoria owners and farmers' cooperatives, the Rotary Club, the swimmers' club, ferry operators, fishing captains, theater companies, artists' collectives, social workers, olive farmers, gelato sellers, winemakers, dockworkers, folksingers, and long-distance truckers. By the time March 8 arrived, even the northern-focused national press had begun to take notice of the scores of anti-'Ndrangheta marches involving tens of thousands of people taking place across Calabria.[3] The story of Lea, Giuseppina, and Concetta was becoming big news. A slogan had emerged: "La Calabria Non Ci Sta!!!" ("Calabria Won't Take It Anymore!!!") And as the women's stories were repeated over and over, their faces printed and reprinted on placards and posters, T-shirts and banners, broadcast on television, and published in international magazines, Alessandra realized that, slowly but steadily, Lea, Giuseppina, and Concetta were becoming the new legends of the 'Ndrangheta.

To the clans, this was catastrophic. Their invincibility was cracking. "These women had rebelled against the 'Ndrangheta's machismo and that act, and the stories of what happened to them, had cost the 'Ndrangheta their control and their system of consensus," said Alessandra. "That was the 'Ndrangheta's whole foundation and its whole essence. This was a huge crisis for them."

On the morning of March 8, it took a full hour in Reggio Calabria's main court to assemble all 127 'Ndranghetisti and their lawyers, as well as the prosecutors, officials, reporters, and three judges. It took another two hours for the presiding judge to read the list of convictions. By the time he had finished, ninety-three 'Ndranghetisti had been convicted. Sentences ranged from eight months to fourteen years. *Capo crimine* Domenico Oppedisano got ten years, probably enough to ensure he would die in prison.

Most important to the prosecutors, in its judgment the court formally acknowledged the 'Ndrangheta as a cohesive global entity with a presence in 120 locations around the world. Once and for all, the true nature of the world's biggest mafia had been established in irrefutable case law. "Today's ruling recognizes the accuracy of our reconstruction of the structure of the 'Ndrangheta as a unified organization, arranged in a complex hierarchy, governed by a top council, rooted in Calabria with branches overseas," Pignatone told reporters. "This represents a crucial step in fighting the 'Ndrangheta in Calabria and wherever it has taken root."

As Pignatone and his team congratulated each other quietly inside the Palace of Justice, Calabrians were dancing in the streets outside. As *Il Quotidiano* had demanded, almost every town in Calabria was holding an anti-mafia parade. In Reggio itself, there were conferences, plays, rallies, workshops, exhibitions, and speeches. As a show of public defiance, it was unique in Calabrian history. The icons of this new movement were Lea, Giuseppina, and Concetta, their faces almost ubiquitous.

None of the women could be present to see their triumph. That morning, however, Alessandra had arranged for a letter from the students of Mattia Preti girls' high school in Reggio Calabria to be delivered to Giuseppina in prison. The girls' words, thought Alessandra, would at least give Giuseppina a flavor of what was happening. "Dear Giusy," it began,

> *We wouldn't have had the strength. We wouldn't have had the strength and courage as women. We wouldn't have had the strength and courage as daughters or sisters. We wouldn't have had the strength and courage in this city and in this country, where so often everything is silenced by fear and shame. But when someone finds the strength and courage to speak, especially as a mother, that fear disappears, and we want to redeem ourselves and remain silent no more.*
>
> *We listened to your story in silence. And these seemingly distant events suddenly became real. You opened our eyes. You opened the eyes of so many young men and women who will not forget your strength and courage. With everything you've gone through, and are still enduring, with these words we wanted to give you back a little of the strength you've given us. You're a beacon for women's emancipation. Your freedom makes possible our own. Your freedom makes possible the freedom of this land.[4]*

Giuseppina was overjoyed. Once, she had dreamed she and Concetta might be the start of something. Now it was happening. Everywhere, it seemed, people were hailing Lea and Giuseppina and Concetta and coming out against the 'Ndrangheta.

In Reggio, Alessandra was equally touched by *Il Quotidiano*'s front page. Above a child's drawing of the three women, the paper had printed a headline that encapsulated what, for more years than Alessandra cared to remember, had been her personal creed: "With

Women, We Will All Break Free." Below it, editor Matteo Cosenza
had written an open letter to Denise Cosco:

Dear Denise,

*I do not know you but you should know the affection and
admiration I have for you. I don't know if you'll be able to read
these thoughts in the secret place where, at this time of liberty and
warmth and celebration, you are forced to live. Your choice, to
testify twice against your father about the death of your mother,
Lea Garofalo, reflects how your mother lived. You had to choose
between your living father and your dead mother and you chose the
triumph of truth, legality, and justice. You've even had to testify
against a man who was your partner.*

*You should know that your mother is proud. She made her
sacrifice for your future, which she dared to imagine as one of
dignity and free of the oppression she was born into. It would be
so easy to give in to hatred. But nothing can be built on hate.
Nobody, either, is born a criminal. These people are part of our
family, our neighborhoods, our schools, our traditions, and our
homeland. Many 'Ndrangheta men did not decide to be as they
are. They never had a choice. Our collective action, if it is serious
and profound, can prick their consciences. It can make new men of
them.*

*My dear Denise, this disease has spread so wide that as long
as the fever doesn't heal, it will continue to infect us. We must
remember the example of the women who broke this so-called code of
honor to proclaim their own right to freedom, respect, and dignity.
The road ahead is long and hard. We know this struggle will
take more than a little festival. But we have your example. Your
testimony gives us confidence that even in the darkest night, even
amid the torment that you, your mother, and the other women have
experienced, there is light ahead. We must build a different future.*

Nothing about the present suffering and violence is either natural or inevitable. This task will take all our commitment. We will have won when you are once again free to stroll the streets of Calabria, enjoying the sun and the sea breeze in peace. It is your right. It will be our failure if you are denied it.[5]

XXIII

THE MAXI-TRIALS, THE marches, *Il Quotidiano*—something was stirring in Calabria. Alessandra and the other prosecutors sensed a moment of possibility, even hope. It was exhilarating, but also disquieting. The state had fought for generations to change Sicily, and that war still wasn't won. The campaign against the Calabrian mafia now had its first convictions but, really, had just begun. Even the cases against the Coscos, the Cacciolas, and the Pesces had years to run through the various appeals and procedural tiers of the Italian justice system. Lea, Giuseppina, and Concetta might be the icons of this new movement, but if Carlo Cosco or the Pesces or the Cacciolas somehow walked free, then the spring of 2012 would be remembered as a brief, bright instant that vanished as quickly as it appeared.

By now, Alessandra knew that the best way to ensure a result in the Pesce case was to end all contact between the family and Giuseppina. Roberto di Bella's juvenile court had already taken care of the children, Angela, Gaetano, and Elisea. Now Alessandra had Giuseppina moved to Paliano prison outside Rome, a penitentiary set aside for mafia collaborators.

Housed in an old fifteenth-century palace on a natural rock fortress with idyllic views of the town and the Apennine mountains, Paliano housed around fifty *pentiti*, men and women. Prison facilities included a library, a theater, a church, a sports field, three workshops, four kitchens, four laboratories, five gyms, and a playroom

for children. Inmates were taught primary and secondary education
in its five classrooms. For the better educated, there were courses in
accounting and business studies as well as vocational training. All
the inmates were encouraged to work: in the prison pizzeria, growing tomatoes and cherries and cavolo nero in the organic garden,
making clothes, or embroidering cushions. There was a choir. There
was Internet. There were private bathrooms with bidets.

The idea, said Paliano's head warden, Nadia Cersosimo, was to
show how life in the mafia was a pale, negative image of reality.
Inside a clan, respect was synonymous with fear, and family with
crime. Paliano taught its prisoners that true respect was about
voluntary admiration, not involuntary deference, and true family
was about love, not mutual defense. Mafia families coached their
children to despise the law and hate the state. Cersosimo said her
own parents had taught her respect for the law and loyalty to the
state—and at Paliano, she attempted to raise her inmates afresh as
she herself had been brought up. It didn't always work. But when it
did, it could change lives. One prisoner gained a degree in econom-
ics. Two inmates, a man and a woman, married in the prison chapel.
"We all share in these new paths," said Cersosimo. "It's a family."
Alessandra was among many prosecutors who were impressed. "She
runs that prison as if it were her home," she said.

At Paliano, Giuseppina was allowed regular visits from her children. She watched the Lea Garofalo trial and the Cacciola arrests on
television. She followed the proceedings against her own family in
Palmi by video link from an underground security bunker set up for
the purpose at Rebibbia prison in Rome. When she turned thirty-
two on September 24, 2011, she was allowed a small party.

As Giuseppina and Alessandra resumed their collaboration,
they also revived their friendship. Between trial days during late
2011 and early 2012, Alessandra would fly up to meet Giuseppina
at Rebibbia and finesse her testimony. Sometimes during the hour-

long drive from Paliano, Giuseppina's protection officers would report being shadowed by cars with blacked-out windows. But Alessandra had insisted on a new team of bodyguards for Giuseppina, and their evident professionalism convinced Giuseppina she was in no danger. Alessandra was pleased to note the tight bond of trust that was quickly developing between Giuseppina and her protection squad. When, in December 2011, Giuseppina began giving detailed evidence for the first time against her father and brother—the two 'Ndrangheta men to whom she was most loyal—Alessandra credited the confidence she now felt able to place in the state.

Giuseppina's main concern remained the happiness of her children. A year earlier, Angela's despondency had derailed Giuseppina's cooperation. Now Angela seemed resolved to support her mother. Gaetano and Elisea, too, appeared happy in the care of Roberto di Bella's youth program. Still, abandoning family and everything you'd been taught from birth was never going to be easy.

In December 2011, realizing that the three children would be apart from Giuseppina for Christmas, Alessandra decided to make sure all three received presents. Out shopping, she spotted a cuddly toy that inspired her to try an experiment with the youngest, six-year-old Elisea. "When these children think of carabinieri, they think of hooded people in black balaclavas who seize their father or uncle in the middle of the night," said Alessandra. Alessandra decided to give Elisea a bear dressed in a carabinieri uniform. "I thought she could see this bear as a more friendly figure and, through my gift, the girl could get used to the idea of the state."

When Alessandra saw Giuseppina in January 2012, she asked if Elisea had liked her present.

"Yes, yes, she liked it," replied Giuseppina. But Alessandra could see she was embarrassed. "I'm afraid she took the carabinieri uniform off," said Giuseppina eventually.

Alessandra told Giuseppina not to worry. "Slowly, slowly," she said. "Let's see if things change."

And slowly, slowly, they did. Each time they met, Alessandra would ask Giuseppina for an update on the bear. In February, Giuseppina smiled and said the bear was now wearing its shoes. "Then she told me it was wearing its trousers," said Alessandra. "Then it was wearing its hat. Very gradually the bear began to wear more and more of its uniform. It took from January to September. But, finally, the bear was completely dressed and Elisea placed it right by the front door. She told her mother it was 'so that the carabinieri can protect us.'"

Alessandra saw the bear's transformation as an extraordinary metaphor for how, with their mother's encouragement, Giuseppina's children were altering their outlook on the world. "It was something amazing, what Giuseppina was managing to do," she said. "Slowly and progressively, she was setting out with her very fragile young children on a new path to something else. It was small steps on a long path. But slowly and surely, she was making them understand that the state can help them."

ALL ALESSANDRA'S EFFORTS with Giuseppina were to prepare her for the trial ahead. The first hurdle came on New Year's Eve, 2011, when a new 180-day deadline for Giuseppina to sign her witness statements fell due. The day before, Alessandra flew in to see Giuseppina, bringing with her several thousand pages of documentation. Eight months earlier, Giuseppina had refused to sign. Now, even on the phone, Alessandra could tell she was nervous again. The prosecutor arrived at Rebibbia fearing a repeat performance. She relaxed when she realized that what she had understood as anxiety was actually excitement. Giuseppina signed then slumped in her chair. She had now officially replaced her family with the state.

A bigger ordeal for Giuseppina would be facing her family in court. The hearings in Palmi weren't scheduled to begin until May 2012, giving Giuseppina and Alessandra months to ready themselves. Once proceedings were under way, however, they would be a marathon. The trial was expected to last a year. Giuseppina's evidence was so detailed that her testimony and cross-examination alone would take a week, Monday to Friday, eight to ten hours a day.

Alessandra arranged for Giuseppina to speak via video link from Rebibbia. When a number of Pesce relatives were given permission to attend the trial in Rebibbia, Alessandra requested a screen in court to block their view. But Alessandra knew her star witness and her family would still be aware of each other's presence and would be feeling each other out, testing each other's will. She decided to train Giuseppina like an athlete. She stressed physical fitness, encouraging Giuseppina to exercise for her stamina and advising her to take chocolate and fruit juice into the hearings to sustain herself. She told her to ask for a break any time she needed it. To prepare Giuseppina's mind, Michele Prestipino began joining Alessandra on her visits to Rebibbia. The prosecutors would put Giuseppina through her paces, spending days going over questions and evidence and likely questions from the defense, so that Giuseppina knew the case and the judicial procedure back to front.

Alessandra had also long understood that if Giuseppina was to betray her family, she would need a substitute to hold on to. Alessandra had given up the habit of a lifetime to become something approaching a mother to her. As Giuseppina's day in court drew nearer, Alessandra was heartened to see their relationship deepening. Once they finished the formal work of taking statements and verifying evidence, the two women found that what remained was warmth and closeness, an acceptance and appreciation of each other. One day, when Alessandra was setting up her tape recorder in their usual room at Rebibbia, Giuseppina entered carrying a gift. Alessandra unwrapped it to find a small hand-embroidered cushion. On it, Giuseppina had stitched the words: "Thank you for everything. With love, Giusy." "I was touched," said Alessandra. "After all, I was the one who had arrested her. Twice. In prison, she couldn't make much but she had done what she could. And the care she took in making this cushion! The tiny stitching. She'd scented it with a flowery fragrance, and the smell filled my apartment for a week. It was a symbol, a token of her gratitude that she was still alive, thanks to my stubbornness. And a very feminine one, which seemed to indicate a particular warmth and regard for me."

WHEN THE FIRST day of Giuseppina's testimony finally arrived on May 22, Alessandra judged that she and Michele Prestipino had done all they could.[1] Giuseppina was determined and confident. In a remarkable reversal of roles, she even tried to soothe Alessandra's nerves. A year earlier, when Giuseppina had suspended her cooperation, Alessandra had told her in parting that she would hold on to the dream that Giuseppina would one day restart her collaboration and face her family in court. Now Giuseppina winked at Alessandra. "Don't worry," she said. "Dreams can come true."

Still, as Alessandra stood in Palmi's main court, watching the video monitor while Giuseppina took her seat in Rebibbia, she was tense. Bringing a collaborator to testify against the mafia in court was a high point in any Italian prosecutor's career. Bringing Giuseppina to testify against her family, perhaps the only time that such a knowledgeable witness would give evidence against so powerful a clan, was the judicial event of the decade. The next few days would be a procedural and bloodless war, but a war nonetheless. On one side, truth and justice. On the other, murderous criminality and intense blackmail. Alessandra found herself simultaneously in thrall to the proceedings and terrified by them. How would Giuseppina cope?

Alessandra began by asking Giuseppina to describe her life as a mafiosa. Giuseppina explained her duties, which included passing messages between the men and managing the Pesce extortion rackets. She gave an overview of the other businesses: trucking, drugs, weapons, and corruption. She laid out the organization's structure, specifying which of her uncles and cousins were its bosses and lieutenants, and the line of succession. She spoke about how the men maintained a legal fund for family members on trial or in jail. She explained how her grandmother Giuseppa Bonarrigo's house served as a meeting place where the men believed they could talk without fear of being bugged.

Giuseppina spoke in detail about the men's fear of surveillance, and how they used detectors to find listening devices in their cars or under the paving at her grandmother's house, even the secret cameras hidden in the walls of a nearby school and hospital. She described how her father, Salvatore Pesce, had lived in a bunker under her grandmother's house, linked to the surface by a passage hidden inside a barrel, before he was arrested in 2005. She talked about the family's links to judges, carabinieri, and government officials. She told the story of how her cousin Francesco would stay outside the polling station on election day, telling voters: "Vote for so-and-so, he's a friend." She ran through Rosarno's history of killings and clan wars, especially between the Pesces and their rivals, the Belloccos. The rules were straightforward, she said. "You killed one of ours, we killed one of yours." The same went for traitors. When a cousin, Rosa Ferraro, discovered that Salvatore had put the Pesce family supermarket in her name, and was using it to launder money and defraud a salami maker, Ferraro had denounced him in the street. To the Pesces, said Giuseppina, such disgrace could only be answered with death. Rosa's imminent murder had only been narrowly avoided by her surrender to the authorities.

Alessandra then led Giuseppina through her own decision to testify against her family. Giuseppina began by saying that her marriage to Rocco Palaia had been loveless. "He never worked and he was never at home if one of the babies was ill," she said. "He wasn't home for a Sunday walk with his family. He didn't even give me money for medicine." She cried when she talked about Domenico Costantino, and how she had finally met a man who loved and respected her for who she was. Still, once her affair was discovered, Giuseppina knew she was dead. Asked who would administer her punishment, Giuseppina replied that her husband, Rocco, had told her that the family had "a pit ready for me" but that it would be her brother, Francesco, who would pull the trigger. "It has to be the eldest son in the family," she said.

This attachment to primogeniture typified the backwardness of mafia life, said Giuseppina. So did the violent misogyny. It had been standard mafia behavior for her family to blackmail her into signing a retraction by holding her children hostage. So was beating and starving her children when she defied the clan and resumed her cooperation. Giuseppina had been able to give the culture of the mafia some thought during her months at Paliano. She now delivered her conclusions to the court. The 'Ndrangheta men turned love and sanctuary into hate, intimidation, and fear, she said. "In a sense, whatever problems we have as a family, it came from that, the whole environment in which we were living," she said. "*That*'s the evil I see." That was the reason that she, her sister, her mother, and others were in jail. For the women, the mafia was evil in the way it made them complicit in their men's crimes ". . . in the sense that this chain doesn't break—this willingness to go on committing crimes." It was the mafia's perversion of family that meant "women are always going to meet with prisoners and now are prisoners ourselves." But that corruption of family love was also "why I couldn't stand the idea of my children without me and why I made this choice: so my children might avoid my fate and have a better life, where they are their own masters and can choose what they want to do. That's also why I cut all contact with my brother. Because as a man, he'll never accept my choice."

As she spoke, Giuseppina could hear coughing from the defendants' dock. It happened whenever she mentioned her brother. Even from hundreds of miles away down a video line, she recognized the voice and understood the message. "Her brother was saying: 'I hear you,'" said Alessandra. "'I hear what you're saying about me.'" To Alessandra's relief, Giuseppina was unperturbed. Turning to Alessandra during a break, she joked, "Does my brother have a sore throat?"

It was the first of several attempts by the Pesces to throw Giuseppina off balance during the trial. Her mother still refused to use her daughter's name, referring to her only as "the collaborator." Through a prison guard, her sister Marina sent her a photograph of the two of them together with their children. "That was very destabilizing for Giuseppina," said Alessandra. "She loved her sister a lot. That was very strong pressure on her, and she just had to find a way to handle it."

Giuseppina found the presence of her father, Salvatore, hardest to bear. She had often told Alessandra that among her family, she was closest to her father. She would cry when she spoke of him, saying he was the only one who ever understood her and that if he hadn't been in jail, he would have protected her from Rocco.

In court, as Giuseppina finished her final day of evidence, her father asked to make a statement. Alessandra sat motionless. As Salvatore walked from the dock to the witness stand, Giuseppina could see him for the first time. He was wearing a white shirt with blue stripes. "Giuseppina started crying as soon as she saw him," said Alessandra. "The shirt was the last present she had ever given him. It was her father's way of reminding her of her blood ties, of telling her who she was. On the screen, I could see Giuseppina's tears streaming down her cheeks."

Quickly and quietly, Alessandra suggested Giuseppina take a break. With Giuseppina safely out of earshot, Salvatore Pesce then began to speak. Initially, he turned his anger on Alessandra, accusing her of abusing her office and forcing Giuseppina to lie by threatening to take her children away and giving her drugs. He said Alessandra had exceeded her powers by arresting Giuseppina's mother and sister, Angela Ferraro and Marina Pesce, in Milan. "You have acted unlawfully," he shouted at Alessandra. "And why? You want to die?"

Alessandra interrupted to request the court transcript be forwarded to the director of public prosecutions in Rome to decide whether Salvatore's threat to her constituted an offense. Salvatore was then allowed to continue. "I want to tell my daughter that everybody loves her," he said. "After this is all over, when all the lights have been turned out and all these careers have been improved and when you're all by yourself, you will find us here waiting for you. We'll be here."

Alessandra marveled at how, in open court, Giuseppina's father could tug at his daughter's heart while threatening her in the same breath. Was there no end to these men's malice?

WEIGHING HERSELF DURING the week of Giuseppina's testimony, Alessandra calculated that she lost two or three kilograms a day. She was surprised to see Giuseppina coping far better. "She carried on through the trial—with great pain and suffering but also with great strength," said Alessandra.

Alessandra knew Giuseppina drew most of her courage from the same source that had always inspired her: her children. A few days before Giuseppina testified, her eldest daughter, Angela, had given her a necklace with a silver cross on it. "That was another message," said Alessandra. "Angela was telling her: 'If you feel afraid, if you feel scared, touch the necklace and think of us.' During the trial, she had a moment or two when I thought she was collapsing. But she immediately recovered, and I know her strength came from thinking about her children and how she was doing this for them. That gave her all the strength she needed."

Alessandra pondered the affection she felt for Giuseppina, once again characterizing their connection as "umbilical." She wondered how it compared with the bond that still existed between Giuseppina and her family. The trial hearings would continue for the rest of 2012, and sentencing wasn't expected until May 2013. Few sights were more likely to rekindle a daughter's love for her parents than the spectacle of them in a cage. The day the case concluded, however, would likely be the last Giuseppina would ever see her parents and her family. Giuseppina needed to come to terms with their inevitable separation.

After the stress of testifying, Alessandra and Michele Prestipino left Giuseppina alone for a few weeks. At Paliano, it was summer and the tomatoes and eggplants were ripening in the penitentiary garden, ready for the *pentiti* to pick in the early evening to make giant trays of parmigiana in the kitchens. One hot July day, when they judged enough time had passed, Alessandra and Prestipino flew up to Rome and took the drive east out into Lazio and to Paliano. The two prosecutors arrived in the early afternoon. In their honor, warden Nadia Cersosimo had organized a surprise supper, attended by all the staff and inmates, cooked using vegetables and herbs from the garden. The guests ate and chatted amiably with the *pentiti*. Afterward, Giuseppina presented Alessandra and Prestipino with pickles and jams whose lids she had decorated with embroidered doilies: a simple design of cherries and apricots next to the initials of Paliano district. Regarding Giuseppina, it struck Alessandra that her witness had changed once more. For the first time, she wrote, "I had the distinct impression that I had replaced her family in her emotions." That family loyalty, that unquestioning bond—it was gone.

If anything, Alessandra began to realize, it was now she who was becoming too attached to Giuseppina. In quieter moments, she would admonish herself for imagining that their bond could ever be more than temporary. She would have to move on to other cases. Giuseppina would need to live her own life. Still, Alessandra's staff were incredulous when, a few weeks after her visit to Paliano and hours before she left on her annual August holiday, she took a call from Giuseppina on her office line, a number that an 'Ndranghetista should never have possessed. Giuseppina was upset over arrangements for her children's custody. Some bureaucrat was messing her around.

Alessandra's staff knew better than to interrupt their boss. Like any good mother, she never stopped worrying.

W HEN THE LEA Garofalo trial collapsed in November 2011, it had seemed like a disaster. Within a week, however, a new judge, Anna Introini, was appointed and immediately added new urgency to the proceedings.

Introini was one of the most senior women in the Italian judiciary. A fifty-nine-year-old veteran of several mafia cases, as well as of attempts to prosecute Silvio Berlusconi, her experience had left her with little patience for defense gymnastics or procedural delays, let alone mafia misogyny. Mindful that Carlo's term of custody expired on July 28, 2012, Introini ruled, over the defense's objections, that no previous hearings need be repeated and that Denise's damning testimony still stood. She also instituted an accelerated timetable of two court days a week.

When hearings resumed in December 2011, the weight of testimony against Carlo and his *'ndrina* quickly mounted. A fellow prisoner at San Vittore in Milan testified—over Massimo Sabatino's shouted denunciations—that he had heard Sabatino describe how Carlo had asked him in May 2009 to dress as a washing-machine repairman and kidnap Lea in Campobasso.[1] A number of Carlo's acquaintances spoke of their fear of him. Others had such trouble with their memories that they unwittingly gave the same impression. Proceedings were further accelerated by Carlo's refusal to take the stand. One day, sending a message to the 'Ndrangheta that he was observing omertà, he cupped his hands over his ears. "The message was: 'There's no problem, don't worry, feel safe, I'm not going to talk,'" said Alessandra. Still, by not testifying, Carlo couldn't help but speed up his trial. By the time Matteo Cosenza wrote his letter to Denise in *Il Quotidiano* on March 8, Judge Introini had said she would announce a verdict and sentence on March 30, 2012.

When the day came, Introini passed word that she would deliver judgment at 8:30 P.M. Outside court, the hall was packed. On one side, relatives of the defendants whispered with their lawyers. On the other, student activists huddled around Enza Rando, passing her letters of support for Denise. Journalists hovered. In the caged dock Carlo, his brothers Giuseppe and Vito, Massimo Sabatino, Rosario Curcio, and Carmine Venturino greeted their relatives through the bars.

Just after 8 P.M., a court official announced proceedings were about to start. As the reporters squeezed into the press seats, Carlo chatted quietly with his *'ndrina*. When Judge Introini entered, the court fell silent. Introini took her seat. "In the name of the Italian people," she said, "the Court of Assizes condemns Carlo Cosco, Giuseppe Cosco, Vito Cosco, Rosario Curcio, Massimo Sabatino, and Carmine Venturino . . ." Judge Introini ruled that all six men had taken part in Lea's murder. She convicted all six of helping to dispose of Lea's body by dissolving it in acid and of pretending that Lea was alive and well and living in Australia. Introini gave life sentences to all. She specified that Carlo and Vito should serve their first two years in solitary, while the other four should serve one. All six men were also ordered to pay a total of €200,000 to Denise, €50,000 each to Lea's sister Marisa and her mother, and €25,000 to the city of Milan.

It was hard to imagine a tougher set of sentences. Alessandra was delighted. The 'Ndrangheta seemed shocked. In the public gallery, Carmine Venturino's mother and sister began to cry. Other relatives screamed in despair. "Are you happy now?" yelled one woman at the activists.

Outside court, Enza read a prepared statement. "The most important part of today is that a young girl of a murdered mother has had the courage to bear witness for justice," she said. "She broke through the fear and silence and made her contribution to justice and truth." Libera's founder, the priest Don Luigi Ciotti, added: "This sentence will go down in history. We must bow before this young girl who found the nerve to break omertà and restore dignity, truth, and justice to her mother."[2]

Denise had testified against a father who had murdered her mother and ordered her own death. By staying true to Lea, she had broken not just with omertà but with her upbringing, her family, and all Calabria. What her mother had started, she had finished. She was only twenty years old. She deserved the widest possible admiration.

When Calabria's prosecutors considered it over the next few months, however, Carlo's conviction felt anticlimactic. Going to jail, even for life, was something an 'Ndrangheta boss like Carlo Cosco accepted as the price of power. Even if the state had punished him, he had punished Lea for her disloyalty. The journalists writing about the case might focus on his sentence, but their stories couldn't help send the message that if you crossed the 'Ndrangheta or Carlo Cosco, you died.

And, of course, the way the 'Ndrangheta worked, Carlo might be in prison, but his stature inside the organization had risen. In the 'Ndrangheta's view, he had done the righteous and honorable thing by killing his unfaithful turncoat wife. He and his 'ndrina had shown discipline in court. They hadn't talked. They'd barely recognized the court's authority. They even managed to torture Denise further by refusing to say how and where Lea had died or what they had done with her body. Carlo had been tested over and again and he had remained steadfast. In the 'Ndrangheta's eyes, he was already a *santista*, literally sanctified. Now he would be recognized as one of the biggest bosses in Italy, free to expand his empire from prison and plan for the day when he settled his score with Denise, just as he had done with her mother. Carlo was unshaken. The 'Ndrangheta endured.

BARELY THREE MONTHS after Carlo's conviction, however, came news that his organization had been smashed. At 9 A.M. on June 21, 2012, seventy policemen in riot gear descended on *il fortino delle cosche* at No. 6 Viale Montello. Breaking down doors, they evicted two hundred residents, including several 'Ndrangheta families and more than fifty Chinese and African immigrant families. In two hours, the mafia's forty-year occupation of one of Milan's most historic buildings was over. Carlo's base of operations was destroyed.[3]

Behind closed doors, other cracks were appearing in Carlo's empire. During their investigation of Lea's death, the carabinieri had discovered a secret diary that Lea had kept throughout her early years with Carlo. "I didn't know it existed," said Denise. "She kept it when she was pregnant with me. Reading it, I learned she was very much in love with my father." Her mother's words gave Denise a new perspective. "Our family's is a story about courage," she said, "but more than that it's about love. Everything began with the love my mother had for my father." To Denise, the way her mother wrote about her father, Carlo must have returned that love. "He had other motives for marrying her," she said. "But I think he did love her."[4]

Facing up to life in prison, Carlo's *'ndrina* was experiencing similarly mixed emotions. In July 2012, the prosecutor in the case, Marcello Tatangelo, received a letter from Carmine Venturino. "I want to confess what I know about the murder of Lea Garofalo," wrote Carmine. He went on to state that he had assisted in Lea's murder and lied about it afterward. He added that while under Carlo's command, he had had to obey "the law that exists in Calabria, which is

different from the one that governs the rest of the world." His lawyers had assured him he would be acquitted since without a body,
there could be no murder.

That had turned out to be incorrect. As a result, Carmine was
now following his own counsel. The trial had taught him, he wrote,
that "I am not a mobster. I am not a monster." He wasn't immune to
suffering, like Carlo and the other men. Rather, "the pain of losing
Denise leaves me no choice," he wrote. "It's a very delicate thing.
But I think everyone would like to know the facts of Lea's disappearance, especially Denise. I do this out of love for Denise. She was
brave. She is an example to me. I have to tell you the facts of what
really happened."[5]

CARMINE VENTURINO WAS thirty-three when he was sentenced
to life. He had been born in November 1978 in Crotone, on the
plain below Pagliarelle. He told Tatangelo in a series of interviews
over the summer and autumn of 2012 that one of his earliest memories was of how his family's attention, and love, was focused on his
brother, who was born disabled.[6] Carmine didn't blame them. He
described his family as "poor but honest." Like most Calabrians,
however, he said his parents would never have thought of crossing
the 'Ndrangheta.

When Carmine fell in with a crowd from Pagliarelle and began
smoking hash, heroin, and cocaine, his family let it happen. They
made no objection either when in September 2006, aged twenty-
seven, he moved to Viale Montello in Milan. At first, Carmine was
a user. Soon he was dealing for one of Carlo's cousins. Within a year,
he was working for Carlo, who had moved back into Viale Montello on his release from prison. With the money he was earning,
Carmine rented his own apartment. One day in 2008 Carlo showed
up at his door with a blanket and a pillow, asking if he could stay.

"He never left," said Carmine. His rapid promotion from drug user to lieutenant in Europe's biggest drug mafia was, said Carmine, "sweetness, followed by bitterness."

Carmine had heard about Lea Garofalo in Pagliarelle. "Everyone was talking about it," he said. "We all knew that Carlo had had to go away because of her and that that was why he wanted to kill her." In their apartment, Carlo told Carmine that Lea was trying to take Denise away from him. He was frustrated that Denise didn't try to fight her mother more. He didn't articulate, yet, what his plans were for Lea. Then again, said Carmine, he didn't have to.

Carlo's chances of exacting his revenge increased significantly in spring 2009 when Lea left witness protection for the second time. She sent a message via her sister, Marisa, asking Carlo if she and Denise could return to Calabria. Carlo had every reason to agree. Lea was playing into his hands. One day in April, said Carmine, "Vito Cosco came to me in Milan and told me that Carlo wanted to buy four sets of camouflage military gear, four balaclavas, and four sets of boots and gave me a note with a set of measurements on it. I asked what they were for, and Vito replied we would need the stuff to kidnap and kill Lea." Carmine added that he already knew where to buy the gear, because he had bought ski masks there for another murder.

Carlo told his *'ndrina* that since he was already suspected of trying to kill his wife, he couldn't risk direct involvement in this new attempt. Instead, he wanted Vito, Carmine, and Rosario Curcio to murder Lea. Carmine duly bought the clothes with cash and loaded them into a stolen red Fiat van, together with an Uzi submachine gun equipped with a silencer and two magazines that he picked up from Viale Montello, all ready for the drive down to Calabria. But the plan was foiled when Carlo, having arrived in Pagliarelle to scout the attack, found that Lea had installed a new steel door on the house where she was staying, and that the police had stationed a car outside.

Carlo returned to Milan with a new plan. He'd spoken to Denise, and she'd told him she wanted to finish school in Campobasso. Carlo had rented her and Lea an apartment there. "That was where we were going to kill Lea," said Carmine. Carlo set May 5 as the date for Lea's murder. He recruited another 'Ndranghetista, Massimo Sabatino, to pretend to be a washing-machine repairman and gain access to the flat. Sabatino was to kidnap Lea. The other men, waiting outside, would then drive her to an isolated spot in Bari in the south, where they would kill her and get rid of her body. But on May 3, Carmine had a car accident. "I was drunk and high," he said. "I was so scared." With two stitches in his head, Carmine told Carlo he wasn't well enough to take part. Rosario Curcio, too, pulled out at the last minute, saying he couldn't leave his business unattended. "Stay well out of this," he advised Carmine. When Carmine told Vito he couldn't come, Vito slapped him across the face, knocking him to the ground. In the end, Carlo dispatched Giuseppe, Vito, and Massimo, only for Massimo to screw up the kidnapping. Carlo was incandescent. "You're all useless!" he shouted at Vito. "Do I have to do everything myself?!"

Evidently, Carlo decided he did. When Lea and Denise moved back to Pagliarelle for the summer holidays, staying with Lea's grandmother, he and Carmine drove down from Milan. Carlo began seeing Denise regularly. One night, he and Carmine took Denise out to a nightclub. They stayed out until 5 A.M. Denise's phone had run out of power, and she couldn't call her mother to tell her she would be home late. "When we dropped Denise back at her grandmother's house, Lea slapped Denise because she'd been so worried," said Carmine. "When we left, Carlo turned to me and said: 'That was totally uncalled for. That bitch has to die.'"

The next day, Carlo called Vito, Carmine, and Rosario Curcio together. He said they were going to kill Lea right away, as soon as possible, and he had a new plan for how to do it. Carmine would watch Lea's grandmother's apartment. As soon as Lea left to fetch water from the square, Carmine would call Carlo on a new burner phone that Vito had given him. Carlo would then arrive on the back of a motorcycle driven by Rosario and shoot Lea dead as they drove past; then he and Rosario would head immediately for the coast, dump the gun, and wash off any powder residue in the sea. In the event, Carmine did as he was told but Lea turned out to be buying cigarettes from the village shop. She was back in her apartment before Carlo and Rosario arrived.

Carlo just couldn't seem to kill Lea. He had tried and failed three times in five months. By now, his obsession was all-consuming. Enough people inside the 'Ndrangheta knew what he was planning so that if he didn't pull it off, he risked losing status. But as August turned to September, Carmine was surprised to observe a new calmness in Carlo. The reason, Carlo confided to him one day, was that he had finally figured out how to murder his wife.

Lea was beginning to trust him again, Carlo said. She was calling him and texting him all the time. "Carlo showed me text messages from Lea in which she had written that Nini—her nickname for Denise—wanted a little brother," said Carmine. "They were messages of love. I was amazed. Later they even went out for gelato together." Carlo calculated that if he could take his wife on a late-night date to Botricello, he could take all the time he wanted. The longer he waited, the more comfortable Lea felt, the easier it would be. "Carlo was very happy with himself," said Carmine. "He said now it would be so simple to kill her. He told me Lea was trapped."

In November 2009, Lea and Denise left for Florence to attend court. Initially Carlo thought he would try to kill Lea there. Then he told Carmine he had a better idea. He had convinced Lea and Denise to spend a few days with him in Milan. Carlo said they would kill Lea in the city where she had first betrayed him. There was a symmetry to the plan that pleased Carlo. He wanted all his men in on it.

———

ONCE LEA AND Denise arrived in Milan, said Carmine, "we followed Lea day and night, all the time." The plan, as in Campobasso, was to wait for the right moment, then kidnap Lea, try to find out what she had told the carabinieri in 1996 and 2002, then kill her and dispose of the body to make it look as if she had disappeared to Australia.

For four days, the gang played cat and mouse with Lea around Milan's streets. On one occasion, Carmine watched Lea enter a laundry and pulled over, ready to snatch her when she emerged, before deciding there were too many security cameras and the street was too busy. Another time, Carlo took Lea out to dinner and told his men to take her when she stepped outside for a cigarette, but it was a cold night and Lea stayed put. The following night, Carlo took Lea to dinner again and told Carmine, Vito, and Rosario to wait for the two of them in a quiet street near an underpass, ready to intercept the two of them and kill her on the spot when Carlo drove past. On the way over, however, Carlo ran a red light and was stopped by a carabiniere, so Carlo called it off. That was also the night that Carmine met Lea for the first time. A few hours after he was meant to have killed her, he found himself driving over to Lea's hotel at Carlo's request and giving her a small block of hash.

Carmine and Rosario began to think Carlo was about to be thwarted one more time. Rosario, for one, still believed that Lea was Carlo's private concern and not something with which the 'ndrina should be involved. Maybe Carlo would kill her this time. Maybe not. Right now it looked like he was dating her. Every 'Ndranghetista knew the clan had its hot and impetuous side, its machismo. But its activities were also based on cold calculation, especially when it came to matters like the murder of a clan daughter. Carlo's planning was all over the place. He affected calmness, but you could tell he was in turmoil. This was the kind of thing that could sink them all, said Rosario. He and Carmine should play no part in it.

But Carlo was insistent. The gang would have their last chance on November 24. Lea and Denise were due to take the 11:30 P.M. train back to Calabria. Carlo told his men he had come up with yet another plan. He had asked his friend Massimiliano Floreale if he could borrow the keys to Floreale's grandmother's apartment on Via San Vittore, on the edge of Milan's historic center. He had also arranged for Denise to have dinner with her cousins so that Lea and he would be alone again. Shortly after 6 P.M., Carlo picked up Denise at the Arch of Peace, near Sempione Park, and dropped her off at her cousins.' Then he set off to fetch Lea.

Around the same time, Carmine drove Vito to the apartment on San Vittore in a Volkswagen Passat he had stolen that day. When the pair arrived, Vito entered the apartment. Carmine's job was to stay outside. If anything was wrong, he was to signal by turning on his hazard lights. While waiting, Carmine called Rosario to arrange a time and a place to pick him up. But when Rosario answered, he said he couldn't come. He was with his girlfriend and she was in one of her moods. Rosario said he couldn't shake her. It was clear he was lying. "You should stay out of it, too," he told Carmine.

Just after 6:30 P.M., Carlo picked up Lea from Sempione Park. After she climbed into the Chrysler, he told her he had to drop in briefly at an apartment a few streets away. Shortly before 7 P.M., Carmine saw Carlo and Lea pull up on San Vittore in the Chrysler. The pair parked and got out. Carlo rang the bell to the apartment. Vito buzzed him in. Lea entered, then Carlo.

Fifteen minutes later, around 7:15 P.M., Carmine saw Carlo exit the apartment, walk quickly to the Chrysler, and leave. "He didn't say a word," said Carmine. Vito left the apartment seconds later and climbed into Carmine's Passat.

"We did it," said Vito, breathing heavily.

Vito gave Carmine a mobile. It was Lea's, he said. "Get rid of it right away before anyone calls," Vito instructed. Vito then left on foot.

Carlo and Vito now had to construct their alibis. Carlo also had to try to persuade Denise that Lea had just upped and left. That left it to Carmine and Rosario to get rid of Lea's body.

Carmine exited the car, ripped the SIM card out of Lea's phone, and threw it into a drain, followed by the phone battery. He threw the rest of the phone in a trash can. He got back into the Passat and phoned Rosario. Carlo had evidently called Rosario in the meantime. Rosario now said he would help after all, and Carmine drove over to pick him up.

Looking for somewhere to dispose of the body, the two men spent more than an hour trying to locate the keys to a warehouse owned by a friend in San Fruttuoso on the outskirts of Monza, about half an hour away by car. Unsuccessful, they drove back to San Vittore and ascended the stairs to the apartment. Carmine opened the door, turned on the light, "and there was Lea Garofalo's body on the ground," he said. "She had a sofa over her."

Carmine wrenched back the sofa. He scarcely recognized Lea. "She had bruises all over her face. Her mouth was bloody, like it had been crushed. There was blood all over her nose and neck and a pool of blood on the floor. The clothes across her chest were ripped. There was a green cord around her neck with which she had been strangled and which had cut into her neck so deeply that it had disappeared. I knew the cord. It was from the curtains in my apartment."

Whatever doubts Carmine and Rosario had once harbored, the ferocity of Lea's killing erased them. They trussed the body with a sheet, just in case Lea was merely unconscious. Then they lifted it into a large cardboard box they had brought along. They scrubbed the floor with hot water and rags. Then they threw the rags into the box, used duct tape to seal it, and heaved it downstairs to the ground floor. Carmine waited in the hallway with the box while Rosario went to fetch the Passat. Then the two men lifted the box out through the apartment block's front door, down the street, and into the back of the car.

With nowhere to dump the body, Carmine and Rosario drove to the home of Floreale's parents. They dropped off the keys to the apartment, left the Passat locked in the street, and went home to change clothes. A few hours later, by which time it was nearly midnight, Carmine called Floreale and asked to meet him at the apartment on San Vittore. Once both men had arrived, Carmine apologized to Floreale that the floor of his grandmother's apartment might be a little dirty. Spotting a piece of the green cord on the floor, Carmine immediately burned it in an ashtray. He then noticed a spot of blood on the sofa and told Floreale that the two of them should dump the couch in the street, which they did, next to some rubbish bins. Floreale asked no questions.

Around 1:30 A.M., Carmine went to see Carlo at the Green Dragon. Carlo said Denise was asleep at Viale Montello. Carmine updated Carlo on the cleanup. Carlo said he now had the warehouse keys and that Carmine and Rosario should take Lea's body there the next morning. Carlo and Carmine then went back to Carmine's apartment. Before they turned in, Carlo asked if he could borrow some antiseptic cream for a cut on his finger. He showed Carmine the mark.

"Lea," he said, smiling.

THE NEXT MORNING, November 25, 2009, Vito and Rosario drove Lea's body in the Passat to the warehouse outside Monza. Carmine went in a separate van. By the time he arrived, Vito had left to clock in for work at a construction site. Rosario and Carmine took Carmine's van to fill up a ten-liter jerry can with gasoline. Then they drove back and lifted the box containing Lea's body out of the Passat and into the warehouse. "We took a large metal trunk that was in the warehouse," said Carmine. "We opened the box with the body in it and shoved the body into the metal trunk. You could just see her shoes sticking out. We shook some of the gas on the body and lit it. We threw the cardboard box on top."

Carmine said he and Rosario watched Lea's body smolder for an hour. "It didn't burn well," he said. "At one point, Rosario said that maybe it wasn't working because there wasn't enough air getting in. So I took an axe and knocked several holes in the bottom of the trunk. But even with the new holes, the body burned very slowly." Carmine left Rosario and went to find Vito to ask him for advice. Unsuccessful, he returned to find that Rosario had moved the body out of the trunk with a section of scaffolding and dropped it on top of some wooden pallets, placed more wood on top, then, after adding more gas, set light to everything again. "The body was much more destroyed now," said Carmine. "The head was almost gone. There was a lot of smoke and a strong smell of burned meat. Next door, there were some gypsies burning leaves and at some point one of them, a woman, came up to the fence and asked if we could give her a pallet for their fire. I passed them one through a hole in the fence. She couldn't have failed to notice the smell of cooking meat. She didn't ask any questions."

Neither Carmine nor Rosario had slept more than a few minutes the night before, and by 1 P.M. exhaustion was setting in. "Before leaving, we put what was left of the corpse in a small pit that had already been dug in the warehouse grounds. Only a part of her chest and her legs were left. But there were many bone fragments, which we collected with a shovel and dumped in the trunk. Finally, I chopped up what was left of the body into small pieces with the axe. It was all blackened bones and flesh. Then we covered it with earth and a metal sheet."

Carmine and Rosario left to sleep for a few hours. They returned that afternoon with Vito, who sent Carmine to buy five more liters of gas. The three men then shoveled what remained of Lea's body back into the metal trunk, loaded some extra wood on it, doused it in gas once more, and set light to it a final time. They watched it burn down to the embers, broke what remained into shards by beating it with the back of the shovel, and left.

That night, Carmine caught up with Carlo in the Green Dragon. He was with Denise. Carmine told Carlo Lea's body was nearly gone. Carlo told Carmine about Denise's five-hour interview with the carabinieri. That was another headache they would have to deal with, he said.

The next morning, Carmine and Vito returned to the warehouse one last time. They scooped the ash and burned embers into a wheelbarrow, washed and scrubbed the metal trunk, and threw all the remains they could find into a nearby manhole. The following day, November 27, Carmine met the friend who owned the warehouse to return the keys to him. "Finished?" asked the friend. "All done," confirmed Carmine.

Carmine never spoke again to Carlo or any of the other men about those three days. The only time Carlo brought up the matter was in March 2010, when he heard that Denise had spoken to the carabinieri and accused him of murdering Lea. If that was true, said Carlo, "then we all know what we have to do."

CARMINE OFFERED TO show the warehouse to Tatangelo and the carabinieri forensics team. It was October 2012, almost three years since Lea had died. The forensics officers took fragments of dust from the warehouse and, using a bulldozer, dug into the soil and excavated the manhole. Over several days, they were able to gather more than three kilos of material, which they transported to their laboratory in Milan. Processing the samples took several more days. But by early November, they were able to confirm the presence of 2,812 bone fragments, as well as a dental screw with which Lea had been fitted in 2007, and microscopic parts of the necklace and braided white-and-yellow gold bracelet that Carlo had given Lea when they first met.

Denise had initially been distraught at the knowledge that she had fallen in love with the man who had disposed of her mother's body. Now she found comfort in his contrition. When Tatangelo brought Carmine and the other defendants back to court in April 2013, Denise listened to his testimony throughout. Carmine didn't spare her feelings with his descriptions of what he had done to her mother's body. But it was clear he felt compelled by devotion to her. "I want to say that this is a very difficult day for me," he said. Carmine said that in prison he had learned that family was nothing without love, and that love conquered any other allegiance. "I am not accusing ordinary people or strangers but people with whom I shared three years of my life, some of them from the same family. I made this choice out of love for Denise. Her father does not love her. Her family does not love her. But she owns my heart. It sickens me to think that I am contributing to her pain, but it is also thanks to her example that I am here today." Carmine said he was aware he was signing his own death warrant by speaking. "I know I'm cannon fodder now," he said. "Sooner or later, Carlo will kill me." Still, he added, he had no choice. "I am really in love," he said.

Carmine's confession was striking as much for the reasons why he had spoken out as what he said. The code stressed discipline and the suffocation of feeling. Hardening their hearts was how 'Ndranghetisti won. By outkilling and out-terrorizing, they could outlast their rivals. And yet here was Carmine, a drug dealer working for one of the 'Ndrangheta's hardest men, speaking out because he couldn't contain his tenderness. Even in the 'Ndrangheta's darkest depths, a faint light still shone.

When Lea's former lawyer Annalisa Pisano read about Carmine's testimony in the newspapers, she found herself reeling for different reasons. For three years, she had dreamed about Lea calling out her name, surrounded by flames in a warehouse. "I thought I had to be wrong," she said. "I'm not the kind of person who believes in that sort of thing. But when I heard this was how it ended for her, in the worst possible way, of course I remembered my dream right away."

Initially, Annalisa was horrified by what her nightmare might mean. Had she deserted Lea? Had Lea died calling for her help? In time, however, she came to think of it differently. According to Carmine's evidence, Lea had died long before the flames consumed her. If there was any truth to her dream, Annalisa began to think it was as a testament to the bond between her and her client. "I began thinking that, in a way, this was some sort of consolation," she said. "If her last moments really were spent thinking about me, then maybe she knew that I loved her."

XXV

G IUSEPPINA'S EVIDENCE HAD led to the arrest and trial of sixty-four members of the Pesce 'ndrina. So detailed was it, and so numerous the charges to which it led, that the trial lasted for a further year after she testified. But shortly after 6 P.M. on May 3, 2013, after seventeen days of deliberation, the three judges filed back into court in Palmi to deliver their verdict.

Twenty-two of the accused were acquitted. Forty-two were convicted. Three-quarters of the sentences were for more than ten years. The most severe went to Giuseppina's immediate family. Her uncle, clan head Antonino Pesce, was sentenced to twenty-eight years. Giuseppina's father, Salvatore, received twenty-seven years and seven months. Her husband, Rocco Palaia, was given twenty-one years and two months; her mother, Angela Ferraro, thirteen years and five months; her sister Marina Pesce twelve years and ten months; and her brother Francesco twelve years. Ten more Pesces, two more Ferraros, and one other Palaia were convicted. Even Giuseppina's eighty-year-old grandmother, Giuseppa Bonarrigo, was sentenced to a year and eight months for receiving stolen goods. The only clemency shown was to Giuseppina, sentenced to four years and four months for mafia association, most of which she had already served.[1] "The Pesces were destroyed," said Giovanni Musarò. "There was barely a single one left walking around Rosarno."[2]

While most of the family absorbed their ruin in silence, a few

Pesces found the humiliation too much. Giuseppina's younger sister, Marina, whom Alessandra described as blessed with "the face of an angel," began howling and screaming and tearing her hair when the sentences were read out. "She completely freaked out," said Alessandra. Outside court, grandmother Bonarrigo—one of the few Pesces allowed bail—growled to reporters that real Pesce women went with their men to the grave. Not long afterward, Alessandra arrived at work at the Palace of Justice in Reggio to find a group of 'Ndrangheta wives from Rosarno staging a protest outside. "It was surreal," she said. "They had signs which read 'Shame on you,' 'The sentences are unjust,' and 'The innocent are in jail.' Some had even chained themselves to the gates." In all seriousness, apparently, Europe's biggest mafia was presenting itself as a victim of the state. Alessandra assumed the demonstration was also designed to send a message. "The idea was to show that real Calabrian women were still with the 'Ndrangheta. But I saw it as a sign of desperation, of weakness. You really need to prove something that you shouldn't need to? You really need to demonstrate something that a few years ago everyone would have taken for granted?"

The Pesces were broken and their rule of Rosarno was over. Two weeks after the verdicts, Giuseppe Pesce, the last *'ndrina* boss still on the run, turned himself in to begin his sentence of twelve years and six months. "Enough," he said as he walked into the Rosarno carabinieri station. "I'm sick of running. Let's finish it here and now."

Still, the people of Rosarno took longer to digest their new reality. The Pesces had ruled the town for decades, and most of the bosses were still alive and still sending their boys to collect *pizzo* from shopkeepers and restaurant owners. But people noticed that the price of extortion was falling. A violent reaction from the Pesces was inevitable but when it came, it was pitiful: a grenade, which slightly injured the brother of Giuseppina's boyfriend, Domenico

Costantino, when he opened a farm gate to which it was strapped. Maybe the Pesces *were* finished. It was hard to believe. But then so was the sight, little more than a year after the end of the maxi-trial, of a bulldozer driving through the front door of Giuseppina's grandmother's old house, the family's former meeting place. The authorities had confiscated the house in 2011 but had struggled for years to find a contractor willing to do the work. Now Gaetano Saffioti, a builder from Palmi, told reporters he was delighted to raze the Pesces' palace to the ground. So happy, in fact, he had done it for free. "The fight for legality is won with deeds, not words," he said.[3]

Watching as one of Europe's most powerful crime syndicates was pulled apart brick by brick, Alessandra found herself wondering whether it was the Pesces' obsession with honor that had ultimately doomed them. It was almost as if the family had died of shame. "If a woman betrays her family, it has a huge resonance," she said. "It means the family is unable to control its women." To an 'Ndrangheta crime family, it seemed there was nothing worse.

LESS THAN A month after the Pesce convictions came new verdicts in the Lea Garofalo case. Carmine's confession had exposed Carlo's lie that Lea was still alive. When proceedings reopened in Milan on April 9, 2013, Carlo made a desperate attempt to regain the initiative, announcing from the dock at the end of the first day: "President, I wish to speak!"

His lawyer, Daniel Sussman Steinberg, appeared stunned. Carlo had been clutching a piece of paper all day. Now it was clear why: he, Carlo Cosco, was breaking omertà. After a brief consultation between Carlo and Steinberg, the lawyer announced that Carlo would like to make a "spontaneous statement," and Carlo was escorted to the witness box.

Speaking in halting Italian, he read: "Madam President, and gentlemen of the court, I accept full responsibility for the murder of Lea Garofalo."

In the courtroom, nothing moved.

"I wanted to do so during the original trial but circumstances prevented me," Carlo continued. "My daughter hates me and deservedly so, because I killed her mother. But I cannot endure the shame of the accusation that I want to kill her. For me, it is inconceivable that my daughter is under anyone else's protection. From whom? I would give my life for her. Woe betide anyone who touches my daughter!"

It was an astonishing outburst. There was, after all, no reason for it. Carlo had already been convicted of Lea's murder. Legally, his confession changed nothing. But psychologically, it changed everything. Carlo, it seemed, had cracked. The hardest of the 'Ndrangheta's hard men had let his feelings show. He was an 'Ndranghetista, a *capo*, a *santista*. He was a drug smuggler, an extortionist, and a murderer. But first and foremost, it now appeared, he was a father. "I hope one day that my daughter will forgive me," said Carlo. "I live in hope of her pardon."

Others, however, perceived an altogether different message. When Carlo began reading his letter, he had scratched his ear. Then he scratched his eye. A little while later, he touched his finger to his lips. To those able to read the signals, Carlo was sending another message to the 'Ndrangheta. *Listen to me*, he was saying. *Watch me. You'll hear and see that I will say nothing.* Carlo wasn't confessing. He was offering reassurance and proposing a bargain. *I am responsible for all this*, he was saying. *Whatever the price, I will pay it. But I will not collaborate. And in return, nobody touches my daughter.*[4]

Now that Carlo had finally opened his mouth, however, he seemed to find it difficult to close. Over the next few weeks, he spoke expansively about his early married life with Lea. He explained the attack in Campobasso by saying he had asked Sabatino to beat Lea to "teach her a lesson" after she threatened his mother. He described meeting his daughter again after seven years. "*This* became my obsession," he said. "To be with my daughter, to know where she was. Not to kill her mother. I never intended that."

Carlo's testimony was all about love. Carlo loved his daughter. Carlo loved his mother. When Lea hurt Carlo's mother, Carlo had only asked Sabatino to slap Lea around a little because, really, Carlo said, he loved Lea, too.

It was the same when Carlo killed her. "I really didn't mean to," he said. "That morning, November 24, 2009, I went to get Denise and her mother in the hotel. When I saw them, I had an idea to surprise Denise. She had told me she wanted to live in Milan. So I thought I'll ask my friends for a key to their apartment to give to Denise as somewhere where she could come and go."

A few hours later, Carlo took Lea to show her the apartment on Via San Vittore where their daughter could stay. But Lea had misunderstood. "When she saw the apartment, she was angry," said Carlo. "She told me I was a liar because I told her I had nothing, no money, and actually I had an apartment. The truth was that it wasn't mine. I lived with Venturino. But Lea told me that I was an asshole and that I would never see Denise again."

Carlo caught his breath.

"I had a fit of rage, Madam President," he said. "I punched her. Twice. She fell and hit her head on the couch. I grabbed her by the shoulders and this time she fell and hit her head on the floor. Even before I saw the blood, I knew she was dead."

It was all just a terrible accident, Carlo was saying. One of those things that happened when a bighearted husband and father was overcome by emotion. "All this happened because I loved Lea," said Carlo. "If I hadn't loved her, nothing like this would ever have happened. But when she threatened me with never seeing my daughter again, I couldn't see my love for her anymore.

Because I love Denise above all else. For me that's the greatest torment. Denise must know that I care for her. She must know the truth." Trying to rationalize his client's intervention, Steinberg, the lawyer, described Carlo as split by a "lacerating internal struggle," which prompted him to lash out at Lea but acquitted him of premeditated murder.

Prosecutor Marcello Tatangelo was unconvinced. "You're only talking now because Lea Garofalo's body has been found," he said. Carlo hadn't shown remorse at the time, he added. Quite the opposite. Days after Lea's murder, Carlo had hosted a party in Pagliarelle to toast her death under the guise of an eighteenth birthday party for Denise. But Tatangelo was curious nonetheless. "Why speak up now?" he asked.

"Eh," said Carlo with a shrug. "People said things that weren't right. You mentioned acid. You said I hated my daughter's mother. How could I let that go?"

Unmoved by Carlo's protestations of love, on May 29, 2013, appeals judge Anna Conforti, another of the most senior women in Italy's judiciary, confirmed life sentences against Carlo and his brother Vito, Rosario Curcio, and Massimo Sabatino.[5] Carmine's sentence was reduced to twenty-five years. Giuseppe Cosco was acquitted but remained in prison, since by now he was also serving an unrelated ten-year sentence for drug trafficking. Five months later, using evidence given by Lea seventeen years earlier, seventeen 'Ndranghetisti were arrested in Pagliarelle, Petilia Policastro, and Crotone, charged with seven murders, possessing illegal weapons, and drug dealing—charges that related to the clan feud that had raged in the Calabrian hills between 1989 and 2007.[6]

Outside court on the day Carlo's life sentence was confirmed, Enza told a crowd of supporters, "Denise thanks you all. That you are all here gives her strength." Denise could now finally bury her mother, added Enza, and the funeral would be in Milan. "This is the city where she was killed," said Enza. "But it's also the place where everyone finally mobilized to fight the mafia."

ONLY MARIA CONCETTA Cacciola's case remained unresolved.

Partial closure came in Palmi in early July 2013, in the same courtroom where the Pesces had been humbled. Giuseppina testified in Concetta's case, breaking down when asked to describe her friend and recalling how "terrified" Concetta was of her brother Giuseppe. "She told me if you knew him, then you knew he could kill her," she said. "She was forbidden to leave the house, to go out, or to have friends. She never went to a party. She was never allowed to have fun."

On July 13, 2013, Concetta's father, mother, and brother were found guilty of provoking her suicide. Michele Cacciola was given six years; Giuseppe, five; and her mother, Anna Rosalba Lazzaro, two.

If Alessandra and Giovanni were unhappy with the lightness of the sentences, the judge was, too. "The court had started doubting that Concetta's death was suicide," said prosecutor Giuseppe Creazzo. The judge indicated he had been dissatisfied at being unable to impose the kind of sentence that a conviction for murder would allow. "So he sent the case back to the prosecutors for them to investigate further if it was murder."

Sandro Dolce, who had interviewed Lea Garofalo in 2002 and was now assistant prosecutor in Palmi, was ordered to investigate the Cacciolas' two lawyers, Gregorio Cacciola and Vittorio Pisani. After seizing their computer terminals, he found proof that Concetta's statement had been through various drafts on their computers before she even returned to Rosarno—proof of a conspiracy to force her to retract. In February 2014, the two lawyers were arrested. On

September 8, Vittorio Pisani sent word that he wanted to confess. Alessandra and Giovanni had him moved to the *pentiti* prison at Paliano. They spoke to him a few days later.

Pisani told the two prosecutors that he had started working for the Cacciolas in June 2011, a few months before Concetta died. He said the family had initially approached him because they suspected Concetta was having an affair with a policeman. They wanted him to use his contacts on the force to investigate. "It was an abnormal request," said Pisani, "but I took it because I had money troubles and I didn't want to lose the chance of working for a family like the Cacciolas."

Later that month the carabinieri discovered one of the Cacciolas' bunkers, then a second. The Cacciolas and Belloccos were convinced the information had come from Concetta. The Belloccos insisted that she be made to return to Rosarno and retract. By this time, the Cacciolas, impatient for a result, had begun threatening Pisani. When Concetta returned to Rosarno, Pisani was under no illusion that she, too, was being coerced. On August 12, he witnessed Concetta record her retraction. When she died eight days later, he knew the family was responsible. For a year and a half, Pisani had tried to bury his conscience. The Cacciolas and the Belloccos were unimpressed, however, and Pisani became convinced he was in danger. "I was scared," he told the prosecutors. "And I needed to be able to look myself in the mirror again."

"Tell us, why was so much attention paid to this one woman?" asked Giovanni.

"As a warning," replied Pisani. "It was to say: 'Enough now.'"

The identity of Concetta's killer remained a mystery. But the case was still open and the prosecutors were inching closer. On July 30, 2015, the Court of Appeal in Reggio Calabria increased Michele's sentence to eight years and eight months, Giuseppe's to seven years and four months, and Anna Rosalba Lazzaro's to five years and six months.

XXVI

I N OCTOBER 2014, Alessandra and her husband packed up their tiny apartment in the roof of the carabinieri barracks in Reggio and moved back to Milan. Alessandra had been promoted to deputy public prosecutor in Italy's financial capital. Most of the rest of the anti-mafia team had already left Calabria. Giuseppe Pignatone, Michele Prestipino, Giovanni Musarò, and Renato Cortese, the flying squad chief, were all taking up more senior positions in Rome.

The reassignments made sense. Some of the biggest 'Ndrangheta clans had been smashed, especially on the stronghold of the Gioia Tauro plain. The cost to the prosecutors of their success was an increased threat to their lives. Alessandra, who like Pignatone and Prestipino had lived inside close protection for years, knew she had added new names to the list of those who wanted to kill her. Of those she knew about, there was Giuseppina's father, Salvatore, who had threatened her in court, and Concetta's mother, Anna Rosalba Lazzaro, who had been bugged cursing Alessandra as "that bitch, that bastard bitch. I want her dead!"

Giovanni Musarò was another prosecutor now forced to make peace with the idea that he was fighting for a nation in which he no longer really lived. In 2010, in an unrelated case, Giovanni had ordered the arrest of the entire Gallico 'ndrina in Palmi, a total of thirty-two 'Ndranghetisti, including an eighty-four-year-old grandmother. Subsequently, clan head Domenico Gallico suffered the humiliation of watching his 'ndrina turn their backs to him in court. In

October 2012, Gallico asked to meet Giovanni in his cell in Viterbo prison, north of Rome. Giovanni was mystified, but agreed nonetheless. "It was a very strange situation," he told a parliamentary inquiry later. "I was shown to a very small room. When Gallico entered, he was alone without an escort and uncuffed. He came around to my side of the desk and said: 'Dottore, what a pleasure that we can finally meet face-to-face. May I have the honor of shaking your hand?'"

When Giovanni extended his right hand, Gallico pretended to do the same, then with his left hit Giovanni across the face, breaking his nose. "I fell from the chair," said Giovanni. "As I lay there up against the wall, he kicked and punched me maybe fifty or sixty times." During the attack, Giovanni remembered thinking: *If I don't block his punches, he's going to break my neck. He's going to kill me.* After thirty seconds, several guards pulled Gallico off, kicking and screaming. "Are you crazy?" asked one, pinning him to the floor. Gallico pointed at Giovanni. "Ask him what he did to me and my family!" he howled. "Ask him what he did to me!"

Bodyguards were posted outside Giovanni's door in the hospital that night. They had not left his side since. Not long afterward Marcello Fondacaro, an 'Ndrangheta informer, told Giovanni that the same Bellocco boss who had ordered Concetta be made to retract had also made a plan to kill Giovanni and his boss, Prestipino. "The Belloccos thought Maria Concetta Cacciola's retraction would have ended the story," said Giovanni. "They were very angry when that didn't happen. Giuseppe Bellocco, in particular, was known as a very dangerous human being who held grudges and harbored great resentment." According to Fondacaro, Bellocco planned to ambush Giovanni and Prestipino with gunmen and explosives as the two prosecutors drove to court. "He knew I drove to Palmi twice a week during a trial I was dealing with," said Giovanni. "He knew the route, the color of my armored car and my escort car, and that

Prestipino would have been following in his armored car, with another escort car with him. He'd even asked permission from the Gallicos to carry out the attack." The double assassination failed only because the trial in Palmi was unexpectedly adjourned. And while, to some, gunmen *and* explosives might have seemed like overkill, to the prosecutors it underlined how serious the 'Ndrangheta were about revenge. "In Calabria they do it well or not at all," said Giovanni.

It was time to get out. None of the anti-mafia prosecutors or their families could expect to live a normal life again. It was, in a way, their own life sentence. But Alessandra, for one, was finding inspiration from an unexpected source. "Giuseppina knows what she did is another death sentence," she said. "Her betrayal has to be punished with death and it has to be her brother, the same blood, who kills her to restore the family honor. And one day, he will get out." But Alessandra said it had been years since she had seen Giuseppina doubt herself. "For Giuseppina," she said, "what she did was an act of love toward her children." In the end, the contest between The Family and her own family had been no contest at all. "She's fine," said Alessandra. "Actually, I think she's happy."

FROM THE MOMENT 150 years earlier when a group of southern criminals met a band of revolutionary freemasons in jail and decided to veneer their thuggish criminality with myth and legend, the 'Ndrangheta had shown itself to be nothing if not adaptable. Calabria would always be the 'Ndrangheta's homeland. There were still plenty of *'ndrine* to pursue there and the trafficking, extortion, corruption, and murder would continue. But as the prosecutors' Calabrian campaign against the 'Ndrangheta began to wind down, new surveillance evidence made clear that the center of gravity for Italian organized crime was moving to the north of the country and even further afield. The change made sense. Italy was the only country in the world that even had a law of mafia association. Few other countries allowed such intrusive surveillance. Plenty of them made it far easier to legitimize criminal wealth by buying assets like bonds, shares, property, and businesses.

And if the 'Ndrangheta was moving, it was also changing shape. The Calabria prosecutors had made a point of mapping and destroying the 'Ndrangheta's command structure. For the organization, the intelligent response was to dismantle it. Prosecutors began reporting the emergence of a more informal, decentralized, diffuse group, a loose association, an ad hoc gathering, even something as ephemeral as a state of mind. They likened its penetration of Italy's legitimate economy and, beyond it, Frankfurt, London, and New York to liquid poured on a sponge.

And you couldn't squeeze the world. In their new positions, many of the prosecutors found their time in Calabria quickly began to feel like the golden years. Like the swordfish hunters of the Strait of Messina, the Calabrian prosecutors had harpooned a monster and forced it to the surface. But now the creature was disappearing back into the deep, vanishing into the folds of an international financial system that not only tolerated secrecy but, in the case of the $20 trillion offshore banking industry, actively depended on it. The prosecutors often felt like they were in a losing race against time. Hundreds of billions of 'Ndrangheta euros and dollars had been already successfully laundered beyond reach or reproach. And to the prosecutors' frustration, in the world of frictionless global money movements, their fastidious objections were often viewed as pedantry. Franco Roberti, head of Italy's anti-mafia and antiterrorism office, lamented the lack of cooperation his investigators received in London or New York or Hong Kong, let alone the centers of secret banking on paradise islands around the world. Foreign governments "don't want to believe that the problem of the 'Ndrangheta is their problem, too," he said. "They want to believe that their money doesn't stink." Roberti was pessimistic about the chances of beating a global mafia in a world where politics was subordinate to business. "Business dictates and politicians follow, and this has facilitated the absorption of mafia money and influence around the world," he said. A world in which any idea of the common good had been replaced with greed and yawning inequality was one, said Roberti, whose gates were wide open to mafiosi. He called it the Snow White syndrome. "Nobody wants to look in the mirror," he said.

That kind of thinking could lead a prosecutor down a dark path, as Alessandra knew. A world where financial and political scandal had become depressingly routine was one in which it was all too easy to conclude that what the prosecutors were really fighting was the night in human nature. The 'Ndrangheta wouldn't be able to corrupt business and politics unless businessmen and politicians already had the potential for it. Hadn't the serpent admirers of Milan understood centuries ago that enlightenment and darkness walked hand in hand? And if family itself was a form of corruption, as the mafia posited, then what chance did legality have in any country, let alone Italy? "We can't fight the 'Ndrangheta just by putting people in jail," said Alessandra. "We need a cultural change. We need a change in people's minds." The prosecutors had no way to assist that effort. Barricaded behind their steel doors and bulletproof windows, all they could do was watch.

NONE OF THAT would diminish what had been accomplished in Calabria. The 'Ndrangheta was reeling. However nimble they were, the clans could not adjust to betrayal. "That's an unacceptable issue for them," said Prestipino. "It's unbearable. It threatens their entire existence." The effect of the Calabrian campaign would be felt for generations. Prestipino's experience in Sicily had taught him that once a mafia's invincibility cracked, the floodgates opened. In Sicily, hundreds of mafiosi had come forward to testify. "They never recovered," he said.

In the hill villages and small towns of Calabria, the 'Ndrangheta was still ruthlessly punishing disloyalty. In February 2012, a thirty-year-old man called Fabrizio Pioli who was having an extramarital affair with a mafioso's daughter was beaten to death with sticks outside Rosarno. In August 2013, Francesca Bellocco and Domenico Cacciola, whose affair had scandalized two of Rosarno's biggest crime families, disappeared. Such violent reprisals discouraged the flow of *pentiti*. But a steady stream was under way. By the end of 2015, the judiciary could count 164 *pentiti* and twenty-nine witnesses who had testified against the 'Ndrangheta. That was hardly a cascade. But given that five years earlier even a single 'Ndrangheta *pentito* was almost unheard of, it felt significant.

Perhaps most remarkable was the number of 'Ndrangheta wives following the three women's example: fifteen, more than had ever testified in four decades of Cosa Nostra trials. Di Bella's youth court, in particular, had become a magnet for dissident 'Ndrangheta women. As sons—more than thirty by the end of 2016—turned against their fathers, mothers chose their children over their husbands. "It's a phenomenon we didn't predict," said di Bella. "Many women realize these measures are not punishing their children but protecting them. They come secretly and ask us to send their children far away." One woman who wrote to di Bella in confidence in November 2015 was typical. Her husband had been convicted of murder. Her father, cousin, and eleven-year-old nephew had all been killed. Her two teenage boys, she wrote, "are rebellious and violent, hanging around with bad guys, and fascinated by the 'Ndrangheta and guns. My son Rosario thinks jail is an honor that will win him respect. Please send my children away. The thought tears me apart but it is the only solution. In my family, there is no one—no one—I can trust."

This first act of rebellion by an 'Ndrangheta mother sometimes grew into something more. Di Bella said the youth courts could add another ten 'Ndrangheta women to the fifteen who had testified in the adult courts. As a result of his success, di Bella's program was being rolled out across Italy. It helped that at the same time, such global figures as Malala Yousafzai and Michelle Obama were making women's emancipation a worldwide issue. Di Bella found himself wondering whether Italy might have finally found its way to a mafia-free future. "We're opening up these disagreements inside families that were previously thought to be impenetrable," he said. "We're a crack in the monolith, a light in the dark, a bright threat to the whole mafia family system."

At times, the momentum was palpable. In June 2014, Pope Francis further splintered the mafia's consensus when he traveled to Calabria and, before a crowd of a hundred thousand, excommunicated all mafiosi, denouncing the 'Ndrangheta as an example of "the adoration of evil and contempt for the common good." Francis later followed his decree by condemning the Camorra in Naples and visiting *pentiti* at Paliano. The change felt seismic, said di Bella, and to the 'Ndrangheta more than anyone. "They can feel the ground moving under their feet," he said.

IN THEIR NEW offices in Milan and Rome, asked by their staff how it had been in the south, Alessandra and Giovanni would tell stories about Calabria.

Giovanni's favorite tale was about hope. He'd been listening to wiretaps of the Cacciolas one day, he said, when he heard them discussing a family called the Secolos, whom the Belloccos were gradually ruining through loan-sharking. It reminded him of a con-

versation he had had with Concetta. She had told him about the
bind the Secolos were in and how the matriarch, Stefania Secolo,
had asked Concetta if she could help them. Concetta had asked her
father to intervene but he had dismissed her pleas. Giovanni wanted
to know more. "So I called Stefania Secolo in for a meeting," he said.
"And in the days before she was due to come in, we also began listening to her phone. Her brothers and everyone else were saying to
her: 'Don't say anything! Don't honor the memory of someone who
cannot come back to life! Don't be a hero! Heroes die!' But on February 28, 2012, she came to me and told me exactly what happened,
and with her evidence, we arrested the Belloccos and put them in
jail." Giovanni sighed. It was "such a beautiful story," he said. "Stefania Secolo spoke out because her friend Concetta had reminded
her how a person should behave and how they could be free. Her
friend had been killed for it. Yet Stefania still spoke." From his five
years in Calabria, "that's the day that stays with me." There was all
the hope in the world in that one day, he said.

Alessandra was happy to talk about Giuseppina. But when people asked, she would often tell them the story of Giuseppina Multari. Just before Christmas in 2012, a few months after Giuseppina
Pesce had resumed her cooperation and was preparing to testify
against her family, a letter addressed to her arrived at the Palace of
Justice in Reggio. The writer "expressed her support for Giuseppina
and urged her to believe in the institutions of the state and the
people around her," said Alessandra. "The letter read: 'Go for it!
Be brave!'" It was signed "Giuseppina Multari, protected witness."

"I was curious," said Alessandra. "Who was this woman who
had sent this very special letter? She was in the witness program
and I'd never even heard of her." Alessandra searched through the
Palace of Justice archives, looking for records of a Multari. Eventually she found a letter Multari had written to the carabinieri in 2006
and some statements she had made in 2008. Alessandra read how

Giuseppina Multari was Concetta's cousin by marriage. Her husband, Antonio Cacciola, was notorious in the *'ndrina* for dipping into his own drug supplies. He was also having an affair. One night in November 2005, Multari and Antonio had a fight, Antonio stormed out—and Giuseppina never saw him again. "Officially it was a suicide, but Giuseppina Multari was convinced his family had killed him," said Alessandra. "And after her husband's death, she was kept at home by his family like a slave. She could not go out. She could not drop off her children at school. She was only allowed to go to the cemetery."

One night, the Cacciola men left the house to go to a wedding. Finally alone, Giuseppina fled. She walked to the coast. "She was going to drown herself in the sea," said Alessandra. "But suddenly her phone went off, and it was her brother Angelo. She told him she was trying to kill herself. He came and found her." By the time Angelo arrived, his sister was suffering from hypothermia. He drove her to the hospital. When Angelo asked her why she was trying to commit suicide, she told him about the Cacciolas and the beatings and how she was living in a virtual prison. "I am going to do something for you," Angelo replied. "I am going to help you."

"The brother left," said Alessandra. "And *he* never came back."

After six more months confined to her in-laws' home, Giuseppina managed to sneak a letter to the carabinieri. As a result, in 2008, she made several statements against the Cacciolas and was taken into witness protection. "But no one ever acted on her evidence!" exclaimed Alessandra. "I decided to go to see her. And when she saw me, she burst into tears. 'I've been waiting six years for someone to come and talk to me,' she said."

Giuseppina described the Rosarno clans and the Cacciolas' empire in a series of statements that eventually ran to several hundred pages. A dozen 'Ndranghetisti were later convicted. But what was especially striking about the case, said Alessandra, was Giuseppina

Multari's faith in herself. Even though the state had let her down, she had held on to her conviction and her courage. "The best part?" said Alessandra. "Some of the men who kept her in that house are now serving time for slavery." It was, she added, a medieval conviction for medieval men.

IT WAS LEA's story above all, however, that moved Italy. If Concetta represented tragedy, and Giuseppina Pesce embodied resilience, then Lea was both. Here was a woman born into the mafia who had tried all her life to escape it. Trapped even deeper by marriage, she discovered the strength to fight in her love for her daughter, before being let down by the state, and trapped by a husband pretending to fall in love with her again. It was an epic melodrama of such unbelievable twists and turns that people seemed to turn up at the commemorations of her life that were held across the country from 2013 just to check that what they had heard was true.

There was something else, though. After her death, a number of pictures of Lea and Denise found their way into the newspapers. There was Lea smiling through long, dark hair, or sitting on a rock by the beach with Denise on her knee, or holding Denise aloft in a city piazza, or smoking a cigarette in sunglasses on the beach, or at the stove in Bergamo on the run with Denise. People began to feel they knew Lea. Before them was a whole life, from girlhood to marriage to motherhood, from love to fear, in the city and on the beach, in the north and the south. In time, Lea's story became one of the few ever to truly unite Italy. Posters of her face became a staple on walls across the country. There were documentaries and anti-mafia rallies, marches and newspaper profiles, plays and books and a television movie. Parks, bridges, piazzas, and roads were named after her. Plaques were erected in Bergamo and Boiano and next to the warehouse outside Monza where she was buried. In Milan, a plot was selected for Lea's remains in the Cimitero Monumentale beside the city's most illustrious citizens.[1] A monument was erected in Petilia depicting a ball splitting a rock in two. In his speech unveiling the statue, the mayor declared Petilia would be forever after a beacon to "women of courage" across Italy.

On October 19, 2013, nearly four years after her death, thousands of Italians gathered on a chilly morning in Milan to remember Lea in the city where, as an expectant mother, she had once hoped for a new life. Buses rented to transport mourners from Pagliarelle and Petilia arrived ominously empty. Among the crowd bearing flowers and waving flags decorated with Lea's face, however, were hundreds of Calabrians who had made their own way. Enza Rando met one 'Ndrangheta wife who, following the service, walked immediately into a carabinieri station to make a statement against her family. "She said: 'Lea taught me to be brave,'" said Enza. "'Lea taught me to have courage.'"

Alessandra, unable to attend such a public event, watched on television. Lea's coffin was carried through the streets around Sempione Park by pallbearers who included the mayors of Milan and Petilia, and Don Luigi Ciotti, head of Libera. It was the size of the crowd that most caught Alessandra's attention. The roots of the 'Ndrangheta went back to 1861 and the unification of Italy. Everything that had followed since had sprung from that first refusal to accept an Italian nation-state. As a result, Italy had never really come together. It had always been north and south, state and mafia, Piedmontese, Lombardian, and Venetian against Campanian, Calabrian, and Sicilian. And it was in those rifts that malevolence and murder had thrived. And yet here, on the streets of Milan, was all Italy together. This was what a modern, lawful, united nation looked like. Was it possible that in the funeral of a mafioso's daughter there were glimpses of a nation finally made whole?

Lea's coffin was placed on a stand in front of the crowd. Over it hung a banner that read "I see, I hear, I speak," a slogan that, along-side images of Lea, Giuseppina, and Concetta, had become a fixture at anti-mafia rallies. Don Luigi then addressed a eulogy to Lea. She needn't worry, he told her. Denise now had a family of thousands to look after her. "Your heart and your conscience will forever be wellsprings of freedom," he said. "You were a martyr to truth. Your spirit will never die."

Don Luigi was followed by Denise.[2] She had been only a girl of seventeen when, a few streets away, her mother had disappeared into the night. Now she was a woman of twenty-one and a govern-ment witness who had sent her father and boyfriend to jail for mur-dering her mother. And finally she was able to say her good-byes. The crowd stood in silence. Denise, close by but hidden from view on her bodyguards' insistence, spoke to the crowd through loud-speakers. "Today is a very difficult day for me," she began. After a long pause, in a gentle voice, she spoke to her mother. "Thank you for all you did for me," she said. "Thank you for giving me a better life. Everything that happened, everything you did, I know now that you did it all for me and I will never stop thanking you for it." Denise's voice was cracking. There was no revenge here, no honor, and no justice. There was just a daughter standing before her mother, telling her she loved her. "Ciao, Mama," Denise said.

ACKNOWLEDGMENTS

AN EXTRAORDINARY SELECTION of people tried to suppress the story of *The Good Mothers*, and many of them did their best to frustrate the reporting and writing of this book. As with any investigation into the mafia, the 'Ndrangheta's violent enforcement of omertà ensured that many of its leading characters were unavailable. By the time I heard their stories, two of the three Good Mothers, Lea Garofalo and Maria Concetta Cacciola, were dead, killed for their courage in standing up to the organization; the third, Giuseppina Pesce, was unreachable in witness protection. Most mafiosi and those intimidated by them were also unwilling to speak. On those occasions when subjects did talk, their answers to my questions often contained warnings or veiled threats. That the book exists at all is due to the courage and determination of a rare few.

Foremost among those who stepped forward to be counted is my agent at Pew Literary, Patrick Walsh. Patrick was the first to spot the potential of this story, and he remains the greatest champion for whom a writer could ask, somehow combining charm and warmth with sage advice and commercial precision. Patrick forms an unbeatable team with Luke Speed, my film agent at Curtis Brown, who immediately saw the promise of *The Good Mothers* and whose consequent effect on my professional life has been nothing less than transformational. Arabella Pike at HarperCollins in London and David Highfill at HarperCollins in New York were both everything a writer wishes for in an editor: gracious in their welcome, generous in the time they allowed me to write, firm in their support against saboteurs, efficient and insightful in their editing—and providers of delicious lunches. In London, Katherine Patrick at HarperCollins UK organized a publicity campaign that could have conquered worlds, Leo Nickolls created the fantastic cover, and Iain Hunt ushered the final text to publication with the skill and collegial civility that has led to his universal acknowledgment as one of the best in the business.

In the U.S., Chloe Moffett's stoicism, precision, efficiency, and unflappable good humor kept me on track when many others might have given up. David Palmer's forensic eye for text saved me from several embarrassments. Lauren Janiec and Libby Collins attracted and corralled extraordinary press interest. And Tavia Kowalchuk made sure every bookseller and book enthusiast, library, and literary institution knew the story of *The Good Mothers*. My deep thanks, too, to publisher, Liate Stehlik.

Elsewhere, Tessa Ross and Juliette Howell at House Productions, who bought the film and television rights before there was even a proposal, let alone a book, have my everlasting gratitude for their brave and early support. I owe a large debt to Nick Trautwein at the *New Yorker* for championing an excerpt in the magazine, as well as gentle, meticulous, and insightful editing; Dorothy Wickenden and David Remnick for their enthusiasm; and Fabio Bertoni, Nick Niarchos, Stephania Taladrid, and Francesca Magnani for their forensic diligence. Thank you also to Philip Gourevitch for the introduction.

I first heard about the women of *The Good Mothers* on my first reporting trip to Italy (for a different story) when Laura Aprati, an Italian journalist whom I had asked to set up a couple of interviews, insisted that as part payment I watch a one-woman play she had written with Enrico Fierro. The play, *O cu nui o cu iddi* (*With Us or with Them*), was being staged entirely in Italian to an audience of teenagers in a run-down, heavily mafia area on the outskirts of

Rome. I picked up on the drama and the tragedy but little more. My confusion—and the audience's—was only heightened when Laura pushed me onstage to answer a few questions through an interpreter about my impression of the play, the mafia, and the past, present, and future of Italy.

Chastened by this exposure of my ignorance, I returned to my guesthouse knowing only the name of the woman on whose life the play was based: Maria Concetta Cacciola. Thus began the process of research and reporting that led me to her story, and those of Giuseppina Pesce and Lea and Denise Garofalo. There was a lot to read. Though the Italian press initially missed the story of the Garofalos, it later made up for its inattention with blanket coverage of Carlo Cosco's trial. By then, Lea and Denise were becoming heroes to a generation of young Italian activists. The arrest of the powerful Pesce clan, by contrast, was a big story from the start, especially when Giuseppina began testifying. As the press watched the unraveling of the Gioia Tauro 'Ndrangheta, Concetta's death also received significant coverage.

Still, many of the newspaper reports were frustratingly brief and incomplete. There are sound reasons for this: Italian journalists who report on the mafia in any depth are routinely forced to seek protection from the authorities. In addition, the 'Ndrangheta is a phenomenon whose scale and threat has only recently begun to be understood. Uncovering the detail of the criminal conspiracy that lies behind the story of *The Good Mothers* and exploring the history of the 'Ndrangheta required a painstaking two and a half years rummaging through the archives of the Italian judiciary, accumulating, translating, and assessing tens of thousands of pages of court documents. These were then supplemented by lengthy and repeated interviews with the participants as well as historians and academics.

Laura was my guide throughout this process, along with Giuliana Clementi, the interpreter who first translated my ramblings that night at Laura's play. Laura's deep knowledge and resourcefulness left few stones unturned. Giuliana's pinpoint and nuanced translation in a world that the 'Ndrangheta would prefer to remain as murky as possible was essential to the accuracy of my understanding. I am forever grateful for their assistance. I also benefited immensely from the insight and generosity of Enrico Fierro, Laura's professional partner for many years and an encyclopedia of mafia knowledge; and from the generosity and expertise of Lucio Musolino, whose contacts in Calabria are unparalleled and who continues to report daily on the 'Ndrangheta in the face of numerous threats to his life. I also owe deep thanks to Teo Butturini, Marta Clinco, and Francesco Creazzo for fixing and translating.

I would also like to acknowledge the generous assistance of Alessandra Cerreti, whose insight into the importance of women to the 'Ndrangheta and how feminism was the key to bringing down Europe's most powerful mafia informed the theme of *The Good Mothers*. Alessandra allowed me to interview her for a total of eight hours over the course of a year.

The openness of the Italian justice system, and its tradition of prosecutors presenting their entire case in official documents that contain transcripts of wiretaps and surveillance videos, as well as transcripts of interviews with key suspects and witnesses, is a treasure trove for any journalist, and those legal and evidential documents form the backbone of this book. As well as to Alessandra, I am indebted to numerous prosecutors in Calabria and across Italy for their assistance in providing the relevant documents and agreeing to lengthy interviews, particularly Franco Roberti, Michele Prestipino, Giovanni Musarò, Giuseppe Lombardo, Sandro Dolce, Giuseppe Creazzo, Roberto di Bella, Federico Cafiero de Raho, Marcello Tatangelo, and Gaetano Paci, and, despite a cold that had taken away his voice, the indomitable Nicola Gratteri. Renato Cortese took time out of his busy schedule to answer my questions. Raffaele Grassi, Reggio Calabria's steadfast police chief, was unfailingly solicitous on my visits to the city and granted me a rare and astonishing tour of the giant floor on the top of the police headquarters entirely given over to wiretapping, surveillance, and bugging. Like many on the Gioia Tauro *piano*, I am also indebted to Antonino de Masi and Antonino Bartuccio, mayor of Rizziconi, who continue to speak out—to me and others—despite the repeated threats to their lives.

Among the lawyers who also assisted me, particular thanks are due to Annalisa Pisano, Lea Garofalo's only contact in the outside world for many years, who broke seven years of silence to speak tearfully and honestly to me in a quiet corner of a courthouse café in Catanzaro. Vincenza "Enza" Rando, one of my first interviewees, dealt patiently with my frequently misjudged questions. Adriana Fiormonti, Giuseppina Pesce's lawyer, was charmingly instructive on her client and the workings of the 'Ndrangheta. Jules Munro at Simpsons Solicitors in Sydney, Beth Silfin at HarperCollins, and Nicola Landolfi in Rome all provided crucial legal advice.

I drew on a host of academic research in my investigation of the 'Ndrangheta. Among those who were especially helpful were Enzo Ciconte in Rome, Ernesto Savona in Milan, and John Dickie and Anna Sergi in London. Anyone interested in pursuing this subject could do worse than to peruse the considerable back catalog belonging to these four experts.

I also relied on a small army of readers to proof and offer suggestions, all of which were invaluable. My deep thanks to Max Askew, Colin Perry, and members of southern England's best book club: Venetia Ellvers, Serena Freeland, Cleodie Gladstone, Wiz Hok, Susie Honey, Cheryl Myers, Millie Powell, Louisa Robertson, Amanda Sinclair, Sally Turvill, and Anna Worthington. Deep thanks as ever to Tess, who read every draft, endured countless discussions, and offered limitless, incisive advice. None of it works without you, Tess.

To the many lawyers and various others on several continents who tried to frustrate this book—and whose tactics bore a marked resemblance to those employed by the 'Ndrangheta—I hope you can still enjoy it. A number of you made the argument that this was not my book to write, because I was neither Italian nor a woman. As someone who has worked as a foreign correspondent for more than two decades, I know the pitfalls of the profession only too well. The outsider is hindered by ignorance, language, and expense. A very fair question is often: who are you to tell this tale? My own view is that these obstacles are formidable but not insurmountable; that distance can sometimes lend perspective; and that empathy, imagining yourself in the shoes of another, is the duty of any writer and the basis of any good writing. If the story of *The Good Mothers* tells us anything, it is that to define human capacity by the accident of gender or skin color, religion, or nationality, is folly. The entire world gained because a small group of southern Italian women sought a different destiny from the one others had marked out for them. It is their example, above all else, that has been my guide in these pages.

NOTES

THE STORY OF *The Good Mothers* relies heavily on official court documents released during the trials of those charged with the murders of Lea Garofalo and Maria Concetta Cacciola, and the cases that followed Giuseppina Pesce's revelations. The Italian justice system is an invaluable tool for the reporter trying to reconstruct a story after the fact. At each stage of the trial process, the prosecutor will release, in printed form, all the evidence he or she intends to rely on in court, including all transcripts of tapped phone conversations and other intercepted communications. These documents are detailed and comprehensive: each set of trial documents for Giuseppina Pesce ran to more than one thousand pages, and more than two thousand in the latter stages of the process. They also carry an unimpeachable legal privilege, as do the trial transcripts. It's hard to imagine a legal system where more trouble is taken to ensure that justice is seen to be done.

For each of the three Good Mothers, as well as for other cases that feature in their story, my method was to digest the official documentation, then follow it up with supplementary interviews with the protagonists. Italy's anti-mafia prosecutors were unfailingly accommodating, and most direct quotations from prosecutors in the text are from those interviews, though I have marked the source where it might be unclear or where that is not the case. (A full list of those prosecutors who assisted me, along with my thanks, can be found in the acknowledgments.) Mafiosi, 'Ndranghetisti, and their legal representatives tended to be less forthcoming: such are the restrictions of omertà. I also interviewed a number of experts— academics, law enforcement officers, judges, lawyers, politicians, officials. Again, any quotations that appear in the text should be assumed to be sourced to my interviews unless I have indicated otherwise. Finally, as part of my research, I read thousands of articles in the Italian and international press, as well as a slew of books and academic articles, and I have indicated in the text where I have relied on them for points of information.

I

1 This chapter is based on official transcriptions of Denise Cosco's testimony in court on September 20 and October 13, 2011, judicial documents from the murder trial that followed, and transcripts of her interviews with the carabinieri on November 25, 2009, and March 5, 2010. I also conducted several supplementary interviews, notably with Denise's lawyer, Vincenza Rando; Lea's lawyer, Annalisa Pisano; and prosecutors Alessandra Cerreti, Giuseppe Creazzo, and Sandro Dolce.

II

1 Interview with the author, May 2016, Pagliarelle.
2 Estimates of the 'Ndrangheta's earnings vary wildly. This is partly because the 'Ndrangheta is such a secretive organization, partly because it is laterally structured, giving no one boss much knowledge of the 'Ndrangheta's finances beyond his own *'ndrina*. Some variation is also accounted for by Italian researchers' habit of focusing only on revenues from inside Italy. Finally, some of the more spectacular figures seem to be explained by researchers, journalists, and prosecutors wishing to draw attention to the group.

Transcrime, a respected criminal research unit run by Professor Ernesto Savona, whom I interviewed at his offices at the Catholic University in Milan, estimates the 'Ndrangheta's annual earnings at $3.49 billion. In a paper published in *Global Crime* in 2014 ("Mythical Numbers and the Proceeds of Organized Crime: Estimating the Mafia Proceeds in Italy"), Transcrime also estimated 'Ndrangheta annual earnings to be in the range of $2.5 billion to $4 billion.

Most other estimates of the 'Ndrangheta's earnings are far higher, in the $40 billion to $80 billion range. In December 2008, for instance, the U.S.

consul general to Naples, Patrick Truhn, returned from a fact-finding tour to Calabria to file a report that began with the arresting opening statement: "If it were not part of Italy, Calabria would be a failed state. The 'Ndrangheta organized crime syndicate controls vast portions of its territory and economy and accounts for at least three percent of Italy's GDP (probably much more) through drug trafficking, extortion and usury" (Wikileaks released the cable: https://www.wikileaks.org/plusd/cables/08NAPLES96_a.html).

The figure of $100 billion comes from anti-mafia prosecutor Giuseppe Lombardo, who is based in Reggio Calabria and has studied the 'Ndrangheta's money, domestic and international, for a decade. Lombardo is not an individual given to exaggeration, and there are few people in the world who know more about the 'Ndrangheta's money. It is his figure that I have used here as an upper limit.

Why the variation in figures? And why use Lombardo's figure, which is one of the highest? Savona was keen to puncture what he considered to be the wilder estimates of mafia wealth, a laudable aim in an area prone to hyperbole. Still, anecdotal evidence such as the value of the European cocaine trade (€4.5 billion to €7 billion a year at wholesale prices, or €22 billion a year at street prices), the embezzlement and defrauding of billons of euros in European Union funds, and the uncovering of mafia money-laundering networks processing tens of billions of euros a year suggests Transcrime's figures are low. Possibly this is because, in its admirable effort to nail the facts, Transcrime focused only on documented domestic seizures and Italian police evidence of criminal revenues, plus academic and media reports. In other words, it concentrated only on the known and local and took no account of the unknown or foreign. It's worth noting that in a separate 2013 study, Transcrime itself estimated that 80 percent of the 'Ndrangheta's money is earned overseas. Lombardo, on the other hand, took a global view and has information on the 'Ndrangheta not available to academic researchers. His figures also accord much more closely with other international estimates of the value of global organized crime.

3 Milka Kahn and Anne Véron, *Women of Honour* (London: Hurst, 2017), p. 77.

4 Although Italian law recognized the imperative of defending honor until 1981, allowing the defense of reputation as mitigation for murder. See Pierfilippo Saviotti, " 'Le donne contro la 'ndrangheta,' Pavia incontra il procuratore Cerreti," Stampo Antimafioso, November 16, 2013: http://www.stampoantimafioso.it/2013/11/16/pavia-procuratore-cer reti/#sthash.zns0zKkt.dpuf.

5 Michele Inserra, "Quaderni del Sud, Locri la giornata della memoria Al cimitero di Rosarno per le donne 'sparite,' " *Il Quotidiano del Sud*, March 17, 2017:

http://www.quotidianodelsud.it/calabria/societa-cultura/2017/03/17
/quaderni-sud-locri-giornata-memoria-cimitero-rosarno-donne.

6 *Amanda Knox*, Netflix, 2016: https://www.netflix.com/title/80081155.

III

1 This section is based primarily on several interviews with Alessandra Cerreti conducted between July 2015 and May 2016, as well as supplementary research.

2 "Profile: Bernardo Provenzano," BBC, April 11, 2006: http://news.bbc.co.uk/1/hi/world/europe/4899512.stm.

3 "Imprenditore arrestato per frode all'erario E' accusato di aver sottratto un miliardo," *La Repubblica*, February 9, 2007: https://www.repubblica.it/2007/02/sezioni/cronaca/arresto-cetti-serbelloni/arresto-cetti-serbelloni/arresto-cetti-serbelloni.html; "Islam, nell'aula del tribunale è polemica fra giudice e imputato sul copricapo," *La Repubblica*, February 26, 2009: http://milano.repubblica.it/dettaglio/islam-nellaula-del-tribunale-e-polemica-fra-giudice-e-imputato-sul-copricapo/1596678.

4 Emanuela Zuccalà, "La 'ndrangheta esiste, che fatica dimostrarlo ogni volta," *Io Donna*, October 9, 2012: http://www.iodonna.it/personaggi/interviste/2012/alessandra-cerreti-pubblico-ministero-mafia-calabria-40999238466.shtml.

IV

1 This chapter is based on official transcriptions of Denise Cosco's testimony and of her interviews with the carabinieri on November 25, 2009, and March 5, 2010, as well as supplementary interviews with Denise's lawyer, Vincenza Rando; Lea's lawyer, Annalisa Pisano; and prosecutors Alessandra Cerreti, Giuseppe Creazzo, and Sandro Dolce.

V

1 John Dickie, professor of Italian studies at University College London, is a rare example of an outsider in a field—mafia history—dominated by Italians. His studies of mafiosi, *Cosa Nostra*, *Mafia Brotherhoods*, and *Mafia Republic*, draw on earlier work by Italian scholars but also Dickie's original research. Alessandra read works by many mafia scholars, most of them Italian. But it was Dickie's research that revealed to her the 'Ndrangheta's early attachment to prostitution. It is a measure of Dickie's stature that Alessandra later struck up a correspondence with him. In this passage,

I quote from Dickie's work as well as from a supplementary interview in London in June 2016.

2 John Dickie, *Mafia Brotherhoods* (London: Sceptre, 2011), pp. 171–74.

3 See for example the founding myths of the Chinese triads, the Japanese yakuza, or the South African prison gangs the 26s, 27s, and 28s.

4 León Arsenal and Hipólito Sanchiz, *Una Historia de las Sociedades Secretas Españolas* (Barcelona: Planeta, 2006), pp. 326–35.

5 Dickie, *Mafia Brotherhoods*, p. 5.

6 Antonio Zagari, *Ammazzare stanca* (Cosenza, Italy: Periferia, 1992; reprinted Reggio Emilia, Italy: Aliberti, 2008).

7 Interview with the author, May 2016, Rome.

VI

1 This section is largely sourced from repeated interviews with Alessandra Cerreti, Giovanni Musarò, and Michele Prestipino between July 2015 and November 2016.

2 Rachel Donadio, "Corruption Is Seen as a Drain on Italy's South," *New York Times*, October 7, 2012: http://www.nytimes.com/2012/10/08 /world/europe/in-italy-calabria-is-drained-by-corruption.html.

3 Interview with the author, June 2016, Gioia Tauro.

4 Alex Perry, "Cocaine Highway," *Newsweek Insights*, November 17, 2014: https://www.amazon.co.uk/Cocaine-Highway-lines-habit-terror-ebook /dp/B00PSI1M42/ref=sr_1_1?ie=UTF8&qid=1481295939&sr=8-1&key words=cocaine+highway.

5 Steve Scherer, "The Mafia and a Very Special Flower Arrangement," Reuters, April 11, 2016: https://www.reuters.com/investigates/special-report /italy-mafia-flowers/.

6 The best description of the 'Ndrangheta's structure and the evidence gathered for it can be found in the judicial documents supporting the case that eventually resulted from these inquiries, code-named Operazione Crimine. Copies can be found at the following web addresses: http://www.casadellale galita.info/doc/sentenza-GUP-CRIMINE.pdf (939 pages) and http://www .casadellalegalita.info/doc/Decreto-Fermo-CRIMINE.pdf (2,681 pages).

These documents also detail the election of Domenico Oppedisano and give further detail on the carabinieri's surveillance methods.

7 For an account of the summit, see this interview with the center's manager, Paderno Dugnano: https://www.youtube.com/watch?v=xGsOuUHH0WA.

8 Stephan Faris, "Italy Braces for a New Mafia War," *Time*, October 14, 2010: http://content.time.com/time/world/article/0,8599,2025423,00.html; "It-

aly: Police Uncover Mafia Drug Ring in Milan Convent," AKI, May 12, 2010 (a reprint of the story, containing details of the government crackdown, can be found on a chat thread of the Gangsters Inc. blog at: http://z14 .invisionfree.com/GangstersInc/index.php?showtopic=1605&st=720); Nick Squires, "Italy Claims Finally Defeating the Mafia," *Telegraph*, January 9, 2010: http://www.telegraph.co.uk/news/worldnews/europe/italy/6957240 /Italy-claims-finally-defeating-the-mafia.html.

VII

1 Much has been written about Lea Garofalo's death. In this account, I have stuck to the official transcriptions of her testimony in 1996, July 2002, and April 2008; Denise Cosco's statements on November 25, 2009, and March 5, 2010, and her testimony in court on September 20 and October 13, 2011; and judicial documents from the murder trial that followed. I also conducted supplementary interviews with Vincenza Rando, Alessandra Cerreti, Marisa Garofalo, and Sandro Dolce in 2015 and 2016.

2 Milka Kahn and Anne Véron, *Women of Honour* (London: Hurst, 2017), p. 107.

VIII

1 The source material for most of this chapter is the same as for chapter 7.

2 I have supplemented quotes from my own interview with Enza Rando with some from this court report: Emanuela Zuccalà, "L'ultimo sms di Lea Garofalo: torno a Milano per ricominciare," *Corriere della Sera*, November 14, 2012: http://27esimaora.corriere.it/articolo/lultimo-sms-di-lea-garofalo -allavvocatotorno-a-milano-mi-rifaro-una-vita/.

IX

1 "Reggio Calabria, bomba al tribunale alto potenziale, danni, nessun ferito," *La Repubblica*, January 3, 2010: https://www.repubblica.it/2010/01/sezi oni/cronaca/reggio-bomba/reggio-bomba/reggio-bomba.html; Nick Pisa, "The Moped Mafia: CCTV Catches Bomb Delivery by Italian Mobster on Scooter Driven by His Moll," *Daily Mail*, January 8, 2010: http://www .dailymail.co.uk/news/article-1241682/The-moped-Mafia-CCTV-catch es-bomb-delivery-Italian-mobster-scooter-driven-moll.html. Though the driver was initially reported as being a woman, Prestipino said later investigations identified a man.

2 "Rosarno, polizia: 'Ndrangheta dietro a scontri. Via 1.100 immigrati,"

Reuters, January 11, 2010: https://it.reuters.com/article/topNews/idIT
MIE60A0AB20100111?sp=true.

3 Reports of the discovery of the car can be found on this Gangsters Inc. chat
thread: http://www.z14.invisionfree.com/GangstersInc/index.php?show
topic=1605&st=720.

4 The passages on the early life and friendship in Rosarno of Maria Concetta
Cacciola and Giuseppina Pesce are based on official court documents, dated
July 13, 2013, released by the Italian prosecutor, Giuseppe Creazzo, who
oversaw the case relating to Cacciola's death, as well as transcripts of Giuseppina's testimony to those proceedings, dated February 7, 2013. Supplementary material is available in official documents relating to the subsequent
trial of lawyers representing the Cacciola family, dated July 30, 2014, and a
custody hearing for Concetta's father, Michele Cacciola, dated February 4,
2012.

X

1 This chapter is based on official transcriptions of Denise Cosco's statements
on November 25, 2009, and March 5, 2010, and of her testimony in court on
September 20 and October 13, 2011; on judicial documents from the murder
trial that followed; and on statements made to police and in court by Carmine Venturino in 2012 and 2013.

XI

1 "Operazione 'All Inside,' colpo al clan Pesce di Rosarno. 30 arresti,"
CN24TV: http://www.cn24tv.it/news/30318/operazione-all-inside-colpo
-al-clan-pesce-di-rosarno-30-arresti.html.

2 Caterina Scaffidi Domianello, "Donne contro la 'ndrangheta," *Narcomafie*,
July–August 2013: http://www.liberanet.org/narcomafie/2013_07.pdf.

3 Julian Gavaghan, "Italian Mob Boss Arrested After 17 Years on the Run Is
Cheered by Crowd as Police Lead Him to Jail," *Daily Mail*, April 27, 2010:
http://www.dailymail.co.uk/news/article-1269304/Italian-mobster-arrested
-17-years-run-cheered-crowd-police-lead-jail.html.

4 Tom Kington, "Italian Police Arrest 300 in Raids on Calabrian Mafia," *Guard-
ian*, July 13, 2010: https://www.theguardian.com/world/2010/jul/13/cal
abria-mafia-arrests-italy; Stephan Faris, "Italy vs. the Mafia: Beheading the
'Ndrangheta," *Time*, July 13, 2010: http://content.time.com/time/world/arti
cle/0,8599,2003598,00.html.

5 Interview with the author, July 2015, Milan.

6 Interview with the author, July 2015, Modena.
7 Interview with the author, July 2015, Milan.
8 Ibid.

XII

1 Stephan Faris, "Italy Braces for a New Mafia War," *Time*, October 14, 2010: http://content.time.com/time/world/article/0,8599,2025423,00.html.
2 Author interview with Alessandra Cerreti, May 2016, Milan.
3 Clare Longrigg, "Women Breaking the Mafia's Rules," Mafiology, October 14, 2013: https://mafiologytest.wordpress.com/2013/10/14/women-breaking -the-mafias-rules/#more-556.
4 Ibid.
5 Cerreti spoke about her conversation with Giuseppina in several forums, such as in Rome in March 2014: "Experts Commend Mafia-Linked Women's Help in Crime Fight," Xinhua, March 15, 2014: http://china.org.cn/world/Off_ the_Wire/2014-03/15/content_31793448.htm. She also gave several accounts during more than seven hours of interviews with the author in July 2015 and February and May 2016. This quotation is a compilation of Cerreti's public remarks and her quotations in interviews.
6 Longrigg, "Women Breaking the Mafia's Rules."
7 Interview with the author, July 2015, Milan.
8 Ibid.
9 Ibid.
10 Interview with the author, February 2015, Rome.
11 Interview with the author, July 2015, Milan.
12 Interview with the author, July 2015, Rome.
13 Giuseppina Pesce's statement to prosecutors was sourced from official transcripts of her testimony included in several subsequent trial documents.

XIII

1 This chapter is based on numerous trial documents relating to the Lea Garofalo case. In the earlier stages of the investigation, the carabinieri made some false allegations and were mistaken over some factual details, which were corrected as their inquiries proceeded at later stages of the investigation and the trial.
2 Author interview with Enza Rando, July 2015, Modena. See also Michele Brambilla, "The Tragedy and Courage of a Mobster's Daughter," *La Stampa in English*, April 17, 2014: https://www.lastampa.it/2014/04/17/esteri/lastampa-in

-english/the-tragedy-and-courage-of-a-mobsters-daughter-lrpU6aQB445i
f2MPCiJM9I/pagina.html.

XIV

1 This section is based on trial documents relating to Operation All Inside, the prosecution of the Pesce clan, and statements made by Giuseppina Pesce both to Alessandra Cerreti and during the subsequent trial.

2 Clare Longrigg, "Women Breaking the Mafia's Rules," Mafiology, October 14, 2013: https://mafiologytest.wordpress.com/2013/10/14/women-break ing-the-mafias-rules/#more-556.

3 *Calabria Ora*'s website has since closed. I am grateful to the veteran journalist Franco Abruzzo, whose website is an invaluable archive on a diverse range of matters, including the *Calabria Ora* controversy: https://www.fran coabruzzo.it/public/docs/palmi-articolicommenti-9fb13.rtf.

XV

1 This chapter is based on official records of statements made by Maria Concetta Cacciola to Alessandra Cerreti and Giovanni Musarò on May 25 and June 28, 2011; trial documents relating to the prosecution of Michele Cacciola, Giuseppe Cacciola, Anna Lazzaro, Gregorio Cacciola, and Vittorio Pisani; and supplementary interviews with Giuseppe Creazzo, Giovanni Musarò, and Alessandra Cerreti. I'm also grateful to Laura Aprati and Enrico Fierro for a transcript of their one-woman play about Concetta, *O cu nui o cu iddi*, which is also closely based on the official evidence.

2 Caterina Scaffidi Domianello, "Donne contro la 'ndrangheta," *Narcomafie*, July–August 2013: http://www.liberanet.org/narcomafie/2013_07.pdf.

3 Interview with the author, May 2016, Milan.

4 Interview with the author, May 2016, Rome.

5 Clare Longrigg, "Mafia Witness 'Forced to Drink Acid,'" Mafiology, February 2, 2014: https://mafiologytest.wordpress.com/2014/02/02/mafia -witness-forced-to-drink-acid/more#572.

6 Interview with the author, May 2016, Rome.

XVI

1 This section is based on the author's interview with Alessandra Cerreti in May 2016 in Milan.

2 Interview with the author, May 2016, Milan.

3 Caterina Scaffidi Domianello, "Donne contro la 'ndrangheta," *Narcomafie*, July–August 2013: http://www.liberanet.org/narcomafie/2013_07.pdf.

4 Various reports of the correspondence between Giuseppina Pesce and her family can be found online. The most complete is Caterina Scaffidi Domianello's account in "Donne contro la 'ndrangheta," *Narcomafie*, July–August 2013: http://www.liberanet.org/narcomafie/2013_07.pdf. Others that proved useful include two reports on strill.it: http://www.strill.it/citta/2011/10/la-famiglia-scrive-a-giuseppina-pesce-le-lettere-ricevute-in-carcere/; and http://www.strill.it/citta/2011/09/le-lettere-di-giuseppina-pesce-collaboro-per-dare-un-futuro-ai-miei-figli/. Excerpts were also included in the judicial documents accompanying the trials that followed Operations All Inside and All Clean. Finally, Alessandra Cerreti read some of the letters to the author in an interview and at other times summarized their contents.

XVII

1 This chapter is based on evidence and transcripts presented in official judicial documents relating to the trial of Michele Cacciola, Anna Lazzaro, and Giuseppe Cacciola, and the subsequent trial of the two lawyers, Vittorio Pisani and Gregorio Cacciola. This material is supplemented by the author's interviews with Alessandra Cerreti, Giovanni Musarò, and Giuseppe Creazzo, as well as reference to the play *O cu nui o cu iddi* by Laura Aprati and Enrico Fierro.

2 Dario Crippa, "Sciolse la mamma nell'acido, nessuna pietà per mio padre," *Il Giorno*, July 4, 2011: https://www.ilgiorno.it/milano/cronaca/2011/07/04/537205-sciolse_mamma.shtml.

3 Santo Della Volpe, "Le donne e la lotta di liberazione dalle mafie," Libera, 2012: http://www.libera.it/flex/cm/pages/ServeBLOB.php/L/IT/IDPagina/6462 (no longer available).

4 The eleven-minute recording of Concetta's "retraction" is on the Stop'Ndrangheta website: http://www.stopndrangheta.it/stopndr/art.aspx?id=1419,La+ritrattazione+estorta+alla+Cacciola.

5 Clare Longrigg, "Mafia Witness 'Forced to Drink Acid,'" Mafiology, February 2, 2014: https://mafiologytest.wordpress.com/2014/02/02/mafia-witness-forced-to-drink-acid/more#572.

XVIII

1 This chapter is based on evidence and transcripts presented in official judicial documents relating to the trial of Michele Cacciola, Anna Lazzaro, and Gi-

useppe Cacciola, and the subsequent trial of the two lawyers, Vittorio Pisani and Gregorio Cacciola. This material is supplemented by the author's interviews with Alessandra Cerreti, Giovanni Musarò, and Giuseppe Creazzo.

2 Interview with the author, May 2016, Milan.

3 Interview with the author, May 2016, Rome.

4 "Orsola Fallara in condizioni disperate al Riuniti di Reggio dopo un tentativo di suicidio," CN24TV, December 16, 2010: http://www.cn24tv.it/news/16616 /orsola-fallara-in-condizioni-disperate-al-riuniti-di-reggio-dopo-un-tentativo -di-suicidio.html.

5 Carlo Macrì, "Il suicidio della testimone anti clan," *Corriere della Sera*, August 23, 2011: http://www.corriere.it/cronache/11_agosto_23/il-sui cidio-della-testimone-anti-clan-carlo-macri_7e7fbc74-cd49-11e0-8914 -d32bd7027ea8.shtml.

6 The full letter can be found here: http://www.sdisonorate.it/wordpress/wp -content/uploads/2014/03/Le-testimoni-di-giustizia-calabresi.pdf.

7 Ibid. *Calabria Ora*'s front page can be seen a few pages further on.

XIX

1 This chapter is based on official transcriptions of Denise Cosco's statements on November 25, 2009, and March 5, 2010, and of her testimony in court on September 20 and October 13, 2011, as well as judicial documents from the murder trial that followed.

2 Milka Kahn and Anne Véron, *Women of Honour* (London: Hurst, 2017), p. 118.

3 Marika Demaria, *La Scelta di Lea* (Milan: Melampo Editore, 2013), p. 26. I am indebted to Ms. Demaria, the only reporter to stay in court throughout the nine months of the trial, whose persistence allowed for a complete, public account to be given.

XX

1 This section is based on trial documents relating to Operation All Inside, the prosecution of the Pesce clan, and statements made by Giuseppina Pesce to Alessandra Cerreti and during the subsequent trial.

2 Much of the Pesce correspondence is also reprinted in full in Caterina Scaffidi Domianello's invaluable articles in "Donne contro la 'ndrangheta," *Narcomafie*, July–August 2013: http://www.liberanet.org/narcomafie/2013_07.pdf. Excerpts from Giuseppina's letter of August 23, 2011, are also reprinted here: http://www.strill.it/citta/2011/09/le-lettere-di-giuseppina-pesce-collaboro -per-dare-un-futuro-ai-miei-figli/.

3 Domianello, "Donne contro la 'ndrangheta."

4 Piero Gaeta, "Condannati a 20 anni Vincenzo e Ciccio Pesce," *Gazzetta del Sud*, September 21, 2011: http://www.calabrianotizie.it/condannati-anni -vincenzo-ciccio-pesce-sentenza-esemplare-del-gup-roberto-carrelli-palombi -che-ieri-sera-condannato-undici-imputati-ordinato-maxi-risarcimento/.

5 Paolo Toscano, "Giuseppina Pesce si è pentita di nuovo," *Gazzetta del Sud*, September 22, 2011: http://www.calabrianotizie.it/giuseppina-pesce-pentita -nuovo-dopo-avere-interrotto-collaborazione-con-magistrati-della-dda-reg gina-figlia-del-boss-salvatore-ripreso-riferire-vicende-della-cosca-figli/.

6 Ibid.

7 'Ndrangheta. "Giuseppina Pesce domani al processo di Palmi," CN24TV, September 22, 2011: http://www.cn24tv.it/news/32497/ndrangheta-gi useppina-pesce-domani-al-processo-di-palmi.html; "Clan pesce, Palaia scrive alla moglie pentita: 'stai rovinando te stessa ed i tuoi figli,'" CN24TV, November 23, 2011: http://www.cn24tv.it/news/32639/clan-pesce-palaia -scrive-alla-moglie-pentita-stai-rovinando-te-stessa-ed-i-tuoi-figli.html.

8 "Operazione 'All clean 2'. I dettagli," CN24TV, October 13, 2011: http://www .cn24tv.it/news/33781/operazione-all-clean-2-i-dettagli.html.

9 "Processo al clan Pesce, la testimone di giustizia sarà sentita da un luogo segreto," CN24TV, October 21, 2011: http://www.cn24tv.it/news/34338/processo-al -clan-pesce-la-testimone-di-giustizia-sara-sentita-da-un-luogo-segreto.html.

10 Nick Pisa, "Judge Hands 1,000-Year Prison Sentence to 110 Mafia Mobsters in Massive Show Trial," *Daily Mail*, November 22, 2011: http://www.daily mail.co.uk/news/article-2063932/Judge-hands-1-000-year-prison-sentence -110-Mafia-mobsters-massive-trial.html.

11 Author interview with Alessandra Cerreti. Also see the account in Francesca Chirico, "Rosarno, donne e 'ndrangheta: il processo del contrappasso," Stop'Ndrangheta, November 25, 2011: http://www.stopndrangheta.it/stopndr /art.aspx?id=1215,Rosarno%2c+donne+e+%27ndrangheta%3a+il+processo- +del+contrappasso.

XXI

1 This section is based on two interviews with Roberto di Bella at his offices in Reggio Calabria in July 2015 and May 2016, as well as a visit to the hostel housing 'Ndrangheta children in Messina and interviews with the staff there.

2 Riccardo Francesco Cordì, "Voglio una vita normale," *Corriere della Sera*, May 8, 2014: http://www.corriere.it/cronache/14_maggio_08/voglio-vita -normale-6f0f1dc2-d672-11e3-b1c6-d3130b63f531.shtml.

XXII

1 Translation from the United Nations Office of Drugs and Crime, *Review of Implementation of the United Nations Convention Against Corruption*, Italy, p. 4: https://www.unodc.org/documents/treaties/UNCAC/WorkingGroups /ImplementationReviewGroup/26-27November2013/V1387842e.pdf.

2 *Il Quotidiano della Calabria*'s front page for February 10, 2012, can be seen here: http://www.stopndrangheta.it/file/stopndrangheta_1381.pdf. The page includes the start of Matteo Cosenza's editorial, as well as stories on Maria Concetta Cacciola, Giuseppina Pesce, and Lea Garofalo, perhaps the first time that the three women and their stories had been reported collectively. The full editorial is here: http://19luglio1992.com/il-simbolo-dell8-marzo-tre-donne -coraggiose/.

3 For example, see Giuseppe Baldessarro, "Lea, Concetta, Giuseppina è l'8 marzo della Calabria," *La Repubblica*, March 2, 2012: https://www.repubblica.it /cronaca/2012/03/02/news/donne_ndrangheta_8_marzo-30721686/.

4 Ilaria Calabrò, "Reggio, 8 marzo: dagli studenti una lettera alla Pesce, 'nel tuo riscatto è possibile il riscatto di tutti,'" strettoweb.com, March 8, 2012: http://www.strettoweb.com/2012/03/reggio-8-marzo-dagli -studenti-una-lettera-alla-pesce-nel-tuo-riscatto-e-possibile-il-riscatto-di -tutti/25999/#07DWLhJEL6JRX3w0.99.

5 Matteo Cosenza, "Vicini a Denise che ha scelto la verità e la giustizia," *Il Quotidiano della Calabria*, March 8, 2012: http://www.stopndrangheta.it /file/stopndrangheta_1485.pdf.

XXIII

1 This section is based on official transcripts of the court proceedings held in Palmi, May 21 to 26, 2012.

XXIV

1 Marika Demaria, "Processo Lea Garofalo, riprendono le udienze," *Narcomafie*, December 2, 2012: http://www.acmos.net/processo-lea-garofalo-ripren dono-le-udienze.

2 "Sei ergastoli per l'omicidio di Lea Garofalo la testimone sciolta nell'acido," *Il Fatto Quotidiano*, March 30, 2012: https://www.ilfattoquotidiano .it/2012/03/30/milano-ergastoli-lomicidio-garofalo-testimone-sciolta-nel lacido/201316/. See also Tom Kington, "Italian Mobster Condemned by Daughter's Evidence," *Observer*, April 1, 2012: https://theguardian.com /world/2012/apr/01/italian-mobster-jailed-by-daughters-evidence.

3　Simona Ravizza, Cesare Giuzzi, and Redazione Milano online, "Viale
　Montello 6, sgomberato dopo 40 anni il 'fortino delle cosche,'" *Corri-
　ere della Sera*, June 21, 2012: http://milano.corriere.it/milano/notizie/
　cronaca/12_giugno_21/viale-montello-fortino-cosche-sgombero-polizia
　-cosco-lea-garofalo-201694845491.shtml. *Corriere della Sera* also has pic-
　tures of No. 6 Viale Montello as it was when Carlo ruled it and how it
　might be renovated here: Elisabetta Andreis, "Una 'corte' moderna nell'ex
　fortino della mafia," August 29, 2016: http://milano.corriere.it/notizie
　/cronaca/16_agosto_29/viale-montello-fortino-mafia-stabile-abbandonato
　-progetto-demolizione-41cb3f10-6d58-11e6-baa8-f780dada92e5.shtml.

4　Michele Brambilla, "The Tragedy and Courage of a Mobster's Daughter,"
　La Stampa in English, April 17, 2014: https://www.lastampa.it/2014/04/17
　/esteri/lastampa-in-english/the-tragedy-and-courage-of-a-mobsters-daugh
　ter-lrpU6aQB445if2MPCiJM9I/pagina.html.

5　This account of Carmine Venturino's confession is based on official court
　documents. There are also numerous press reports of Carmine Venturi-
　no's letter. See for instance Sandro De Riccardis, "Il verbale dell'orrore sulla
　pentita Garofalo: 'Bruciai il suo corpo finché rimase cenere,'" *La Repubblica*,
　March 20, 2013: http://repubblica.it/cronaca/2013/03/20/news/il_verbale
　_dell_orrore_sulla_pentita_garofalo_bruciai_il_suo_corpo_finch_rimase
　_cenere-54945861/?ref=search; Alessandra Coppola and Cesare Giuzzi, "Uc-
　cisi Lea Garofalo, il coraggio di Denise mi ha spinto a collaborare," *Corriere della
　Sera*, December 4, 2012: https://www.senzatarga.wordpress.com/2012/12/04
　/lea/; Marika Demaria, *La Scelta di Lea* (Milan: Melampo Editore, 2013).

6　This section relies chiefly on official records provided by prosecutor
　Marcello Tatangelo of his interrogation of Carmine Venturino on Octo-
　ber 3 and 11, 2012, as well as later transcripts of Carmine's questioning
　by Tatangelo in court. Once again, I am also indebted to Marika De-
　maria of *Narcomafie*, who doggedly followed the case and published in-
　termittent reports as well as her book, *La Scelta di Lea*. Also useful were
　various other press reports, as indicated.

XXV

1　"All Inside, il dispositivo della sentenza (I grado)," *Narcomafie*, May 3,
　2013: http://www.stopndrangheta.it/stopndr/art.aspx?id=1709,All+In
　side%2c+il+dispositivo+della+sentenza+(I+grado).

2　When the final sentences were delivered four years later, on March 29, 2017,
　sentences were confirmed against thirty-four accused: "'Ndrangheta, diven-
　tano definitive le condanne inflitte al clan Pesce di Rosarno," Zoom 24,

March 29, 2017: http://www.zoom24.it/2017/03/29/ndrangheta-pesce-con
danne-rosarno-45842/.

3 Giuseppe Baldessarro, "'Ndrangheta: nessuno demolisce la casa del boss, ac-
cetta solo l'imprenditore sotto scorta," *La Repubblica*, September 16, 2014:
https://www.repubblica.it/cronaca/2014/09/16/news/calabria_ndran
gheta_boss-95872877/.

4 Barbara Conforti, *Mafia, la trahison des femmes* (documentary), Canal+,
March 2, 2014.

5 "Omicidio Lea Garofalo, in appello confermati 4 ergastoli. Un assolto," *Il
Fatto Quotidiano*, May 29, 2013: https://www.ilfattoquotidiano.it/2013/05/29
/omicidio-lea-garofalo-in-appello-confermati-4-ergastoli-assolto/610120/.

6 Vincenzo Ruggiero, "Omicid di 'ndrangheia. 17 arresti a Crotone e in altre
4 regioni. Decisive le dichiarazioni di Lea Garofalo," CN24TV, October 29,
2013: http://www.cn24tv.it/news/77515/omicidi-di-ndrangheta-17-arresti
-a-crotone-e-in-altre-4-regioni-decisive-le-dichiarazioni-di-lea-garofalo
.html.

XXVI

1 Vincenzo Ruggiero, "Omicid di 'ndrangheia. 17 arresti a Crotone e in altre
4 regioni. Decisive le dichiarazioni di Lea Garofalo," CN24TV, October 29,
2013: http://www.cn24tv.it/news/77515/omicidi-di-ndrangheta-17-arres
ti-a-crotone-e-in-altre-4-regioni-decisive-le-dichiarazioni-di-lea-garofalo.
html.

2 There are several videos of Lea's funeral online that include Denise's
short speech. See https://www.youtube.com/watch?v=4oR9kFYFVcs or
https://www.youtube.com/watch?v=I9jxIMRQlT8.

ILLUSTRATION CREDITS

Lea Garofalo. The picture is undated but seems to capture Lea in her early twenties, just after she became a mother. The image became iconic. (*http://www.wikimafia.it*)

Lea, on the left, and Denise captured by CCTV in Milan in their last minutes together on the evening of November 24, 2009. (*Milan Carabinieri*)

Alessandra Cerreti, pictured in her office in Reggio Calabria. (*FILIPPO MONTEFORTE/AFP/Getty Images*)

Reggio Calabria, as seen from the hills to the southeast of the city, looking northwest across the Strait to Messina. (*Anna Quaglia/Alamy Stock Photo*)

San Luca. For decades, the 'Ndrangheta have convened an annual meeting on September 2 in this Aspromonte hill village, using a religious festival as cover. (*ROPI/Alamy Stock Photo*)

Carlo Cosco in a police mug shot taken after his arrest in February 2010. (*Lanese/Epa/REX/Shutterstock*)

Giuseppina Pesce the day after her arrest in April 2010. (*ANSA*)

Domenico Oppedisano being driven through the streets after his arrest in Rosarno in July 2010. (*Franco Cufari/Epa/REX/Shutterstock*)

Giuseppina Pesce in her mug shot after her arrest. (*ANSA*)

Maria Concetta Cacciola. As she was confined to the family home for weeks at a time, only one other picture of her has ever surfaced. (*ANSA*)

The gate of the warehouse in San Fruttuoso, Monza, where Lea's remains were discovered in October 2012, three years after her death. (*Fabrizio Radaelli/Epa/REX/Shutterstock*)

Breaking a lifetime of omertà, Carlo speaks in court on April 9, 2013. (*Corriere TV*)

Giuseppina's mother, Angela Ferraro, and sister, Marina Pesce. (*ANSA*)

Concetta's mother, Anna Rosalba Lazzaro, and father, Michele Cacciola. (*ANSA*)

Lea's funeral on October 19, 2013. Thousands from all over Italy turned out for a woman who, four years after her death, united the nation against the mafia under the slogan "I see, I hear, I speak." (*Marco Aprile/NurPhoto/Corbis via Getty Images*)

INDEX